Jane Green is the author of *Straight Talking*, *Jemima J.*, *Mr Maybe*, *Bookends*, *Babyville*, *Spellbound*, *The Other Woman* and *Life Swap*. She lives in Connecticut with her husband and four children.

JANE GREEN

Perfect Partners

JEMIMA J.

MR MAYBE

PENGUIN BOOKS

PENGUIN BOOKS

Published by the Penguin Group
Penguin Books Ltd, 80 Strand, London WC2R 0RL, England
Penguin Group (USA) Inc., 375 Hudson Street, New York, New York 10014, USA
Penguin Group (Canada), 90 Eglinton Avenue East, Suite 700, Toronto, Ontario, Canada M4P 2Y3
(a division of Pearson Penguin Canada Inc.)
Penguin Ireland, 25 St Stephen's Green, Dublin 2, Ireland (a division of Penguin Books Ltd)
Penguin Group (Australia), 250 Camberwell Road,
Camberwell, Victoria 3124, Australia (a division of Pearson Australia Group Pty Ltd)
Penguin Books India Pvt Ltd, 11 Community Centre,
Panchsheel Park, New Delhi – 110 017, India
Penguin Group (NZ), cnr Airborne and Rosedale Roads, Albany,
Auckland 1310, New Zealand (a division of Pearson New Zealand Ltd)
Penguin Books (South Africa) (Pty) Ltd, 24 Sturdee Avenue,
Rosebank, Johannesburg 2196, South Africa

Penguin Books Ltd, Registered Offices: 80 Strand, London WC2R 0RL, England

www.penguin.com

Jemima J. first published by Penguin Books 1998
Mr Maybe first published by Penguin Books 1999
This combined edition published 2005

1

Copyright © Jane Green, 1998, 1999
All rights reserved

The moral right of the author has been asserted

Printed in England by Clays Ltd, St Ives plc

ISBN-13: 978-0-141-02733-3
ISBN-10: 0-141-02733-9

JEMIMA J.

For David
My real-life romantic hero

ACKNOWLEDGEMENTS

This book would not be the book it is if it weren't for so many people who helped and encouraged me throughout those long months.

My agent, Anthony Goff, whose wisdom, integrity and humour made the road to hell and back almost fun . . .

For her friendship, guidance and determination, my editor, Louise Moore, without whom, quite literally, I would not be where I am today . . .

Angela Martin, my talented PR, and, more importantly, my friend.

Ami Smithson for her fabulous covers, and the entire team at Penguin for having faith and putting their money where their mouths are.

Graeme Weston, who showed me the real side of Santa Monica; my brother Charlie for being such a titles whizz; and of course my parents for their continuing love and support.

And finally Judith Murray, whose kindness, help and editorial skills have been incomparable.

Thank you.

CHAPTER ONE

God, I wish I were thin.

I wish I were thin, gorgeous, and could get any man I want. You probably think I'm crazy, I mean here I am, sitting at work on my own with a massive double-decker club sandwich in front of me, but I'm allowed to dream aren't I?

Half an hour to go of my lunchbreak. Half an hour in which to drool over the latest edition of my favourite magazine. Don't get me wrong, I don't read the features, why would I? Thousands of words about how to keep your man, how to spice up your sex life, how to spot if he's being unfaithful are, quite frankly, irrelevant to me. I'll be completely honest with you here, I've never had a proper boyfriend, and the cover lines on the magazines are not the reason I buy them.

If you must know, I buy them, all of them, for the pictures. I sit and I study each glossy photograph for minutes at a time, drinking in the models' long, lithe limbs, their tiny waists, their glowing golden skin. I have a routine: I start with their faces, eyeing each sculpted cheekbone, heart-shaped chin, and I move slowly down their bodies, careful not to miss a muscle.

I have a few favourites. In the top drawer of my chest of drawers in my bedroom at home is a stack of cut-out pictures of my top super models, preferred poses. Linda's there for her sex appeal, Christy's there for her lips and nose, and Cindy's there for the body.

And before you think I'm some kind of closet lesbian, I've already told you the one thing I would wish for if I rubbed a lamp and a gorgeous, bare-chested genie suddenly appeared. If I had one wish in all the world I wouldn't wish to win the lottery. Nor would I wish for true love. No, if I had one wish I would wish to have a model's figure, probably Cindy Crawford's, and I would extend the wish into having *and keeping* a model's figure, *no matter what I eat.*

Because, tough as it is to admit to a total stranger, I, Jemima Jones, eat a lot. I catch the glances, the glares of disapproval on the occasions I eat out in public, and I try my damnedest to ignore them. Should someone, some 'friend' trying to be caring and sharing, question me gently, I'll tell them I have a thyroid problem, or a gland problem, and occasionally I'll tack on the fact that I have a super-slow metabolism as well. Just so there's no doubt, just so people don't think that the only reason I am the size I am is because of the amount I eat.

But you're not stupid, I know that, and, given that approximately half the women in the country are a size 16 or over, I would ask you to try and understand about my secret binges, my constant cravings, and see that it's not just about food.

You don't need to know much about my background, suffice to say that my childhood wasn't happy, that I never felt loved, that I never got over my parents' divorce as a young child, and that now, as an adult, the only time I feel really comforted is when I seek solace in food.

So here I am now, at twenty-seven years old, bright,

funny, warm, caring and kind. But of course people don't see that when they look at Jemima Jones. They simply see fat.

They see my enormous breasts – particularly bloody builders, it's got to the stage where I actively avoid walking past building sites of any description – they see my large, round stomach, the thighs that rub together when I walk.

Unfortunately they don't see what I see when I look in the mirror. Selective visualization, I think I'll call it. They don't see my glossy light brown hair. They don't see my green eyes, they don't see my full lips. Not that they're anything amazing, but I like them, I'd say they were my best features.

They don't notice the clothes either, because, despite weighing far, far more than I should, I don't let myself go, I always make an effort. I mean, look at me now. If I were slim, you would say I look fantastic in my bold striped trousers and long tunic top in a perfectly matching shade of orange. But no, because of the size I am people look at me and think, 'God, she shouldn't wear such bright colours, she shouldn't draw attention to herself.'

But why shouldn't I enjoy clothes? At least I'm not telling myself that I won't bother shopping until I'm a size 12, because naturally my life is a constant diet.

We all know what happens with diets. The minute you cut out certain foods, the cravings overtake you until you can't see straight, you can't think properly, and the only way to get rid of the craving is to have a bite of chocolate, which soon turns into a whole bar.

And diets don't work, how can they? It's a multi-

million-dollar industry, and if any of the diets actually
worked the whole caboodle would go down the toilet.

If anyone knows how easy it is to fail it's me. The
Scarsdale, the High Fibre, the F-Plan, the six eggs a day
diet, Slimfast, Weight Watchers, Herbalife, slimming
pills, slimming drinks, slimming patches. You name
them, I've been the idiot that tried them. Although some
have, admittedly, been more successful than others.

But I have never, even with the help of all these diets,
been slim. I have been slimmer, but not slim.

I know you're watching me now with pity in your eyes
as I finish my sandwich and look furtively around the
office to see whether anyone is looking. It's okay,
the coast is clear, so I can pull open my top drawer and
sneak out the slab of chocolate hiding at the back. I tear
the bright orange wrapper and silver foil off and stuff it
into the dustbin beneath my desk, as it's far easier to
hide a slab of dull brown chocolate than the glaring
covering that encases it.

I take a bite. I savour the sweet chocolate in my mouth
as it melts on my tongue, and then I take another bite,
this time furiously chewing and swallowing, hardly
tasting a thing. Within seconds the entire bar has disappeared, and I sit there feeling sick and guilty.

I also feel relieved. My bad food for today has just
been eaten, which means that there's none left. Which
means that tonight, when I get home and have a salad,
which is what I'm now planning to eat for dinner, I can
feel good, and I can start my diet all over again.

I finish reading my magazine, then tuck it into my bag,
ready to attack the pages with scissors when I'm safely
at home in my bedroom, and I glance at the clock and

sigh. Another day in my humdrum life, but it shouldn't be humdrum. I'm a journalist, for God's sake. Surely that's a glamorous, exciting existence?

Unfortunately not for me. I long for a bit of glamour, and, on the rare occasions I do glance at the features in the magazines I flick through, I think that I could do better.

I probably could, as well, except I don't have the experience to write about men being unfaithful, but if I had, Jesus, I'd win awards, because I am, if I say so myself, an expert with words.

I love the English language, playing with words, watching sentences fit together like pieces of a jigsaw puzzle, but sadly my talents are wasted here at the *Kilburn Herald*.

I hate this job. When I meet new people and they ask what I do for a living, I hold my head up high and say I'm a journalist. I then try to change the subject, for the inevitable question after that is 'Who do you work for?' I hang my head low, mumble the *Kilburn Herald*, and, if I'm really pushed, I'll hang it even lower and confess that I do the Top Tips column.

Every week I'm flooded with mail from sad and lonely people in Kilburn with nothing better to do than write in with questions like, 'What's the best way to bleach a white marbled lino floor that's turned yellow?' and 'I have a pair of silver candlesticks inherited from my grandmother. The silver is now tarnished, any suggestions?' And every week I sit for hours on the bloody phone ringing lino manufacturers, silver-makers, and, apologizing for taking up their time, ask them for the answers.

This is my form of journalism. Every now and then I have to write a feature, usually a glorified press release, a bit of PR puff that has to be used to fill some space, and oh how I revel in this seemingly unexciting job. I pull the press release to pieces and start again. If my colleagues, the news reporters and feature writers that mill around me, bothered to read what I'd written they would see my masterful turn of phrase.

It's not as if I haven't tried to move up in the world of journalism. Every now and then when boredom threatens to render me completely incompetent, I drag myself into the editor's office and squeeze into a chair, producing these few cuts and asking for a chance. In fact today yet another meeting is due.

'Jemima,' says the editor, leaning back in his chair, putting his feet on the table and puffing on a cigar, 'why would you want to be a news reporter?'

'I don't,' I say, restraining myself from rolling my eyes, because every time I come in here we seem to have the same conversation. 'I want to write features.'

'But Jemima, you do such a wonderful job on Top Tips. Honestly, love, I don't know where we'd be without you.'

'It's just that it's not exactly journalism, I want to write more.'

'We all have to start at the bottom,' he says, the beginning of his regular monologue, as I think, yes, and you're still there, this isn't the *Guardian*, it's the *Kilburn* bloody *Herald*.

'Do you know how I started?'

I mutely shake my head, thinking, yes, you were a bloody tea boy for the *Solent Advertiser*.

6

'I was a bloody tea boy for the *Solent Advertiser*.' And on, and on, and on he goes.

The conversation ends the same way too. 'There may well be a vacancy on features coming up,' he says with a conspiratorial wink. 'Just keep on working hard and I'll see what I can do.'

And so I sigh, thank him for his time and manoeuvre myself out of the narrow chair. Just before I get to the door, the editor says, 'By the way, you are doing that course aren't you?'

I turn to look at him in confusion. Course? What course? 'You know,' he adds, seeing I don't know what he's talking about. 'Computers, Internet, World Wide Web. We're going on the line and I want everyone in the office to attend.'

On the line? Doesn't he mean online, I think as I walk out with a smile on my face. The editor, desperate to show off his street credibility, has once again proved he's still living in the 1980s.

I march back to my desk, idly wondering why he won't give me a chance. It's fine for me to do a stupid bloody computer course, but it's not fine for me to use my brain. Go figure.

I pass the news reporters, all busy on the phone, my eyes cast downwards as I pass my secret heart-throb. Ben Williams is the deputy news editor. Tall, handsome, he is also the office Lothario. He may not be able to afford Armani, this being, as it is, the *Kilburn Herald*, but his high street suits fit his highly-toned body, his muscular thighs so perfectly, they may as well be.

Ben Williams is secretly fancied by every woman at the *Kilburn Herald*, not to mention the woman in the shop where he buys his paper every morning, the woman in the sandwich bar who follows his stride longingly as he walks past every lunchtime. Yeah. Don't think I hadn't noticed.

Ben Williams is gorgeous, no two ways about it. His light brown hair is floppy in that perfectly arranged way, casually hanging over his left eye, his eyebrows perfectly arched, his dimples when he smiles in exactly the right place. Of course he is well aware of the effect he has on women, but underneath all the schmooze beats a heart of gold, but don't tell him I told you. He wouldn't want anyone to know that.

He is the perfect combination of handsome hunk and vulnerable little boy, and the only woman who isn't interested in him is Geraldine. Geraldine, you see, is destined for greater things. Geraldine is my only friend at the paper, although Geraldine might not agree with that, because after all we don't socialize together after work, but we do have little chats, Geraldine perched prettily on the edge of my desk as I silently wish I looked like her.

And we do often have lunch together, frequently with Ben Williams, which is both painful and pleasurable, in equal measure, for me. Pleasurable because I live for those days when he joins us, but painful because I turn into an awkward fourteen-year-old every time he comes near. I can't even look at him, let alone talk to him, and the only consolation is that when he sits down my appetite disappears.

I suspect he thinks I'm rather sweet, and I'm sure he knows I've got this ridiculous crush on him, but I doubt he spends much time thinking about me, not when Geraldine's around.

8

Geraldine started here at about the same time as me, and the thing that really kills me is that I started as a graduate trainee, and Geraldine started as a secretary, but who's the one who gets to write features first? Exactly.

It's not that I'm completely cynical, but with her gleaming blonde hair in a chic bob, her tiny size 10 figure squeezed into the latest fashions, Geraldine may not have an ounce of talent, but the men love her, and the editor thinks she's the biggest asset to the paper since, well, since himself.

And the thing that kills me even more is that Geraldine is the one woman here that Ben deems worthy of his attentions. Geraldine isn't interested, which makes it just about bearable. Sure, in a vaguely detached way she can appreciate Ben's good looks, his charm, his charisma, but please, he works at the *Kilburn Herald*, and by that fact alone would never be good enough for Geraldine.

Geraldine only goes out with rich men. Older, richer, wiser. Her current boyfriend has, amazingly, lasted eight months, which is a bit of a record for her, and Geraldine seems serious, which Ben can't stand. I, on the other hand, love hearing what I think of as 'Geraldine stories'. Geraldine is the woman I wish I was.

For now my feast is finished, and I settle down in my chair and pick up the phone to call the local veterinary practice.

'Hello,' I say in my brightest telephone voice. 'This is Jemima Jones from the *Kilburn Herald*. Would you have any idea how to remove the smell of cat spray from a pair of curtains?'

*

Jemima Jones pulls open the front door and immediately her heart sinks. Every day as she goes home on the bus she crosses her chubby fingers and prays her flatmates will be out, prays for some peace and quiet, a chance to be on her own.

But as soon as the door opens she hears the music blasting from the living room, the giggles that punctuate their conversation, and with sinking heart she pushes her head round the door.

'Hi,' I say to the two girls, one lying on each sofa, swapping gossip. 'Anyone fancy a cup of tea?'

'Ooh, Mimey, love one,' they both chorus, and I wince at the nickname they have taken it on themselves to bestow upon me. It's a nickname I had at school, one I tried to forget because the very mention of it, even now, brings back memories of being the fat girl in the class, the one who was bullied, the one who was always left out.

But Sophie and Lisa, in their vaguely patronizing way, continue to call me Mimey. They may not have known me at school, but they do know I hate the name because I once summoned up enough courage to tell them, but the fact that it irritates only seems to amuse them more.

Do you want to know about Sophie and Lisa? Sophie and Lisa lived in this flat long before I came on the scene, and most of the time I think they were probably far happier, except that they didn't have a permanent tea-maker in the evenings. Sophie is blonde, a chic, snappy blonde with an inviting smile and come-to-bed eyes. Lisa is brunette, long, tousled locks and a full, pouting mouth.

Meeting them for the first time you'd probably think they were perhaps fashion buyers, or something similarly glamorous, because both have perfect figures, ready smiles and wardrobes of designer clothes, but, and this is the only thing that makes me smile, the truth is far less interesting.

Sophie and Lisa are receptionists. They work together at an advertising agency, and spend their days trying to outscore one another with dates. They have both, in turn, worked through all the men in the agency, most of them eligible, some not so eligible, and now they sit behind their polished steel and beech desk, and hope for a dishy new client to walk through the door, someone to set their hearts alight, their eyelashes afluttering.

It's not unusual for them to be at home now, but it is unusual for them to be at home all evening. They arrive home at 5.30 p.m. on the dot then lounge around reading magazines, watching television, gossiping, before jumping into hot baths at 7 p.m., hair at 7.45 p.m. and make-up at 8.15 p.m.

Every night they're out the front door, dressed up to the nines, by 9 p.m. Teetering on the highest heels, they totter out, giggling together, instructing me, and I'm usually either in my room or watching television, to behave myself. Every night they seem to think this is hugely funny, and every night I want to smack them. It's not that I dislike them, they're just completely inconsequential, a couple of chattering budgerigars who constantly amaze me with their stupidity.

Off they go to Mortons, Tramp, Embargo. Anonymous

places where they pick up anonymous men, who might, if they're lucky, wine, dine and drive them around in Ferraris before disappearing off into the night.

Don't be ridiculous, of course I don't go with them, but, as contemptuous as I am of their lifestyles, a part of me, just a tiny part, would love to have a taste of it too.

But it's not worth even thinking about. They are thin and beautiful, and I am not. I would never dare suggest going along, and they would never dare ask me. Not that they are nasty, you understand, underneath the glitz and glamour they're nice girls, but a girl has to keep up appearances, and fat friends, I'm afraid, do not come into the equation.

Their diet, such as it is, seems to consist of bottles of champagne fuelled by lines of cocaine provided by the men they meet. The fridge at home is always empty, unless I've been shopping, and in the eight months I've lived here I have never seen them eat a proper meal.

Occasionally I've seen one of them come in announcing 'I'm starving!', and then Sophie, or Lisa, will pull open the door of the fridge and walk into the living room munching on a tomato, or half a slice of pitta bread with a hint of pink – the thinnest spreading of taramasalata I've ever seen.

You doubtless think we make an odd trio. You're probably right. The Italian man in the deli at the end of the road was flabbergasted to discover we lived together. The two beauties he flirts with at every opportunity, and the sad, overweight girl who probably reminds him of his fat mother always dressed in black.

But Mr Galizzi has got it wrong, because for all my

faults I'm not sad. Miserable a lot of the time, yes, but those who bother to get under the layers of fat know that not only does there beat a heart of gold, I'm also bloody good fun to be around, providing I'm in the right mood. But nobody really bothers to look for that, nobody really bothers to look beneath the surface appearance.

I stand in the kitchen, dropping three teabags into three oversized Habitat mugs. I pour in the water, add semi-skimmed from the fridge, and out of habit drop in two heaped teaspoons of powdered sweetener for myself. Good girl, I tell myself, good girl for resisting the sugar, nestling quietly yet ominously in the cupboard above the kettle.

I bring the tea into the living room, and Sophie and Lisa cry their thanks, but the lazy cows don't move from the sofas, don't clear a space for me to sit down, so what else can I do but hover in the doorway, clasping my burning hot mug and wondering how soon I can go up to my room.

'How was today?' I eventually venture, as the girls stare at the television set, some American sit-com featuring perfect-looking people with perfect white teeth and perfect figures.

'Hmm?' says Sophie, eyes never leaving the screen, even while I sip my tea.

'We're in love,' offers Lisa, looking at me for the first time this evening. 'We've got the most amazing new client.'

Now Sophie looks interested, and I lower myself to the floor, sitting cross-legged and awkwardly in my role as agony aunt.

'Honestly, Mimey, this guy *was* gorgeous, but we don't know which one of us he fancies.'

Sophie shoots a fake filthy look at Lisa, who smiles broadly.

'He definitely fancied one of you then?' I don't really need to ask the question, because who, after all, would not fancy one of these beautiful girls at first sight?

'Oh yes,' said Lisa. 'After his meeting he stood at the reception desk for ages chatting.'

'I think he was chatting up Lisa,' says Sophie.

'No,' says Lisa. 'Don't be ridiculous, sweetie. He was interested in you.' But it's completely bloody obvious she doesn't mean it, and even I can see that he was mesmerized by Lisa's pouting lips and tumbling, just-out-of-bed locks.

'So did he ask you out?' I ask, wishing for a fleeting second that some handsome stranger would stop at my desk and chat me up. Just once. Just to see what it feels like.

'No,' Lisa says ruefully. 'But he did ask if we'd both be there next week when he comes in for a meeting.'

'We were sitting here before, planning what to wear,' says Sophie, turning to Lisa, 'so, what about the red suit?'

'I'm just going upstairs,' I say, feeling well and truly left out as I heave myself to my feet and edge out the door. I'm no longer needed, the courtesies of greeting have been dealt with, and I would never be asked an opinion on clothes, because as far as Sophie and Lisa are aware I haven't got a clue.

I climb slowly upstairs, stopping at the top to catch my breath, walk into my bedroom and lie on the bed, staring at the ceiling, until my breathing becomes slower, more regular.

I lie there and spin out an elaborate fantasy about what I would wear if I were thin. I would have my hair cut into a super-trendy shaggy style, and perhaps, if I dared, would have a few blonde highlights, just at the front.

I would wear sunglasses a lot of the time. Occasionally they would be big Hollywood film-star tortoiseshell ones, but the rest of the time they would be cool, smart little round glasses, glasses that spelt sophistication, glamour.

I would wear tight cream trousers, lycra crop tops, and the bits of flesh exposed would be taut and tanned. I would, I decide, even look fantastic in a bathrobe. I look at my old white bathrobe hanging on the back of the door, huge, voluminous. I love wrapping it around myself for comfort, trying desperately to ignore the fact that I resemble a balloon with legs.

But when I'm slim I'll keep that bathrobe. It will, being a man's bathrobe, gather in folds of fabric around my athletic new body. The sleeves will hang down, obscuring my hands, and I will look cute and vulnerable.

Even first thing in the morning I will look gorgeous. With no make-up and tousled hair, I imagine meeting Mr Perfect, and curling up in an armchair with the bathrobe wrapped around me, exposing just my long, glowing legs, my bony knees, and naturally he will be head over heels in love with me.

I think about this for a while, and then I remember my magazine. I draw it out of my bag and once again study the pictures, reaching into my bedside drawer to pull out the scissors and add the latest models to my collection.

And as I put the scissors back I notice, at the very back of the drawer, a packet of biscuits. My God! I actually forgot about them, I actually forgot about food in the house.

No. I won't. I'm being good now. But then surely it's better to eat them, make them disappear, so there's no more bad food in the house. Surely it's better to finish them in one go than to eat them slowly and steadily over the course of a week. That way there won't be any left after tonight, and then I can really start my diet. The one that's going to work. The one that's going to fulfil my fantasies.

Yes, I'll eat them now and start again tomorrow.

And this is how we leave Jemima Jones for the evening, just as we leave her every evening. Sitting on her single bed in her afterthought of a room, gazing at magazines and cramming a packet of biscuits into her mouth.

CHAPTER TWO

Can somebody turn the sunshine off? It's shining directly in my eyes as I roll over in bed and groan. I can't get up yet, it's so warm, so comfortable, so I just lie here for a few minutes, waiting for the tinny pop music to start playing from my radio alarm clock, and I wish, oh God how I wish, that I could stay in bed for ever.

Look, Jemima, see how when you roll over on your back your stomach feels, well, not quite flat, but certainly not fat. See how your breasts roll over to either side, giving the distinct illusion of a vast expanse of flatness in the middle.

Jemima lies there and rubs her stomach, half affectionately, half repellently, for there is something innately comforting in the bulk that is her body. But then she rolls over to her side, and tries to forget her stomach weighing down, sinking into the mattress. She tucks the duvet in tightly around her and wishes she never had to get up.

But today is the course day. Today is the day she is, as the editor put it, going 'on the line'. And, much as she is looking forward to the course, for her brain, being active and large, is constantly on the look-out for new information, she cannot help but feel more than a little anxious because she will be breaking her daily routine.

From Monday to Friday Jemima's routine is as follows: she wakes up at 8.45 a.m., lies in bed and listens to Sophie and Lisa getting ready for work. Listens to the door slam as they clatter up the path at 9 a.m., and then hauls herself out of bed.

Avoids the mirror in the bathroom, for it is full length and she really does not want to see herself in all her glory. Starts running a bath, and pours at least five capfuls of bubble bath in to hide her flesh.

While the bath is running, goes to the kitchen and pours herself a bowl of cereal. Healthy cereal. Slimming cereal. (Except you're not supposed to have quite as much as that, Jemima, the bowl is not supposed to be so full the cereal is slopping out over the sides.)

Jemima eats the cereal in a hurry, comes back upstairs for the bath. Heads back to the bedroom and gets dressed, and only then, when she's covered in the comfort of her clothes, does she look in the mirror and quite like what she sees. She likes her intelligent green eyes, and she applies the tiniest bit of eyeliner and mascara, just to accentuate them.

She likes her full pouting lips. But they tend to disappear in the round moon-ness of her face, so she paints them pale pink.

She likes her glossy hair, and she brushes and brushes until it gleams back at her in the glass. She preens in the mirror, pouting her lips, sucking in her cheeks, pushing her neck forward until her chins almost, almost, disappear.

I could be beautiful, she tells herself every morning. If I lost weight I would be beautiful. And as she looks in the mirror she tells herself firmly that today is the start of the rest of her life. Today is the start of her new diet.

And what happens next, Jemima?

Feeling virtuous, positive, excited at the prospect of your new life, you leave your flat at 9.25 a.m. and catch the bus to work. You stand at the bus-stop with the same people you see every day and you don't say a word to them, nor they to you.

You find a seat on its own, and sit there, your thighs spreading on to the seat next to you, and you pray that no one will sit beside you, forcing you to hold your breath, squeeze in your thighs, suppress your resentment at their audacity.

And then you alight at the corner of Kilburn High Road, a short walk from your office, and every morning as you walk up the road, just as you pass the shoe shop with its window display of rather nasty shoes, your nostrils start quivering.

There is nothing in the world quite like the smell of bacon frying, I'm sure you will agree. Together with dill, fresh lavender and Chanel No. 5, it is one of Jemima's favourite smells. If it simply remained a favourite smell then all would be fine, but Jemima's nostrils are stronger than her will-power.

Your steps become slower as you approach the working man's caff, and with each step the picture of a bacon sandwich, rashers of greasy bacon, awash with fat, oozing out of thick white sliced, becomes so vivid you can almost taste it.

Every morning you battle with yourself, Jemima. You tell yourself that today you started your diet, but the smell becomes too much to bear, and every morning you find yourself queuing at the counter and requesting two bacon sandwiches.

'He likes his bacon sandwich doesn't he, love?' says the woman behind the counter, a woman called Marge whom Jemima Jones has got to know. Once upon a long time ago Jemima told Marge the bacon sandwiches were for her boss.

Poor lass, thought Marge, *I know* they're for her. But Marge, being a kind-hearted soul, pretends to believe her.

'Lovely day,' says Marge, handing the sandwiches to Jemima, who tucks them in her bag, continuing the charade, before walking up the street. A few yards away the bacon sandwiches start calling you.

'Jemima,' they whisper from the depths of your bag. 'We're lovely and greasy, Jemima. Feel us. Taste us. Now.' And you plunge your hand in, the craving fast overtaking any anxiety about eating in public, and in one, two, three, four bites the sandwiches have gone.

And then to the office, wiping your mouth with your sleeve and stopping at the newsagent to buy some sugar-free mints to hide the smell of bacon.

Your mornings are spent sorting out letters, and watching the clock until 11.30 a.m., when it is time for tea. 'I'm starving,' you say to Alison, the secretary who sits opposite you. 'I haven't had breakfast,' and it is your way of apology for the egg and bacon sandwich you bring up from the canteen together with a cup of tea and three sweeteners.

And then at 1 p.m., every day, you head back down to the canteen for lunch. A salad is what you have, every day, except the salads you choose from the salad bar are as fattening as a cream cake.

Coleslaw, rice salad, pasta salad, slabs of cheese and potato salad swimming in mayonnaise, you pile them on your plate and tell yourself you are being healthy. A wholemeal roll, covered in two slabs of butter, completes your meal, except you are not really full. You are never really full.

The afternoon is spent writing up your Top Tips, before nipping down again at teatime. Sometimes you have a cake, sometimes crisps, sometimes biscuits, and occasionally, well, around twice a week, you have another sandwich.

And finally at 6 p.m. your day is over. Waiting for the bus home, you nip into the newsagent and buy a couple of bars of chocolate to sustain you on the journey, and then that familiar feeling of dread pours over you as you approach your house, and your two perfect flatmates.

And your evenings blend together into one. Alone again, a blessed relief as Sophie and Lisa are out partying, you eat your evenings into oblivion. You watch television, game shows, sit-coms, documentaries. There are few with such eclectic tastes as you, Jemima, and few with your knowledge.

Or you might read, for you have hundreds of books to quench that thirst for knowledge. And a lot of the time you spend lying on your bed, daydreaming about romance, which is something you have little experience of.

Don't misunderstand me, Jemima isn't a virgin, but her virginity was lost during a quick tumble in the dark with a boy who was so inconsequential he may as well stay anonymous.

And since then she has had the odd fling with men

who have a penchant for the larger lady. But she has never really enjoyed sex, has never tasted the pleasures of making love, but that doesn't stop a girl from dreaming does it?

But today, the day of the course, the day of learning how to surf the World Wide Web, is a break from that routine, and Jemima Jones hates breaking her routine. No bacon sandwiches for Jemima this morning, because the course is in the West End, many miles away from her familiar caff.

But at least she will not have to go on her own, because Geraldine, Geraldine of the perfect figure and rich boy-friend, will be picking her up.

'I'm not getting the bloody tube,' said Geraldine yes-terday afternoon, when I asked how she was getting to the course.

'I've got a perfectly good car,' she added, fully aware that the entire office was envious of her shining new black BMW, the car paid for partly by her boyfriend and partly by her parents, although she doesn't tell people about the parents' contribution. She only told me because I wouldn't let the subject drop and eventually she had to admit it.

'What about you?' she asked. 'Why don't we go together?' I couldn't believe it, going to the course with Geraldine! Walking in with someone else, for once not being on my own. 'Are you sure?' I asked. 'You wouldn't mind?' Because why would Geraldine want to befriend someone like me? It's not that I dislike her – she, after all, is one of the few to have always treated me like a human being – it's just that I can't help but be intimidated by her perfection.

''Course not,' said Geraldine. 'The damn thing doesn't start until 10.30, so I'll pick you up at 10. How does that sound?'

It sounded fantastic, and here I am now, sitting in the living room flicking through the pages of a book on container gardening but not really looking at the pictures, just waiting for the hum of Geraldine's car.

There is no hum, there are two short beeps of the horn, and pulling the curtain aside I can just about see Geraldine's elbow resting on the door-frame as she taps her fingers to the music I assume she must be playing.

Geraldine and her car go together like apples and honey. They're both sleek, chic, with glossy exteriors and purring engines. Geraldine, as usual, has done herself proud. She's wearing a beautifully cut navy suit, the jacket just skimming her thighs, the lapels showing off a white silk T-shirt. On her head is a pair of large black sunglasses, keeping her highlights off her face, and she's holding a cigarette langurously, sexily, out of the window.

I feel like an ungainly oaf next to Geraldine, so I lumber into her car and just as I put the seat belt on – Geraldine, incidentally, isn't wearing one – she offers me a cigarette, which I take. You didn't know I smoked? Of course I smoke because way back when, in the murky teenage years, all the cool people smoked, and even then I wanted so badly to be cool.

Now admittedly, more often than not it's a pain in the arse because everywhere I go I'm surrounded by virulent anti-smokers, but it still makes me feel, well, not quite cool, but certainly less awkward.

My first cigarette was in the back row of a cinema, in the days when everyone was allowed to smoke in the back row. I was fourteen years old, with a group of girls and boys from school, and, although I never really fitted in, they didn't care if I tagged along because they thought I was 'a good laugh'.

Naturally I was never fancied, but I was always able to put a smile on their faces, and so I became one of the gang. And in the back row of that cinema, while the others kissed loudly and longingly, at that stage not quite aware of what desire feels like but desperate to emulate it anyway (that knowledge came with hindsight, none of us knew that at the time), I sat and smoked.

I remember unwrapping my pack of ten Silk Cut, the first pack of cigarettes I'd ever bought, and drawing out my first ever cigarette. I lit it with a match and sat back to watch the film, feeling impossibly cool and grown up.

'You're smoking!' said one of my friends loudly, in both horror and respect, and all the others stopped kissing and turned to watch me.

'So?' I said, puffing away on my cigarette, holding the smoke in my mouth then releasing it in one big gasp.

'So, where d'you get them?'

'I bought them, dumbass.'

'But you don't smoke.'

'I do now.' I carried on puffing, painfully aware that six sets of eyes were watching my every move.

'You're not inhaling!' said one of the boys, loudly

enough for an older woman sitting in front of us to turn around, a look of anger on her face, and say, 'Ssshhh!'

'Ssshhh! Ssshhh! Ssshhh!' my friends echoed, falling about with laughter, while I felt slightly sorry for the woman, who did, after all, want to watch the film.

'But you're *not* doing it properly,' he insisted. 'My mum smokes and it only comes out in a puff of smoke when you don't inhale. I bet you can't blow it out through your nose.'

I tried, and failed, I snorted but nothing happened.

'See, told you. You can't inhale.'

'I bloody can,' I said, and, in a gesture I had seen hundreds of times on television, sucked the smoke into my mouth and breathed in. The smoke filled my lungs, a burning, acrid smoke, and almost instantly I started to feel dizzy. But see how cool I am! See how sophisticated I look! I exhaled the smoke in a long, slow stream from my nostrils, and turned to my friends with a smile.

'Who says I can't inhale?' The others were too impressed to speak, and I finished my cigarette, feeling more and more dizzy and nauseous. Deep breaths, I told myself, deep breaths. I. Am. Not. Going. To. Be. Sick. And I wasn't. Not until later, anyway.

But amazingly enough that didn't stop me. For years cigarettes made me feel sick but it didn't stop me. And now, after years of practice, cigarettes have stopped making me feel sick, and they have become a habit, an addiction that, much like food, is proving impossible for me to break.

Sitting here in Geraldine's car, when I compare Geraldine's seductive long drags to my short ones, I feel all wrong smoking. I look awkward, awkward fingers grasping the cigarette, exhaling all too quickly. I still, unfortunately, look like a fourteen-year-old trying out her first cigarette.

'So how's everything at work?' says Geraldine, flicking the butt out the window and checking in the rear-view mirror that her lipstick is still perfectly applied.

'Same really,' I say with a shrug. 'I went to see the editor again and surprise surprise, there aren't any vacancies at the moment.'

'Oh poor you,' says Geraldine, but I think she's probably relieved. Geraldine knows I can write, Geraldine wouldn't be anywhere if it weren't for me because whenever she has a deadline I'm the one she comes running to asking for help. At least once a week I sit in front of my computer reading Geraldine's haphazard copy, before ripping it apart and putting it back together again so it makes sense.

And I don't mind, really, I don't, and perhaps in a strange way this is why, sitting in her car, I'm feeling less bad, less intimidated by her, and I'm starting genuinely to like her. And perhaps it's also because I know, beyond a shadow of a doubt, that when it comes to words I am infinitely more talented than Geraldine, however slim and beautiful she may be.

For if I were promoted, who would help Geraldine?

'Oh well,' she continues, 'never mind. Your time will come.' She lifts her hand and puts her sunglasses on, groaning. 'God, what a hangover.'

I look at her in amazement, for Geraldine obviously does not know the meaning of the word. A hangover means bloodshot eyes, pale skin with a hint of grey, lank hair, deep shadows under the eyes. Geraldine, as she always does, looks perfect.

A gurgle of laughter emerges from my mouth. 'Do you ever look anything less than perfect, Geraldine?'

Geraldine flicks her hair back and says, 'Believe me, I look a mess,' but she's pleased because, like all girls who are perfectly groomed, below the perfection is a writhing mass of insecurity, and she likes to hear that she's beautiful. It helps her to believe it.

'So what happened last night?'

'Oh God,' Geraldine groans. 'Dimitri took me out for dinner and I drank so much champagne I was positively comatose.'

'Where did you go?'

'The Collection.'

'I haven't been there yet,' I say, knowing full bloody well that I'll probably never go there, being, as it is, a restaurant for the rich and the beautiful, but I know all about it. I know about the bright young things from the magazines who go there, and I know about it from Sophie and Lisa, who naturally have been wined, dined and seduced in both the bar downstairs and the restaurant above.

'I suppose it was filled with the famous and beautiful?'

'Actually,' says Geraldine, 'actually, it was filled with lots of people who looked as if they ought to be famous, except neither of us knew who anyone was.'

'Bloody wannabees,' I say with a deep sigh. 'They're just everywhere these days,' and we both laugh.

Geraldine suddenly turns right and pulls up outside a large mansion block. 'Sorry,' she says, turning to me.

'Ben Williams was bugging me for a lift so I said we'd come and get him. You don't mind do you?'

'No,' I say, heart suddenly pounding. 'I didn't know he lived here.'

'Me neither until he gave me his address yesterday, but even a rat must have a home.'

'Who does he live with?'

'Two other guys, apparently. God, can you imagine what their flat is like?'

'Ugh,' I say, even though I haven't got a bloody clue. Me? How the hell would I know what a bachelor pad is like, but then again I've watched *Men Behaving Badly* and even I can pretend. 'Stinking socks draped over all the radiators.'

'Porn mags piled up in the corridor,' Geraldine says, grimacing.

'Sheets that haven't seen a washing machine in six months.'

'Piles of filthy washing-up overflowing the sink.' We both clutch our stomachs and Geraldine makes gagging noises. I laugh, but suddenly I see Ben running out the front door and the laughter stops as my stomach does its usual lurch on sight of this gorgeous man.

'Make him sit in the back,' whispers Geraldine. 'I don't want to sit next to him.'

So Ben walks over to the car and I climb out, trying to be dainty, delicate, feminine. 'Morning girls,' he says, 'both looking particularly lovely today.' He doesn't mean me, he's just being polite, so I stand awkwardly on the pavement and Ben looks at me patiently, waiting for me to climb in the back.

'Ben,' shouts Geraldine from the driver's seat. 'You don't mind getting in the back do you?'

'Oh,' says Ben. After a pause, in which I wish more than anything in the world that the ground would open and swallow me up, he says, 'Sure.' And in a swift and graceful movement he climbs in.

I buckle up my seat belt while Ben leans forward, resting his arms on either seat in front. 'So girls,' he says, as Geraldine pulls out. 'Good night last night?'

'Yes, thanks,' says Geraldine, while I stay quiet.

'What did you do?'

Geraldine tells him, and I start playing this little game I play a lot of the time. I do it when I'm in a car and we pull up to traffic lights. If the light stays green until we pass, then I will find true love. Sometimes I add within the next six months. I don't know why I carry on playing it, as it never comes true, but I do it again now. I think, if you ask me what I did last night, then it means that we will end up together. Please ask me, Ben. Please. But then if he does ask me, what will I say? That I stayed at home and ate chocolate biscuits? Oh God, how can I make myself sound interesting.

'What about you, Jemima?' Oh Christ. The question's out there before I've formulated an answer.

'Oh, I went to a party.'

'Did you?' Ben and Geraldine ask the question simultaneously.

'You didn't mention that,' says Geraldine. 'Whose party?'

Quick, quick. Think, Jemima.

'Just an old friend.'

'Wild night, eh Jemima?' says Ben with a wink.

'Yup,' I say finally, deciding to throw caution to the wind. 'I got very drunk, slightly stoned and ended up shagging some guy in the toilet.'

A silence descends on the car, neither Ben nor Geraldine knows quite what to say, and I feel sick. I know I've said the wrong thing. It doesn't come out as funny as I had intended, it comes out as peculiar, so I take a deep breath and tell the truth. Well. Sort of. 'Actually, I'm lying. I stayed in and watched *World in Action*.'

Ben and Geraldine get the joke and they laugh. Except unfortunately, at least if you're sitting where Jemima Jones is sitting right now, it really isn't very funny. It's actually rather sad.

CHAPTER THREE

I'd heard about the Internet, read about the Internet, talked about the Internet, but I never really understood what it was all about, and even Ben's presence doesn't distract me from the computer screen where we're being shown how to use the World Wide Web.

And it's fascinating. I never thought I'd be able to grasp it, but Rob, the man who's taking the course, is explaining so clearly, so concisely, that I'm beginning to understand exactly what the big deal's all about.

I can see that Geraldine's bored, and to amuse herself she's flirting with Rob, who seems delighted that someone like Geraldine would even look at him, but Ben's my ally in this, Ben's as enthralled as me, and together we're visiting newsgroups, sites, forums.

Rob shows us how to create a page, and explains that this is the Web: that all over the world people are designing pages filled with whatever information and pictures they choose, and from those pages there are links to hundreds, often thousands, of other pages.

He shows us how to search for a topic, and then how to follow those links until we find what we're looking for, and it's like a completely new world opening up for me.

And as the day carries on, the more we learn, the more I start to relax with Ben, the less he seems to intimidate me, maybe because we've got something in common now, I don't have to struggle for something to say.

At 5 p.m. Rob says we're done, and I catch Geraldine's eye as she rolls it to the ceiling. The three of us walk out together, and as soon as we're out the door Geraldine digs into her Prada bag and pulls out her cigarettes.

'God, I needed that,' she says, inhaling deeply as we stand on the corner. 'That was the most boring thing in the world. I knew most of it, for God's sake. Talk about Internet for idiots.'

'I thought it was really interesting, actually,' says Ben. 'What did you think?' He turns to me and I nod vigorously, because I would agree with Ben no matter what I thought, and it's just a happy coincidence that I happen to feel the same way.

'I loved it,' I say. 'I still can't get my head round it.'

'I know,' echoes Ben, 'there's so much it's almost impossible to take it all in.'

'Oh shut up you two,' says Geraldine, as a little glow lights up inside me because, stupid as it may be, she has linked me with Ben. 'Look,' she says, gesturing up the road. 'There's a really nice bar up here. If you promise not to talk computers all night, why don't we go for a drink?'

Who? Ben? Me? Both of us? She was looking up the road as she said it and I just stand there in silence because she can't mean me, she wouldn't want to have a drink, socialize *after work*, with me. Surely?

'Good idea,' says Ben, and they start walking off while I stand there feeling like an idiot, unsure of what to do.

'Jemima?' says Geraldine, turning round. 'Come on,' and I almost want to kiss her as I race to catch up.

CHAPTER FOUR

Drug addiction; food addiction; alcohol addiction; cigarette addiction. The funny thing is no one ever talks about Internet addiction.

But Internet addiction is the scourge of the nineties. All over the world men and women are going to bed on their own, curling up miserably while their partners lock themselves away in their studies and tap, tap, tap away into the early hours of the morning.

The Internet is another world, where people can be anyone they want, and, even as you read these words, marriages are disintegrating through lack of communication, thanks to a little coloured screen tucked away in a corner of the house.

But of course Jemima Jones knows nothing of this. Jemima Jones doesn't have to worry about partners getting pissed off, or miserable marriages, or even yet another addiction to add to her list.

All Jemima knows, right now as she's on her way home from work, is that the Internet seems like fun, and she can discover all she wants about cleaning silver, fraying curtains, removing cat spray smells, just by tapping a few keys.

And what's even more exciting is that the information she receives could be coming from anywhere in the entire world. She walks along the pavement, lost in thoughts about the Internet, so deeply immersed that before she knows it she's at her front door, and guess what? She completely forgot to buy some chocolate on the way home.

Good girl, Jemima. *Well* done. Today is the day of the first diet that's actually going to work. I'm going to really try this time. No chocolate!

I walk upstairs and can already hear Sophie and Lisa giggling away in Sophie's bedroom as I tentatively push open the door.

Lisa's lying back on the bed, clutching her pillow. 'I'm in love,' she sighs as I walk in. Oh shut up, I think, but I don't say that. I say, 'Let me guess. A new guy started at work and he's devastatingly handsome and he wants to marry you?'

'No, don't be daft. It's the guy we met last week, the new client. He asked Lisa out.' Sophie's trying to look pleased, but envy is written all over her face. I don't believe that stuff about blondes being stupid, at least I didn't before I met Sophie, but I know that she believes blondes ought to have more fun, and she can't believe this guy went for Lisa.

'His name's Nick Hanson, he's thirty-three, single and I love him,' sighs Lisa dreamily. 'Lisa Hanson. What do you think? Mrs Nick Hanson, Mrs Lisa Hanson.'

'I think you might be jumping the gun a bit.' I'm not bitter, I promise you, it's just that I've seen this so many times before and I know exactly what will happen. At the end of their first date Lisa will come home and will spend the evening sketching wedding dresses and drawing up guest lists.

'So when are you going out?'

'Tomorrow night. Oh God, I love him, he's the most divine man I've met in ages.'

I sit down on the bed, something I'd never normally do, but I didn't see Sophie and Lisa last night, and yesterday something actually happened. I have something to talk about. Or perhaps I should say *someone*.

'I did my course yesterday. The Internet one.'

'Great,' says Lisa.

'Really?' says Sophie. 'That's funny, I was just reading about the Internet in one of my magazines. Did you know that loads of people are dating on the Internet?'

No, I didn't know, and quite frankly I don't really care, but at least Sophie's showing a vague interest, so I encourage her.

'What was the article about?' I say.

'Honestly, it sounds amazing. You go to these dating places and there are pictures of single people, and you can write to each other, e-mail over the computer. But people are meeting from all over the world. There have even been marriages because of it.'

Lisa sits up and looks at Sophie. 'Yes, but you wouldn't think of doing it would you?'

'I don't know really,' says Sophie. 'I mean, I don't think I'd ever be able to work out how to use it, but it sounds quite exciting. You could pick up a gorgeous American hunk and live happily ever after in his mansion in Dallas.'

'Sounds a bit sad to me,' says Lisa.

'Well,' says Sophie, turning to me. 'Did you learn how to meet people on the Internet then?'

'Not really, it wasn't that sort of course, but it's amazingly interesting, you can find out pretty much anything.

And afterwards I went for a drink, that's why I wasn't home last night.'

I'm so desperate to tell someone, anyone, about Ben Williams, I'm practically bursting.

Are you sure you can't hold it in any more, Jemima? Go on then, tell them all about it.

'Who with?'

I can see I've got them, they want to know and I don't blame them. I mean, it's not often I talk about my social life, probably because I don't exactly have what you'd call a social life, and they can see that something's happened.

'With Geraldine,' I pause. 'And Ben.'

'Who's Ben?' Naturally they don't know, because up until now my crush has been secret, but I have to tell someone, and far better to tell Sophie and Lisa, who would never meet him, than to confide in, say, Geraldine.

'The deputy news editor at work.'

'And???'

'And . . .' Should I tell them? Should I keep it secret? Oh, what the hell. 'And I think he's completely wonderful.' There. A deep breath. It's out there. No going back.

Sophie and Lisa sit in shocked silence. I've never talked about men before, and as I watch them I can see their eyes glaze over as they imagine what this Ben looks like, and I can see they've got it completely wrong.

*

Jemima Jones is absolutely right, they have got it completely wrong.

Lisa thinks he is probably 5'7", has messy brown hair, thick glasses, and dresses in ill-fitting suits in shades of brown. She thinks he is the type of man who would still live at home, and his idea of an exciting night out is probably going to the movies to see subtitled films.

Sophie thinks he is probably 5'7" tall, and 4'6" wide. She thinks he has to be overweight, incredibly dull, and a complete computer nerd. She suspects that his idea of an exciting night is spent down at the pub drinking pints of lager with his nerdy friends.

If only they knew.

For Ben Williams is the sort of man that both Sophie and Lisa would fall head over heels in love with. Little do any of them know, including Geraldine, that Ben has a golden future ahead of him. That his post at the *Kilburn Herald* is merely a stepping stone to the heady world of television presenting. That he will start as a reporter on the news, and will graduate within a frighteningly short space of time to anchorman, by virtue of his dimples and white teeth. That every woman in the country, including Sophie and Lisa, will, at some point in the not too distant future, go to bed dreaming about meeting Benjamin Williams, because by then, naturally, he will be Benjamin, an air of gravitas attached to his devastating good looks and little boy vulnerability.

'So come on then, what's he like?'

Now it's my turn to sigh. 'He's very funny, he makes

me laugh. And he's bright, and charming, and he knows how to treat women.'

'But what does he look like?'

'I don't know how to describe him, really. He's about 6'2".' Sophie and Lisa catch one another's eyes and each suppresses a smile, and I know they think I'm lying. So what? I carry on. 'He's got dark brown hair, and beautiful eyes, but I'm not sure what colour they are. Green maybe?' Yup, thinks Lisa, looking again at Sophie, she's describing some model she's seen in one of her magazines.

'And he's got these amazing dimples when he smiles,' I conclude, smiling happily at the very thought of Ben Williams.

'And does he like you?' ask Sophie, gently, patronizingly, because she doesn't want to hurt me by telling me she knows I'm lying, so she'll humour me. Silly cow.

'No,' I say wearily. 'I mean, he likes me, but he doesn't *like* me. He likes Geraldine, but she doesn't like him.'

'Well maybe that can grow, him liking you, I mean,' says Sophie. 'When he gets to know you he'll realize what a lovely person you are.' She stops suddenly, aware of what she's just said. 'Not that he wouldn't be attracted to you anyway,' she stammers. 'You've got the most beautiful face.'

I can't believe Sophie doesn't see how transparent she is. I know exactly what she thinks of me. She thinks I am huge, vast, the fattest girl she's ever met, and I don't blame her. When I look in the mirror, if I look beyond my face, I see exactly the same thing.

'I haven't,' I say, for what else could I say? 'He'd *never* fancy me, but I can dream.'

38

'So what about Geraldine?' asks Lisa. 'If he's so gorgeous, how come she doesn't fancy him?'

'He's probably not rich enough for her,' says Sophie, who has come out with this uncharacteristically bitchy comment because she is jealous of Geraldine. She has never actually met Geraldine, but she has seen her on the rare occasions that Geraldine has come to pick me up or drop me off. She's never said anything directly to me but I know she has seen Geraldine's air of confidence, her BMW, and she is as jealous as hell.

'That's not really fair,' I say, although it happens to be true, and I feel guilty at talking about Geraldine, the one person whom I could perhaps call a friend, so I add, 'Geraldine's a lovely person when you get to know her.'

'Hmm,' says Sophie. 'Anyway, you never know. Maybe he's sitting in his flatmate's bedroom at this very moment telling his flatmate all about you.'

As it happens, at this very moment Ben Williams is watching the news. He's sitting on his black leather and chrome sofa, feet up on the glass coffee table which is covered with magazines, newspapers, an overflowing ashtray, a few empty cans of Heineken and bits of torn-up Rizla packets. He's drinking a beer, but not Heineken, those belong to his flatmates. He's drinking Budweiser Budvar, the original, and he's studying the news.

When the reports start he pulls his feet off the coffee table and leans forward, elbows on his knees, dangling the bottle of beer idly between his legs, but his eyes are fixed on the television screen, and as the reporter speaks, so Ben mimics him, over and over again, until Ben's voice is almost indistinguishable from the reporter's.

'Until late last year, this derelict building in one of London's more fashionable districts was ignored by the council, and the surrounding residents in this leafy street,' said the reporter. Said Ben.

'This is Jeremy Millston for the *Six o'Clock News*,' ends the reporter, as the cameras switch back to the news studio.

'This is Benjamin Williams for the *Six o'Clock News*,' echoes Ben, standing up to turn off the television. Perfect. All the inflections in exactly the right places. He checks his watch, and wanders into the kitchen to get another beer, he won't be meeting his flatmates at the pub for another half hour.

Ben takes his beer into the bedroom and fishes under the bed, pulling out a large box stuffed with papers. Oh I'm sorry, you want to know what Ben's bedroom is like? Well, not what you expect, for starters. Geraldine and Jemima may have been right about the rest of the flat, the socks draped over radiators and the porn mags piled up in the living room, but Ben's bedroom is his haven, his sanctuary, and a quick look around may tell us exactly what we need to know about Ben Williams.

It may be a rented flat, but Ben and his flatmates were given permission to redecorate. Needless to say they haven't done a thing, except for Ben. Ben has painted his bedroom walls a dark bottle-green. His blind is navy, green and burgundy check, and his duvet cover and pillow cases match.

Dotted around the wall are original cartoons, which Ben collects. A number of the cartoons on his wall have appeared in national newspapers, and all are of a satirical nature. Before you ask, Ben doesn't have the money to afford this, not yet, but he is careful with the small amount he does earn, and half the cartoons were bought from his savings, the rest gifts from his parents.

An old armchair, picked up by Ben for £20 in the junk shop down the road, sits in one corner of the room, facing an old French cherrywood table, also from the junk shop, a bargain at £50. Piled on top of the table are books. Autobiographies, biographies, cook books – for Ben loves to cook – fiction, non-fiction. The latest titles, together with some old favourites, are in this corner of the room.

Next to the books is a silver photo frame containing a picture of Ben smiling happily with his parents on graduation day. He is proudly wearing his gown and mortar-board, and a quick glance at his parents shows us where Ben got his looks.

His mother is tall, slim and *soignée*. She is wearing a slim cream skirt, a navy jacket and high cream shoes with a navy toe. On her head is a hat, a designer hat, a hat that most women dream of owning. Ben's father is significantly older than his wife. Tall, handsome, with thick grey hair. All three are beaming into the camera with shining smiles and open faces. They look like a nice family. They are in fact a delightful family.

Ben's father is a wealthy businessman and his mother is a housewife. Being an only child, Ben has been doted upon, but he has always insisted on making his own way in the world. After university Ben turned down his father's offer to work in the family business, and joined the local paper as a junior reporter on a pittance.

He rented a hovel of a flat, far far worse than this one, and lived with five other boys in similar situations. He allowed his parents to provide the odd treat, such as a beautiful watch on his birthday, or a pair of cufflinks, or a suit, but on the whole he paid his own way.

Ben Williams loves his parents and his parents love him. They are a normal, healthy family. The only thing that is slightly abnormal is perhaps how well they all get on. Because Ben's parents have always treated him as an equal. Even when he was a child his parents would stop to listen to what Ben had to say. He was never patronized or ignored, but listened to and related to as an adult. His father now makes the odd offer to come and work in the family business, because his father does not understand the media world at all, but Ben has nearly got where he wanted, and he knows this is the right thing for him to be doing.

Oh Geraldine, if only you knew about Ben's background. You would discover he is, or at least his family is, wealthy enough even for your *nouveau riche* tastes. But you can't help but judge the superficial, and you will only see as far as Ben's beaten-up Fiat Panda.

So back to Ben's bedroom. In the recesses next to his bed he has put up pine shelves, and stained them to remove that orangey patina that looks so cheap. He sanded down the shelves himself, then bashed them a bit with a hammer to make them look old before rubbing in the stain with wads of cotton wool.

And on the shelves are more books, more photographs.

Books piled high, almost overflowing, and photographs of Ben's friends, former girlfriends, lovers.

Look, there's Ben at university with Suzie, the girl he went out with for the best part of his three years there. She's not classically beautiful, not model material, but see how pretty she is, how her skin glows, how white are her teeth, how glossy her long auburn hair.

And there's Ben with Richard, his best friend. The pair of them on holiday, Greece perhaps, sun-tanned faces, shorts and T-shirts, sunglasses and arms flung over one another's shoulders, grinning widely into the lens.

And in pride of place is a photograph of a celebrity, a genuine star of one of Britain's most popular soap operas. Cheesy as it may well be, this is the photo Ben is most proud of, for she is Laurie, one of his conquests, but we'll save the story of Laurie until later.

Ben lies back on his bed, crumpling the jacket of his suit, which he flung on the duvet when he got home from work, but this is a good sign, for while we know from his bedroom that Ben isn't a slob we can now assume that neither is he anally retentive.

He lies back holding the piece of paper he dug out of the box he pulled from under his bed. It is a script from the news, a script that Ben painstakingly transcribed in his shorthand, scribbling down everything the newsreader said, and now he lies back and reads the first words in his television voice.

'Good evening.'

Practise, practise, practise, Ben. All over the world there are thousands of young men and women, people just like Ben, who dream of being a television presenter.

They ache for their fifteen minutes of fame, long to be famous for the sake of being famous.

If they're lucky, if they have the requisite long blonde hair, flirtatious nature and penchant for being wild, the girls may just make it on to the screen as presenters of some wacky new show. The men may, if they have the right contacts, also land on our screens as children's presenters. But few have the dedication to do what Ben's doing.

Ever since Ben was a child Ben has dreamt of reading the news. At university, studying for his English degree, Ben sat down with Richard and worked out how he was going to do it. He decided his greatest advantage (other than the dimples and white teeth, because Ben, although he is aware of them, doesn't really think about them all that often) would be a background in journalism. He knew he could have got on one of the graduate trainee schemes that all the national newspapers seem so keen on running these days, but he also knew, from speaking to people who had already gone down that route, that most of their time was spent doing dogsbody work.

And so he decided to look for a local paper. A local paper that wouldn't pay very well, but would give him the required news training. A local paper where the news editor might have the time to take Ben under his wing and show him how to sniff out a news story, how to doorstep members of the public, celebrities, and win an exclusive interview through charm alone.

A local paper where Ben might have a chance to rise quickly in the ranks, before moving to regional television. And from regional television he would move to network television. He would be an anchorman. He would present the news.

Admittedly, at twenty-nine, Ben's career hasn't progressed quite as quickly as he had planned, but nevertheless he's on course, and changes, he rightly suspects, are afoot.

Naturally he didn't tell the editor of the *Kilburn Herald* any of his plans when he turned up for an interview. He sat there and told the editor he was a newspaper man, he loved newspapers, loved the *Kilburn Herald* (for Ben had moved to Kilburn for the express purpose of working for the *Kilburn Herald*, a paper, he decided, at which he could make changes), had in fact spent years dreaming of working for the *Kilburn Herald*.

He told the editor he was happy to start as a junior reporter, but that at some time, not too far away, he would be news editor. And the editor, being a rather vain and stupid man, was flattered by Ben Williams, and won over by the smile and the dimples.

But he wasn't as stupid as all that. He realized the effect Ben's good looks would have on the people he had to doorstep. And sure enough, from the very first day Ben and Ben alone was the reporter to land the stories that everyone wanted. His future had started. Ben was on his way.

And now, in this large rented flat in a wide, tree-lined street in Kilburn, Ben puts aside the piece of paper and gets up off the bed. A cursory glance in the mirror tells him he looks fine, not that it matters tonight, it's only the boys at the local pub, but you never know. You just never know.

CHAPTER FIVE

It may be lunchtime, but Jemima Jones is sitting at her desk wondering how she can find out what to do with terracotta pots filled with candles once the candles have burnt down. She could, quite easily, telephone a candle shop and ask them, and it would, of course, be easier, not to mention quicker, than logging on to the Internet, but the course is still fresh in her mind, and she wants to test the Internet, to find out whether she can do it on her own.

She double-clicks on the sign on her computer and then clicks on CONNECT, listening to the computer dial up the modem and put her through. And here she is, the Internet at her feet.

Where should she go first? What should she do? She tries to remember what they taught on the course . . .

'Hey, quick work.' I turn round and of course it's Ben, jacket off, shirt-sleeves rolled up, dimples at the ready.

'Just thought I'd see if I could work it by myself.'

'I keep meaning to try it too, but I haven't had the time. Do you mind if I join you?'

Mind? Mind? Is he mad? I would move heaven and earth for you to join me, Ben. I would cut off my right arm if it meant you would join me.

'Sure, why don't you pull up a chair.'

Ben pulls up a swivel chair and sits close to me, and I never thought I'd say this but it's almost too close for comfort, certainly too close to breathe comfortably. I can feel my breath coming out in short, sharp bursts, but Ben doesn't notice a thing. He doesn't even notice how I involuntarily catch my breath as he puts his hand on top of mine on the mouse, and clicks on the Internet.

'What are you looking for?' he says to me, keeping his eyes fixed on the screen.

'Nothing special,' I lie. 'Just exploring, really.'

'Is everyone at lunch?'

I look around at the empty desks, listen to the phones ringing out with no one to answer them, and turn back to Ben. 'I think so, it seems pretty dead in here.'

'Good.' He turns to me with a wink. 'Let's explore the sex sites.'

I smile broadly to hide my embarrassment. It's not that I don't want to see them, although I'd never dare admit it, I just don't want to see them sitting with Ben, but it will keep him here for a while, so what the hell.

'I just did a story about kids downloading porn from the Internet on to disk, then selling it at St Ursula's. Let's see what all the fuss is about,' Ben says nonchalantly, but I'm sure that's just an excuse to see what it's all about. St Ursula's is the local comprehensive with a reputation so bad that on the rare occasions I have to walk past at the time when the children are coming out, I cross the road or, better yet, find an alternative route. It's not quite as bad as the building sites but nearly. Nearly.

Ben's concentrating hard on the screen, and I have to smile. St Ursula's indeed! You must think I'm stupid,

Ben, but good excuse, though. I have to admit I wouldn't have thought of that one.

'How do you find them?' I ask, ever the innocent.

'God knows, let's try and find out.'

Ben clicks until there's a box on his screen saying SEARCH. 'Right,' he says. 'Here goes. What do you think, sex or porn?'

'Try sex first,' and Ben leans across me, without realizing that as he does so his right arm brushes my left breast and I think I've died and gone to heaven. There is no expression on his face other than intense concentration as he types in the letters SEX, then presses SEARCH.

Nothing happens for a few seconds and Ben looks at me and grins. 'Wouldn't it be a nightmare if the editor came past now?'

I grin back. I would suffer any humiliation just for the pleasure of feeling Ben's arm lightly touching my breasts.

'We'll just tell him we're doing some research,' I say with a wicked smile.

Ben laughs. 'He'd probably want to pull up a chair himself. One of my friends just got a computer at home and he says that all his friends, even the girls, have been coming over and asking him to show them the Internet. Every time he asks them what they want to see, they all say sex. So there you go, we're not abnormal after all.'

You mean you're not abnormal, Ben, because to be completely honest I'm really not that bothered about scouring the sex sites, in fact, I think I'd rather not, but I'm not going to dwell on the potential embarrassment involved in surfing sex sites with the man of my dreams, I'm just going to sit here and enjoy being with you.

Suddenly the computer screen changes, and there's a

list on the screen, all of them sexual names, each urging you to click on them, see what they have to offer. I am not going to blush. I am going to be cool, calm and collected. Even as I sit here reading about oral, anal, sucking, fucking, I am not going to show Ben that I am anything other than a woman of the world.

'Brilliant,' says Ben, as I'm concentrating on keeping my face its normal colour. 'Let's go and see HOTSEX.'

Jemima isn't concentrating, but Jemima, we have to warn you, in just a few seconds you're going to want the ground to open and swallow you up.

Ben clicks on HOTSEX and nothing happens, the screen just goes completely black. Talk about anti-climax. 'Do you think it's not working?' Ben says, disappointment written all over his face.

'I think it probably just takes a long time. Look! Something's happening.' And sure enough, a series of lines starts appearing on screen. I'm watching Ben out of the corner of my eye, and Ben's watching the screen.

Welcome to the hottest, dirtiest, horniest site on the Internet

We have everything to satisfy your tastes

10 gigabytes of adult GIF files

Download dirty video clips from Amsterdam

Have live interactive sex with the horniest chicks around

Porn, sex, fucking, oral, anal, lesbian, gay

Join Hotsex for just $29.95

If you're a visitor click here to see the special visitor's site

'We did it, we did it!' says Ben in jubilation, clicking on the visitor's site. 'We found sex on the Internet!'

'Bearing in mind this is *research*, you're sounding incredibly excited,' and I can't help but smile at Ben's reaction.

'Oh yes, sorry, I forgot. Research. Yes, this is research. Of course.'

The screen goes black again and then more words of welcome, next to which are three tiny little boxes of a bright blue and green universe, surrounded by a red circle.

And nothing else happens.

'Jesus, what a waste of time,' says Ben. 'Where are the bloody pictures?'

'Maybe you have to click on a universe?'

Ben tries, but nothing happens. 'Shit, shit, shit. Look, I've gotta go for a pee, let's try and sort it out in a sec. Won't be a minute.' He walks off and I idly pick up a magazine lying next to the computer while I wait for him to come back.

God, yet another model breaking into the big league and isn't she gorgeous. I study her platinum-blonde hair and perfect eyebrows, and then make a mental note to add her to my collection when I get home.

'SHIT!' Ben shouts as his footsteps come running up behind me.

'OH MY GOD!' I look up at the screen and clap my hand over my mouth and both of us, just for a split second, seem to freeze in horror. As soon as we've pulled ourselves together, we frantically turn around, breathing sighs of relief that no one else is in the office. Because there on the computer screen, what was a little box containing a universe is now a massive colour picture of a naked woman, legs spread, with her mouth wrapped around one man's penis, while another is standing behind and screwing her.

The picture is crystal clear, every detail shines from the screen, and Ben, once he is sure there is no one other than Jemima to see him, is practically salivating. And Jemima? Well, I was right. Jemima wants to die.

Jemima has never seen porn before, not proper hardcore porn, and, sitting next to Ben, she blushes furiously, a hot red rising up and covering her face. Don't look round, she thinks, don't look at me, Ben, don't see what I look like.

'What are you two up to?' Geraldine's striding towards us, as immaculate as ever in a crisp camel suit, large gold earrings and the omnipresent sunglasses on top of her head.

'Research,' I bluster, feeling more and more stupid even as the colour starts to fade from my face.

'Shit,' whispers Ben, but before he can get rid of the picture Geraldine's in front of the screen.

'Oh my God!' she says, almost under her breath. 'Where did that come from?'

'Hotsex,' I mutter.

'Hot what?'

'Hotsex,' repeats Ben. 'We found this site on the Internet.'

'You'd better not let anyone see what you're doing.'

'Really?' says Ben. 'Tell me something else I didn't know.'

Geraldine muscles between us. 'Let me have a go,' she says, french manicured nails reaching for the mouse on the table.

'What's this then?' she says, clicking on to DOOR ONE. 'What's behind Door One, I wonder?'

None of us has to wonder long, as the picture disappears and more lines start appearing, another picture. This time a man, head arched back in ecstasy as a semi-naked girl, on her knees in front of him, is shown in graphic detail giving him a blow job.

'God,' whispers Geraldine. 'This is hysterical, it's so, well, so unsexy.' I start to laugh because she's absolutely right. There is nothing, but nothing, sexy about looking at a pornographic picture on a computer screen. Then Ben starts to laugh, and soon the three of us are clutching our sides and wiping the tears from our eyes. This stuff is far too clinical to turn anyone on.

'Oh dear,' gasps Geraldine, wiping the tears carefully away so as not to smudge her MAC mascara. 'What else can we look at?'

'What, more sex?' Even Ben's surprised.

'No, idiot. I mean aren't there any other interesting places?'

'I don't know. I don't know what else to look at.'

'Oh Ben, for God's sake. Here, let me.' Geraldine gets rid of the sex and clicks a few times, finally coming across HOT SITES ON THIS NETWORK.

'That's probably more sex,' I moan, clutching my heart, which I don't think can take the strain of another full-colour graphic porn picture on the computer screen at work.

'No, it's not,' says Geraldine, 'it's just sites that are popular.'

And sure enough a new list of sites appears on screen.

'There, that looks good,' says Geraldine, gesturing at a site called LA Café. Geraldine reads out loud. 'LA Café. The coolest virtual café on the Internet. Grab a cappuccino, the latest articles from the American magazines and meet other single people, all looking for that one special person.'

'LA Café, here we come,' says Ben, as Geraldine clicks on the site.

'Jesus, this thing takes for ever,' says Geraldine, while we wait for the site's logo to load.

'Oh well, at least we're not paying for it,' I say, just as the logo comes on screen.

LA Café

The coolest site for the seriously single

and the cappuccinos you've been surfing for all your life

'We have to join but it doesn't cost anything,' says Geraldine, clicking the JOIN logo. A small box appears saying NAME: KILBURN HERALD.

'Oh forget that,' she says, 'we won't be pulling anything as the *Kilburn Herald*. What shall we call ourselves?'

'How about the Three Musketeers?' offers Ben, who's now genuinely excited.

'No. Too obvious.'

'We're only messing around, let's come up with a name that sounds suitably sexy,' I offer, really quite curious to see what's going to happen. I think for a minute. 'What about Honey?'

'Brilliant,' says Geraldine, deleting KILBURN HERALD and typing in HONEY.

'Hey, that's not fair,' says Ben. 'If we join as Honey they won't know there's a guy involved. How am I going to pick up women?'

'Be quiet,' says Geraldine, 'too late now,' and so it is. We've joined the LA Café, or rather Honey has joined the LA Café.

'What do we do now?' I ask, after we've sat there for a couple of minutes staring mutely at the logo. 'Why don't we click on one of those boxes on the side?'

'Okay,' shrugs Geraldine, as she clicks on a picture of three heads together.

Who is Here, it says, as a box flashes up on screen with a load of names.

```
Suzie 24
=^..^= Cat
Scott Shearer
Honey
Ben the invincible
Todd
Luscious Lisa :-)
Ricky
Tim@London
Brad (Santa Monica)
```

Geraldine reads the names. 'Well, what the hell's Tim doing at the LA Café if he's in London?' she says.

'Same thing as us, presumably,' laughs Ben.

'Let's find out.' She clicks on his name and immediately another box appears on screen. The box is divided into two. The top half has Tim@London over the top, and the bottom, smaller half says Honey.

'Hello, fellow Londoner,' types Geraldine, the words appearing in the small box at the bottom. 'What are you doing at the La Café?' She presses RETURN and the words disappear from the bottom box and reappear at the top, ready for Tim@London to read.

'Picking up luscious Californian babes, of course. Why are you here?'

'Just checking it out. Looking for some Californian hunks. Any recommendations?'

'Lol. I'll have a think.'

Geraldine turns to Ben. 'What does Lol mean?'

'Dunno,' he says. 'Ask him.'

'What does Lol mean?'

'Laugh out loud. You're new to this then?'

'First time. Any other tips?'

'Sure. :-) means happy. :-(means unhappy. ;-) means a wink, but also (w) means wink. (g) means grin, (s) means smile, and ROFL means rolling on the floor laughing.'

'Thanks,' types Geraldine. ';-)'

'God, this is amazing.' I am truly flabbergasted. 'It's a whole other language. Can I have a go?'

Geraldine moves the mouse over to me and I move my hands quickly over the keyboard. 'So, have you found your Californian dream babe yet?'

'Yup, talking to her at the moment. Suzie, she's blonde, she's twenty-four, she's a hardbody and a total babe.'

'How do you know she's not lying to you?'

'She said she'll e-mail me her photo.'

'I hope she's not lying.'

'We'll soon find out (s). So where in London are you?'

I turn to the other two and make a face. 'We can't say Kilburn, it's too naff.'

'Say West Hampstead,' says Geraldine, 'it's the next best thing.'

So I do as she says and type in West Hampstead.

'Wowowow,' Tim@London types back. 'I'm in Kilburn!!!'

The three of us start laughing.

'Hi, Honey! So how old are you?' suddenly flashes up on the screen from Todd, and I abandon my conversation with Tim@London.

I type twenty-seven, but Geraldine stops me just as I'm about to press RETURN, to send the words to him.

'Don't say twenty-seven,' she urges. 'You don't have to tell the truth on this. Tell him you're nineteen.' So I do, realizing she's absolutely right. I don't have to tell the truth on the Internet. About anything.

'Just the right age for me!!!'

'How old are you?'

'Thirty-two.'

'That's a bit old for me isn't it?'

'You know what they say about older men . . .'

'Yes. That they should know better than to chat up nineteen-year-olds.' I press RETURN then add a ':-)' to show that I'm joking. Don't want to annoy him. Not yet, anyway.

'Ouch. Not fair.'

'Sorry. But do fill me in, what do they say about older men?'

'Older, wiser, more experienced. In every department (w).'

Geraldine shrieks with laughter. 'Go on,' says Ben, 'see if you can get him talking dirty.'

'Oh yes ? ' I type. 'Why not tell me EXACTLY what you're better at.'

'I don't believe this,' says Ben. 'This is sick.' But he's grinning.

'Okay, Honey. You want to know what would happen if you went out on a date with me?'

'Darling, I can't wait to hear.'

'Well first of all we wouldn't bother going to a restaurant, I'd want you all to myself at home, so I'd cook a gourmet meal, and we'd eat by candlelight on my terrace overlooking the swimming pool to the sounds of soft jazz playing on the stereo.'

Geraldine makes gagging noises.

'Go on.'

'After dinner I'd lead you into my bedroom and I would give you a massage. I'd unbutton your shirt, and dribble some baby oil on to my palm. I'd warm the oil between my hands and then I'd make you lie on the bed while I slowly rub the baby oil into the smooth, tanned skin of your back.'

'How do you know it's tanned?'

'Sssh. You're spoiling the atmosphere. After you're completely relaxed, I'd move my hands lower, pulling down your skirt until I'm rubbing my palms over your bare buttocks. I'd move lower and lower, pulling your panties down as I go, slipping my hand in between your legs, where it's warm, dark and moist with longing.'

'Oh my God!' I don't believe this!'

'What a perv!' shrieks Geraldine.

'Let the guy finish!' says Ben.

'Then I'd turn you over, and slowly stroke the oil on to your bare breasts. Your nipples would be erect by now, aching for me to take them between my fingers and rub them gently.'

Geraldine and I shriek with laughter, and for the first time in my life I stop feeling intimidated by her, and start to think that actually she's really very nice. Ben doesn't say anything. He's smiling, but one look at his face and we can tell he wants to hear more. Unfortunately, he won't.

I sit there and cover my face in mock horror. 'I can't do this any more,' I say, 'this is too horrible,' and I quickly type in, 'Okay, thanks for the massage. Must do it again some time. Bye.'

'Sorry. Did I put you off?' Poor Todd, he's blown it and he's hardly started yet.

'Just ignore him,' says Geraldine. 'Let's try someone else.'

'My turn, my turn,' says Ben, reaching for the mouse. 'Hi Suzie,' he types. 'I'm Ben. I'm with two female friends. Now it's my turn.'

'Oh. Okay. How are you, Ben?'

'Good, thank you. But the burning question is, what are you doing with Tim@London, who evidently has no money because he lives in a really grotty area, when you could be with me.'

'Ben!' I start laughing. 'Like you live in a palace?'

'Sssh,' he says. 'What difference?'

'Are you rich then, Ben?'

58

'Richer than Tim@London, and better looking.'
'LOL.'
';-)'
'How do you know what he looks like?'
'Trust me. I know these things.'
'So what do you look like?'

Geraldine groans at me. 'God, he's off. Shall we go and get a coffee?'

And they do. They go downstairs to the canteen and leave Ben sitting at the computer, chatting animatedly to Suzie, the babe of his dreams. The babe that's as different to Jemima as, well, as a typewriter and a computer linked up to the Internet.

CHAPTER SIX

It has been two weeks and call me a coward but I haven't dared venture back on to the Internet, terrified that a pornographic picture will leap on to my screen, or some mad American will start talking to me.

But I can't get the bloody thing out of my head, and I can't get over how fantastic it is, the way you can communicate with anyone you wish, wherever you want. Truth to be told, I think it's brilliant, everything. The World Wide Web, the chat forums, the possibilities.

Not that I'm looking for anyone, I mean, it's me, for God's sake, the woman who never has any boyfriends, and, although I know what a nice person I am, I'm not the most sociable of creatures. I wish I were, I wish I could be more like my flatmates at times, but unfortunately my size dictates my social life, and my size is the one thing I can't control. I know what you're thinking, go on a diet, but it's not as easy as that, I just can't stop the cravings when they come, and somehow living on the Internet seems a far easier option than giving up chocolate.

I mean, this could open up a whole new life for me, a new life that doesn't care about looks, about weight, about expanses of flesh.

Or perhaps I should say, doesn't *know*, because I'm not stupid, if I had described myself accurately to Todd, he would have been off faster than you can say megabyte.

But I really can be anyone I want on the Internet. After all, who could ever find out? What harm could there be? And, let's face it, up until now the only fun thing in my life has been fantasizing first about being thin, and then about Ben Williams, but even those fantasies have been so tame that they're hardly worth repeating.

Are we interested? Okay, let's take a peek into Jemima's daydreams. When Jemima Jones goes to bed and closes her eyes, this is what she sees: she sees herself struck down with gastroenteritis, a bad bout, not so bad as to be seriously threatening, but bad enough for her to lose huge amounts of weight.

She sees herself decked out in little suits, tight fitted jackets, short skirts just skimming her thighs. She sees herself bumping into Ben Williams, who has by now left the *Kilburn Herald*, as in fact has she.

She sees herself going up to Ben at a crowded party, and saying hi, with a cool look in her eyes and a casual flick of her now blonde hair. She sees Ben's eyes widen in shock, replaced seconds later by admiration, respect, lust. She sees Ben driving her home, and coming in for coffee. She sees her flatmates fall over themselves trying to flirt with him, but she sees that Ben only has eyes for her.

She sees Ben moving closer towards where she sits on the sofa, unable, even for a moment, to take his eyes off her face. She sees his mouth in close-up detail, as he bends forward to kiss her. When they have kissed, and, incidentally, it is a kiss that instantly propels her up to

61

a cloud, Ben looks in her eyes and says, 'You're the most beautiful woman I've ever seen. I love you and I want to be with you for the rest of my life.'

Ridiculous, isn't it, but Jemima Jones never gets beyond that first kiss and the declaration of love. Occasionally the kiss takes place elsewhere, sometimes at the party, sometimes in the car, sometimes on the street, but his words are always the same, and, as far as Jemima's concerned, those words are the beginning of her happy ever after.

So I think we all agree that right now, at this stage in her life, Jemima Jones deserves a bit of fun.

The first step in my new life is to stop at the bookshop on the way home from work. Actually it's not really on my way home, it involves a massive detour to Hampstead, but, despite this being a break from my daily routine, I'm beginning to realize that my life is changing, and by the looks of things so far it would appear to be getting infinitely better.

The evidence? Well, as far as I can see, seven important, life-changing things have happened this week. First, I went on a course to learn the basics about the Internet. Second, after the course I went for a drink, *I actually went out for a drink*, and, not only that, the drink lasted all evening. This, as far as I'm concerned, is the definite beginning of a social life. Third, it wasn't just any old drink, it was a drink with Geraldine and Ben Williams. Geraldine, with whom I had never, until that drink, socialized after work, and Ben, about whom I fantasize every night. Fourth, I was actually able to relax in Ben's company! I wasn't the tongue-tied teen-ager he occasionally joins for lunch in the canteen, I was almost, almost, myself. Fifth, I had a good time. No, forget that, I had a *great* time! Sixth, Ben joined me on the Internet today, and yes I was embarrassed by the sex, but more importantly I showed Ben I have a sense of humour, at least I hope I did. Seventh, I haven't had any chocolate for two whole weeks.

Is it any wonder that Jemima Jones feels that life is taking a definite turn for the better? Never mind that the drink she shared with Ben Williams and Geraldine was two weeks ago. Never mind that she hasn't seen Ben Williams properly since their brief sojourn on the Internet. Never mind that neither Geraldine nor Ben has suggested a repeat drink. That one evening was enough to set a chain of events in progress. Cause and effect, except Jemima doesn't quite know the full effect just yet. Nor do we.

But nevertheless, two weeks have passed and still Jemima's feeling so happy, so high, so full of excitement at her new life, she treats herself to a taxi to Hampstead. She stands on the corner outside the *Kilburn Herald*, eyes full of hope, hands full of bags, and she hails a black cab.

'Hampstead, please,' I tell the driver, climbing awk-wardly into the back.

'Whereabouts, love?' he says, a middle-aged man with a kind face.

'Do you know Waterstone's?'

He nods, and off we go. Up through West Hampstead, passing the hordes of young people on their way home from work, zippy suits, designer briefcases, aspirations in their eyes. Up across the Finchley Road, up Arkwright Road, cut through Church Row as I stare with envy at the houses that once contained bohemian artists and writers, and now contain wealthy businessmen, and right at the tube, down Hampstead High Street, he pulls up, double-parking, for of course there are no spaces in which to park, and clicks his meter.

'Keep the change,' I say, handing him £6, for today is the beginning of my new life, and I can afford to be a bit extravagant. I might even do a little shopping, because it's only 5.45 p.m., and the shops will be open for a while yet, tempting me with their glamorous window displays.

But first into Waterstone's, dark, cool, calm, I breathe in the air of reverence and feel a sense of calm wash over me. Books may be my special treat, but I hardly ever buy more than one at a time, and it's even more rare for me actually to venture into a bookshop to buy it. I'm a member of a paperback club, a club that sends me a catalogue every month, from which I choose a book at a discounted price, but it's not quite as good as it sounds. As well as me choosing the books I want, they also send me a book I don't want, the editor's choice, and I'm supposed to send it back after twenty-eight days if I don't want it. Needless to say, I never seem to get round to it, so half the shelves in my bedroom are groaning from the weight of books I didn't want and wouldn't read.

But today I'm going to treat myself. I've decided that

I'm going to buy at least three books, and I'm going to browse for hours and soak up the atmosphere, enjoy the anonymity, revel in the fact that no one in here is looking at me or passing judgement on my thighs rubbing together as I walk because they too will be immersed in books.

I start with a table near the front, and gently brush the piles of hardbacks. No, I tell myself, that really would be extravagant, and today is a paperback day, so I walk over to another table. Covers, so many covers, so many different, delectable pictures, and although, metaphorically speaking, it is the thing I hate most, when it comes to literature I always judge books by their covers. First the cover will catch my eye, then I read the back of the book, and then finally the first page. I pick up one, a new novel I've read about in a magazine. 'A love story of the nineties,' says the back cover. 'A modern romance that puts all other romances to shame.' I open it up to the first page and start reading. Yes. This is the first book I'll buy.

Then I pick up another book. No picture, just a bright yellow cover with large purple letters, the author's name and the title. Hmm, interesting. I read the first page, where I meet Anna, an eighteen-year-old girl about to embark on a university degree. She is going to meet her future lecturer, who will, she suspects, quiz her about her reasons for taking an English degree. It is beautifully written, the sentences so clear, so concise, so vivid, I almost forget about adding it to my pile. I forget I'm in Waterstone's, to be honest I seem to forget about everything, and, as I read on to the fourth page, the fifth, I become Anna's invisible acquaintance, a secret

65

shadowy figure who lurks silently in the background, looking in on Anna's life, holding her hand as she meets the gruff professor.

Jemima is so immersed in Anna's world she doesn't see that on the other side of the room, standing almost exactly parallel to where she is now, is Ben Williams. Ben is also immersed in a book, back to the room, facing the bookshelf; he is reading the first few pages of a thriller, rocking gently on the balls of his feet as he reads.

But before we start assuming this must be fate, I have to point out that although Ben likes Jemima, he doesn't *like* Jemima, so perhaps now is not the time to start jumping to conclusions.

But it is rather strange that both of them should be in Waterstone's at exactly the same time. Ben, it has to be said, comes to Waterstone's once every couple of weeks, but rarely does he take advantage of the fact that Waterstone's is open until 10 p.m., rarely does he venture into this bookstore after work. Ben usually makes his journey on a Saturday, he will pop in on his way to meet some friends for a drink at a pavement café.

Tonight, however, Ben is not going out. Nor is he watching the news. Tonight Ben has nothing to do, and this is why he is in the same place as Jemima Jones, at the same time. And because Ben didn't jump in a cab, he got the tube, Ben has only just arrived.

So here they are, Jemima and Ben, these two colleagues, both with their backs towards one another, both lost in their respective hand-held worlds of academia and dodgy dealing in the City, both completely unaware of their proximity.

All it will take for Jemima to turn around and see Ben is a tiny twist of fate, a decision to buy the book, to add it to the first, to perhaps turn and look for another one, and, in turning, note that the man of her daydreams is standing opposite her. But fate can be cruel, or possibly in this case understanding, because what, after all, would Jemima do if she saw Ben?

We can be sure that her mouth would drop open, that her heart would skip at least one beat, probably two or three, and that she would not know what to do next. Perhaps she would clumsily go over to say hello, joy and love written all over her face. Perhaps she would be too embarrassed to approach him, and would merely set her books down and quietly skulk away.

And Ben? Ben would be surprised and pleased to see her, as he would if he bumped into any of his colleagues unexpectedly. He might suggest a coffee for, as we already know, he has nothing better to do, but that would be the sum of it.

Luckily we don't have to worry about what either will do, because neither has the slightest idea the other is there. Jemima carries on reading, while Ben closes his book firmly and takes it to the till. He gives the dowdy girl behind the till a winning smile, and she takes the book and places it in a plastic bag, melting while she does so. Please come back in again, she thinks, please come back tomorrow, when perhaps we'll have a conversation, which may lead to coffee, which may lead to . . . anything. Everything.

But Ben just pockets the book and walks out, with

not a backward glance. Jemima decides to buy the book, and then looks around for one more. She goes to yet another table and suddenly her eye lands on the perfect book: *The Idiot's Guide to the Internet.*

Well, I may not be an idiot, but flicking through the book I realize that there are hundreds of things I don't know, thousands of sites I might want to visit. Yes, this is the final book. Time to go.

I wander over to the till and hand my pile of three to the dowdy girl looking bored. I try and catch her eye to give her a friendly smile, but she's not interested, she doesn't even look at me when she hands me my books, safely encased in a plastic bag, and when I thank her she just scowls and turns away. Honestly. Some people are just so rude.

I walk back outside, and linger for a moment on the pavement, because I'm not ready to go home and it's such a beautiful evening, and for the first time in ages I don't care that I don't look like the beautiful people milling around me, I want to do something, go somewhere, have a life.

I don't know quite where to go, so I wander down the hill, looking in every window I pass, all the high street chains that line the high street, and even though the windows are filled with garish, high-fashion clothes, size 8 bits of cloth that would normally serve only to emphasize my inadequacies, tonight I don't care, and anyway, a girl can dream, can't she?

*

On the other side of the road strolls Ben Williams. He too is looking into shop windows, admiring the shirts, the suits, wishing he had a bit more money so he could afford them, but not wishing with quite the same zeal as Jemima, because after all he is a man, and men do not share women's excitement about clothes. Have we ever heard of a male shopaholic? Exactly.

Ben turns round and stops, about to cross the road, and there, standing exactly opposite him on the other side of the road, is Jemima. Ben looks to his left, Jemima looks to her left. Ben starts to cross as a big lorry trundles up then stops, sitting slap-bang in the middle of the road, obstructing the view because the road has become too narrow for the lorry to pass down due to the early-evening shoppers double-parked.

But Jemima doesn't cross, because surely then they would meet in the middle. Jemima sees a crêperie stand on her right, and instead of walking into Ben, of whose presence she is unaware, she turns right and walks down to the crêperie.

And so once again they miss one another. But Jemima's being a good girl, she decides against the thick crêpe dripping with butter and oozing chocolate sauce. She heads instead for a café, which, to her delight, is almost empty.

She squeezes into a corner table by the window and orders a cappuccino, then pulls out the first of her books and submerges herself, in comfort this time, in Anna's world.

Ben, meanwhile, is dying for a drink. He walks past a café and stops, peering in the window to see what it's like. Nope, he thinks, too empty, I need something busier, buzzier, and of course he is looking too far into the restaurant, well beyond the corner table by the window, the corner table at which Jemima is sitting, head buried, lost in another world.

So close but yet so far, Jemima. I wish we could tell you that Ben Williams is standing but feet away from you, but it's not our place, I'm afraid. Fate will just have to continue taking its course.

And fate, as usual, is shining on Ben Williams. He crosses the road and walks into a bar that's more his scene. Large plate-glass windows on to the street, a smooth polished cherrywood bar sweeping round the centre of the room, with young, good-looking barmen chatting idly by the glasses. Small round wooden tables with cast-iron legs and twirly iron chairs contain Hampstead's better-looking people, and right at the back is a sofa, a couple of old, beaten-up leather armchairs, and a huge fireplace which is not yet roaring, too early in the year for that, but is alight, casting a golden glow on the people sitting near the back.

Ben pushes open the door, immediately assaulted by noise, heat, animated chatter. Yes, he thinks, this is where I'll have a drink. He goes up to the barman and orders a bottle of designer beer, then looks around for the most comfortable place to sit, and heads towards the sofa at the back.

He's slightly out of place in his dark navy suit, but he sinks into the sofa, drapes his jacket along the back, and exhales loudly. Good place, he thinks, looking around. He takes a swig of beer, pulls the book from his pocket and settles back, one elbow leaning on the arm of the sofa, his hand resting just above his forehead, pushing his hair back, the other holding the book. The beer rests on the table.

If a photographer from *Vogue* were to walk in now, he would not be able to resist this little tableau. For Ben looks quite amazing, his right ankle resting on his left knee, long legs, well-built body, handsome face. He looks like a set-up, too good to be true, too good for any woman to resist.

So can we blame the tall, slim brunette sitting at one of the tables for taking the initiative? She's with her two girlfriends, all equally stunning, all dressed in the latest fashions, the clothes that Jemima Jones can only dream of wearing. Hip-hugging trousers with tiny bootleg flares at the bottom. Soft leather boots with square toes and centre stitching, tiny little vest tops squeezed over perfect, pert breasts.

The brunette and her friends noticed Ben the moment he walked in. Too much of a suit? they asked themselves. 'With a face like that,' said the brunette, 'who cares.'

They sit there watching Ben, who is completely unaware of their presence, of their giggles as they try and decide what he does for a living. 'Way too handsome for an estate agent,' they decide, 'maybe an investment banker?'

The brunette, who is killing time by working in a shop until she finds a husband to sweep her off her feet and carry her into the sunset on his white charger, calls over one of the waiters, whom naturally she knows, because every evening she is in this bar with her friends.

'Do you know that guy?' she whispers, pointing to Ben. The waiter shrugs. 'Never seen him before.'

'Look,' she says. 'Do me a favour. Will you take him

over another bottle of beer, I'll pay for it, and tell him I'm buying him a drink.'

The waiter smiles. The brunette's girlfriends laugh at her audacity, but with looks like hers, she can afford to be audacious.

The girls watch in silence as the waiter takes a bottle of beer over to Ben on a tray. The waiter bends down in front of Ben and murmurs something, pointing at the brunette, before walking away while Ben, bless him, blushes.

He stares at the bottle, too embarrassed to look around the room, to look at the brunette, and the brunette, much like the dowdy woman in Waterstone's, melts.

'Oh my God,' she whispers to her girlfriends. 'Did you see that? He blushed! I think I'm in love!'

Ben's face cools down and he looks at the brunette, amazement in his eyes, for she is truly gorgeous, and he smiles and raises the bottle to her, a silent toast.

'Guys,' she says to her girlfriends as she stands up, 'I'm going in there.'

'Good luck,' they say, unable to take their eyes off Ben. 'Don't do anything we wouldn't do.'

She walks, no, sashays over to where Ben's sitting. 'Do you mind if I join you?'

'Um, no,' says Ben, thinking this doesn't happen in real life, surely? Surely this only happens in the movies. 'Please sit down. Thank you for the drink.'

'I bet it's not the first time a woman's bought you a drink.'

She's wrong. It is. 'Um, actually, yes. It is.'

'Oh.' She shrugs her shoulders and laughs. 'Oh well, there's a first time for everything. I'm Sam,' she says, extending her hand, using the handshake as an excuse to get closer to him.

'I'm Ben,' he says, shaking her hand.

'My favourite name,' she laughs, and Ben laughs back.

Jemima Jones finished her cappuccino a long time ago, but she stays in her little café for a while, reading, except she is not comfortable, squeezed into this tiny hard chair, and after a while she thinks she would be far more comfortable at home, lying on her bed.

She pays, walks out of the café, and starts down the hill, feeling ridiculously happy for no reason at all. She goes past the bar and looks in at the beautiful people, thinking that one day she will be slim enough to join them.

And then she sees them. Ben and Sam, sitting on the sofa at the back, and she freezes, her mouth open in a gasp of shock. Ben and Sam are getting on as famously as two people who have nothing in common other than a mutual attraction can get on. Sam is flirting outrageously, and Ben is enjoying having a gorgeous woman flirt with him. Already he knows that he will not be going out with her, because already she has proved to be indescribably stupid, but Jesus does he fancy her.

He realizes he may have to take her out a couple of times before getting her into bed, but he is sure it will be worth it, and so they sit, closer and closer, touching one another more and more, Sam resting her hand on his arm as she talks to him, Ben leaning in towards her to hear more clearly. It is only a matter of time.

*

How can your moods change so suddenly? I mean, I was feeling so good, so happy, so optimistic, and now I'm rooted to the spot, trying hard to suppress a growing wave of nausea. It's Ben. The love of my life, and he's with a woman, and she's beautiful, and she's skinny, and I hate her, and I love him. I love him, I love him, I love him.

And I can't move, but I have to, because I don't want him to see me, and as I turn and walk away the cloud I've been floating on for the past two weeks disappears into thin air, and in its place it feels like there's a large black rain cloud. I walk slowly down the high street, and call me pathetic, call me a loser, but I can't help it. I can't stop the two fat tears that work their way slowly down my cheeks.

CHAPTER SEVEN

Jemima Jones is not having a good day. The rain cloud followed her home last night, dropping tears into her eyes, removing the hopes from her heart.

She trudged down the high street, aware that people were looking at her, and not caring whether they were looking at her size or her tears. Nobody dared ask what was wrong, and Jemima had never felt so alone in her whole life.

She went home, back to an empty flat, lay on her bed and cried, and when the tears had passed she just lay, staring up at the ceiling, wondering why nothing good ever seemed to happen to her.

I know I'm overweight, she thought, but I'm not a bad person. I love animals, and children, and I'm kind to people and why does no one ever fall in love with me, why can't Ben see through the weight and fall in love with me as a person.

Because Jemima knows that Ben is a good person. She knows better than most about judging books by their covers. She knows that people judge her instantly on her appearance, and she knows that people do the same thing with Ben.

Single women of an appropriate age do one of two things when they meet Ben. They either fall instantly in lust with him, or, if they suspect Ben is the kind of man they could never hope to attain, they choose the second option and hate him instead, hate him for being arrogant, vain, self-important.

But we know that's not true because we've got to know Ben a little bit, and Jemima knows it's not true because she looked through his dimples and blue eyes (for she got it wrong when she described him to her flatmates, his eyes are actually the colour of the English sky on a hot summer's day) and saw that Ben, like her, was not a bad person.

Ben too makes time for people. Even Jemima. He has the same winning smile and easy charm with everyone he meets, regardless of what they look like. In fact, the only time Ben is awkward is when he meets a woman he fancies, and then he's not entirely sure of how to behave.

Take last night, for example. Ben was wrong about having to take Sam out a couple of times before he would manage to sleep with her. Sam was a sure thing. Sam made this blatantly clear. Too blatant. Too clear. Her aggression, which became more and more apparent as the evening wore on, suddenly started to turn Ben off. He still fancied her, but could he be bothered, he wondered? Did he really want to go through the whole procedure of waking up in bed with a stranger who may or may not become obsessive? Ben got bored, and Ben said goodnight to Sam, although not without a long, slow kiss goodnight, because, let's face it, Ben isn't *that* much of a new man. Not yet, anyway.

And he was absolutely right not to have gone home with her, for Sam is exactly the kind of girl to get obsessive. She's the kind of girl who regularly sleeps with men on the night she meets them and then wonders why they don't call afterwards. But she doesn't stop there. She phones them, and phones them, and phones them. She offers them tickets to concerts, dinner invitations, parties.

At first they are flattered, what man, after all, wouldn't be, with a stunning girl like Sam chasing them. But then they become bored. Where is the challenge? Where is the thrill of the chase? And inevitably they start making excuses, and Sam does what she always does. She shouts and screams at them on the phone, calls them bastards, like all the bastards she's ever met. Ends with telling them she thought *they* were different, as if guilt, somehow, will make them come back, and then finally she slams the phone down.

Then she goes out and repeats the whole scenario with someone new.

Ben is perceptive enough to realize the sort of woman Sam is. A 'bunny boiler' is how he would describe her to his friends, and they would all groan in recognition.

But because Ben's a nice guy masquerading as a bastard, Ben let her down gently by asking for her number after they kissed and promising he would call. This was perhaps not exactly the right thing to do because Sam wrote down her home number, her work number and her mobile number. At this very moment Sam is doing what thousands of women in her position have done. She is watching the phone at work and willing him to call. Every now and then she picks it up to check it's still working, and she has been hovering by the phone all day, leaping on it should it dare to ring.

But Ben won't call, not least because girlfriends are not exactly a priority at the moment. The type of women Ben goes for are high-maintenance. They require picking up, being paid for, presents. Ben, at this very moment in time, has neither the funds nor the inclination to think about high-maintenance women in anything other than an abstract way.

So while he fancies Geraldine, he knows that right now she'd never give him a chance, and quite frankly that's okay with Ben. It's enough that she brightens up his days at work. He's happy not to take it further.

Ben is far too busy thinking about his career to think about women. Sure, if someone uncomplicated came along who would be willing to fit in with Ben's life, and just see him occasionally, i.e. on the occasions when he's not working, working out or seeing his friends, then great. But Ben hasn't met this woman yet.

So Jemima's having a bad day, and Ben's interviewing a local woman whose thirteen-year-old son has just stabbed a schoolteacher. Normally he wouldn't, as the deputy news editor, be writing the stories himself, but this is the *Kilburn Herald* after all, and everyone has to muck in.

Jemima has spent all day hoping for a glimpse of Ben, and each time footsteps come her way she turns, but it would appear that Ben is out of the office. She has spent the day making phonecalls. She has discovered the best way of drying your nail varnish quickly (dip the nails into a bowl of icy cold water), the best way of keeping lettuce fresh (put the lettuce into a bowl of iced water, add a slice of lemon and put it in the fridge) and the best way of storing tinned foods in the cupboard (buying plastic shelves, £5.99). Jemima is bored. Bored, fat and unhappy. Not a good combination, I think we all agree.

So it is a welcome relief when her phone distracts her with an internal ring.

'It's me,' says Geraldine, which is ridiculous really because she knows full well that her extension number is flashing on my telephone. 'Do you want to meet me in the canteen for a cup of tea?'

Anything to break the monotony of this work, the pain of Ben not wanting me. Of course I want a cup of tea, just to get away from this desk, from this miserable bloody office.

'Have you lost weight?' is the first thing Geraldine says to me as I walk over to her by the hot-water machine, pouring the water over the teabags in two plastic cups.

For the first time today I perk up. I don't know, I haven't weighed myself for the last few weeks, I haven't even thought about it, which, miraculous as it may sound, must be because I've actually started having fun. I've discovered the Internet, and in Geraldine and Ben I've finally found two people who seem to be real friends, although I hadn't realized I might have lost weight before Geraldine mentioned it just now. But, thinking about it, I haven't been eating as much, and my clothes might just possibly be feeling less tight.

'Your face definitely looks slimmer,' says Geraldine, picking up the cups and carrying them to the table.

Jemima could kiss Geraldine, because Geraldine is right, she has lost weight. She hasn't thought about her weight for two weeks, and the minute she stopped thinking about it, stopped worrying about it, stopped feeling guilty about her binges, was the minute she started to lose it.

Until last night, however, because lying on your bed feeling fat and miserable is inevitably the beginning of a binge, and last night, when Jemima had composed herself, she phoned the local pizza delivery company. They brought round a large pizza, although huge might be a more appropriate description, garlic bread and coleslaw. Jemima opened the front door and pretended she was having a load of friends round. Just to make sure they believed her she also ordered four cans of diet coke.

But today is another day, and, although she may have put on a couple of pounds after last night's binge – and yes, it is quite possible for Jemima to put on two or three pounds overnight – in general she has lost weight.

We sit down and Geraldine sighs, running her fingers through her hair.

'Is everything okay?' I say, even though I can see quite clearly that everything is not.

'It's just Dimitri,' says Geraldine. 'He's getting on my nerves at the moment. I feel a bit funny about things.'

Uh oh. I know exactly what this means. This is Geraldine's pattern. This means that Dimitri has fallen head over heels in love with Geraldine, which in turn means that Geraldine is rapidly cooling off, and poor old Dimitri will soon be finding out that she is not the woman of his dreams after all.

'Funny how?'

'I don't know,' she sighs. 'He's just always *there*.'

'But isn't that how boyfriends are supposed to be?' I mean, for God's sake, Geraldine. 'Isn't that what every woman wants?'

'I suppose so.' Geraldine shrugs. 'But it's all getting a bit on top of me.'

Just in case you're interested, here's what will happen next. The more Geraldine backs off, the more keen Dimitri will become. It will probably end with a marriage proposal, which Geraldine will turn down, because by the time the proposal comes around she will be desperate to get away from him. She will, however, keep the ring. As she always does.

'Maybe you should just wait and see what happens.'

'Maybe I should start dating other men.'

No! Oh God, no! That might mean Ben, she might go out with Ben, and I couldn't stand that. It's bad enough seeing him with a stunning stranger, horrible but just about bearable, but if Ben and Geraldine got together it would kill me. Find out now, find out what she thinks now.

'Who?'

'No one in particular,' says Geraldine. 'But if I started going out again with the girls I'm sure I'd meet someone soon.' She has the confidence of those with unnatural beauty, for who else could be so certain? Other women stay in relationships, miserable, horrible, destructive relationships because the alternative is far too horrendous to even consider. Being on their own.

But of course Geraldine could never begin to understand this. Geraldine has always moved onwards, and upwards. Occasionally sideways.

'What about Ben?' I say in such a casual tone it sounds fake, even to me. 'He likes you.'

'Ben? Ben? You are joking aren't you?'

Of course I'm not joking, Geraldine, can't you see how I am when he's around? Can't you see the effect he has on me? How could I be joking when I think he is the most perfect male specimen ever to have set foot on the planet?

'No. Why?'

'Well, Ben's just Ben. He's very handsome but what is he? He's a deputy news editor on the *Kilburn Herald*. And Ben isn't exactly the type of guy who's going places is he? I mean, what will he achieve in his life? He'll become the news editor, then the editor, and that's it. He'll stay on a crappy local paper for ever.

'He'll marry some pretty local girl who wants to be a wife and mother, and if they're lucky they'll live in West Hampstead and have 2.4 children and a Volkswagen.

'Ben,' she repeats, shaking her head with a laugh. 'I don't think so.'

Thank you, God. Thank you for being on my side. I don't give a damn what Geraldine thinks of Ben as a person, and anyway I think she's wrong. I don't think he'll be here for ever, I think he's far too good for this, but that doesn't matter right now. All that matters is that Geraldine and Ben will never be a 'they' or an 'us'. They will always be Geraldine and Ben, and I suddenly feel so relieved I could cry.

'So,' says Geraldine with a sigh. 'Enough about me. What's going on in your life?'

She says this regularly, and I do what I always do – I move the conversation straight back to Geraldine because what would I tell her? Would I tell her about my trip to the bookshop perhaps, and turn it into an exaggerated adventure where I tripped over handsome men every step of the way? Would I tell Geraldine about seeing Ben with that girl last night? Would I laugh to cover up the pain and ask Geraldine if she knew anything about her? Or would I perhaps tell Geraldine about ordering a huge pizza and crying all night? No. I think not.

So I stir my tea for a few seconds, then look up, 'But what *are* you going to do about Dimitri?'

By the time we venture back upstairs the *Kilburn Herald* has significantly emptied. The news desk is still buzzing, just in case, but features, the area at the back where Geraldine and I sit, is quiet.

'Jemima,' whines Geraldine just before walking back to her desk. Here we go. I know exactly what this whine means.

'I need some help.'

'Go on,' I say with an exasperated smile, although I'm not exasperated, I'm actually delighted at any chance I get to do some proper writing.

'I'm writing this piece about dating again after you get divorced for the woman's page. I'm a bit stuck, could you have a quick look at it?' Which means, if you are as expert at reading between the lines as I am, 'Could you rewrite it?'

Geraldine runs back to her desk and picks up a proof then dashes back. 'God, you're an angel,' she says. 'I owe you big time,' and she leaves, not turning round but waving just as she walks out the door.

Sometimes I can't believe Geraldine's writing, I can't believe how someone can find it so difficult because it never seems to take me long to rework her copy. I start by rewriting the intro, adding some colour, crafting it into something the readers will want to continue reading.

'STANDING at the aisle, reading your wedding vows, you hoped and prayed your marriage would last for ever,' I tap. 'But years later your vows of loving and honouring your husband are as distant a memory as the happiness you once shared.

'Divorce in the nineties is sending thousands of women back to a game they thought they would never see again – the Dating Game.

'And women all over the country are discovering that no matter how wise, how experienced, how old they may be, no matter how much the rules may have changed, when it comes to excitement, disappointment, pain, nothing has really changed at all.'

Eyes glued to my computer screen, I type. I lose myself in the writing, and then tidy up Geraldine's 'Case Studies' – three women who have agreed to tell their story in the *Kilburn Herald*. When I've finished I send the copy back to Geraldine's basket, so no one will know I had anything to do with it. So that's what friends are for.

It's going home time, but just as I'm about to leave I suddenly remember something. I remember that I haven't taken the books I bought out of my bag, and now would be a perfect time to try out the Internet.

I reach down and pull out *The Idiot's Guide to the Internet*. Right. Time to explore, and turning back to the screen I double-click on the sign on the left that will take me to the Internet. As the machine is connecting, I flick through the little guide.

Now this really is incredible. I learn about Web sites, about art galleries on the Internet where you can post your own pictures or download those of others. I learn of alternative medicine sites, where you can learn how others have fared by trying cures not recognized by traditional medicine. I read about estate agents sites, where wide boys in suits have posted pictures of properties they're trying to sell. I read about museum sites, music sites, dating sites.

I read about newsgroups, bulletin boards for every hobby, interest and obsession you can think of. Places where people can post a message, a question, a thought, and scores of like-minded people can reply.

And then I read about Tarot, a site where you can have your fortune told, and that's when I stop reading and start clicking. I want my fortune told. I want to know whether I'll find true love. I want to know if Ben is the man for me. Don't worry, though, I promise I'll take it all with a healthy pinch of salt. At least, I'll try to.

The page appears on the screen, with a choice of Tarot card decks, and me being me I click on the Tarot of the Cat People, simply because I've always wanted a cat, and suddenly three small boxes appear asking for my name, gender and age.

I type them in, and then another box comes up, this time asking for my question. A quick check round the office shows that I'm safe, there's no one around to see what I'm doing, so here goes . . .

`'Will Ben Williams fall in love with me?'` I type, before clicking the button saying RESULT.

Three cards appear at the top of the screen, with the translations beneath. Card number one represents the past. It is the King of Wands (reversed). 'Severity. Austerity. Somewhat excessive and exaggerated ideas. Dogmatic, deliberate person.'

Card number two represents the present. It is The Empress (reversed). 'Vacillation. Inaction. Lack of interest. Lack of concentration. Indecision. Delay in accomplishment or progress. Anxiety. Frittering away of resources. Loss of material possessions. Infertility. Infidelity. Vanity.'

What a load of bollocks! Infidelity? I should be so lucky. Vanity? Please!

But I carry on reading anyway, the final card, the Knight of Wands, representing my future. 'Departure. A journey. Advancement into the unknown. Alteration. Flight. Absence. Change of residence.'

Well, this *is* a load of rubbish, but I don't want to go home just yet. Maybe I'll go back to the LA Café, at least I know how to find the bloody thing. Ah, who's here today.

```
Suzie 24
=^..^= Cat
Honey
Candy
Explorer
here4u
Luscious Lisa
Ricky
Tim@London
Brad (Santa Monica)
```

Who first? Should I talk to Tim@London, given that I sort of already know him, or should I be adventurous and start chatting to someone I don't know? Luckily the decision is taken out of my hands, because the computer suddenly bleeps three times and a box flashes up, with Brad (Santa Monica) written at the top.

'Hi, Honey.'

'Hi,' I type back. Now *this* is more exciting.

'Do you have time to chat?'

'Sure thing.'

'So where are you, Honey?'

'London,' and then I think, hang on, he's American, he might be a bit thick, so I add 'England', just in case.

'Really? I was just there!'

'Oh? Whereabouts?'

'In London. I stayed in the Park Lane Hotel. It was business.'

Now this *is* more like it.

'What kind of business?'

'I'm your typical Californian beach bum who's made a living out of what he loves best. I own a gym.'

'So you're revoltingly fit then?' Oh God, I'm feeling inadequate again, but this is the Internet, I mean, this guy could never know what I really look like.

'LOL. Revoltingly. I like that. What about you?'

Oh God. This question was bound to come up sooner or later.

'I'm pretty fit but I work too hard to exercise as much as I'd like.'

'What do you do?'

'I'm–' I stop. Why be a boring journalist when I could be anything in the world? 'I'm a television presenter.'

There. Glamorous, exciting, and conveying that I'm probably pretty stunning if I'm on television.

'You must be stunning. You sound like an O:-).'

'What's an O:-)?'

'An angel! Unlike myself. I consider myself more of a }:-). That means a devil.'

'LOL. I'm no angel, but I don't do too badly.'

'Are you new to this?'

'Yes, I'm new, is it that obvious? Are you here a lot then, if you know I'm not here all the time? You can't be that fit if you're sitting on the Internet all the time (s).'

'Ah ha! Actually, the computer's in my office and I just sit here and mess around if I'm stuck at my desk. It keeps my mind off work!'

'What time is it there?'

'10 a.m. I've been in the office two hours. Before that I went running, and this afternoon I'm going roller-blading.'

'I love rollerblading.' Careful, Jemima, don't get too carried away.

'Yeah. It's a great sport. Good exercise and sociable at the same time.'

'You must be meeting hundreds of gorgeous California babes if you're out rollerblading all the time. What are you doing trying to pick up single women here?'

'Who says I'm trying to pick up single women?'

'Oops. Sorry. Aren't you?'

'Maybe just this single woman. You are, aren't you? Single?'

'Yes.'

'How come? You sound way too gorgeous to be on your own.'

If only you knew, I think, suddenly deciding to borrow Geraldine's life for a little while.

'I just ended a long relationship,' I type. 'He wanted to marry me but he wasn't the one.'

'How do you know he wasn't the one?'

'Good question. I suppose, naïve as it might be, I just think that when I meet the right one I'll know.'

'I don't think that's naïve. I think that's probably right. I feel the same way and I'm still waiting for that bolt of lightning to strike. But poor guy. He must be devastated. But lucky me (g).'

'Indeed.'

'So what kind of show do you work on?'

Think, Jemima. Think.

'It's like a British version of *Entertainment Tonight*.'

'No kidding! Are you like the Leeza Gibbons of British television?'

'No.' Even in this world of make-believe I know this would be pushing it. 'I'm a senior reporter.'

'That's still fantastic.'

'So what about you? How did you get into the gym business?'

'Left college, studied business, didn't know what to do, and moved to LA to hang out. Hardly anyone in LA is a native Angeleno, we're all from someplace else.'

'Did you want to be in the movie business?' I remember what Geraldine said about people who live in Los Angeles.

'LOL. No way. Too much pressure. I just wanted to

89

find something I loved doing that would make me a lot of money. I started going to a run-down gym every day, and the owner told me it was up for sale. I managed to raise the money, bought it and haven't looked back.'

'So do you make a lot of money then?'

'Put it like this. I'm *very* comfortable.'

'What kind of house do you live in?' Now, before we go any further, I think I just have to make it clear that I'm not being a gold-digger here. I just find it incredible that I'm talking to this man in Los Angeles of all places, somewhere I've never been, somewhere I've always dreamt of going, and I want to know everything about his life. I want to know if he really does live in a world of golden sands, palm trees and open-topped cars blaring rock and roll.

'A nice house! What kind of house do you live in?'

'A not so nice house. I was going to buy last year,' Lord, forgive me for stepping into Geraldine's shoes once again, 'but then it all fell through, so now I'm renting until I find somewhere nice again. I live with two girls.'

'I think I've died and gone to heaven! Any space for a guy?'

'Afraid not.'

'So how old are you, Honey?'

'I'm twenty-seven and I have to tell you, Honey's not my real name. My real name is JJ.'

'I like JJ. I like twenty-seven even better. I'm thirty-three.'

'So how come you're still single, Brad? Or do you have another name too (s)?'

'No. Brad's my real name. I date quite a lot, but, as I said, just haven't met the right woman yet.'

'What kind of woman would be the right woman?'

'I wish I knew. I keep hoping I'll know when I meet her.'

'I know what you mean!' **Except, naturally, I don't.**

'Oh damn. The phone's going. Listen, I have to go now, but I've really enjoyed talking to you, JJ. Can we meet here again?'

Call me cheesy but my heart skips a beat. 'I'd love to. How about tomorrow?'

'Same time?'

'Perfect.'

'Okay. I'll bring the sunshine, you bring the smiles. Take care.'

'Bye.' **I sit back and turn off the computer, and crazy as it may sound I'm excited about this and it takes the longest time to wipe the smile off my face.**

CHAPTER EIGHT

Ben had a hell of a week this week. Really, we wouldn't wish Ben's job on anyone. First of all he had to interview a woman who had the misfortune to have a thirteen-year-old crack addict tearaway as a son, trying to coax the story of his upbringing out of her.

She, poor cow, started off by merely answering Ben's questions with a yes and a no, intimidated beyond belief by this tall, good-looking, well-spoken journalist. Actually it wouldn't have mattered if Ben had been short, fat and balding, she would have been intimidated anyway, and she hates all journalists.

But in the end his charm won through, and finally he walked away with a story. He could have gone back to the office, but luckily he chose to file the story straight to the copy-takers from a payphone. I say luckily, because by the time Ben had got back it would have been at the very point Jemima Jones was asking her computer whether he would fall in love with her.

Then he was out on other stories for the rest of the week, he hardly saw anyone at all, didn't have time for chats, just kept his head down and kept working.

But Wednesday night was a bit of a bonus. Ben was home earlier than usual and both flatmates were out, so he had the place to himself. He could kick off his shoes, read the media *Guardian* he'd saved from Monday, and the latest issue of *FHM*, *and* watch the news. Just generally chill out.

He was settling back into the sofa, the television on to provide background noise, some early-evening quiz show that Ben would never dream of watching, and he was flicking through the media *Guardian*.

An ad on page 16 caught his eye but, perhaps more importantly, caught his imagination.

TELEVISION REPORTER

London Nights is a new daily show from London Daytime Television. Entertaining and informative, we need three reporters for on-screen work. A minimum of three years' journalism experience is required, with no television experience necessary. An interest in showbusiness and entertainment, news and politics, or health and beauty is essential.

Screen tests will be held.

Please send your CV, a covering letter and a showreel or photograph to . . .

This is it! thought Ben, sitting up with excitement. This is my big break. A reporter specializing in news and politics, this job has my name written all over it. He didn't hesitate, because Ben, after all, is a doer rather than a thinker. He reached for his pen and scribbled down the first draft of a letter.

A photograph, he thought, where can I get a decent photograph? Ben only has decent photographs, but a picture of him in sunglasses and a baseball cap is hardly the right image to project, and, as Ben well knows, a television image is essential.

He pulled a box from under his bed and sifted through the hundreds of photographs. Eventually he found one that was perfect, a photograph he sneaked out from the picture library at work. A photograph of him in a suit standing next to a local celebrity.

Screw the celebrity, Ben, this is your career, and Ben duly whisked the scissors out of the kitchen drawer and snipped the photograph cleanly in half, the celebrity gently floating to the grubby grey carpet.

He finished his letter, attached his CV, and slipped the photograph into the envelope. Now all he can do is hope.

Funny how my appetite seems to have decreased recently. It's lunchtime and I feel no desire to have a huge plate of food. This salad, a proper salad, is fine, and I'm quite happy sitting in the canteen with my nose buried in a magazine.

I bought this magazine this morning. Not my usual glossy fashion mag, I grant you, but one of the cover lines was about Internet dating, and I'm just really curious about this, so I bought it and I'm learning all about Internet cafés.

I didn't even know these places existed. This café, Cyborg, is in the West End. The picture shows metallic surfaces, banks of computers around the walls, and beautiful people sitting at the tables in the centre, sipping cappuccinos and eating ciabatta rolls stuffed with sun-dried tomatoes, mozzarella and fresh basil.

Internet dating, apparently, is the hottest thing since, well, since the Internet. According to this article, and it has to be said I take it with a slight pinch of salt because I know you can't believe everything you read, but according to this people are meeting and falling in love all over the world.

And not only that, Cyborg has become an in place, a place to see and be seen, a place where, should you not be lucky enough to find your soulmate on the Internet, you might just meet his eyes gazing at you over the top of your computer.

'That looks interesting,' says Ben Williams, towering above me as he puts his tray on the table opposite. 'I've heard about that.'

My heart starts pounding and already I can feel the faint flush on my neck. Surely this is the perfect opportunity, how can I ask him whether he wants to go, how can I make my voice sound casual when I'm all choked up inside?

'We should go down there one night,' says Ben, lifting a forkful of stringy roast beef to his mouth. 'The three of us should go. It would be a laugh.'

'I'd love to,' I gush. 'I mean, it sounds really interesting, I'd love to learn more about it.' A cooler tone to my voice now, I keep my excitement in check.

'We'll have to find out when Geraldine's free, although it's a bit of a quiet week for me, I could go any time.'

'And why is my name being taken in vain?' Geraldine sits down, a plateful of lettuce, tomatoes, cucumber and no dressing for lunch.

'Ben was just saying we should go to this place.' I gesture to the article. 'It sounds like fun.' But I'm thinking, why Geraldine too for heaven's sake? Why not just you and me, Ben? Not that I wouldn't want Geraldine there, it's just that I'd die to spend an evening alone with Ben. Die.

'Yup,' echoes Ben. 'In fact I'm not doing anything tonight. You?' He looks at me and I shake my head. Of course I'm not doing anything tonight. 'You?' He looks at Geraldine, who shakes her head, then makes a face. 'Sorry, guys, but count me out.'

'But why?' asks Ben.

'A computer café? I don't think so. It'll be full of computer nerds and strange men in anoraks.'

'That's where you're wrong.' The words are out of my mouth before I can stop them because the last thing I'm trying to do is persuade her to come, but my mouth seems to have a life of its own and I push the magazine towards her. 'Look at the people in that picture. They're all gorgeous.'

'Hmm,' says Geraldine, who has to concede that the people are, indeed, better than average-looking. 'They're probably models brought in to disguise the computer nerds and anoraks.'

'Oh Geraldine,' I say, again pretending I want nothing more than for her to join us. 'Just come.'

'Nope,' says Geraldine, picking up a slice of cucumber with her fingers and munching away. 'I'm busy washing my hair.'

'God, you're pathetic,' says Ben, but he doesn't say it nastily, he can't help it, it is so obvious that he wants her to come. 'Even if they are computer nerds it won't matter because we'll be there.'

'Nope.' She's refusing to budge and an involuntary

sigh of relief escapes my mouth. Luckily, neither of them notices.

'Well we're going anyway aren't we, Jemima?' And I beam away as I nod my head.

They sit and eat, and chatter about work, and in Ben's pocket is the job advert burning a hole, making him itch to tell someone. He's planning on sending off the application today, but he doesn't trust himself, he wants a second opinion before he actually posts it through the letterbox next to the bus-stop.

He wants to tell Jemima and Geraldine, he wants to know what they think, whether he stands a chance, whether they could see him on television, but he's not entirely sure Geraldine can be trusted.

Jemima, he knows, wouldn't breathe a word, and Geraldine, he suspects, wouldn't intentionally repeat anything, but it may just come out by mistake, and he doesn't want to risk word getting round the *Kilburn Herald* that he is looking for another job.

Also, Ben, not that it's any of our business but isn't it slightly bad karma to talk about a job before you get it?

So Ben keeps quiet, Jemima keeps quiet, too busy dreaming about tonight, and Geraldine rattles on about Dimitri, the boyfriend that was, although she hasn't quite managed to tell him that yet.

They finish their lunch and walk to the lift. Please, don't forget, prays Jemima, don't forget that we have a date tonight.

*

'So, shall we go straight from work?' Ben's looking at me.

Damn. I promised that guy Brad that I'd meet him tonight and I suppose I could go 'online' at Cyborg and talk to him from there, but Ben would be with me and I don't want him looking over my shoulder. I have a choice here. Ben or Brad. As if there's any question.

'Fine,' I say. 'Definitely.'

'Great,' says Ben, smiling warmly at me, because, I suspect, even though he would prefer to be with Geraldine, he would never be mean enough to cancel me, not when we've made this arrangement.

Later that afternoon Geraldine sends a message to my screen.

'Careful,' she says, 'word might get out about you and Ben . . .'

'What do you mean?' I send back, knowing exactly what she means, and praying that it does somehow get out, because perhaps if people thought something was going on, something might, in fact, go on.

'You know what people are like round here. If they see you leaving together they might just jump to conclusions!' As if! Geraldine knows this would never happen with me. Yes, the *Kilburn Herald* is a hive of gossip, and anyone seen, ever, with a member of staff of the opposite sex is immediately presumed to be having an affair. But nobody in their right mind would ever think I might be having an affair with Ben Williams. In my dreams, perhaps, but that's about it.

'Oh please!' I write, playing along with Geraldine's game. 'He's not my type!'

'What, with all those dimples, not to mention the

gorgeous hair that always flops in exactly the right
place? Are you serious?'

It's not always in exactly the right place, and so what
if it's floppy? It's gorgeous. Bitch.

'Absolutely,' I type back. 'We're just friends.'

'Well have a nice friendly time then, and don't do
anything I wouldn't do . . .'

At six o'clock I am so excited I'm practically bursting.
I've been to the loo, I've put on some make-up, although
truth to be told I can't really see any difference, and I'm
sitting at my desk trying to stop the urge to jump around
the room.

I'm sorry, Brad who?

And then Ben walks over and as soon as I see him at
the other end of the room I know he's going to cancel
me. How? He hasn't put his jacket on, his sleeves are
rolled up, and he looks tense and worried. Shit.

'Are you ready?' I say nervously, knowing full well
he's about to say he's not coming.

'I'm really sorry, Jemima,' says Ben, and to give him
some credit he looks as if he means it. 'I've just been
given a story to do on edition. I'm going to be here all
night.'

'Don't worry.' False gaiety brightens up my voice. 'We
can go another time. I've got loads to do at home
tonight anyway.' Like watch television. Read. Listen
to music.

'I'm sorry.' I start to feel sorry for him because he
really does look as if he doesn't want to be here. 'It's
fine,' I say again. 'We'll do it another time.'

'Look,' he says, and I'm convinced he can see the
disappointment in my eyes. 'You don't live far from me.

If I finish early enough maybe we could meet up later for a quick drink?'

'Great!' I say, too quickly to hide the enthusiasm in my voice, and mentally kicking myself under the desk for not being a bit more cool.

'Okay. What's your phone number?'

I write it down and, idiot that I am, while I'm writing I try to keep the smile from my face. Unsuccessfully.

'I'll give you a ring when I'm finished,' says Ben, who is looking more and more pissed off at the prospect of having to work late. 'Are you leaving now?'

'In a little while. I've got a few things to clear up first.'

He's phoning me! He wants to take me out for a drink! I have a date with Ben Williams! I'm seeing Ben Williams by myself after work! He didn't have to ask me but he wants to see me! Yes! Yes! Yes! Yes! Yes!

But before I go home, before I allow myself completely to give in to the excitement that's taken over my body, I have to meet Brad, and before I meet Brad I have to play my game, remember?

If I connect to the Internet within 45 seconds, then Ben Williams will fall in love with me. Please, please, please connect within 45 seconds.

I watch the little clock on the bottom right of the screen. 33. 34. 35. 36. Still not connected. I can't bear to look. I squeeze my eyes shut, praying that when I open them again I'll be connected. I open my eyes. 42. 43. Connected.

Phew. Thank you, God.

`'I thought you weren't going to make it :-('` flashes up on my screen, as soon as I enter the LA Café.

'I'm sorry. I was working on a big story.'

'Can you send me a videotape? I'd love to see you in action.'

'I'll try,' **and miracles will happen,** 'but everything's a bit busy at the moment.'

'So how was your day, JJ?'

'Superb.' **Now at least I'm telling the truth.**

':-) That's so English of you! I just came back from a workout which I didn't feel up to at all. I had a late night last night.'

'Did you have a hangover?'

'No. Nobody in California gets drunk. Ever. Do you drink?'

'No.'

'Smoke?'

'No.' **Forgive me for I am sinning, but a little white lie never hurt anyone.**

'Good! Me neither. I can't stand smoking, it's the one thing I really hate.'

'So tell me about your friends,' **I ask to get him off this line of conversation, and is it just me or does he sound ever so slightly boring? Nah, must be just me, I mean he's a genuine Hollywood hunk, for God's sake, what's boring about that?** 'What do you do socially?'

'Just kinda hang out, I guess. I have friends from all walks, and a lot in entertainment.'

'I'm surprised. I would have thought all your friends would be body-builders.'

'LOL. No, I meet all types through the gyms. We have a load of celebrities who work out here, and some of them have become friends.'

'Names, names, give me names.'

'Okay (S), but don't hold it against me. I know Demi and Bruce quite well, and a lot of the cast from *ER*. But a lot of my friends just work in the business, they're the guys behind the scenes. What about you?'

Think Geraldine, think Sophie and Lisa. Think anything but your own life.

'I go out for dinner an awful lot, usually quite smart places, and occasionally to clubs, but not that often, I did that when I was younger.'

'I'm trying to get a feel for who you are. What are you wearing right now? (I don't mean underwear (g), I mean what is your style).'

Shit. I look down at what I'm wearing. Massive stretchy black leggings and a huge voluminous orange shirt.

'An Armani shirt,' I type. 'Fitted jacket, short skirt, and cream shoes. I have to look smart for when I'm on screen.'

'Mmm. You sound just my type. I'm wearing my oldest pair of Levi's, a faded blue Ralph Lauren polo shirt (it matches my eyes!!) and sneakers. I keep a suit in the office for when I have meetings, but most of the time I'm real casual.'

'So what's Los Angeles like?'

'I love it. I love the climate, the buildings, the people. It's unlike anywhere else in America. Have you ever been here?'

No. I've never been anywhere, really. When I was younger, when my parents were still together, we went to a campsite in France a couple of times. I remember the soft sand, the palm trees in Nice, the warm water, but as I grew older, as my mother tried to cope with being a single-parent family, the foreign holidays stopped, and the French campsite became small hotels in Dorset, Wales, Brighton. What I wouldn't give to go to somewhere like Los Angeles.

'I haven't but I'd love to.'

'You should come out here. I bet you'd love it.'

'Is that an invitation? (g).'

'Sure! You could come and stay with me.'

Blimey, that's a bit quick, thinks Jemima, but then being as naïve as she is, Jemima doesn't know that Angelenos have a habit of extending the arm of friendship, before whipping it back again as soon as you try and take hold.

'But we hardly know each other,' I type, wondering whether Brad is ever so slightly insane. I mean, who in their right mind would extend this sort of an invitation to someone they don't know?

'We'd get to know each other pretty quick (g).'

'LOL.' I'm getting the hang of this.

'So when are you planning your next vacation?'

'I hadn't really thought. Some time soon, though.'

'Just don't go anywhere without speaking to me first! What are you up to tonight?'

At least now I can tell the truth. 'I'm going out for a drink with a friend.'

'A male friend?'

'Yes.'

': - ('

'Why :-(?'

'I'm jealous.'

I know this is ridiculous but reading those words suddenly makes me feel good. Stupid, really, because he's never seen me, but nobody has ever had cause to be jealous before. Of me! Jemima Jones! Going out with another man! This is amazing. New, but nevertheless amazing.

'Don't worry, he really is just a friend.'

'Tell me he's fat and forty.'

'Okay. He's fat and forty.'

'(vbg). Good. Just remember little old Brad sitting in California thinking about you. Can we meet again tomorrow?'

'I don't know if I can. I think I'm going out.'

'Okay. I'll e-mail you instead. How's that?'

'Perfect. I'll look forward to it.'

'Will you e-mail me back?'

'Promise.'

'Okay, JJ. Take care, and a big hug from me.'

'Same here. Bye.'

I gather up my stuff and while I'm getting ready to leave I'm trying to picture Brad in California, which is tough bearing in mind I haven't been there, but I have seen it in the movies. I wonder whether he really is a golden-haired, blue-eyed Californian god, or whether he is merely doing what I've been doing, and reinventing himself over the Internet.

Either way, it's going home time, and only a couple of hours, I hope, until I see the love of my life all by myself.

'I had a great day today.' God knows why I'm bothering

telling them, but I need to talk to someone, so instead of simply hovering in the doorway of Sophie's bedroom, which is what I usually do before disappearing up to my own room, I walk in and sit on the bed, which I know must seem slightly strange to them.

'Oh,' says Sophie, and then Lisa. 'Great.' I can see they're both flummoxed, having never heard me volunteer any sort of information, and never, in the history of our living together, have I walked in and sat on the bed.

'Why?' Sophie, at least, has the decency to be polite.

'No real reason, just a good day. And . . .' I pause for dramatic effect. 'And,' I continue, 'I've got a date tonight.'

'A date?' The two girls chorus, looking at me in wide-eyed amazement. 'Who with?'

'With the most gorgeous man in the world,' I say dreamily, in a tone remarkably similar to theirs. 'With Ben Williams.'

'Oh,' says Sophie.

'Ben,' says Lisa. And I know that each of them is simultaneously picturing a fat/ugly/boring/computer nerd in an anorak.

'Where are you going?' says Lisa.

'I don't know. Just out for a drink.'

'Well that's great! Good for you!' Sophie is being patronizingly kind.

'What time is he coming?' says Lisa.

'He's calling me when he's finished work. He's stuck in the office.'

'That's brilliant,' says Lisa. 'We'll be here for a while yet. We're going to a new club tonight so we won't be leaving until later. Maybe we'll meet him?'

'Oh.' Shit, no. Not if I can help it. 'Maybe.'

'Anyway,' says Sophie, all smiles, 'any chance of a cup of tea, Mimey?'

'Nope.' Abso-bloody-lutely not, my slaving days, I have just decided, are over. 'Not tonight. I've got to get ready.'

I can see Sophie and Lisa look at one another, and from the expression on their faces I suspect they have just realized that the gentle equilibrium of our household could well be about to change.

But Jemima doesn't care, why should she? She's got more important things on her mind, Ben Williams for one. She saunters out of the room, and doesn't let the fact that she can hear Sophie and Lisa whispering about her bother her for a second.

Jemima Jones flings open the doors of her wardrobe and desperately looks for something new. Something exciting, something inviting, something that might make her look slim, or at least slim enough to attract the advances of a certain Mr Williams.

But it's not easy to hide the flesh of someone as large as Jemima, and in the end she settles on a long black jumper and black trousers.

Jemima lies back in her bath, bubbles stretching to the ceiling, and loses herself in her usual daydreams. This time she sees herself out for a drink with Ben, in a small wine bar in West Hampstead.

Jemima will be on sparkling form, sharp and witty enough to have Ben wiping the tears of laughter from his eyes.

'I never realized you were so funny,' he'll say, clutching his stomach with mirth and looking at her in a whole new light, for even Jemima isn't stupid enough to think he'll fall for her beauty.

But perhaps if she is funny enough, charming enough, he may take a second look at the emerald green of her eyes, or the fullness of her ripe lips, or the shiny swinginess of her mousy but ever so glossy hair.

At the end of the evening he will walk her to the front door, and he will look at her very seriously, then shake his head, shaking away the crazy thought that he might be attracted to her. But the thought will not go away, and he will bend his head and kiss her, a gentle kiss on the lips.

'I'm sorry,' he'll say. 'I don't know what came over me,' but then he'll lose himself in her eyes and kiss her again. That's enough for tonight, a happy ever after would be inevitable after that.

'Jemima?' A gentle knock on the door.

'Yes?'

'I've brought you a cup of tea. I'll just leave it out here shall I?'

'Oh thanks, Sophie. That's lovely.' Now *that* really is a first. A smile spreads across my face as I hold my nose and duck my head under the water.

At ten to nine the phone rings.

'Jemima? It's Ben.' But of course. Who else could it be?

'Oh, hi.' He phoned! He phoned! He phoned! 'How was the rest of your day?'

'Fraught. But thank God it's finished now. Listen, I'm

just leaving the office so shall I come straight to you?'

There's a silence while I digest what he's just said. He hasn't cancelled! He's coming here!

'Hello? Jemima, are you still on for a drink?'

'Yes, yes. Sure. Fine. I'll see you soon.'

'Just give me your address again.' And I do.

'God, you really do like him don't you?' says Sophie, who's sitting on the sofa manicuring her nails with spiky spongy things sticking up all over her head, wrapping her hair into tight little knots in preparation for this evening.

I nod happily as I suddenly realize what will happen when Ben comes over, that there's no way on earth he could fancy either of them in the state they're in at the moment, and with any luck they'll still be like this when he arrives.

'Well, you look lovely,' offers Lisa, sitting there in her dressing-gown with curlers in her hair and a face pack looking incredibly like someone who's been dragged through a hedge backwards. Ha!

I can't help myself, I'm so excited I dance round the living room, whirling round and laughing, and Sophie and Lisa actually join me, and the three of us leap up and down in a rare state of happiness and unity. I don't think we've ever felt this before and we probably could carry on for hours except the spell is broken by the doorbell ringing. And me feeling sick.

I freeze. We all freeze. 'I'll get it,' says Sophie, and I don't even try to stop her as she runs down the stairs and opens the door. I peek my head round the landing. I'm going to enjoy this.

'Hi,' says Ben, leaning against the door-frame in his beautiful navy suit. 'Is Jemima in?' He smiles, and I can see what Sophie's seeing. What I see every time I look at Ben. Dimples, white teeth and blue eyes.

Ben's face falls. 'Have I got the wrong address? Damn, I'm so stupid, I must have written it down wrong.'

'No!' Sophie recovers her composure, simultaneously remembering that she looks terrible, that she has spiky spongy sticks in her hair, and no make-up, and is wearing a grotty old dressing-gown, and I literally have to hold my hand over my mouth to stifle the laughter that's bubbling up inside.

Sophie doesn't say anything. She can't say anything. She's absolutely, one hundred per cent gobsmacked, and she stands aside and gestures upstairs with a look of shock on her face.

Ben smiles his thanks and starts walking upstairs, as I start walking down. We meet in the middle.

'Have a lovely time,' shouts Lisa, who at that moment appears at the top of the stairs to see what Ben looks like. She can't see, for she hasn't got her contact lenses in, so she runs downstairs, still caught up in the excitement of dancing round the living room, for a closer look.

'Oh,' she breathes, one hand coming up to try and hide her face, the other frantically covering the curlers. 'Oh.'

'Oh?' Ben raises an eyebrow, grinning in amusement at the sight of thse two strange creatures, and I think I'm going to burst.

Lisa runs back upstairs, followed swiftly by Sophie.

'Bye, girls,' I shout as I follow Ben out the door. 'Have a good evening.'

*

There's no reply. Sophie and Lisa have collapsed on the sofa, each groaning with embarrassment.

'Oh my God,' shouts Sophie.

'Oh my God,' groans Lisa. 'Did you see him?'

'Did I see him? Did I see him? I've just seen the most gorgeous man I've ever set eyes on in all my life and you're asking me if I saw him? Jesus Christ, look at me.'

'Jesus Christ,' echoes Lisa. 'Look at *me*.'

'I'm in love, I'm in love,' moans Sophie softly, leaning back against the cushions.

'No, I'm in love,' says Lisa, putting her head in her hands at the thought of this gorgeous man seeing her like this.

'Shit,' announces Sophie.

'Shit,' announces Lisa. 'We have to see him again. Where do you think they've gone?'

'You're not thinking what I'm thinking are you?' says Sophie, a sudden glint in her eye.

'We could try.'

'Fuck it,' says Lisa with a grin. 'What have we got to lose.'

CHAPTER NINE

'You don't mind walking do you?' says Ben Williams, as the front door closes behind them. 'I thought we'd go to that bar on the main road.'

'No, that's fine,' I say quickly, because I'm already struggling to keep up with Ben's large strides, and consequently already trying not to lose my breath.

'Strange flatmates you've got there,' Ben volunteers after a silence. 'I take it they don't always behave like that.

'Or look like that,' he adds, as an afterthought.

'No. They're on their way out. That's them looking their best.'

Ben laughs. 'What are they like?' Not that he's interested, he's just trying to make conversation.

'They're okay,' I say, praying he's not interested, praying he couldn't see beyond the face masks and spiky spongy things in their hair. 'They're nice girls, really, but I wouldn't say we're friends.'

'What do they do?'

'They're receptionists at Curve Advertising Agency.'

'What, together?'

I nod.

'Do they ever get any work done?'

'I don't think their job is that stressful.' I silently muse on the conversations Sophie and Lisa constantly have about men.

'In fact,' I add out loud, 'I don't think they ever talk about "work" at all.'

'I bet they're the sort of girls who go out with very rich men, with very fast cars, who have very short relationships.'

I laugh in disbelief as I look at Ben. 'Very good. How could you tell?'

Ben smiles. 'I just can.'

Ben can tell because Ben has done that scene. Not as a rich man with a fast car, but as himself, because Ben can intrude on any social scene by virtue of his looks.

Ben had just left Durham University, where he had been hugely in demand, both as a boyfriend and as a friend. He was the golden boy of the campus, and his best friend, Richard, who had been down in London already for two years, had infiltrated the Chelsea set of bright young things, and welcomed Ben home with open arms and lavish parties.

Ben met heiresses, minor aristocracy, Eurotrash, minor celebrities. He went to dinner parties with people he had only ever read about on the rare occasions he had picked up a girlfriend's magazine, and he sat next to them and talked to them as an equal.

Most people wouldn't want to enter these circles. And even if they did, most people wouldn't have a clue how to get in. There was one occasion where Ben found himself spending all evening talking to the star of one of the most popular soap series in the country, a girl who, with her olive skin, long dark hair and petulant lips, was, at the time, the most adored girl in the country.

When Ben walked into the room – a party held in one of London's smartest restaurants – he spotted her and his heart turned over. Only that morning he had been reading about her in a newspaper, how she had just split from her equally famous boyfriend, a star of a rival soap, and how she was enjoying some time, probably about five minutes, on her own.

Ben was dying to meet her, but how can you approach someone so beautiful and so famous? Not even Ben had the balls to do that.

'Have you met Laurie?' said Richard casually to Ben, after Richard had himself kissed her on both cheeks and been enveloped in a warm hug by the delicious Laurie.

'We haven't met,' said Laurie, fixing her gaze on Ben and beaming a smile as she held out a hand to shake his, a smile that spread up through her face and gave her eyes, or so Ben thought at the time, the most amazing warmth.

'I'm Laurie,' she said, shaking his hand.

Ben nearly said, 'I know,' but luckily he didn't, because it's not the done thing in those circles to show you recognize someone, not unless you are equally famous. 'I'm Ben,' he said, smiling a perfect smile and struggling not to lose himself in her big brown eyes.

They spent the rest of the evening laughing softly together, and after a while Ben forgot she was Laurie, the most lusted-after woman in Britain, and she became Laurie, a gorgeous girl he was talking to at a party.

He didn't ask for her number. Not because he didn't want it, because Ben wanted nothing more, but because he thought she would be so used to being chatted up, she would never be interested in him. Admittedly, they

113

did get on, but no, she couldn't have been interested in him, Ben Williams, trainee news reporter.

But wonder of wonders, Laurie called him. She got his number from Richard, called and invited him to a party. A party where they didn't so much fall in love as consummate their lust for one another, a lust which continued for three months, three months of whirlwind jet-setting and partying.

Ben accompanied Laurie everywhere. They went to film premières, to restaurant openings, to exclusive nightclubs, and this in fact was the problem. Towards the end of three months, much as he liked being with Laurie, he was starting to feel that if there was the opening of an envelope, Laurie would insist on going.

With Laurie he mixed with the beautiful people. He even brushed shoulders, on the odd occasion, with Sophie and Lisa, who were never actually invited themselves, but who would be there with their latest glamorous men, not that Ben ever noticed, he was far too busy being Laurie's boyfriend.

And that, you see, was the beginning of the end. 'So *you're* Laurie's mystery man,' people used to say, instantly forgetting his name. 'So *this* is Laurie's boyfriend,' they'd say, greeting him distractedly before turning away to someone more famous, and consequently, at least in their eyes, more interesting.

He was bored, and it showed. On the few occasions he tried discussing this with Laurie, she'd smother him with kisses and tell him not to be ridiculous, that he was being silly, that none of these people mattered.

But you see it did matter. It mattered that Laurie had to be the centre of attention, wherever she went, and in the end Ben went to her flat one night and told her it wasn't working. He said he wasn't happy, that he really liked her, but he didn't like her lifestyle.

Laurie, being the actress that she is, cried for a while, and tried begging him to stay, promising things would be different, but Ben knew they wouldn't be, and he put his arms around her and kissed her softly on the forehead as he wished her good luck and goodbye.

Ben walked out of Laurie's flat, out of her life, and out of the whirlwind of parties, and truth to be told, although he missed Laurie, particularly at night, he was filled with a huge relief.

Because Ben isn't much good at pretending and, try as he might, he never felt he fitted in with the jet-setters, nor did he want to. It didn't take long for Ben to see beyond the glitz and glamour, to the heart of insecurities, pretensions and inadequacies that people tried to cover up.

He hated the fact that on the rare occasions people asked what he did for a living – and I say rare because most of these people were far too self-absorbed to be interested in anyone else – their faces would cloud over with boredom when he told them he was a reporter on the *Kilburn Herald*.

Ben never tried to disguise his job because he didn't have to. He was, is, secure and confident enough to not care what others think, and this is what he hated most of all, how he was judged by his job, not himself.

So yes, Ben is more than familiar with women like Sophie and Lisa, with the men they go out with, the parties they go to, and he wouldn't touch their lifestyles with a barge-pole. But of course Jemima doesn't know this. Nor do Sophie and Lisa, who, at this moment in time, are buzzing round the flat, pulling spiky, spongy things out their hair, washing off face masks, expertly applying make-up.

They are going out later, but they have decided to do a pre-clubbing pub and bar crawl. They watched Jemima and Ben walk up the road, and they know they won't have gone far, and they will soon be off on a search.

Ben and Jemima reach the bar, slightly incongruous for this part of Kilburn, for it looks like it ought to be in Soho or Notting Hill.

Large picture windows look out on to the street, and a huge bust of a woman, the sort of bust that used to be on the front of ships in pirate movies, stares fondly down from the top of the door-frame.

Ben holds the door open for Jemima as they walk in, and Jemima instantly wishes they had gone somewhere else, somewhere less trendy, somewhere where she didn't feel out of place.

For despite being in Kilburn the bar is filled with beautiful, fashionable people. A different sort of fashion to Soho or Notting Hill, more of a street fashion, less a designer label fashion, but nevertheless fashionable. The air is filled with smoke and soft laughter, and Jemima follows Ben to the bar, her shoes clip-clopping on the scrubbed wooden floors as she walks.

Antique mirrors and mismatched paintings cover the wall, and in a small room off the main bar are a couple of beaten-up leather sofas and armchairs. It is to this room that Ben carries their drinks – a pint of lager for him and a bottle of Sol for Jemima.

Jemima isn't a drinker, has never particularly liked

the taste of alcohol, nor has she ever quite known what to order in a bar when asked what she wants to drink. Vodka or gin and tonic sounds too grown up, too much like her parents, Malibu and pineapple, which is the only drink she loves, is too downmarket, and pints or even half pints of beer are too studenty.

Thank God for designer bottled beers, because these days Jemima never has to think. She'll just order a bottle of Sol, or Becks, or Budweiser, knowing that at least she will fit in.

Ben sits down on a brown leather sofa covered in cracks just under the window, then slides up to allow room for Jemima, who is about to settle herself in the armchair adjacent to the sofa.

Jemima squeezes in next to Ben, feeling more than a touch faint-hearted at such close proximity, and she pours her beer into a glass, because although we all know it's far more cool to drink designer beer straight from the bottle, Jemima can't quite get to grips with it.

'What do you think?' says Ben, looking around the room. 'It's nice here isn't it.'

'Lovely,' I practically choke as I gulp my designer beer through nerves and wonder why places like this always make me feel so awkward.

'So how's work?' Ben opens with the standard question, the question you always ask when you don't know someone very well, but quite frankly I don't care. It's enough that he's here. With me. Tonight.

'Boring as hell,' I say, my stock answer. 'I keep thinking I should really start looking around but then I still have this ridiculous hope that they're going to promote me.'

'They should,' said Ben. 'I know you rewrite most of Geraldine's stuff and you're very good.'

'How did you know that?' I can't believe he knows that!

'Oh come on,' says Ben with a smile. 'Geraldine's a good operator but she can't write to save her life. I saw that piece you wrote for her today, the one on dating, and there's no way Geraldine would have written an intro like that. I don't think she could write an intro of any sort.'

'But she's so nice.' I always feel vaguely guilty whenever anyone says anything negative about Geraldine. 'We shouldn't really be talking about her like this.'

'Like what? As I said, she is very talented, just not at writing. That's your problem, Jemima, you're a very good writer but you haven't got the confidence to be a good journalist. There's a huge difference. Journalism means digging, it means making hundreds of phonecalls, doorstepping if necessary, to get your story. It means operating on hunches, chasing leads, not stopping until you've got what you want. You haven't got that instinct, but Geraldine has. I know she's not a news reporter, but she could be.' He looks at Jemima carefully. 'You, Jemima, are a wonderful writer, far too good to be wasted on a newspaper, any newspaper, never mind the *Kilburn Herald.*'

'So what could you see me doing?'

'I think you should be going for a job on a woman's magazine.'

I look down at the half-empty bottle of designer beer and idly start picking off the foil around the rim of the bottle. I know Ben is absolutely right, even though I'm not sure I like hearing it from him. I mean, it's one thing recognizing your own weaknesses, but quite another hearing that someone else can see them that clearly, particularly when that someone happens to be Ben Williams. But, having said that, I'd kill to work on one of the glossy magazines I love so much, but I also know the type of women who work there, and I know quite categorically that I'd never fit in.

The type of women who work on glossy magazines are pencil-slim. They have highlighted hair, and hard faces covered in too much make-up. They always wear designer black, and always, like Geraldine, have sunglasses pushing their hair off their faces.

They go out for long liquid lunches, and network every evening in the trendiest bars in town. I could never look like that nor live like that, but of course I can't tell Ben this, so I shrug. 'I don't know, maybe you're right. What about you then, Ben? Are you a writer or a journalist?'

'Actually,' says Ben with a shy grin, 'I think I'm kind of neither.' Confusion crosses my face as Ben reaches into his pocket and pulls out a crumpled piece of paper.

'Here,' he says, handing it to me. 'What do you think of this?'

I skim-read it quickly then double back and read it again more slowly. 'What do you mean, what do I think?' Horror suddenly courses through my veins. No! Don't leave! My God, if you left the paper what would I have to look forward to? I would be completely desperate and I would not want to carry on.

'What do you *think*?' Ben repeats, a different emphasis on the words. 'Could you see me on television?'

'Yes, of course!' I say, because Ben needs to be reassured, and the truth is I could see him on television. Absolutely. 'You'd be brilliant on television, you'd be perfect!'

Ben sighs with relief. 'Do you think I'd get it?'

'Well they'll be nuts if you don't. You'll definitely get an interview, and I'm sure you'll be in with a chance. You've got a background in journalism *and* perfect white teeth, what more would you need?' Listen to me. I'm actually teasing Ben! I, Jemima Jones, am teasing the gorgeous Ben Williams! Ben laughs, showing off those teeth, and I suspect he's surprised at this side of me he's never seen.

Ben bares those beauties in a rictus, a great big false cheesy smile, and says, 'This is Ben Williams on *London Today*.' I start laughing, he looks ridiculous, and he raises one eyebrow and says, 'There, what do you think of that?'

'Too much white teeth,' I laugh. 'Even for you.'

'Can I read you my application letter?' he says. 'I'm sending it tomorrow, but would you tell me what you think?'

'Sure.'

'But you mustn't tell anyone. I know I can trust you but I wouldn't want anyone else at work to know about this.'

I watch as Ben pulls a copy of the letter out of his briefcase and as he hands it to me I feel totally honoured that he's trusting me.

'Dear Diana Macpherson,' I read silently. 'Re: Vacancy for television reporter as advertised in last Monday's *Guardian*. I am currently working as the deputy news editor on the *Kilburn Herald* but would love to move into television . . .' My eyes glaze over as I finish reading what can only be described as a completely bog-standard letter, and definitely not a letter that would even get him an interview, let alone a job.

I put the letter down and, trying to be as honest as I know how, I say, 'It's a great letter. It says everything you need to say, but if you want my honest opinion I don't think it's going to cut it. I think you need something more dynamic, more creative.'

'Oh God, do you think so?' Ben's face falls. 'I was trying to write something interesting but I was in such a hurry I just wrote down the first thing I could think of. You wouldn't . . .' His eyes light up as he looks at me.

'Of course I would!' I laugh, because I've been dying to since I read the first sentence, and grabbing a pen out of my bag I turn the letter over and start scribbling on the back.

'Health and beauty may not be my strong points,' I write, speaking the words out loud so Ben can hear, 'although I do have a bathroom cabinet fully stocked with men's cologne (freebies passed to me by the women feature writers at the *Kilburn Herald*), and my interest in showbusiness and entertainment may be limited – I have a healthy interest because of my work as the deputy news editor, but offer me the chance of a film première ticket and I'll run a mile. However, my knowledge of news and politics is exemplary.

'I am, as I briefly mentioned, currently working as the deputy news editor on the *Kilburn Herald*. Not, I'm sure you'll agree, the most prestigious of papers, but nevertheless the perfect place for a solid background in journalism. I started as a trainee reporter and have now been with the paper for five years. Needless to say, it is now time for a change, and I firmly believe that the future for all good journalists lies in television.

'I am, naturally, addicted to news and politics, and am an avid viewer of programmes not dissimilar to yours. I'm afraid I do not possess a showreel, however, I enclose a photograph together with my CV, and look forward to hearing from you.'

'There,' I say, slapping the pen down as Ben shakes his head in amazement.

'God, Jemima,' he says, rereading the words. 'You're amazing.'

'I know,' I sigh. 'I just wish someone else would notice.'

'That is just so inspired,' he says, a wide grin spreading across his face.

'At the end of the day, Ben, they're either going to love it or hate it, but either way they'll definitely notice it.'

'Do you really think so?'

'I really think so.'

While Ben and Jemima sit there chatting, mostly about work, it has to be said, Sophie and Lisa have got dressed – the pair of them in almost identical black lycra dresses, knee-high boots (Sophie's are suede, Lisa's are leather), with little black Chanel bags over one shoulder. Sophie is wearing a soft black leather jacket with a fur collar, and Lisa is in a cape. These are their pulling outfits – the clothes they wear when they venture to an unknown club to attract potential millionaire husbands.

They do look wonderful. They also look completely

out of place in Kilburn, tottering down the street in their smart clothes, leaving bystanders open-mouthed at these two exotic beauties.

They've already been in to the Queen's Arms, a bit of a mistake, they realized as soon as they walked in. They had to wave their arms to see through the smoke, and when they did they saw hundreds of men, all propped up against the bar, who went completely silent, presumably in admiration at the sight of Sophie and Lisa.

'I think I've died and gone to heaven,' groaned a builder, clutching his heart while his mates laughed.

'Looking for me, love?' said one to Sophie, as she looked around the pub, wishing fervently she was somewhere else.

'Will you marry me?' said another to Lisa, who kept her nose in the air and kept walking.

Both girls, to their credit, ignored the men, and walked out, heads held high, while the men jeered, and a couple ran to the door to try and jokingly persuade them to come back.

'God, what a nightmare,' says Sophie to Lisa as they walk up the road. 'Are you sure this is worth it? Shouldn't we just jump in a cab and go into town?'

'Are you mad?' Lisa turns to her in horror. 'When we've just met the best-looking man we've seen in ages.'

'He is gorgeous,' agrees Sophie, 'but he works at the *Kilburn Herald*. I mean, he's hardly in our league is he?' Sophie, bless her, has forgotten that she is a receptionist, because in her dreams she is a rich man's wife.

'With looks like that I couldn't give a damn. I don't want to marry him, but I'd kill to have a fling with him,' says Lisa, adding, 'Phwooargh,' with a faraway look in her eyes.

'Okay,' says Sophie. 'One more try.' They walk past the picture windows and into the bar, taking note of the beautiful and fashionable people, and feeling instantly superior. They, after all, are not only fashionable, they are also wearing designer labels, and both make sure the gold intertwined C's on their Chanel bags are facing outward just so that everyone can be sure of this fact.

'They *must* be here,' says Lisa, looking slowly at each table.

'I can't see them,' says Sophie, walking past the bar and into the room at the back. 'Nope,' she says as she surveys the room. 'Where the hell can they be?'

Doesn't time fly when you're having fun? Both our glasses are empty, so I stand up to get some more drinks, hoping to prolong this evening for as long as possible, praying that Ben won't stand up and say it's time to go. 'I'll get this round,' I say as nonchalantly as I can. 'Same again?'

'Are you sure?' says Ben, who, being the perfect gentleman I think he is, would probably be more than happy to pay for the second round. And the third. But I insist and he agrees to the same again.

But as I stand up I suddenly have a horrifying thought. From the front, I am passable. I can just about hide my size, and hope that people look at my eyes or my hair, but from the back even I admit that I'm huge. Can I back out of the room? Would Ben think I was completely mad?

124

Should I risk turning round and allowing Ben to see me from behind?

As I stand there in this dilemma, Ben starts rereading his application letter, so with a huge sigh of relief I walk, front first, out of the tiny room and into the main bar. BLOODY HELL! WHAT THE HELL ARE THEY DOING HERE?

I don't bloody believe this. Sophie and Lisa never, ever, come to places like this. Drink in Kilburn? Are you mad? Those evil little cows, I know exactly what they're doing. Look at them, tarted up to the nines and standing by the bar looking for something, and don't think I know exactly what they're looking for. Me. Or to be more precise, Ben. Bitches.

What am I going to do? I can't let them see me, I can't let them join us, because look at them now, Ben wouldn't recognize them as the two girls he met earlier this evening, and he might, just might, fancy them. Shit, shit, shit. I turn around and rush back to Ben.

'Ben,' I say, thinking, thinking, thinking.

Ben looks up. 'Hmm?'

'I just wanted to ask you, before I forget, um. Well, it's just that I wanted to ask you, do you have a showreel, because the ad said send a showreel.' Jesus, I sound like a total idiot but it's the best I could come up with, given the urgency of the situation.

'I'm going to send a photograph. Why, do you think I should send a showreel?' Ben is, as I knew he would be, looking at me as if I'm a bit strange.

'Well,' I say, sitting down. 'There are pros and cons, I suppose. I mean, a photograph doesn't show them exactly what they want to see, i.e. what you'll be like on television, but then a showreel is probably bloody expensive to put together.'

'Right,' says Ben, now looking completely confused as to why I'm sitting down again minus the drinks.

I look over Ben's shoulder and – thank you, God – see Sophie and Lisa walk out of the bar. Highly unusually, bearing in mind this is Kilburn, a black cab with an orange light shining happens to be driving down the road just as they leave, and both girls, on reflex, leap into the road with arms held high.

I can feel Ben watching me as I watch the cab drive off.

'Right,' I echo Ben, standing up purposefully. 'Drinks,' and off I go to the bar.

CHAPTER TEN

Jemima really doesn't want to get out of bed, not when she can lie here daydreaming about last night with Ben Williams.

Unfortunately for Jemima, her daydream didn't come true, but it was the next best thing, because, after Ben had insisted on walking her home, he leant down and kissed her on the cheek.

Jemima blushed bright red, and silently thanked God for being shrouded in darkness so Ben wouldn't see. 'I'll see you tomorrow,' he shouted as he walked up the road, and Jemima nodded mutely on the doorstep, too happy to speak.

She didn't have time to think about him last night – the three beers had gone straight to her head, and as soon as she touched the pillow she was out like a light, but now, now that it's morning, Jemima has time. Time to go over every word, every sentence, every nuance.

She has time to think about what happened, what could have happened, and what will, she hopes, happen in the future, and in all her fantasies Jemima is thin.

Jemima lies there for too long, and when she looks at the clock she knows that she'll be late for work if she doesn't get a move on. She hurries to the bathroom to run her bath, and completely forgets, yes really, completely forgets about her cereal.

And then, while she's waiting for the bath to run, she

decides to do something she hasn't done for months. She stands on the scales. Holding her breath, she balances her weight carefully, not daring to look down until she is perfectly still. And when she does, she starts smiling, because Jemima Jones has lost ten pounds. There's still a long way to go, but Geraldine was right, Jemima has finally managed to lose some weight.

Jemima stands there for a while and then she puts her hand out and holds on to the towel rail. She presses down hard and watches her weight plummet. The harder she presses, the more the weight goes down on the scales. I wish, she thinks. I will, she thinks.

And then, as she is about to get in the bath, she hears voices downstairs and realizes that Sophie and Lisa haven't left for work. She looks at her watch. 9.10 a.m., and they are never usually here at this time, they will be late.

'Jemima,' says Sophie from outside the bathroom door.

I lift my head out of the water. 'What are you doing here? You're going to be late for work.' Subtext: you're an evil cow and I haven't got anything to say to you.

'I know, we're just leaving but we both overslept.'

'Did you have a good time last night? How was the club?' I try my best to be nice, and I don't mention I saw them, that I know what they were up to.

'It was brilliant,' says Sophie. 'But how was your evening?'

'Lovely.' I'm smiling.

'So that was Ben?'

'Yup.'

128

There's a pause.

'He is gorgeous.'

My smile widens.

'Why don't you invite him over for dinner one night?' says Sophie, a hint of pleading in her voice.

As if! 'Maybe I will.' In your bloody dreams. I will keep Ben as far away from Sophie and Lisa as I possibly can.

'Okay, I gotta go. Have a good day.' I lie back in the bath and listen to both their high heels clatter down to the front door, the clicking punctuated by whispers and giggles.

Poor Sophie and Lisa. They really think I'm stupid enough to propel Ben into their arms? How wrong they are.

'So how was last night?' Geraldine sashays over, sipping from a cappuccino in a polystyrene cup she bought on the way to work.

'Fine.' I fight to keep the grin off my face, the grin that would give my feelings away.

'Did you go to that computer café?' Geraldine's tongue snakes out to her top lip and licks away the smudge of foamy chocolate that sits there.

'No, Ben had to work late so we just went for a drink.'

'Ooh, very cosy.' Geraldine looks at me closely. 'Jemima? You're not blushing are you?'

'No,' I say quickly. Possibly a little too quickly, and I feel a hot flush cover my neck and cheeks.

'Jemima! You are!' She lowers her voice and smiles. 'Do you fancy Ben?'

'No!' I say, wishing to Christ I didn't blush half as easily as I do.

'You do!' says Geraldine, 'I don't believe it.'

The flush starts to fade away. 'Geraldine,' I say firmly, with a conviction that comes from God knows where. 'There would be absolutely no point in me fancying Ben Williams, which, incidentally, I don't, because he would never, ever, be interested in someone like me. I don't particularly enjoy wasting my time, on anything, and certainly not on fancying someone who is so obviously unattainable.' I think, in my embarrassment at Geraldine guessing, I think I have come up with an argument so convincing that Geraldine immediately backs down.

'Okay,' she says, 'I believe you, but he is good-looking, everyone else seems to fancy him. Except me,' she adds with a sigh. 'I've got enough bloody problems of my own.'

'So how is Dimitri?'

'A nightmare. He's been coming round to the flat every night, begging me to go back to him. I've tried ignoring him but he just stands on the doorstep shouting up at my window, or bangs on the door for hours. The neighbours are going crazy and I don't really know what to do.'

'You could move,' I say, smiling.

'I think I might have to.' Geraldine smiles back, before looking across the room. 'Well, well,' she says. 'Speak of the devil.'

'Oh yes?' says Ben Williams. 'And what were you saying?'

'Jemima was just telling me you were a lousy shag.'

'I thought I was pretty good, actually, Jemima. You certainly seemed to be enjoying yourself.'

I laugh, fighting the urge to blush at the very thought. If only. If only.

'I just came over to say thanks for having a drink with me last night. I had a really nice time.'

'I've got to get some work done,' says Geraldine. 'See you guys later,' and she walks back to her desk.

'I also wanted to say thank you for looking at the job stuff. I really needed to talk to someone about it, and I know I can trust you.'

'Absolutely,' I say. 'My lips are sealed.' With a loving kiss perhaps? In my dreams.

'We must do it again some time,' says Ben distractedly, looking over at the newsdesk.

'Great!' Calm down, Jemima, calm down. 'What about next week?'

'Sure,' he says looking back at me with a smile. 'Maybe next week we'll manage to get to that computer café.'

How is a girl supposed to work when she's fallen in love? She's not, that's how. I do practically nothing for the rest of the day, unless you count floating on a large fluffy cloud called number nine, as work. I do manage to get my boring phonecalls done, though – soak greying underwear in Biotex before washing to make it sparkling white again; never open the oven door while cooking a soufflé; rinse hair in chamomile tea to bring out blonde highlights – and every time I catch a glimpse of Ben I lose myself in a massive fantasy.

At 4.35 p.m. I remember Brad. He said he'd send me an e-mail, and even though there are more important men to think about, it's so boring I log on to the Internet to see what he sent.

Yup, bang on time. As I connect a voice comes out of the speakers. 'You have new mail waiting,' it says in an

American accent, and a little box with a picture of an envelope in it says '1'. I click on the box, and after a few seconds Brad's e-mail comes up.

Hi, JJ!

I decided to send this just after we spoke – I couldn't wait until tomorrow, so here's a little surprise. If you press VIEW, you'll see a picture of me, it was taken a couple of months ago so it's pretty accurate – I haven't changed all that much, just had a haircut.

I'm on the beach at Santa Monica with my dog, Pepe. She's a schnauzer and the one true love of my life, but I had to send her home to my parents recently because I just don't have the time to look after her. I hope you like what you see, and I can't wait to see a picture of you. Will you e-mail me one by return? You have to get it scanned in to the computer, but I'm sure you'll find a way. If you can, meet me on Friday at the same time to let me know what you think!

I hope you had a good evening last night, and I hope you were good – you have to save yourself for me (g).

Big hug, Brad. xxx

Now this should be interesting. I move my cursor on to VIEW, and click once. Brad's letter disappears and the outline of a picture comes on to the screen. Just the outline, because the picture takes a while to appear. First, a few lines of sky emerge at the top of the screen then I can just about see the ocean, and suddenly the top of a head of blond hair.

The lines continue, and I'm amazed that I'm actually holding my breath, and when the whole picture is on the screen I exhale loudly. Bloody hell. He's one of the best-looking men I've ever seen in my whole life.

He's crouching, squinting slightly at the lens because the sun is in his eyes. One hand is around his dog, and the other is on the sand. He is very tanned, with blond hair and smiling blue eyes, and his teeth make Ben's look like those of an old hag, so gleaming, so perfect, so capped are they.

He is wearing a green polo shirt and faded Levi's, just as he said, and his arms are muscular and strong, covered with fine blond hair. He looks like an advert for the perfect male product of California. In fact, he looks so perfect that for a minute I can't help but wonder whether this is some cut-out from a magazine, but it looks like a photograph, and the dog is exactly as he described. Jemima Jones, your luck is changing.

'Phwooargh,' says Geraldine, coming up to stand behind Jemima. 'Who's that?'

'That's Brad.' I don't even bother looking round, I'm way too busy drinking in his unbelievable looks.

'Who's Brad?'

'The guy I've been chatting to on the Internet.'

'I didn't know you'd been chatting to anyone.'

'Yeah. I met him at the LA Café, remember the place you found?'

Geraldine nods. 'He is absolutely gorgeous. Too gorgeous to be true. How do you know it's him?'

'I don't. I mean, he did describe himself, but I have to agree, he does look too perfect, but on the other hand this is a photograph, it's not a cut-out from a maga-zine.'

'So what happens now?' asks Geraldine, who can't

quite believe that of all the people Jemima could have chatted to in the LA Café, she picked one who looks like a god.

'Oh God.' My voice is a horrified whisper. 'It's awful. He wants to see a picture of me.'

'Oh,' says Geraldine, who, nice as she is, is still probably thinking that he would never fancy me in a million years if he saw me. She doesn't say anything else. She doesn't have to.

'Exactly,' I say with a sigh. 'Oh.'

'Well why don't you cut a picture out of a magazine? What's the difference, he'll never know.'

I shake my head. 'I can't do that. I know I'll probably never meet him but I can't be that dishonest.'

'I've got it!' shouts Geraldine, clapping her hands together. 'I've got it, I've got it, I've got it.'

'What?'

'Right. There is a picture of you in the picture library isn't there?'

'Forget it, Geraldine. That picture is disgusting, it makes me look like a great big blimp.'

'Not when I've finished with it,' says Geraldine with a smile. 'Or rather, when Paul's finished with it.'

Paul is the man who works in the graphics department. Young, shy, sweet, the whole office knows he's got the most enormous crush on Geraldine. Paul is one of the few people I really like here. Not that I know him that well, but he's always calm and always takes the time to ask how I am, when people are screaming at him to get pages drawn, titles put into place, pictures put on to his Apple Mac. Paul is the man who always designs leaving cards should anyone at the *Kilburn Herald* be lucky enough to move on. Paul, in other words, as well as being a very nice guy is also a genius.

'Ring the library,' says Geraldine, 'and tell them to send up your picture.'

Ten minutes later a messenger troops towards my desk with a file containing my disgusting picture. I pull it out and feel sick as I survey my double chins and huge fat cheeks.

'No looking yet,' says Geraldine, whisking away the picture. 'I'll come and show you later.'

Geraldine runs off, a woman with a mission, putting her arms around Paul and babytalking to him in a way that turns him to jelly.

'Paaaauuul,' she says, arms wrapped around his neck. 'I need a favour.'

'Sure,' says Paul, who at that minute would have given Geraldine the earth.

'Jemima needs to look thin.'

Paul looks confused.

'Look. See this picture?' Paul looks and nods. 'You're so clever you could make her look thin couldn't you? You could airbrush out her chins and shade her cheeks and make her look thin.'

Paul smiles. 'As a favour to you, Geraldine, I'll do it. When do you want it?'

'Wellllllllll,' she says, looking up at him with huge blue eyes. 'You couldn't do it now could you?'

Paul sighs happily, anything to keep Geraldine near, and he sits down and scans the picture of Jemima into the computer. The photograph comes up on screen, and

Paul, with a few clicks of his mouse, shades out Jemima's chins.

'That's amazing,' gasps Geraldine. 'Can you do anything with her cheeks?'

Paul narrows her face, and then chooses the exact same shade of Jemima's skin. With incredible precision, he shades her cheeks in carefully until she has cheekbones. Perfect, beautiful, protruding cheekbones.

'God,' he says, staring at the screen.

'God,' says Geraldine staring at the screen.

'She would be beautiful if she lost weight. Look at that face, she's absolutely stunning, who would have thought.'

Of course we know that Jemima would be beautiful, but Paul and Geraldine have never even dreamt of what Jemima would look like if she were thin.

'Her hair looks a bit dull. I know it's mousy brown but can you put a few blonde highlights in, lighten it up a bit?'

'Who do you think I am? God?' laughs Paul, but just a few clicks and Jemima has golden honey-blonde highlights.

'What about her lipstick? Can you change the shade, that red's too harsh.'

'What colour do you want?' Paul brings up a colour chart on screen and Geraldine points to a natural pinky brown. 'There!' she says pointing at the tiny little square. 'That's the colour.'

Jemima, gazing out from the computer screen, looks absolutely stunning, but Geraldine knows it's not enough.

'Just wait there,' she says to Paul. 'We haven't quite finished. I'll be back in two secs.'

Geraldine runs back to her desk and quickly spreads out the pile of glossy magazines threatening to topple over on one side. *Vogue*? No, too posed. *Elle*? No, too fashion victim. *Cosmopolitan*? Perfect.

She grabs *Cosmopolitan* and runs back to Paul, flicking through the pages as she runs.

'That's the one!' she says, stopping at a picture of a girl on a bicycle. Her skin is fresh and glowing, her body is encased in the briefest of lycra cycling shorts and vest. Her hair is the same colour as Jemima's on the computer screen. She is standing astride the bicycle, looking into the camera, with one foot on the pedal. She is leaning forward and laughing. It doesn't look like a model, it looks like an exceptionally pretty girl on a summer's day who's been caught by her boyfriend's camera.

'You know what I'm going to say don't you,' says Geraldine smiling.

'I know what you're going to say,' says Paul, taking the picture of the girl on the bicycle and scanning it in.

He cuts and pastes. Clicks and shades. And there she is. Slim, stunning Jemima Jones, standing astride a bicycle, with one foot on the pedal, on a hot summer's day. Paul puts it on a floppy disk, and prints out the photograph, handing it to Geraldine. He has to admit he's done an incredible job.

'You are a genius,' says Geraldine, giving Paul an impromptu kiss on the cheek.

'And *you* are a persuasive woman,' he smiles. 'Now go away, I've got work to do.'

Geraldine runs over to Jemima, who's on the phone,

and without saying a word lays the printed-out photograph in front of her.

'Sorry,' I say to the caller on the other end of the phone, because Geraldine's leaping up and down next to my desk and making faces at me. 'Call I call you back?' I put the phone down and pick up the piece of paper Geraldine's been flashing in front of my face.

'So?' I say. 'I don't want to use a model's picture from a magazine. I told you that.'

'It's not a model, you idiot,' grins Geraldine. 'It's you.'

'What do you mean, it's – ' And as I look at the photograph I can feel my eyes widen in disbelief as my mouth drops open. 'Oh my God,' I whisper. 'Oh my God.'

'I know,' says Geraldine. 'Aren't you beautiful?'

I nod silently, too shocked to speak as I trace my cheekbones, my heart-shaped chin with my index finger. 'How? I mean, when? How . . .'

'Paul did it,' says Geraldine, 'so it's not really my doing, I just told him to add the blonde highlights, change the lipstick, and I found your body. What do you think?'

'I never realized.' I didn't, I swear to God, I never realized I could ever look like this. I can't take my eyes off the picture. I want to enlarge the picture and stick it on my face, show people I am beautiful, show them what's underneath the fat.

'Send it, send it,' says Geraldine. 'This picture is more than a match for Brad's. Send it and see what he thinks.'

Geraldine stands behind me as I log on to the computer again and send an e-mail.

'Dear Brad, I got your picture and you look perfect, better than perfect, too good to be true. Are you sure you didn't cut your picture out of a magazine?

'Anyway, I got the boys in graphics to scan in a picture of me taken . . .'

I look at Geraldine. 'When shall I say it was taken?'

'Say it was in the summer. Say you were cycling through Hyde Park with friends.'

'Okay.' I continue, '. . . in Hyde Park when I was with some friends in the summer. I hope you like it, I'm not looking my best.'

I grin at Geraldine. Geraldine grins back.

'I'm out again tonight but I'll meet you tomorrow (Friday) same time, same place. Take care, JJ. xx.'

' JJ?' asks Geraldine.

'That's what he calls me. Jemima Jones.'

' JJ. I like that. I think I might start calling you JJ.'

I put the disk in the computer, the disk that's got the picture of me on it, and press the ATTACH button at the bottom of the e-mail. I attach the picture to the letter, and press SEND. When the message comes up saying it's been sent, I breathe a sigh of relief and look guiltily at Geraldine.

'Wouldn't it be a nightmare if he wanted to meet me?'

'Don't be daft. He's thousands of miles away, you're safe as houses. Come on, let's go and get a cup of tea.'

'Your mum phoned,' shouts Sophie from the confines of her double bedroom when I get home. 'She said can you call her when you get in.'

'Thanks,' I yell up the stairs, grateful that I don't have to make small talk as I head for the living room.

'Hi, Mum,' I say, as she picks up the phone in Hertfordshire and says hello in her posh telephone voice. 'How are you?'

'Not bad,' says my mother. 'How are you?'

'Fine. Work's going well. Everything's fine.'

'And what about the diet? Lost any more weight?'

Here we go again. 'Yes, Mum, I've lost ten pounds in the last two weeks.' For once I'm not lying, and hopefully this will keep her happy for the moment.

I knew this was too much to ask. 'Careful,' she says. 'You don't want to lose it too quickly or it won't stay off. Why don't you join a slimming club, like me?'

My mother was slim and beautiful when she was young. She was the belle of the ball, or so she always says, and I know from the old black and white photographs that she was something special. Before she was married, she looked like Audrey Hepburn, with a beauty and elegance that betrayed her background.

She started putting on weight when my dad left sixteen years ago, and now, since hitting middle age and the boredom that comes with it, she's ballooned, but of course Mum being Mum she doesn't quietly accept it, she turns it into a bloody event. She's joined a slimming club, made a brand-new circle of friends, all of them larger ladies with shared dreams of taut tummys and firm thighs, and it's now the only thing she has to look forward to in life.

'Honestly, Jemima, it really works. I lost another two pounds this week, and I've made so many new friends. I think it would do you good.'

'Okay, Mum,' I say wearily. 'I'll try and find one in my

area.' Which of course I won't, because as far as I'm concerned a slimming club would be a living hell.

Conversations with her mother always seem to go the same way. Her mother never seems to ask about Jemima's work, her friends, her social life. She always asks about her weight, and Jemima immediately jumps to the defensive, suppressing it carefully with a weary sigh.

Her mother, you see, thinks she wants what's best for Jemima. In fact, her mother wants what's best for her mother. Her mother wants a slim, beautiful daughter who will be the envy of all her neighbours.

Her mother wants to take Jemima shopping, and show her off proudly as she squeezes into size 8 leggings. Her mother wants to turn to shop assistants and say smugly, 'The things young people wear today. Honestly, I don't know how they do it.'

Her mother wants to walk down the street with Jemima and feel immeasurably proud, she wants to soak in the admiring stares, bask in her daughter's beauty. What she doesn't want is what she's got. A daughter she loves, but of whom she's ashamed.

Because at this moment in time Jemima's mother tries her damnedest not to take her daughter shopping. She tries to avoid the pitying stares of shopkeepers, the humiliation of having to shop in outsize stores, of people staring at them walking down the street.

Jemima's mother loves Jemima, deeply, as only a mother can love her daughter, but she wishes Jemima looked different. If Jemima's mother could have seen the picture Geraldine has just constructed, Jemima's mother would have wept.

'And how's your social life?' my mother finally asks.

Should I tell her I had a drink with the most gorgeous man in the country last night? Should I tell her I've met the most gorgeous man in America on the computer? Should I tell her about the photographs?

'Fine,' I say finally. 'It's fine.'

'So what else is new?' says my mother, who always ends the conversation this way.

'Nothing, Mum.' I say what I always say. 'I'll call you next week.'

'All right, and well done with the diet. Keep up the good work.'

I put down the phone and pull the picture of myself out of my bag. Careful not to let Sophie and Lisa see it, I make cups of tea for all of us then go upstairs and lie on my bed, and gaze at my picture for a very long time.

CHAPTER ELEVEN

'YOU ARE BEAUTIFUL!!' says the e-mail on my screen. ' I couldn't believe it when I got your picture, you said that I was too good to be true but you look like a model! I didn't even know English girls could look that good! I'd really love to hear your voice, how would you feel about chatting on the phone? I understand if you don't want to give me your number, but I'll give you mine. Maybe you can call me later today. 310 266 8787. Hopefully I'll hear from you later, JJ. Take care. Brad. xxx.'

'Well,' says Geraldine, standing behind Jemima reading the words.

'Well,' I echo, feeling incredibly guilty. 'That's another fine mess you got me into.'

Geraldine laughs. 'It's not a mess, it's fun. The only way it could become a mess would be if he wanted to meet you, and he's so far away I'm sure that will never happen. So, are you going to phone him?'

'Why not?' Nothing to lose. 'I'll give him a call later.'

'I bet he's got a really sexy voice,' says Geraldine. 'As long as he doesn't punctuate every sentence with "like" and "rilly".'

I laugh. 'You are so cynical, Geraldine, I don't understand you sometimes.'

'I may be cynical but you, my dear Jemima, are an

innocent, and that's why you need fairy godmothers like myself to keep your best interests at heart.'

'Ben Williams, please,' says a voice at the end of the phone.

'Speaking,' says Ben, cradling the phone in one shoulder and looking through a pile of papers on his desk.

'Hello there,' says the girl, sounding young, sounding like someone not very important. 'This is Jackie from London Daytime Television.'

'Oh hello!' says Ben, attention suddenly riveted to the voice on the other end of the phone.

'I'm Diana Macpherson's secretary. We got your application this morning and Diana was wondering when you could come in to meet her.' As Jackie says this she's looking at Ben's photograph, and laughing to herself because she made a bet with Diana that his voice wouldn't be nearly as sexy as his face. She's laughing because she is wrong. Boy is she wrong.

'Oh!' says Ben. 'That's fantastic!' Calm down, he tells himself, play it cool, this doesn't mean anything. 'Well, things are a bit quiet this week, when do you want to see me?'

'We've had thousands of applications and we're trying to see the people on our shortlist as soon as possible. Any chance you could pop in this afternoon?'

Any chance? Any chance? Ben will create the chance. 'This afternoon's fine. Would three-ish suit you?'

'Three-ish would be perfect,' says Jackie, making a mental note to reapply her make-up after lunch. 'Ask for me at the main reception and I'll come and get you.'

'Do I need to bring anything?' asks Ben.

'No,' she laughs. 'Just yourself.'

Ben puts down the phone and looks around him. Shabby, he thinks. This room is filled with shabby desks, shabby computers, and people in shabby suits. Soon, he thinks, I will be working in television, where everyone is smart and stylish, where I will never again have to deal with the daily dross of the *Kilburn Herald*.

Careful, Ben, remember that old expression, don't count your chickens before they're hatched, but then again, if you received a picture of Ben you'd interview him too.

If the truth be known, had it not been for Jackie, Ben Williams would not have been seen. It is true that London Daytime Television received thousands of applications, and it is true that most of them went straight to Personnel, where they were sorted out into three piles: Yes, No, and Maybe.

Ben, however, was clever. Ben addressed his envelope directly to Diane Macpherson, so his application bypassed Personnel and ended up on Jackie's desk. Jackie has had a few of these applications, for there are several potential television presenters who possess as much common sense as Ben Williams, but none of the others has caught Jackie's eye in the way Ben did.

Jackie was pushing them all into an internal envelope to send straight up to Personnel when she spotted Ben's photograph, and as soon as she read his letter she went to see Diana.

'Diana,' she said, walking through the doorway, for this is television and the formalities normally associated with the hierarchy of blue-chip companies do not exist here. 'I think you should look at this.'

'Not another bloody job application,' said Diana. 'Send it up to Personnel.'

'Actually,' said Jackie, sitting down and drawing her legs up under her, 'actually I think you should have a look at this.'

'You fancy him then,' smiled Diana, reaching first for the photograph. 'Mmm,' she said, licking her lips. 'I see exactly what you mean.'

Diana Macpherson is a tough woman, as she would have to be to reach the position of executive producer on a show as big as *London Nights*. She is also single, and happens to have a particular penchant for pretty young boys like Ben. Diana Macpherson is a rough diamond – brought up on a council estate, she was the only girl on the estate to win a scholarship to a good girls' school, and then go on to university.

She is a bleached blonde, who at forty-one may not be as young as she used to be, but still turns heads by virtue of her micro mini-skirts and mane of hair. Everyone is terrified of her, and few have earnt her respect, but those who have have also won her undying loyalty.

Jackie, she respects, because Jackie comes from the same side of the street as Diana, and Jackie is bright. Jackie may be working as a secretary now, but when the time is right Diana will make her a researcher, and from there the world will be her oyster.

'So who is he then? Has he got any TV experience?'

'No,' says Jackie, 'but he's the deputy news editor on some local paper, and he sounds perfect for the news and politics reporter.'

'News and politics? Shame to waste that face on news and politics. Nah, he might be better for showbiz. Then again he might be crap on screen.' Diana sits in silence for a while, thinking.

'Why don't I get him to come in?' says Jackie. 'Then we'll see whether he's as good as he looks.'

'Yeah,' says Diana, 'I could do with a pretty boy round the office again.'

Jackie laughs, for the last pretty boy around the office went on to become the presenter of his own chat show, thanks to his affair with Diana.

'Go on,' says Diana. 'Give him a call and see if he can come in this afternoon.'

But Ben of course doesn't know any of this, although it obviously won't be the first time his looks have got him through the door. Ben is far too excited to analyse exactly why he has been chosen to meet the people at London Daytime Television, far too excited to get any work done.

'Jemima,' he says on the internal phone when he has said goodbye to Jackie. 'It's Ben. Can you meet me for lunch?'

'When? Now?'

'Yup, I'll see you down there. I've got something to tell you.'

'I've got an interview,' says Ben as we're queuing in the canteen. 'Can you believe it? I'm going in this afternoon!'

'That's amazing!' Of course I'm happy for him, I'm not that bitter, but even as I try to share his excitement I can feel my heart sink. 'See,' I say brightly, trying to cover it up as I nudge him playfully, 'I told you they'd know you were too good to pass up.'

'I know,' sighs Ben. 'But I really didn't think they'd give me a chance.' His face falls. 'Maybe they won't. Maybe I'll get on really badly with this Diana Macpherson and that will be it.'

'Do me a favour. You're being interviewed by a woman? You're in. All you have to do is charm her socks off and boom, you're on television.'

'Do you really think so?'

'Yes,' I nod. 'I really think so.'

'Oh God, I hope I get it,' he says.

'You will,' I say, knowing that I am probably right, that the gods will be shining on Ben Williams because of his good looks and easy charm.

We carry our trays to a table and sit down, me with a plate of salad, real salad as opposed to salads swimming in mayonnaise and calories. I'm with Ben, remember? Ben has invited me to lunch, and anyway these last couple of weeks my appetite doesn't seem to be what it once was.

I know I've only lost ten pounds, but I can see the difference already. My clothes are slightly baggier, my trousers no longer cut into the place where my waist should be, nor are they straining at the seams when I sit down.

I had forgotten how good this feeling was. For the time being, the cravings have subsided, and for the past couple of weeks I've only had a small bowl of cereal for breakfast, and I've bypassed my daily bacon sandwiches completely. The smell still gets me every day, but somehow I've managed to learn to live with it, not to give in to the temptation.

'Can you imagine if I were on television?' Ben says, looking as if he's lost in a world of cameras and fan mail. 'It would be amazing.'

'I've never understood people who wanted to be on TV.' I look at him in astonishment. 'I can't think of anything worse.'

'Why?'

'Well, for starters think of the lack of privacy. Suddenly everywhere you go people recognize you and want your autograph or your time.'

Ben grins. 'Fantastic!' he says.

'And then,' I continue, rolling my eyes, 'there's the press invasion. I mean, you know yourself what it's like. As soon as you're on screen you become public property, and that means newspapers have a licence to dig up as much dirt as they can find.'

'Are you suggesting I may have sordid secrets?' says Ben with a grin.

'Doesn't everyone?' I look at the ceiling thinking I should be the one on television, because I am probably the only person in the world with no skeletons in her closet. 'And anyway, they don't have to be that sordid. Think of the number of times you've opened the Sunday tabloids and seen an ex-girlfriend or boyfriend of someone famous spill the beans on their steamy sex life. I'd hate that. All sorts of awful people would come crawling out of the woodwork.'

'I hadn't thought of that,' says Ben. 'But I don't think any of my exes would do that.'

149

'It's amazing what people will do when there's money in it.'

'God, if someone wanted to offer one of my exes money to talk about our sex life together good luck to them. I don't think they'd find anything interesting.'

I blush, can you believe it? Ben mentions sex, and I blush. Never mind that it wasn't that long ago I was sitting looking at hard-core porn pictures with him on the Internet. Nope, all he does is say the word and I bloody blush. 'Oh well,' I say. 'That only seems to happen to people who become famous for no reason at all, and I suppose they enjoy all the attention. They probably wouldn't bother with London Daytime Television reporters.'

'What about BBC newsreaders?'

'Is that what you want to do?'

Ben groans in mock ecstasy. 'I would kill to be a BBC newsreader.'

I'm stunned. 'Well you are a dark horse. I never realized.'

'There are a lot of things about me you don't know,' says Ben playfully, as he tucks in to his lunch.

'So,' says Geraldine, squeezing in next to them. 'Is Jemima telling you about her latest boyfriend?'

'Geraldine!' Shut up! I don't want Ben to know about Brad. But, on the other hand, if he thought someone else found me attractive maybe he'd start looking at me in a new light. What do you think, worth a try?

'Well?' says Geraldine. 'Are you?'

'What boyfriend?' says Ben.

'The gorgeous Californian hunk on the Internet.'

'No,' he says, 'I don't know anything about this. I don't

150

believe you, Jemima Jones, you've been pulling on the Internet?'

'Not exactly. I just went back to the LA Café, I was messing around and I've been chatting to this guy, Brad.'

'Brad!' Ben laughs. 'God, how typically American.'

'But Brad is completely, drop-dead gorgeous. A hunk. No two ways about it,' says Geraldine.

'How do *you* know?' Ben's curious.

'He e-mailed me his picture,' I say, wishing we'd never brought the subject up because however you look at it dating on the Internet sounds as naff as answering Lonely Hearts adverts, and before you ask, no, I've never done that.

'And,' adds Geraldine, munching on a mouthful of crisp iceberg lettuce, no dressing, 'she's calling him this afternoon.'

'Good for you,' says Ben distractedly, looking at his watch and jumping up. I look at my watch and see that he's got to make tracks if he's going to be on time for his interview. 'Sorry, guys,' he says, standing up. 'I've gotta run.'

'Good luck,' I shout, as Ben runs off.

'Good luck?' Geraldine's looking quizzically at me. 'What for?'

'Oh, some interview he's doing this afternoon.' Good girl, Jemima, that's what I like to see, thinking on your feet.

'So when are you going to call the hunk?'

'I don't know.' I sigh dramatically. 'This could all end rather nastily, I'm not sure I want to.'

'Oh what the hell,' says Geraldine, 'what have you got to lose?'

She's right. I know she's right.

We walk back upstairs together and Geraldine tells me about a man she met last week, Simon, who drives a top-of-the-range Mercedes, works in investment banking and is taking her out for dinner tonight.

'Right,' she says, perching her tiny bottom on the edge of my desk. 'Pick up that phone and call Brad.'

'I can't,' I say, smiling.

'Jemima! Just do it.'

'No.' I shake my head firmly.

'Honestly, I despair of you sometimes. Why not?'

'Because.' I pause for dramatic effect. 'Because it's six o'clock in the morning in California and I don't think he'd be very happy.'

'Oh,' says Geraldine. 'In that case I'm going to come back over here at five o'clock, and I expect you to be on that phone. Long distance. Agreed?'

I nod my head. 'Agreed.'

Sure enough, at five o'clock on the dot Geraldine walks over to my desk. If I didn't know better I'd think she'd set her alarm.

'Okay, okay,' I laugh, picking up the phone. 'I'm phoning him.' I dial the number without really thinking of what I'm doing, just laughing at Geraldine, who's pulling faces at me as she disappears down the office.

'B-Fit Gym,' says the American voice brightly on the other end of the phone. 'Good morning, how may we help you?'

'Good morning,' I say, suddenly wondering what the hell I'm doing. 'May I speak to Brad, please?'

'Certainly, ma'am. May I say who's calling?'

'It's Jemi – ' I stop. 'It's JJ.' Ma'am?

'Please hold the line.'

I sit and wait, and I come incredibly close to putting the phone down but just before I do someone else comes on the line.

'Good morning,' says another bright female voice. 'How may I help you?'

'Oh hello. May I speak to Brad, please?'

'May I say who's calling?'

'It's JJ.'

'Please hold the line.'

'Hello?' A deep, sexy, male Californian voice. 'JJ?'

'Brad? It's me. JJ.'

'Oh my God, you called me! I can't believe you called me. It's so good to speak to you.'

'Thank you,' I say, not knowing what else to say.

'I just got in to the office, what a great surprise.'

'Well it's five o'clock here, so I'm wrapping up.'

'God, your voice is as sexy as your picture, which, I have to tell you, is now pinned to the wall. In fact, I'm looking at you as we speak.'

'I'm really flattered.' If only you knew.

'So JJ, did you have a good day?'

'It was fine. I did a bit of filming this morning, which was fun.' Don't ask me what it was, please don't ask.

He doesn't. 'I can totally understand why you're on television, you look so groomed, I think is the word.'

'What, even on my bicycle on a hot summer's day?'

'Absolutely. I had to show your picture to everyone here, and boy, let me tell you, you have a fan club already in California.'

'God, that's so embarrassing,' I groan audibly.

153

'Don't be embarrassed. I think it's great that you work out and keep healthy, you're exactly my type of woman.'

'Good,' I say, recovering my composure. 'I aim to please.'

Brad laughs. 'So listen, Jemima, what I don't understand is how come you don't have a boyfriend. I mean I know you said you just broke up with someone, but you must have men falling at your feet.'

'I wouldn't put it quite like that. I do meet a lot of men through work but I suppose I'm picky.'

'Well I am honoured that you liked my picture enough to call me. So, talk to me some more, I love your accent. Tell me everything about yourself.'

'God, where do I start?'

'Okay, tell me about your parents, do you have any brothers or sisters?'

'No brothers or sisters. I'm an only child and my parents are divorced.'

'Oh that's tough,' says Brad. 'Mine are too. Did yours divorce when you were young too?'

'Yup,' I say, wondering why on earth I'm telling all this to someone who is practically a stranger, when not even those closest to me, well, Sophie, Lisa and Geraldine, know anything about my past. 'My mother is not a happy woman. She bitterly resents being on her own, and tries to have far more input to my life than is healthy, which is mostly why I moved to London.'

'You're not from London then?'

'No, I was brought up in the country. In a small town on the outskirts of London, which I suppose is really suburbia.'

'And did you ever get lonely as a child? Did you want brothers and sisters?'

I wasn't just lonely as a child, I was achingly, heart-breakingly lonely. I used to go to bed at night and clasp my hands together, praying to God to deliver a baby brother or sister, not fully understanding that without a father, there was little, if any, chance of that happening. But although I have already revealed more than I planned, this would be too much, so I take a deep breath and say breezily, 'Sometimes, but not often. I was fine by myself.'

'Look,' says Brad after I've filled him in on the finer details of my childhood, the pain-free details. 'This might sound crazy, because this is the first time we've actually talked and we hardly know each other, but I have a feeling that we could have something special here.' He pauses while I try to digest what he has just said, because truth to be told the only reason I've been doing this is through boredom, not because I thought there could be something special here.

And for God's sake, this man is practically a stranger. Admittedly, a particularly good-looking one, but this seems bizarre. We've never met, this is our first phone conversation and he could be some psychotic killer. And how does he know I'm who I say I am? Oh. Perhaps I'd better get off this train of thought.

'JJ? Are you still there?'

'Yes, sorry. Carry on.'

'Well, it's just that I know it sounds kinda crazy to meet on the Internet, but then people are meeting like this all over the world, and sometimes it does work out. Look. I think you are great. I think you're funny, and

155

honest, and beautiful and I love your accent and I don't want to scare you off but I'd really like to meet you.'

Thank God Brad cannot see me, see how my face has paled, how I am thinking seriously about killing Geraldine because I knew, I just bloody knew that this would happen.

'I'm not suggesting you come over here, I mean I know that would be a big step for you and you're probably really busy in your career, but how would you feel if I were to fly over to meet you?'

'Um,' I say imaginatively, stalling for time, praying for divine intervention, which of course doesn't come. 'Um,' I repeat.

'Okay,' says Brad. 'I can hear that I've thrown you a bit, but would you just think about it?'

'Okay,' I lie. 'I'll think about it.'

Then, as if that isn't enough, I do the unthinkable. I give Brad my telephone numbers, both home and my direct line at work (because I wouldn't want to blow my cover as a top TV presenter), and when we say goodbye I put the phone down and go into the loo to look at myself in the mirror.

I look at my chins, my cheeks, my bulk, and as I stand there I make a decision. A huge decision. A decision so momentous that even in this split second I know that it will change my life. I run back to my desk, well, run/lumber, grab my bag, and run down the stairs.

I'm not going far. I'm walking, almost sprinting, up the Kilburn High Road to the brand new fancy gym that just opened. I pass it every day, barely registering its existence because what, after all, would a gym mean to me.

But today is the day I'm going to change my life. And pushing through the double doors I approach the pert blonde receptionist with as much determination as I can muster.

'Hello,' I say. 'I'd like to join.'

CHAPTER TWELVE

'I'll just get you a form,' says the blonde behind the reception desk, looking at Jemima Jones with more than a touch of curiosity, because she can't quite understand why someone the size of Jemima would want to join a gym.

Of course she should have realized that she wants to lose weight, but the fact of the matter is that this brand-spanking-new gym isn't just any old gym. The joining fee is £150, and the monthly fee after that is £45. A lot of money, precisely to keep out people like Jemima Jones.

It's a good job Jemima doesn't wander around before joining, because had she seen the type of people who do frequent this gym, she would have been off faster than you can say Stairmaster.

She would have seen the beautiful people glowing prettily on the treadmills, a hint of sweat showing their suntans off to maximum potential. She would have seen the women in the changing room carefully applying their make-up before they ventured out, just in case the man of their dreams should happen to be cycling beside them.

She would have seen the middle-aged housewives, wives of high-flying businessmen, who drip with gold as they step up and down and up and down and up and down to keep their figures perfect for the round of dinner parties they attend.

She would have seen the muscle-bound men, all young, all fit, all good-looking beyond belief, who go to the gym partly to keep in shape and partly to eye up the women.

And Jemima Jones would have been far too intimidated to set foot through the door, but luckily the manageress isn't around, and there's no one who can show Jemima all the facilities the gym has to offer, so Jemima just takes the form and sits down in reception to fill it out. She blanches slightly at the price, but then it's a small price to pay for being thin, and this gym is so close she won't have any excuse not to go, so with pen in hand she starts ticking the boxes.

As anyone who is currently spending each night in front of the television eating take-aways will know, the hardest part of an exercise regime is taking the first step. Once you find the motivation to start, exercise can be strangely addictive, much like, in fact, the Internet.

When the form has been filled in and she has written down her bank details for the direct debit, she goes back to the desk.

'Um, I've never actually been to a gym before,' I say, feeling faintly ridiculous as the blonde hands me a stack of papers, timetables for classes, information about the gym.

'Don't worry,' says the blonde with a bright smile. 'Many of the people here haven't been before. We need to get you in for a fitness assessment and they'll work out a regime for you.' My body tenses as I wait for her to look me up and down with a withering glance but she doesn't, she just smiles and opens a large diary on the desk and flicks through the pages. 'You normally have to wait around three weeks for a fitness assessment, but we've had a cancellation tomorrow morning. Could you make it at 8 a.m.?'

8 a.m. tomorrow? Is she mad? 8 a.m. is the middle of the night.

'Eight o'clock's fine,' I hear myself say, the words hanging in the air before I've had a chance to think about what I've just said.

'Lovely,' says the blonde, pencilling in my name. 'You won't need a leotard, just a T-shirt and shorts . . .' She takes a look at me and sees my face fall at the prospect of wearing a leotard. 'Or sweatpants would be fine. And trainers, you need to wear trainers.'

'That's fine,' I say, wondering where the hell I'll get all this equipment, but in for a penny, in for a pound, and looking at my watch I see it's 6.15 p.m., and I know there's a sports shop in a shopping mall in Bayswater that will still be open.

I leave the gym and, crazy as this may sound, I'm convinced that already my step feels lighter, my frame seems somewhat smaller, and in my mind's eye I can already see myself as I'm going to be. Slim. And beautiful. As I once was, I suppose, when I was a child, before my father left, before I discovered that the only thing to ease the pain of being abandoned by an uncaring father was food.

I hop into a taxi – my, my, Jemima, you are being extravagant these days – and instruct the driver to take me to Whiteleys, where I ignore the clothes shops, the shoe shops, even the book shop, and go straight up the escalator to the sports shop.

Half an hour later my arms are being dragged down to the floor with shopping bags. I've bought a tracksuit, two pairs of lycra leggings, three pairs of socks and a gleaming pair of Reebok trainers. I have spent so much money today that there's no way now I can change my mind. That was the idea.

And as I walk out of the shopping mall I stand for a few minutes looking at the bustling crowds, listening to the mix of voices from every part of the world. I could go straight home, that is what I would have done a few weeks ago, but look at this street, look at the last rays of the sun. It's a beautiful evening and I'm not ready to go home and sit watching television, not just yet.

And as I wander down Queensway, pushing through the crowds of tourists, I start to feel like I'm on holiday, and what better to do on holiday than to sit at a pavement café and enjoy a drink.

Normally I'd order a cappuccino, and scrape the chocolate off the top before adding three sugars, but things are about to change, and I find a small round marble table outside a patisserie, and order a sparkling mineral water.

She doesn't have anything to read, nor does she have anyone to talk to, but Jemima is feeling happier than she has felt in a long time. Happier, perhaps, than she has ever felt in her life. She sits in the fading sunshine and without realizing it she has a huge smile on her face because for the first time she starts to feel that life isn't boring. Life is the most exciting it has ever been.

Jemima Jones's life has been rumbling for a while now, but today is the day it finally turned over.

Ben Williams has just got home to find the answering machine winking three messages at him. Two are for his flatmates, and the last one is from Richard, his oldest friend. We would say best friend, but we can't say that too often because men, after all, are not supposed to have best friends, they are supposed to have mates.

Nevertheless, Ben picks up the phone and calls his best friend, his oldest friend, his best mate, because (a) he wants to talk to him as it's been a while, and (b) he has to tell someone about his interview today or he might possibly burst.

'Rich? It's me.'

'Ben! How are you, boy?' This is the way they talk to each other.

'I'm fine, Rich, how 'bout you?'

'Rolling along, Ben. Rolling along. I haven't seen you for ages, what have you been up to?'

'Actually, I've got some news.'

Richard's voice drops to a whisper. 'I know a good doctor.'

'What?'

'You've got some bird pregnant.'

'Don't be ridiculous.' Ben starts laughing. 'I haven't got anyone pregnant, chance would be a fine thing! No, I had a job interview today.'

'That's great, what for?'

'Come on, Rich, you can do better than that. What's my dream job?'

'No! You had a job interview as a newsreader? No way, that's serious.'

'It wasn't for a newsreader, but it is for television. I went for a job interview with London Daytime Television as a reporter on a new show.'

'Good work. When d'you hear?'

'I'm not sure. They seemed keen but I have to do a screen test.'

'Good luck, I'd like to see my best mate on television. Think of the pulling you could do then.'

Ben just laughs, because Ben wants to tell Richard everything. He wants to tell him about walking in and sitting in the huge domed glass atrium of the TV company. He wants to tell him how it felt sitting surrounded by pictures of the stars of the company, and how a very famous presenter of the morning show came and sat next to him.

He wants to tell Richard about going up in the lift, about stepping out feeling sick with nerves, and waiting just outside for the secretary to come and get him. He wants to tell him how friendly the secretary was, if anything slightly too friendly, but how he assumed that is how they all are in television.

He wants to tell Richard about walking in to meet Diana Macpherson. About her micro mini-skirt and high heels, about how she kicked her shoes off after a few minutes and put her feet on the desk.

He wants to tell Richard how Diana fixed him with a cool gaze and said, 'Well fuck me, Jackie was right, you're even prettier in the flesh.'

He wants to tell him how he made her laugh, how they ended up talking about the nightmares of being single, about how he pretended to equal her horror stories with stories of his own, because he really felt there was some sort of a bond.

He wants to tell him that they didn't really talk about television, or about work. That she seemed far more interested in him, and that it didn't feel like an interview, that it felt more like having a chat with a friend, and did Richard think that was a good thing or a bad thing.

And he wants to tell Richard how, at the end of their 'interviews', Diana shook his hand and said, 'All right then, Ben Williams. I won't say you're in 'cos I don't know what you look like on screen, but our viewers would fucking love those pretty-boy looks of yours, and I want you in on Thursday to have a screen test.'

But of course he can't say any of this, because Richard is a bloke, and as well we all know blokes don't *do* detail, they do facts, and Richard would probably fall asleep with boredom.

So they sit and chat, and all the time Ben's mind is far away in the land of London Daytime Studios, and as soon as he says goodbye to Richard, he picks up the phone and dials Jemima, because who better to listen to the details than Jemima Jones, his new-found friend.

'Hello, is Jemima there, please?' Listen to how well spoken he is.

'Sorry, she's out at the moment. Can I take a message?'

'Um, yeah. It's Ben from work. If I leave my number could you get her to call me?'

Sophie nearly drops the phone. 'Oh hi, Ben!' she says enthusiastically. 'It's Sophie, we met the other night.'

'Were you the one with the face pack or the one with strange things in her hair?' Ben's laughing.

Sophie groans. 'Please don't remind me. We both looked awful, but for the record I was the one with the strange things in her hair.' Lisa looks up from the magazine she's reading on the sofa. Her eyes widen as she mouths, 'Is it him?' Sophie nods.

'Ah,' says Ben, who can't think of anything else to say.

'But I don't usually look like that,' adds Sophie, who wants to keep Ben talking, who wants this conversation to develop into the sort of hour-long conversation women always try to have with men they have only just met, and who they fancy madly.

'I should hope not,' says Ben. 'I wouldn't have thought Curve would appreciate it.'

'Jemima told you where I work?'

'She mentioned it,' says Ben, wondering why this message is taking so long to deliver. 'Look, can I give you my number?'

'Sure. Sorry. I'll just get a pen,' she says, flying back to the phone in an instant. 'Okay, shoot.'

Ben leaves his number and asks if Jemima could call him back as soon as possible, and they say goodbye.

'Guess what I've got,' she says to Lisa, waving the piece of paper in the air then clutching it to her chest.

'You bitch,' says Lisa, who sort of does mean it, but sort of doesn't. 'You can't keep that, you have to give it to Jemima.'

'I will,' says Sophie, 'but first I'm going to copy it down for myself.'

'But what excuse will you use? You can't just phone him, and he wasn't exactly on the phone with you for long,' she says triumphantly. 'It didn't sound like he was that interested.'

'Not yet,' says Sophie. 'But I think we should invite him somewhere, maybe a party or a club, and if we have to we'll invite Jemima too, but we are going to see him again, and this time we are going to look better than we've ever looked before in our lives.'

Lisa grins, happy now that she has been included, and confident that, given the choice, Ben would opt for her tumbling curls.

The girls hear the front door slam, and Jemima comes upstairs, dumping her bags on the living room floor.

'Oooh,' say the girls in unison. 'You've been shopping. Show us what you've bought.'

'It's not very exciting,' I say, when in fact I'm very excited, I'm so excited I don't think I'll be able to sleep tonight. 'I just bought some gym stuff. I joined a gym today.'

'You're kidding,' says Sophie, looking completely shocked.

'I kid you not,' I say happily.

'But what for?' says Lisa.

'To get fit, what do you think. I am going to lose all this weight and get fit, and in a few months' time you won't recognize me.'

'Is this for that guy at work, Ben?' says Sophie slyly.

'No,' but of course it's for that Ben at work, although now it's also for Brad in Santa Monica. 'It's for myself,' I say, and you know what? As I say it I realize it's true. Sure, Ben and Brad are the catalysts, but I'm going to lose weight for me.

'Oh by the way,' says Sophie, just as I'm walking upstairs. 'Ben called. His number's by the answerphone.'

Everything stops, only for a few seconds, but in those few seconds all I can hear is my heart-beat thundering in my ears, and when my world starts again it goes spinning into overdrive. I pick up the phone, and when Ben picks up the receiver at the other end I – ridiculous creature that I am – am almost completely breathless.

'Ben?' I try to calm myself, to take deep breaths. 'It's Jemima.'

'Hi!' he says, and I start to relax, because I never expected Ben to sound so happy to hear from me. Please let him ask me out, please let him have phoned me because he can't stop thinking about me.

'Aren't you going to ask me?' he says.

Ask him? About what? I remember. 'I forgot, oh I'm so sorry, I forgot. How was it, how did it go, did you get the job?'

Ben settles back into his sofa and tells Jemima Jones everything. He tells her all the things he wishes he could have told Richard, and he can hear from her gasps of amazement and sounds of encouragement that she is glued to the phone, one hundred per cent completely rapt. *This* is the kind of reaction you only get from women. This is why Ben phoned Jemima.

'I can't believe you're going to be on television!'

'I don't know if I am,' says Ben, but of course he does know, he's always known.

'So when's the screen test?'

'Day after tomorrow.'

167

'So soon!'

'Yup,' says Ben. 'They'd like someone to start in about two weeks, so if I gave in my notice on Monday I'm owed two weeks holiday so that would be it, I could start in two weeks.' He pauses. 'If I get the job, that is.'

'You'll get the job,' I say.

'Do you really think so?'

'Yes,' I say again. 'I really think so.'

When my alarm goes off at 7.15 a.m. I groan, roll over, and decide that this is madness. I'll go another time. But no, says a little voice inside my head, if you don't go now you'll never go and think of the money you've spent.

So I crawl out of bed, half asleep, and go to the bathroom, where I splash my face with cold water to try and wake up. I throw my clothes for the day into a bag, and pull on an old T-shirt, my new tracksuit bottoms and the new trainers.

Stumbling out the door, I walk to the bus-stop in a complete daze, amazed at how quiet London is at 7.30 in the morning, so when I reach the gym, I can't believe how many people are already there, puffing and panting through their pre-work workouts.

'Hi,' says a big brawny bloke in reception, walking over. 'You must be Jemima. I'm Paul, and I'm your fitness instructor.'

Paul takes me upstairs, through the gym where I look straight ahead, trying to ignore the bodies beautiful, and into a small room designed specifically for the purposes of fitness assessment.

'Right,' he says, putting a form on the table. 'You have to fill this out, but first I have to check your blood pressure.' He does this, and then I wince as he pulls out what looks suspiciously like a surgical instrument.

'Don't worry,' he laughs. 'This isn't going to hurt. This,' he says, pointing to the pincer-like instrument, 'is to measure your fat ratio. That way we can keep track of how much fat is turned into muscle.'

Shit! This is a mistake. This is my biggest nightmare. No one's ever measured my fat before, Jesus, no one even knows how much I weigh, and my eyes suddenly fall upon the scales in the corner of the room. Shit, shit, shit.

But what can I do? I can't run away, so I just pretend I've left my body, I'm somewhere else, as Paul measures the fat on my arms, my waist, my stomach and my hips. He doesn't say anything, just writes the results on the form.

'Okay,' he says when he's done. 'If you slip your shoes off I'll just weigh you.' Shit.

I stand on the scales looking miserably at the wall as Paul juggles with the scales until he has my exact weight. Fourteen stone, eight pounds. He writes it on the form, as I try and control my embarrassment, the only relief coming when I remember that had I come a month ago, I would have been nearer fifteen and a half stone, because somehow I have managed to shed almost a stone in the last few weeks.

'So,' he says, sitting down and gesturing for me to sit down too. 'That wasn't too painful, was it?' I smile at him gratefully, because he didn't shrink with horror at my size, he's being so matter of fact that at last I'm starting to relax.

'What are your aims?'

'You mean apart from getting fit?'

Paul nods.

'I want to be slim. I want to lose all this weight and I want to be fit. And healthy.'

Paul nods sagely. 'Good. I'm glad you're here, because the biggest mistake people make is to crash diet and do no exercise, which means that yes, in the short term they lose weight, but they inevitably put it back on again, plus you'd be horrified at what serious dieting and no exercise can do.'

'What do you mean?' I'm intrigued.

'You wouldn't want to be left with great huge folds of flabby skin would you?'

I shake my head in horror.

'That's why you need to exercise. You have to tone up and firm up, and that's just as important as what you eat. Speaking of which, have you thought about a food plan?'

'I've cut down what I eat, but no, other than that I haven't really thought about it.'

'How would you feel about me working out a diet for you?'

I nod enthusiastically as Paul starts explaining about proteins, carbohydrates, fat groups, food combinations.

'Food combining is the best way for you,' he says and, pulling a blank piece of paper out from a drawer, he starts writing. For breakfast every day, he writes, I will have fruit, as much as I want, but no melon because it's harder to digest. I will always wait for twenty minutes before eating anything else to allow the fruit to digest.

For lunch I will have salad with only one of the food groups, because I will never mix protein with carbohydrate. For example, he writes, salad with cheese, salad with a jacket potato, salad with bread. I could have, he tells me, an avocado and tomato sandwich on wholemeal bread with no butter. Avocado is fine, he says, when it's eaten in the right combination.

For dinner I will have vegetables with grilled fish, or chicken, and again I can have as many vegetables as I want.

'And,' he says, looking up, 'you will need to drink lots of water every day. At least one litre, preferably more.'

'Will I lose weight quickly?'

'You'll be amazed,' he says. 'But it's better that you don't lose it too quickly because the quicker you lose it the quicker it will climb on again. But this isn't a diet, Jemima, it's a way of life, and once you understand that you'll find that your entire shape starts changing.

'I want you to have regular assessments,' he says, standing up and walking towards the gym, 'every six weeks or so you should come in to see me to check your progress.'

I follow him meekly into the gym and Paul starts by showing me the warm-up exercises. He leads me to the bike, and says, 'Five minutes on the bike, I think, just to warm you up.'

So I sit and I pedal, and within two minutes sweat is pouring off my brow and dripping on to the floor. 'That's it,' says Paul. 'You're doing great, nearly there.' Jesus, I want to stop, I can already feel the muscles, what muscles there are, in my legs cramping up, but if Paul says I can do it, I can do it. And I do.

'Stairmaster next,' he says, pressing some buttons on

the Stairmaster. Fat burner, he enters, then my weight, then ten minutes. I start climbing.

After two minutes I'm thinking this is really easy, what's all the big fuss about? After five minutes I think I'm going to die.

'I. Don't. Think. I. Can. Carry. On,' I manage to get out in spurts of breath.

''Course you can,' says Paul with a smile. 'Think of the tiny, pert bottom you'll have.' I picture a tiny, pert bottom in my mind, and motivation, inspiration, floods my body and drives me on. I manage nine minutes, and then I really can't do any more.

'Don't worry,' says Paul. 'Next time you'll do ten, but you have to break the pain barrier. Once you've done that it's easy, and every time you come here you'll find it gets easier and easier.'

After the Stairmaster I row 1,500 metres, then finish off with a one-mile powerwalk on the treadmill.

'You've done brilliantly,' says Paul, who seems to believe in the power of motivation and isn't letting the fact that he is talking to a bright red, puffing, sodden lump put him off. 'I'm not going to give you any weights just yet. First of all we'll concentrate on the cardiovascular stuff to burn some fat, and then we'll work on building muscle.'

I stagger down to the changing room, where I shower on shaky legs before going in to work. But you know the strangest thing? The strangest thing is that, tired though I am, walking along the road on my way to the office, stopping briefly to buy a bottle of still mineral water, I don't think I've ever felt better in my life.

CHAPTER THIRTEEN

'I'm going to a leaving party tomorrow night,' I type in my e-mail to Brad. 'One of my closest friends at work is leaving to work for another television company so I'm pretty sad. I know it will be a good night, but I don't know who I'm going to talk to any more, other than you, of course, whom I seem to be becoming more and more dependent on.

'Anyway, I won't be able to talk to you later as I'm going straight to the gym, but call me tomorrow when I get home after the party and I'll tell you all about it.

'Big hugs and kisses as usual, JJ. xxxxxxxxxx.'

Good heavens, let us just stand here and take a look at Jemima, because the transformation, in just a month, is completely remarkable. Paul, the trainer, is quite frankly amazed, but he is also slightly worried because the weight has dropped off at an alarming rate, and he suspects that Jemima is eating far less than he told her to.

His suspicions are right. Jemima took his diet sheet home with her, put it in a drawer, and promptly ignored all the good advice, and for the last month this has been her daily routine.

Jemima Jones gets up in the morning at 7 a.m., and has a glass of hot water with a slice of lemon in it. She pulls on her tracksuit, shoves her clothes for work into a training bag and is in the gym by 8 a.m. She has doubled the routine Paul devised for her, and has added some movements of her own. She spends fifteen minutes on the bike, twenty-five minutes on the Stairmaster, fifteen minutes on the rowing machine and half an hour on the treadmill, mostly powerwalking but with the odd spurt of running.

She then does floor exercises and sit-ups, and just about manages to get to the office by 10 a.m., completely ignoring bacon sandwiches on the way there.

She sits at her desk and swigs still mineral water all morning, and then for lunch she has a side plate of plain lettuce, tomatoes and cucumber, while Geraldine shakes her head in amazement, still unable to comprehend Jemima's will-power after all this time. Once lunch is finished, Jemima will feel ever so slightly guilty at having eaten anything at all, because Jemima has taken this dieting business to extremes.

She drinks another litre of mineral water during the afternoon, finishes work at around 6 p.m., chats to Brad on the phone usually for at least half an hour, and occasionally an hour, and then goes back to the gym.

She does an exercise class for an hour at the end of the day, and then relaxes in the steam room or the sauna. She still thinks she is huge, although she is infinitely less huge than she was a few months ago, and refuses to watch herself in the mirrors of the gym, except to think that one day all this excess weight will be gone. One day she will have a hard body. One day she will *be* a hardbody.

If Jemima had any choice at all she would eat nothing in the evening, because she has started this new regime and she is determined to lose the weight, but she knows that if she eats absolutely nothing, she will not have the energy to exercise, and she needs protein, so dinner is a small plate of steamed vegetables and a plain-grilled chicken breast.

The food she eats is boring and plain, but for once she doesn't care. She doesn't have cravings, she feels too good at having lost this weight. She likes the feeling of her clothes being large and, although she hasn't as yet bought anything new, she knows that if she carries on being as good as she has been, it won't be long before she will be able to wear whatever she wishes.

Jemima Jones has been losing between five and six pounds of weight a week. Add her weight loss this last month – twenty-two pounds – to the thirteen pounds she lost in the previous month, and we will see that Jemima Jones now weighs twelve stone.

Paul has told Jemima that, at 5'7", she should aim to get down to ten stone, but Jemima Jones has ignored this and has decided that she will weigh eight and a half stone, even if it kills her.

Jemima stands in the bathroom, takes off all her clothes and looks at herself in the full-length mirror. She still feels revulsion at the cellulite on her thighs, the bulges on her hips, but even she has to concede that the change is miraculous.

For, despite being twelve stone, Jemima Jones now has a waist. She has knees. She has a small double chin, rather than a quadruple one, and her face is almost unrecognizable for it has slimmed down so much. JJ is slowly emerging from the fat of Jemima Jones and, although she is not yet the JJ on a bicycle on a hot summer's day, there is no question that she is getting there. She is finally getting there.

And tomorrow night is the night she has been dreading, Ben's leaving party. Everyone has been amazed, because nobody has ever left the *Kilburn Herald* to go on television. Some have left to join national newspapers, regarded as heroes by the colleagues they have left behind, but those are few and far between, and nobody has ever dreamt of knowing someone who started at their crappy local paper and went on to be famous.

'Next thing you know we'll be interviewing *you*,' guffawed the editor, clapping Ben on the back after it had sunk in that he was losing his star reporter. 'Don't forget us when you're rich and famous, eh?' And Ben just smiled, mentally ticking off the days on his fingers.

For all his diligence and hard work, Ben has been far too excited these last weeks to concentrate on the paper, but he has been forgiven, and his normal daily duties have already been delegated to others, his presence at the office now being a mere formality.

Ben was at the office when he received the call telling him he got the job. He knew the screen test was the best he could have possibly done, but he didn't know whether it was good *enough*, and the days of waiting were some of the worst of his life.

'It's fate,' he kept saying to Jemima. 'Either it's meant to be or it's not.'

'Que sera, sera,' she would echo back, hoping that fate would smile upon him, but hoping too that fate would smile upon her, that perhaps it wouldn't mean taking him away from her, because she was absolutely sure that once Ben left the *Kilburn Herald* he wouldn't look back, he wouldn't remember the friends he left behind.

And it is safe to say that Ben and Jemima are friends. They weren't, when we first met them, they were merely colleagues, but as so often happens in times of need friendships are forged, and Ben needed a confidante, more than ever during the week of the long nights, as he dubbed it.

But friendships can be a transient thing, as Jemima well knows, and their friendship, as much as it is based on trust and admiration, is equally based on convenience, and Jemima is certain that once Ben is immersed in the glamorous world of television she will no longer hear from him.

But Jemima wants Ben to be happy, more than she wants him to be at the *Kilburn Herald*, and she was the first person he told when he heard he got the job.

'Ben,' said a sharp voice on the phone. 'Diana Macpherson here.'

Ben's breath caught in the back of his throat, and Diana's laugh cut through the silence. 'Well,' she said, 'I suppose you want to know what I thought of the screen test?'

'Yes,' said Ben, not sure what to make of her tone.

'I've just watched it,' she said, 'and I had to phone to tell you that you. Are. Fucking. Amazing.'

Ben gasped. 'You're joking!'

'I never joke about things like this. This is one of the best screen tests I have ever seen, and I can't believe you haven't presented before. Are you sure you're telling the truth?'

Ben laughed.

'I've shown it to the head of features and we both agree that you're the right man for the show, but there is one problem.'

Ben's heart sunk. 'A problem?'

'Yeah. It's not a big one, but when we spoke you said you wanted to do news and politics, and I'm afraid that's not what we're offering. We'd like to offer you a year's contract on *London Nights* as the chief showbusiness reporter.'

There was a silence while Ben tried to digest what she had said.

'You still there, Ben?'

'Yes, sorry. It just wasn't what I expected.'

Diana sighed. 'I know, but I've been in this game long enough to know what people's strengths are, and although I know that news and politics are what you really want to do, I also know that you'd be wasted on that. You need to be much more high profile, and quite frankly, Ben, with this as a stepping stone the world's your oyster.'

'I know.' Ben nodded his head, still not quite sure what to say. Of course it was a wonderful opportunity, but did he want to be seen as a showbusiness reporter? As a fluffy, flim-flam celebrity interviewer?

'Can I just have a few minutes to think about it and then I'll call you right back?' asked Ben, unaware that nobody, no first-time presenter, had ever had to think about an offer from Diana Macpherson before.

'Okay,' she agreed. 'I'll be in the office for another ten minutes, and if I don't hear from you I'll ring up our second choice. Sorry to be brutal, but that's television for you.'

'Don't worry,' said Ben. 'I understand.'

Ben went running round to Jemima's desk, and they sat there, heads huddled together, while Ben told Jemima what had happened and what his reservations were. Don't be ridiculous, said Jemima, it's the chance you've spent years waiting for, you wouldn't be pigeon-holed, and all it took in television was to get your foot in the door. 'If you screw this up,' she said seriously, 'you don't know when the next opportunity will arise. Or indeed if,' she added ominously, 'it will arise.'

That was what did it for Ben. He checked his watch, two minutes to go before the ten minutes were up, kissed Jemima on the cheek, picked up her phone and dialled London Daytime Television.

'Diana?' he said in a much firmer voice. 'It's Ben Williams. I've thought about it and I'm phoning you to tell you I'd love to work for you, and as soon as we organize the dates, I'll be in the office.'

'Phew,' said Diana Macpherson, who was smiling. 'You gave me a right fucking scare, especially because we didn't even have a bloody second choice!'

And with just one phonecall Ben's fate was sealed. It may not be the job he always wanted, but it's certainly a start, and a very good one at that, but before a new beginning must come an ending, and tomorrow night is the last night of his time at the *Kilburn Herald*.

Jemima Jones feels sick at the thought, so sick, in fact, that she commits an unforgivable sin and confides in Sophie and Lisa, only because she has no one else to talk to, and she doesn't mean to say anything, it just comes out by mistake.

*

'You seem a bit down,' says Sophie, as they walk in. 'Is everything all right?'

'Fine,' I say, and before I can help it a huge sigh has escaped my lips. 'I think I'm just overdoing it a bit maybe.' I try and cover it up.

'You *are* spending a huge amount of time at the gym,' agrees Lisa, 'maybe you should cut it down, I mean, no one needs to exercise as much as you.'

Shall we take a look at what's going on here? Lisa is beginning to see that the Jemima Jones of old is well on her way to being the JJ of the future, a JJ that could well be the unthinkable. A threat. Because Lisa, as addicted as she is to the superficialities of life, can see that as the weight is dropping off, a real beauty is emerging, and Lisa doesn't like this. Not one tiny bit.

'Maybe,' I say, but actually I'd like to be spending a lot more time in the gym. If I had my way I'd move into the gym, I'd work out all day every day, but I can't expect her to understand this, I can't reasonably expect anyone to understand this. I know what this is, I've seen it on a daytime show. I'm addicted to exercise. Ha! Me! If someone had told me six months ago that I would become addicted to exercise I would have rolled on the floor laughing. But I know about this, I know that this addiction is more or less the same as being addicted to alcohol or drugs. I know my body is now overflowing with endorphins, and I feel fantastic almost all the time.

I once, just once, missed an evening class when I went

out for a drink with Ben, and the next morning I felt so damned guilty I doubled my workout, and nearly collapsed with the strain.

'There is another reason, I suppose,' I say because I have to say it. I have to tell someone and I can't tell Geraldine. 'Ben's leaving tomorrow.'

Sophie and Lisa perk up. 'What?' says Sophie. 'Not the gorgeous Ben that we met?'

I nod miserably.

'Where is he going?' asks Sophie.

'He's going to London Daytime Television. He's going to be a reporter on a new show.'

'You mean he's going to be on screen?' Lisa's eyes are wide, and they're so bloody superficial I can see exactly what they're thinking. Pulling a handsome man is all well and good, pulling a rich man is even better, but pulling a famous man almost goes off the Richter scale, and Ben is not only gorgeous, he's about to be famous. They're so impressed they can hardly speak.

'Yes, he's going to be on screen, and I'm just a bit down about it. I mean I'm thrilled for him, really, I am, but I'll miss him. He's become one of my closest friends at work, so maybe that's why I'm feeling a bit low tonight.'

'Where's the leaving do?' says Sophie nonchalantly. As if I'm that stupid. As if I'd tell her. Honestly. As if!

'I can't remember,' I say, shrugging, standing up and heading out of the room. 'Some wine bar somewhere.'

Jemima Jones walks upstairs to her room while Sophie looks at Lisa. 'Thank you, God,' she says with a smile, 'for providing me with this golden opportunity.' For

Sophie has kept Ben's number, just hasn't had the bottle to call him. Until now.

'What are you going to do?'

'Watch me.' Sophie digs her Filofax out of her bag, pulls out Ben's number and picks up the phone.

'Hello, is that Ben? Hi, it's Sophie, Jemima's flatmate. Yes, the one with the hair. I just phoned to say good luck, Jemima just told me about your new job and I've never met anyone who's been on television before. You must be really excited.'

'Er, yes,' says Ben, who can't imagine why this girl he hardly knows is phoning. 'I am.'

'I just wanted to say well done, because now you're practically famous you probably won't be coming round here too much, so just in case we don't meet again, good luck.'

'Thanks,' says Ben, with a smile. 'Really, that's ever so nice of you.'

'Have you had a leaving do then?' says Sophie innocently, winking at Lisa.

'No, it's tomorrow night.' There's an awkward silence where neither of them knows what to say, but Ben fills the gap first. 'Come along if you like.'

'I'd *love* to!' she breathes. 'Where is it?' She writes down the address as Lisa jumps around in front of her, pointing at herself and making faces.

'Is it okay if I bring my friend Lisa?' she finally says grudgingly.

'Sure,' says Ben, thinking what the hell, he'll be far too out of it to notice.

'Wonderful. We'll see you tomorrow night.'

Hi Sweetie

Thanks for your e-mail, it always brightens my day to come in to work and find a message on screen from you. I can't believe how close I feel to you and we've never even met, but as soon as you're less busy you'd better come straight to LA, although I'm not too sure I can wait another three months!

I'm already planning all the things we can do together once you come over here. There are so many things in Los Angeles I want you to see. I'll have to take you to Universal Studios, rollerblading down Venice Beach, to all my hang-outs so you can meet all my friends.

I know this sounds crazy but I've been telling everyone all about you, and I made a copy of your picture which I carry around so everyone's seen you too and they can't wait to meet you.

I'm sorry your friend is leaving, but you seem to have so many friends one less probably won't make that much difference. Wear something beautiful tonight, I'd like to picture you in a black silk dress, cut so it swings around your legs as you walk, and if you have any high-heeled strappy sandals, wear them tonight and think of me.

On second thoughts, if the weather in London's as bad as I think it is you might be better off in a sweater and boots!

Anyways, my darling, take care and don't be too sad. I'm sitting here in the sunshine thinking of you, and I'm still here for you.

Call me when you get home and I'll call you straight back, and have a good time.

Huge hugs and kisses, Brad. xxxxxxx

I'm not sure I like this familiarity, and something about the words might just possibly put me off if I stopped to think about it. It's not that there's anything nasty about them, about his letters, I think it's just that he seems a bit bland, but maybe that's just a cultural difference. Anyway, I'm sure he's completely different in the flesh. He's probably just not very good at writing letters. That's all.

'That was nice of your flatmate to call.'

'What?' I turn from my screen and look at Ben in horror. 'What are you talking about?'

'Your flatmate. Sophie. She phoned last night after you told her about the job to wish me luck.'

Little cow. I don't believe her. 'But I didn't give her your number. Where did she get it from?'

Now it's Ben's turn to look surprised. 'I don't know,' he says, shrugging. 'I assumed you gave it to her.'

'Strange.' I'm wondering what she's up to.

'Anyway,' said Ben, 'I said she could come along tonight.'

'Oh.' So that's what she's up to. 'What did you think of her? Is she your type?'

'Jemima!' he admonishes. 'The only time I've ever met the girl she looked a complete state, plus you know that she's not the type of girl I'm interested in.'

'Sorry,' I say, smiling a little inside. 'I just thought maybe it was time you had a girlfriend.' Careful, Jemima, this is a dangerous game you're playing.

'Girlfriend?' says Ben laughing. 'What would I do with a girlfriend at this time in my life? I'm far too busy being famous. By the way, do you know who I am?'

'Yes,' I laugh. 'You're Ben Williams, the amazingly large-headed man, whose head is growing by the second.' I shake my head in mock disbelief. 'God knows what you're going to be like when you're actually on television.'

'I will be marvellous,' says Ben, throwing up his arms in a dramatic gesture. 'I will be a stupendous presenter of rubbish. I will be Ben Williams, panderer to the stars, arse-licker of the famous.'

'Ben!' I giggle, thrilled that our friendship has reached this stage of easy teasing. 'You won't forget me, will you?'

'But you are lowly Jemima Jones, of the crappy *Kilburn Herald*. I have to forget you, I know no one from anything as downmarket as the *Kilburn Herald*!' Ben is speaking in his luvvie tones, but he stops as he sees a shadow of doubt cross my face. He couldn't be serious. Could he?

''Course I won't forget you, Jemima. You're my only real friend here, how could I possibly forget you?'

I smile, and adjust my rapidly shrinking bottom on the chair as I turn to reveal a cheekbone that's only just starting to emerge, but Ben doesn't notice the cheekbone. Ben doesn't seem to notice my weight loss at all, which means only one thing: I'm not thin enough yet.

Perhaps in an abstract way he has noticed I'm looking better, but I suppose when you're with someone for long periods of time it's very difficult to perceive any change in their size. You would instantly notice if they had a drastic haircut, or wore something they never normally wear, but weight is something you rarely notice. Particularly if you're a man. At least that's what I hope.

The only way Ben will notice that Jemima has lost weight is if he doesn't see her for a while, which would be Jemima's idea of living hell, a living hell that, she suddenly realizes, could become a reality.

'So you will stay in touch?' ventures my insecurity, refusing to let the subject drop.

'Only if you promise to respect and adore me.'

'But of course, oh-famous-one,' I say, when of course I, unbeknownst to Ben, already do.

CHAPTER FOURTEEN

At lunchtime Jemima watches Ben walk up the road with his colleagues from the newsdesk. She stands on the corner, holding on to her gym kit, and feels as if her heart is going to burst with sadness.

She had been invited to join them for lunch – the pre-leaving-do-lunch at which Ben will be forced to drink far more than he should in the middle of the working day – but she had declined because tonight is the proper leaving do, and since it is starting straight from work Jemima would not have been able to make it to the gym tonight, so she skips lunch and exercises during her lunch break instead.

Who would have thought that exercise would ever be a higher priority than the opportunity of spending time with Ben Williams? Might it be thus assumed that Jemima has become just a touch obsessive . . .

For when she has finished in the gym, when she is certain there is nobody around to walk in on her, she stands gingerly on the scales in the ladies' changing room, squeezes her eyes shut and then looks down. Eleven stone, twelve pounds. Jemima steps off and steps on again, just to check, because Jemima Jones has never been eleven stone *anything* in her entire life.

Cause for celebration, I think we all agree, but on a Friday lunchtime on the Kilburn High Road there is, unfortunately, very little that Jemima can buy to celebrate. She would like a dress, the dress that Brad described last night, but even though she is eleven stone something (eleven stone something!) she doesn't want to spend the money just yet.

'When I'm ten stone,' she tells herself as she walks back to the office after her workout. 'When I'm ten stone I shall treat myself properly.' And as she walks along she stops outside the chemist and peers through the doorway at the make-up counters. Oh what the hell, she thinks. I may as well give myself a small treat now, and I do want to look the very best I possibly can for tonight, so in she goes.

At 5.15 p.m. I clutch my new make-up and walk into the loo, not really surprised that Geraldine's already there, pouting in the mirror as she dusts some bronzer on her already golden cheeks.

'Hello stranger!' says Geraldine. 'Getting ready for the party?' She stands back from the mirror and admires her red dress, which makes me think of Brad immediately, because it's just like the black dress he wanted me to wear – a short, flippy soft dress that hugs her curves and shows off her legs, snugly encased in shimmery, sheer natural stockings, with flat red suede pumps on her feet. Bitch. No, sorry, only joking, but to be a bit more serious I look at Geraldine and feel as dowdy as hell.

'I just thought,' I start, feeling self-conscious and ridiculous. 'I just thought maybe I'd put some . . .' I tail off as Geraldine grabs my make-up bag.

'What have you got here?' She pulls out the make-up,

silently, and lays it next to the sink. 'Well,' she says, looking at me. 'Some of this will suit you but some of it won't, but if you borrow some of mine then it will all be fine.'

'Don't worry,' I mumble, trying to keep the dejected tone out of my voice because I'm suddenly rethinking the whole idea. 'I'm not sure I can be bothered.'

'Jemima!' says Geraldine in exasperation. 'You are hopeless sometimes. I've been dying to get my hands on you for days. What you need, now that you're losing all this weight, is a serious makeover, and tah dah!' She holds her arms up in the air. 'Guess who's the perfect person to do it.'

I can't help it, I start laughing, and I lean back against the counter, careful not to sit on the wet patches around the sinks. 'Okay,' I say with a smile. 'You can start by making me up.'

'Jemima Jones!' says the big, booming voice of the editor as I walk into the dark smoky vaults of the Wine Cellar a little after six o'clock. Geraldine is standing next to the editor, and Geraldine smiles with delight when she sees me, not to mention the look of amazement on the editor's face.

'What have you done to yourself, young lady?'

I shrink in horror as a hand comes up to my face. Have I smeared my lipstick? Do I have mascara running down my cheeks? Is there spinach in my teeth?

The editor carries on. 'Jemima Jones, you are a shadow of your former self.'

Thank God! I suppress the rising giggle and smile with delight, trying to be nonchalant, trying to look as if I'm not thrilled that someone has finally noticed, even if it is just the editor. 'I've just lost a bit of weight, that's all.'

'Lost a bit of weight?' booms the editor. 'Young lady, you are half the size you were. And not only that,' he leans forward conspiratorially. 'You're also a bit of a looker, aren't you?'

Oh my God, I can feel the blush coming, but luckily I catch Geraldine's eye and I can see that she's also holding back the giggles, and the blush fades away.

Geraldine is trying to suppress the giggles, but she's also smiling broadly at her handiwork, for Jemima Jones does, truly, look like a different person. Admittedly, thinks Geraldine, her clothes aren't great, but she doesn't know that Jemima is waiting to be even slimmer before she buys some new ones.

What she is looking at is Jemima's face. She is looking at the creamy skin, given a hint of gold with the help of Geraldine's supremely expensive foundation. She is looking at Jemima's green eyes, large and sparkling with the help of Geraldine's expert knowledge of eyeshadows, eyeliners, and eye drops to turn the whites of her eyes brighter than snow. She is looking at her full pouting lips, made to look even more full with the help of Geraldine's lip liner, lipstick and lip gloss. And finally she is looking at Jemima's hair, which Geraldine has gathered up in a french twist, soft tendrils falling about her face.

'You look gorgeous,' Geraldine mouths to me, as she

reaches up and wipes off a tiny smudge of lipstick from my cheek, which, quite frankly, no one other than Geraldine would have noticed.

'Jemima!' My heart skips a beat as Ben comes rushing over and puts an arm around me. 'For a minute there I thought you weren't going to come.' He thought about me! He actually worried about me, he spent time worrying whether I was going to come. Now this, surely, is a result.

I recover my composure and look Ben in the eye, willing him to notice how I look, to see the new Jemima Jones, to like what he sees and fall in love with me. But Ben just says, 'Here, have a glass of champagne,' and as he hands it to me he looks over my shoulder and says, 'Diana! You made it.'

'Couldn't let my new star reporter down could I?' says Diana Macpherson, striding through the room as people part to let her through, because, after all, Diana Macpherson is famous in the media world.

And I can't help it, I watch with a mounting sense of horror as Diana almost gives Ben a kiss on the cheek, but then evidently thinks better of it and straightens up, extending her hand, which Ben shakes warmly. Phew.

'Let me introduce you,' he says, turning first to the editor, who is so impressed with Diana Macpherson that his mouth, once open, is captured in a fish pose, the editor having forgotten to close it. Diana shakes hands with him, then with me, but just as Ben's about to introduce her to Geraldine she turns to Ben and says, 'Come with me to get a drink,' and Ben shrugs us and allows himself to be propelled by her towards the bar.

'What a bitch!' says Geraldine, who, quite understandably, feels snubbed by the great Diana Macpherson, and only Geraldine would say what everyone else is thinking but would never dare voice out loud.

'Don't worry,' I soothe, 'I'm sure it wasn't personal,' but of course it was personal, I'm not stupid, I saw the way Diana Macpherson's eyes swept over Geraldine with a cold, flinty stare, and from what I've heard Diana Macpherson is not a woman's woman, even more so when the woman happens to be as attractive as Geraldine.

'God, I'm really sorry about that,' says a voice next to us. 'Diana is a law unto herself, and sometimes she can seem rude.' We both turn to look at a young, good-looking guy, dressed in an old pair of Levi's and a brushed cotton shirt. 'Sorry,' he says again. 'I'm Nick. I'm here with Diana.' Nick holds out his hand to Geraldine as he says this, and holds her gaze for longer than is altogether necessary, before shaking my hand and making me feel more of a spare part than I do already.

'Here with Diana?' asks Geraldine with a raised eyebrow. 'Does that then mean that you are her' – she pauses coolly – 'other half?'

'Hardly,' laughs Nick. 'I'm more like her occasional date.'

'And this is where she brings you?' Geraldine's teasing him, but neither Nick nor I misses the flirtatious tone in her voice.

'Yes, but I've promised to take her out for dinner later on.'

'Do you, er, work in television?' I venture, trying to be polite but feeling more and more unwanted.

'No,' he laughs, shaking his head. 'Do you know Cut Glass?'

Everyone knows Cut Glass. Initially a small, funky optician's shop that specialized in hard-to-find trendy glasses that couldn't be bought elsewhere, Cut Glass is now one of the largest, if not in fact *the* largest, optician chain in the country.

'You're an optician.' It's a statement, not a question, and Geraldine's eyes instantly dull as she starts thinking of ways to get away from him. I know her so well, I smile to myself. Cute, she thinks, but boring, boring, boring.

'No,' laughs Nick. 'Not exactly.'

Oh God, I can see Geraldine think, this gets worse. He's not even an optician, he's a bloody sales assistant.

'It's my company,' he says reluctantly, after a pregnant pause.

'What do you mean it's your company?'

'It's my company,' he repeats.

'Oh my God!' Geraldine suddenly pales. 'You're Nick!'

Nick's looking at her in confusion. 'I told you I was Nick.'

'No.' she shakes her head. 'But you're Nick Maxwell, I know all about you.'

'What do you mean, you know all about me?'

'I'm a friend of Suzie.'

'What?' he says, his smile growing larger. 'Suzie Johnson?'

'Yes,' says Geraldine, who cannot believe her luck because Nick Maxwell, all six foot one of him, is not only gorgeous but hugely wealthy, very nice, and enormously eligible, and Geraldine knows all about him already. 'Suzie's one of my oldest friends, I've been hearing about you for years.'

'Oh my God!' Now it's Nick's turn. 'You're Geraldine Turner!'

I've been feeling more and more surplus to requirements, and finally I can see that it really is time to leave these two to get on with it. 'Drink?' I say, but they both shake their heads, already lost in the geography of discovering who else they have in common, so I wander off to the bar.

Everyone is having too good a time to remember that they are at this party to bid farewell to their much loved deputy news editor. The lights have got dimmer, the music's been turned up, and Jemima is leaning against the bar sipping her cheap white wine – the champagne finished a long time ago – and surveying the room.

She sees Ben standing with Diana Macpherson and the editor, Diana in mid-flow, pressing her hand on Ben's arm every now and then to emphasize a point. Funny, thinks Jemima, how she isn't touching the editor in the same way. In fact, she doesn't seem to be touching the editor at all.

She's far too old and far too rough for Jemima to feel truly threatened – surely she is not Ben's type in the slightest – but nevertheless every time she places a long manicured finger on Ben's sleeve, Jemima feels her heartstrings tug a little bit more. Leave him alone, she thinks. He's not yours.

Nor, Jemima, is he yours, but Jemima, having rarely, if ever, had a crush on someone before, does not see this. Most women, it must be admitted, spend their teenage years falling in and out of love. They are more than familiar with the pain of going to a party and watching the object of their young desires end up with another girl. They are well versed in talking to their girlfriends about 'the bitch' that stole him, and they are equally well aware that, although it might feel it at the time, it is not the end of the world.

But Jemima didn't have an adolescence like most teenage girls. While her classmates were at parties, experimenting with make-up, clothes, and fumbling in darkened bedrooms on beds piled high with coats, Jemima was at home with her mother, eating, watching television and daydreaming.

Jemima didn't go to any parties until she went to university, and even there she rarely ventured to large social occasions once Freshers' Week was over. Jemima Jones found a group of friends who were, she thought, as inadequate as herself. The social misfits they called themselves, pretending to delight in their difference, but each of them wishing they belonged elsewhere.

And up until recently Jemima had shown very little interest in the opposite sex. Yes, she had lost her virginity, but she had never felt what it was like to pine for someone, to lie awake all night praying they will notice you, to wince with pain when you realize they will never reciprocate your feelings.

'Mimey!' My reverie is interrupted by a voice I know well, and I turn slowly, trying to figure out why I am hearing this voice at a work do, and as I turn I know that the cheap, white wine I have been gulping all evening to relieve my nerves has gone straight to my head, and I am, how shall I put it, slightly woozy with alcohol. Oh all right then, I'm slightly pissed.

And when I see them, Sophie and Lisa, standing together, I smile broadly, grin, actually. I'm pretty damn sure I'm doing about as perfect an impression of a Cheshire cat as I know how. 'You both look . . .' I pause as I look them up and down, head to toe. 'Wonderful!' I exclaim magnanimously, despite the silence that appears to have descended upon the room at their arrival.

For Sophie and Lisa have really gone to town, except they've done it in Kilburn, and somehow what would look magnificent in Tramp looks completely ridiculous in the Wine Cellar just off the Kilburn High Road. They look extraordinary, extraordinarily out of place.

Lisa has obviously been to the hairdresser, who has sent her away with hair so big she almost has to watch her head walking through doorways. She is wearing a tiny piece of black fabric masquerading as a dress, and high, high, strappy sandals.

Sophie has caught her hair in a french twist, much like mine, and has squeezed herself into a sparkly black cocktail dress, which shimmers and shines every time she moves.

They look like a bloody parody of themselves, and I can't, I just can't wipe the grin off my face, and as I say hello to them I see that over their shoulders both Geraldine and Nick Maxwell are also grinning, and just for a second I feel a wicked, wicked glee that they should be so awkward.

Except, of course, Sophie and Lisa don't feel awkward, they feel beautiful, and they have obviously done it for Ben. Bad move. Big, bad move. Ha! Serves them right.

'So where is the clever boy then?' asks Sophie, looking around the room to try and find Ben.

'See that tall blonde woman over there?' I point out Diana Macpherson, knowing that Diana, should Sophie or Lisa break in on her territory, will make mincemeat out of them. 'He was talking to her a minute ago, he's probably just gone to get her a drink.'

'God,' says Sophie, smoothing down her dress and giving Diana Macpherson the once-over. 'Talk about mutton dressed as lamb. Who is she?' Sophie doesn't turn back to me, just keeps her eyes glued to Diana as Ben walks back and hands Diana a glass of wine.

'Dunno,' I shrug, trying desperately to hide an evil grin. 'She's not from the paper and I haven't seen her before. Maybe she's a friend of Ben.' I stop talking and the three of us watch in silence as Diana brushes a bit of lint off Ben's jacket in a gesture that is way too intimate for simply a boss.

'Maybe she fancies him,' I say, wondering exactly what the outcome of this peculiar conversation will be.

'She should be so bloody lucky!' says Sophie indignantly, before she evidently remembers that I, her flatmate, have a crush on Ben, and she shouldn't be quite so obvious.

'Tell you what, Mimey,' she says in a confiding tone. 'Why don't I go over there and get rid of the old bag then you can come over and talk to him. I bet you haven't said a word to him all night.'

I can't hide the evil smile any longer, and as the grin

spreads across my face I say, 'Would you? That's so amazing of you.'

'What are friends for?' says Sophie, who's already started striding through the tightly packed people to reach her prey.

'I'd better go with her,' says Lisa, tottering behind her.

'What *is* going on?' Geraldine comes to stand next to me. 'What are your flatmates *doing* here, and, more to the point, what the hell do they *look* like?'

This is too much for me. I start laughing, and the more I laugh, the harder it is to stop, but I'm not that pissed, okay? Just slightly. Eventually I manage to gasp, 'Just watch. I think this is going to be one of those Kodak moments.'

'Does your flatmate know who Diana Macpherson is?' says Geraldine in confusion.

'No,' I splutter. 'And nor does she know what she's like, but she fancies Ben and she thinks that Diana is mutton dressed as lamb and Sophie's going to drag him away from her, come what may.'

Geraldine looks shocked, but swiftly realizes she's in on a classic moment. 'Classic!' she whispers in awe, as she watches Sophie's approach.

Sophie, being the rather silly girl that she is, seems to have decided, in the space of less than a minute, that Ben has obviously been cornered by this overblown, overaged blonde, and as she walks purposefully towards them she is already planning her strategy. Ben, she has decided, is looking as if he doesn't want to be there, so Ben will probably be eternally grateful to anyone who has the presence of mind to take him away from this woman who is, Sophie assumes, ruining his leaving do.

I am, she thinks, as she draws closer and closer, infinitely younger than this blowzy blonde, and far more attractive. Plus, she notes, as she finally walks over, I have better legs. Ben, she decides, now has a girlfriend who will send this woman scarpering. This girlfriend, she thinks, is me. Brilliant! she tells herself. He will never be able to thank me enough!

'Ben!' she shouts, as Ben looks up from his conversation with Diana and stares at her blankly, primarily because he finds it hard to focus on her, she appears to have two, if not three, heads, and secondly because he does not recognize her in the slightest.

His blank stare swiftly becomes mild alarm, because she certainly seems to know him, indeed to know him very well.

'Darling!' she exclaims, grabbing his face between her hands and planting a big wet kiss on his lips. 'I'm so sorry I'm late. Have you missed me?' she adds, in a kittenish purr.

'I . . . er . . .' Ben is completely and utterly flummoxed. Who is this strange woman, is she perhaps some PR girl he might have spoken to on the phone?

'Hello,' says Sophie, turning coolly to Diana Macpherson, whose face has suddenly turned as hard as steel. 'I'm Sophie.' She holds out a hand as Diana just looks at her. 'Ben's girlfriend.'

'My what?' slurs Ben, who has suddenly realized who she is.

'Don't be coy, darling. It's hardly a secret any more

is it?' Sophie reaches up and affectionately ruffles his hair.

'But . . .' Ben splutters, 'but we've only met once. You're Jemima's flatmate, aren't you?'

Sophie hesitates, but only for a split second. 'Is this a little game, darling? Do you want me to play along? All right then, we've only met once.' She turns to Diana and rolls her eyes, while Ben stands there looking flabbergasted.

'Sorry,' she says to Diana, who, it has to be said, is far, far brighter than Sophie, and is slowly getting an inkling, thanks to the expression on Ben's face, that this is not quite what it seems. 'We just have these little games we play,' continues Sophie, blissfully unaware that her plan is not going to, well, to plan.

'Oh?' says Diana, switching on the charm and smiling a smile that her colleagues know means only one thing – she's going in for the kill. 'So you're Ben's girlfriend? I've heard so much about you.'

Sophie's smile fades for a second before she recovers. 'Nice things I hope,' she offers, because as far as she knows Ben doesn't have a girlfriend, and, if he does, she might be here, and if she's here then Sophie's in big trouble.

'Oh wonderful things,' says Diana. 'I was so sorry to hear about your sister,' she says, now knowing beyond a shadow of a doubt that Sophie is some stupid tart who fancies Ben, who thought that she could drag him away from her.

'My sister, yes, it was a shame. I'm surprised Ben told you,' says Sophie, who's beginning to think that the sooner she gets away from here the better.

Jemima and Geraldine have inched forward until they are feet away, and both are straining their ears to hear what's going on.

'Mmm,' says Diana confidently. 'Ben tells me a lot of things. I'm his psychiatrist.'

'What?' says Sophie, who's completely unsure of what to do next.

'Well you know,' says Diana, leaning forward and lowering her voice. 'After the problem last year with *the voices* and the schizophrenic tendencies, Ben and I have been seeing one another three times a week. He didn't tell you?'

'Yes, come to think of it he did mention it, but you know how private Ben is.'

'Absolutely,' agrees Diana. 'Just as long as you keep your kitchen knives well hidden, if you know what I mean.' She nudges Sophie. 'I shouldn't really say this,' Diana says, 'but do be careful, I mean we wouldn't want you to end up like his last girlfriend would we.'

'Er, no.'

'No, exactly. Anyway, Ben tells me you're an osteopath. Come with me to get a drink and tell me all about your work.' Before Sophie has a chance to protest, Diana has grabbed her by the arm and propelled her to the bar, while Geraldine and Jemima collapse in tears of laughter.

'What the fuck?' says Ben, who has temporarily, perhaps due to shock, sobered up somewhat. He turns to me, slurring slightly. 'Was that my girlfriend?'

'No, Ben,' I smile gently. 'You haven't got a girl-friend, remember?'

'That's what I thought,' says Ben, looking into his wine glass in confusion. He looks back up at the girls. 'Jemima,' he says, downing his glass in one. 'Geraldine,' he says, swaying gently and looking at Geraldine. 'What am I going to do without you both?' He flings his arms around both our shoulders while Geraldine, who has not touched a drop all night, rolls her eyes in disgust and disengages herself.

'You'll be fine, Ben,' she says. 'You'll doubtless find thousands of gorgeous young women at *London Nights* who will fall in love with you. And speaking of love . . .' She looks up until she catches the eye of Nick Maxwell, who has just returned from getting Diana Macpherson's coat. 'I have got a date with one of the most eligible men in London.'

'Who?' says Ben, who, by the looks of things, is far too drunk to care.

'Never you mind.' Geraldine, being sober as a judge, has thankfully realized that Ben is the last person she should be telling, because you never knew how Diana Macpherson would take it.

'Excuse me,' she says, checking that Diana isn't around so she can go and say goodbye to Nick. 'Back in a sec.'

But Ben's arms are still around my shoulders, and I'm so nervous that I seem to have suddenly sobered up, and I can see everything in minute detail, and feel every pressure of Ben's arm on my body.

'You're my only friend,' he says to me, turning and burying his face in my shoulder. 'I love you, Jemima,' he mumbles into my shirt, and I freeze.

And the world stands still.

'What did you say?' I ask haltingly, convinced I misheard.

Ben focuses on me for a few seconds then, much in the manner that Sophie, who has now left the party, kissed him, kisses me. It is a big, wet, sloppy kiss on my lips, and thank you, God, thank you, thank you, thank you. It lasts a good four seconds, and when it's over Ben stumbles off, leaving me rooted to the floor, shaking like a leaf.

'I love you too,' I whisper, watching as he's pulled to one side by the editor, who's just about to make a speech. 'I love you too.'

CHAPTER FIFTEEN

Before we take a look at JJ – for Jemima Jones exists now in name alone – we need to know that she has rarely been home since we last saw her. A whole three months has passed and we need to be warned, just so that we recognize her, just so that we don't get carried away and think that Jemima Jones is nowhere to be found.

She has been to work, which has been thoroughly miserable without Ben Williams, and she has been to the gym. She has done her best to avoid her two flatmates after the fiasco of Ben's leaving do, and she has buried the pain of Ben not calling her during this time.

She has become increasingly friendly with Geraldine, who, incidentally, is now firmly ensconced with Nick Maxwell, and she is running up enormous phone bills to Brad in California, who, despite being many, many miles away from her, is proving to be the one light in her life.

Jemima feels she knows Brad pretty well by now. She has given him her time, her thoughts and her energy, because she no longer has to save any of the aforementioned for Ben, who has disappeared from her life and reappeared on her television screen.

Brad is investing the same in Jemima, soon to be known full time as JJ, but perhaps it is fair to ask the question, how well can you really know someone whom you've never met? How close can you be to someone whom you talk to via the Internet, fax and telephone? How do you know they are who they say they are?

It probably doesn't matter. After all, those conversations are the one thing Jemima has to look forward to because food no longer offers the consolation it once did, and Ben phoned three times during the first month he left to say what a great time he was having, and she hasn't heard from him since.

Food. Jemima is eating just about enough to give her the energy to exercise, to watch her skin regain its taut elasticity, to rediscover bones and muscles she didn't think she had. In the first couple of weeks after Ben left Jemima still had cravings, which took all her energy to fight, but fight them she did, and binges are now a thing of the past.

Jemima, when we last saw her at the party, was eleven stone, twelve pounds, but now Jemima Jones weighs eight stone, nine pounds. Jemima Jones has lost almost a whole person's worth of weight. Jemima Jones looks exactly like the girl in the picture.

'I can't believe it,' says Geraldine, standing in the living room, watching Jemima as she whizzes around looking for her coat. 'I just can't bloody believe it.' Can any of us, in fact, believe that Jemima, our beloved Jemima Jones, can whizz *anywhere*?

'Believe what?' says Jemima distractedly, spying her huge old black coat lying behind the sofa. She pulls it on and wraps it around herself to keep warm, for Jemima Jones is frequently cold these days, not having the padding to warm her bones.

'I mean look at you,' says Geraldine. 'You're skinny.'

'Don't be ridiculous,' says Jemima, 'I'm hardly skinny,

and I still have this weight here.' She grabs what's left of the fat on her thighs, and let me tell you, there isn't a lot.

'What weight there, for God's sake?' says Geraldine. 'Trust me, you're skinny. You're the same size as me.'

'I wish,' says Jemima, who actually is the same size as Geraldine, more or less, only she can't quite get her head round that yet. She knows she *looks* different, she knows she *feels* different, she's just not entirely sure how she should be feeling about it.

'Anyway,' she continues. 'Where are we off to?'

'An expedition,' says Geraldine mysteriously. 'You are in my hands today, and all you need to bring with you is a chequebook.'

'Oh God,' says Jemima nervously. 'If you're thinking of taking me shopping you can forget about your designer stores. This trip to LA is wiping me out, I haven't got a penny.'

'Don't worry,' says Geraldine. 'What do you think credit cards are for?'

'I know,' sighs Jemima. 'But I'm almost up to the limit on mine now, and I don't know how the hell I'm ever going to pay it off.'

'Darling,' says Geraldine. 'Just think about it logically. We're only here for a hundred years or so, which, in the grand scheme of things, is nothing, therefore nothing's really very important, and certainly not money. So you'll pay it off when you get back.'

'Geraldine, I don't have rich parents who'll bail me out whenever I get into trouble. How am I going to pay it off on my salary?'

'Jemima, for starters my parents *hardly ever* bail me

out. And anyway, what do you spend your money on? Before now you've never really spent anything.'

'I know,' moans Jemima, thinking about all the restaurants she's never been to, the clothes she's never bought, the holidays she's never had, 'but that's no reason to go and spend everything now.'

'We're not spending *everything*,' says Geraldine. 'We're not going to Armani, but if we do happen to see some nice clothes I'm afraid we might have to have a look. Anyway, you can't go to LA in your old clothes. For starters they're not the sort of things Brad expects JJ to wear, and secondly even if they were they're all swimming on you now. I mean this in a caring, sharing sort of way, Jemima, but quite frankly, darling, you look ridiculous.'

Jemima looks down at herself, at the black sweatshirt she is wearing that hangs in folds of fabric on her new body, at the tracksuit bottoms that look like balloon pants, so large are they on her new frame, and she looks up again uncertainly.

'Okay,' she concedes. 'I suppose you're right.' She raises her eyes to the ceiling. 'May God and my bank manager forgive me,' and they walk out the door.

'First stop is Jeff,' says Geraldine, manoeuvring her car through the back streets of Kilburn and up into West Hampstead.

'Jeff?'

'My hairdresser.'

'Why?' I start to feel ever so slightly nervous, because my long, glossy hair, after all, has always been one of my favourite features, and yes, I trust Geraldine, but do I really trust her this much?

Geraldine pulls a cigarette out and lights it from the car lighter, then offers me one, but I shake my head. 'No, thanks. I've given up.'

'You've given up?' Geraldine looks as if she's both amazed and impressed.

'Yeah. Brad hates smoking, so I figured I may as well give up before I actually get there.'

Geraldine nods.

'Anyway,' I continue, 'why are we going to your hair-dresser?'

'Jemima,' says Geraldine with a sigh. 'Do you trust me?'

'Yes.' Reluctant but true.

'And do you think I have good taste?'

'Unquestionably.'

'And do you think I would do anything to you that you wouldn't like?'

'No.'

'Exactly. So just sit back, relax, and let me take charge. I promise you this, by the end of the day you will not recognize yourself.'

So I sit in silence and look out the window, tapping my foot to the music Geraldine has put on, trying not to feel sick to the stomach at the prospect of some strange man called Jeff being given free rein with my lovely hair.

Eventually we pull up outside a hairdresser's in Hampstead. Peering through the large plate-glass windows, I can see it's a hive of activity, that the hairdressers and their clientele are equally beautiful, and that this is not your ordinary hairdresser. Even through the window I can see it's expensive. The mirrors, in front of which preen the clients, line each wall, but in between are two beautiful round antique tables, on top of which are Chinese vases overflowing with enormous white lilies. There are huge plush sofas facing one another, on which sit nervous people awaiting their appointments, flicking through designer magazines to try and find the perfect haircut before they meet the scissors.

Geraldine marches straight up to a young, slim, dark-haired man, his glossy brown hair slicked back into a ponytail.

'Geraldine!' he says in a rich baritone, turning the hairdryer off and turning away from the client. 'How are you?' He kisses her on both cheeks, and it is obvious that Geraldine is a favoured client, that she has been coming here for years.

'This is Jemima,' she says, as I feel the need to beat a hasty retreat. 'Remember our phone conversation?' Phone conversation? What phone conversation?

Jeff nods.

'What do you think? Can you do it for her? Will it look good?'

Jeff stands back and looks at me, then lifts up my hair, feeling it, weighing it, thinking about it. 'It's not going to look good,' he pauses. 'It's going to look unbelievable. You were absolutely right.'

Geraldine gives Jeff a warning look. 'Just don't tell her what you're doing.'

Jeff sighs. 'You do realize that is completely unethical, Geraldine. I can only not tell her if she agrees.' Eventually he seems to notice me, and he sighs dramatically as he looks at me and says, 'Jemima, would you mind if I cut and coloured your hair to Geraldine's instructions without telling you what I'm going to do first? God.' He shakes his head. 'I've never done *this* before.'

Oh what the hell. I nod. 'It's fine, Jeff. Believe it or not I trust her.' But I can't help pleading for a tiny clue.

'Okay,' sighs Geraldine. 'Not a clue but a question. Do you or do you not want to look like your picture?' I nod. 'Do you or do you not like the colour of your hair in the picture?' I nod. 'Leave it to Jeff then. He's a miracle worker.'

'I'm not going to take too much off,' says Jeff, lifting my hair again. 'Just an inch or so to give you a blunt cut which will take off all these split ends, and I think – ' He pulls some hair down over my forehead. 'How would you feel about a fringe?'

Can you have feelings about a *fringe*? I look at Geraldine, who nods. 'A fringe is fine,' I say with a grin.

An hour later I'm having severe second thoughts. Surveying my space age-ish head in the mirror – hundreds of tiny bits of silver foil sticking up all over – I turn to Geraldine with a severe tone and say, 'You'd better be sure about this.'

'Just relax, for God's sake.' She turns to Jeff and asks him how much longer it will take.

'Okay,' she says. 'I'll come back in an hour.'

When Geraldine comes back into the salon she actually walks past Jemima, and, when she sees her mistake, she stands rooted to the spot, with a hand clamped over her mouth in amazement.

Remember Jemima's hair, long, glossy, mousy brown?

210

Now look at it, see what Geraldine is staring at, this streaky golden mane which catches the light as Jeff flicks her hair around.

See how cleverly different shades of honey, of ash, of pale, pale copper have been woven together to create a sheath of liquid gold. And see how it spreads behind Jemima's shoulders, bobbing gently as she talks.

Take a closer look. See how the fringe stops just above her green eyes, how the green is accentuated by the gold above it, how the fringe shows off her heart-shaped face perfectly.

'Jesus,' says Jeff, standing back and surveying his handiwork. 'You look absolutely beautiful, if I say so myself.'

'Jesus,' echoes Geraldine softly, when she finally finds her voice. 'Jesus,' because she can't seem to think of anything else to say.

'I look disgusting don't I?' I haven't dared look in the mirror, I just buried my head in a magazine, and now I don't want to look. But I can see from their faces that I don't look disgusting, and so reluctantly I raise my eyes to my reflection and I gasp. And I can't help reaching out a hand, corny as it may sound, and touching my face, my hair, in the mirror, and almost without thinking I find myself whispering in agreement. 'Oh my God!' I say quietly, turning to Geraldine in amazement. 'I'm the woman in the picture.'

'No, you're not,' says Geraldine in awe. 'You're far more beautiful.'

Geraldine insists on paying. 'It's my treat,' she says,

and as we leave Geraldine keeps looking at me, and she keeps going on about how beautiful I am.

'Shut up, Geraldine!' I say eventually, after the fourth person we've passed has turned round and given us an odd look. 'Everyone will think you're my lesbian lover, for God's sake!'

'Sorry.' Geraldine snaps out of it, and we both start laughing as she pulls me into a boutique down a little side alley, but just before we go in I turn to Geraldine.

'Seriously,' I say. 'I can't believe everything you've done for me. Everything you're doing for me. I honestly don't know how to thank you.'

'Jemima!' she sighs, rolling her eyes. 'This is the most exciting thing I've ever done. This is like the world's biggest makeover, and trust me, I'm getting as much out of it as you. You,' she says in a German scientist-type voice, 'are my creation!' And with that we both giggle and step inside.

'Right,' she says, sizing up the room. 'Step number two is clothes. These,' she says, rubbing the fabric of my sweatshirt between her fingers, 'have got to go.'

What's wrong with my comfortable baggy clothes I wonder, as I start idly flicking through the rails of perfectly co-ordinated clothes. Although I thought I'd be ready for this, the moment I've always dreamt of, what if I don't look the way I'd envisaged? Because as much as I want to try this new look, I'm terrified that somehow I'll still look like a blob.

But something strange starts to happen to me as I continue breathing in these strange textures and colours, and suddenly I'm dying to try them on and go for it. Suddenly I understand what all the fuss is about.

Now I understand why Geraldine dresses so beautifully. You want to know why? Because she can. And for the first time in my life, so can I.

I keep flicking through, loving every texture, every colour. Black fades to chocolate brown, fades to camel, fades finally to cream, with a touch of navy thrown in for good measure. I see some beautiful trousers and, ignoring Geraldine, who is piling armfuls of clothes for me into the shop assistant's eager arms, I go to the changing room to try them on.

'What do you think?' I ask Geraldine, wondering why the trousers feel a bit big, and holding them up at the waist so they fall better.

'Too *big* for you, darling. What size are they? I'll get you a smaller size.'

'Size 14,' I say. Oh my God, I can't be smaller than a size 14. Can I?

'Try these,' says the shop assistant, handing me the same trousers in a smaller size. 'I think you're more like a size 10.'

The trousers fit. The beautifully tailored jacket fits. The short, flippy skirts fit. The little silk T-shirts fit, more importantly, the little black dress fits. The camel suede shoes fit. The soft leather boots fit. And more to the point, *I* fit. And I cannot believe that the smart, sophisticated woman, grinning like a Cheshire cat in the mirror, is me. Me! Jemima Jones! Once again, I am completely speechless.

'*Now* you're ready to go to LA,' says Geraldine triumphantly, as I dig in my bag for my purse, trying not to feel sick at the extraordinary amount of money I'm about to hand over. Oh fuck it. This is a once-in-a-lifetime experience. These clothes will last me for ever, and at the end of the day they are what Brad expects me to wear.

'Let's have a coffee. All this shopping and hairdressing is just exhausting!' Geraldine loops an arm through mine and we troop off down the high street, two slim (slim!) blondes, laden down with fabulous goodies.

'Look,' whispers Geraldine, as a zippy red sports car joins the end of the traffic jam, just parallel to where we're standing.

'What?' I whisper.

'Look in the sports car.' So I do, and sitting in the driver's seat is a dark-haired, blue-eyed, handsome man. He stares coolly at me, holding my gaze then dropping it to take in my new clothes – because, sorry, I couldn't resist, I had to wear those gorgeous trousers right now – then back up to my eyes. And I know what this looks means, I've seen this look in countless Hollywood films. This look means he fancies me! He fancies *me*, Jemima Jones!

As the traffic moves off he smiles at her, a small smile of regret that he was not able to talk to her, for she is what he could only describe as a looker and a half. He drives through the lights and stares at her in his rear-view mirror. Now she, Richard tells himself as he turns the music up, was gorgeous. He reaches over, picks up his mobile phone and dials his best friend.

'Ben? Rich! I think I've just fallen in love.'

'Did you see that? Did you see that?' If she wasn't going out with Nick Maxwell, Geraldine would be green with jealousy, but as it is she's just over the moon. 'He fancied you, he fancied you!' she choruses. 'And he was gorgeous!'

Jemima's in a daze. Jemima has never had a look like that before from a man who looks like that, from anyone in fact, if the truth be known. Jemima will not forget that look, not for a long time, because that look finally confirmed what she has just discovered this afternoon. Jemima Jones is beautiful. She is slim, she is blonde, she is beautiful, and, because of Geraldine's help, she is also chic, stylish and sophisticated, although admittedly she hasn't quite yet realized it.

'Mimey,' calls Lisa, as she opens the front door and dumps the bags in the hallway. 'Your mother called.'
'Thanks, I'll call her,' says Jemima, walking upstairs and pushing open the living room door.

'Fucking hell!' says Lisa.

'Oh my God!' says Sophie. And they both sit on their respective sofas with their mouths hanging open.

'Well?' says Jemima, giving her head a little shake. 'What do you think?'

'It's . . .' Lisa stops.

'Just . . .' Sophie stops.

The pair of them are speechless with envy, dysfunctional with disbelief. They had, up until now, vaguely registered that Jemima was losing weight, but so what? Being slim doesn't automatically make you beautiful, and Jemima was never a threat to them, but standing in the doorway of the living room, in her new tailored trousers and understated chocolate-brown shoes, Jemima Jones looks exactly like the sort of woman

Sophie and Lisa have always tried to be. Except they've never quite made it. They've always got the jewellery wrong, or the shoes wrong, or the make-up wrong. They have always looked glamorous, but neither has ever had an ounce of class. Standing in the doorway in a haze of gold, camel and cream, Jemima is a vision of loveliness.

'It's fine,' says Lisa eventually.

'It suits you,' says Sophie eventually, and both bury their heads back in their magazines, while Jemima feels herself slowly coming down off the high. Couldn't they be nice, she thinks, just this once? Couldn't they have told her she looked great, just to make her feel good?

Jemima hovers, then goes back into the kitchen to call her mother, and as she walks out of the room she can already hear the girls whispering. She stops for a second, straining to hear them, and hears the tail-end of one of Sophie's whispers. ' . . . bound to put the weight back on.' And then hears Lisa, ' . . . being blonde doesn't make up for being a loser.'

Back in the old days Jemima would have gone to her room and eaten her way through a packet of biscuits for consolation, but things have changed, and Jemima can see through the bitchy comments to the jealousy that lurks behind. Bitches, she quickly tells herself, before she can get upset. They don't matter. And she goes into the kitchen to call her mother.

'Mum? Hi, it's me.'

'Hello! How are you, darling?'

'I'm fine. I've just got back from the hairdresser's.'

'Nothing too drastic I hope?'

216

'It wasn't really cut, but I've had some highlights.' No point in telling her I've gone blonde, she'd only disapprove and call me brassy.

'Not blonde, Jemima?'

'Not really, Mum. Streaky.'

'I hope it's not brassy. I've always thought blonde lights can look really cheap.'

'No, Mum,' I raise my eyes to the ceiling. 'It doesn't look cheap.'

'Hmm. Anyway, how's the weight?'

I smile, because at least I know she'll be happy with me now, she has to be, I've become the daughter she always wanted. 'You won't believe this, Mum. I'm eight stone, nine pounds!' There's a silence on the other end of the line.

'Mum?' Surely she can't find something negative to say about this? Surely she'll be happy for me? But that silence is one I've come to know well. She still disapproves.

'That's too thin for you, Jemima,' she says finally and belligerently. 'You must look like a scarecrow.'

'I look fine,' I sigh, instantly wishing I'd never bothered to pick up the phone.

'I hope you're eating enough,' she says, as I roll my eyes at the ceiling. God knows I've tried. I mean, I've achieved the one thing that I always thought she wanted, but no, it's still not enough, and I suddenly realize that, for whatever reason, I will somehow never be good enough for her. I will never make her happy. I am either too fat or too thin. There is no middle ground. Nothing I ever do is destined to please her.

'Yes, Mum. But what about you? Been out with the girls from the slimming club again?'

'Oh yes!' she giggles, delighted at the opportunity to talk about herself. 'Jacqui, remember I told you about Jacqui? Well, Jacqui's getting married and it was her hen night on Saturday. We went to a nightclub! Can you imagine me in a nightclub? Actually, I did myself proud . . .' I switch off as my mother giggles along to her little story and eventually I say goodbye and go upstairs to my room.

I sit in front of the dressing table and put on my make-up, copying the way Geraldine made me up for Ben's leaving party, and, even though I should be used to it by now, I still can't believe that this is me, that the woman staring back at me in the mirror is Jemima Jones.

And then I brush my long, blonde hair, watching as the spotlights in the ceiling pick up the golden lights, and eventually I stand up, go to the bathroom and grin widely in the full-length mirror, with one hand seductively pressed on my hip, although it feels completely ridiculous for me to pose in this way.

'Goodbye, Jemima Jones,' I say firmly, not giving a damn if either of my flatmates should hear. 'Hello, JJ,' and with that I laugh, flick back my new hair, and go to phone Brad.

CHAPTER SIXTEEN

Hi Darling,

I can't believe you're coming, you're actually coming! My friends are even more excited than I am, if that's possible. But seriously, I will come to the airport to pick you up because it's kinda out of the way, so from there we'll go straight back to my house. Don't worry about anything - I've already made up the spare room for you and I think you'll be very happy in there - you have your own TV, video and bathroom, and I've filled the whole house with flowers for you!

If you're not too tired, it would be really nice to take you out for dinner, but let's see how you feel. I'm just looking forward to actually meeting you, and I know I should be worried but I'm not, I really have a good feeling about this, although I probably shouldn't be saying that yet!

Have a great flight, darling, and I'll see you in two weeks' time! (Oh my God - two weeks!)

Huge hugs and kisses, Brad, xxxxxx

'Well that's it now,' I say, turning to Geraldine, who's reading my e-mail over my shoulder. 'Like it or not I'm going.'

'What do you mean like it or not? You sound so unhappy about it. Tell you what, I'll go.'

I smile, because I *am* excited, but, if you really must

know, the only person I desperately want to see looking like this is Ben, but Ben, as you already know, seems to be long gone, and Brad, I suppose, is the next best thing.

'I'm sort of serious,' adds Geraldine. 'Most women would give their right arm to be flying off to meet a hunk like Brad.'

'No, I do want to.' And it's true, I do, and I know that I don't have anything to worry about any more on the looks front, it's just that I'm seriously nervous, I've never done anything this, well, this adventurous in my life. 'But what if it's awful?'

'Look at you, Jemima,' says Geraldine forcefully. 'You're still worried that he's not going to like you aren't you?'

I shrug, because, although I can see that I've changed, that I look like a completely different person, underneath I still feel the same, I still feel fat.

'That's not going to happen,' Geraldine continues. 'You are *gorgeous*, will you just get used to it and get on with your life?'

'Okay, okay,' I say, smiling. Anything to get her off this track, because ridiculous as it may sound I'm getting a bit sick of people telling me how beautiful I am, I just can't take it all that seriously, and I don't feel beautiful. Not yet. Well, maybe I do occasionally, but it only seems to last a few minutes at the most. If anything I feel a bit of a fraud. 'I suppose I'd better go and see the editor and ask for the time off.'

'You mean you booked your ticket without checking to see if it was okay?' Geraldine is horrified.

'Yes.' It wasn't exactly forefront in my mind, what with having to lose about a billion stone in three months.

'I've booked the ticket so now I just have to make the time.'

'Talk about flying by the seat of your pants,' and Geraldine walks off muttering under her breath.

'Come in, come in,' says the editor, leaping out of his seat and coming to open the door for me, which is astounding because he has never, ever done this in the past. 'I'm glad you came to see me,' he says, except he's not looking into my eyes as he says this, the old lech is eyeing my body up and down. 'There are a few things I've been meaning to talk to you about.' I just bet there are.

I sit down in the chair he's proffering and try to cross my legs slowly in the way I've seen Sophie and Lisa do so many times before, my right ankle tucked sensually behind my left calf, both legs at an angle, and I suppress a laugh at how I, Jemima Jones, can finally use my looks to further my career. The editor certainly looks as if he approves. In fact, he's so bloody busy approving my legs he seems to have forgotten what it was he wanted to talk to me about. I cough.

'Yes, yes. What was I saying?' He reluctantly drags his eyes up to my face. 'Good Lord, Jemima,' he says after yet another pause. 'I'm sorry, love, I just can't believe it's you.'

I smile benignly, now used to getting compliments from men who have known me for years, who before never seemed to notice me in the slightest.

Only this morning the internal phone rang yet again. Yet another news reporter wondering if I could do a story for him, and would I mind meeting for a drink at lunchtime to discuss it further. At first I wondered what the hell was going on, but according to Geraldine I'm now the office 'babe', and I know I should be flattered, delighted, but actually I'm slightly pissed off that no one ever bothered with me before. But it's not all bad. At least the work has improved.

For the first time last week I was sent on an interview, and not just a crappy, boring interview, I was sent to interview the new star of a London soap, who conveniently lives around the corner from the *Kilburn Herald*, not having, as yet, earnt enough money to move to a better area.

The interview went fantastically. A little too fantastically perhaps, as I ended up trying to manoeuvre myself out of the way of this admittedly cute man who seemed to have sprouted a thousand hands, all of which were trying to paw me.

Life, I now realize, is certainly different when you're thin. Even the gym has now become a place of excitement, for wonder of wonders, I seem to have been welcomed into the crowd of beautiful people, and even in my leotard – yes, I replaced my huge tracksuits a long time ago with tight black leotards and cycling shorts (even slim I don't quite have the confidence to wear the brightly coloured lycra crop tops and thongs I once dreamt of) – with no make-up on at all and my hair scraped back into a ponytail, there's always some bloke who decides he's going to chat me up. Amazing.

'Working hard?' they usually start, as I smile, nod and try to continue my workout, but they still stand there, trying to make conversation, and if Paul, my trainer, happens to be around, he usually steps in and steers them on to another machine. Thank God for Paul.

*

Thank God indeed, for Paul is the one person who is worried about Jemima. He can't help but smile when he sees these muscular hopefuls chat her up. If only they had seen her before, he thinks, but of course these men had, only they hadn't ever noticed her. Paul has been trying to monitor Jemima's routine, for although she does look amazing, he is worried about how quickly the weight has come off, and he is convinced that under the golden skin – she has been using Clarins fake tan regularly on Geraldine's recommendation – Jemima Jones may not be as healthy as she looks.

He has tried to broach the subject with Jemima, but she is instantly dismissive. 'Of course I'm eating enough, Paul!' she keeps saying. 'Anorexic? Me? Don't make me laugh.' For the record Jemima isn't anorexic, merely obsessed, which is definitely equally unhealthy, and possibly nearly as dangerous. We shall see.

And now, sitting in the editor's office after my lunchtime workout, I watch as he picks up the phone and rings his secretary. 'Laura,' he barks in his gruff Northern accent, 'we'll have two coffees and a plate of biscuits.' He puts the phone down and says to me, or should that be, leers, 'I don't suppose you'll be eating the biscuits. Must be hard to maintain that figure.'

And more fool me, I blush. 'I manage,' I say firmly.

'Now then, Jemima. The reason I wanted to talk to you was because I think you are destined for greater things. I always told you your time would come, and now that you've proven yourself with that interview, I think we're ready to move you on to features.'

Funny that. Funny how, now that I'm slim and blonde, he suddenly wants to promote me. I know I should be grateful, he probably expects me to gush my thanks, but all I can think of as I sit here looking at his expectant face, his chubby cheeks and his little piggy eyes that keep straying down to my legs is, you bastard. You big bloody bastard. You would never have given me this chance if I didn't look like this. If I hadn't lost weight I would have carried on doing the Top Tips page for the rest of my bloody life.

'Well?' says the editor, doubtless expecting me to be overjoyed.

'Well,' I say, completely torn, because, bastard though he may be, this is the chance I've been waiting for for years, but then it's also sexist, and really, I'm speechless, and half of me wants to tell him to stuff his offer, while the other half wants to pounce on it. 'Why now?' I say eventually, after the editor has started to sweat somewhat.

'It's just a question of timing,' he says. 'We always knew you were an asset to the paper, and now, with Ben gone, we need another bright young thing to do all the big interviews, and let's face it, Jemima, the fact that you've turned into a stunning young woman doesn't do you any harm.'

There. He said it. He actually admitted that he was a sexist bastard. And I sit and look around his office. I look first at the threadbare grey carpet, stained with coffee, the odd cigarette burn. I look at the framed front pages on the wall, big stories that have got into the nationals, and I look at the editor sitting behind his cheap formica desk in his cheap nylon shirt with his fat fingers and nicotine-stained smile, and my over-

224

whelming feeling is that I want nothing more than to turn on my heel and run. I want to run far, far away from the *Kilburn Herald*. And the mention of my beloved Ben's name is like a knife through my heart because he still hasn't called, and the best thing I can do is get away from here, from him, from all the memories.

But I don't say that. I can't say that. Not just yet.

'I'd love the job,' I say finally, forcing a smile. 'But on one condition.'

'Condition?' The editor wasn't expecting any conditions.

'I need a holiday. I'd like to go away in two weeks' time for a fortnight.'

The editor sighs with relief, and I know exactly what he was thinking during the silence. For a minute there he thought I was going to be telling him I'd only take the job at a massive increase in salary.

'No problem, love,' he says. 'Geraldine can do your page while you're gone, and while you're away we'll take on someone new to take over the Top Tips. How does that sound?'

'Fine,' but shit, Geraldine will go mad. 'Oh,' I add, getting up to leave. 'One more thing. I'm assuming that there will be an increase in my salary commensurate with my new job?'

The editor is almost speechless, probably amazed at the confidence losing weight can bring, for the Jemima Jones of old would never have dared to say anything like that, and, I have to admit, he has a point.

'Naturally,' he blusters. 'I'll talk to the financial people and we'll work something out. Don't worry, love, leave it to me. Where are you off to anyway?'

'Los Angeles,' I smile, closing the door behind me and relishing the look on his face, for the editor's idea of a holiday is Brighton, or, at an absolute push, a week in Majorca. And as I walk down the corridor I start to feel, for the first time, a small buzz of excitement in the pit of my stomach. 'Oh my God. I'm going to Los Angeles!'

'You can't wear that!' Geraldine lies back on my bed and flings her hands dramatically over her eyes. 'Jemima! for God's sake, haven't you heard of airoplane chic?'

'Airoplane what?' I'm being practical, I'm waiting in my tracksuit, a pair of comfortable trainers and a T-shirt for my long-haul flight. But I want to look good for Brad, so in my hand luggage I've put a mini skirt, a linen shirt and knee-high boots which I'm planning to change into just before we land. Just in case you're wondering, the last two weeks have positively flown by, and today's the day, I'm actually going. Geraldine – and what would I now do without Geraldine – is driving me to the airport, as caught up in my adventure as I am myself.

'Airoplane chic,' she repeats. 'You know, the glamorous look that all the celebs and models employ when they fly anywhere.'

'But Geraldine,' I say smiling, 'I think you're forgetting that, er, I'm not a celeb or a model. I'm a journalist on the *Kilburn* bloody *Herald*. And anyway' – I open my bag and show her the contents – 'I've packed clothes to change into, I don't want to be uncomfortable on the flight.'

'First, Brad doesn't know you work on the *Kilburn* bloody *Herald*,' she reminds me. 'He thinks you're Miss Snazzy Television Presenter, and while I'm not suggesting you wear a suit or knee-high boots on the flight, at the very least employ a bit of glamour.' She clicks her teeth. 'Those clothes,' she gestures to my overnight bag, 'are completely wrong for a flight. Even if they are only to change into at the end.'

I shrug as she opens my suitcase and starts rifling around. 'This,' she mutters, pulling out a crisp white T-shirt. 'This,' she says, holding up a pair of black stretchy trousers and nodding approvingly. 'And this,' she says, digging out an oversized black sweater, 'to loop casually over your shoulders. You can still wear the trainers but this is LA, now all you need are the accessories to complete your look of airoplane chic.'

'Accessories?'

'I knew it!' she says. 'After all my lessons you still haven't learnt about the importance of accessories. Jemima, my darling, accessories are everything. But Auntie Geraldine came prepared so you don't have to worry. Be back in a sec.'

I get changed into the clothes Geraldine chose as she runs to the car. A minute later she runs back holding a Louis Vuitton vanity case, which even I, Jemima Jones, know costs an absolute fortune.

'Now Jemima,' she says, looking at me very seriously. 'This vanity case was a present from Dimitri, and although Dimitri and I are no longer, this is my pride and joy. I am lending it to you now, but guard it with your life.'

'Geraldine, I'm speechless. But what do I need it for?'

'To look the part. Everyone carries a Louis Vuitton vanity case when they're travelling. And now,' she says, 'for the *pièce*, or *pièces*, *de résistance*.' She opens the vanity case and pulls out a pair of large, tortoiseshell Cutler & Gross sunglasses. 'These were used in a fashion shoot a couple of weeks ago and I lost them. I feel terrible, I phoned the PR and she's just about forgiven me. I can't think where they've got to.' She grins wickedly as she hands them to me. 'You don't actually need to wear them on the flight. Wear them at the airport, and when you're not wearing them on your eyes, wear them on top of your head.' She shows me how to loop my hair back perfectly with the glasses, which, it has to be said, do seem to add a touch of instant glamour.

'Hmm,' she says, rifling around in the vanity case. 'What else have I got here?' She pulls out two bottles of Evian water and a can of what looks like hairspray, followed by a selection of exotic-looking jars. 'The water is obviously for you to drink on the plane. Whatever you do, avoid any alcohol, it will only make you retain even more water than you already will. The can is a spray of Evian water, which you have to use as follows.' She flicks back her hair and, with a flourish of her hand, sprays the mist finely over her face, breathing a sigh of relief when she's done. 'There,' she says. 'It's what all the models do, as it stops your skin drying out. These,' she adds, gesturing to the pots, 'are also freebies. I phoned the company and told them I was writing a piece about their products so they sent me the whole range. They're super-duper moisturizing products, and I would suggest you use them every couple of hours. Darling, you have no idea how flying dries out your skin. And finally,' she says, pulling out a tiny little white plastic bottle, 'eye drops to give you those bright, white, sparkling eyes, even after an eleven-hour flight. God,' she adds, almost to herself, 'someone should pay me for this.'

'Geraldine,' I say, shaking my head but unable to stop smiling, 'you, are a godsend. What would I do without you?'

'What you'd do, Jemima, is look like every other wannabe flying to Los Angeles with stars in her eyes. Now you look like a there.'

'A what?'

'A there. A made-it, whatever you want to call it.' She looks at her watch. 'Jesus, we'd better leave if we're going to make it. Are you all set?'

'Nearly. I've just got to write a note for Sophie and Lisa.' Geraldine rolls her eyes. 'I have to, Geraldine. Just in case there's an emergency.'

'I bet you're glad to see the back of them.'

'I don't mind. They don't bother me much, they're quite amusing in a sad sort of way.'

'Yup, an ugly sisters sort of way.'

'Exactly,' I laugh.

'So how do you feel?' Geraldine asks, as we lug my cases to the front door.

'Nervous as hell?'

'Don't be. I wish it was me. You're going to have a blast.'

Jemima Jones is getting a lot of attention at the airport, although she hasn't really noticed, too caught up in the excitement of her trip to take in the admiring glances. Perhaps it's the fact that she does indeed look like a made-it, particularly when she puts the sunglasses on to hide her exhilaration, perhaps it is simply that, with the help of her fairy godmother Geraldine, she seems to have perfected the art of looking impossibly cool, not to mention beautiful. Whatever the reason, the package-tour people are nudging one another and whispering, 'Who do you think it is?' 'I'm sure she's famous.' 'Isn't she the girl from that film?'

'I'm going to miss you,' says Geraldine, putting her arms around me and giving me a huge hug. 'Who's going to make my days bearable for the next two weeks?'

'Who's going to rewrite your copy, you mean.' I grin, hugging her back and completely forgetting to mention that Geraldine has the joy of writing the Top Tips column in store for her.

'That too,' says Geraldine, 'but seriously, I really am going to miss you. Have the most fantastic time. Will you call me?'

'Of course I will.'

'As soon as you get there? I'm dying to know what he's like. God, he might be short, fat and balding.'

'Don't!' I admonish, because I'm nervous enough as it is. 'That would be awful,' and then I remember that although I've never been short and balding, I was once fat, and in a split second I remember how people judged me, how they misjudged me, more like. 'But it would be okay if he was a nice person,' I add, although I'm crossing my fingers and praying he has a full head of hair. 'Anyway, we've seen his picture, I'm sure it really is him.'

'If you're sure, I'm sure,' says Geraldine, 'but whatever

he's like you've got a ticket to Los Angeles. Are you absolutely certain you can't fit me in your suitcase?'

We both look down at my suitcase, so full all the sides are positively bulging. 'Quite certain,' I laugh, 'although what I wouldn't give to have you come with.'

'Take care,' says Geraldine, giving her another hug, and as Geraldine leaves Jemima she realizes that she really will miss her, that Jemima has become very important in her life, that Jemima has helped her to rediscover the joys of female friendship, for, up until recently, Geraldine always considered herself a man's woman, a woman with no time for female friends. Isn't it strange how things change . . .

And that's it. I'm on my own. I walk up to the Virgin check-in, a bottle of mineral water in one hand, the Louis Vuitton vanity case in the other, and a pile of glossy magazines, 'to keep you from getting bored', from Geraldine under my arm. I hand my economy ticket over the counter, and someone, somewhere, must be smiling upon me today, or perhaps Geraldine's ploy is working, but whatever it is the check-in girl seems to think I might be a made-it as well, and although she tells me it's not airline policy to upgrade those who simply look the part, the economy class is full, and Virgin would like to upgrade me to upper class.

What a result!

'Gosh! Really? That's fantastic!' I say, forgetting to act like a famous film star, like someone who would naturally be upgraded. 'Actually, I've never even flown before! And now I'm flying upper class! Thank you, thank you so much.'

Needless to say the check-in girl looks shocked, she realizes her mistake, but lucky me, it's too late, and I don't even care that I've been desperately uncool because I'm the one with the upgrade! I'm the one flying upper class!

And then I have two hours to kill in the airport, and I buy books at the airport bookstore, splash myself with perfume in Duty Free, and look longingly at the jewellery shops, picking out what I would buy if I had the money.

I also spend far too much time looking longingly at the Silk Cut, but no, I do not smoke any more. Not even when I'm so nervous I could be sick. No. I'm fit and healthy. I do not need to smoke. So, when a voice comes over the tannoy telling me my flight is boarding, I bounce down to the departure gate, trying to control the urge to shout with excitement and joy.

Eleven hours is a hell of a long time to spend on a flight, but eleven hours can pass incredibly quickly when you're Jemima Jones and you've never flown before. Eleven hours can pass incredibly quickly when you are sunk in the height of luxury, when you are fed and watered at the drop of a hat, when you have your own personal video screen and can choose any film that takes your fancy. Jemima Jones is far too excited to sleep, and when the stewardesses pull down the shutters on the aeroplane windows and the rest of the people in upper class pull on their eye patches and gently snooze, Jemima

Jones watches videos, reads her magazines, and spends a disproportionately long time with her head leant back, thinking about her life.

She thinks about the way her life has changed. She thinks about Brad, about what he's going to look like, what he's going to think of her, what she will do in Los Angeles. And she thinks about Ben, but she tries not to think about him too much, for every time she does she cannot help but feel a physical pull, a pang perhaps. Try as she might to get on with her life, the fact remains that she misses him, that she suspects she'll never feel quite the same way about anyone ever again, and this is something that she doesn't think she'll get over for a very long time.

So she sits in upper class and sprays her can of Evian on her face, drinks her mineral water, and religiously rubs moisturizer in to stop her skin dehydrating. An hour before they arrive she goes to the loo to put on her make-up, and as she stands there, as she brushes her mascara on, the butterflies suddenly start flying around her stomach and she looks at herself in the mirror and says disbelievingly, 'Jemima Jones, what the hell are you doing?'

CHAPTER SEVENTEEN

They always say that you're supposed to feel tired after a long-haul flight. I don't feel tired, I feel excited, and happy, and nervous. It's almost as if up until now it's been a big game. There I was, playing around on the Internet, having this make-believe romance with someone I'd never met, and it was fun, it gave me something to look forward to, but now, now that I'm actually here, I'm so frightened.

Not because he could be *anyone*, he could be an axe-murderer, a paedophile, a rapist, although that had crossed my mind, but more because I've come all this way and what if he doesn't like me. I know what Geraldine would say, what if I don't like him, but that's kind of irrelevant, I mean, I've never been in a situation where I've had a choice. And I know things are different now, I know I don't look like I used to, but it still seems ridiculous that I might not like someone who likes me.

What if I'm not what he expected? What if he sees through the illusion and sees the fat unhappy girl lurking beneath? After all, it wasn't that long ago that I was a laughing-stock. It hurts me to even say that, but I know it's true. I know that despite the few people who saw through, who were kind to me anyway – people like Geraldine and Ben – most of the people I knew simply felt sorry for me.

And although I look in the mirror and I don't recognize

myself, in a weird sort of way this feels like a game too. It feels like it can't be real, that I'm playing at being thin, and that at some point I will be fat again. I know I'm thin because I'm buying size 10 clothes (even they are slightly big on me) but I still feel the same, and I'm so scared that Brad will see that. And, more to the point, where the hell is he anyway?

I've got my suitcases, I've walked through customs, and I can't see Brad, or even anyone who looks remotely like him, anywhere. I thought he'd be standing right at the front, I suppose, if I'm honest, I had stupid daydreams about this gorgeous hunk running over to me and scooping me up in his arms, but although there are many, many people here, none of them looks like Brad.

What if he doesn't turn up? What if he's not in? Where will I go? What will I do? As the panic starts to set in I realize that now I really do want a cigarette more than I've ever wanted one before in my life, but even as the thought crosses my mind I notice that all around are signs saying that it is a no-smoking airport, implying that anyone caught smoking will be hanged, drawn and quartered, so I just sigh deeply and try to look like a woman who knows what she's doing.

'Excuse me?' I turn, breath catching in my throat as I see a short, fat, balding man standing in front of me.

'Brad?' Sorry, sorry, sorry, but I haven't got a hope in hell of hiding the disappointment in my voice. Oh my God, I'm thinking. You lied to me, you lied about your picture. I conveniently forget that I also lied about mine because that is hardly relevant now. Shit, I think next,

I've got to spend two whole weeks with this revolting man, and then I think no! I'm not going to judge him, he might be really nice, but even as I stand here thinking that I'm looking at him and wishing I hadn't come. Wishing I'd left it as a game.

'No.' He shakes his head as I exhale loudly in a sigh of relief. 'I'm Paul Springer. I'm a film producer.'

'Oh?' I say uninterestedly, wondering what on earth he wants.

'I hope you don't mind me asking, but you're very beautiful, I assumed you had to be an actress.'

'Thank you,' I say, with a genuine smile this time, because when compliments have always been things that other people get, you do feel ridiculously thrilled when you start getting your own. 'But I'm not,' I add, and I start to turn away, because at first I thought he might have been Brad's driver, or someone he sent to pick me up, but he quite obviously doesn't know him, or me either.

'A model then?' He grabs my arm.

'No. Afraid not.' I try and shake off his arm.

'Well you should be. Are you new in town?'

'Yes.' I'm now wondering how to get away from this man without seeming rude but I'm not entirely sure how to do it because his hand appears to be stuck to my arm.

'I'd be very happy to show you the sights.'

'Thank you, but I'm here staying with a friend.'

'Here's my card.' He stands there holding out a business card with a chubby hand, and as I reluctantly take it he comes up with what is obviously his number one pulling line. 'I know you don't act, but I have a part in my next movie that I think you'd be perfect for.' I'm amazed that Geraldine was so right, I'm actually speechless, and I look at him open-mouthed because it is so obviously a line, but what is most bizarre is that this line must work, but not, obviously, on me.

'Thank you,' I say uncertainly, 'I'll be in touch,' and with that he licks his lips slowly and repeats, 'Perfect, just perfect,' and this time I forget my British reserve and politeness, pick up my bags, and move to the other end of the hall.

I'm looking at my watch when a voice says in my ear, ' JJ?' and this time my heart starts pounding as I turn around and look into the eyes of the most beautiful man I've ever seen.

Oh my God, oh my God, oh my God! His picture didn't do him justice, nothing could do this man justice. Can a man be beautiful? Can anyone be as perfect as this man standing before me, looking at me hopefully, doubtfully, for I still haven't said anything.

'Brad?' I say eventually, when I've got my breath back, and he doesn't say anything, just nods before sweeping me up in his arms and giving me a hug, a huge, enveloping hug, and, in those few seconds that I'm in his arms, I feel like this is the moment I've been waiting for all my life.

'I can't believe you're here!' he says finally, when he releases me, and we stand there trying to take one another in, remembering our pictures, trying to work out whether we are the respective people we thought we were. I look at him and think, you could not like me, you could not be with me, you are far too beautiful to be with me, but he hasn't backed away as I thought he might, there is nothing on his face that is showing disappointment, and I am the first one to tell him he is not what I expected.

'Your picture doesn't do you justice,' I say nervously, so scared he'll see through me to the fat girl I've fought so hard to hide.

He smiles, perfect white teeth which I look at with amazement, because I have never seen teeth more perfect, nor lips more sculpted, nor eyes so blue. 'Neither does yours,' he says, and I feel a familiar heat rise up my face, the blush that Jemima Jones so hated, the blush that JJ is supposed to have banished for ever. I stand and I blush, and all the while I cannot take my eyes from his face, and I cannot believe my luck.

Brad laughs and pushes his hair, his sun-streaked blond hair, out of his eyes and he shakes his head. 'You are so much better than I expected. You're gorgeous, JJ, you really are.' He reaches down with a sun-tanned arm, an arm covered in fine blond hair, and my stomach twists in an unfamiliar feeling, a feeling which, it slowly dawns on me, must be lust, pure and simple lust, and he stands tall, taller than me, and says, 'C'mon, let's get out of here.'

And as we walk out of the airport to his car, I allow myself to exhale with relief, because I am good enough, and as I lower myself into the tan leather seats of his sleek black convertible Porsche, I cannot wipe the smile off my face and I surreptitiously pinch myself, just to confirm this isn't all a dream.

He turns the ignition on and looks over at me with a grin, and I still cannot wipe the smile off my face, and I still cannot quite believe this is reality. Thank you, God, I pray silently, closing my eyes for a brief second. Thank you for making me slim. Thank you for delivering me this perfect man.

*

What a couple they make, Brad and JJ. Even before they've hit the highway everyone is staring at them, drinking in their beauty, this vision of the Californian dream. Two beautiful people, in a beautiful car, on a beautiful day. They drive on to the Santa Monica Freeway, the wind whipping their hair back, sunglasses protecting their eyes, and Jemima Jones tips her head back in her seat and gazes at the sky, at the tips of the palm trees that rush past her, and she thinks that for the first time she understands about being happy. She keeps sneaking a peek at the vision sitting next to her, still unable to believe that she will be spending the next two weeks with him. They don't talk, the noise of the engine and the cars rushing past make it too difficult to hear each other speak, so the music is turned up, and every now and then these two beautiful people look at one another and smile. When something looks this good, how could it possibly go wrong?

'This is Santa Monica Boulevard,' says Brad, pulling off the freeway. We stop at a traffic light and a sports car I don't recognize pulls up next to us. I turn to look at the driver and it's a young, good-looking guy who, much to my astonishment, gives me an appreciative glance before shouting to Brad, 'Nice car, man. Nice babe.'

Brad smiles and puts his foot down as we drive down this huge, wide road lined by huge shops that are far bigger, far brighter than any at home. Right at the end I can see palm trees, and beyond a hazy blue, and just as I'm about to ask him where this leads, he turns to me and says, 'This road takes us all the way down to the ocean. We'll drive down there, then take Ocean Boulevard to my place. I think you'll like it a lot, it overlooks the water.'

Like it a lot? I'm already in love with the air here, the sunshine, the beautiful people, although to be perfectly honest I haven't seen that many yet, but this is, after all, the mecca of the rich and famous, and I'm already trying to celebrity spot as we drive along this road that seems to have no pedestrians whatsoever.

'How are you feeling?' Brad turns to me, raising perfect eyebrows.

'Fine, great, this is fantastic.'

'Are you tired?'

'Not really, although I'm waiting for it to hit me.'

'How about stopping for a coffee?'

'That would be great.'

We turn right past more shops, but this time there are hundreds of people milling around, then left into a picture-perfect road, palm trees on either side *and* down the middle. I sit there marvelling at how clean everything is, how wide the roads, how perfectly pastel the tiny boutiques, how different to Santa Monica Boulevard, because this is obviously where the smart people live. Brad pulls up outside a corner coffee shop calling itself Starbucks, and as he's parking I sneak another look at him, still unable to believe how incredibly blond, and gorgeous, and perfect this man is.

He jumps out the door, and runs over to my side to let me out.

'This,' he says, gesturing to the coffee shop, 'believe it or not is one of the in places to go. There are Starbucks all over Los Angeles now, it's the only place to get a decent cup of coffee, and all the movie people congregate here on the weekends.'

Being a weekday the place is quiet, the green iron tables and chairs scattered on the street outside are almost all empty; at the one exception sits a lone blond man in a baseball cap and sunglasses sipping a cup of what looks like coffee and reading a copy of *Variety*. His dog lies disconsolately under his chair, nose on paws, eyes closed, doubtless dreaming of dog-food commercials.

We walk in and up to the counter. 'Hi,' says the man behind the counter, 'what can I get you?'

'Jemima?' Brad turns to me.

'Um.' What can I order, what would be sophisticated? I look beyond the counter at the board and I'm stumped. There are mochas, frappuccinos, lattes, a million things I've never heard of. 'I'll have a cappuccino.' Both Brad and the man behind the counter look at me strangely. 'Would that be decaf or regular?'

'Um, regular, please.'

'How many shots?'

'I'm sorry?'

'How many shots?' The man looks pleadingly at Brad, who evidently decides to take the matter in hand. 'Don't worry,' he says to him, 'she just got here from England. We'll have two tall skinny lattes with a shot of almond.'

'We will?' I look at Brad with a raised eyebrow. 'Skinny?'

'Don't worry about it,' he says with a laugh. 'It means fat-free with a shot of almond syrup. You'll like it.'

Our coffee comes in paper cups which we take outside, and we sit down at one of the tables and Brad smiles at me. 'You're really here,' he says, while I think, yes, I'm really here, and yes, you've already said that. On several occasions, but that thought doesn't last very long, it's pushed aside almost instantly by the thought that Brad is most definitely the best-looking man I have ever had the pleasure of being with.

'This is so weird,' he says. 'Meeting someone like you on the Internet, then actually meeting, and most of all seeing that you absolutely fulfil my expectations. More than fulfil. For a minute there' – he laughs at whatever he's about to say – 'for a minute there I was worried that you'd cut the picture out of a magazine and you'd turn out to be really fat or something.'

I laugh politely with him, thanking God I lost the weight, that I didn't have to put up with the humiliation of turning up looking like the Jemima of old, but a part of me wishes he hadn't said that, wishes he hadn't sounded so superficial, so like a person I would have hated had we met six months before. But I manage to push the feelings aside and I merely smile and say, 'I know.'

'I thought the same thing about you,' I continue, 'and this guy started talking to me at the airport and I thought it was you.' I tell Brad the story and he listens attentively before saying, 'That's what everyone in LA is like, trust me, you'll get used to it.'

'You mean everyone just hands out business cards to complete strangers?'

'Well yes, there is that, but more that men have no problem approaching women they find beautiful.'

'But he was revolting!' I counter.

'That doesn't matter,' says Brad. 'Some of the most

242

beautiful women in Los Angeles are with some of the ugliest men.'

'But why?'

'You have to understand that nobody actually comes from Los Angeles. Everybody flocks here hoping to fulfil a dream. The men all want to be film producers, and the women all want to marry film producers. It's not like New York, where the women go to become successful in their own right. Here the women want to marry success, and for the men, the ultimate status symbol is having a beautiful, hardbodied woman on their arm.'

'But don't these women feel sick at the thought?'

'You are naïve aren't you?' Brad looks amazed before smiling to himself. 'That's so refreshing. No, these women don't feel sick because power is a tremendous aphrodisiac.'

'But surely anyone could go around picking up women and saying they were a film producer?'

'Sure. That's exactly what happens.'

'You mean this guy could have been a floorsweeper.'

'In this case it's unlikely because he gave you a card with a company name on it that's well known, so you could easily check up on him. But I've heard a lot of stories where guys get business cards printed, and anyone could set themselves up as a freelance film producer or director.'

'How extraordinary.'

Brad laughs. 'So I take it you won't be following this up?'

Now it's my turn to laugh. 'Not bloody likely.'

'I love hearing you talk,' he says. 'I know I've heard your voice on the phone, but it's a completely different experience being here with you, watching you, watching the way your hands move.'

'Thank you.' I'm suddenly embarrassed, and I keep thinking he's made a mistake. He shouldn't be with me, he should be with one of these beautiful models, or actresses. Not me, dull Jemima Jones from the *Kilburn Herald*.

'So were they okay about letting you have time off work?' he says, moving the conversation back on to more neutral, comfortable ground.

'Fine, and they're going to promote me when I get back.'

'Promote you? What can they promote you to?'

Shit! Nearly gave the game away. Remember, Jemima, you're now JJ, a television presenter.

'They're giving me a much bigger slot on the show.'

'I can really see you on television,' he says. 'Maybe you should talk to some people over here, that British accent would drive them wild.'

'Maybe I should,' I say, feeling a warm glow spread inside, already enjoying the fact that Brad is thinking I might be staying, that already he likes me enough to think we may have a future.

I know you're probably thinking I'm mad, but trust me, if you were here, if you were sitting opposite this earthly version of a god, you would have thought the same thing too.

Would we, Jemima? Would we really? Well, maybe Jemima Jones is right, because it is oh so very easy to be blinded by what people look like, and yes, she's right,

Brad is the ultimate specimen of the perfect man. But let's be honest here, they hardly know each other, and although they like the look of each other, which is, as we all know, a good start, looks – and Jemima of all people should be remembering this – aren't everything.

We finish our Starbucks coffee – and incidentally, it *is* delicious – and then we climb back in his car and drive home, and what a home! Brad lives in a gorgeous house overlooking the beach. A modern, box-like house; inside the rooms are enormous, bleached wood floors stretch as far as the eye can see, and french windows open out on to a large wooden deck.

'I bought it because the space reminds me of a loft,' says Brad, as I just stand in the centre of this room that's about ten times the size of my whole flat, completely blown away by the beauty of the light, the sound of the ocean, the sparkling, fresh *Californianness* of it all.

He shows me around, shows me the modern, stainless steel and beech kitchen, points out the huge modern canvases on the walls, makes me sit in an oversized white linen sofa that's so deep it practically swallows me whole.

'I thought I'd cook dinner here tonight,' says Brad. 'I figured you'd be too tired to go out.' I nod my assent, saying that would be lovely, and Brad takes my things up to the spare room, and shows me the bathroom. 'I'll be in the kitchen when you're ready,' he says, as he closes the door and I breathe out a sigh of relief.

Everything is perfect. Not only is he perfect, but he didn't assume we'd be sharing a room, and although I hope, oh God how I hope, this becomes more than just friends, I'm not ready for that yet.

So I stretch my arms behind my head as I lie on the white damask bedcover and watch the ceiling fan circle overhead. The last of the day's light is filtering through the wooden slatted blinds, and I can't help it, I'm smiling a huge, self-satisfied smile. And after a while I get up to go into the *en suite* bathroom, and as I do I pass an old gilt mirror on the wall. I know you probably think I have a thing about mirrors, and you're probably throwing up with my vanity, but it's not that. It's just that if you looked the way I used to and then lost all the weight too, you'd need some sort of affirmation of who you are. You'd also need to keep checking that you're still here, it's still you.

So I walk up to the mirror and look at myself, watch my face as it breaks into a big smile.

'I've made it,' I say quietly, and yes, okay, slightly gleefully. ' JJ, you've bloody well made it.'

CHAPTER EIGHTEEN

There's a brief knock on the bathroom door which I don't hear for a few seconds, being, as I am, submerged under the water.

'Jemima?'

I sit up with a start, and frantically look around the room for a towel before remembering that I have locked the door.

'Yes?'

'I just wanted to check that everything was okay. Do you need anything?'

'No, I'm fine. Thank you, though.'

'Oh. Okay. I'll go and start preparing dinner.'

'Brad?'

'Yes?' I hear his footsteps come back to the door.

'There is one thing?'

'Sure.'

'Would you mind if I made a phonecall to England?'

'Of course not. That's fine. There's a phone in your room next to the bed. Do you know the dialling code?'

'Don't worry, I've got all these instructions on my AT & T card.' Once again Geraldine came to the rescue, insisting I apply for this card so my progress reports to her would be cheaper.

'Okay. Fine. See you in a little while.'

I walk out of the bathroom enveloped in a fluffy white towelling robe which Brad had thoughtfully hung on the back of the door, another huge white fluffy towel wrapped around my wet hair, and I dig into my bag and pull out a little booklet of instructions from AT & T. I read the instructions then sit on the bed and pick up the receiver.

1 800 225 5288. 'Hello and welcome to AT & T. To place a call, press 1.' I follow the instructions and wait with bated breath as a phone starts to ring.

'Hello?' The voice is half asleep.

'Geraldine?'

'Oh my God, it's you! Hang on, let me wake up.'

'What time is it there?'

'Two o'clock in the morning.'

'Oh I'm really sorry, I didn't realize. Look, why don't I call you tomorrow . . .'

Geraldine interrupts. 'Are you crazy? I've spent all day thinking about you and hell, it's only sleep. I want to hear everything. What's he like, how's it going, is he gorgeous?'

I laugh and lower my voice to a whisper. 'Geraldine, you would not believe what he's like.'

'Uh oh. You mean he's awful, he's not like his picture, he's short, fat and balding.'

'No way. He is, and I mean this absolutely seriously, he is the most beautiful man I've ever seen.'

'You're joking!'

'I swear. He is about a million times more perfect than his picture. I just can't take my eyes off him.'

'And what did he think of you? Were you what he expected?'

'That's the amazing thing. He said that the picture I sent him didn't do me justice either. I mean, I don't want

248

to sound big-headed or anything but I think he likes me, I really do.'

'Jemima, that's not being big-headed, that's being honest. That's fantastic. So, have you decided what to name your children?'

I laugh. 'Not yet, but wait until the end of the evening.'

'What are you doing tonight? Let me guess, he's taking you somewhere really snazzy like Spago, or that other place, Eclipse, and your dinner guests are Tom Cruise and Nicole Kidman.'

'Somehow I don't think so. No, we're staying in and he's cooking me dinner.'

'He cooks too! Jemima, whatever you do don't let this one get away.'

'I'm not going to, if I can possibly help it, but every time I look at him I wonder what he's doing with someone like me.'

'Don't be ridiculous, Jemima. He's lucky to have someone like you.'

'Hmm. Maybe,' I say, even though I don't really believe it.

'So, do you think tonight's going to be the big seduction?'

'Christ! I hadn't even thought about that. It's almost as if he's too perfect to even imagine touching, let alone sleeping with.'

'Sounds too good to be true.'

'I think he probably is.'

Geraldine stifles a yawn. 'Sorry, Jemima, I'm getting sleepy.'

'Don't worry, I'll let you go back to bed. Thanks for waking up.'

'Don't mention it, darling. I'm delighted to hear everything's going well. Give me a call in a few days and let me know what's happening.'

'Okay. Take care.'

'Yeah.' Geraldine yawns again. 'You too.'

I put the phone down and pull my suitcase on to the bed and start to unpack, in a funny sort of way feeling much more secure now that I've spoken to Geraldine, now that I have her approval.

Brad, very quietly, puts the phone down in the kitchen, careful not to bang the receiver, careful not be heard. He stands back and slowly a perfect smile spreads over his face as he hits the air in an imaginary high five. Yes, he says to himself. Yes.

What should I wear? What should I wear? I've pulled all the clothes out and hung them up, and now I'm having a major clothes crisis. I don't want to look too sexy, but nor do I want to look as if I've made no effort at all. I need Geraldine now, not on the end of the phone but here, in this room, smoking a low-tar cigarette and pulling out the perfect outfit with her perfectly manicured nails, although I don't need her encouraging me to spend any more money than I already have.

I just don't know. I try on a little black dress, and, although I stand for a while marvelling at how it hugs my flat stomach and tiny waist, I know it's far too dressy, and I pull it off and carefully hang it back up. I try on a pair of cream silk trousers and a white T-shirt, and it looks great, but then I think, what if he does try to seduce me, trousers aren't exactly sexy.

In the end I settle on a white T-shirt and a short, A-line, tan suede skirt. Suede. I know, I know, I must be crazy bringing anything suede to Los Angeles, after all, it's so hot here, but it's my newest acquisition and I love it, I love the sensuality of the butter-soft suede. Yes. I look in the mirror. This is it. Perfect. I clip on some chunky silver earrings and slip my feet into flat white sneakers. Casual, sexy, perfect. Maybe, by osmosis, some of Geraldine's style has rubbed off on me after all.

'Wow,' says Brad after I eventually emerge, having spent what felt like hours perfecting my make-up, blow-drying my hair into a glossy, gold mane. 'Wow.'

'You like it?' I do a little twirl and Brad grins as he hands me a glass of champagne.

'You look great. Really, I love that skirt.' He gently strokes the fabric and smiles his appreciation, while, I have to say, my stomach does a mini flip, but I calmly sip the champagne as if I'm the kind of girl who drinks champagne every night of the week, a girl, in fact, much like Geraldine.

'Come into the kitchen and talk to me while I finish off,' says Brad, and as I follow him through I can't help but notice that the lights have suddenly become far, far dimmer than they were when I arrived, and in the huge stone fireplace there's now a fire crackling away, which, even though it's probably seventy degrees outside, does give a cosy glow to the room.

I pass the dining table, wrought iron and glass, and see that Brad has already set the table, fresh flowers in the middle and two tall candles on either side, waiting to be lit.

251

Naïve as I am, even I can see that Brad has aimed for romance, and just to confirm this he flicks on the music by remote control, and soft, sexy, soulful sounds emerge from every corner of the room.

'Quadrophonic speakers,' he explains, seeing me look around, trying to work out exactly where the music is coming from. 'It cost a heck of a lot, but it's worth it for the effect.'

I bet, I think, but of course I don't say that, and I can't help but wonder, as we walk into the kitchen, how many times he's done this before, but as soon as I think it I try and banish it, because at the end of the day it's here and now that matters, that I'm here and he's doing it for me now.

'How's the champagne?' he asks.

'Delicious.' I take another sip, before realizing that my glass is empty. Damn. Must be my nerves, I obviously gulped it down without even tasting it.

'Here.' He laughs, proffering the bottle and filling up my glass. 'I don't usually drink, but this is a special occasion.' He laughs again, and I watch him over the rim of my champagne glass, still unable to get over how incredible-looking this man is.

The effect? Jemima is absolutely right. Brad is well used to creating effects, and well versed in creating seduction scenes. Jemima may think he's a superb cook, that he's doing all this for her, but Brad has done this many times before. And what is he cooking? He is starting with goats' cheese, placed perfectly on a round slice of walnut bread that has been lightly toasted, warmed in the oven, and drizzled with walnut oil and a hint of lemon juice, all resting on a bed of rocket. For the main course he is preparing chicken breasts marinaded in rosemary and garlic, served with butternut squash and a selection of fresh vegetables, and for pudding he has created an exotic fruit salad with fat-free ice-cream to go with it. Not perhaps the most adventurous menu, it's true, but remember that this is a man obsessed with keeping the calories down, and truth to be told it's a wonder the goats' cheese got in there at all.

Brad isn't a marvellous cook, but he has six marvellous recipes that he brings out over and over again. He carefully notes which he has served to whom, just in case he makes the terrible mistake of serving the goats' cheese twice in a row. Luckily, he hasn't had to worry about this with Jemima.

Admittedly, he hasn't gone out of his way like this for a while, and we shall discover the reasons why later on, but for now let us see whether the effect is working . . .

'You know what I can't believe?' says Brad, chopping carrots and courgettes – or zucchini as he calls them – into julienne.

'Hmm?' I'm feeling more than a little bit woozy, the champagne combined with jet-lag is having a complete knock-out effect, but I can't seem to stop drinking it, anything to calm my nerves.

'I can't believe that someone like you doesn't have a boyfriend.'

'Well.' I sway ever so slightly on my stool. 'I can't believe that someone like you doesn't have a girlfriend.'

Brad smiles. 'How did I know you were going to say that?'

'Kismet?' I say sarcastically, instantly regretting it, because I didn't mean to be sarcastic, it just kind of came out. I mean, what was I supposed to have said? But Brad, thankfully, seems to have missed the sarcasm.

'Yeah!' he says enthusiastically. 'Kismet! I'm a big believer in fate, what about you?'

Okay, we can talk about this. This is something we have in common. This is good. Maybe we'll find hundreds more things we have in common, maybe there is a foundation there on which to build something different and special. God, I hope so.

'Absolutely,' I say. 'I do believe in fate, but I also believe that we control our own destinies, and I'm not sure which I believe in more. I think that mostly I believe that life is a bit like a tree, and that there are several branches we could take. I think that's where the controlling our own destiny bit comes in. If we choose a certain branch then our life will go one way, and fate will throw things at us from then on.'

Brad nods his head sagely. 'So,' he ventures after a pause. 'Do you think that this is fate?' He puts his glass down and looks at me very intently.

'I certainly believe there's a reason for us meeting.' God, can you believe how cool I sound? 'And I'm sure that everyone comes into our life because they have something to teach us.'

'So what lessons do you think you could learn from me?' A hint of a raised eyebrow, a touch of flirtation in his voice?

'How about I tell you tomorrow morning?' Well *done*, Jemima, finally I've had enough champagne to give me the confidence to flirt.

'How about I give you your first lesson now?' Brad starts moving towards me, and, stupid cow that I am, I jump up in a panic.

'Let's eat first,' I say brightly. 'I'm sure I'll be in far more of a learning mood once I've had some food. Anyway I'm starving, mmm, this looks delicious. I never realized you could cook too, you kept that very quiet. So, is the food ready?' Shut *up*, Jemima. You're making a fool of yourself. I shut up.

Brad laughs and reaches over to ruffle my hair. 'You're funny, JJ, did you know that?'

'It has, er, been mentioned in the past.' What? Does he think that all blondes are brain dead? I resist the urge to say something even more sarcastic, but I suppose I can't hold this against him. I mean, he hardly knows me, and I can't blame him for jumping to conclusions, for not knowing what I'm like, whether I'm funny or not. 'Well, the food is ready,' he says. 'Why don't you light the candles while I bring it out.'

So I duly do what I've been told, and when Brad walks in, holding two plates, he flicks a switch by the door with his elbow and plunges the room into darkness, all except for the two candles on the table and the flickering light of the log fire.

'That's better,' he says, sitting down.

'Much,' I agree.

'Now I can hardly see you,' I add. It's a joke, that old sarcasm just won't stay down tonight, and once again I thank my lucky stars that for Brad, being (a) American, and (b) Californian, sarcasm is as alien to him as Marks & Sparks knickers.

'Oh,' he says, sounding wounded. 'I'm sorry if I disappoint you.'

'No, Brad,' I appease him, daring to place a hand on his, 'I'm joking. British humour. Sorry.'

'Right,' he says, attempting to laugh but failing. Never mind, a man this beautiful could never believe that someone wasn't interested in him for long, and he's almost instantly back to his usual self.

We make small talk during the goats' cheese salad. We start laughing together in the interval between the hors-d'oeuvre and the main course, and by the time the chicken's on the table we're starting to relax, and I can't speak for Brad, but I'm definitely beginning to feel that we might well have something here.

'So what are you looking for in a relationship?' I venture eventually, numerous glasses of champagne having given me more than a hint of Dutch courage.

'What am I looking for? I'm looking for someone who's honest, sensitive, feminine. Someone who isn't necessarily into having a career, who'd be a great wife and mother.' He pauses at this point and gazes into my eyes, and it feels really, I don't know, really intense, and after a few seconds which feel like a few hours I start to feel *really* uncomfortable, so I look away.

'I want someone who makes me laugh, who enjoys the good things in life, who has integrity and depth.

'I want someone . . .' Oh God, just how long is his list going to be? I mean, I expected a couple of pointers, not an hour-long monologue about his expectations. Stop it, Jemima, stop being so negative.

' . . . who's self-aware, who is open to loving and being loved. And I need someone who looks great; who looks after herself, who doesn't drink or do drugs, who is slim, and fit, and healthy.'

Strange, that, or am I just being difficult? How come he kept telling me what he wanted and then finally told me what he needed? Is there a difference? Maybe, maybe not. Is this important? Maybe, maybe not. Whatever, right at this moment I'm too damn busy trying not to fall asleep at the table to worry about it any more. I am soooo tired and, exciting as this is, as gorgeous as he is, I really don't think I can keep my eyes open for too much longer.

Brad finishes his litany, and finally, thankfully, he notices my drooping eyelids.

'Oh you poor baby,' he says gently, 'you're tired.'

I nod, because quite frankly I don't think I can speak. The combination of alcohol and tiredness would definitely make my words come out all wrong.

'Why don't I put some decaf coffee on, we can sit by the fire while you drink it, then you can go to bed.' I nod again, gratefully this time, and on surprisingly (or perhaps not) unsteady feet I walk over to the fire and pretty much collapse in front of it.

Brad goes to make the coffee, and when it's ready he sets it on the coffee table behind me. He sits on the floor next to me, and strokes the hair out of my eyes. I know I should feel nervous, in any other circumstances I'd probably be throwing up, but I'm way too far gone to feel nervous, to worry about what to do, what to say. I just sit there and find myself concentrating on his hand, his big, strong hand softly brushing the hair out my eyes, then stroking my cheek, and finally resting on my chin.

'C'mere,' he says softly, and I don't have the energy or, to be honest, the inclination to resist. I mean, please, here I am in this unbelievable house in Los Angeles, LOS ANGELES!, with this stunning man and I'm supposed to say no? I don't think so. And anyway, I'm curious, I want to know how it would feel to lie next to someone this beautiful. I want to know what his skin would feel like, taste like, what it would *be* like. Let's face it, the brief interludes I've had in the past haven't exactly been anything to write home about. But this would be more than something to write home about, this is movie-making time, this is so unreal I almost feel as if I'm in a film. Even the way he gently cups my chin as his face moves closer and closer to mine feels as if it's happening in slow motion.

And finally those perfect lips are on mine, and he's kissing me, and I would go into more detail but I'm, quite frankly, slightly embarrassed. I mean, it's never happened like this before, it's never been this slow, or gentle, or lovely, if you want to know the truth.

And I don't feel the way I've felt before. I don't want to do it with the lights off, or lying flat on my back so my stomach's almost flat, because now it *is* flat, and I don't have to feel self-conscious, or worry that he's not going to be able to do it because my size will turn him off.

Now, wonder of wonders, I'm semi-naked with a man who's bigger than me! His chest is bigger than mine! His arms are bigger than mine! And, more to the point, what a chest! What arms! Oh my word, I thought bodies like this only existed in the pages of glossy magazines. Look at these pecs, look at these biceps and triceps and every-thingceps.

And then all our clothes come off (and I don't even mind!), and I'm watching him as he does things to me that no one has ever done to me before, and after a while I have to close my eyes because I'm seriously embarrassed, but a little while after that I stop being embarrassed because this unbelievable feeling suddenly starts spreading throughout my whole body, and the next thing I know he's lying on his back, inside me while I rock on top of him, and I'm screaming the whole house down. I don't even know where this scream is coming from, all I know is that it sounds guttural, animal, and I couldn't stop it even if I wanted to. Which I don't, because this is so gooooood. Mmmmmmmmm, this is so gooooood.

'That was incredible.' Brad rolls on to his side and gazes at me, planting soft butterfly kisses down my cheek.

'That. Was. Incredible!' I murmur, still trying to come to terms with what just happened. I think I just had an orgasm! For the first time in my life I know what all those magazines have been writing about, and, while I'm feeling wonderful, I also feel a bit shellshocked by the whole thing, it was just so amazing, and so unexpected.

'No, I mean, that was seriously unlike anything I've experienced,' says Brad.

You think? What about me? I've never experienced anything so completely deliciously mind-blowing in my entire life.

'I know,' I say, before I suddenly get hit with this

irrational thought that he's going to think I'm cheap, I hardly know the guy, after all. 'You don't think I'm cheap do you?' I say, before I can help myself. 'I mean I don't usually do this, I never usually do this. This isn't like me at all . . .'

'For someone who never usually does this,' he says, taking my hand and curling it up inside his masculine palm, 'you're awfully good at it.'

I laugh, for he's put me at my ease. 'That's not what I meant.'

'I know,' he says. 'And I also know that you're not the kind of girl to take lightly. This was one of the best nights of my entire life.'

'Mmm,' I say, really falling asleep now. 'Me too,' I just about manage to murmur, and that's as far as I can remember.

Brad very gently picks her up – can you imagine *anyone* picking up Jemima Jones a few months ago – and carries her to bed. He bypasses the spare room completely, and tucks her up on the left side of his huge king-sized bed. He pulls the bedcovers up and tucks them under her chin in case she gets cold from the air-conditioning, and Jemima murmurs and turns over, still fast asleep.

'Thank you, God,' Brad whispers as he kisses her softly on the nape of her neck. 'Thank you for making her so perfect,' and with that he goes to the bathroom to take a shower.

CHAPTER NINETEEN

'Morning, sleepyhead.'

I peel open my eyes, which is a hell of an effort, I can tell you, and for a split second I'm completely disorientated. Where am I, who's talking to me? And then I remember and as I shield my eyes from the sunlight streaming in through the blinds I remember that this beautiful man standing at the side of the bed is Brad, and that last night we made love, and that it was the greatest experience of my life to date.

He sits on the bed and I drink in his looks, the fact that even in a T-shirt and running shorts and sneakers he looks positively delicious, and he leans over to kiss me good morning, and I keep my lips sealed tightly shut because I'm so worried about having morning mouth when he smells so clean, so masculine, so sexy.

'What time is it?' I venture when he leans back, out of breath shot, as it were.

'Nine o'clock. I didn't want to wake you so I just went out for a run.'

'Jesus, nine o'clock? I never sleep till nine o'clock.'

'That's because you're never jet-lagged.'

I want to get out of bed and brush my teeth, wash my face, make sure my make-up isn't all over the place because I can feel already that my skin is gritty, that I definitely didn't wash it off last night, but I can't get out of bed because I don't appear to be wearing any clothes, and, slim as I may now be, walking around naked in front of someone I hardly know – despite the fact we have been as intimate as any two people can be – is not an experience I think I can deal with right now.

I wipe my fingers under my eyes, hoping to remove any stray mascara or eyeliner that may have worked its way down there during the night, and smile at Brad in a way that I hope he'll find sexy.

'So what are you in the mood for this morning?' he says, and I think about my morning mouth and then I think, screw it, and I pull him down towards me and kiss him. Properly. Tongues and everything.

I didn't think it could get better than last night. Really, I thought I'd hit the height of orgasmic experiences, but today, this morning, in the bright sunlight of day, it was even better. Warmer, softer, funnier. I never thought you were supposed to talk during sex, at least, I've never said anything before because it always brought me back to where I was, and made me feel almost shameful. But Brad and I talked to each other this morning, very gently. Before, during and after. And we laughed, which was a complete revelation, because before today I've never thought sex was supposed to be funny. Not that it was ha, ha, funny, just intimate I suppose, and maybe that's what was such a revelation for me.

'Jesus,' says Brad, lying back on the bed, breathing heavily. 'You really are something, JJ.'

I lean over him, my hair trailing over his face as I kiss him softly on the lips, slowly coming to terms with the idea that this man is mine. At least for the time being.

'So now what?' I say, wondering how we're going to spend the rest of the day.

'What do you mean?' says Brad, with a panicked look on his face, and I start to laugh because I realize he thinks I'm asking 'now what' about the relationship.

'What are we going to do today?' I say.

'Oh. Right. Well, I have to check in to the gym later on this afternoon, but how about this morning we go for breakfast then maybe rollerblading?'

'That sounds fantastic,' I say, trying not to let on that I lied about rollerblading and that I'll probably make a complete fool of myself. But then again, rollerblading is the perfect exercise to keep my thighs slim and toned. 'But can I work out at the gym later on?' Rollerblading, I'm afraid, isn't enough to keep the guilt at bay.

'Sure you can,' says Brad. 'In fact, this afternoon there's a spinning class which you might enjoy.'

'Spinning?'

'Yeah,' he laughs, seeing I haven't a clue what he's talking about. 'It's cycling on the spot, but real fast. It's kind of a killer but you feel great afterwards.'

'Maybe,' I say, because, although it does sound great, I think at this stage I'd rather stick to what I know.

We get up, shower, and climb in Brad's car, and he takes me for a short drive around Santa Monica, just to give me a feel for the place, and, driving along, with his right hand resting on my left leg, I am truly in heaven.

There seem to be hundreds of people milling around, and, although some of them are beautiful, quite honestly I'm surprised at how ordinary most of them are. I somehow expected all of Los Angeles to look like something out of a film, but for every gorgeous person there seem to be ten more who aren't.

'That's 3rd Street Promenade,' says Brad, pointing to a cobbled street lined with shops and restaurants, 'it's famous in Los Angeles for the street performers, especially on the weekends.' As we stop at the lights I can hear Frank Sinatra playing, very loudly, and I can't figure out where it's coming from.

'Hang on,' says Brad. 'You gotta hear this,' and he parks the car round the corner and takes my hand as we walk down to where the music's coming from.

In the middle of the street is a man in his sixties. He's wearing a fedora, a black jacket and a bow tie. He's holding on to a microphone and swaying slightly while crooning along to the huge Karaoke machine that sits behind him. It's all Frank Sinatra, and what I can't believe is that this man sounds more like Frank than Frank himself. Everyone milling past seems to stop, at least for a few seconds, before leaving with smiles on their faces, and the bucket resting on the ground in front of him is slowly filling up with dollar bills.

'Isn't he great?' says Brad, putting his arm around me as we stand next to one of the benches that line each side of the street. I nod, because it is great, and as I turn to look at Brad I notice that sitting on the bench is an old homeless woman. You can tell she's homeless, her grey hair is long and matted, her raincoat is ripped and torn, and strewn around her feet are a dozen plastic bags. Her eyes are closed, and she's humming along, and suddenly she opens her eyes and sees me.

She stands up, collects her bags, and as she walks off she touches my arm and says, 'You gotta hear "New

York, New York". He does it last. It's wonderful,' and with that she disappears.

'Now that,' I say, looking at Brad, 'is bizarre.'

'Not really,' says Brad. 'This guy's an institution. He's here practically every week.'

'But that woman . . .'

'Right. Santa Monica seems to be a mecca for the homeless. Listening to this guy is probably the highlight of her week.'

'But how did she get here?'

'Who knows,' he says, shrugging. 'How did any of us get here?', and with that he leads me to the bucket, throws in a couple of dollar bills, and we go back to the car.

We drive through wide residential streets, huge roads lined with grassy verges and large houses, and eventually we hit Montana, a quiet road that reeks of money, simply because the small boutiques and restaurants on either side are so quaint, and Brad pulls up outside a small coffee shop which looks packed. Outside, on the street, there's one spare table, and Brad tells me to grab it while he gets breakfast.

Don't think I'm being egotistical, please, but I can't help but notice that three – three! – men put down their papers, stop their conversations and turn to stare at me, and although my initial thought is that it must be because I have something on my face, I soon realize that it's because I look good.

Tutored by Geraldine, I'm in my new second-hand Levi's, 26 waist, a white shirt and brown suede loafers, and when I put them on this morning I thought that, perhaps for the first time, I really do look like the woman I wanted to become.

'One coffee,' says Brad, placing the cup in front of me as the men look away, because one look at Brad and they know they couldn't compete, 'and one fat-free blueberry muffin.'

It's delicious. He's delicious. This life is delicious. I think I could stay here for the rest of my life.

I suppose this is the time when we ought to be talking, getting to know each other, but we did so much of that last night, and now that we've slept together all we seem to be doing is staring at one another and grinning. Brad holds my hand, only allowing me to have it back to pick up my muffin and take the occasional bite, and even as I'm eating he strokes my leg, or my arm, or something. It's as if we have to have permanent contact with each other, and everyone seems to be staring at us, or perhaps that's my imagination.

But in my imagination I imagine that they're staring because they wish they had what we had. I have no idea what it really feels like to be in love. I loved Ben, it's true, but I never *had* Ben, and, as I sit here with this man I've just made love to, I wonder whether perhaps it wasn't love with Ben, it was merely infatuation.

Not that I love Brad, not yet, of course not. But I feel so high, I can't stop smiling, and I'm sure that my glow is lighting up the whole of America.

'You're so beautiful,' Brad says to me again, and I bask in the glory of his admiration. He checks his watch and says we should go blading because he'll have to do some work when we get to the gym.

And so we stop at the hire shop and pick up some blades for me then we drop the car home, Brad picks up his blades, and we walk, in sock-clad feet, down to the promenade.

'Um, there's something I have to tell you,' I start nervously, as Brad looks concerned. 'I lied about roller-blading. I've never done it before in my life.'

Brad throws his head back and laughs. 'Why on earth bother lying about that? Don't worry, you'll be fine.' He continues chuckling as I shakily put the boots on and stand still, too terrified to move.

'Here,' he says, taking my hand, 'This is how you blade,' and he shows me how to start with my feet at right angles to one another, how to push off with the right and glide forward with the left, and wonder of wonders, me, clumsy, oafish Jemima Jones, can do it. I'm not very good, admittedly, but Brad keeps hold of my hand, and with those strong arms he balances me every time I threaten to tip over.

It takes a while, but soon we're blading side by side, on this wide tarmac boardwalk that runs alongside the beach. I don't even care that every few minutes these gorgeous women pass, headphones on, perfect figures gyrating to the music that's filling their ears. And I don't even care that these women all eye Brad up and down as they approach, because he's not looking at them, he's looking at me. And I don't even care when one of the blonde bombshells turns to her friend skating alongside her, also with headsets on, and mouths 'gay', gesturing at Brad, who doesn't see. I don't care. Actually, I think it's funny, and in a way I know what she means. It's almost as if Brad is too damn perfect to be straight. It's not something I would ever have thought in England, but here, where the gay culture seems to be so much bigger, here I can understand why she would have said that.

I laugh to myself, especially when I picture what Brad was doing to me at ten past nine this morning, and then I stop laughing to myself and I start shivering with pleasure at the memory.

'This is so much fun,' I shout, as we pick up speed and head down towards the Santa Monica pier.

'I thought you'd never done this before,' he says, and with a grin I shoot off in front of him, amazed that I'm so confident on these wheels.

'I lied,' I shout back and he grins and blows me a kiss as he races to catch up with me.

Jemima and Brad look like the perfect couple, like they've just stepped out of a romantic love story, and even though they're not really talking, they're giggling together and teasing one another in a way that is increasingly like two people falling in love with each other. Or could that be two people falling in love with love itself?

Two hours of rollerblading has completely done me in, and when we've finished we stop at a deli and help ourselves to salad, which we put in a container and take to Brad's gym to eat in his office. Just in case you're wondering, I'm even more conscious of keeping my figure here, so I bypass the salads of rice and pasta, which, delicious-looking as they are, are not what I need to maintain my figure. I opt, instead, for mounds of exotic salad leaves, piled high with roast vegetables and sesame seeds, not, according to the woman in the deli, roasted in oil. Completely fat free. Aren't I good? Aren't you proud of me?

The gym, just off 2nd Avenue, when we get there, is much like I expected. A sun-filled reception houses a huge desk, behind which sit two gorgeous women in perfectly co-ordinated aerobic gear. One is wearing a pink bodysuit with tight, tiny orange lycra shorts, and the other is in an orange bodysuit with pink shorts, both with tiny thongs at the back. They are extremely tanned, extremely fit and extremely friendly, which surprises me somewhat, because back at home, when women look like this, they usually turn out to be class A bitches.

'Hey, Brad!' says one enthusiastically as they walk in.

'Hey, Brad!' says the other, looking up in her wake.

'Hey, Cindy, Charlene. I'd like you to meet JJ.'

'Hey, JJ,' they both say at the same time. 'It's so great to meet you.'

'And you.' I suppress a laugh, because what could be so great about meeting me?

'You're JJ!' says Cindy suddenly. 'Oh my God, we've heard so much about you. We've even seen your picture. Wow, you're here.'

'Yup.' Is anybody over here ever going to say something that makes sense? 'I'm here.'

'And you're from England?' It's Charlene's turn.

'Uh huh.'

'That's so great. I had a boyfriend from England once. He was from Surrey. Gary Tompkins?' She's looking at me expectantly, as if I might know him. As if. I shake my head and shrug my shoulders. 'Sorry,' I apologize. 'It's a big place.'

269

'Don't worry,' says Charlene, 'he wasn't so hot anyway. But welcome to Los Angeles. Do you think you'll stay?'

'I'm here for two weeks,' I say. 'Then I have to get back to work.'

'That's too bad,' says Cindy. 'It's a great place. Maybe you could come back.'

'Maybe,' I say, wondering if everyone here is so friendly. I mean, I've heard Americans are like this, but I never really thought it would be true.

'They're really nice,' I say to Brad, as we pass through the reception area and through the actual gym, and then I stop because I have never in my life seen a gym so well equipped, nor people so perfect. The gym is buzzing. Heavy hip-hop music, a song I vaguely recognize, is bursting out of every corner, and although everyone in here is sweating up a storm, they all look fantastic, the sweat only seems to set off their glistening tans and perfect bodies.

'God,' I whisper in bewilderment, because it's worlds away from my gym, where most of the people are either there because they're at the before stage and they look terrible, or because it's a place to see and be seen, and they'd never let something as mucky as sweat mess up their make-up or hair-do.

'You like it?' asks Brad, obviously proud of this thriving business. 'Meet Jimmy, one of the personal trainers here.'

Tall, bronzed and buff, Jimmy shakes my hand. 'It's so great to finally meet you, JJ. Welcome to Los Angeles, and if you need any help here, *anything* at all' – looks at me meaningfully – 'don't hesitate to ask.'

'Hands off, Jimmy,' says Brad, pushing him playfully.

'Whoah, Brad,' says Jimmy, holding up his hands with a cheeky grin on his face, 'you can't blame a guy for trying.'

'Hello?' I say. 'I'm here.'

'Sorry, JJ,' says Brad. 'But boys will be boys. C'mon, we'll go to my office and eat lunch.'

So we do, and ridiculous as this may be – seeing as it's the middle of the day and we're eating salad out of plastic containers – we start feeding one another, and soon food is everywhere but in our mouths and we're kissing furiously when the door bursts open and we leap apart.

Brad, for the record, leaps furthest, but then it is understandable, after all, he is the boss, and we both look up to see a large girl standing in the doorway.

'Oh' says the girl. 'I didn't realize you were here.'

'I just got here,' says Brad, dusting the food off himself and trying to straighten himself out, while I take a good, long look at the girl, partly to try and work out who she is, and partly because, and it's a hell of a shock to see it, partly because the girl standing in the doorway looks an awful lot like the girl I used to be. She's small with dark, glossy hair, and I can see that she would be pretty, she could be pretty, all she has to do is lose a few stone. Because this girl is huge, she has two, no, three chins. She is wearing a smock-type shirt to hide the huge bulk of her breasts, she has her arms crossed to hide as much of her body as she can, and she has that slightly wounded look in her eye. She could be me, I think as I carry on staring at her. I could be her.

'This is JJ,' says Brad. 'And this is Jenny. My personal assistant.'

'Hi, Jenny,' I'm determined to be friendly, to make an

effort, to show Jenny that her size doesn't bother me, it doesn't make me think Jenny's any less a person just because there's more of her. I stand up from my sitting position on the desk and walk over to Jenny with arm outstretched to shake her hand, but as I get closer I feel instinctively that she won't be shaking my hand, that, for some strange reason, there's a strong air of hostility in the room. And I'm right. I come to a standstill because Jenny doesn't move. Jenny just nods hello. Jenny doesn't say anything, and Jesus Christ, how I remember what it was like to be Jenny.

I remember how I felt when someone skinny and beautiful was introduced to me, how inadequate I felt, how I couldn't look them in the eye, and I try desperately to think of a way to make Jenny feel at ease.

'That's a beautiful shirt,' I say finally. 'Did you buy it here?'

'No,' says Jenny, forced to speak, and then she turns to Brad. 'I have some files here for you. Shall I just leave them on your desk?' Her voice is as cold as ice, and I recoil, but then I think how much worse it would be, how magnified those feelings of inadequacy would be if you worked somewhere where you were surrounded by bodies beautiful all day, so I try again.

'Have you worked here long?' I say, trying to offer her my friendship.

'Yes,' says Jenny, refusing, this time, to look at me, and with that she turns and walks out of the office.

'I'm sorry,' says Brad, running his fingers through his hair. 'She can be difficult sometimes.'

'Don't worry about it, I suspect I understand far better than you know,' I say without thinking.

'What on earth do you mean?' Brad's voice sounds slightly harsh, and I wonder what he would think if he knew I used to be the same size as Jenny. I'm tempted, just for a second, to tell Brad how I used to be, but then I decide against it. Too soon.

'It's just that I imagine it's very hard for her, working somewhere like this, being surrounded by skinny people all the time. What I don't understand is why she does work here. Surely it would be easier for her to work somewhere less . . .' I pause, wondering how to put it. 'Less body-conscious.'

'I think you're probably right,' says Brad, 'but you see Jenny's been with me for years, she's like my right arm, and to be honest I think that's the only reason she stays here, out of loyalty to me.'

'You're sure she hasn't got an eensy weensy crush on you?' I tease, too taken with Brad to remember that it's no laughing matter being the fattest girl in the office and having a crush on the most beautiful man in the building.

'Jenny?' Brad snorts with derision. 'No. She's more like my sister.'

Hmm. Once upon a time that was what Ben would have said about me. 'Well, I know someone who definitely does have a crush on you.' I reach out my hand and place it on Brad's thigh.

'If I lock the door will you promise to tell all?' Brad's moving over to the door and shutting it gently.

God forgive me for acting like a brazen hussy, but I can't help it, he's just too irresistible. I cross my hands over my chest and slide my shirt off my shoulders revealing nothing underneath except bare flesh. I push

Brad into a chair and straddle his lap while slinking my arms around his neck. 'Promise,' I purr, 'swear, and cross my heart.'

CHAPTER TWENTY

I stretch luxuriously in bed and fall back against the mound of pillows, thinking about my life. I think about Brad making love to me this very morning before going to the office and arranging to meet me later. I think about the life I've left behind, the sheer dross and drudgery of working at the *Kilburn Herald*, and I think about what my friends would say if they could see me now, because, even though it's only been just under a week, I know already that I could get used to this.

How can I go back there? Back to dreary old London, when Los Angeles is so warm, so exciting, so inviting.

And then, I can't help myself, I start thinking about Ben. Funny how he crops up at the strangest moments. I can go for ages without giving him a thought, and suddenly he'll pop into my head. And when he does, of course I still miss him, but these days only when I remember him, which thankfully isn't all that much of the time because I'm having far too good a time.

Another thought creeps in, one I don't want to think about, one I'm hoping I'll be able to forget about, but no, the harder I try not to think about it the more I can't help it. Okay. I give in. Last night we were at the Mondrian Hotel, a huge, minimalist designer haven on Sunset Boulevard. A place that Brad insisted I see, even though I'm really not that bothered about in places, it's not as if I frequent them at home.

But it was spectacular. I've never been anywhere like it. The vast, minimalist lobby, stark glass doors leading on to a wooden deck lit by candles. I loved it. I loved the oversized terracotta pots, the large Indian mattresses strewn with cushions scattered by the side of the pool. And I'm trying not to think about what happened after that, about what Brad said, because every time I think about it, all sorts of negative thoughts start flooding in, and I don't want anything to go wrong, I don't want to shatter this perfection. Not now.

But it was bizarre. Okay, here goes. I'll tell you. There we were, sitting at a table in the bar of the Mondrian, the candlelight throwing flattering shadows on the faces of the beautiful people, but none more beautiful than Brad, in my opinion anyway. We sat, and we kissed, and we talked, and the more we talked the more we revealed about our lives, our loves, our hopes, our dreams, and the more we revealed the more I thought that this was it. Sorry. This is it.

'I'd like to live in a house on the beach,' I said, pictures fresh in my mind because earlier that evening I'd sat scanning the property section of the *Los Angeles Times*, escaping into a fantasy world of swimming pools, sand between my toes, crashing waves.

'I think I'd be happy anywhere,' said Brad, 'as long as I was with you.'

Jemima, oh, Jemima. Didn't you think it just a little strange that Brad was being quite so forward in just under a week? Were there no warning bells going off in your head? Would it not perhaps have been sensible to sit back and wonder whether he might just perhaps have an ulterior motive?

But no. It seems that Jemima Jones wasn't ready to spoil her perfect world just at that moment. Instead she sighed with happiness, and the conversation moved on, twisting and turning, until finally they were left only with the practicalities of her stay.

'Are there any bookstores around here?' I asked, knowing that is the one thing that would really make me feel at home, to have the luxury of browsing among my beloved books.

'The best ones are probably the Barnes & Noble or the Borders on 3rd Street Promenade,' said Brad. 'If you'd have told me earlier we could have gone in there before. You really do like reading don't you?'

I nodded.

'So what kind of stuff do you read?'

'Everything.' I smiled mysteriously. 'I have completely eclectic tastes and I'll read pretty much anything. What about you?' I asked, realizing I had no idea of his literary tastes, and, although it might not be important to you, I think it says a hell of a lot about a person.

'I don't really have the time,' he admitted, taking another sip of champagne. 'I kind of like science fiction when I do read.' He paused for a while before adding, 'I read more when I was at high school. I remember reading a book by that guy, oh, you know, what's his name.' He looked at me for help while I shrugged my shoulders and shook my head. 'You *do* know, the one that wrote *Romeo and Juliet.*'

Did I hear that? Was he joking? My eyes widened in disbelief, but then I thought, he must be joking, he's going to laugh any second now. 'Shakespeare?' I said slowly, expecting him to crack up.

'Yeah,' he nodded vigorously. 'That's the guy. Great book.'

He didn't laugh. He didn't even smile. What could I say? I wouldn't mind if his taste ran only as far as trashy cops and robbers books, but to forget the name of the greatest playwright ever? I was completely, utterly speechless, and it suddenly became blindingly obvious what was wrong with Brad, and that it is absolutely true that nobody is perfect. Brad, gorgeous, beautiful, kind, sweet Brad, I thought, with more than a hint of dismay, is thick. Thick as pigshit. Oh my God, why did he have to say that.

But no, I tried to tell myself. Just because he doesn't have the same interests as you doesn't mean he's necessarily stupid, just ... different. And that doesn't mean he's a bad person, or he's not going to treat you well.

I'll try and forget it, I decided, put it out of my head. And I did try, really I did, but somehow it sounds a lot easier than it is.

And my dismay, concern, pissed-offness, whatever you want to call it, must have shown on my face, because Brad suddenly said, 'Is everything okay?'

'Yes,' I smiled. 'Fine,' and he leant forward and gave me a long, sumptuous kiss on the lips, and I relaxed a bit, and then I decided that I really didn't care about the other stuff because this kiss made it all worth while. That this was what I had been waiting for. This man was who I had been waiting for. And this stuff, this feeling of being cared for, being looked after, being protected, is surely what it's all about.

But now, lying in bed this morning, I can't help but wonder if that *is* enough. Don't be ridiculous, of course it's enough. It has to be enough, but, just to be completely reassured, I pick up the phone and dial.

'*Kilburn Herald* features.'

'Geraldine? It's me.'

'Jemima? Hi! I miss you, and, you nasty old bitch, guess who's got to do your bloody column while you're away. Thanks a lot.' She doesn't mean it, although she finally understands why I've been so unhappy writing the Top Tips.

'I miss you too.'

'You can't be missing me. You're probably having a fantastic time. I want to hear everything. How's the gorgeous Brad? Are you in love? Have you done it yet?'

'Fine, not sure, yes.'

'Yes?'

'Yes.'

'Oh my God! How was it, how was it? Tell me everything! I want all the gory details.'

'It was unbelievable, Geraldine. Seriously, truly, unbelievable. I have never had such amazing sex in my life. He is just so gorgeous. Every time I look at him I can't believe I've got him.'

'So is he completely voracious?'

'Completely. We even ended up having sex on his desk in his office.'

'Oh,' sighs Geraldine. 'I'm so jealous.'

'Why? Don't tell me it's all gone horribly wrong with that guy you met at Ben's leaving do, Nick Maxwell?'

'No, it hasn't gone wrong at all. In fact, it's probably more right than ever before. But we haven't slept together yet.'

'You're joking?' This is most unlike Geraldine, who regularly uses her body to control her relationships.

'I wish I was. It's not that I don't want to, or that he hasn't tried to get me into bed, but this is different, Jemima. I really like him. I mean *really* like him, and I don't want to blow it by jumping into bed with him too soon.'

'Oh.' Shit. Does that mean I've blown it with Brad? 'Does that always blow it?'

'According to *The Rules* it does.'

'What's *The Rules*?'

'It's all about how to play hard to get to hook the man of your dreams.'

'And you believe it?'

Geraldine sighs. 'I never did, but I decided to give it a whirl just to see, and I think it really works. And,' she continues, 'the cardinal sin is to sleep with them. At least, you're not supposed to until they're madly in love with you and you know they're definitely not going to disappear the next morning.'

'But it's been ages, Geraldine.'

'I know,' she sighs again. 'I'm practically climbing the walls. I even passed Ann Summers yesterday and seriously thought about going in and buying a vibrator.'

'Geraldine!' I don't want to hear about vibrators, for God's sake, I've only just had an orgasm, and it's hard enough to talk about that, let alone vibrators. I love Geraldine for this, though. I love the fact that she's never embarrassed, but the only thing I'd change is her self-centredness. Although I know she's probably the only true friend I've ever had, she always, always, brings the conversation back round to herself as soon as she can. Still, that's not such a bad thing, and at least I know I can rely on her. Even if I don't want to talk about vibrators with her.

'Don't worry,' Geraldine says. 'I didn't, but only because I didn't have the nerve to go in there by myself. I wish you were here, Jemima.'

'I don't.'

'Well, you know what I mean. It just kills me hearing you're having sex all over the place and I'm being Miss Born-Again Celibate.'

'It's not all perfect, you know,' I admit. Finally.

'How can it not be perfect?'

'Well, I don't know how to put this . . .'

'Just say it.'

And I do. I tell Geraldine about the conversation last night, about the Shakespeare situation, and Geraldine hoots with laughter.

'So what?' she says, when she's recovered her composure. 'So he's not Mr Intelligent. Darling, he's rich, he's gorgeous, and he's crazy about you. Who gives a stuff about anything else.'

'Maybe you're right.' I'm starting to feel better about it.

'When,' says Geraldine dramatically, 'have I ever been wrong?'

'So I should just ignore the fact that – '

'That he's stupid? Yes. And anyway, just because he doesn't read Shakespeare hardly means he's stupid does it? He does, after all, appear to have a thriving business.'

'Yes, that's certainly true.' I'm feeling much better now.

'So. No problems. Right?'

'Right. Thanks, Geraldine. What would I do without you? Have you spoken to Ben recently?' Where did that question come from, Jemima?

'No. Why? Have you?'

'No, I just wondered how he's doing.'

'I've seen him on the box if that's any consolation and he seems to be doing fine. If the truth be known, he's turning into a bit of a heart-throb as far as the public are concerned.'

'Hmm.' Why does this piece of knowledge make me feel uncomfortable?

'Anyway, my darling, this must be costing you a fortune, and I've got to file the copy on those bloody Top Tips. I'll call you in a couple of days, how does that sound?'

'That sounds wonderful.'

'Okay, I'm out with Nick tonight. God knows if I can hold off much longer. I'll let you know next time we speak.'

We say goodbye and I put down the phone. Geraldine's absolutely right, I'm being ridiculous. I go into the kitchen and open the fridge. A few fat-free yoghurts, some fruit and several bottles of mineral water, and I examine the aforementioned while shaking my head in amazement. Open any bloke's fridge at home and you're likely to find a six-pack of beer, some left-over Indian take-away and, if they're extremely lazy, a pile of pre-packaged meals for one from a designer food store.

Right, I decide, closing the fridge door with a bang.

Gym first then supermarket, because tonight I will be cooking dinner for Brad. I put on my gear and get ready to leave when the phone rings.

'Hi, sweetie.' Brad has taken to calling me sweetie. 'I miss you. Are you coming in?'

'Yes, I'm just about to leave. Listen, how would you feel if I cooked you dinner tonight?'

'I'd love that. Do you want to go shopping this afternoon?'

'No, don't worry, I'll go by myself. I want to surprise you.'

'I can't believe how much work there is to do, and while you're here. I feel so bad, I really wanted to show you Los Angeles, all the fun stuff like Universal Studios and Disneyland.'

'Brad, I'm not interested in all that touristy stuff.' Which isn't quite true, but, as much as I would like to see it, I'm also quite happy in my role as Los Angeles wife. 'I'm just really happy to do what you do, it gives me a better sense of who you are, what your life is like.'

'Are you sure?' The relief in his voice is obvious.

'Yes, I'm sure.'

'Okay. Leave now, I can't wait to see you.'

'I'm leaving, I'm leaving!' I laugh, blowing him a kiss before skipping out the door.

'Jenny!' What a coincidence, to bump into Jenny in this juice bar, but then again, it is just down the road. I will make her like me, I will make this girl my friend, even if it kills me, and it looks like it might, because Jenny just eyes me up and down in a seriously unfriendly fashion before giving a grudging 'Hello'.

'How funny seeing you here!' No one could say I wasn't trying. 'I just finished my workout. Let me get you something to drink.'

'No, that's okay. I have to get back to the gym.'

'So why did you come in here then?' I gesture round the little coffee shop down the road from the B-Fit Gym.

'Okay,' sighs Jenny. 'I'll have a mineral water.'

Poor thing, I know exactly what she's up to. She'll probably have a mineral water here then go home later and eat three packets of biscuits. 'Why don't you sit down?' I pull out a chair for her. 'I'll bring the drinks over.'

I pay for both mineral waters, and carry them over to the corner table where Jenny's sitting glumly, chin resting on her hand.

'Thanks,' says Jenny.

'It's my pleasure,' I say warmly, honestly, trying so hard. 'Brad says you've worked for him a long time?'

'Yes.' Her answers are still monosyllabic and I can tell this is really going to be hard work.

'Do you enjoy it?'

'I guess.' Jenny shrugs her shoulders.

'You must know Brad very well by now.' I'm trying to keep it light, but the strangest thing happens. Jenny blushes, and it's so like how I used to be with Ben that I suddenly see that she obviously has the most enormous crush on Brad and I've just put my foot in it big time. 'I didn't mean . . .' I say lamely.

'That's okay,' says Jenny, as the blush starts to die down. 'It's fine.'

'Look.' Let's try and start all over again, Jemima. 'There's obviously some kind of tension between us which I don't understand, because I'd really like us to be friends.'

Jenny looks at me in horror. 'I can't be friends with you.'

'Why ever not?'

Jenny shrugs. 'It just wouldn't work.'

'I think you'd be surprised, Jenny,' I say gently. 'I think you'd find we have a lot more in common than you think.'

'I don't think I'd be surprised at all,' says Jenny bitterly.

'No, I'm serious,' and it dawns on me that the only way I'm ever going to make this girl like me, or trust me, is to be completely honest with her and tell her the truth. 'Can I tell you a secret?'

Jenny looks up without interest and shrugs her shoulders.

'Okay. You see me now and I'm slim, I'm fit. A few months ago I was seriously overweight. Far, far bigger than you.'

'Yeah, really,' says Jenny, getting up to leave. 'Don't bother. Number one, I don't appreciate being patronized. Number two, I don't believe you. And number three, even if I did, it wouldn't make any difference to me. As far as I'm concerned you're my boss's new girlfriend and that doesn't mean *we* have to be friends. Thanks for the drink. I'll be seeing ya.'

'But Jenny – ' It's too late, Jenny has picked up her bag and walked out. What did I say? What did I do? I probably shouldn't let this bother me, but it does, I can't help it. I know people used to feel sorry for me, but no one ever disliked me. I'm the girl who gets on with everyone, and I hate the fact that Jenny doesn't like me. Maybe if I knew why, I could deal with it, but she just seems to have taken an instant dislike to me, and I so want us to be, if not friends, at least on pleasant terms.

I constantly go over this conversation and wonder what exactly I have said to upset her. I act like a paranoid idiot, peering round corners before walking anywhere so I don't bump into her again, and when I get to the gym Jenny, luckily, is nowhere to be seen, and Brad's in his office.

'The weirdest thing just happened,' I tell him, after he's kissed me hello, and not just a peck on the cheek, a long, passionate kiss, and I physically have to push him away, because although it seems I can never resist him, at this very moment in time I have to get this Jenny business off my mind. So I tell him, only missing out the bit about the size I used to be, and it does cool Brad down. Completely.

'I'm sorry,' he says, sitting back down behind his desk. 'You mustn't let it upset you, she's just very protective about me.'

'But it's crazy.' I'm beginning to get slightly annoyed about this now. 'I'm really trying to befriend the girl, and if I didn't know better I'd say she absolutely hated me.'

'She doesn't hate you,' sighs Brad.

'How do you know?'

'I just know. She's threatened by you.'

'But surely you've had other girlfriends before. Is she like this with all of them?'

Brad shrugs. 'I haven't really had serious girlfriends before. Look,' he says, standing up and coming round to massage my shoulders, 'it really doesn't matter. It's not important, but I'll talk to her, okay?'

He won't discuss it any more, so I reluctantly agree and, as I do, I feel that Brad's massaging hands are going AWOL, and they've left my shoulders and they're moving down, past my collarbone, down to my bra.

'Brad,' I plead, because I'm really not in the mood, but somehow I haven't got the strength to resist him, or the way he makes me feel, and it's a good job his phone rings a few seconds later, or there would have been a repeat performance of a week ago, which is all well and good, but I'm still trying to prove to myself that there's more to this budding relationship than simply a great sex life.

'Can I borrow your car?' I mouth to Brad as he talks on the phone, and he nods and throws his car keys on the desk, not thinking about insurance, or whether I can even drive. I can, luckily, drive, despite not owning a car in London, but never, in my wildest dreams, did I think I'd be driving a convertible Porsche.

Now I really have died and gone to heaven, this car isn't a car, it's sex on four wheels.

'Hey, babe,' yell two young guys pulling up alongside me. 'Where are you going?'

'Shopping,' I yell back with a huge grin.

'Can we come?' one shouts, hand over his heart to show he's fallen in love.

'Sorry,' I yell. 'Only room for me and my bags.'

'We love you,' they shout, as I press my foot down to the floor and zoom off, and, presumably to demonstrate this love at first sight, they try and follow me, but the car is way too fast for them and within seconds they've disappeared.

'Hel-lo,' says a good-looking man crossing the road at the traffic light. 'Now this is what I like to see in Los

Angeles. A beautiful single blonde driving a Porsche.'

'How do you know I'm single?'

'A man can dream can't he?'

I smile and shoot off. I pull in to the first place that looks like a supermarket, park in the car park and grab a shopping trolley. In a tight T-shirt, leggings and Reeboks, with my sunglasses on top of my head and my hair in a sleek ponytail, I'm delighted to note that I look like every other hip, young Santa Monica housewife doing the weekly shop, except of course that I'm walking down every aisle shaking my head with disbelief.

Never in my life have I seen such a choice of low-fat, non-fat, fat-free, cholesterol-free food. There are fat-free healthy scones, caramel popcorn rice cakes, low-cholesterol lemon snaps, reduced-fat ginger snaps, fat-free cholesterol-free chocolate fudge brownies, the list goes on and on and on, and despite saying goodbye to my binges a long time ago, I have to seriously resist the urge to sweep everything off the shelves and into my trolley.

'Excuse me?' says a masculine voice, and I turn with a raised eyebrow.

'I hope you don't mind me bothering you but I was wondering whether you knew the best way of cooking zucchini.'

Now this, I don't believe. I mean, I'd heard about people being picked up in supermarkets, I'd even helped Geraldine write about people being picked up in supermarkets, but I never *really* thought it happened, and certainly not to me, but perhaps I'm wrong, perhaps this is a genuine query.

'You could try steaming it, I suppose. Or go Italian and coat it in egg and flour and fry it.'

'You're English!' he says, his pose relaxing. 'Where are you from?'

'London.'

'Welcome to Los Angeles. Say, you wouldn't want to *show* me how to cook this would you?' Now it's his turn to raise an eyebrow.

'I'd love to.' It is a pass! 'But my boyfriend would hate it.'

'Oh I'm sorry,' he says. 'I knew someone that pretty would have to have a boyfriend.'

I shrug and carry on down the aisle, taking the most ridiculous amount of time to get my shopping done, first because the lay-out is somewhat different to my local Sainsbury's, and second because I have never seen such choice.

And when I've finished and I've loaded up the car, I sit for a minute, unable to believe quite how forward everyone here is, and how easy it seems to be to meet men if you're in Los Angeles and on your own. Sophie and Lisa would have a field day. Maybe I should phone them and tell them to come out. Then again, maybe not.

CHAPTER TWENTY-ONE

Jemima may well wonder about the divine Ben Williams every now and then, but she would never dream he's as famous as he now is. Sure, she's heard about it, she even saw his first foray on television when she was back in London, but she can have no idea of how Ben fever seems to have gripped the nation.

It doesn't happen all that often, but sometimes a new television presenter will appear, more often than not a woman, and soon every newspaper in the country is writing about them, every person in the country is wishing to be them, and their career takes off in leaps and bounds until you can barely leave your house without seeing huge billboards advertising their presence.

This is how it is for Ben Williams. Those first days on *London Nights* left him breathless with excitement, not only because of his immediate increase in salary but also because, even then, even after a handful of appearances on television, he was recognized.

The very first time he was asked for his autograph he was in a supermarket. He'd had a great day but he was tired, and all he could think of was getting home, putting his feet up and having a nice, cool beer.

But, walking down one of the aisles, lost in a world of his own, he gradually became aware that he was being followed. At first he thought he was going mad, that his senses were deceiving him, and he kept turning round to find no one there. But eventually he spotted two women standing staring at him, whispering to one another behind their hands.

'It *is*!' he heard one say, as the other gave her a shove and propelled her in Ben's general direction. Ben didn't know what was going on, so he ignored them and carried on shopping, until he had no choice.

'Excuse me,' she said, a brow-beaten housewife in her mid-forties. 'I hope you don't mind, but aren't you that man on television?'

'I'm not sure,' said Ben, not quite knowing what to say. 'Which man?'

'Oooh you are! I recognize your voice. You're the new bloke on *London Nights* aren't you?'

Ben, to his credit, blushed slightly, and although part of him wished she would keep her voice down because he didn't want everyone to hear, part of him wished she'd shout a bit louder, so everyone *would* hear.

'Um, yes,' he mumbled, smiling the bashful Ben smile that would soon ensure his already burgeoning heart-throb status.

'My friend and I think you're fantastic!' The words came out in a rush, and as she said it she started rummaging around in her bag, producing a pen and a torn-up scrap of paper.

'Honestly,' she continued. 'You brighten up our house every night. Doesn't he, Jean?' she shouted over to her friend, who looked as if she were trying to work up the nerve to come over.

'Would you mind?' She offered him the pen and paper, which Ben looked at for a moment wondering what he was supposed to do with it. The woman sidled up next to him and said, 'I'm Sheila. Could you just put "To Sheila, with lots of love".' She tailed off, trying to remember Ben's name. 'Is it Tom?' she asked, as Ben felt a fit of nervous giggles coming on.

'No,' he managed to contain himself. 'It's Ben. Ben Williams.'

'That's it!' she said. 'Ben Williams.'

Ben balanced the piece of paper on the handle of his shopping trolley, aware that passing shoppers had stopped to see what was going on, were looking at him in a way, he realized, that meant they too had recognized him, but thankfully no one else was going to do what Sheila was now doing.

'Oh thank you,' she breathed heavily, tucking the paper very carefully into the front pocket of her bag. 'We'll be watching you tomorrow.'

'No, no,' said Ben, recovering his composure. 'Thank *you*, and enjoy the show.'

As Sheila and Jean wandered off, heads together like a couple of lovesick teenagers, Ben understood, for perhaps the first time, how his life was about to change.

He went home and phoned Richard to tell him what had happened, and Richard nearly wet himself with laughter.

'You know what this means don't you, Ben?' he said, when he finally stopped.

'What?'

'You can't go anywhere without your full make-up on now,' and with that he started laughing so hard he had to put down the phone.

Richard thought it was funny that night, but six weeks

later, when they decided to go out for a few drinks, he thought it was fantastic.

'Let's just go to a local pub,' suggested Ben.

'Not on your life, mate,' said Richard. 'You're famous, you don't go to local pubs, you go to bars and restaurants where the women are gorgeous.'

And so it was that they ended up at Fifth Floor, on the top of Harvey Nichols, one Friday night, and Richard was right, the women were gorgeous. They bought champagne, and within minutes found themselves surrounded by stunning women, model figures encased in the latest fashions. Nobody actually asked for Ben's autograph, nobody would be that uncool, but it was blindingly obvious from the stares, the whispers, the flirtatious looks, that everyone knew exactly who Ben was.

'Fantastic!' said Richard at one point. 'I must remember to bring you out with me more often.'

'Yeah,' laughed Ben, who was enjoying himself, but still wasn't completely comfortable with his new-found fame.

'What about the redhead?' Richard nudged Ben, and they both watched her perfect undulating backside as she went to the loo to apply more lipstick.

'What about her?' said Ben, admiring the way she carried off a skirt that short, that clingy.

'She's up for it, Ben. What about you?'

Of course Ben was up for it, what red-blooded young man wouldn't have been? But Ben, remember, is not just a dizzy television presenter. Ben's a journalist, and Ben has met many women like this, and he knows perfectly well how they operate.

'Rich, do you really think I want to wake up next

Sunday and read all about my bedroom exploits in the *News of the World*?'

'She wouldn't!' said Richard.

'She bloody well would.'

'How do you know?'

'Trust me.' He almost added, 'I'm a journalist,' but he restrained himself at the last minute. 'I just know.'

So Richard went home with a blonde, and Ben went home alone, and the next day Richard phoned him with tales of the blonde, all related in a very bad Monty Python pastiche. 'Did she go, eh? Did she go?'

And that was merely the beginning of Ben's journey into celebritydom, a small stepping stone. For now, just a few months down the line, Ben is well and truly established. No longer is he a mere reporter, he's now a presenter. *The* presenter. The public know he's single, they know he lives with two flatmates (although with his new large income he's started looking for a flat of his own), they know his likes and dislikes. But to be fair, none of them *really* knows him. They don't know what his sense of humour's like, they don't know what makes him tick, what he thinks about when he lies in bed at night, because Ben, being the journalist that he is, has perfected the art of putting on a face for the press, and, charming as he is to the other journalists who now clamour to interview him, he never shows them who he really is.

Only his close friends know that. Only people like Geraldine. Richard. And Jemima Jones. But Ben hasn't had too much time on his hands to think about his former work colleagues. He tried to keep in touch, really he did, but he was swept up in such a whirlwind it was difficult for him to find the time, and the longer he prevaricated, the harder it was to pick up the phone. And now his life is work, parties, launches, interviews. Never has he been so busy.

And never has London Daytime Television had such a bright star. Everywhere she goes Diana Macpherson is patted on the back, congratulated on her brilliant discovery.

Diana, as far as she's concerned, made Ben, and that means one thing in Diana's book. He owes her. Big time. And she's simply waiting for that day when she can call in her debt, because Diana Macpherson, like so many other strong, successful, scary women, always wants what she can't have. And she wants Ben Williams, not only because he's gorgeous, but because he's shown no interest in her whatsoever.

Diana Macpherson is well used to bedding rising stars, wannabe celebrities who hang on her every word, feed the aura of power that surrounds her. What she's not used to are men like Ben, men who are polite, charming, friendly, but make no response whatsoever to her overt flirtations.

Just last week she called him in and told him they ought to have a drink, just to discuss how the programme was going, to see whether they could come up with any other ideas.

Ben thought it was a bit strange, but, television being television, he'd already heard all the gossip about Diana and her toy boys, that her nickname was the Piranha, and he could tell from the way she looked at him that the last thing on her mind was the programme.

'Rich,' he whispered into the phone, checking there was no one around to overhear.

'What's the problem?'

'It's Diana. I don't think I can hold her off much longer.'

'How many times, Ben? How often have I told you not to shit on your own doorstep?'

'*I* don't want to,' Ben said emphatically, 'but we're going out tonight for a drink and I'm running out of excuses.'

'Whoa,' Richard laughed. 'Better put your chastity belt on.'

'For God's sake, Rich. I need advice.'

'Tell her you've got a girlfriend.' Richard was already sounding bored.

'She knows I haven't.'

'Well, I don't know. Just say you've got a headache.' He laughed at his joke.

'Forget it,' said Ben. 'I suppose I'll cope.'

Diana turned a business drink into dinner at a small French bistro in Chelsea, a dark, cosy, candlelit restaurant, perfect for romantic trysts.

'It's my local,' she told Ben, who tried to ignore the fact that she had transformed herself into a complete dog's dinner between the last time he saw her in the office and the time she reappeared to tell him she was ready to go. She was wearing a plunging, see-through, fitted shirt, a black Wonderbra more than visible underneath, with a very tight skirt and very high heels.

'You look nice,' Ben said, aware that she was his boss, that he had to flatter her, but trying to keep things as professional as he could.

'Oh thanks,' she said, preening like a schoolgirl and trying to sound surprised. 'This old thing?' she said, brushing her shirt, the shirt she'd bought at lunchtime with the express purpose of finally seducing Ben.

They sat down and Ben did his damnedest to talk about work. The wine was flowing, and he tried to drink as slowly as possible, to stretch out every drop, while Diana kept topping up their glasses – his always half full, hers always completely empty.

So they made small talk about work through the hors-d'oeuvres, while Ben tried, unsuccessfully, not to get too drunk, and to give him his credit he did manage to stretch work talk until halfway through the main course, when Diana put down her knife and fork, and leaned forward.

'Ben,' she said in what she hoped was a husky voice. 'I don't often meet men as charismatic as you.'

'Thanks, Diana. Shall we get some more mineral water?'

'Ben,' she said again. 'What I'm trying to say is —'

'Waiter?' Ben looked around frantically for the waiter while Diana sighed and sat back in her chair, for Ben had spoilt the moment. Her moment.

Ben declined pudding, at which Diana was delighted, for she had already decided that Ben would be coming back to hers for a nightcap. Then the timing would be right. The timing would be perfect.

'My house is just round the corner,' she said as they walked out, her having paid, for Diana Macpherson probably has the largest expense account in the country.

'Okay, fine. Thanks for a lovely evening,' said Ben, backing off.

'You don't mean you'd let me walk home by myself?' said Diana, mock indignantly. 'A girl on her own at night?'

Girl? thought Ben. In your dreams. 'Sorry, sorry,' he apologized, now not knowing what the hell to do, because, much as he didn't want to sleep with her, he didn't want her to sack him either, and, despite being famous and sought after, Ben knows exactly how transient the television world is, and he knows perfectly well that today's Ben Williams is tomorrow's David Icke.

They walked along, side by side, and when Diana took Ben's arm he resisted the urge to flinch. Oh fuck, he just kept thinking. Oh fuck.

And when they reached the door, Diana turned to him, a playful smile on her lips. 'Now how about that nightcap?' she said.

Ben silently prayed. If you help me now, God, I promise I'll go to church, and he heard the sound of an engine, and as he turned round he glimpsed the orange light of a black cab that was free. 'Taxi,' he yelled, sticking out his arm, while Diana looked crestfallen.

But the taxi driver had been working all day, and he was off home to his wife and kids. He shook his head at Ben as Diana smirked. 'Why don't you come in and I'll call you a minicab?' she said.

But she didn't pick up the phone, and Ben was so impressed with the minimalist grandeur of her flat and, by this stage, so drunk that he forgot to ask why not. She placed a large whisky in his hand, and a firm hand on his thigh.

Oh fuck, Ben thought again, but before he had a chance to think up a strategy Diana was kissing him, and, although he knew he shouldn't, in a funny sort of way he was quite enjoying it. This was Diana Macpherson! Oh what the hell, thought Ben in his drunken state, why not?

And so Ben and Diana finally consummated their professional relationship. Ben, drunk though he was, ensured he gave the performance of his life, which probably wasn't such a good thing, because Diana, having experienced the most overwhelming orgasm of *her* life thanks to Ben's proficiency at oral sex, thinks she has fallen in love.

The oral sex was Ben's way of proving to Diana that he was a good lover, for the sex, at least in Ben's eyes, was pretty damn average. Sure, he made all the right moves and did all the right things, but, as far as he was concerned, he could have been fucking a shop-window dummy, and yes, he managed to do it, but no, it wasn't good for him. And, perhaps most importantly, Ben has remembered why he doesn't have meaningless sex with faceless women. Because it's not worth it.

There's only one problem. The sex may have been meaningless but the woman has a face. And a name. Diana Macpherson. His boss. Oh shit.

And after this night of passion, when Diana took the lead and Ben just thanked God he didn't suffer from Brewer's Droop, Diana has decided that Ben is the best thing that's ever happened to her. Her constant gazes at Ben have not, unsurprisingly, gone unnoticed in the office, and rumours of a suspected affair have already started flying around.

But Diana would never confirm them. No one would

ever dare ask her to her face. And anyway, one night of passion hardly constitutes an affair, except Diana doesn't plan on leaving it at one night. No siree.

'I just knew he had that star quality the minute he walked in the door,' she tells Jo Hartley, a freelance journalist who's writing a huge piece about the rise and rise of Ben Williams for an upmarket tabloid. 'Presenters like Ben are few and far between, and it's my job to spot them then develop them and realize their full potential.'

'Was it a conscious move, to employ someone who was single, because so many of the other presenters are married? And presumably with Ben and his obvious sex appeal you're attracting a much younger audience.'

'Mmm,' nodded Diana, thinking about Ben's obvious sex appeal. 'I'd say you'd just about hit the nail on the head.'

The piece runs over a double-page spread, with several pictures of Ben as a child, as a teenager, and finally in all his current glory.

'Un. Be. Lievable,' says Geraldine as she sips the cappuccino she picked up on the way to work and reads the paper. One of the news reporters walks past her desk.

'I see you're finding out all about our old deputy news editor,' he says as he passes.

'Who would have thought?' she says, eyes hardly able to leave the page, and then she shrieks with laughter as she reads the next quote.

'Even Diana Macpherson, the feisty head of programming at London Daytime Television, seems won over by this man's charm. At the very mention of his name her eyes glaze over like the rest of the female population.

' "I love his obvious sex appeal," she says. "I chose him, initially as a reporter, and even then I knew that I could develop that."'

When Geraldine finishes the piece, she sits back and lights a cigarette, trying to postpone that bloody Top Tips column. But then her eyes sparkle as she grabs the paper again, pulls out the two pages covered in Ben Williams, carefully folds them up and slips them into an A4 brown envelope.

'Darling Jemima,' she writes on a compliments slip. 'If I had time I'd write a letter, but I wanted you to see this. Can you believe it?!! Ben Williams splashed all over two pages!! Wish I'd known then what I know now . . . maybe I would have taken him up on his offer after all!! Hope you're having a spectacularly marvellous time, and give Brad's pecs a lick from me. Speak to you very, very soon, all my love, Geraldine.'

Smacking her lips, she seals the envelope and addresses it to Jemima, and on her way to the post-tray she smiles with delight at the thought of Jemima's surprised face when she gets it.

Ben's sitting at the breakfast table about to tuck into a bowl of cereal when he hears the thud of the paper on the mat. Shit, he thinks. Today's the day the interview goes in. He hates doing publicity, but Diana, in her professional mode, has told him he has to do everything, because everything depends on the ratings and good PR means better ratings.

For the last few weeks Ben has had daily conversations with the head of publicity at the TV station, who's constantly arranging for Ben to see journalists, or to take part in one of those rent-a-celeb pieces in which Ben's opinion on complete crap sits alongside other celebrities' opinions on the selfsame complete crap. But never has he had a profile this big. He agreed to the interview, under duress, and it was only afterwards that he discovered they were doing more than just talking to him, they were ringing up all his friends as well. 'A colour piece,' Jo Hartley had said. She didn't say stitch-up, but then Ben supposed she wouldn't, would she.

So with heavy heart he opened the paper, immediately cringing with embarrassment as he saw the pictures. Now where in the hell did they get *those* from?

I can't believe I said that, he thinks, starting to read the piece, before realizing that he didn't say it, that Jo Hartley had taken what he *had* said and paraphrased it into more tabloid-friendly language.

He carries on reading, shocked at what they'd found out about him. Nothing spectacularly juicy, just stuff that he'd forgotten about. They'd dug up people he'd vaguely known at university, and there are several paragraphs devoted to his life as a rugger bugger, but luckily no real kiss and tells, just mentions of previous girlfriends.

'Jemima was right,' he murmurs, scanning the rest of the page. 'Being famous isn't quite what it's cracked up to be.' Bloody hell, he thinks. Jemima Jones! Now why the hell didn't I think of Jemima. She'll give me advice about Diana, he thinks. She'll tell me what to do. And then he thinks of how long it's been since he last called her, and how she had always known just what to do.

Jesus, Ben, he thinks to himself, you've been a real bastard not calling Jemima. Geraldine, he thinks, he could live without. Yes, he fancied her, but there was never the connection that he had with Jemima. You should never have left it this long, he thinks, and with that he picks up the phone and dials her home number.

'Hello. Is Jemima there, please?'

'No, she's on holiday in Los Angeles for a couple of weeks.'

'She's what? What's she doing there?'

'Who *is* this?' Lisa vaguely recognizes the voice.

'This is Ben Williams. Is that Sophie?'

'No,' says Lisa, mentally rubbing her hands together with glee because Sophie's popped out to get some cigarettes and she'll go ballistic when she finds out Ben Williams phoned. 'This is Lisa,' she laughs. 'The brunette.'

'Oh hi. How are you?'

'Just fine,' she says. 'And I don't need to ask how you are, all I have to do is switch on my television.'

'Yes,' Ben laughs, because what is he supposed to say? There's a silence while Lisa tries to think of something clever to say next, but she can't think of anything at all, and the silence stretches on.

'Sorry,' says Ben, finally. 'I thought you were going to say something.'

'Oh. No.'

'What's Jemima doing in LA?'

'She's staying with her new boyfriend.'

'You're joking!' Ben's flabbergasted. 'Not that Internet guy?'

'Yes, that's the one.'

'You haven't got her number by any chance have you?'

'Hang on,' says Lisa, reaching for the pad by the phone.

303

She reads the number out to Ben, and then says, 'Um, you should pop in some time. Have a drink with us.' Which of course means have a drink with me.

'Yeah, sure. I'll do that,' says Ben, which of course means he'll forget about her the instant he puts down the phone. Which he does. He also neglects to phone Jemima in LA, because Diana Macpherson is next on the line, presumably hoping to soothe his furrowed brow. But he will phone Jemima, he honestly will. As soon as he remembers again.

CHAPTER TWENTY-TWO

A week can pass incredibly quickly when you're having fun. A week can also pass incredibly slowly when you find that you're actually quite lonely, you're not surrounded by the safety network of your friends, your home, familiar surroundings.

Not that Jemima Jones isn't having a good time, how could she not? Her evenings are a riot of new sounds, tastes, smells, and naturally the whirlwind of passion that she's having with Brad.

But her days aren't quite what they could be, and even after a week Jemima Jones is discovering that being on your own, in a strange city, albeit a city where the strangers treat you like old friends, is not quite the same as being on your own at home. Particularly when you're as strapped for cash as poor Jemima is now. The *Kilburn Herald*, as we already know, pays her a pittance, and all the money she saved by not having a life has almost trickled away. For now she's just about okay with Brad paying for everything, so let's just hope he *continues* to treat her as well as he has been . . .

Her daily routine here has changed enormously. She and Brad wake up at 8 a.m., and thus far they have had wild, wanton sex before both getting up and going for a run along the beach, which is sheer bliss for Jemima, so unused to living near the water, to the warm, early-morning sun, to the friendly smiles of passing people.

They stop for breakfast on the way back, a glass of

vegetable juice, a fat-free, sugar-free blueberry muffin or cranberry scone, and then Brad climbs in the shower at home. He kisses her goodbye, and Jemima showers, makes herself some coffee and climbs back into bed, poring over the magazines that are scattered all over Brad's coffee table, but no longer does she tear out the pictures of models. She doesn't need to, she's fulfilled that dream, and, while she's still interested, that degree of desperation has disappeared.

At around 11 a.m. she puts on her tiny lycra leotards, her leggings, her trainers, and she goes to do her workout at the gym. If Brad's not too busy, he'll take her out for lunch, or she may go wandering by herself, although it's hard for her to get around, because Brad needs his car, and Los Angeles, even Santa Monica, is not a place to be without a car.

But Jemima is slowly running out of places to wander. She has been up and down 3rd Street Promenade more times than she cares to mention. She has been into the bookstores, and has emerged with nothing, because all of the titles seem to be geared to those working in the film world, and Jemima, frankly, has no interest in books telling you how to write a film script, which director did which work, and why the film industry is so wonderful.

She has been into all of the shops lining 3rd Street Promenade. Repeatedly. She has been into the Santa Monica mall, into the eating section, and stood for a while, completely flabbergasted at all the stalls offering every type of food you could imagine. Chinese, Japanese, Italian, gourmet coffee, croissants, Ethiopian, Thai, and in the hundreds of tables planted in the middle of the mall were hundreds of people, all tucking into oversized portions in polystyrene containers. She stood there, and she thought how six months ago, had she walked in here, she would have worked her way round all the stalls, but now, despite enjoying all the exotic smells mingling together, the thought of actually eating anything slightly repels her.

She has been up and down Montana, into all the smart, expensive boutiques and coffee shops. She was even extremely tempted to buy a cream designer suit that looked like a dream on her newly skinny body – which, incidentally, much to her delight is getting skinnier by the day thanks to a completely fat-free diet and an exercise regime that would make Cher jealous – but she didn't buy the suit, because where, after all, would she wear it? How, after all, could she afford it?

She has discovered that people don't dress up in Los Angeles, that anyone wearing a suit with anything other than trainers on their feet is regarded as somehow strange, an outsider, someone not to be trusted. So she is living in her jeans, and if she and Brad go out in the evening, she teams the jeans with a cream body, a brown crocodile belt and a jacket.

She has sat by herself at a long wooden trestle table in Marmalade, and flicked through the *Outlook* – the local Santa Monica paper – while eating a selection of three salads, and trying not to look as if she is desperate to talk to someone.

She has been to every Starbucks coffee outlet that she can find, and she has perfected the art of ordering coffee, American style, be it latte, mocha or frappuccino.

She has walked up and down Main Street, past the New Age bookstore, which she is sorely tempted to try, but hasn't, as yet, had the nerve to go into. She has, however, been into the designer aerobic shops and has finally succumbed, kitting herself out in the very latest exercise wear. Now Jemima looks more like an Angeleno than most Angelenos.

She is constantly meeting people, or should we say, people, men, are constantly meeting *her*. Wherever she goes she is accosted by someone offering to buy her coffee, take her out, show her around, and although there have been times when she has been tempted, she has never said yes, because that, as far as she's concerned, would be tantamount to infidelity. So she smiles sweetly and tells them she has a boyfriend, before wishing them a nice day and walking off.

She has discovered American television, and, although she feels slightly guilty, a large part of her afternoon, when not rollerblading by herself with Brad's Walkman attached to her waist, is spent watching shows that she's never heard of. She thinks she has just about got the plot of *The Bold and the Beautiful*. She is addicted to *Days of Our Lives*. She adores *Rosie O'Donnell*, and *Seinfeld*, as far as Jemima Jones is concerned, is a positive gift from heaven.

Yesterday she found that the best place to have lunch, on those occasions when Brad could not make it out of the office, is a large, bustling restaurant called the Broadway Deli. She hit upon the deli by accident, and, while she was standing there, scouring the restaurant area, wondering if she had the nerve actually to sit at a table by herself when everyone around her was in couples, threesomes, foursomes and moresomes, she noticed a lunch bar on the right.

And not only that, there was a spare stool, and she squeezed in next to a man who was just leaving, and picked up the paper he'd left behind.

'Coffee?' said the man behind the bar, as I nodded vigorously. As he placed a huge white cup and saucer in front of me and poured the coffee, I smelt a smell I hadn't smelt in what felt like years, a smell that instantly propelled me back to London, back to Geraldine, back to Ben, back to the *Kilburn Herald*.

Bizarre as it may be, I suddenly realized that the Broadway Deli was the first restaurant I had been into that allowed smoking, albeit only at the bar, and as I sat there sniffing I have never wanted a cigarette more badly in my life.

And as if the gods were listening, there, just in front of me, a little to my right, was a pack of cigarettes, calling me, tempting me. Nothing strange about that, I know, but they weren't just any old cigarettes, they were Silk Cut. King Size. Ultra Low. My brand.

'Excuse me,' I said to the girl sitting next to me, 'but are those your cigarettes?'

'Yes, help yourself.' The girl watched as I greedily pulled a cigarette out of the pack and gratefully bent my head as she held out a light. I closed my eyes and inhaled deeply, feeling the smoke hit my lungs, and, partly because it was so forbidden, so naughty, the acrid taste was at that moment in time possibly one of the greatest tastes of my life.

'You look like you really needed that,' said the girl in amusement.

309

'God, yes. You'd never believe this is now my only vice would you?'

'Sounds boring.'

'I have a horrible feeling you might be right.' I stuck out my hand. 'I'm JJ.'

'I'm Lauren. You're English too aren't you?'

I nodded. 'Where are you from?'

'London.'

'Me too. Whereabouts?'

'Kilburn.'

'You're joking! What road?'

'Mapesbury. Do you know it?'

'Know it? That's unbelievable, I'm in the Avenue.'

'God, what a small world.'

'Wouldn't want to paint it.'

'What?'

'Nothing,' I mumbled, feeling a bit stupid. 'Just something I heard someone say once, but I can't believe we're from the same place.'

'I know,' echoed Lauren. 'Bloody incredible.'

As we sit there smiling I suddenly breathe a sigh of relief because for the first time in Los Angeles I think that I may have found a friend. You know how sometimes you just know that you're going to be friends, sometimes within seconds of meeting someone? That's kind of what it was like with Lauren. She was just so natural that she put me at ease instantly.

We ordered our food, a plain salad, no dressing, for me, and Lauren ordered the Chinese chicken salad, and as soon as the waiter behind the bar disappeared we turned to one another in amazement.

'So what are *you* doing here?' I asked, assuming

Lauren must live in Los Angeles because she looked so tanned, so fit, so healthy, so LA. But then I took a closer look and saw – this is Geraldine's influence on me – that her trousers and belted cardigan were, if I'm not mistaken, definitely designer, that her shoes were definitely expensive, and that her bag was definitely a Bill Amberg. Just how much more stylish can you get?

'I came out here about a month ago to be with this man, and now it's all gone horribly wrong and I can't face going home again because I told everyone this time I'd met The One, so I'm stuck here in this grotty little apartment, and every night I dream of curling up in one of the sofas at the Groucho, or drinks at the Westbourne, or dinner at the Cobden, and I miss home but I just have to sit it out. What about you?'

'This is more and more weird,' I laughed, shaking my head. 'I mean, I came out here to meet a man too, but I've only been here just over a week, and so far it's going fine. I think. He is gorgeous, and he's being lovely to me, but . . .' I tailed off and shrugged my shoulders. Do I want to reveal my doubts to this stranger? Not just yet, I have to see whether I can trust her.

'So where is he now?' asked Lauren.

'At work.'

'Didn't he take time off to show you the sights?'

'He wanted to, he just has too much on at the moment.'

'What does he do?'

'He owns a gym. B-Fit Gym, I don't know whether you know it?'

'Oh my God!' Lauren's eyes opened wide, filled with admiration. 'You're the one who came out to meet the hunk. I know exactly who you are. I can't remember his name. Damn,' she said, almost to herself.

'Brad?' I was feeling slightly nervous, did she really know all about me, and if she did know, how did she know?

'Yes! Exactly. The most perfect specimen of manhood I'd ever seen. Bloody hell. Congratulations!'

'I don't understand how you know all this.' Still feeling a bit bemused.

'Oh don't worry,' said Lauren breezily. 'Nothing sinister. I go to the B-Fit Gym, I've been going every day since I got here, and you get to know the people. Not that I know your gorgeous Brad, he's never even looked at me, but I overheard someone saying he was flying out an English girl that he met on the Internet or something.'

'That's me, I'm afraid.' I cringe as I admit it.

'Why sound so embarrassed about it?'

'It's just it sounds so naff, meeting on the Internet.'

'Nah, not at all. Us single girls have to go wherever the opportunities are. So what's he like then? I've got to be honest with you, I really am impressed. He's just so perfect.'

Do you know what's weird? If Lauren wasn't so open, so friendly, so natural, I probably would have been intimidated by her and I would almost certainly have taken offence at this candidness, but just then I was so relieved to have found an ally. To have found someone who, despite the long dark hair and slight cockney lilt, was somehow reminding me more and more of Geraldine with every word she spoke.

'He *is* gorgeous isn't he,' I said, smiling like the cat

312

that got the cream at the thought of his gleaming white teeth, the softness of his hair, the hardness of his muscles.

'Phwooargh, is he ever.'

And then I couldn't stop this sigh escaping. 'I know, I know. I just think that everything should be perfect, and I suppose I had this vision of us spending all this time together and doing all these things together, and although I see him in the evenings I'm starting to feel a little bit lonely.'

You might think it strange that I'm being so open with a girl who's practically a stranger, but then isn't it sometimes easier to pour out your heart to someone you hardly know, who doesn't matter, who won't judge you?

'Don't worry about that,' said Lauren, giving me a friendly shove. 'You've got me now. I'll be your friend. God knows I could do with a reminder of home right now.' She looked dreamily into space. 'Keep talking. I'll close my eyes and pretend we're at the K bar.'

I laughed.

'So,' she carried on. 'Friends? How about it?'

For a moment there I was so happy I could have hugged her.

'Tell me about your man then,' I asked. 'How did it all go wrong?'

Lauren sighed and handed me another cigarette before lighting one for herself. 'Okay. Here goes. Are you sure you want to hear the full story?'

I nodded. 'Sure as I'll ever be.'

'Okay. I met Charlie in London about six months ago. Actually I wasn't supposed to be meeting him, I was supposed to be meeting one of his associates to try and set up an interview with some woman they look after.'

'Hang on.' I put a hand on Lauren's arm, trying not to start laughing. 'Sorry to interrupt but what do you do for a living?'

'I'm a journalist. Anyway, so there I was – '

'No!' I said. 'You're not going to believe this.'

Lauren looked at me and her mouth dropped open. 'Don't even think about telling me – '

'I bloody am!' I laughed out loud.

'No fucking way. Who do you work for?'

'Don't ask,' I groaned. 'The *Kilburn Herald*.'

'Hey, it's a starting point,' she said. 'I used to work for the *Solent Advertiser*.'

And then I started laughing even harder.

'What's so funny about that?' said Lauren.

'Don't worry. It would take too long to explain. So where do you work anyway?'

Lauren named one of the top glossy magazines, a magazine I would have killed to work for, a magazine of which several cut-out pages, even as we speak, are nestling in the top drawer of my bedside table at home.

'Now it's my turn to be impressed. Don't tell me you're something really important like editor,' I said.

'I bloody wish!' said Lauren. 'But actually I am the style editor.'

'So how come they let you come here?'

'I've taken a three-month sabbatical. The plan was to come here, realize that this was true love, get married so I can get American citizenship and then move husband and myself, and naturally by that time at least three babies, back home to Blighty.'

'But I take it your plans have changed?'

'Too bloody right. So where was I? Ah, yes. Charlie.

So Charlie turned up instead of this guy I was supposed to be meeting, and sat in on the interview.'

'Was this in London?' I interrupted, trying to get the full picture.

'Yup. They'd flown over for a ten-day publicity tour, and this was right at the beginning. So Charlie walked in, and I thought he was nice. Nothing spectacular, but nice, you could tell he was a good person, and he is attractive. He wears these little round tortoiseshell glasses which I completely adore, and he was really sweet after the interview. Anyway, the interview was fine, and the next day he phoned me to check everything was okay, and he asked me out.

'We went out that night, and he was so nice to me I suppose I started to fall for him, and we spent pretty much every night together.'

I raised an eyebrow.

'Not like that,' Lauren grinned, before grimacing. 'Although now I wish we bloody had, I wouldn't be sitting here if we had.'

'Uh oh, is that the problem?'

'It sounds so shallow doesn't it? I mean, here's this wonderful man whom I did find attractive, and he was convinced he'd met the woman he was going to marry.'

'So why on earth didn't you sleep with him?'

'I was reading this new book about how to play hard to get . . .'

I shook my head and sighed. 'Not *The Rules* by any chance?'

'Yes! You've read it?'

'No,' I laugh, 'but a friend of mine is doing it at home.'

'Well, all I can tell you is it bloody well works. On the day he left Charlie told me he'd never felt this way about anyone before, and he wanted me to come out to California. So basically we spent the next few months with him phoning me every day, and I suppose I convinced myself that this time it really was going to work, and I completely fell in love with the idea of being in love.' She paused to take a bite of salad.

'And?' I prompted, dying to hear the end.

'And, I finally got the time off work, came out here, he picked me up at the airport, he was exactly as I remembered him, and we spent all afternoon kissing and cuddling and it was fantastic.

'And then,' she exhaled loudly, 'and then, we went to bed.'

'Do I want to hear this?'

'No. You don't. It was a bloody nightmare.'

'Just no chemistry or was he just awful?'

'Well this is the weird thing. Up until then I had this theory that there was no such thing as being bad in bed. I always thought that it was just a question of having the right chemistry, and if the chemistry wasn't there then it would be awful.'

'Tell me about it,' I nodded, remembering the terrible sex I'd had before I met Brad.

'Christ, was I wrong. I now believe that there is such a thing as being completely crap in bed, and Charlie was completely crap in bed.'

'But what do you mean, how can anyone be that bad?'

'I know. I wouldn't have believed it myself. But,' she said leaning forward confidingly, 'his dick was about this big!' She held out her little finger.

'Uh oh,' I said. 'A no-hoper then?'

'A no-hoper. I mean, he really should have come with a warning. You get to know someone, you think they're perfect, and then boom! You discover they have the dick of a ten-year-old.'

'So what did you do?'

'I put up with it for about two weeks, because I kept hoping that it would get better, and I tried not to think about it. Also – ' She paused. 'Also, it wasn't just that. He was bloody crap at going down on me.'

'Oh.' What was I supposed to say? Hardly the sort of thing you discuss with strangers, is it, no matter how friendly they seem.

'Yeah,' she nodded. 'You know how it is, he couldn't find my clit if it had a big red arrow showing him the way.' I blushed, and I'm still blushing at the memory of the language she used, but she didn't seem to notice.

'Then I started coming up with excuses, I was really tired, I had my period.'

'And he believed them?'

'Nah.' Lauren shook her head and laughed. 'Eventually, the last time we had sex I just knew as an absolute certainty that this was the most pointless experience of my life. I could hardly feel anything for God's sake, and if it wasn't for his balls banging against my – '

'I get the picture,' I interrupted, not wanting to hear any more.

'Sorry.' She paused and shrugged her shoulders. 'So anyway, the next day I told him I was moving out.'

'How did he take it?'

'Nightmare.' Lauren raised her eyes to the ceiling. 'He was so upset he didn't speak. I sat there for three hours

317

talking at him and he didn't say one single word. He just sat and looked at the floor.'

'God. Nightmare. Did you tell him why?'

'What? Tell him his dick wasn't big enough? No, I couldn't do that. I just came out with all this shit about how I wasn't ready for a relationship, we lived too far apart from each other to ever really make it work, and eventually I sealed it by telling him I thought I had a problem with commitment.' She drifted into silence, obviously lost in memories.

'And now you're here, picking up strange women in the Broadway Deli,' I said, breaking the silence.

'Exactly,' laughed Lauren. 'So please tell me the sex with Brad is out of this world, because I've forgotten, I really have.'

'You will be delighted to hear it's out of this world.'

'Really?'

'Really.'

'Give me the details, go on.'

I shook my head, because nice as she is, I'm not the sort of person who finds it easy to talk about sex, and certainly not in the sort of language she's used to. As you've probably noticed.

'So is this true love? God, how I need to hear a story with a happy ending.'

'I don't know. I'm not sure I'd even know what true love is.'

'What? You've never been in love?'

'Well ... There was this guy in London I was crazy about, I'd never felt that way about anyone before, and I always thought I was madly in love with him. Not that anything ever happened, we were just friends.'

'Why? Is he blind?'

I love this woman! 'No. I didn't look like this when I was in London.' I thought for a moment, wondering whether to tell Lauren, and what the hell. I'd been so honest up until then, why stop? 'If you want to know the truth I was the size of a house.'

'No way.' Lauren looked me up and down in disbelief. 'No way.'

'I swear,' I swore.

'So how the hell did you get to look like this?'

'Lots of hard work. Masses of exercise and no food.'

'It was obviously worth it. You look fantastic.'

'Thank you.'

Lauren looked at me curiously. 'So has your life changed, now that you're thin?'

I shrugged, thinking about how invisible I felt before I lost weight, and how much that had changed. 'In some ways of course,' I said slowly. 'You can't even begin to imagine what it was like being . . .' I paused, wondering whether I could now say the F word out loud, and after a deep breath I managed it, 'fat. It colours your whole life. Nobody wants to be seen with you, nobody notices you, or if they do it's because they think you're worthless.'

'Why were you that size?'

A good question, and one I'd thought about many times since losing the weight. 'I suppose in a way I wanted to hide from everyone. Even though I hated it, it was my protection, it kept people away and a part of me was very frightened of people, especially of men, and my size made me feel safe.'

Lauren nodded. 'I can understand that. But what about men?'

'What about them?' I laughed. 'I never really had any boyfriends, just the odd fling which makes your Charlie look like an Adonis. Men were never really an issue.'

'So what about this guy in London?'

'You might know who he is actually. When I knew him he was the deputy news editor of my paper, but now he's moved into TV. Ben Williams. He's a reporter on – '

'Fucking hell! Gorgeous Ben Williams! I know exactly who he is, I was completely hooked on the show before I left. I've been trying to get a bloody interview with him for weeks.'

'But you're the style editor, surely you don't do interviews?'

'Not usually, no, but pass up the opportunity of meeting Ben Williams? Not bloody likely! God,' she said, shaking her head. 'You're something, JJ. All these gorgeous men!'

'Yeah, but Ben was never interested in me.'

'But you know him! He's your friend! What's he like, tell me everything.'

So I did, and before we knew it, four hours had passed, and by the time we left, we were firm friends. Lauren gave me her phone number and said if there was anything I needed, just give her a call, and I gave Lauren my phone number, saying there was no reason why either of us should be lonely any more. Corny isn't it, but not so corny if you think how lonely I've been. We walked out together and said goodbye, and spontaneously both of

us reached over at the same time and gave one another
a hug. A hug that said thank God we've found each other,
thank God we've finally found a friend.

CHAPTER TWENTY-THREE

The phone rings as I walk through the door.

'Sweetie, where have you been?' Bless Brad for sounding so worried.

'I met the most amazing girl today.' The excitement is still in my voice, the thrill of having someone to talk to when Brad's not here. 'And we just sat and talked for hours.'

'Where did you meet her?' Brad sounds a bit, well, a bit perturbed. It crosses my mind that maybe he thinks I'm lying, so I tell him the whole story, just leaving out the bit about the small dick because men don't appreciate that kind of thing.

'That's great,' he says, although if I'm honest he doesn't sound all that interested. 'Honey,' a slight digression from his usual pet name, 'I'm coming home early tonight. Wanna try a yoga class?'

'That sounds . . . interesting,' I say cautiously, because let's face it, yoga doesn't mean losing weight, and if it doesn't help me maintain my new slim figure then what is the point? Really?

'Okay. I'll be home soon, and then maybe tonight we'll go out for dinner. I thought we'd try this restaurant on La Cienega.'

'You mean, we're actually leaving Santa Monica?'

Brad laughs. 'Don't make it sound such a big deal, you're making me feel guilty.'

'I didn't mean to. Sorry.'

'Hey, don't worry about it. It'll be nice. I want to make a fuss of you tonight, and I think you'll enjoy this restaurant, it's French, so it should remind you of home.'

'Darling, I'm English.'

'I *know* that,' he laughs, 'but France, England, Italy, they're all Europe.'

'I know *that*,' I laugh back, and we say goodbye.

We don't really need to join Brad and Jemima at yoga, just a quick peek perhaps. Suffice to say Jemima finds it strange, and more strange is the fact that there are equal numbers of men and women, all decked out in the latest lycra, all deep breathing and contorting their bodies into strange positions.

'I'm not sure whether I can keep this up,' puffs Jemima, lying on the floor with her legs over her head, straining to make her toes touch the floor just above her hair.

'You're doing great,' Brad says smoothly, lying next to her, looking as if he does this every day of the week. 'You'll feel great afterwards. Now ssshhh. Breathe.' And Jemima does, trying to forget that she, like everyone else in the packed room, looks completely ridiculous.

'There,' Brad says when the group has finished and are standing round talking to one another. 'How do you feel now?'

'Fantastic,' lies Jemima, who feels pretty much the same, has been bored throughout and finally understands why she has never been to a yoga class before.

'Told you so,' he says, kissing her on the nose. 'Let's get out of here.'

*

We go home, and, as Brad is showering, as I'm brushing my teeth, he opens the glass door and pulls me in the shower.

'See?' he says, rubbing the soap gently all over my body and setting every nerve I have on fire, 'never say I don't look after you,' and before I have a chance to reply he bends his head and kisses me.

Quickies, I think ten minutes later, can be just as exciting as long, luscious, langorous sex.

'Mmm,' says Brad, enfolding me in a towel. 'Maybe we should cancel tonight and just spend the evening in bed.'

'Haven't you had enough yet?' Does this man never stop?

'I could never get enough of you,' he says, looking deeply into my eyes until finally I break away with a kiss and go to get dressed.

We go to Le Petit Bistro, a busy, bustling restaurant, and I spend the whole evening marvelling at the mix of weird and wonderful people surrounding us. Opposite us is a table of six of the best-looking men I've ever seen, presumably gay, because each of them stops talking when we walk in, and, instead of looking at me, which I'm slowly getting used to, they all, one by one, look Brad slowly up and down from head to toe.

At the far end is a woman like no woman I have ever seen, and for a moment I think she might be a man in drag. Throughout dinner she keeps her white fur coat on, which matches her white stetson and the enormous diamonds glittering in her ears and around her throat.

'Is she someone famous?' I whisper to Brad, pointing

her out. 'Nope,' Brad says, shaking his head. 'Just some rich old woman with no fashion sense at all, darling!' and we both laugh. But I can't believe what this woman looks like. She must be seventy if she's a day, and she obviously doesn't give a damn that she looks ridiculous. Part of me thinks, good for her, but the other part thinks, does she honestly look in the mirror before she goes out and say, yes! I look good.

And then I look over to the right, and I nearly squeal with excitement. Finally, I finally see what I've been waiting to see since I arrived. A real-life celebrity. And not just any old celebrity, George Clooney! The man I used to sit and fantasize about, when, that is, I wasn't fantasizing about Ben.

'Oh my God,' I whisper, 'that's George Clooney.'

'Where?' Brad doesn't seem very interested, but I gesture slightly with my head and Brad turns to look.

'Oh yes,' he says uninterestedly, and immediately looks away and goes back to eating his endive and heart of palm salad.

'Now he,' I say, trying to look, but trying to look as if I'm not looking, 'is gorgeous.'

'Why don't you talk to him?'

'And say what? I love you?'

'You could just tell him you admire his work. People don't generally bother celebrities here, you see them all over the place, but if you are going to talk it's better to be cool and just say something flattering. I love you probably wouldn't go down too well.'

'I couldn't say anything,' I say, which is true. I'd be far too embarrassed to approach him, but think what

Geraldine will say! Think how jealous Sophie and Lisa will be!

'Speaking of love . . .' Brad finally puts down his knife and fork while I start shaking because, inexperienced though I may be, I know what's coming next. I know because Brad suddenly has a very serious look on his face, serious but soppy at the same time. He reaches over and takes my hand, which he holds very gently, stroking my fingers with his thumb, and I watch him doing this and I wonder why I'm not feeling completely and utterly happy.

'JJ,' he says, and I look up, into his eyes. 'I never thought I'd say this. I never thought this would happen, but you do know I love you.'

Well I didn't know, actually. I mean, I know that Brad certainly says and does all the right things, and that most women probably would have thought, even after just over a week, that he really is in love, but I can't get rid of this feeling that something isn't completely right.

And I still can't put my finger on it, and I want it to be right, I want it so badly to be right, so most of the time I try not to think about it. I know I said those things about him being stupid, but, as Geraldine said, that's not it. I just have this feeling that this can't be real, this is like a play, like a couple of actors, but maybe that's my insecurity kicking in. Maybe it's just that I can't believe someone this gorgeous could love me. Plain old Jemima Jones.

But you see, every now and then I catch Brad sitting, staring at nothing, and he looks as if he's in another world, miles away, thinking about someone else, and even though when I interrupt these reveries of his he's all over me, covering me with kisses which usually end in us making love, I can't help but wonder where he's been when he's gone. Mentally, that is, because physically I know he's either at the gym or with me, he definitely wouldn't have the time to actually be with another woman. I just sometimes think his thoughts are. That's all.

And so when he sits here and tells me he loves me, I try to push that feeling away, because no one's ever told me before that they loved me, unless you count Ben's drunken mumblings at his leaving do, which I don't, and therefore nor should you.

And surely when someone like Brad is in love with you, you have to love them back? So what if he's Californian, so what if he's not as intellectually capable as some of my friends back home, that doesn't mean he's not my soulmate. And he loves me. *Me!* Jemima Jones!

But my other concern, if you can call it that, is what are you supposed to say when someone tells you they love you? Are you supposed to be ultra-cool and say 'I know' or are you supposed to say 'I love you too'? I can't decide, so I don't say anything at all.

'I know this must seem very quick.' Brad looks at me earnestly. 'But they always say you know when you know, and I know. I really do. I feel like I've found my soulmate.' I know I just thought the same thing, but it sounds so ridiculous spoken out loud, so naff, and for a minute I look at him wondering if he is on another planet after all. I don't really know what to say, and, although the silence probably isn't very long, it feels very long. It feels like hours.

'I think I feel the same way,' I say eventually and, much as I hate to admit it, I think I say it partly to make Brad

327

feel better, and partly to fill the silence. I mean, someone has to say *something*, don't they?

'You are just what I've been looking for,' he continues. 'You're just so perfect. *We're* so perfect together.'

'But I'm going home in a few days,' I say. 'What are we going to do?' And I think about Lauren, and wonder whether I could cope with a long-distance relationship, but then I stop comparing myself to Lauren because, after all, I know the sex with Brad is fantastic. Probably the best thing about the whole relationship.

'That's what I wanted to talk to you about,' he says slowly.

'What, you mean stay?'

'Not for ever.' He obviously sees the panic in my eyes. 'But maybe you could change your ticket and stay for, say, three months. It would give us a chance to see if this really would work.'

'But what about my job at home? What would I do here? What about all my *stuff*?' Thoughts start whirling round my head, how would I do this, how could I do this?

'Okay,' says Brad. 'Let's work this out. First of all you'd need to phone your work and see if they would let you have the time off. The worst thing that could happen is they say no, in which case you'd have to make a choice. Do you just leave and try for another job when you get back home, or do you go straight back home?'

I nod, thinking, again, about Lauren, and wondering whether she might just possibly consider finding me some work, or at the very least putting me in touch with people who could. I mean, hell, it's not as if I'd be leaving some fantastic job, some fantastic magazine, it's only the *Kilburn* bloody *Herald*.

'Second,' continues Brad, 'you don't have to worry about what to do out here. I know hundreds of people in the television industry, so if you decided to stay I'm sure we could find you something. In the meantime you don't have to worry about working, or about money. God knows I've got enough for both of us, so that shouldn't be a problem.'

'But Brad, I need to work. Much as I love being here, I'd get so bored with nothing to do all day.' I don't bother mentioning that I'm bored already.

'I know it's not a long-term solution, but in the short term, if you were bored, you could always work at the gym.'

'Doing what?' I have this ridiculous vision of myself teaching an aerobics class.

'What about PR? I don't have anyone except Jenny, and I know she has a hard job coping all by herself.'

Yeah, really, I think. Jenny would love that. But of course I don't tell Brad that working with me would be Jenny's idea of hell because she hates me, because I know he'd tell me she doesn't and I am being ridiculous, so I don't say anything, I just sit and wait for what he's going to say next.

'And third, what *stuff* do you mean?'

'I'm still paying rent on my flat at home, and all my stuff is there, my things.'

'Don't you have a friend who could look after it for you?'

'But I'm not sure I want to give it up. If,' and I kiss the palm of his hand as I say this, 'if things don't work out, and I'm not saying they won't, I think it's far more likely that they will, but if they don't I don't want to have to go back to London with nowhere to live.'

'So sublet your room.' Brad leans back as if it's all so easy, and, as I watch him watching me, I realize that it is easy. He is absolutely right. Life should be an adventure, and this is the biggest adventure of my life. I've started it, so I may as well go with it and see where it takes me.

'Okay,' I say, smile, and take a deep breath. 'Let's do it.'

'You'll stay?'

'I'll stay.'

'Jemima Jones,' he says, leaning forward, taking my face in his hands and giving me the hugest kiss on the lips, 'have I told you how much I love you?'

A few minutes later we're rudely interrupted by the sound of applause. I blush furiously as the table of six men all hoot and cheer, and even our bloody waiter joins in. 'Would you like to see the menu,' he asks, one eyebrow raised, 'or are you covered for dessert?'

I phone Geraldine the next morning, and she's over the moon.

'You lucky cow!' she keeps saying. 'I hope you've got a spare room because I'm coming to visit.'

'I wish you would,' I say, realizing how much I miss her, how much more fun this would be if Geraldine were here.

'I'm serious,' she says. 'I'll be packing my stuff before you know it. The only thing is you've got my bloody Louis Vuitton vanity case.'

'I'm sorry,' I groan. 'Do you want me to send it back?'

'Don't worry,' she laughs. 'I'm sure I can live without it. Anyway, I can get Nick to buy me another one.'

'Ah. Nick. So?'

'So?' And I can tell instantly that she's not doing *The Rules* any more.

'So I take it you're no longer a *Rules* girl?'

'I most certainly am a *Rules* girl,' she says indignantly. 'Just because I slept with him doesn't mean I'm going to stop.'

'You slept with him!'

'I figured it was about time, and, bless him, he really went to town. Flowers, champagne, everything.'

'And did it warrant fireworks as well?'

'Mmm. It was absolutely, one hundred per cent delicious.'

'I don't believe this, Geraldine. You're in love!'

There's a long pause. 'You know what, my darling Jemima? I think I bloody well am!'

And I know I shouldn't be, but I'm jealous. I'm supposed to be in love too, so why can't I muster the same enthusiasm, the same dreamy tone in my voice?

'I'm really happy for you,' I say. 'I hope you get everything you wish for.'

'Mmm,' she says. 'An eight-carat diamond engagement ring *and* Nick Maxwell. My life is perfect.'

I'm shocked. 'You mean he's given you an engagement ring?'

'Don't be silly. I'm just planning my future.'

I laugh. 'Listen, this is costing me a fortune and I need to speak to the editor. Can you put me through?'

'Good luck,' she says, blowing me kisses. 'With everything.'

'And how's the land of Hollyweird?' booms the editor down the phone.

'It's weird,' I laugh, 'but actually I'm in Santa Monica, which is not quite the Los Angeles you see in films. It's a bit more down to earth.'

'Never been myself,' says the editor, 'but wouldn't mind taking the wife and kids. Life's too short to be taken slowly,' he adds, yet another one of his boring clichés. 'So you're back in next Monday then, Jemima?'

'Er, well, actually. That's why I was phoning.'

'And I thought it was because you were missing me,' he says with a sigh. 'Go on then, love. This is going to be bad news, I knew it the minute they told me you were on the phone.'

'The thing is that I'd like to stay for a bit.'

'Not found a job on the *Hollywood Reporter* have we?'

'No, nothing like that.'

'Must be love then.'

'I think it might be.'

'Look, Jemima,' he says, and from the tone of his voice I know he's going to agree, he's actually going to agree! 'I wouldn't normally agree to this, but, seeing as you're one of our best reporters, I'm going to have to say yes. How long are you proposing to stay?'

'Three months?' I can't help it, it comes out as a question.

'All right, Jemima, but there is a condition.'

'Yes?' I'm doubtful.

'The *Kilburn Herald*, great as it is, needs a touch of glamour. I'll agree to you staying out there if you agree to do a weekly page on Los Angeles. I want our readers to get some Hollywood gossip firsthand. I want to know who's doing what, where, with whom. And, more to the point, I want to know it first.'

'I'd love that!' I gasp, because this is my dream job. A column! All of my own! 'But I have a condition of my own.'

'Yes?' says the editor warily.

'I want a picture byline.'

'No problem there, love. Have we got a decent picture of you?'

God, no. The only picture of me in the office is a fat picture. 'I'll send you one from here,' I say, thinking on my feet.

'Okay, Jemima. Let's see how you do.'

'Thank you so much,' I gush. 'It's going to be great.'

'I'll expect your copy every Wednesday morning, first thing. And Jemima, love?'

'Yes?'

'I hope he's worth it.' And chuckling to himself, he puts the phone down.

Jemima Jones used to believe that she was born with a wooden spoon in her mouth. Jemima Jones used to believe that there was such a thing as an exciting, glamorous life, only that it would never happen to her.

But what Jemima Jones never understood was that sometimes, in life, you have to make things happen. That you can change your life if you're willing to let go of the old and actively look for the new. That even if you're on the right track you'll get run over if you just sit there. And heaven knows Jemima Jones hasn't been sitting anywhere for a long time now. Jemima Jones is now running with the winds, and suddenly, for the first time in her life, everything seems to be going right.

In fact, at this very moment in time I would say that Jemima Jones is an inspiration to us all.

CHAPTER TWENTY-FOUR

'I'm sorry, JJ,' says Cindy, coming back on the line, 'but I'm afraid Brad's in a meeting and can't be disturbed. Just hold the line and I'll put you through to Jenny.' Before I can yell no, I'm put on hold and I can't put the phone down because that would be childish, and anyway, why can't Brad be disturbed? Since when has he been too busy to talk to me? I've been here for four and a half weeks, and I've never had a problem getting through before.

'Hello?' Jenny comes on the line and even in one word I can hear the exasperation in her voice.

'Jenny? It's JJ. How are you?'

'Fine.'

'Look, I know Brad's in a meeting but can you just let him know I'm coming in about three o'clock.'

'Certainly. Oh by the way, he said that in case you called I should let you know that he has another meeting tonight and won't be home as planned.'

'Fine. Thank you, Jenny.'

'You're welcome,' she says, sounding as if she means the very opposite, as if I've once again pissed her off royally. Call me crazy, call me paranoid, but don't I detect the tiniest hint of triumph in her voice? Must be my imagination.

And now I'm the one who's pissed off. Not only will I be

on my own all day, it looks like I'll be on my own tonight as well, and the thought fills me with dread. Oh God, have I made a terrible mistake, should I have just got on that flight home and gone back to where I belong?

No. I'm determined to be positive, to make the best of the time I have here, to make the best of the relationship I have with Brad. Damn it, I think, as I pick up the phone and rifle through my address book to find Lauren's number. I'm going to go out tonight and have some fun.

'Lauren? It's JJ.'

'Hi!' She sounds extraordinarily pleased to hear from me. 'I was just thinking about you!'

'That's lucky,' I say, 'because I was just thinking about you.'

'So what's the plan, Stan?' she says.

'What are you doing tonight?'

'I was looking forward to yet another miserable bloody take-out from the local deli, and stuffing my face in front of the TV.'

'Does that mean I can't tempt you with a girlie night out?'

'Tempt me, tempt me,' she laughs.

'It's just that Brad's got a meeting so I'm on my own, and I thought maybe we could check out that new restaurant on Main Street.'

'Cool, schmool in the pool,' she says, in a perfect Californian accent as I laugh, wondering where on earth she gets her expressions from. 'I'm there. Listen, what are you doing now?'

I look at my watch. 'I'm off to the gym.'

'Me too. Why don't we meet at the gym, grab some

lunch after the workout and then we can arrange what to do later?'

'Perfect,' I say. 'Oh, by the way. Lots to tell you.'

'I can't wait,' she says, and we put down the phone.

It's only when I arrive at the gym that I realize that I'm actually excited about seeing Lauren again. For the first time since I arrived, I'm starting to feel more at home. I've got a home, a boyfriend, and now, finally, I'm starting to find friends. Lauren may be the only friend I have out here right now, but it's a start, and it's starting to compensate for missing Geraldine. I'm even missing Sophie and Lisa – although they can be bitches, at the end of the day I'm probably closer to them than to anyone. I mean, I live with them. They're practically family.

But Lauren's someone who could become a real soul-mate. Isn't it funny how sometimes you can instantly connect with people? How, despite being almost strangers, you can feel that you have known someone all your life? The ideal is for this to happen with a man, a potential soulmate, life-partner, but it can, honestly, be just as gratifying when it happens with a friend, someone like Lauren.

And thank God I've found her, because the more I think about it the more I realize that it really wouldn't have been much fun, spending so much time on my own, particularly as Brad seems to be starting to take me slightly for granted. I mean, think about it. I've flown all this way to be with him, I've even changed my flight for him, and he hasn't had the decency to take time off work.

Admittedly, he's busy, but he seems to be getting busier

and busier with every passing day, which doesn't seem to be exactly fair on me, but before I get too pissed off he is the greatest lover ever, and he is sweet to me. Hell, he loves me, for heaven's sake. What could be better than that?

So I meet Lauren at the gym, and we work out together, which is much more fun than working out alone, and truth to be told I'm starting to get the eensiest, weensiest bit bored with the gym, and on the way out we bump into Jenny, who, it seems, is starting to make an effort.

'This is my friend Lauren,' I say to Jenny, partly to be friendly and partly to goad Jenny, to see whether she'd still be rude to a friend of mine. 'And this is Jenny.'

'Hi,' says Lauren with a friendly smile.

'Hi,' says Jenny warmly, or at least warmly for her. 'Nice to meet you.'

'Working hard?' I try, still stuck for conversation with this difficult woman.

'God, it's gone crazy in here,' says Jenny, rolling her eyes to the ceiling. 'Your poor boyfriend's run off his feet.'

Now that is a result. It's the first time Jenny has referred to Brad as my boyfriend, and is this just because Lauren's here or is some of the frostiness disappearing?

'Poor you.' I say warmly. 'Don't let him work you too hard.'

'Don't worry,' says Jenny. 'It's all part of the job. Anyway, have a good day.' She smiles as she disappears, and I turn to Lauren with my jaw practically on the floor.

'Was it my imagination or was she reasonably friendly?'

Lauren shrugs. 'She seemed fine to me. Why? Isn't she normally?'

'Maybe it's just me, but the last couple of times we've met she's been the bitch from hell.'

'She's probably just jealous of you,' says Lauren as we walk to the changing room. 'She's not exactly a goddess is she?'

'Yeah, but neither was I, and I know what it's like.'

'Have you told her that you used to be like her?'

'I tried, but she didn't want to know.'

'It's tough isn't it? Looking at you now, I have a problem believing you used to be fat.'

I sigh and run my fingers through my hair. 'Me too,' I say with an uncomfortable laugh. 'But I was, and I know how unhappy it makes you, and I can see so much of me in Jenny.'

'What if you tried to help her?'

'I don't think she'd accept it.'

'Maybe she's one of those people who's happy the size she is.'

'Next you'll be telling me she's got a gland problem.'

'Maybe she has.'

'Bollocks. The only reason anyone's that size is because they eat too much. Trust me. I know.'

'Look,' says Lauren. 'Why are you getting so worked up about her? She's only Brad's bloody PA isn't she?'

I nod.

'Exactly. She doesn't have anything to do with your life, and, while I admit that it's always a good idea to get their secretaries or PAs or whatever on your side, she seems perfectly fine now, so just relax about it.'

'Maybe you're right.' And I should relax and I should

forget about it, but during lunch, even as I'm laughing with Lauren, and Lauren whoops with joy, I can't quite get Jenny out of my head, and I can't quite figure out why.

'So come over to me at seven tonight, okay?' I scribble down my address.

'Bloody hell,' says Lauren, simultaneously taking the piece of paper and looking at her watch. 'It's four o'clock! Where on earth did the afternoon go?'

'Who cares,' I laugh and kiss her on the cheek. 'At least it went. See you later,' and I wave as we walk off in opposite directions.

When I get home there's a message from Brad on the answerphone. I call him back, miraculously he's not in a meeting, and he apologizes profusely for not being around in the evening. 'What will you do?' he asks.

'I think I'll just pop out for a quick drink with Lauren. What time will you be home?'

'Not late,' he says. 'Around nine?' It's a question, and I say that's fine.

'I love you, baby,' he says, his voice as smooth as honey. 'I'll make it up to you.'

'That's okay.' I say.

'I love you too,' I add. As an afterthought.

So I glue myself to the television set for the rest of the afternoon, and finally at six o'clock, I start getting ready to go out, and I know this must sound crazy but I feel more excited than I've felt in ages. I shower, dry my hair, take an incredible amount of time putting on my make-up, and choose a little black number for tonight. 'What the hell,' I say out loud, modelling in front of the mirror. 'Why not?'

At seven on the dot the doorbell rings, and there, on the doorstep, is Lauren, equally done up, and we both laugh.

'Thank God,' says Lauren. 'I thought I'd gone a bit OTT, but you obviously had the same idea. Now we can go clacking off to take this town by storm.'

'Do you think everyone can tell we're English?' We're standing side by side in front of the mirror in the hall.

'Dunno really,' says Lauren. 'I'd say from the neck up we look like two Californian babes, but from the neck down, tarted up like this, we're as English as tea and scones, which can only be a good thing.'

'What do you mean?'

'The Americans love our quaint accent. How posh can you be?'

I put on my best Queen's English accent. 'The rain in Spain stays mainly on the plain.'

'In Hertford, Hereford and Hampshire, hurricanes hardly ever happen,' says Lauren, and we both give each other high fives in the classic American style.

'Before we go you've got to show me round,' says Lauren, already peering round doorways, so I naturally give her the full guided tour.

'I'm not surprised you're staying,' says Lauren, when she's inspected every room, every gadget, every appliance. 'It's bloody gorgeous.'

'You're right,' I smile. 'It is bloody gorgeous. And I'm bloody lucky.'

'That you are,' says Lauren, and linking arms we leave the house.

*

341

The restaurant's so well hidden from the paparazzi we almost miss the bloody place. Eventually, after trooping up and down the road, Lauren spies a lone doorman standing outside a huge pair of cast-iron doors.

'Maybe that's it?' she says doubtfully, because there are no signs, no windows, nothing.

'Let's go and ask.' Where did this new-found confidence come from? We troop up to the doorman, but before we can even open our mouths he has said good evening to us, and swung open the door.

'Are we in the right place?' I whisper, as Lauren strides down the hallway through to the double doors at the end.

'I bloody well hope so,' she whispers back. 'I haven't got the nerve to ask, it sounds so naff. We'll soon find out,' she says, pushing open the next set of doors, and, sure enough, we step into the restaurant. At least I hope it's *the* restaurant. It could be any restaurant, except when we look at the other side of the room we see a huge, stainless-steel bar running along the whole length of one wall, and we know this must be it. Even this early in the evening there are scores of people crowded around, all busy talking to one another and scouring the room at the same time, just to check that someone more interesting hasn't arrived.

'Thank God,' says Lauren with a sigh. 'This, finally, feels like home. In fact, if I close my eyes I could almost pretend I'm in Saint.'

'Saint?'

'You must know Saint. The bar?'

'Oh of course,' I lie. 'Saint.'

'Please allow me to buy you a drink,' says a smooth,

swarthy man with chiselled cheekbones and come-to-bed eyes.

'No, thank you.' I drag Lauren away before she gets the chance to completely melt away. 'We're fine,' and I pull her to the other end of the bar.

'What did you do that for?' pouts Lauren. 'He was delicious.'

'He was disgusting! Lauren, for God's sake, talk about being in love with himself.'

'With those cheekbones I'd be in love with myself too,' she says, looking over my shoulder and trying to find the guy, trying to give him meaningful eye signals.

'You can do much better than that,' I say purposefully, leaning over the bar and trying to catch the barman's attention, which doesn't take long at all because he's staring at Lauren like it's his birthday, Christmas and Thanksgiving all rolled into one. 'Ladies,' he says, with a well-practised smile. 'What can I get you?'

'Phwooargh,' whispers Lauren, eyes glued to his well-muscled torso as he pours us cocktails, and, I have to say, she has a point. 'Now he's much more my type.'

'You are incorrigible!' I laugh, but if I didn't have my gorgeous Brad I'd be thinking the same thing.

'It's all right for you,' says Lauren, reading my mind. 'You've got a man. And he's divine. I've only had the crap-in-bed Charlie, and I'm still on the look-out.'

'Can you just try and make it a bit less obvious?' I whisper. 'Nothing puts a man off more than a woman who's desperate.' I'm interrupted by the barman, who places the drinks in front of us and holds Lauren's eye for about twenty seconds longer than is altogether necessary.

'What were you saying about men being put off?' smirks Lauren, sipping from her cocktail and checking out the barman's bottom.

'Oh shut up! Cheers.'

'Here's to men!' says Lauren, clinking her glass to mine.

'Here's to friendship!' I say.

'Here's to both!' And we take a good, long swig.

The cocktails are a lot stronger than Jemima and Lauren realized, and two hours later they're both rip-roaringly drunk. Men surround them all evening, and Jemima, despite despairing of Lauren's hunting earlier on, is having the time of her life. Never has she felt more beautiful, more desirable, and she's flirting and laughing as if she's looked this way, had this much attention, all her life.

'I've gotta have a piss,' says Lauren, half falling off her stool and stumbling off into the distance. Funny, she thinks, as she holds the door open for a girl who looks very familiar as she scuttles off with her head down. 'Isn't that girl that Jenny?' But no, she thinks. It can't be. What would someone like that be doing among all these beautiful people here?

At 10.30 Jemima looks at her watch. 'Shit!' she shouts. 'I'm supposed to be home.'

'Don't worry about it,' giggles Lauren. 'Play the *Rules*! Be hard to get for a little while!'

'I've got to go,' says Jemima, who's slightly more sober than Lauren, 'and you'd better go too.'

'No!' says Lauren, banging her fist on the table to emphasize her point, except she misses the table and ends up banging her thigh. 'We're staying,' except it comes out 'shtaying'.

'Nope.' Jemima gets up and pulls Lauren to her feet. 'I'm putting you in a taxi.'

'Just give me one sec. Oh shit. Shit.' She turns to Jemima. 'What's my phone number?'

'I don't know,' says Jemima. 'Can we just go?'

'Not until you've looked up my phone number.'

Jemima digs out her address book and shows Lauren her phone number, and as Lauren tries to focus on it she shouts the number out to the barman, who's hovering near by with pen and paper in hand.

'Got it,' he mouths. 'I'll call you.'

'All right,' says Lauren, as the pair stagger out. 'Well would you bloody believe it? Now *that's* what I call a result.'

Amazing how quickly you can sober up when there's a crisis. Not that Jemima's having a crisis exactly, it's just that she expected Brad to be home waiting for her. She didn't expect to come home to an empty house.

'Brad?' she calls, after fumbling at the door with the key for what feels like hours. She manages to get in, dumps her bag, and slowly climbs up the stairs. 'Sweetie?' she says softly, pushing open the bedroom door. 'Oh,' she says, seeing the bed's empty. She checks every room in the house, but he's not there, and she's not feeling good about this. Not feeling good at all.

*

Why does everyone else seem to have a hangover the next day, whereas I get the headache, the nausea, later on that very same evening. There's only one thing for it, coffee, and, trying very hard to focus on everything in the kitchen, I make myself a strong black coffee, which, fifteen minutes after drinking, seems to have the desired effect and I feel a lot more sober than when I first walked in.

But where the hell is Brad? Didn't he say he'd be home around nine? Why isn't he here? The more I think about it, the more I start worrying that something terrible's happened, because for all his busyness, he's not unreliable, he wouldn't just turn up late, not when he knows I'm waiting. Surely.

Car crash? Accident? What? Where is Brad and why isn't he home? I check my watch again. It's 11 p.m., two hours after he said he'd be home. Maybe he came home, realized I wasn't here and went out again. He'll be home any minute. I'll wait up for him.

But by midnight there's still no sign of him and now I'm starting to feel sick with worry. If I were at home I'd know what to do, but here I don't even know what the hospitals are called, and anyway I'm probably being silly, maybe something came up.

I get into bed and watch television to try and take my mind off things, but every time I hear something, some little noise, my ears prick up and I expect to hear his key in the lock. Except I don't. So I keep flicking, and suddenly I find myself watching a travel programme, the featured destination today being London, and this huge wave of homesickness washes over me as the camera pans over Big Ben, the Thames, the Houses of Parliament.

Ben works near there, near the Thames, near the South Bank. I wonder what Ben's doing now? And that's my very last thought before falling fast asleep.

CHAPTER TWENTY-FIVE

I thought my hangover would be over by this morning, I thought the headache and nausea of last night was it. Jesus, was I wrong. It takes me a few seconds to orientate myself, to remember where I am, why my head's pounding, and then, when I roll over and see the other half of the bed hasn't been slept in, I start to feel even more sick and I remember that Brad didn't come home last night, and by the looks of things he hasn't been home at all.

My heart starts to pound, and a wave of nausea washes over me as I shake my head, trying to clear it, to work out what is going on. And then I hear noises from the kitchen, plates clashing together, the scrape of cutlery.

I pull on a dressing-gown, and, with hand to my head to protect my hangover from any more of the brutal noise from the other end of the flat, I slowly make my way to the kitchen and stand quietly in the doorway, watching Brad, wondering what to do next, what to say.

He's humming to himself as he stirs scrambled eggs on the stove, and on the counter next to him is a wooden breakfast tray, immaculately laid for breakfast for one. There's a basket of muffins, a glass of orange juice, coffee, and a vase filled with huge, dewy red roses.

What is all this about? I don't say anything for a while.

Just lean against the door-frame watching him, and after a few seconds Brad turns round and jumps as he sees me.

'Hi, baby,' he says, coming over to kiss me on the lips, and I can't do this, I can't pretend that everything's okay when it quite obviously isn't. I feel as if he's broken my trust so I turn my head away, leaving Brad to skim my cheek.

'I'm sorry,' he says. 'I am so sorry about last night.'

'What happened?' Even I'm surprised at how cold my voice is. How stern. 'Where were you?'

'The meeting just went on and on, and it was so late I ended up sleeping at the office.'

'Where in the office?'

'I swear,' says Brad, seeing that I don't believe him. 'I slept on the couch in the lobby. The maids couldn't believe it when they walked in this morning.'

'Why didn't you phone, at least let me know where you were?' It comes out like a whine and I have to remember to be more angry, less pleading.

'I knew you were going out, and by the time the meeting finished it was so late I didn't want to worry you.'

'So you just let me think you'd been in a car crash or something?'

'Oh I'm sorry, baby, I didn't think for a moment you'd be that worried. I figured you'd be fast asleep and by the time you woke up in the morning I'd be home.'

'I can't believe you've been this selfish.' Careful, careful. I don't really want to be angry, because this is the first time I've ever had a proper boyfriend, and look how gorgeous he is, and if I really do lose my temper I might scare him away, and if that happened what would happen to me?

'JJ, I'm sorry. You're right, I was selfish, but it won't happen again, I promise you.' Brad looks sorry, he looks like he means it, and with his head hung low he looks so contrite, so like a little boy, so completely vulnerable and gorgeous, I have to forgive him. What else can I do?

I know you probably think I shouldn't forgive him, I should make him feel guilty a bit longer, but the story is plausible enough as long as you don't look too deeply, and I don't want to look too deeply, I want to believe him. Despite the fact that more and more problems with this relationship seem to be emerging every day, I want to at least pretend that everything's rosy, because look at us. We look so good together. We're the perfect couple.

'Okay,' I say, shrugging.

'Okay?' His face lights up. 'Does that mean I'm forgiven?'

'I suppose so.'

'God, I love you, JJ,' he says, putting his arms around me and kissing me on the nape of the neck, the one place he knows is guaranteed to send shivers shooting down my spine.

I lean into him, smelling his smell, feeling the light stubble on his face with my cheek, and slowly I allow myself to feel better. Brad circles my back lightly, moving his hand slowly down until it's sliding in between my legs, and I can't help the small gasp that comes out of my mouth, and then the pair of us are sliding down the wall to the kitchen floor, and soon the breakfast has been forgotten, and the only sounds emerging from the kitchen are our soft whispers and groans of pleasure.

'I do love you,' I say to him afterwards, after possibly the best sex we've ever had, when I'm feeling guilty at making him feel guilty, when he obviously loves me so much. 'And I'm sorry for being a bitch.'

Oh Jemima, stop being such a wimp, you weren't a bitch in the slightest. Perhaps you should have been, but more importantly you offered Brad the information that you love him, and you said it first, it wasn't a reply to him. Do you really, Jemima? Do you really love him?

Lying on that floor, feeling the muscles in his back, for the first time Jemima starts to believe that she might love him, that everything may well work out after all.

'I'm taking the day off today,' says Brad, as he goes in to take his shower. 'I want to spend the whole day with you, with no interruptions.' He kisses my shoulderblade as I walk past him, naked, to the bedroom, with, and you'll be very glad to hear this, no inhibitions whatsoever.

'Really? The whole day?'

'Really,' he says, turning away. 'I thought we could have lunch, maybe go blading later. Whatever you'd like.'

'I'd love that. I don't mind where we go, as long as I'm with you. The only thing I have to do is get started on the column I was telling you about. Maybe we could go star-spotting? I've got to work out exactly what I'm going to write about.'

'Celebrity gossip is the last thing you should be worrying about in this town,' Brad says with a smile.

'All you have to do is pick up a copy of *Daily Variety* and the *Hollywood Reporter* and you've got everything you need.'

'Well.' I'm doubtful. 'Maybe if we got back in the afternoon I could do some work later on.'

'Good,' he says, closing the bathroom door. 'That sounds perfect. I'm just going to take a shower. Won't be long.'

The phone rings as I'm lying dreamily on the bed, going over every inch of Brad's body in my mind. I don't normally pick up the phone here, it still feels a bit strange, answering the phone in a house that isn't yours, but Brad's in the shower, and there seems little point in letting the machine pick up. It might be important.

All I hear is a long groan then, 'JJ, it's me, Lauren. Just tell me, are you feeling as disgusting as me?'

I laugh. 'No, not even a fraction as disgusting as you. You had far more than me to drink, remember?'

Lauren groans again. 'I wish I *could* remember. I can't remember a bloody thing. How did we get home?'

I tell her about our ride home in the taxi, about her leaning out of the window and singing old Abba songs at the top of her voice, about her very nearly throwing up in the back seat.

'I really disgraced myself didn't I?' she says.

'Absolutely!'

'Really?' Lauren's voice picks up. 'Tell me, tell me. Did I pull? Did I give out my phone number to any gorgeous men?'

'Actually, you did. You screamed it from one side of the restaurant to the other for the barman, but I think every man in the place was writing it down.'

'Oh my God! It's coming back to me. The barman, I remember the barman! Was he as handsome as I think he was?'

'You are a complete nightmare!' I laugh. 'Yes, he was as handsome as you remember. You scored better than me.'

'You weren't out to score. You've got the gorgeous Brad. So was he tucked up in bed wondering what you were up to?'

'No, he wasn't.' I don't know whether to tell Lauren or not, because I've got a sneaky feeling I know what she'd say, which would, in fact, probably be the same thing Geraldine would say. In other words, they'd both tell me to be careful, not to accept things at face value, not to believe him, and, stupid as this may sound, I don't want to hear this right now, I want to believe everything's fine, that he was telling the truth.

I listen to check the water's still running, Brad's in the shower so he won't be able to hear, and then I tell a tiny white lie. 'He wasn't in when I got back, his meeting ran on, but he came home when I was in bed.' Not quite a lie, I just omitted the fact that it happened to be this morning.

'Hmm,' says Lauren. 'How late was he?'

'Not very. Everything's fine. I'm not worried so why should you be?'

'Okay. If everything's fine with you then it's fine with me. So what are you up to today? How about lunch?'

'I can't today, Brad's taken the day off work and we're going out.'

'Sounds like a guilty man to me.' Now that's exactly what I didn't want to hear.

'Sounds like a man in love to me,' I say with a false ring of confidence, hoping to convince her, hoping to convince myself.

'Well, have a good day,' says Lauren. 'Don't worry about me, all by myself.'

'Come with!' I say, trying to sound as if I mean it, because even though I think Lauren's fantastic, I'm so looking forward to spending a whole day with Brad, just the two of us, on our own, I don't mean it at all. 'I'd love you to come with and Brad won't mind, he'd love to meet you!' Which isn't exactly true, because Brad has shown surprisingly little interest in what I do or who I meet when I'm not with him.

'Yes,' says Lauren, with a hint of sarcasm in her voice. 'Because I really love playing gooseberry.'

'You wouldn't be.' Even I can hear that I don't sound sincere. 'Brad and I aren't like that.'

'Brad and I. There you go. That's a sure sign if ever there was one.'

'So you're not coming?' I think I've just about managed to hide the relief.

'Nope. But thanks, JJ, it's really nice of you to ask me.'

'Will you be okay? What are you going to do?'

'I might catch a movie this afternoon. Oh, hang on, my call waiting's going.'

I sit on the phone and wait. And wait. And wait. I hate this, I hate people who leave you hanging on the line for hours. Just as I'm about to put the phone down Lauren comes back.

'JJ? Oh my God! I'm so sorry, but that was him! He called!'

'Who?'

'Bill! The barman!'

'And?'

'And I now have plans for today. We're meeting for lunch.'

'Just behave yourself,' I laugh. 'We don't want you getting into trouble.'

'I will. Behave, that is. I don't plan on getting into trouble just yet.'

We both laugh and say goodbye as Brad walks out of the bathroom.

'Who was that?'

'Lauren.'

'Who's Lauren?' Typical. That's how much attention Brad has been paying to my life.

'Brad!' I hit him playfully. 'You know exactly who Lauren is. She's my new friend, the one I met at the Broadway Deli, the one I was out with last night.'

'I totally forgot you went out with her last night. Where did you go?' Brad's towelling his hair as he talks.

'We went to that new restaurant on Main Street.'

Brad stops towelling for a second then starts again, but slower, more thoughtfully. 'Which restaurant?' he asks, his voice sounding slightly strained.

'The Pepper,' I tell him. 'It was fantastic.'

'Oh,' says Brad, picking up speed.

'Have you been there?' I ask.

'Is this a trick question?' Brad asks, putting down the towel, and maybe I'm going crazy but I could swear he's paled underneath his golden tan.

'What on earth do you mean?' I ask, trying to work out whether he has gone pale, and if he has, why.

'You know I've been there,' he says carefully.

'No, I don't,' I say, completely bewildered, I mean, what is going on here?

'I thought I told you I went there.'

'No, silly,' I laugh, relieved that I must have been imagining it, that there's nothing sinister going on. 'You didn't.'

'Oh, I thought I did,' Brad says, adding, 'I went on the opening night.'

'Nope, you didn't tell me that. Fabulous isn't it?' I say, sitting down at the dressing table and picking up a hairbrush.

'Mmmm,' says Brad, as he crosses the room, takes the hairbrush from my hand and stands behind me, watching me in the mirror as he brushes my hair.

'That feels so nice,' I murmur, as I close my eyes.

'It's supposed to,' says Brad, as a thump down the hall makes us both start.

'Mail,' he says, putting down the brush, and a few seconds later he calls out, 'JJ, there's something here for you.'

'For me?' What could have come for me? I feel a buzz of excitement as I run down the hall to the front door, where Brad hands me a letter addressed in Geraldine's distinctive handwriting.

'It's from my friend Geraldine in London,' I tell Brad, who's not really listening, and I smile as I rip open the envelope and draw out these newspaper pages. I read the compliments slip and laugh, thinking that Geraldine never changes, and wondering how she's getting on with the Top Tips column, and then I open the pages that are clipped on to the slip, wondering what they are.

'Jesus Christ!' My hand starts shaking and I have to put my hand over my heart to stop it pounding.

'What's the matter?' Brad looks at me in alarm.

'Nothing, nothing.'

Brad walks over and looks at what's written on the pages. 'Who's Ben Williams?' he says.

'Just someone I used to work with.' I can't take my eyes off the page, I scan all the pictures, read the headlines, go back to the pictures. It's Ben. My beloved Ben. Oh my God, I'm not supposed to feel like this. I look at Brad in alarm, but his back's turned to me, he doesn't see the expression on my face. So I stand there and I start to read, with my heart tumbling around at the sight of the man I thought I'd forgotten about or, at the very least, put firmly in my past.

'Sure he's not some old boyfriend of yours?' Brad's smiling, but I don't return the smile, I can't look up from the pictures of Ben, and I don't say anything at all, I just walk into the bedroom and collapse on to the bed, trying to stop the pages trembling as I devour every single word.

I'm not entirely sure how I manage to calm down, but I do, and I even resist the urge to pick up the phone and call Geraldine. I'm not sure how I feel. Confused might be the best description. I really thought I was over Ben, I really thought that I'd finally found happiness with Brad, and that I'd always think Ben was good-looking but that it would be in an objective way, that it wouldn't actually affect me personally.

And I'm confused because I can't believe that the mere sight of him, simply reading about a man whom I know, a man I thought I once loved, can make me feel like the

357

Jemima Jones of old, the Jemima Jones I thought I'd said goodbye to.

But Ben's not here, I tell myself, and even if he were there would be no guarantees. Okay, so I look completely different, but he was never interested in the past, he probably wouldn't be interested now.

And I look at Brad, at this huge, golden lion of a man, and I know that he could have his pick of women, but he has chosen me, which must mean I'm very lucky. And okay, sometimes I worry that maybe we don't have as much in common as perhaps we should, and occasionally I do find myself comparing him to Ben and, apart from the looks front, he seems to fail pretty miserably, which is why I try not to do it all that often, and we may not have the same sort of teasing friendship I had with Ben, but then Ben never wanted me and Brad does.

And he is good to me, he treats me well. Okay, so last night he slipped up, but work is work, and I have to try and understand that side of his life. I am lucky. I must be. I mean, look at him.

Oh yes. One more thing. The sex, of course, is amazing.

And we do have a blissful day. We go for a long, leisurely walk right up to the end of the Santa Monica pier, where we sit on a bench facing the ocean, and Brad tries to persuade me to go on a fairground ride, but I decline because I'd feel too much like a tourist and right now I'm trying to feel like a native, like Brad's wife, and, considering it's only been four and a half weeks, I think I'm doing a pretty good job.

We walk back along the pier, hand in hand, and I smile to myself as I watch the other women watching Brad, and

Brad makes me laugh when he points out one bizarrely dressed woman and whispers, 'Would you look at that? What *is* she wearing? God, cowboy boots with those awful legs and that dreadful mini-skirt.'

And I try very hard to shove Ben to the very back of my mind, I try to keep reminding myself how lucky I am to have a man like Brad.

We kick around in the ocean like a couple of kids, yelling and screaming as we splash one another with water, and then, after smooching in the sand to yells of encouragement from a group of boys sitting around a ghetto blaster, we continue walking until we hit Shutters on the Beach, according to Brad the best hotel in the area.

We walk through the lobby and it is beautiful. The polished wood floors, the over-stuffed white damask sofas, the beautiful bowls of fresh roses that sit on the antique furniture, and we walk through to sit on the terrace overlooking the water, feasting on delicious food, feasting on one another.

And after lunch we go back home, pick up the car, and Brad drives me up to the Pacific Palisades, where we park the car and take a two-hour hike into the mountains. Now this, breathing in the clean, fresh air and striding alongside my gorgeous man, is what life should be about.

And when we get back we share a bath, and naturally one thing leads to another and we end up having frantic wet, soapy foreplay in the bathtub, when the phone rings.

'Leave it,' I murmur, just on the brink of orgasm.

'I can't,' moans Brad, standing up and going to the phone in the bedroom, as I groan and roll over. 'Hello?'

I hear him say. 'Oh, hi.' There's a silence for a bit, while I assume he's listening to someone and I pull a towel off the rail and wrap it around myself, still basking in the delicious glow of afterlove, and wondering how on earth I could have missed out on this incredible feeling for so many years. And then, I know this is crazy, but I'm sure I hear Brad whispering.

Eventually he puts the phone down, but he doesn't come back to the bathroom, he goes to the kitchen, so I follow him in there wondering whether I'm going mad.

'Who was on the phone?' I say, trying to make it sound like a casual inquiry.

'The phone? Oh, just work.'

'Why were you whispering?'

He looks at me as if I *am* crazy. 'What are you talking about?' he says. 'I wasn't whispering.' And I believe him.

We would have thought this strange. Actually, we probably would have thought it a hell of a lot more than strange, but Jemima doesn't think like this. Jemima refuses to think like this, and when Brad leaves, half an hour later, to sort out a problem at work, he tells her he loves her and she believes it.

And when she eventually sits down at Brad's desk to do some work of her own, she reads the piece about Ben Williams again. Ben was a fantasy, she thinks. Brad's a reality. I'm much happier with Brad than I could ever have been with Ben, and with that she opens the *Hollywood Reporter* and starts scouring the page for stories.

CHAPTER TWENTY-SIX

Ben meant to call Jemima, really he did, but when you're a celebrity and you have a work schedule that means you're working pretty much all the time, and when you're not working you're going to launches or opening supermarkets or giving interviews to the press, it's very easy to forget to do things like call old friends.

It's even easier to forget to call them when you're good-looking and single and you've slept with your boss, which seems to have caused the two of you to have entirely different reactions. You think it's the biggest mistake of your life and you're trying to forget about it, but your boss is spending all her time trying to figure out how to orchestrate a repeat experience.

For the last three months one of the producers on the show, Simon, has been trying to arrange an interview with Alexia Aldridge, the hottest actress in Hollywood. The producer and his team of researchers have made hundreds of phonecalls to her agent, her publicist, her assistant. They've sent hundreds of faxes, promising her huge amounts of airtime, promising to pay for her flight, her accommodation, if only they can have an exclusive interview when her new film opens in London.

The agent said yes, it was a good idea, could they put it on a fax, which they did. They never heard from him again, despite sending numerous additional faxes. The publicist for the film said yes, it was a good idea, could they put it on a fax, which they did. They never heard from her again. The assistant said yes, it was a good idea, the best person to talk to was the publicist. The publicist, when they finally managed to get hold of her, apologized for not getting back and said she'd spoken to Alexia, who would love to do it, it's just that things were a bit busy at the moment, and perhaps they should talk to the film publicist nearer the time. This time the film publicist said yes, it was a good idea, and thousands of faxes later they had agreed a time, a date and a place, not mutually convenient, merely convenient for Ms Aldridge.

There was just one problem, and this problem was becoming Diana Macpherson's problem. Alexia had been in London recently, and she happened to have watched *London Nights*. There was only one person she'd allow to interview her. Ben Williams. Who else?

Under normal circumstances, the production team at *London Nights* would have told Alexia Aldridge that the interview was going to be done by their showbiz reporter – funnily enough, the job that Ben was doing when she spotted him – and that it would be impossible for the main presenter to do it.

But Alexia Aldridge rarely gives interviews. Not quite in the same league, or the same age, as Streisand, nevertheless she is something of an enigma, and that she has agreed to talk at all makes it something of a worldwide scoop, irrespective of what she may or may not actually reveal.

And Diana Macpherson, who should be over the moon at this brilliant coup, is actually not very happy. Not happy at all. Usually she would be buying champagne for the whole crew, but just recently she has started to think more about her personal life. She's started watching mothers in the park, and once or twice she's even stopped to coo at particularly attractive babies. Diana Macpherson has never thought of herself as a woman, more of a working machine, but for some strange reason she's started fantasizing of late about relationships, marriage, babies.

Not sex. That's always available when you're as powerful as her, but Diana wants more than just sex now, and, despite initially targeting Ben as a new shag, Diana now sees him in a completely different light. Diana now thinks that Ben might just be the man she's been looking for. And think what beautiful babies he'd make. She does. Frequently.

And she was convinced that she pulled it off the other night. Ben may have been trying to avoid her ever since – or is that her imagination – but it must have meant something to him, and anyway, she forgives him because after all, he is young, he doesn't yet know what's good for him. And Diana Macpherson would be very good for him. In every way.

The last thing she wants is to send Ben to Los Angeles, but it looks as if, this time, she really has no other choice.

So now we can understand why she's not happy. Plus, of course, there's the additional problem of finding someone to replace Ben while he spends the best part of a week in America. Plus there is the cost of sending an entire film crew to the other side of the world. Plus she could be left with egg all over her face if Alexia Aldridge changes her mind, or throws a wobbly, or decides to clam up on film. And Alexia Aldridge is young, single and tremendously beautiful. But no, Diana tells herself, she might want Ben to interview her, but she'd never bother getting involved with someone as lowly as a television presenter from England.

Allow me to let you into a little secret here to help you fully understand why Diana is allowing Ben to slip from her grasp. Diana Macpherson is scared of one thing. Ratings. Diana Macpherson has reached her position of power by being clever, by making good moves, and securing an exclusive interview with Alexia Aldridge, albeit a very expensive one, is a good move, and she's not about to let her get away, even if it means letting Ben Williams get away. Temporarily.

So Diana calls Ben into her office to tell him the news, and ignores the fact that Ben walks in looking as if he's been called into a torture chamber.

'We've got the interview with Alexia Aldridge,' she tells him.

'Great,' says Ben, looking at the door and wondering how quickly he can get out of there.

'But she'll only do it on one condition.'

'Hmm?'

'That you do the interview.'

'Okay. Fine,' says Ben, standing up and getting ready to go. 'Is that all?'

'No, Ben. Sit down. She can't fly over here because she's getting ready to start her next film, which means we have to fly you over there.'

'Over where?' Now Ben's interested.

'Los Angeles.'

His face lights up. 'I've never been to Los Angeles! God, how exciting.'

'It's not going to be fun, Ben,' Diana says sternly. 'I'm sending you out in two weeks' time with Simon and a film crew. You're there to work, and it will be hard work. And' – she pauses – 'I want the best fucking interview I've ever seen. Got that?' Diana, hackles raised at Ben's rejection, is being more professional than Ben has ever seen her.

'Yes, Diana,' he says meekly. 'I'll deliver the goods.'

'I bet that's what you say to all the girls,' she says, smiling, unable to resist the temptation to flirt just a little.

Shit, thinks Ben, who just smiles sweetly, laughs at her little joke and backs out of the office.

He runs over to Simon. 'Have you heard?' he says, enthusiasm and excitement written all over his face.

'Yeah. Bloody brilliant isn't it?'

'But we're there to work, Simon, and it will be fucking hard work.' Ben does an impersonation of Diana that's frighteningly accurate, and Simon falls about laughing.

'Fuck that, mate,' he says. 'It's gonna be interview in a day, then birds and booze the rest of the week.'

'Simon,' says Ben, in a serious tone. 'You're a man after my own heart.'

Ben spends the rest of the day trying to keep his excitement in check. 'Lucky bastard,' says each researcher as they pass his desk, for Ben is not a celebrity to them, he is merely a work colleague, someone to have a laugh with. By mid-afternoon he's calm enough to get some work done, and he spends the rest of the day ploughing through press cuttings about Alexia Aldridge. If he weren't such an avid video-watcher he'd have to start watching her films, but luckily for Ben he's seen them all, and the only thing he has to do tonight is phone Richard to make him green with envy.

The two weeks have flown by for Ben. The night before he's due to leave, while he's throwing clothes into a suitcase, he suddenly remembers Jemima. Should he call her now? Will she still be in Los Angeles? Should he tell her he's coming? No, he decides, he'll take a chance and surprise her when he gets there.

Coincidence perhaps? This mini-excursion of Ben's might seem little more than another coincidence, particularly given that, thanks to Geraldine, Ben has stomped back into Jemima's consciousness with a bang, but maybe it is more than that. Maybe fate is finally working to give Ben and Jemima the happiness for which they've both longed, the happiness they each thought they'd found, Ben in his dream job, Jemima in her dream man.

Perhaps neither of them has been quite as fulfilled as they'd hoped, and perhaps fate will sort that out once and for all. On the other hand, that could be quite wrong. Ben and Jemima might miss each other completely. After all, Ben's going to be doing all that hard work, and he's only there for a few days. And Jemima may make it work with Brad, because on the face of it he certainly looks like her dream man, but at this precise moment in time Jemima Jones isn't having a particularly good day. Admittedly, these things are relative, and perhaps it is just because yesterday, the day she spent with Brad, was so perfect that she was bound to be on a bit of a downer today.

At least she's found some stories. She's just putting the finishing touches to her column, for which she's managed to cobble together stuff from the local papers, together with a review of the Pepper, and as she finishes reading it she decides that actually it's quite good after all. If you didn't know, you'd never dream that Jemima was spending most of the time on her own, because Jemima has painted Los Angeles as the epitome of glamour and excitement. Which I suppose it can be. It's just that it isn't like that for her.

When she finishes she puts her head in her hands and sighs, thinking about what happened earlier today, when she went to the gym, wondering why on earth Jenny seems to blow so hot and cold.

'Hi, Jenny,' I said, when I passed her in the hallway. Jenny ignored me.

'Jenny?' That's it. I'm not taking this shit any more, and I stopped feeling sorry for her a long time ago. Well, this morning, anyway. Jenny turned round with a sigh.

'What?' Jenny said, sounding bored.

'What exactly is your problem?' I'd had enough and I was determined not to let her get away with this.

'I'm really likely to share my problems with *you*,' Jenny said sarcastically.

'Look, I'm really trying to be friendly, and you're just—' – I was practically spluttering with rage – 'bloody rude.'

'Bloody rude am I? Well I don't remember anyone saying I had to be nice to you.'

'I'm your boss's girlfriend, for God's sake, it's not that you have to, it's just that I've never done anything to hurt you and it would be nice if you were nice.'

'Being Brad's *girlfriend*,' Jenny said, putting a nasty emphasis on the word, 'means shit, as far as I'm concerned. You think you can fly over here, with your blonde hair and your skinny legs, and just take over. Well you can't.'

'What the hell are you talking about? I'm not trying to take over, I'm only in here once a day.'

'Forget it,' said Jenny, shaking her head. 'I don't like you, and I'm never gonna like you. Let's just leave it at that.' And she started walking away.

'No.' I couldn't help myself, I grabbed her arm. 'I won't just leave it at that.'

Jenny looked with disdain at my hand on her arm before shaking it off, marching back up to me and saying very slowly, 'Why don't you just go screw yourself.' She stood for a few seconds, evidently enjoying the shock on my face, and then she walked off, leaving me standing there shaking like a leaf.

If I'd been able to find Brad I would have told him what had happened, told him to sort it out, sack her, something, but Brad wasn't around, and Lauren wasn't at home, and I've just had to live with this all day, and yes, I'm upset. I'm hurt and upset that someone should hate me for no reason at all, and even though I've chucked all those plans for befriending Jenny out the window, I hate confrontation. However, I can only be pushed so far, and this, as far as I'm now concerned, means war.

*

I go to the kitchen, where I pour myself a diet coke, and then I walk back into the bedroom, climb on the bed and reach for the remote control, but, as I reach across, the glass tips over and spills diet coke all over the white linen sheets.

Shit! I run to the kitchen for the cloth, but no amount of wiping seems to get rid of the stain and I know Brad will go mad because he likes everything to be perfect, but do I know where the sheets are? Do I hell. In a total panic I desperately search the hall cupboards, the bathroom cupboards, the bedroom armoire for spare sheets, but I can't find anything, so eventually, feeling faintly ridiculous, I pick up the phone and dial the gym.

'Charlene? It's JJ. I'm fine. You? Is Brad there? Oh? He's in a meeting? Can you do me a favour, can you just ask him where the clean sheets are, it's an emergency.' I wait for a few minutes, watching the stain, mentally urging Charlene to hurry up.

'In the cupboard at the top of the wardrobe?' I look around the bedroom and see where she means. 'That's great, Charlene. Thanks. Yes, you have a good day too,' and I put the phone down, and just as I'm about to get up the bloody phone rings again and it's Lauren.

'I've just spilt diet coke everywhere, can I call you back? I've got to change the sheets.'

'Bugger the sheets,' says Lauren. 'I've got to tell you about my day from heaven. I'm in love.' She starts to tell me all about 'Bill the horny barman' and screw the sheets, this is much more important, this is my friend for God's sake and the sheets will have to wait.

'You know those times when you meet someone and everything is absolutely perfect?' Lauren asks me.

'You mean, like it was with Charlie?'

'No,' laughs Lauren. 'I mean like when you're a teenager and you have these incredibly romantic experiences which feel like something out of a film, and sex is never really an issue because neither of you is doing it yet.'

'Yes.' And I sort of understand what she's trying to say, even though I never experienced anything of the sort when I was a teenager. My teenage experiences were confined to comfort eating and not being invited to the parties that all the cool people were invited to.

'I swear, that's what it was like with Bill. We just had the most perfect day,' sighs Lauren. 'We met up for a coffee first at that place on, I think it's 2nd Street, the Interactive Café?'

'Yes,' I nod. 'I know the one.'

'And then we went for a walk along the beach, and I felt like a teenager again, we were splashing around in the sea like a couple of kids.'

I smile, because Brad and I were doing exactly the same thing, probably at exactly the same time.

'And then we went for lunch.'

'Don't tell me you went to Shutters on the Beach.'

'No,' says Lauren, bemused. 'Why would we go there?'

'Don't worry about it. So where did you go?'

Lauren continues telling me, and, trying hard not to worry about the stain, I encourage her with snorts of laughter and approval, and then after a few seconds I vaguely become aware that those bleeps that have been bleeping for the last few seconds don't mean the phone is faulty, they mean call waiting.

'Hang on,' I interrupt Lauren. 'I've got another call coming through. How do I work this bloody thing?'

Lauren explains, and I do as she says and press the buttons she tells me to.

'Hello?'

'Still me,' says Lauren.

'Shit. Hang on, let me try again.'

'Hello?'

'Nope, still me.'

'Oh, I give up. It's probably someone really boring for Brad anyway. I'll just ignore it, carry on telling me what happened.' And Lauren does.

What Jemima could never know is that the person trying to get through is Brad. Brad who has lost all his cool, calm, Californian composure. Brad who at this moment is in a blind panic, and is frantically redialling his number, only to be told the person is on the other line and his call will be answered shortly. Which it isn't. 'For fuck's sake, pick up the god-damned phone!' he screams, drawing worried glances from the staff who are milling around outside his office.

'Oh shit!' he shouts, grabbing his car keys and running for the door.

'Brad?' says Jenny, who's been having a meeting with him about new marketing plans. 'Brad? What's the matter?' She stands up, obviously worried, and puts a hand on his arm, but Brad ignores her and just keeps running.

He tears out of the building, jumps in his car and puts his foot down. Ignoring the pedestrians, ignoring his fellow drivers, ignoring the speed limits, Brad shoots off, looking suspiciously like he's about to have a heart attack.

'All right, darling,' says Lauren. 'I'll see you tomorrow.'

'Do you know where he's taking you tonight?'

'No, and I don't care. Can you believe he's changed his shift for me? Thank you, Lord, for finally introducing me to a decent man.'

'I don't want to put a dampener on things,' I say, putting a dampener on things, 'but doesn't this sound vaguely familiar? I mean, what if he's crap in bed?'

'He won't be,' says Lauren. 'You can always tell what a man's going to be like by the way he kisses, and he's the best kisser in the world.'

'I thought Charlie was a good kisser.'

'Yeuch, eurgh, yeuch.' Lauren makes choking, vomiting noises down the phone as I start laughing. 'I was lying. Charlie was a crap kisser.'

'Brad's a great kisser.'

'Yeah, well. He would be.'

'What do you mean?'

'Someone that good-looking must have had loads of practice.'

'He's not the promiscuous type,' I say indignantly.

'I didn't mean that. I just meant he probably spent all his time at school snogging behind the bike sheds. Do you think they have bike sheds here?'

'Nah. I think they probably did it under those things you watch baseball on.'

'What? Oh, you mean those bench things.'

'Mmm. I think they're called bleachers or something.'

'You're probably right. So what are you up to tonight?'

'Don't know. But whatever it is it won't be nearly as exciting as your night.'

'I hope you're right,' says Lauren, laughing. 'Listen, I've gotta go. I've got legs to wax, facials to prepare, moustaches to bleach.'

'You haven't got a moustache!'

'Ah ha! It works then?'

'You're going to do it aren't you?'

'You bet your damn life I am. I'm fed up with playing hard to get and then discovering they can't satisfy you when it's too late. This time round I'm going to make sure he's good at sex right from the beginning.'

'Just make sure you use a condom.'

'Condom? This is California, babe. I'm cutting the fingers off Marigold gloves and using those instead!'

I snort with laughter at the thought. 'Have a good time.'

'I will! I'll call you first thing.' And we both say goodbye, and I look at the stain again, which, much to my horror, looks as if it may well have seeped through to the mattress. I go over to the cupboard in a panic and reach up to try and open the door, but I can't quite reach it, so I drag the chair by the dressing table over, and, balancing precariously on the chair, I just about manage to get the door open.

I reach into the cupboard then cover my head with my arms because a pile of stuff comes out, just missing me, to land on the floor.

'Ouch,' I shout, because it didn't quite miss me, a magazine caught me on my forehead and it bloody well hurts. Right, sheets. I can see them at the bottom and I carefully pull one out before climbing off the chair to gather up the stuff that's now on the floor.

What is all this shit anyway? I start picking up the papers, and then something catches my eye and I kick some papers aside with my foot to see what it is. And I freeze.

No. This cannot be happening. For a few moments the whole world seems to stand still, and I have to close my eyes because maybe, maybe, this is a bad dream and when I open them again this *stuff* will have disappeared and I won't have to deal with it because I'm not sure whether I can, I'm not sure whether I'm experienced enough, or strong enough, and even if I were I don't know whether I could, and oh fuck. Why me. Why is this happening to me?

And I open my eyes and it's not a dream, it's real, and I think I'm going to throw up, but somehow curiosity kicks in and instead of running to the bathroom I put my hand on my heart, which is beating about a million beats to every second, and I sink down on to the floor without even thinking about it and I start looking through the pile.

CHAPTER TWENTY-SEVEN

'Now this,' says Ben, turning to Simon and raising a glass of champagne, 'is the life.'

'Better buckle up,' says Simon with a grin. 'We're about to land.'

'I don't want to land,' groans Ben. 'I want to stay on this plane for ever and ever.' The stewardess walks past and smiles at Ben, who gives her his most charming smile and turns back to Simon. 'See what I mean? Beautiful women, free champagne, delicious food.'

'You can afford to fly first class,' grunts Simon. 'On my measly pay I'd end up in cattle class with crappy seats and crappy food.'

'I didn't pay for this,' says Ben.

'Yeah, but you got upgraded because you're famous. I don't somehow think that they'd automatically upgrade overworked producer Simon Molloy just because I have a nice smile.'

'But they did,' grins Ben.

'Only 'cos I'm with you.'

They do up their seat belts and prepare to land.

'Where are we staying again?' asks Ben.

'Ah,' says Simon, reaching into his briefcase. 'Now here, I really have done us proud. London Daytime Television wanted to put us up in some grotty cheap hotel, but I managed to wangle this place called Shutters on the Beach.' He pulls a brochure out of the case and hands it to Ben. 'Nice isn't it?'

'Nice?' says Ben, as the plane starts to descend through the sky. 'It's bloody gorgeous.'

'Bloody gorgeous,' he says again, as they walk through the reception area, the very same reception area Jemima has only recently walked through herself. Ben, being a man, doesn't notice the details in the way Jemima did, but nevertheless he can appreciate the quiet beauty of the place.

'I've got to make some calls, and then I've got to meet the publicist,' says Simon, as they follow the porter up in the lift. 'How about we meet a bit later on?'

'Let's speak,' says Ben, looking at his watch. 'I'm not sure I'm up for a night out tonight, I can feel a serious bout of jet-lag coming on.'

'Okay,' agrees Simon, who's not feeling so hot himself. 'If you bail out on me tonight then tomorrow, after we've done the interview, we have to do some heavy drinking.'

'You're on,' says Ben with a grin.

'Good.'

Ben is tired, but he's also excited, and he hasn't got any calls to make, any people to meet, and after half an hour of flicking through hundreds of television stations, he decides to go for a walk.

He has no idea where he's going, but he doesn't care. Just the fact that he's able to walk around in nothing more than a pair of jeans and a T-shirt is enough, the fact that within minutes of leaving the hotel he passes three of the most beautiful women he's ever seen is enough, the fact that he's actually here, in Los Angeles, is enough.

Ben doesn't know about jaywalking. He doesn't know that in California, should you be stupid enough to cross at the lights before the sign changes to a green pedestrian, you can be fined. So here he is, standing at the street corner with a crowd of people, wondering why no one's crossing the empty road. He strides across as a black, convertible Porsche screeches past him, missing him by centimetres, and as the car roars off the driver, an impossibly handsome blond man, screams, 'Asshole!' Ben stands for a few seconds, shaking, as a young man with long hair and baggy clothes walks up to him.

'Don't cross until it says so, man,' he drawls, walking off.

'Oh' says Ben, recovering his composure. 'Thanks.'

I don't know what to feel. I don't know whether to be horrified or whether to be fascinated, whether to laugh with relief because it wasn't my imagination that something was very wrong, I wasn't mad, or whether to throw up.

Everything seems to be standing still. The only thing I'm aware of at this very moment in time is the pile of photographs and magazines in front of me. I feel as if I'm in a daze, but somehow I can't stop myself from looking, it's as if I need to see this because if I don't look at everything it may not be real.

I reach across and pull over one of the many magazines from the pile. 'Big and Bouncy!' it proclaims on the cover, a lurid headline over a picture of a woman who's not so much a woman, more a mountain of flesh. She's completely naked, grinning into the camera and spreading her legs, presumably to help the viewer see what they would otherwise miss due to the rolls of skin, the acres of fat that would otherwise completely obliterate her genitalia.

Jesus Christ. Who buys these things? What are they doing *here*? In Brad's apartment.

I turn the first page and read the note from the editor, addressed to those men who like larger ladies. I turn every page, and you know what I can't believe? I can't believe that someone like Brad could get turned on by these enormous women, so what the hell are they doing in his apartment?

The horrified part of me doesn't want to look, wants to run crying into her mother's skirt and hope the big, bad, nasty world will go away, but that other part of me, the fascinated part, can't stop turning the pages because these women are me. They're what I used to be, except I never knew what I looked like then because I never dared look in the mirror properly. I used to pretend that if I couldn't see the fat then no one else could either.

Except looking closely I can see that these women aren't really me. They have pouting, glossy smiles, they lick their lips seductively as they look into the camera, they seem proud of their size, their bulk, their excess weight, but they shouldn't be proud. Or should they?

Am I going mad? Is it possible that men would have found me attractive then, despite being hugely over-weight? I love the attention I get now that I'm slim and blonde, but has my life changed all that much? Yes, I feel better, more confident, but I'm still the same person inside, and if I'm being really honest with myself I wouldn't say I'm that much happier now, and all the insecurities I had when I was fat are still there, they haven't gone away, even though that sounds ridiculous.

The weird thing is that people judge me by my looks as much as they did before, only now they just come up with a completely different conclusion, and yes, I have a boyfriend, but my life certainly isn't the fairytale I thought it would be. Most of the time, even though I'm in Los Angeles, with Brad, most of the time, I suddenly realize, I'm desperately lonely. Far, far lonelier than I ever was back home in Kilburn.

And the more I think about it, the more I realize that I really haven't felt myself since arriving in Los Angeles. I feel almost as if I'm playing a role, that I've become so immersed in being Brad's girfriend I've forgotten who I really am. In fact, it's not even since I arrived in LA. If I'm totally honest about it, I haven't felt myself since I lost weight and I never understood before how much I used the excess weight to protect myself.

I finish reading the magazines and then I pick up the stack of photographs, and slowly, methodically, I go through them. Each of them features a huge woman, and, just as I think I've had enough shocks to last a lifetime, I see the one thing that suddenly explains everything, and I can't help it. Clichéd as it sounds, I cover my mouth with my hand and gasp.

Because there, in all her naked glory, is Jenny. Jenny, lying on Brad's bed, smiling seductively into the camera. On the bed where Brad and I make love so often. Lying there as if it's hers. No wonder. No wonder she hates me. And everything becomes horribly clear.

And as everything starts falling into place, I'm left with one overwhelming thought. What the hell is Brad doing with me? Why did he tell me he loved me? Why does he want me to stay? Why me?

I sort of feel as if the connections are there, in my mind, they're just not quite fitting together. But I don't have to think about this for very long, because suddenly the bedroom door opens, and Brad's standing in the doorway.

I know it's him, I don't even bother looking up, I don't need to, and I wait for him to say something but he doesn't, all I can hear is the sound of his heavy breathing. He's out of breath, he's been running, he's rushed to get here, and eventually, after this long silence, I do turn to look at him except I don't look him in the eyes, I just look at the trickles of sweat which are just beginning to slide down his forehead.

'They're not mine,' is the first thing he says. I don't say anything, I just start shaking. It's almost like a freeze-frame in a film, nobody moves, and finally I find my voice.

'I suppose you're looking after them for a friend.'

'It's a long story,' he says. 'But they're not mine.'

'Brad,' I say quietly. 'I'm not stupid.'

Brad runs his fingers through his hair and sits down on the bed, head in his hands, and all I can think is that he looks guilty. Guilty. Guilty. Guilty.

'Perhaps you ought to tell me what this is all about,' I say, only my voice doesn't sound like mine, it's far too collected, far too calm, and this situation doesn't feel like my own, it feels like an out-of-body experience, like something I'm watching in a cinema.

Brad's silent for a long time, and I don't bother pushing him. I just sit and wait, still flicking through the magazines, as if I'm in a dream.

'I don't know what to say,' he says.

'Okay.' My voice is as cold as ice. 'I'll help you. Am I right in assuming these pictures are yours?'

Brad nods.

'So presumably you have them because you find these women attractive.'

Brad shrugs.

'Do you?'

He shrugs again.

'Do you?'

'I guess.'

'So now would you like to explain this?' I pull out the picture of Jenny and put it in front of Brad, who groans and drops his head in his hands, like I did before, like that child, like everything will disappear if he closes his eyes, that if he can't see me or the incriminating evidence, perhaps I won't be able to see him either. I know how he feels.

'At least I understand why she hates me,' I continue. 'No wonder she bloody well felt threatened, she couldn't pose for your sick porn collection while I was here could she.'

'It's not like that,' says a voice from the doorway. Jesus Christ. It's not my day. There, in the doorway, is Jenny. Brad groans again and covers his eyes.

'Oh really,' I say. 'Seeing as Brad seems to have lost

the power of speech, perhaps you'd better tell me what it *is* like.'

'I'm sorry, Brad,' says Jenny, walking over to stand next to him and putting her hand on his shoulder. 'I came over because I knew something was wrong when you ran out of the office. Are you okay?'

'Is he okay?' This is unbelievable. 'Excuse me? Hello? Never mind about him, for Christ's sake. I want you to tell me what these are.'

Jenny gives a cursory glance at the pictures. 'Okay,' she says to me, not even having the decency to show the slightest hint of embarrassment. 'You really want to know what's going on?'

'Yes.' Although suddenly I'm not so sure.

Jenny looks at Brad. 'I'm going to tell her,' she says, but Brad doesn't say anything, he doesn't even bother looking up, he just carries on sitting there with his head in his hands.

'Brad and I were at high school together—'

'You what?' I say. 'I don't believe this.'

'Well believe it,' says Jenny. 'We weren't together,' she pauses. 'Then.' She shrugs. 'I looked pretty much the same as I did now. I was the overweight kid that everyone laughed at. Sure, I had my friends, the social misfits, the geeks, the nerds that no one else wanted to know.' Her voice softens as she looks at Brad.

'Brad was the high school hero. He was the golden boy, the star of the football team. He went out with the head cheerleader, and I fell in love with him the moment I saw him.

'He never noticed me, of course, not in that way, but I remember how he was always nice, he never made cruel comments about my size, or laughed and shouted Big Bird when I walked into the room. He used to tell the others to shut up, not to go on about my size, he'd tell them to leave me alone, which only made me love him more.

'It wasn't until we left school that I understood why he stuck up for me. He'd long gone by then, left for college, while I stayed and took a secretarial job. There was a woman I worked with, Judy, whom I became very close to. She used to say I was just like her when she was a girl, and Judy certainly looked like me, we were the same size.

'We were at work one day when I mentioned what school I'd been to. "You must know my son," she said, and she pulled a picture of Brad out of her wallet. I remember staring at his photo in disbelief, and, although I admitted I knew him, I never told her how I felt about him.

'Even when I left that job I kept in touch with Judy, and she'd always tell me how he was getting on. I never really had boyfriends, I never felt that anyone would be interested in me, but I never let go of the dream that Brad and I would somehow, some day, be together.'

I've stopped looking at the pictures. I can't take my eyes off Jenny, and I know I should hate her, she's ruined my life, but I can't hate her because sitting here listening to her voice I'm hearing the story of my life.

'Judy used to tell me about his girlfriends,' she continues. 'But they never seemed to last, and then a few years ago she told me he was in LA, he'd started this gym, and he was looking for an assistant. I thought about it and thought about it, and I knew I had to come out here, I had to be with him.

'Even if nothing ever happened, I knew the only way I'd be happy was if I was near Brad, so I left my hometown and caught a Greyhound bus to Los Angeles.

'I didn't think Brad would even remember who I was, but I went to the gym, and his mouth dropped open when he saw me' – a small smile plays on her face at the memory – 'and I started working for him that day.

'Two months later we had an office party, and Brad drove me home. He came in, and that was that. We fell in love.'

Jenny pauses, and I stop her from continuing, I don't think I want to hear any more, I don't want to hear about them being in love. I just want to hear the answers to the questions that haven't been answered, but it's finally beginning to sink in, this whole sordid thing, and my voice comes out in a whisper. 'So why am I here?'

Jenny's voice hardens again. 'You think it's easy to look the way I do in a town like this?' she says. 'You think I don't know what people think of me, what people would think of Brad if they knew he and I were together?' You know, strange as it seems, I start to feel sorry for her. I start to understand, because, even though I haven't been here long, already I know how superficial Los Angeles is, how people will only accept you if you're beautiful. And slim.

'So that's why you're here,' Jenny sighs. 'Because Brad needed a trophy girlfriend. He needed someone who's blonde and skinny.' The disdain in her voice hits me like a slap in the face. 'He needed someone like you to prove that he'd made it.'

'But why do you put up with this?' I'm still whispering, and I'm not sure why. Maybe because I can't believe what I've just heard, or maybe because I can't believe the pain this is causing. Not just for me, but for Brad. And Jenny.

'Because I love him,' says Jenny simply, as a tear starts rolling down her cheek. 'I love him, and I know what this town is like, and I understand why he needs someone like you. I have to understand. I have no choice.'

'I'm sorry.' Brad's words come out in a whisper and he looks up, up into Jenny's eyes. 'I'm sorry, Jenny.' He looks at me. 'And I'm sorry, JJ. I never meant to hurt you, I never meant for you to find out.'

'What?' I really don't believe this. 'You thought you could spend the rest of your life with both of us?'

He shrugs. 'I didn't know what else to do.'

'I can't believe I'm here,' I say, the words out before I can even think about them. 'I can't believe I'm hearing this.' I look up at the ceiling. 'Why me?' I ask softly. 'Why did this have to happen to me?' I look at Brad. 'This is true isn't it?' I say, because for a moment there I thought that maybe Jenny had made it all up, maybe she found a way of hurting me beyond belief, of winning the war. But I don't really have to wait for an answer from Brad. I can see in his eyes that it's true, and I can see from the way Jenny takes his hand and he doesn't pull away that it's true.

I stand up and walk to the wardrobe, ignoring them both, and, as I start pulling my clothes off the hangers and flinging them on the bed, I'm vaguely aware that Brad and Jenny leave the room. Brad and Jenny. Even the words, their names, make me feel sick.

But other than the sickness, there really isn't any other feeling. No rage, no grief, not even much pain. Numbness. I just feel numb. I pull out my suitcase and start piling in clothes, throwing things on top of one another, not bothering to fold, or smooth, or press. Suddenly I have this overwhelming urge to get out of here. Fast.

Brad comes back into the bedroom. 'Jenny's gone,' he says softly.

'I'll be gone too,' I say curtly. 'As soon as I've packed I'll be out of here.'

'You don't have to go,' he says.

What? Did I just hear what I think I heard? 'Are you completely out of your mind?'

'I mean, I do have a spare room. You can stay there.'

'Don't be ridiculous.'

'Where will you go?'

'I don't know.' And even though I'm planning to phone Lauren as soon as possible, I don't intend to share that with him. 'Look,' I say to Brad. 'I'd like to be on my own if that's okay.'

'Okay,' he says. 'Will I see you again?'

'I very much doubt it.' And as I look at him I realize that actually this is the first time I'm really seeing him. Despite the pain, the deception, the lies, he is still the best-looking man I've ever seen. But looks mean nothing. So he's good-looking. So what? And I suddenly see that that's all Brad ever was to me. A handsome man. I fell for his looks, not for who he is.

And, most importantly, I fell for him because he wanted me. He was the first man to show any interest in me, and I was flattered, and I think, oh God why didn't

I realize this before, I think I felt I had to love him back.

Brad leaves and I pick up the phone to ring the airline.

'I'd like to change my flight to London,' I tell the reservation girl on the other end of the phone.

'Certainly, ma'am. Just tell me which flight it is and when you were thinking of flying.'

'LAX to London Heathrow. As soon as possible. Can you get me on the flight tonight?' I give her the flight number and hold my breath.

'I think that flight is full, ma'am. Can you hold the line while I just check my computer?'

I hold, and my foot taps the floor impatiently as I wait for what feels like hours for the woman to come back on the line. 'I'm sorry, the flight is full, but we do have a seat on the flight tomorrow.'

'Thank God.' I breathe a sigh of relief.

'You do realize that will be full fare.'

'What?' She's got it wrong, she must have got it wrong. 'But I changed my flight a few weeks ago for $100 and I understood that that was the cost.'

'I'm afraid that the inventory is now full, we are unable to do that any more.'

'So how much is full fare?'

'That will be $954 plus tax.'

I can't have heard right. I clutch the phone and whisper, 'What?'

'$954 plus tax.'

'But I can't afford that!' In my head I'm mentally calculating how much that is in pounds, that's about £700! No way, I haven't got that sort of money.

'I'm sorry, ma'am, that's the best we can do.'

'So you mean I have to wait here until I'm booked to

go home? I can't change my flight again for $100?' I can't believe this is happening to me, I really can't.

'I'm afraid not.'

'Forget it,' I sigh. 'I'll just have to stay in this godforsaken place then, won't I? Thanks.' And I put down the phone, feeling as if I'm going to cry.

Lauren, I'll have to call Lauren, and surprise, surprise, she's not there. Probably out with her barman, I think, and that's when it hits me. I'm on my own. Again. I came out here to be with Brad and now he's left me and that's it, I'm in a strange town, with one friend who isn't home, and I'm all by myself.

I can't help it, I can't stop the tears that start rolling down my cheeks and within seconds I'm gulping huge pockets of air, sobbing like a baby. I pull my knees up to my chest and cradle them with my arms, crying as if my heart is going to break. Stop it, I try and tell myself. He's not worth it, but even as I think that I know that this isn't about Brad. This is about me. This is about finally thinking you've found someone to share the rest of your life with, and not being good enough for them. It's about thinking that being blonde and slim and perfect will automatically bring you happiness, and then discovering that life is full of as many disappointments as there were before.

It takes about an hour to cry myself dry, and when I've finished I leave a message on Lauren's machine. 'It's JJ,' I say, hiccuping a little. 'Something terrible's happened, I need a place to stay. Whatever you do, don't call me at Brad's. I'm going out and I'll keep ringing you until I get you. Speak to you soon.' And I put the phone down.

CHAPTER TWENTY-EIGHT

I lug my suitcase down the hall, thanking God that Brad didn't change his mind and decide to see me off. It's so heavy I'll probably do my back in, but I'd rather be laid up than accept any help from him now.

I take the case to the front door, and the taxi driver runs out and picks it up for me.

'Where to?' he asks, when I'm settled in the back seat.

'I haven't got a clue.'

He turns round and looks at me quizzically. 'You don't know where you're going?'

I shake my head, and as I do the first tears come, but not in a torrent, just a single tear rolling down my cheek.

'Are you okay?' he says gently.

'Yes.' I try to smile. 'I'll be fine.' And we sit there for a bit as he waits for me to compose myself, and as I wipe my eyes I remember the Santa Monica mall, the food hall, and my nostrils are filled with the mingling smells and I know as an absolute certainty that the only thing that will make me feel better right now is food. Lots of it. As much as I can eat.

Cravings. I'd forgotten about cravings, but now I'm getting the strongest craving of my life, and for your information I'm not sitting here thinking about lettuce, or rice cakes, or even, gasp, a loaf of bread. I'm sitting here thinking about spare ribs. About Singapore noodles. About pasta. About biscuits. About cakes dripping with sugar and cream.

And the more I think about it, the more vivid the pictures become until I can almost smell the food, taste the food, hear it beckoning me from afar.

'Santa Monica mall,' I instruct the driver, not giving a stuff about my fat-free, cholesterol-free, obsessive diet. I don't give a damn, I just need to stuff my face.

'Are you sure you'll be okay?' he says, as I start to lug the suitcase up the steps of the mall. 'I'm sure,' I tell him, and push open the doors.

Where do you start when you're about to have the biggest binge of your life and you have a choice of practically every type of food from around the world? It doesn't matter really, because I plan to sample everything, and I start with a sandwich from the deli.

I don't bother sitting at one of the tables, I stand just next to the deli counter cramming a pastrami-on-rye sandwich into my mouth, barely tasting it.

Next I hit the hamburger stall, where I bypass the burgers and go for the fries instead.

I stop at the Chinese and order Singapore noodles and spare ribs, at which point I do sit down because it's far easier to tear the flesh off the bone with your teeth when you're sitting down.

Sweet things, sweet things, sweet things. I go to the bakery and buy a bag of six hot, fresh cinnamon rolls, and I stuff them into my mouth within minutes.

Now what? I look around, stomach full, but I know I haven't even started if I'm hoping to fill the huge, gaping hole in my heart. The candy store. I fill a huge paper bag with sweets, every kind imaginable, and even before I've left the shop I'm cramming handfuls into my mouth without even tasting them.

I leave the mall and lug the suitcase to a phone box outside, undoing the top two buttons on my tiny denim shorts, which are now painfully pressing into my flesh, and as I dial I rub my stomach to try and dispel the ache from so much food, and I curse myself for wearing a short white crop top instead of a voluminous shirt to hide my sins.

'Lauren?'

'I've been so worried!' shouts Lauren down the phone. 'Don't tell me now, just get your arse over here.'

'Oh thank you, thank you, thank you.'

'Don't be stupid,' says Lauren. 'What are friends for?'

Ben has been walking around Santa Monica for what seems like hours. He's discovered that the busiest street seems to be the 3rd Street Promenade, and he's still trying to get over the fact that there's a Virtual Supermarket, a computer shop where you go in, log on, and order whatever you need from the computer.

He stops for coffee at the Barnes & Noble café, and sits for a while, enjoying the cappuccino and the people. He was going to buy a book, but he couldn't find anything other than film books, so he picks up the local paper that someone left on the table next to him, and idly flicks through.

After a while he decides to get back to the hotel. He turns the corner and passes a phone box, and, being the boy that he is, he keeps his eyes glued to the perfect rear view of the woman on the phone. Why don't they make women like that in England, he thinks, taking in the curve of her well-toned buttocks and tanned, muscular thighs, the golden skin set off by faded denim shorts and a white crop top. Ben walks past and turns back, hoping to see the face behind the mane of streaky blonde hair, but the girl has turned away, and Ben smiles to himself and walks back to the hotel.

'Christ, you look awful,' says Lauren, opening the door.

I feel awful, and, as I push past Lauren, clutching my hand to my mouth, I catch a glimpse of myself in the mirror and my golden skin is no longer golden, it's a rather peculiar shade of green.

'Through there,' says Lauren, pointing down the hallway. 'Quick.'

I stumble past her and collapse on my knees in front of the toilet. Up comes the pastrami-on-rye. Up come the Singapore noodles and spare ribs. Up come the fries. Up come the cinnamon rolls. And finally, up come the sweets.

And when it's all finished, when there's nothing left, I rest my head on the toilet seat while my eyes and nose continue streaming, and I'm aware that Lauren's standing behind me, gently rubbing my back.

'Here,' says Lauren, handing me some tissues. 'I'll just get you a glass of water.'

She comes back and helps me to my feet. 'Oh you poor thing,' she says. 'You're shivering.' She leads me to the sofa, then runs back to her bedroom and comes back with a blanket, which she tucks around me.

Lauren doesn't say anything, she just sits beside

me and puts her arm around me, and I lean my head into her shoulder as the pain and the shock finally hit, and this is what I need, to be looked after, to be treated like a child, to feel safe and secure for the first time in ages.

'How about a cup of hot, sweet tea?' she says eventually, and I nod.

'You're so English,' I manage with a small smile when Lauren comes back with two steaming mugs.

'I'm not *that* English. You won't find any milk or sugar in there. It's fat-free dairy substitute and sweetener. So,' she says sitting down, 'what happened?'

I tell her. Everything. Lauren sits there open-mouthed, and when I've finished I look for her reaction, but she can't speak.

'Say something,' I plead.

'I can't,' says Lauren. 'Fucking hell.'

'I know.'

'Fucking hell,' she says again.

'Yeah.'

'Fucking hell.'

'Lauren!'

'I'm sorry, I just don't know what to say. I can't believe it. This doesn't happen in real life, surely?'

'That's what I thought, but I'm afraid it does.'

'What a bastard,' sighs Lauren.

'Yes.'

'And what a bitch.'

'I don't know,' I shrug. 'You'll probably think I'm completely out of my head, but you know what? I actually feel sorry for them. I mean, I feel completely sick that I got caught up in it . . .'

'I noticed,' says Lauren, with a smile.

'Yeah, well. But think how awful it must be for her.'

'You *are* out of your head,' says Lauren in disbelief.

'Maybe, but I know what it's like to be her. The only thing I can't believe is that he treats her like that.'

'Hello? JJ? What about the way he treated you?'

'That too.'

'Well. Good riddance to bad rubbish is all I can say.'

'You're right. You're right. I know you're right.'

'Shall I come out with some more clichés?'

I nod.

'Plenty more fish in the sea.'

'Men are like buses.'

'You can lead a horse to water.'

'What's that got to do with anything?'

Lauren shrugs. 'Dunno, but just bear in mind that too many cooks . . .'

'Oh Lauren.' I shove her and she grins, because she knows I'm feeling a little bit better already.

'See,' says Lauren. 'There is some light at the end of the tunnel,' and we both start laughing.

'That's better,' says Lauren. 'You can stay here for as long as you like.'

'That's the other thing,' I say disconsolately. 'I tried to change my flight today but I can't get back any earlier without paying full fare.'

'So how long are you staying?'

'About two months.' Now this really does scare me. 'I can find somewhere to stay, an apartment maybe, or a cheap hotel.' Which of course I can't, because I don't have the money.

'What? When I've got a perfectly comfortable sofa

394

bed? You're staying here, for free, because I've got more than enough for both of us. End of story.'

Thank God. That's exactly what I hoped she'd say. 'Lauren, what would I do without you?'

'More to the point, what would I do without you?' Lauren says with a smile.

'But what am I going to do for money? I mean, I've got the column on the *Kilburn Herald* and my paltry salary from them but that's hardly enough.'

'You're a journalist, JJ. Money is the least of your worries. First of all, I can get the features editor at the magazine to commission you.'

'What?'

'Yup. You can write a piece for the magazine on good-looking bastards.'

'You mean, tell my story?'

'Not exactly. You can mention the basics, but we'll save the full story for an in-depth feature, which, unfortunately, wouldn't be right for us. For this piece you can write a bit of first-person stuff, but expand on the theme, how we're taken in by looks, how we're blinded by lust, how easy it is to fall for what someone looks like, not who they are.'

'For your magazine?'

Lauren nods.

'Are you sure they'll want it?' She nods again and already I'm thinking about opening the magazine and seeing my byline, my name in big letters, and the thought has the desired effect because I'm starting to feel that there is something to look forward to after all.

'No worries. I know you can do it. Next,' she says, picking up her phone book, 'I'm going to ring

Cosmopolitan in London and you're going to offer them a story on Internet romances, and that's when you tell your full story. Warts and all.'

'Can't they sue me?'

'Like bastard-features and bitch-face are likely to read English *Cosmopolitan*? Anyway, all you have to do is change the names and you're sorted. JJ, you don't have to worry about money. There are thousands of pieces you could be writing out here and filing back to magazines and newspapers in London. Think about it, you're in Los Angeles. You're in the place where all the stars live, so just get on the blower and set up some interviews. It's as easy as that.'

I really am starting to feel better. A whole lot better.

'And meanwhile, when we're not working, which will be most of the time, you and I are going to have a blast. Screw them. We're two gorgeous single English girls, and the world is our oyster.'

'Yes,' I raise my mug. 'The world is our oyster. I'll drink to that.'

'So,' Lauren says, 'how about starting tonight?'

'Starting what?'

'Starting to have a good time.'

'You mean you're not seeing Bill the horny barman?'

'I'm going to cancel him. You and I are going out.'

'Lauren.' I shake my head, still unable to believe that anyone can be so kind. 'I don't want you to cancel him. To tell you the truth this has really taken it out of me. All I want to do tonight is curl up and watch the box.'

'Okay,' says Lauren. 'So we'll curl up and watch the box.'

'No.' My voice is firm. 'I know how you feel about Bill

396

and there's no way you're cancelling him. In the nicest possible way, Lauren, I want to be on my own tonight.' A total lie, but I know I'll cope and there's no reason why I should spoil Lauren's evening as well.

'Are you sure?' Lauren's doubtful, but pleased.

'I'm so sure,' I say.

'Okay. I've got plenty of food in the fridge so just make yourself at home. I'm going to jump in the shower, and then how about I run you a nice hot bath?'

'That sounds lovely,' and it does, except I have to really force myself not to think about the last time I had a bath, with Brad, and what we ended up doing.

Before she leaves Lauren lines up an assortment of pots, jars and tubes.

'These,' she says in a serious tone, 'are my babies. Use them well,' and she blows me a kiss and disappears.

I unscrew each pot, each jar, each tube, and sniff deeply. I examine the packaging, read how each one will give you younger skin, thicker hair, firmer flesh. I pour half a bottle of almond-scented bubble bath in the water and lie back, cucumber slices on my eyes, a hot damp towel wrapped around my deeply conditioning hair.

And when I've towelled myself dry with one of Lauren's huge fluffy towels, I walk into the kitchen and open the door of the fridge. Hooray. For someone as skinny as Lauren, there's an extraordinary amount of food. Without thinking, I pull out a tray of sushi, a carton of yoghurt, a cellophane package of pre-cooked chicken.

But I don't stop there, even though I know I should. I pull out packets of ready-made salads, cheese, fat-free cookies. I spy the bread jar and dig down to where half a loaf of wholemeal bread is temporarily residing.

And then I sit at the kitchen table and I eat. And eat. And eat. And eat.

'Oh hello,' says Ben, hoping he's got the right number because there's a male voice on the answering machine, and he doesn't exactly trust those flatmates of Jemima, even though Lisa, the one he spoke to, sounded more normal than that other blonde nutcase. 'I hope I've got the right number. I'm trying to get in touch with Jemima Jones. This is Ben Williams, an old friend of hers from London. I'm in Los Angeles for a couple of days, and I'd love to meet up with you, er, with her, so if this is the right number and Jemima's there, could she please call me at Shutters on the Beach. Thanks,' and he puts down the phone.

I lie in bed and I know I should feel guilty at the amount I've eaten today, but I don't. The food at the Santa Monica mall doesn't count because as far as I'm concerned I threw it up before it had a chance to convert into fat, and tonight, well, tonight. Yes, I'll admit I was tempted to throw it up again, to stick my fingers down my throat and get rid of all the food, but that's not the answer. And eating isn't the answer either.

And anyway, the throwing up earlier wasn't just about the food, I think it was about the shock today, the combination of both, and I do feel better. I still feel alone, but

I've got Lauren, thank God, and I believe her, I believe that everything will be fine.

I rub my hands over my stomach, feeling how it's bulging slightly, and thanking God that I've exercised as much as I have, that I don't have folds of flabby skin anywhere on my body, and then I remember a time at home, back in London, when my stomach was huge. When it used to take about ten minutes to rub from one side to the other. Well, not exactly, but you know what I mean. I remember how I used my size and my flesh to hide away from the world, to hide my sexuality, to hide who I was, and I know that, despite in a strange way feeling comforted by my size, I won't get that way again, I don't *need* to be that size again.

My stomach is nothing like it used to be, but as I stroke I can feel that neither is it concave, the way it's been since I arrived in Los Angeles, and actually, if I'm being completely honest here, I quite like the fact that it curves slightly. Okay, I know that with a triple workout for the next couple of days it will soon be back to its flat self, and that this bulge is just the temporary result of tonight's binge, but the more I stroke it the more I like it. It feels rounded, feminine, womanly.

I get up in a while, curious to see what it looks like in the mirror, and I go into Lauren's bedroom and pull the full-length mirror around to face me. I lift my T-shirt up over my head and stand there, naked, just looking at myself.

I look at my taut, muscular figure, so lean now that I look more like a boy than a woman. I run my hand over my flat breasts and remember how pendulous they used to be, how like the women I saw in the pictures today.

399

How like Jenny. No. I'm not going to think about that.

I skim my waist, marvelling at how tiny it is, and I try to pinch an inch, except I can't, all I can manage is a few millimetres of skin.

So I get into bed and I decide that I'm not going to binge any more, but I'm not going to stay obsessed with being as skinny as I can be. I think it's high time I just relaxed and lived a little. And I suppose my weight will just settle at whatever it's supposed to settle at. How's that for a revelation?

CHAPTER TWENTY-NINE

'Who *are* all these people?' Ben whispers to Simon, as they're led into a room that is apparently known as the Den.

'The film publicist, the assistant, the agent. God knows.'

'But why are they all here?' whispers Ben. 'I mean, this is only a bloody TV interview.'

'I know,' Simon whispers back. 'Anyone would think we were out to murder her.'

'Where is she anyway?'

'The assistant said she'd be down in a minute.'

'Jesus. Can you imagine how much money she must make? Look at this place!' Ben is gazing around the building in awe, at the huge, Mexican-style villa set high up in the hills above Santa Monica.

'This is *the Den*?' says Ben, laughing, because he'd pictured a small, cosy room, a bit like a library, the very opposite of the enormous white room in which he and Simon are now standing. Simon creeps across the flag-stone floors to the french windows at the far end.

'Get a load of this, Ben,' he says, looking out at a heart-shaped swimming pool cut into the side of the hill, complete with rocks, statues and fountains.

'I think I'm in the wrong business,' says Ben, walking over to join him.

'I think you are,' says Simon. 'I think I am too.'

'Can I get you something to drink?' The boys turn round as Alexia Aldridge's assistant walks in the room.

Simon nudges Ben and says under his breath, 'Double scotch on the rocks?'

'That would be lovely,' says Ben.

'Iced tea?' she says.

'Perfect,' he says.

'Iced tea?' says Simon, looking at Ben in disgust. 'Iced tea? No bloody alcohol in iced tea is there?'

'Somehow I don't think alcohol would be appropriate,' Ben laughs.

Simon checks his watch. 'I'd better go down to the front door, the crew should be arriving any minute.'

Ben walks over to the bookcase, looking for clues to some inner life of Alexia Aldridge that the public might not know, although he thinks it's unlikely. Ben is sure that there's very little chance of him finding out some fantastic fact about her, something guaranteed to make the front page of every tabloid.

Ben reread his cuts last night, and the more he read the more he started to read between the lines. He suspects that Alexia Aldridge hates playing the Hollywood game. That she's actually fiercely bright, and very few men are strong enough to match her. He suspects that she's extremely private, and that were it not for the publicity value of the occasional hand-picked interview, she would lock herself away in her beautiful house and never come out, unless she were making a film. And he suspects that she's fantastically insecure, which is surprising for one so young, so beautiful and so talented, and that she hides those insecurities with the arrogance for which she's so famed.

Finally he suspects that he's going to leave this house having fallen deeply in love with Alexia Aldridge.

The bookcase is an eclectic collection of art books, psychology books, contemporary literary fiction. Ben's not surprised, it's the standard stuff of everyone he's ever interviewed. What does surprise him, as he pulls out a book on the artist Egon Schiele, is that it's been read. That the pages are dog-eared and slightly bent, and that someone has obviously pored over it, cover to cover.

Ben turns as he hears someone walk into the room.

'Sorry I took so long,' says Simon, leading the cameraman and soundman into the room.

'God.' Ben puts a hand on his heart. 'For a minute there I thought it was her.'

'I could pretend,' says Simon, pouting and fluttering his eyelashes.

'Where is she anyway?' says Ben. 'What's taking so long.'

'Hollywood luvvies,' says Simon, sitting down and pouring himself some iced tea, 'are even worse than theatrical luvvies.' He drinks it down in one gulp before adding, 'Darling. Mmm,' he says, looking at the glass. 'That's bloody nice, that is.'

An hour later the crew have set up their equipment and they're standing around, looking at their watches. The door opens. It's the assistant again.

'I don't want to trouble you, but any chance we could get to see Miss Aldridge soon?' says Ben politely.

'Like, this year,' mutters Simon, softly so she can't hear.

'Oh, I'm sorry,' says the assistant. 'She should be with you shortly. She's just finishing getting dressed.'

Half an hour later they're still sitting there.

'This is definitely happening isn't it?' says Ben.

'Of course it is,' says Simon, except he's not sounding half as cocky as he did earlier on.

And then twenty minutes later, just as they're giving up hope, the assistant rushes in and clears the glasses and jug away. 'She's on her way,' she says, and they stand up to greet her.

Nothing could have prepared Ben for the sheer magnetism of Alexia Aldridge. She is beautiful but not classically so. Her mouth is slightly crooked, her nose has a bump on it, but the aura around her is such that none of the men can take their eyes off her.

She's wearing tight lime-green trousers, a white sloppy jumper, a huge amount of make-up that makes her look as if she's wearing no make-up at all, and her hair is perfect. *She*'s perfect, thinks Ben, who, for a few seconds, is so mesmerized by meeting a real-life Hollywood star he can't move, can't speak, can't do anything at all other than stare at her.

'Miss Aldridge?' Simon is first to recover his composure. 'It's a pleasure to meet you. I'm Simon Molloy, the producer and director. And this,' he says, 'is Ben Williams, our presenter.'

'I'm delighted to meet you,' says Ben, shaking her hand.

'And I, you,' she says coyly, looking up at him from under her eyelashes as Simon looks at the crew and raises his eyes to the ceiling.

And so they start running the tape, and Ben starts

asking her questions. He sits in a large white armchair opposite Alexia, who curls up on the sofa, one hand resting on the arm, the other protectively curled round her knees.

'So tell us about your latest film,' he starts, keeping it professional, trying to put her at ease before he starts asking her any personal questions, because she has to trust him, and Ben knows that it may take some time to build up this trust, but he's finding it hard to concentrate on anything, she's just so beautiful.

Alexia starts talking, in her famous throaty voice, and Ben sits there and nods his head, but he's not listening to a word she's saying, he's losing himself in her big, brown eyes.

They talk about the film – why she decided to do a low-budget film and waive her usual multi-million-dollar fee; what she felt when she first saw the script – the story of a single girl who's trying to find love, but can't tell the difference between passion and love, and nearly loses out when she doesn't realize what she's found, and how she feels at the superb reviews; the film, like all other American-made films, has opened in the States already and is not due to open in England for months.

'I know you're very private about your own love life,' Ben ventures, as Alexia nods encouragingly, 'but would you say you related to the character?'

'You mean, do I go for passion rather than love?'

Ben nods.

'I think relationships are very difficult, especially in this industry,' she starts. 'And I think it's very easy to get swept away with glamour, excitement, passion. But look at Hollywood marriages, they so rarely last, and I think the trick is, just as my character in the film does, the trick is to look for friendship rather than passion.'

'So are you attracted to your male friends?'

Alexia laughs. 'Now there's the tricky bit. Unfortunately I've yet to have a friendship with a man which turns into something more, but I'm still looking.'

'So you're not in a relationship with anyone now?' Ben almost blushes as he says this, because it sounds so personal, and the question isn't for the benefit of the viewers, it's for him.

'No.' She shakes her head and leans forward, giving him a flirtatious smile. 'And to be honest I'm happy with that. I'm very busy with work, and I have a lot of close friends, and I really feel, for the first time in my life, that I don't need a man to fulfil me.'

'So obviously you related to your character quite a lot.' That's it, Ben, bring it on to more comfortable territory.

'Absolutely,' she nods. 'I suppose when I was younger I did go for that initial passion, but you change as you get older, and now I'd like to think I look for something more substantial.'

'How do you think you've changed?' I love her, Ben's thinking, still mesmerized by her beauty, she is my perfect woman.

'I'm much more aware as a person. I think I've finally found self-fulfilment. I'm more relaxed with who I am, I do yoga, I meditate, I believe in the power of visualization and I use it. Frequently.' She pauses and looks at the ceiling for a few seconds. 'But I think the main thing is I've learned how to nurture my inner child, and that's the thing that's really made a difference.'

'Your inner child?' says Ben, feeling slightly stupid, for he doesn't have a clue what she's talking about.

'Absolutely,' she nods again. 'My inner child. The lonely, scared, insecure child that lives inside all of us.'

'Er, yes,' says Ben, with typical British reserve. 'Quite. So how did you come to find your, er, inner child?'

'I did these fabulous rebirthing classes,' she says earnestly, 'and taking me back to the trauma of birth, actually being able to feel the shock and terror of emerging from the womb into this world, completely changed my life.'

Ben's just sitting looking at her, not quite open-mouthed, but the look of love that had been in his eyes since the beginning of the interview is rapidly disappearing. There's always a bloody catch, he thinks. She's beautiful, she's single, and she's full of psychobabble bullshit. Damn.

'But surely someone like you doesn't have to go through something like, um, rebirthing?' he ventures.

'This is all image,' she says, 'and actually I'm very ordinary. I go to the supermarket, I go shopping, I go for walks. I'm just like everybody else.'

Yup, thinks Ben, and that's why it's taken us months to set up an interview with you. That's why, in fact, we're bothering to interview you at all. Because you're just so ordinary.

'Do you get recognized when you go out?'

'Occasionally,' she says, 'but, believe me, when I'm walking around with no make-up on and a baseball cap I look very different. It's lovely when people come up to you and tell you they admire your work, but sometimes

407

it can be bothersome if they just want to touch you and get close to you.'

'Has it ever worried you?'

'There was a recent incident, which I haven't talked about before. A guy started following me,' she says slowly. 'He knew where I lived and started sending me letters. First of all he told me he liked me then he loved me, and eventually they got more and more bizarre and he thought he was married to me.'

Thank you, God, thinks Ben, knowing that this is the story that will make the papers, that Alexia Aldridge has her very own stalker.

'Were you frightened?'

'Yes,' she nods, 'and finally he started sending packages and saying that he knew where I was, who I was with, and what I was doing, and he was going insane with jealousy. In the last note I got he said if he couldn't have me, no one would, and he was going to kill me.'

'What happened to him?'

'He's being held for questioning, and it's the first time I've slept in months. But it'll take a long time to get over that feeling of always looking over your shoulder. I guess' – she shrugs her shoulders and smiles – 'it's kind of an occupational hazard.'

Ben catches Simon's eye, who winks and gives him the thumbs-up.

'I think it's time to wrap it up,' says the assistant, standing up. 'Miss Aldridge has a meeting.'

'It's okay, Sandy,' says Alexia Aldridge, waving her away. 'I have a few more minutes. Do you want to carry on?'

Ben looks at Simon, who shakes his head. 'I think

we've got enough,' says Ben. 'If we could just finish by
wishing you luck.' And they do, and Alexia smiles her
famous smile and thanks them, and they get ready to
pack up.

'It's been a pleasure,' she says, shaking Ben's hand for
rather a long time when the interview is over and the
crew have walked out of the room. 'I wish I had more
time.'

'You were wonderful,' says Ben, still trying to figure
out whether she's flirting with him, but suddenly not
really caring. Although it would be an ego trip, all this
rebirthing talk has changed his view of her completely.

'Maybe we'll meet again in London?' she says.

'Oh absolutely. That would be great.'

'Here,' she says, handing him a card. 'These are my
numbers. You should call me.'

'Oh.' Ben's shocked. 'Okay.'

'In fact,' she continues, 'I was wondering whether you
were free tonight. I'd love it if you stayed for dinner.'

'You mean the crew?' says Ben, who's just checking.

'No.' She smiles her pussycat smile and taps him on
the nose. 'Don't be silly. Just us. You and me.'

A million thoughts seem to go through Ben's mind at
once. She's Alexia Aldridge! She fancies me! What a
story! I could dine out on this for years! But I promised
the crew I'd go out with them! They wouldn't mind! She's
full of shit! But she's Alexia Aldridge! But what would
be the point!

'Um, I'd love to,' he says finally. 'But I'm taking the
crew out, and they've worked so hard I can't let them
down.'

Her smile hardens. 'Okay. Never mind. But look, you

409

should call me, I'm spending more and more time in London and I'd love to see you. I know a great healer in London who I think would really help you learn to love yourself. I must introduce you.'

Alexia, unknowingly, has banged the final nail in her own coffin.

'That would be so great,' he says, and he kisses her on the cheek, pockets her card, turns away and rolls his eyes at Simon as she walks out of the room.

'Are you fucking crazy? says Simon in disbelief, who had been surreptitiously listening to the entire conversation. 'She wanted you, mate. You turned down Alexia Aldridge. You're fucking nuts.'

'Simon!' admonishes Ben in a whisper. 'You heard her, all that rebirthing, healing shit. She may be Alexia Aldridge but she's a woman from another planet.'

'So fucking what? I can't believe it,' Simon shakes his head. 'Alexia Aldridge and you turned her down.'

'Okay,' says Ben, gathering up his stuff. 'She's gorgeous. She's beautiful. But she's full of crap. Even if I did stay for dinner, what would we talk about? Past-life regression therapy? I don't think so. All she would have been is a great story to tell your friends, and I'm not interested in that.'

'You're not interested in a shag?'

'Not with someone I can't even talk to.'

Simon frowns at Ben. 'You know what? You're weird, you are. Anyway, that stalking story was the business. Well done.' He claps Ben on the back. 'I think, after that, we all need to go and get very drunk indeed. Sandy?' He walks over to the assistant, who's still hovering in the room. 'Do you have any suggestions for bars or restaurants where we could go tonight?'

'Surely. What kind of thing are you looking for?'

'Somewhere fun, somewhere laid back.'

'Where are you staying?'

'Santa Monica.'

'Why don't you try Schatzi on Main? It's Arnold Schwarzenegger's restaurant and it's really fun, and I hear the food's great.'

'Great. Thanks.' And with that they thank her for her trouble and leave Alexia Aldridge's house.

'I still don't understand you,' says Simon, driving back to the hotel.

'What's to understand? At first I thought she was gorgeous, but as soon as she started talking that drivel I went right off her.'

'Still.' Simon thinks for a minute. 'She is supremely shaggable.'

'If you're into that whole celebrity shagging bit.'

'Which I am.'

'In your dreams.'

'That's about the only place,' Simon admits, as Ben laughs. 'And tonight we're going to get very drunk and try and shag some celebrities.'

'You mean *you*'re going to get very drunk and shag some celebrities.'

'Yup. Female, though. Before you get worried I'm not interested in you.'

'Bloody glad to hear it.'

'How are you feeling now?' We just got back home after

a heavy dose of retail therapy. For Lauren, that is. I, needless to say, couldn't even afford a baseball cap at this precise moment in time, and, even though Lauren offered to buy me a sweater I fell in love with, I declined. She's been far too good to me already.

'Lauren, will you stop asking me how I'm feeling every five minutes!'

'I'm just worried about you, that's all.'

'I'm fine. Really, I'm fine.'

'So you're up for going out tonight?'

'Definitely.'

'Okay. You know where I thought might be fun? Schatzi on Main. It's Arnold Schwarzenegger's restaurant, and apparently it's a good place for single women.'

'But you've got Bill the barman.'

'Which still leaves you. And anyway, just because I slept with him last night.' She stops talking, closes her eyes and licks her lips. 'Mmm, but just because of that it doesn't mean I'm attached.'

'You mean you haven't planned your wedding day yet?'

'No, but after all, tomorrow is another day.'

The crew have opted out of Schatzi on Main. 'Too posh,' they moaned, when Simon told them where they were headed, so the cameraman and soundman have discovered an authentic British pub, and they're jumping for joy at the prospect of authentic British ale.

Simon's not happy. He doesn't want to let his crew down, but on the other hand he goes to authentic British pubs every night of the week at home, and he just can't see what the big deal is.

'Don't worry,' says Ben, when Simon knocks on his door to tell him they're leaving. 'We can always go to the other place later. I'm nearly ready,' he says. 'I just have to make a phonecall,' and he picks up the phone and leaves another message for Jemima.

'Who's the bird?' asks Simon.

'You wouldn't be interested,' says Ben with a smile. 'She's just an old friend who's out here,' and as he puts down the phone he suddenly has a very clear picture of Jemima in his head, and he realizes just how much he wants to see her.

They leave the car behind and walk to the pub, and within minutes they're hugging their pint glasses and sitting in a cluster around a chipped round oak table in the corner.

'This isn't so bad,' says Ben, who's beginning to like it here.

'It's fine,' says Simon, who knows he doesn't have a hope in hell of spotting any stars, let alone shagging them, in a place like this.

So, four men together, they sit and talk about Alexia Aldridge, and then fill in the rest of the time with TV gossip. They talk about Ben's co-presenter, fellow researchers, producers, even Diana Macpherson, and, although they tease Ben about the rumours, he keeps his mouth very firmly shut.

And every twenty minutes or so one of them gets up, goes to the bar, and gets another round for the boys.

At ten o'clock the cameraman starts yawning. 'Bloody jet-lag,' he says, rubbing his eyes. 'I'm heading back.'

'How about it?' Simon asks Ben. 'Still up for Schwarzenegger's place?'

'I don't think so,' says Ben, who's caught the cameraman's yawn. 'I think I'm about ready for bed too.'

'Oh come on, Ben,' says Simon. 'You can't let me down now.'

'Okay,' says Ben reluctantly. 'But just for a quick drink.'

It is a quick drink, because truth to be told Simon's not feeling so hot either. They stand at the bar, unable to get barstools, and have a quick whisky.

'God,' says Ben, looking round the room. 'The women here are amazing.' Simon follows his glance as it rests on two women sitting in the corner of the room. Both have their heads down, deep in conversation, and then the blonde, this gorgeous, tanned, smiling blonde, throws back her head and laughs.

Funny, thinks Ben. I'm sure I've heard that laugh somewhere before. He shakes his head, trying to remember what's so familiar about the laugh, but he doesn't remember, and there's no way he knows this woman. Unfortunately. He keeps glancing back at her anyway, because she is truly lovely, but she doesn't look up at him, not once, far too immersed in the conversation with her friend. Probably got a boyfriend waiting at home, thinks Ben, because she is so obviously not there to pick up men.

'Right,' he says, finishing his drink. 'Shall we make a move?'

I'm not as fine as I say I am, but I'm not that bad either.

Amazing how spending some money, especially when you haven't got it, can perk you up. And being with Lauren is fun, actually, it's a hell of a lot more fun than being with Brad, and every time I think about the way he held me, the way he kissed me, I then have to think about how one-dimensional he actually was, how he never felt like a real person.

And tonight, sitting here at a corner table in the bar of Schatzi on Main, is perfect. Exactly what I needed. I know Lauren planned to get as drunk as we were the other night at the Pepper, but it's turned out to be a far more mellow evening. Yes, we've had some stares, but I suppose two single women in a busy bar will always get attention, but no one's bothered us, and it's nice to just sit, have a few drinks and chill out, as they say.

And the more time I spend with Lauren, the more I like her. She's so open, so warm, so loyal, and I honestly feel as if I've known her for years. She seems to understand exactly what I'm thinking, as if she picks up my mood before I've even opened my mouth, and she always seems to know exactly the right thing to say and do.

Take tonight, for example. Given her drunken debauchery the other night, I was worried she'd spend the night flirting, but to be honest she's hardly looked at any of the men in here, and there have been some gorgeous ones. I know, I'm facing into the room. Not that I'm paying that much attention, I'm too busy laughing at her stories and telling her stories of my own.

But then the weirdest thing happens. I've just finished telling her about the Sophie story, the night of Ben's leaving do and how Sophie pretended to be Ben's girlfriend, when I look up and see two men, just walking out of the restaurant.

My heart completely stops because one of them, the taller of the two, looks exactly like Ben.

'What is it?' Lauren asks me. 'You look like you've seen a ghost.'

'No, it can't be.' I stand up and try and see him more clearly, but there are so many people, and by the time I manage to get a good viewpoint all I can see is his back disappearing through the door. Same build, same hair, but of course it's not Ben. Ben's busy being a television star at home. 'It's nothing,' I sigh, sitting down again and wishing with all my heart it *was* him. 'I just thought I saw someone I knew, but I was wrong.'

CHAPTER THIRTY

Ben Williams slept like a baby last night, and this morning he wakes up feeling fantastic. The only vague blot on his horizon is that Jemima hasn't called him back. He knows he's been remiss in their friendship, he knows he should have kept in touch, and, although part of him worries he's got the wrong number, the other part worries that perhaps she hasn't forgiven him for just walking out of her life.

But he's not *that* worried, it just would be nice to see her, and he's leaving tomorrow. He wonders whether to call again, but three phonecalls, he decides, would be just a touch excessive.

So today is his free day in Los Angeles, and he knows what he should be doing, he should be doing something incredibly touristy like Disneyland or the Universal Studios tour, but when he asked at the front desk they said he'd definitely need a car to get there, and Simon's taken the car to an edit suite, so he's a bit stuck on his own.

This is ridiculous, he thinks, when he's had his shower. He's in the most glamorous city in the world and he doesn't know what to do, so in the end he decides to go down to the beach.

The rollerbladers are out in full force, and Ben wonders whether to hire blades and try it out for himself, but making a fool of yourself in Hyde Park on a Sunday morning when everyone else is also an amateur is one

417

thing; making a fool of yourself in Los Angeles when everyone on skates looks as if they've been born on them is another. So he just walks along the beach, and goes down to the pier.

On the way back he walks past a bookstore, and, despite his bad luck the other day, something about this bookstore says it's much more his kind of place, that there is likely to be decent fiction, and Ben walks in and within the first three minutes he has found two books – two first-time novels by young American writers that he cannot wait to get stuck into.

And, as he walks over to the desk and waits for the cashier to check his Visa card, he does a double-take. Surely not, it can't be . . . But of course, it is. The very same beautiful blonde he saw last night, this time on her own, just leaving the bookstore. He almost wouldn't have recognized her, but he saw her smile, and it's a smile that, even after a brief glimpse last night, he can't seem to get out of his head.

Hurry up, hurry up, come on, come on, he thinks, as the cashier dawdles behind the desk. Ben looks impatiently at her, then back at the blonde, who's stopped just by the door to pick up a book on display. This is fate, he thinks. Of all the bookstores in all of Los Angeles she has to be in this one. And more to the point, a bookstore! She likes books! She could be brainy as well as beautiful! He looks up again. She's gone.

Ben grabs his books, grabs his card, and runs out the door. There she is, those gorgeous thighs striding along the street. He dodges the people meandering along, just in time to see her climb into a car, and in a way it's probably not a bad thing because why is he following her so frantically, what would he say to her if he stopped her, caught her? Damn, he curses. That's it. I'm never going to see her again.

'Thanks for lending me your car,' I shout, tossing the car keys on the table in the living room.

'No problem. Did you get what you wanted?'

'I just went browsing in the bookstore, bought a couple of new novels.'

'Hey, JJ?'

'Yup?' I walk in to Lauren's bedroom and sit on the bed as Lauren tries on the new outfits she bought yesterday.

'Remember that scarf you were wearing when I first met you?' Her voice has a pleading tone in it already.

'Which one? The green silk one?'

'Yes . . .' Lauren whines hopefully.

'You want to borrow it tonight?'

'Yes . . .' Another whine, with a cheeky smile.

'Okay, but guard it with your life, it's one of my favourite possessions. I suppose you want me to get it for you now so you can see what it looks like?'

'Would you mind?'

I open my suitcase and dig through the pile of clothes. It's not there. I open the drawer I'm using for my underwear. It's not there. I look in the bathroom, the bedroom, and the kitchen. I look under the sofa, over the sofa and behind the sofa. It's not there.

'Oh shit.' With a sinking feeling, I realize I know exactly where it is. It's hanging behind Brad's bedroom door.

'Have you lost it?' Lauren walks in from the bedroom.

'No. The bloody thing's at Brad's.'

'Don't worry,' Lauren's face falls. 'I don't really need it.'

'Never mind about you! That's my favourite scarf.'

'Do you want me to call him?'

'Oh my God, you're such an angel. Would you?'

Even knowing that Lauren's going to be talking to him makes me feel slightly sick, and as I watch her walking over to the phone I start shaking. She has a brief cool conversation with him in which he says he does have the scarf and he'll leave it at the gym for her. I hear her say, 'Uh huh. Uh huh. Uh huh. Okay. I'll tell her. Bye.'

'What did he say? What did he say?'

Lauren has a huge smile on her face. 'Jemima Jones, this must be your lucky day.'

'Why?' I'm still shaking.

'You've had a message, you've had a message,' Lauren starts singing, getting up and dancing round the living room in time with her odd little tune.

'Who from?'

Lauren stops and pauses for dramatic effect before announcing in her best Johnny Carson impersonation, 'From . . . Ben WILLIAMS.'

My mouth drops open.

'And not just that. HE'S IN LOS ANGELES! And not just that, HE'S AT SHUTTERS ON THE BEACH!'

'I knew it,' I scream. 'I bloody knew it. I'd know that haircut and that back anywhere. He's here. He's round the corner. Give me that phone. NOW!'

The shakes, if anything, have got worse, but Ben's

here! My Ben! My love! I wait for the hotel to put me through, praying that he's still there, that he won't have gone back home, because I have never wanted anything more in my life than I want to see Ben Williams right this second.

And the phone rings, and rings, and rings. And just as I'm about to give up hope the receiver's picked up and a breathless voice, a voice I used to know as well as my own, says, 'Hello?'

I swallow, feeling my heart pounding, wondering why I'm so out of breath when I haven't been anywhere, and I try to speak slowly, calmly.

'Ben? It's Jemima.'

'Jemima! You're still here!' And is it my imagination or does he truly sound delighted to hear from me?

'I can't believe you're here!' I say, for want of something better.

'I can't believe I haven't spoken to you for so long,' he says, for want of something better.

And then we both start talking at once, I'm so excited, he's here! He's here! He's round the corner.

'What are you *doing* here?' we both say in unison, before stopping and laughing.

'I'm not telling you on the phone,' says Ben. 'Look, are you around this afternoon?'

'Yes.' I'm around for you anytime, Ben.

'How about meeting up?'

'I'd love to.'

'How about meeting up now? We could spend the rest of the day together.'

'I'd love to.'

'Where shall we meet?'

I think for a minute, then suggests a café round the corner from his hotel. 'See you there in fifteen minutes?' I say.

'Done.'

Oh my God, I'm whirling round Lauren's tiny apartment like a dervish. What to wear, what to wear? I pull on some skin-tight black trousers, a crisp white linen shirt and a pair of white trainers. I loop a crocodile belt around my waist and tip my head upside-down to give my hair that sexy, tousled, just-got-out-of-bed look.

'I'm seeing Ben!' I keep shrieking to Lauren, who seems to have caught my enthusiasm, and at this very second is bouncing up and down on the bed and clapping her hands.

'Has he seen you like this?' Lauren suddenly says, while I apply the finishing touches of lipstick.

'Like what?'

'Thin.'

No. Oh God. He has no idea. I'm so nervous, what will he think, what will he say. I just shake my head.

'He'll be gobsmacked,' she laughs. 'I'll drop you off. Come on. You'll be fine. Remember, it's only Ben, he's your friend.'

'Exactly. It's Ben!'

We jump in the car and Lauren puts her foot down, and three minutes later I climb out of the car, seriously worried that the butterflies in my stomach are making me feel nearly as sick as my binge the other night.

Ben's not there. I sit at a corner table for a while and look at my watch, putting my sunglasses on to hide the nerves, to stop Ben seeing right through to the churning emotions inside, and eventually, after I'm bored of sitting with nothing to do, I walk over to the counter to order a cappuccino. I'm standing there as I hear the creak of the door opening and I turn my head slowly to see who it is and it's him. It's Ben. And my heart turns over.

Is it possible that Ben has got better looking? That television has groomed him, given him an air of confidence that he was missing before? For one tiny moment at Lauren's flat I thought that perhaps, once I'd actually seen him in the flesh, perhaps I wouldn't feel the same way, perhaps I'd just look at him, admit he's good-looking but not have it affect me, but no, sod's bloody law. I feel exactly the same way as I did six months ago, and all of a sudden I know I'm going to act like a lovestruck teenager. I'm not going to know what to say, how to be.

And I can't go over to say hello, my feet are rooted to the spot, so I just watch Ben looking round the café, ignoring the guy behind the counter who's trying to hand me my cappuccino, which I can't take because I can't bloody move!

And then finally, finally, Ben sees me, and when he does he starts to smile.

He knows me, he's recognized me! I start to walk towards him, the sunglasses still shielding my eyes, not breaking his gaze for a second, and I forget everything around me except for Ben, my love. Then suddenly he's standing right in front of me and we're both smiling. I don't say anything. I don't have to.

'I never usually do this,' says Ben, as confusion crosses my face. 'But I saw you last night in Schatzi on Main, and again today in the bookstore. I'm meeting a friend here in a few minutes, but I just wanted to tell you that

I think you're the most amazing woman I've ever seen.'

Is this a joke? What is he talking about? What's going on?

Ben blushes. 'I'm really sorry,' he mumbles. 'I didn't mean to embarrass you,' and with a shrug and a smile he turns away and sits at the table I was going to sit at, and I don't know what to do, how to tell him it's me.

'Excuse me? Excuse me? Your cappuccino?' The words float over my head, and I know that I can't go over there, not after what he's just said, I can't just say, actually it's me, Jemima Jones, and as soon as I realize this I also know that I have to leave, except my legs are still shaking, and Ben's buried his head in a newspaper and I have to leave.

And eventually, on auto-pilot, I walk slowly out the door and go home.

'What happened?' Lauren asks. 'What are you doing back here?' And I tell her.

'Go back, you've got to go back there.'

'I can't,' I moan. 'What would I say?'

'Are you completely nuts?' Lauren's shaking her head in disbelief. 'The man you were completely in love with, you're still completely in love with, has just told you he thinks you're the most amazing woman he's ever seen and you didn't have the balls to tell him it was you? This is unreal. Get your arse back there.'

I point to my watch. 'He won't still be there.'

'You are going to see him and, more to the bloody point, talk to him, if it kills me.'

Lauren paces up and down for the next hour, and then she picks up the phone and hands it to me. 'The poor sod will be back at his hotel now, wondering why you didn't turn up. Get on this phone NOW, and arrange to meet him for dinner.'

'What will I say?'

'Tell him you had an emergency and you tried to get through and you couldn't. And for God's sake apologize. Profusely.'

Please don't be there, I pray as I dial Shutters on the Beach, but he picks up the phone in his room after the first ring.

'Jemima?'

'Ben, I'm so sorry.' I tell him the story Lauren came up with and wait for him to say something.

'Don't worry,' he says finally. 'I understand. These things happen. Anyway, I'm leaving town tomorrow so I probably won't get a chance to see you. It would have been nice, that's all.'

'What about tonight,' I say quickly, as Lauren gives me a very sharp nudge in the ribs. 'I could definitely see you tonight. We could have dinner.'

'You really want to?'

'I really want to.'

'And you won't stand me up?'

'I swear on my life, Ben. I won't stand you up.'

The rest of the afternoon seems to pass in slow motion, every second making the anticipation stronger and stronger. Lauren insists I do some serious beauty treatments 'just in case', and she rushes around helping me look the most beautiful I've ever looked in my life.

And finally it's 6.45, just fifteen minutes to go before we're due to meet, and I can't stop pacing up and down, and Lauren keeps telling me off because I keep rubbing my damp palms on my dress and she's right, I might stain it, but I don't know what else to do with my hands so I just pace around, wringing them constantly.

'Well?' I say, for about the hundredth time. 'How do I look?'

'You look fucking incredible,' says Lauren, and, although I would never describe myself as incredible, I do know I look good in my red halterneck sundress, tightly fitting at the top, then flaring out at the hips into a short, swinging skirt. The postbox-red sets off my tan, and I no longer need all the make-up that Geraldine taught me expertly to apply, just the merest hint of mascara and lipgloss. I look healthy, happy, confident and, most of all, I look like a true Californian. To be honest I'm not surprised that Ben didn't know me because looking in the mirror I don't even know myself.

But, because I've had all afternoon to prepare for this, I don't feel that nervous any more. In a weird sort of way I feel more in control, I've already faced him, I know what I'm up against, and I know, beyond a shadow of a doubt, that I still love him.

And that knowledge has sort of given me a power, a power I never thought I had, and I know I can face him this time, I won't run away, and, although of course I'm still nervous, I'm excited now too.

This time I'm a few minutes late. I don't want to be waiting for Ben to arrive, I want to walk in when he's there, feeling strong, powerful, beautiful.

And she does walk in, and he's there, and she does feel all of the above, and she also feels brave, which is, it has to be said, a completely new feeling for her. Once again he stares at her, thinking that this must be fate, that it is ridiculous how he keeps seeing his perfect woman, how she keeps turning up wherever he is, but he looks away after a few seconds because he made a fool of himself earlier on today, and he doesn't want to do it again. But God, is she beautiful. No, he buries his head in a book. He's not going to talk to her again. He's just going to immerse himself in the book and wait for Jemima.

And as he looks at the words, for he can't possibly read when he knows this vision of loveliness is in the room, he sees a pair of taut, tanned legs standing just in front of him, and he looks up at her, and sees that this time she is giving him a warm smile, and he curses the fact that he's meeting Jemima, because right now he wants to spend the rest of his life basking in this woman's smile.

'I can't believe it's you,' he says softly, frowning slightly as I smile.

'Yes, it's me,' and Ben frowns, and he keeps frowning as I lean down and give him an awkward kiss on the cheek, before pulling out a chair and sitting down.

'What are you doing here?' he says, looking confused.

'What do you mean, Ben? We arranged to meet,' I tease in an American accent, because I know what this is about and I'm finally starting to enjoy it.

Ben looks at me and says slowly, 'How do you know my name?'

'Ben!' I burst out laughing. 'It's me, you dumbass.

427

Jemima Jones.' And as I watch I see it register on his face, see the confusion replaced by sheer and utter amazement, and I'm loving this, I'm loving every single second.

Ben tries to speak, but no words come out. He just stares at me, and I can see what's happened slowly dawning on him. That I'm not fat any more, that I've turned into the amazing woman he keeps seeing around, and through his shock and confusion I can slowly see admiration starting to emerge, and this is the best bloody feeling in the whole world.

'Jemima,' he whispers, as the smile leaves my face, and then, without planning it, thinking about it, we both stand up at exactly the same time and fall into one another's arms.

Let this moment carry on for ever, let the whole world disappear, leaving just me and Ben. Ben and me. I want to remember this for the rest of my life, the feel of his chest, his arms wrapped around me, his heart-beat against my cheek. I close my eyes and just cling on to him. Let me stay here for ever and ever and ever.

But for ever only lasts about a minute, and then, reluctantly, I pull away and sit down.

'How?' Ben starts, looking at me in amazement. 'I mean, when?' He can't take his eyes off me. 'It's . . .'

I laugh. 'How did I look like this?'

Ben nods.

'It was after you left. I lost the weight and Geraldine made me over, as she would say.'

'Oh God,' Ben groans. 'I made such a fool of myself today. No wonder you walked out.'

'You didn't make a fool of yourself. It was lovely to hear.'

'But I *knew* there was something familiar about you, I just never dreamt, never thought . . .' He tails off again, still staring at me. 'You just look so beautiful. I mean, you look nothing like *you*. I'm sorry,' he continues, stammering, 'I didn't mean . . .'

'That's okay,' I say smiling. 'I know what you meant, and thank you. You look great too. I've seen you on television. Being a star obviously suits you.'

'I'm not really a star,' says Ben. 'Just a presenter.'

'Bullshit,' I tease. 'Geraldine sent me that double-page spread they ran on you. You're a star, Ben. Take it from me.'

'I can't believe she did that, that's so embarrassing,' says Ben. 'Now you know all about me.'

'Your murky past,' I laugh.

'I know,' he sighs. 'You did warn me.'

'And I'm always right.'

'Yup,' he laughs. 'You always are. God, Jemima. I've missed you,' and I can hear the sincerity in his voice and I know that he means it, and I realize how much I've missed him, and not just because I love him. I've missed this, the easy banter, the friendship, and, even though I haven't seen him for months, it's almost as if barely a day's gone by, I mean, we're so relaxed we could almost be sitting in the canteen of the *Kilburn Herald*.

And how is it for Ben? The longer Ben sits in this restaurant with this beautiful woman, the less she becomes a gorgeous blonde, and the more she becomes

Jemima Jones, for Ben looks past the legs, the dress, the hair, and he sees his old friend, a friend, he suddenly realizes, he never wants to walk out on again.

I'm teasing Ben about work and we're laughing and he tells me about Diana Macpherson, grudgingly, admittedly, and even though I feel a red-hot poker of jealousy stabbing me as he tells me about his drunken mistake, I don't really mind because he's relaxed enough to confide in me, and anyway he doesn't want her, plus he tells me confidentially that he's been offered a far better job with another TV station, which solves the problem. But the funny thing is that actually I feel a little bit sorry for Diana Macpherson, this media ogre, because I know what it's like to want someone that badly, to want them even though they don't want you.

I tell him about Brad, about what it was like to finally have a boyfriend that everyone else wanted, and about how it all went horribly wrong. And yes. Okay. I did tell him about the porn pictures, I tell him very slowly and very seriously, waiting for sympathy, waiting for concern, but when I look up Ben's trying to suppress a smile.

'It's not funny, Ben,' I say sternly.

'No,' he says. 'You're right. It's not,' but he can't contain himself any more, he starts giggling, and it's so infectious and I suppose the story is so bizarre that I start giggling too, and the giggling soon becomes hysterical laughter, and the pair of us are rocking back on our chairs, clutching our stomachs in pain and crying with laughter.

430

'Oh God,' I scrabble around for a napkin to wipe the tears of laughter away. 'I never thought I'd see the funny side of that.'

'Jemima, it's *classic*. It's one of the greatest stories I've ever heard,' and we both start laughing again.

Neither of us eats very much. The food sits on our plates while we pick at it, raise the odd mouthful to our lips, but there's just so much to talk about, so many things to catch up on, and we hardly have a chance to breathe, we don't even let one another finish a sentence, we just let them tumble and twist, and eventually, when the waiters bring the bill, we stand up and smile at one another.

'I've had such a good time,' says Ben, as we walk out.

'So have I. I can't tell you how good it is to see you.' And as I turn to look at him, suddenly, the easy camaraderie of the evening disappears and we both stand awkwardly on the pavement outside the restaurant, and why do I suddenly feel nervous, what does this mean?

Ben's arm reaches out, and suddenly, and oh God I didn't plan this, but suddenly I'm in his arms and we're hugging but it's not like before, it's not just a friendly hug, and I'm very aware of Ben's breathing, of his touch, and as I stand there wrapped around him I feel him stroke my hair and I lean my head back to look at him and then everything becomes slow motion as he bends his head and kisses me, and I know it sounds naff, I know it sounds unreal, but I honestly feel that every fibre in my body is about to melt.

CHAPTER THIRTY-ONE

How do you know when you've found love? How do you know when you've met the person with whom you want to spend the rest of your life? How do you know it's not just two people lusting after one another, and consummating that lust in a night of unbelievable passion. How do you know it's not going to be just a one-night-stand? How do you know whether your wishes will come true?

I wish I knew. All I do know, right now, when I open my eyes to the morning sunlight and Ben Williams fast asleep next to me, is that, even if I never set eyes on Ben again, this has been, and will always be, the happiest night of my life.

I know because I never dreamt that love-making could be so passionate, and yet so tender. I know because no one has ever cupped my face and looked deep in my eyes, and whispered how wonderful I am while moving gently inside me.

I know because I've never felt so comfortable with anyone in my life as I felt with Ben last night, because I'v never felt *any* of the feelings I felt last night.

And finally I know that I will never forget what it is like to be so happy you are frightened you're going to burst.

So I just lie in bed and soak up this joy. I don't move, I'm too frightened of waking Ben up, too frightened of the magic disappearing, but as I watch him sleep he slowly opens his eyes, stretches, and then turns his head to look at me.

What should I do? I want to smile, to say something, but I can't, because I haven't got a clue how Ben is feeling, and when he blinks, smiles sleepily and holds his arm out to me, the relief is so overwhelming it practically sweeps me away and I snuggle into his chest like the proverbial cat that got the cream.

He kisses my hair, and then my shoulder. 'Thank you,' he says huskily, and I just smile, making small circles on his chest with my index finger.

We stay there for a little while, kissing, cuddling, completely comfortable with one another, and then Ben looks at the clock. 'Shit!' he jumps out of bed. 'I've got a flight to catch.'

There's a knock on the door as I sit up in bed.

'Ben? It's Simon. We're leaving in ten minutes. Are you ready?'

'Nearly,' shouts Ben, tripping over his shoes. 'Shit!' he mutters, running around the bedroom.

'I'll help you pack,' I say, climbing out of bed without a second thought, even though I'm completely naked. Ben stops and looks at me then drops his clothes and puts his arms around me, groaning, 'I can't believe it's you. I can't believe last night.' We start kissing again, and then Ben pulls away. 'I can't. We can't. No time. Shit!'

There's no time for lazy post-coital kisses and cuddles, and within ten minutes Ben is packed and dressed, and I follow him downstairs, terrified at how we're going to say goodbye, what's going to happen next.

'He-llo,' says a man I don't recognize, walking over to

Ben but keeping his eyes firmly on me with a bit of a leer. 'Who's this?'

'This is my friend Jemima,' says Ben. 'This is Simon,' and I shake Simon's hand, not missing the look that he gives Ben, which Ben, being the gentleman that he is, tries to ignore.

'Simon, I'll see you by the car,' he says, and Simon reluctantly walks out, probably dying to fill in the rest of the crew on the gossip.

'How long are you here?' Ben says, tucking my hair behind my ears.

'About two more months,' I say, already trying to think of some way to get home, to be with Ben.

'What am I going to do for the next two months?' he says, as my heart lifts.

'I'd love to come home but I can't.'

'Why not?'

I know it's crazy, but I don't want to tell him I haven't got the money, that I'm over my limit on my credit card, that in truth I no longer have a penny to my name. It sounds too sad, too like the Jemima Jones of old, so I think on my feet and come up with the perfect excuse.

'I'm doing a column for the *Kilburn Herald* and you know what the editor's like, I have to stay here, otherwise I'll lose my job.'

'I'll miss you,' he whispers eventually, pulling me close and kissing my forehead.

'We can write,' I say in desperation. 'Or phone.'

'Definitely,' he nods. 'Can you write down your address and number?'

I pull away from him, reluctantly, and scribble down Lauren's address and number, and just as I hand it to him Simon reappears and says testily, 'Ben, we've *got* to go.'

We do hug, and kiss, and then Ben starts walking away. Just before he reaches the door he turns around and runs back, scooping me up in his arms and kissing me. 'I'll phone,' he says. 'As soon as I get back home.'

'What time will that be?'

'God knows. But don't worry, I'll call,' and he leaves, turning back to wave as he climbs in the car, and I float back home on a cloud of sheer, unadulterated bliss.

'Well?' Lauren opens the door before I even get a chance to put my key in the lock, and I don't have to say anything, she can see from the ridiculously soppy grin on my face that last night was unbelievable.

'You did it! You did it!' She leaps up and down and throws her arms around me while I start giggling. 'I want to hear everything.'

'I'm so tired,' I moan, collapsing on the sofa, still smiling.

'I don't want to hear that crap, I want to hear about Ben.'

'I love him,' I say simply, and then I say it again, just to hear the words, just to make sure it's true. 'I love him.'

'Start from the beginning,' she commands, and I do.

I tell her about meeting him, about him not realizing it was me, and how it was like we'd never been apart. I tell her about his stories, his work, his life. I tell her about leaving the restaurant and practically leaping on one another as soon as we got outside. And I tell her about making love with him, what it was like, how I felt.

I tell her word for word, action for action, and all the

time I'm talking this stupid grin doesn't leave my face, and I feel like I'm swimming in happiness.

'So you've got over Brad then?' she says, when I've finished.

'Brad who?' I laugh. 'No, seriously, Lauren. It was so completely different to being with Brad. I mean, the sex was amazing with Brad, but last night made me realize how that's all it was, just great sex. There was no tenderness, no love, just passion, and at the time I thought it was enough. But Ben was so different, maybe because I know him, maybe because we're friends, but I think it's more than that. I know, beyond a shadow of a doubt, that I'm still totally in love with him.' I stop and sigh.

'Do you think he feels the same way?'

'I don't know,' I sigh, as the insecurities threaten to strike. 'I know that he was incredibly caring, and giving, and loving, but I don't know whether that means he feels the same way, but there's no point thinking about that. Anyway, he's going to call as soon as he gets home.'

'What time?'

'I don't know, but I know he'll call. Oh God, Lauren. I just want to be with him. I want to go home.' And I do, and two months feels like an eternity and I don't know how I'm going to cope for the next few weeks with just the memories of one night to keep me going.

'He's going to call,' she says, 'and you're going home in just over seven weeks. It's nothing. It will pass in a flash. Now,' she says looking at her watch. 'How about a celebratory brunch?'

'Perfect,' I say. 'I'm starving.

We go to the Broadway Deli and I tuck into french toast and bacon and strawberries, and it's delicious and we go over every detail all over again, and I feel as if I'm bathed in love, as if everyone's looking at me with envy because I am a woman in love and they wish they were me.

And then afterwards we get some Ben & Jerry's frozen yoghurt and some old videos from Blockbuster and we spend the rest of the afternoon and evening watching our favourite love stories, and I try to concentrate, I really do, but I'm trying not to jump every time I hear a noise because it might be the phone, except it's not, and by 10 p.m. I'm looking at my watch and starting to feel slightly sick because it's six o'clock in the morning at home and I know, I just know, that with the time difference he must have been home for ages now, and even if his luggage took for ever to come through, and even if it took hours to get through customs he would still be home and he hasn't called.

And by midnight I feel the last shreds of happiness drift away from me and I think I'm going to cry.

'Anything could have happened,' says Lauren, finishing off the last of her tub of Chocolate Chip Cookie Dough. 'The flight might have been delayed, he might have had to work. Don't worry, he'll call.' But I do worry and I am worried, and even though I know this morning I said that it wouldn't matter if I never saw him again, that the one night with him would last me the rest of my life, I know that's not true, and I know that the pain that suddenly attacks me like a knife is something I'm going to have to learn to live with, because he hasn't called, and he won't call, and this is how it's going to be for the rest of my life.

*

JANE GREEN

A week later I'm still trying to learn to live with the pain. Sure, I'm putting on a brave face, trying to get on with my life. I don't go to the gym any more, but I go out with Lauren, pretend to have a good time, and then every morning when I wake up the first thing I think is, something's wrong, what is it? And then I remember and the black clouds descend and the bloody things follow me around until the next morning.

You'd think I'd find some peace at night, fast asleep, but even there the pain's still present. I dream about Ben. Constantly. A mixture of memories and surreal fantasy, and, without wishing to sound over-dramatic, I think I understand what it's like to be bereaved, to lose someone you love with all your heart, to know there's no possibility of ever seeing them again.

Brad was bad. That whole Brad and Jenny thing was bad. But it was nothing, nothing, compared to this. A mere drop in the ocean of grief I now feel every moment of the day, and there are days when I don't want to get up at all, I just want to lie in bed and drift into nothingness, just get it all over with.

Ben Williams cannot believe he has been so stupid. He cannot believe that the scrap of paper on which Jemima had scrawled her number and address has gone missing. He cannot believe that he has no way of getting in touch with her. He's left countless messages at Brad's, but he assumes they haven't been passed on because they haven't been returned. He phoned Geraldine, but the only number she had for him was at Brad's, and Sophie and Lisa weren't much use either. He even tried the editor at the *Kilburn Herald*, but he was more interested in moaning about Jemima's missing copy, and again she hadn't been in touch to tell him she'd moved.

Ben's been through his clothes, his bags, his cases with a fine-tooth comb, but he can't find the bloody thing at all.

And although he's only been back a week, he's been thinking about Jemima Jones. A lot. In the middle of a broadcast he'll suddenly lose his train of thought as a picture will flash up in his mind of Jemima's face as she looked trustingly into his eyes when he pulled her on top of him. Or he'll suddenly remember the feel of her skin when he's in a meeting with the production team.

And there are times, late at night, every night, when he just wants to hear her voice, and he keeps hoping that she'll call him, she'll realize something's wrong, but the phone doesn't ring, and when it does it's not her. Eventually Ben – and who would have thought the divine Ben Williams had an ounce of insecurity within – starts to worry that maybe, for Jemima, it was just a one-night-stand. Maybe she doesn't care about him at all. Maybe she's met someone else.

When a week goes by and he hasn't heard from her and he hasn't been able to get in touch, he tells Richard about her. He tells him against his better judgement, for Richard, as we know, is not the best person to tell your troubles to.

'She could call *you*,' says Richard. 'Let's face it, Ben, she knows where you work and all she has to do is pick up the phone. You should just leave it as a brilliant one-night-stand and get on with your life.'

'Hmm,' says Ben, who sees a grain of truth in what

Richard just said. After all, Jemima *could* call him, and she hasn't, so maybe he should just forget about it.

'Oh no,' says Richard, looking at Ben intensely.

'What's the matter?' Ben asks in alarm.

'You're not? You can't be?'

'What?'

'You're bloody in love with her aren't you?'

'Absolutely not.' Ben shakes his head.

'You are. I recognize the signs.'

'I'm not,' says Ben. 'No way,' and he looks at his watch. 'I've gotta go,' he says, standing up. 'I'm doing an interview with the *Daily Mail*.'

'What? Another interview?'

Ben sighs. 'I know. After the last one I thought I'd done enough, but you've got to keep that publicity ball rolling.'

'Don't tell them *anything*,' says Richard dramatically.

'No,' says Ben firmly. 'I won't.

But Ben can't quite help himself. The journalist is so *nice*, a warm, caring middle-aged woman to whom Ben immediately wanted to open his heart, and before he knows it he tells her far more than he should.

'Please don't put that stuff in about not being able to find her,' he pleads, as he says goodbye. 'That's off the record.'

'Don't worry,' she says laying a reassuring hand on his arm. 'You can trust me.'

Ben refuses to think about this for the rest of the evening. How could he, when all he can think about is Jemima Jones and how to find her.

*

I wasn't going to phone anyone at home. I didn't want anyone to know what happened, and I knew that if I dared call anyone to tell them I'd moved, they'd want to know why, and I haven't got the strength to tell people about Brad, about Jenny and, mostly, about Ben.

But a week is a bloody long time when your heart has broken, and Lauren, great as she has been, is starting to get on my nerves. She doesn't mean to, she's lovely, it's just that sometimes I want to be on my own, to just sit and reflect on the one perfect night of my life, on the future I could have had if Ben had called me, but she won't leave me alone, and I know she's trying to cheer me up but sometimes the jokes wear a bit thin, that's all.

And then, finally, it becomes too much. I have to talk to someone who *knows* Ben. Someone who can tell me what to do. Someone who might, just might, know what he's thinking, why he hasn't called.

'Geraldine? It's me.'

'Jemima Jones! Am I glad you called. Where the hell have you been?'

'Are you sitting down?'

'I most certainly am. What on earth is going on there?'

'Oh God, Geraldine. It's awful. I don't know where to start.'

'At the beginning,' she says quietly, so I do. I tell her about Brad, and Jenny, and Lauren, and food, and everything. And then, eventually, I tell her about Ben.

'But he called me!' she says, not even waiting for me to finish describing my pain. 'I knew there was something up because I hadn't spoken to him since he left. He phoned last week to see if I had your number. Jemima,

441

you idiot! He must have lost your number. Why the hell didn't you call me sooner?'

'He called you?' Slowly, slowly, my heart starts piecing itself back together again. 'He called you?'

'Yes! Last week! I knew from his voice that something had happened. I just knew it.'

'What did he say? Tell me exactly what he said.'

'He didn't tell me anything, he just said he'd seen you in Los Angeles and he meant to call you to thank you but he couldn't find your number.'

'What should I do? Should I call him? Oh God, Geraldine, I just want to come home.'

'So why don't you?'

'I can't,' I moan. 'It'll cost me $954 plus tax to change my flight and I've run out of money.'

'Did you tell Ben that?'

'How could I? I didn't want him to feel sorry for me, so I just said I was stuck out here writing the column.'

'Oh for heaven's sake, Jemima. Why didn't you tell him the truth?'

'I don't know,' I murmur. 'Would it have made any difference?'

'I don't know,' she echoes. 'But I'm planning to find out.'

'What are you going to do?'

'Just leave it to me,' she says firmly.

'What? Tell me. Shall I ring him?'

'No,' she says. 'Absolutely not. You just sit tight and let me sort it out.'

'Geraldine, please don't say I haven't got the money to come home. Anyway, he's probably changed his mind by now.'

'Jemima, if it was as incredible as you say it was, he won't have changed his mind. Trust me. I know men.' And I breathe a sigh of relief because no one knows men better than Geraldine.

'JJ? I forgot to tell you, a letter came for you this morning.' Lauren dumps the shopping on the kitchen table.

'Hmm? Where is it?'

'I left it on the coffee table.' Lauren comes out and lifts a magazine to reveal a large brown envelope with a London postmark. My heart stops as she hands it to me but it's not from Ben. It's Geraldine. I'd know that writing anywhere.

I tear open the envelope and pull out a newspaper clipping and a compliments slip.

Jemima Jones! As usual Auntie Geraldine has come to the rescue, and I'm sorry, I know you didn't want me to tell Ben about being stuck out there but I had to. Plus, it gave me a chance to call him a stupid bastard which I've been dying to do for years!!! (no offence . . .)

Anyway, I don't think you'll mind once you've opened this envelope, and it's not from me, it's from Ben, AND, I think you'll find the enclosed interesting reading!!! (I certainly did . . .) Lucky, lucky you!! Things still going great guns with me and Nick, will tell you all when I see you. Soon. Very soon. Ha! Loads of love and kisses, Geraldine. xxxxxxxxxx

I'm smiling because I can almost hear Geraldine speak, and then I read it again and I wonder why Geraldine's written to me, why not Ben, and, if the clipping that's attached is from Ben and not her, why did she bother writing at all, and oh my God, I don't feel too good about this and that small light at the end of the tunnel starts getting smaller, so I pick up the clipping and then I have to sit down very quickly.

'What is it?' says Lauren, sitting next to me, so I start to read it out loud, haltingly, disbelievingly.

'Ben Williams is cagey on the subject of love,' I read. 'He's "had his fingers burnt", as he puts it, and doesn't want to reveal who it is. But millions of women will be devastated to hear that the gorgeous presenter of *London Nights* has fallen in love. "She's an old friend," reveals Williams, "whom I hadn't seen for a while, and then we met up recently and we became more than friends. I don't think I even knew it was love until we were apart, and now I'm just killing time until she comes home." So who is this mystery woman of his? "No one famous," he laughs. "Her name's Jemima Jones."'

I start shaking. I don't know whether to laugh or cry, and neither of us speaks, I think Lauren's as shocked as I am. After a while Lauren frowns and picks up the envelope, and, instead of putting it in the bin, she looks inside, smiles, and then gives it to me. I look at her, then feel the envelope, and there's something else in there, and when I pull it out I see something that looks suspiciously like an air ticket, and why has Geraldine sent me an air ticket? And then I notice there's writing on the cover and I remember that writing, and it says, 'Come home. I miss you. Ben.' And I know why Ben and Geraldine met up, and I know that this was probably Geraldine's idea because it's so typical of her and I don't care, and Ben misses me and he wants me to come home.

And slowly I look closely at the ticket and I gasp when I read it's a one-way flight from LAX to Heathrow for the day after tomorrow. The day after tomorrow! I'm going home!

'See?' says Lauren, throwing her arms around me and hugging me tightly. 'I knew he'd come through for you.'

'He has.' I whisper, as the tears start rolling down my face. 'He has.'

CHAPTER THIRTY-TWO

And so here I am, suitcases in hand, not to mention of course the Louis Vuitton vanity case, and thank God I made it through customs – not that I have anything to hide, I just always feel so damn guilty walking through there, and, as I pile the cases on a trolley and wheel it out to the waiting crowds of people, I know just how much I've missed London.

''Scuse.' A young woman pushes past me and rushes up to her waiting friends, and I never thought I'd be so pleased to hear a British accent.

Ben, I know, won't be waiting, because I phoned him before I left, in a fit of nerves and excitement, gushing my thanks at his generosity while he apologized profusely, told me he couldn't stop thinking about me, and said he just wanted to be with me. With *me*!

My Ben. Back home. I still can't quite believe that in just a few hours' time I'll be seeing him. I know I'll be jet-lagged to hell by the time I actually walk in, but I also know that the adrenalin of seeing him will keep me going well into the night.

But, amazingly enough, even though it's all I've been thinking about since I got the air ticket – seeing him again – I still managed to sleep on the plane. I suppose I was exhausted from all the emotional trauma, but nevertheless I abided by Geraldine's advice and spritzed my face, covered myself with moisturizer and fell fast asleep until I was woken by the stewardess placing a breakfast tray in front of me.

And I realize now there aren't many things I'll miss about Los Angeles, although I will miss Lauren. She drove me to the airport, and we hugged for ages while she cried and kept asking what she would do without me. I felt like crying too, but my excitement at coming home was stronger than the sadness at leaving Lauren, so I just hugged her back tightly, told her she'd be fine, and made her promise to keep in touch.

And I do think she'll be fine, because she's a survivor. She still says she's planning to come home, but I'm not so sure. She and Bill seem to be going strong, and I've got a feeling she may well stay out there after all, but either way she's sworn she'll be back, even if it's just for a holiday, and I want her to meet Ben, and Geraldine, to see how happy I am in the place I belong.

And the funny thing is I've realized that Lauren and I aren't so different after all. That I'm a survivor too; that the experiences I've had over the last few months would surely have broken someone weaker than me. It's not that I feel terribly strong on the surface, but I know, as an absolute certainty, that deep down I have an amazing reserve of strength, which all in all is pretty comforting really.

Although standing here, looking for the taxi sign, I'm not feeling that strong. And I know it's only been six weeks, but I'm not even sure where I belong any more. I know my home's in London, but I feel that I can't take steps backwards, go back to the life I had before. I assumed I'd go back to living with Sophie and Lisa, and in many ways I was dreading it, that really would have felt like moving backwards, but luckily that's changed too.

I phoned them last night, thinking that perhaps I'd just stay there until I found somewhere else, and – stupidly, I know – I was surprised, and slightly disappointed, when Sophie said a friend of Lisa's was staying in the room, and that they'd put my things under the stairs. They weren't expecting me back for ages, and they were really sorry but they couldn't kick this girl out.

I know it's a good thing, but I panicked for a few minutes, until I rang Geraldine, who once again came to my rescue. She's moved into her new flat, which, needless to say, is 'absolutely gorgeous', and the spare room, she said, would be perfect for me.

'But what about Nick?' I asked.

'What about him?' she laughed. 'You won't mind if he stays here sometimes, will you? Plus, you'll have Ben, and just think Jemima, we'll have the most amazing time. I'd love to have you as a flatmate, it's going to be brilliant. I can run out to Habitat this afternoon and get some curtains, and then the room's done. It's yours.'

How could I argue with her?

I clutch the piece of paper with Geraldine's new address, and queue, loving the fact that the cabs that are slowly lining up and pulling away are so familiar, so solid, that they are London, that they, more than anything else, tell me I'm home.

And I wait in line until finally it's my turn to climb into the cab, and as it pulls out of the airport I rest my head against the window and watch the lights on the motorway whizzing past, and the closer we get to home, the more excited I start to feel.

This is a whole new start, Jemima Jones. A whole new

chapter: mine to write however I choose. And the first step is not going back to the *Kilburn Herald*. If Ben can do it, so can I. I'm going to fulfil that dream, work on a glossy magazine, and that's just the beginning. Once upon a time this would have terrified me, but now I can't wait to get started, to set off on a new journey, this time surrounded by people I love, who love me in return.

And on we go. Through Hammersmith Broadway, up to Shepherd's Bush, along the Westway. We pull off and make our way up Maida Vale, through Kilburn, to Geraldine's flat in West Hampstead.

And I look around me, and I can see that London's smelly, and dirty, and that the people look, if anything, slightly tired and harassed. The sun's nowhere to be seen, and as we drive drops of rain start slowly splattering on the windscreen, and the sky darkens with rainclouds.

No one I've seen has the remotest hint of a tan, and all along the Kilburn High Road there are people bundled up in anoraks, hurrying to get their shopping home before they get soaked.

And I love it. I'm safe here. Safe, happy, and secure. I don't care that it's the antithesis of California. I don't care that the weather's always shit. I don't care that no one, ever, says, 'Have a nice day now.' It's wonderful, and vibrant, and real. And most of all, it's home.

EPILOGUE

Jemima Jones is no longer skinny, no longer hardbodied, no longer obsessed with what she eats. Jemima Jones is now a voluptuous, feminine, curvy size 12 who is completely happy with how she looks. Jemima Jones now eats what she wants, when she wants, as often as she wants, as long as it's reasonably healthy.

And Jemima Jones is no longer lonely. Jemima Jones no longer dreams of the perfect romance with a man she can't have. She no longer believes that true love only exists outside herself.

Because Jemima Jones never dared to believe in love. Jemima Jones never dared to believe in herself. She never dared to believe that one of these days fate would actually take the time and trouble to pick her out from the crowd and smile upon her.

But fairytales can come true, and just like Jemima Jones, or Mrs Ben Williams as she's known outside of the glossy magazine where she now works, if we trust in ourselves, embrace our faults, and brazen it out with courage, strength, bravery and truth, fate may just smile upon us too.

MR MAYBE

Acknowledgements

Once again there are a million people who should be thanked profusely, only a handful of whom can be mentioned here.

As last time, the wonderful trio of my Editor Louise Moore, Agent Anthony Goff, and PR Angela Martin

Helen Fraser, Tom Weldon, John Bond, Peter Bowron, Sophie Clark, Ami Smithson, and everyone at Penguin for being so incredibly supportive and making this whole process an absolute delight.

Donna Poppy, who has spotted every typo and misspelt name, and edited both *Mr Maybe* and *Jemima J.* superbly.

Michael Monroe – this book might well have been *Mr Something Else* if not for him.

And David Burke. Just because.

Thank you.

Chapter One

Nick was never supposed to be The One, for God's sake. Even I knew that. And yes, I know those that are happily married often say you can't know, not immediately, but of course I knew. Not that he sounded wrong – Nick spoke the Queen's English slightly better than myself, but nothing else was right, nothing else fitted.

There was the money thing, for a start. My job as a PR might not be the highest-paying job in the universe, but it pays the bills, pays the mortgage, and leaves me just enough for the odd bit of retail therapy. Nick, on the other hand, didn't earn a penny. Well, perhaps that's a bit of an exaggeration, but he wasn't like all the other boyfriends I'd had, wasn't rolling in it, and, although that's not my main motivation, what I always say is I don't mind if he can't pay for me, but I do bloody well mind if he can't pay for himself.

And though Nick occasionally offered to go dutch, it was with such bad grace and I used to feel so guilty, I'd just push his hand away, tell him not to be so silly and drag out my credit card.

And then there was politics. Or lack thereof, in my case, might be more appropriate. Nick was never happier than when he was with his left-wing cronies, arguing the toss about the pros and cons of New Labour, while I sat there bored out of my mind, not contributing just in case anyone asked me what I voted and I had to grudgingly admit I voted Conservative because, well, because my parents had.

Speaking of pros and cons, it might be easier if I showed you the list I drew up soon after I met Nick. I mean, if I sit here telling you about all the reasons why he wasn't right for me, it would take all day, and I've still got the list, so you may as well read it. It might help you to see why I was so adamant that he was just a fling.

Pros

I fancy the pants off him.

He's got the biggest, softest, bluest eyes I've ever seen.

He's very affectionate.

He's fantastically selfless in bed. (Make that just fantastic.)

He makes me laugh.

Cons

He's got no money.

He lives in a grotty bedsit in Highgate.

He's left-wing/political.

He likes pubs and pints of beer.

I hate his friends.

He's a complete womanizer.

He's allergic to commitment.

He says he's not ready for a relationship. (Although neither am I.)

So there you have it – far more cons than pros, and, if I'm completely honest, the cons are much more important, I mean, how could I have even thought of getting involved with someone whose friends I hated? I have always,

always thought you could judge a person by their friends, and I really should have known better.

But then again, I suppose you can't help who you fancy, can you? And that was the bottom line. I fancied Nick. Fancied him more than I'd fancied anyone in years, and somehow, when someone gives you that tingly feeling in the pit of your stomach, you stop thinking about the rights and wrongs, the shoulds and should nots, and you just go with it.

You're probably wondering how I met Nick, because, let's face it, our paths were hardly destined to cross. I'd known him for a while, actually. He was one of those people I used to see at the odd party when I went out with my friend Sally, Sal, and I never took much notice of him, I didn't see him enough to take much notice of him because I didn't see Sal all that much.

I used to work with Sal, indirectly. Years ago, when I first started as a lowly PR assistant, Sal was a journalist on one of the magazines, and she was about the only person who didn't treat me like shit, so we formed a friendship on the basis of that.

Not that I dislike her. She's a great girl. She's just different. To me, that is. She's more like Nick, and I vaguely remember her having a crush on him. That's probably the only reason I did remember him, she'd ask me to watch him to see if he stared at her, all that sort of stuff, and I did, because she was my friend and it gave me something to do, which was better than standing around bored, wishing I were somewhere else.

She used to drag me along to these parties, student parties I'd think snootily, except no one had been a student for years, but they were always in dilapidated houses, held by the four, or six, people who lived there, and they were never my scene.

Not that I could have afforded the lifestyle I wanted. Not then. Champagne tastes and beer pockets, my mother always used to sniff, if I made the fatal mistake of wearing a new outfit when I went round to see my parents.

'What's that?' she'd say, in a disapproving tone of voice.

'What? This old thing?' I'd learn to say, dismissing my fabulous designer outfit that I loved so much I was wearing it for about the sixth day on the trot. 'I've had this for ages.' Or, 'It was lying around the fashion cupboard at work, so they gave it to me. Do you like it?' It took me a while, but eventually I learnt that, as long as I didn't admit to it being new, my mother would like it. If I ever told her I had actually bought something, she'd raise her eyebrows and say, 'How much was that?' And I'd mumble a price, usually knocking off around a hundred pounds, and she'd roll her eyes again and shake her head, making me feel like an errant child.

I used to have these dreams about being a career woman. I wanted shoulder pads, briefcases and mobile phones. I wanted designer clothes and a fuck-off flat which had wooden floors and white sofas and enormous bowls of lilies on every polished fruitwood table. I wanted a Mercedes sports car and chunky gold jewellery.

Unfortunately, life in PR is probably not the best way of going about it, because PR seems to be one of the worst-paid professions in the world. I know what I should have done, I should have gone into the City, because I graduated at the tail-end of the eighties boom, and I could have made a mint, but I never had a very good brain for money, or numbers, and I would have been hopeless. And PR seemed like the easiest option. It sounded glamorous, exciting, and I wouldn't have to start as a secretary, which I was loath to do, because I would have hated people asking me what I did for a living. In PR I was able to start as a Public Relations Assistant, which, at the ripe old age of twenty-one, made me feel like I'd won the lottery.

I answered an ad in the *Guardian*, and when I went along for the interview I decided that if I didn't get this job I would die. The offices of Joe Cooper PR were in a backstreet in Kilburn, not the most salubrious of areas, I know, and from the outside it looked just like a big warehouse, but inside it was magnificent. A huge loft, wooden floors, brightly coloured chairs and velvet cushions, and a constant buzz of phone conversations from some of the most beautiful people I'd ever seen in my life.

And I looked completely wrong. There they were, everyone in jeans, super-trendy T-shirts and big motorbike boots (which was the look at the time), and there I was in my little Jigsaw two-piece cream suit, with matching high heels and a briefcase clutched in my hand to look more professional.

Shit, I remember thinking when I walked in. Why oh why didn't I research this before I came, but then Joe Cooper came to shake my hand. 'You must be Libby,' he said, and as soon as I met him I knew I'd like him, and, more importantly, I knew he'd like me. And he did. And I started the following week on a pittance, but I loved it. God, how I loved it.

Within a month all my friends were green with envy, because I was already on first name terms with some of the hottest celebrities on TV, and I spent my days helping the actual executives, typing press releases, occasionally babysitting those celebrities on their excursions to radio and television shows where they plugged their latest book, or programme, or film. And it was so exciting, and I met so many people, and my Jigsaw suit was placed firmly at the back of my wardrobe as I dressed like all the others and I fitted in.

My budding champagne tastes were brought to full fruition at Joe Cooper PR. Admittedly, not in quite the way I'd planned. Instead of Yves Saint Laurent I wanted Rifat Ozbek. Instead of Annabel's I wanted Quiet Storm. Instead of Mortons I wanted the Atlantic Bar, or whatever the hell was in at the time, I can't actually remember. A lot of the time I was 'entertaining' clients, so it was on expenses, but when you throw a girl into that sort of lifestyle at work, you can't expect her to be happy with takeaways in the evenings, can you?

And now, finally, I can just about afford to fund my lifestyle, with the help of a very understanding bank manager who agreed to give me an overdraft facility 'just in case'. Just in case of what? Just in case I should ever not need it? Because I fill my overdraft facility pretty much all the time, but hell, it's only money, and as far as I'm concerned we're only here for about eighty years if we're lucky, so in the grand scheme of things nothing really matters very much, and certainly not money. Or even men, when it comes to it.

Friends are what matter, that's what I've decided. My social life is swings and roundabouts. Sometimes I'm on a social whirl, out every night, grateful for the odd night in watching television and catching up on my sleep. But then everything will slow down for a while, and I'll be in every night, flicking through my address book, wondering why I can't really be bothered to talk to anyone.

Well, not quite anyone. I talk to Jules every day, about five times, even if we don't really have anything to say to one another, which we don't usually, because what news can you possibly tell someone you last spoke to an hour ago? We usually end up talking shit. She'll phone me up and say, 'I've just eaten half a packet of biscuits and a cheese and pickle sandwich. I feel sick.'

And I'll say, 'I had a toasted bagel with smoked salmon, no butter, and one stick of Twix,' and that will be it.

Or I'll phone her and say, 'I'm just calling to say hi.'

And she'll sigh and say, 'Hi. Any news?'

'No. You?'

'No.'

'Okay, talk to you later.'

'Okay.'

We never, ever, say goodbye, or talk to you at the weekend, or even tomorrow, because, unless we're speaking to each other late at night when we're in bed (which we do practically every night), we know we are going to talk to each other later, even when we've got nothing to say.

What's really surprising about this is not how close we are, but the fact that Jules is married. She married James, or Jamie as he's more commonly known (good isn't it, Jules et Jim), last year, and I was terrified I'd never see her any more, but if anything the reverse has happened. It's almost as if she isn't married, because we hardly ever talk about Jamie. He never seems to be there, or if he is he's shut away in his study, working, and for a while I was worried, concerned that perhaps she'd made a mistake, perhaps their marriage wasn't all it should be, but, on the rare occasions I see the two of them together, I can see that it works, that she's happy, that marriage has given her the security she never had, the security I long for.

And meanwhile, I've still got my friend, my touchstone, my sister. Not that she is, of course, she just feels like it, and Jules is the wisest woman I know. I'll sit and bore her with my latest adventure and she'll listen very quietly, wait for a few seconds when I've finished before speaking, which really used to bother me because I thought she was bored, but actually what she's doing is thinking about what I've said, formulating an opinion, and when she does give me advice it's always spot-on, even if it might not be exactly what I want to hear.

She's what my mother would call a true friend, and I know that no matter what happens we'll always be there for each other, so even on those nights when I'm cocooning, when I decide that I'm not quite ready to face the world, Jules is the one person I always phone. Always.

And at least my flat's comfortable for those solitary periods of takeouts and videos. Not quite the flat I've always dreamt of, but I've made it pretty damn nice considering most of my furniture has either been inherited from my parents or bought second hand from junk shops.

But if it hadn't been for my parents, bless them, I'd never have been able to afford to buy somewhere. I'd probably be sharing some dilapidated house with four, or six, other girls and spending every evening arguing about the washing-up or just resenting them even breathing. I may not have ever had to do it, but I've got enough friends who have, and quite frankly I got sick of them ringing me to ask if they could crash on my sofa because they needed some space.

My flat is tiny. Tiny. The tiniest flat you could ever imagine that's actually a flat and not a studio. It's in a basement in Ladbroke Grove, and you walk in the front door and straight into the living room. But, surprisingly, for a basement it's quite bright, and I've tried to emphasize this by keeping it as neutral as possible. Except I can't help the clutter, the shelves of books, and photographs, and cards, because I never throw anything away, you never know when you might need something.

There's an L-shaped kitchen off the living room, a galley kitchen, open plan, and opposite the large window there are french doors leading into a bedroom. It's so small there's a bed that folds up into the wall, except I never bother putting it up unless I have a party, and then off the bedroom is a minute bathroom, and that's it. Perfect for me, although I haven't lost sight of my dream of huge spaces and high ceilings – I've just about accepted that working in PR is most unlikely to buy me what I want, and I'll just have to marry a rich man for the lifestyle to which I want to become accustomed.

So. Men. Probably the one area of my life that's a complete disaster. Not that I don't meet them, God, it seems as if they're crawling out of the woodwork, except the ones that crawl out to meet me are always worms. Typical, isn't it. Jules can't understand it. I can't understand it. Every time I think that this time it might be different, this time they might treat me well, look after me, but every time it ends in tears.

I thought Jon was the one. Yeah, yeah, yeah, I know I

say that every time. But I really did. He was everything I'd ever been looking for. He was a property developer, which is a bit boring, I know, but he wasn't boring. He was handsome, well dressed, had a beautiful flat in Maida Vale, a Mazda MX-5, knew brilliant people, was great in bed . . . Well, the list goes on and on, really. The only problem was he didn't like me very much. I mean, sure, he fancied me, but he didn't *like* me, he didn't want to spend time with me, and I kept thinking that if I were perfect, if I acted like the perfect girlfriend, he'd fall in love with me. But he didn't. The more I tried to be the perfect girlfriend, the more awful he was to me.

In the beginning he used to call me, but the phone calls practically dwindled away to nothing, and then eventually people used to call me up and ask why I wasn't at that party last night that Jon went to. And he used to go away for weekends without telling me, he'd simply disappear, and I'd spend all weekend in floods of tears, ringing his answering machine and banging the phone down before the end of his message.

My parents met him. Big mistake. Huge. They loved him. They loved the fact that I had finally met someone who could take me off their hands, look after me, and, amazingly and unusually, the more they loved him the more I did. But eventually I couldn't do it any more. I couldn't deal with the stress of being treated like shit, and, I'm quite proud of myself for this, I ended it.

The bastard didn't even seem to care. He sort of shrugged and said he was happy with the way things were, and, when I said I needed more, he just shrugged again and said he was sorry that he couldn't give me more. Bastard. BASTARD.

But no, that was a long time ago. I was apoplectic with

grief for about a week. I kept bursting into tears at work, and everyone was massively sympathetic without actually saying anything. Every time I cried at my desk I'd feel a hand on my shoulder, and a cup of tea would be placed in front of me, wordlessly, which was so sweet. My colleagues' way of showing me that they cared.

Then after a week Jules said I had to get my act together and she knew from the beginning that he wasn't for me and that he was far too arrogant and I deserved better and that there were plenty more fish in the sea and blah blah blah. But I began to see her point.

I started putting myself 'out there' again. Going to bars, parties, launches. And even though I felt like shit I pretended to have a good time, and after a couple of months I realized that I actually was having a good time, and that was when I decided that I'd had enough of men. At least for a while.

Yup, I thought. No more bastards for me. But then about six months on I started getting withdrawal symptoms. Not from Jon, but from cuddles, affection and, all right, I'll admit it, from sex. Now I know there's a cut-off point. I know that when you've been used to having regular sex with someone you miss it for about six months, and that after that you don't really think about it any more because it's just not a part of your life, and then when you finally do it again you're astounded that you went without it for so long because it's so damn nice. I know this because I've had two BIG dry periods in my life. One for ten months and one for . . . God, I don't even know whether I want to tell you. Okay. One for two years.

I know. Twenty-seven bloody years old and I went without sex for two years. Sad, isn't it?

I was probably just about to reach the cut-off point where sex stopped being important, when, instead of waiting for those horny moods to disappear, I decided I'd have a fling. I don't want a relationship, I thought. I just want sex. That's all.

I was in that rare state of mind that women always tell you to aspire to, but which you usually find impossible to reach. That state of mind that is completely happy without a man, isn't looking for anyone, is completely fulfilled by work and friends.

And I really was. I realized, post-Jon-trauma, that I definitely didn't want to be in a relationship with someone unless they were absolutely right, and, let's face it, how often do you meet someone who you really fancy and really like? Exactly.

I do what most women do. I meet someone and some of it's right, maybe he looks right, or has the right job, or the right background, and, instead of sitting back and waiting for him to reveal his other bits, I make them up. I decide how he thinks, how he's going to treat me, and, sure enough, every time I conclude that this time he's definitely my perfect man, and all of a sudden, well, not so suddenly perhaps, usually around six months after we've split up, I see that he wasn't the person I thought he was at all.

So that's where I'm at when Sal phones, and I haven't seen her for ages, and she invites me out, breathless with excitement about her new boyfriend, and when I arrive at the bar Nick is there and he remembers me, and that's that.

Well, not quite, but more of that later. So you would have thought I'd have learnt my lesson after Jon, but have I? Have I? Have I hell. Except with Nick I know from the beginning that I'll never be able to fill in the blanks and reach a conclusion I'll be happy with. And so that night, that night in the bar when there suddenly seems to be this amazing chemistry, I decide that Nick will be my fling, that he'll be perfect for a few weeks of brilliant sex, that I won't get involved, and that we'll probably stay friends.

And I feel really strong. I feel, for the first time in my life, that I can actually do this. That I can have sex with someone and not get emotionally involved, not suddenly start dreaming of marriage and babies and a happy ever after. I feel like a woman. I feel like a grown-up.

Chapter Two

'Libby!' cries Sal, flinging her arms around me in a huge bear-hug. 'God, it's been ages. Look at you! You look fantastic!' This, incidentally, is the way Sally speaks. In exclamation marks.

'Thanks,' I say, believing her because who, after all, wouldn't look fantastic in their brand-new, super-expensive, long, pale-grey, cotton-ribbed cardigan, teamed with grey flannel trousers and sexy high-heeled black boots. 'So do you,' I add, although Sal always looks the same to me. With her natural auburn hair in a sort of fluffy medium-length layered bob, she always looks good in a timeless sort of way because Sal doesn't believe in following fashion, she believes in finding the look that suits you and wearing it until you die.

So, as I said, she always looks pretty much the same. Long, flowing skirts, occasionally jodhpurs, riding boots, fitted jackets and a silk scarf knotted casually around her throat. Tonight it's the turn of the jodhpurs, and I see why.

'Jesus, Sal,' I say, stepping back, because there is something different about her tonight. 'You've lost so much weight.'

'Have I!' she says, with a cheesy grin, because of course she knows she has. She'd never dare wear those camel-coloured skin-tight jodhpurs if she hadn't. 'Must be love!' she whispers loudly, taking my hand and leading me to a table in the corner. 'You must come and meet the others.'

What an, er, eclectic, bunch. This is something that I've always admired about Sal: her choice in friends, her willingness to mix and match, just to throw people together and not worry about the consequences. I, on the other hand, spend my life in a constant panic about whether people will get on with one another, desperately trying to keep my groups of friends separate. There are my trendy media friends, mostly people I've met through work; my university friends; my oldest friends from school; and my art class friends, except I haven't been for ages so I haven't really seen them recently. And then there's Jules, who's my take-anywhere friend, because she's the one person who fits in with everyone.

But Sal doesn't discriminate, and I can see that there are a few familiar faces.

'Hi,' I say with a smile to Kathy, Sal's oldest friend, a tall stunning blonde who oozes style and sophistication and seems to have a constant stream of equally gorgeous men at her side.

'Libby,' she says, stretching out a smooth tanned cheek to kiss the air next to mine. 'How are you? It's been so long. You must meet Phil,' and she gestures to the drop-dead gorgeous hunk at her side.

'Delighted to meet you,' he says, in possibly one of the poshest voices I've ever heard, and holds out his hand to shake mine, which floors me for a few moments because outside the office nobody I know shakes hands, but then I realize why he's holding out his hand, so, surreptitiously trying to wipe my damp palms on my cardigan, I shake his hand firmly and say a businesslike 'How do you do', because I can't be too friendly to someone this gorgeous in case Kathy thinks I'm flirting with him, which I'd never do, and as soon as I say it I turn away to see who else I know.

'You remember Paul,' says Sal, putting a stool down next to a baby-faced scruffy young man sipping from a pint who I know is her latest boyfriend, but I'm not sure why I should remember him.

'Umm.' I'm not sure I do, actually.

'Of course you do,' she says. 'Paul worked with me on the *Sunday Mail*.'

'Oh, Paul!' I say. 'That Paul. Sorry. God, finally I can put a face to the name.'

He grins at me. 'I know what you mean. You must spend all day talking to journalists and never knowing what they look like.'

'Unless,' I say, grinning cheekily, suddenly remembering that I have seen him before, 'unless, the journalist in question has been out for the day wearing a miniskirt to test the latest men's fashion.'

'Shit,' he groans. 'I thought I'd lived that one down.' And we both laugh.

'And Nick,' says Sal, making big eyes at me which I don't quite understand, but then I turn to Nick and realize that he's the one she used to fancy and that she's trying to warn me telepathically not to say anything. 'You must remember Nick.'

Nick turns to look at me, and nods. 'Hi, Libby,' he says, and somehow the way he says my name makes it sound really intimate, and I feel a tiny shiver at the base of my spine.

Hello? What's this all about, then? And I look closely at Nick and it's as if I'm seeing him for the first time. God, I think. I never realized his eyes were that blue.

And he's had his hair cut. It's not in a straggly pony-tail any more, it's a short buzz cut that brings out these incredible sculpted cheekbones, and Jesus, he's handsome, and in an instant I remember what that shiver is. Lust. Pure and simple.

This could be my fling, I think, settling back into my chair and switching into flirt mode. Nick. Perfect.

'So what have you been up to?' he says, giving me what is definitely an appreciative glance.

'Working hard as usual,' I say, instantly regretting how dull it sounds, and racking my brain for an amusing story.

'I like your hair,' he says, and another shiver goes through me. 'You've changed it.'

And I have. I'd had long hair, dead straight, and a fringe the last time I saw Nick. Now it's shoulder-length, no fringe, and flicking up at the bottom.

'You're not supposed to remember hair,' I laugh. 'You're a bloke.'

'You'd be surprised at what I remember,' he says with a smile.

'What do you mean?'

'The last time I saw you was at Sal's party two years ago,' he says.

'Nope.' I shake my head. 'Not impressed. Any bloke would remember that.'

'You had your hair up,' he continues, still smiling. 'And you were wearing black leather trousers, trainers, and a bright orange T-shirt which said "Bizarre" on it.'

'Jesus Christ.' My mouth is hanging open. 'Now I am impressed. How the hell do you remember what I was wearing?'

He shrugs. 'I told you you'd be surprised.'

17

'No, but seriously,' I push, 'how did you remember that?'

'Let's just say I have a very good memory for things I want to remember.'

'Oh,' I say in a small voice, as it dawns on me that maybe he wasn't being stand-offish all those times I had met him. Maybe he fancied me? Maybe?

'So the exciting world of PR is still as exciting as ever, then?' he says.

'I know you think PR's a complete waste of time,' I start, even though I don't know, I just suspect, 'but it suits me. I like it.'

'I don't think it's a waste of time.' He sounds surprised. 'And when my novel becomes a best-seller you'll probably be the first people I come to.'

'You've got a deal?' My voice is high with excitement. This is getting better and better. If Nick's signed a deal, then he's got money, and if he's got money that instantly makes him eligible, and if he's eligible, then, and only then, can I imagine us together.

'Nah,' he sighs. 'Still trying.'

'Oh. What's the book about?' I'm being polite, okay? I think he'll just give me a two-minute synopsis, but ten minutes later he stops, seeing my eyes glaze over.

'Shit, I'm sorry. I've bored you.'

'No, no,' I say quickly, shaking my mind awake. 'I just don't know all that much about politics, so it doesn't mean a great deal to me.

'But it sounds excellent,' I add enthusiastically. 'I can't believe it hasn't been published.'

'I know,' he says sadly. 'Neither can I.

'What are you drinking?' He stands up, and I tell him a Sea Breeze if they've got it, and if they haven't got any cranberry juice then a vodka and soda with a dash of lime.

'Well,' says Sal in a knowing voice when he's gone off to get the drinks. 'You and Nick seem to be getting on rather well.'

I shrug. 'He seems nice, that's all. I never realized.'

'You should go for it,' she says. 'I could see you two together.'

'You don't fancy him any more then?' I whisper.

'Don't be daft,' she laughs. 'I've got Paul now. I don't know what I ever saw in Nick – ' She stops, realizing what she's just said. 'I didn't mean that, he's gorgeous, it's simply that I see now we would never have been right together. You, on the other hand – '

I laugh. 'Sal! You're crazy. I can't see us together at all.'

'Why not?' She looks startled, and I remember how she doesn't think about the important things, about our lifestyles, how different we are.

'Just look at us,' I say, feebly gesturing at my designer clothes, and then pointing at Nick, at his dirty jeans, his scruffy loose jumper with holes in the sleeves, his scuffed Doc Martens.

'What?' she says again, brow furrowed because she isn't getting it. 'What am I looking at?'

'Oh, never mind,' I laugh. 'He's definitely not the one for me, but he is nice. He's really quite sexy.'

'Maybe you should just get together and see what happens,' she says, smiling, leaning back to make way for Nick, who's returning with a fresh round of drinks.

'Maybe I should,' I say, thinking that the getting together bit would suit me just perfectly right now, but I know what would happen. We wouldn't fit, is what would happen. But that's okay, I remind myself. I don't want a potential husband or even a boyfriend. I just want some fun. No strings attached.

'What are you two gossiping about?' says Nick, and I can tell from his smile his ears were burning.

'Er, just work,' says Sal, who is completely crap at lying.

'I see,' he says, sitting down and sliding my vodka over to me. 'Not discussing men, then, were you?'

'No!' says Sal, giving me a hugely indiscreet thumbs-up and turning to snuggle into Paul's shoulder.

Nick and I talk all evening, and, once the book is out of the way, it turns out that he really is interesting, and funny, and different.

'If you won the lottery what would you do?' he asks at one point, and I practically squeal with pleasure because I love questions like this.

'How much?'

'Whatever,' he says.

'No, no. You have to do it properly. You have to name a figure.'

'Okay,' he says, grinning. 'Five million pounds.'

I sit back, thinking about all the lovely things I could buy with five million pounds.

'Well,' I start. 'I'd buy a house.'

'What kind of house and where?'

'One of those huge white ones in Holland Park.'

'You do realize that would set you back about three million quid.'

'Oh. Okay. A small white one in Maida Vale.'

'For how much?'

'Five hundred thousand?'

He nods. 'And how would you decorate it?'

I describe my dream house, except I get a bit lost after I've done the living room, the bathroom, the kitchen and the bedroom, because I've never had to think about any other rooms.

'What about the dining room?' Nick asks. 'What about bedroom number four? What about your second bathroom? What about the study?'

'Oh, God,' I finally groan. 'Too many rooms. Maybe I'll just settle for an amazing two-bedroom flat with huge rooms and a split-level galleried bit to work in.'

'So. You've got four and a half million left.'

'No, a bit less. I'd probably spend about a hundred thousand doing it up.'

He looks at me as if I'm crazy, then shakes his head and laughs. 'Okay, 4.4 million pounds to go. What else?'

'I'd buy a holiday home in the Caribbean.'

'You're big on homes, aren't you?'

'What do you expect? I'm a child of Thatcher's generation.'

'Hmm,' he sniffs. 'Don't tell me you voted for her?'

'No,' I lie expertly, saying what I always say. 'I voted for the Green Party.'

'Did you?' He looks, well, if not impressed, at least not completely pissed off, and for a moment I think of telling him the truth, that I don't give a stuff about politics and the only reason I voted Tory was because my parents had, that it could have been anyone leading my country. I just didn't care.

I decide to keep lying.

'Yes,' I say, nodding. 'None of the other parties seemed to offer anything, and you know what politicians are like. They're all untrustworthy bastards.' This last line

I'd heard at a party, and I thought it sounded rather good, like I knew what I was talking about and it works. Nick nods in agreement, as if I've just said something very sensible.

'Anyway,' I continue, bringing the conversation back on to more familiar footing. 'My house in the Caribbean.'

'Ah, yes,' he says, smiling. 'That's far more important than politics.'

'Absolutely.' I go on to describe the house I would build on the tiny island of Anguilla.

'So we're about a million down,' he says. 'What else?'

'I'd probably take about a hundred thousand and go on a mad shopping spree,' I admit.

'A hundred thousand? Jesus Christ. What would you be shopping for? Diamonds and pearls?'

'Nope.' I shake my head. 'Far too old for my youthful years. I'd go to Armani, Prada, Gucci . . .'

'Top Shop?' asks Nick. 'Oasis?'

'Are you crazy?' I say. 'I'd never demean myself by stepping foot in anywhere like that.'

'Oh, right.' He grins. 'Of course. How stupid of me,' and he holds out his hand, which I slap very gently.

'Anyway,' I say, 'how come you know about 'Oasis?'

'I know a lot of things,' he laughs.

'You're not really a bloke, are you?' I say, narrowing my eyes and squinting at him. 'You're a girl.'

'Damn,' he says, shaking his head and laughing. 'And I hoped you hadn't noticed.'

At about three million pounds I run out of ideas. I have, by this point, two homes, a wardrobe that would make Oprah Winfrey jealous, a convertible Porsche 911, a live-in cleaning woman who doesn't actually live with me, but in the granny flat I stick on to the basement of my house and numerous investments in property. I don't know what to do with the rest.

'I'd, er, give the rest to charity,' I say magnanimously, hoping he won't ask which ones, because I couldn't name a charity if my life depended on it, and anyway I might give a bit to charity, but I honestly can't see me donating two million quid. No matter how worthy.

'Which charity?' he asks. He would.

'I'd give to a few. That breast cancer one. The . . .' – I think hard. – 'NSPCC.' I remember those little blue plastic collection boxes they used to give you at school. 'AIDS Research, lots to them. And animal charities! Yes, I'd give loads to animal charities so no more little ponies and horses in my cat food.

'What about you?' I look at Nick. 'What would you do?'

He sits and thinks about it for a bit. 'I don't think I'd move,' he says. 'There's no real point because I'm quite happy.'

'Where do you live?'

'In Highgate.'

'Do you live by yourself?' But that isn't what I'm asking. I'm asking whether he owns his own flat, whether he is responsible, whether he can support a wife. But no, I stop myself, I'm not going to be his wife. He's not going to be my husband. It doesn't matter.

'Mmm,' he nods. 'I've got a bedsit, and I suppose I could get a one-bedroom flat, but I'm happy where I am.'

'You'd have to buy somewhere,' I say sternly. 'You've got to get your foot on the ladder.' Another phrase I've picked up somewhere that I always use when talking about property.

'Do I? Why?'

'Because . . .' I suddenly don't know why, other than that I've been brought up to believe that everyone should own their own house if they possibly can.

'Because you're one of Thatcher's children, right?'

'Well, so are you,' I say in my defence.

'Ish,' he says.

'Ish?'

'I may be only a couple of years older than you, but my parents were dyed in the wool Labour supporters.'

'But you grew up during Thatcher's time.'

'So does that mean I was supposed to believe in her?'

'No, it's just sometimes hard to go against what you've been brought up to believe in.'

'It wasn't what I was brought up to believe in.'

I'm getting out of my depth. I stand up. 'Another pint?' and he laughs.

'So okay, you won't buy a mansion,' I say when I come back.

'No, no,' he says. 'I've been thinking about it and you're probably right. I should buy somewhere, but it wouldn't be anything amazing. I might even buy the flat I'm living in.'

I look at him in horror. 'A bedsit?'

'Okay,' he laughs. 'I'll buy a one-bedroom flat.'

'What else, what else?'

He sits deep in thought. 'I know!' he suddenly exclaims, his eyes lighting up. 'I'd buy a proper computer.'

'You mean you're writing a novel and you haven't got a computer?' I say slowly.

'I've got one of these typewriter things that has a tiny

24

screen and you can see about three lines of what you've written on it.'

'You must be spending a fortune on Tipp-Ex,' I say.

'There we go,' he grins. 'I'd buy a lifetime's supply of Tipp-Ex.'

'But you wouldn't need Tipp-Ex if you had a computer.'

'I might get nostalgic.'

'For your battered old typewriter that takes for ever and can't go back and correct?'

'How do you know it's battered?'

'It is, isn't it?'

'Yes, slightly. But it has character. Computers seem a bit clinical.'

'Okay,' I sigh. 'We've probably spent less than a hundred thousand so far. You're not doing very well.'

'I could donate a sizeable amount to the Labour Party,' he says sheepishly.

'How much?'

'A million?'

'You can't give a million quid to bloody politicians!' I say in horror. 'You're hopeless.'

'Sorry,' he says, looking it. 'I'm just not very money-oriented.'

'Evidently,' and luckily he laughs, and when he does I can't help but notice how white his teeth are, how his face softens, how goddamned gorgeous he looks.

'So,' says Sal, leaning over and interrupting us. 'Have you got any good stories for me, then, Libby?'

I sit and think. 'Not really stories, but maybe you'd be interested in an interview with Sean Moore?'

'Sean Moore!' Her eyes light up. 'Are you doing him?'

I nod. 'We're doing the PR for his new TV series, and I'm setting up a round of interviews in a couple of weeks.

You should have got the press release, I sent it to you last week.'

'Oh,' says Sal, looking guilty. 'I probably did get it, but I get so many press releases, half the time I don't even look at them.'

'What?' I say in mock dismay. 'You mean I go to all that trouble to think up something witty and clever, and it goes in the bin?'

'No,' she says. 'It joins the towering pile on my desk that's threatening to topple over and knock someone out.'

'You're forgiven . . .' I pause. 'As long as you give Sean a good show.'

'Double-page spread?'

'That would be brilliant.'

'One condition.'

I know what's coming.

'Can we have it exclusively?'

'I hate it when journalists say that,' I groan.

'But you know why we do,' she says. 'There's no point in running an interview with Sean Moore after it's appeared everywhere else.'

'Tell you what,' I say. 'I can't promise you an exclusive because we have to try and get as much coverage as possible, but what I can do is give it to you first, but, and I mean this, Sal, you have to run it when you say you will.' I'm sick to the back teeth of giving newspapers exclusive interviews, running out to buy the paper in the morning and finding it isn't there because another story was deemed to be more important. I then have to chase the journalist for days, and they usually keep telling me it's going in, they just don't know when, and before you know it the whole thing has been forgotten about.

'I will,' she nods. 'Promise.'

'Okay,' I say. 'Ring me in the office tomorrow.'

At eleven o'clock everyone starts getting up to leave.

'You know how it is,' says Kathy. 'School night.' And we put on our coats and wander outside, standing around in a big huddle to say goodbye.

'Where do you live?' asks Nick, just as I'm wondering how to say goodnight to him, and if, in fact, I want to say goodnight to him at all.

'Ladbroke Grove.' The regret is obvious in my voice. I mean, there's no way I can offer him a lift back to Highgate, it's just too damn unsubtle. 'Are you driving?' I say.

He shakes his head. 'No. I don't drive.'

'How do you get around?'

'I cycle.'

'So where's your bike?'

'I got the tube.'

'Oh.'

And then I have a brainwave. 'Do you want a lift to the tube?'

His face glows. 'I'd love one.'

And as we walk off I can see Sal grinning at me, and I can't help it. I start grinning too.

Chapter Three

We walk to my car in silence. I stride along next to him, wondering why my heart is pounding, why I suddenly feel slightly sick, but once the engine is on and the music comes blaring out of the stereo, I start to relax a bit. I mean surely this is the perfect fling?

Not that I want a one-night-stand with Nick, just maybe a few weeks of delicious sex before saying goodbye with no broken hearts. One-night-stands aren't my style. I don't think they're anyone's style, are they? Sure, we've all done it, but even when you can't stand them, even when it's just a drunken mistake after a party, you still want them to call, don't you, even if it's just so you can turn round and tell them you never want to see them again.

It's an ego thing. Definitely. I don't want you, but I want you to want me anyway. So, I don't want a one-night-stand with Nick, but then there's always the worry that it'll be taken out of your control. You think there's going to be a repeat experience and you sit by your phone and wait for weeks for them to call and they don't, and unwittingly you've added another bloody one-night-stand to your list.

But as far as I'm concerned true one-nighters only really happen with strangers. When it's someone you know, particularly someone who's connected to you by friends, they usually do call again, and I sort of know, even while driving in the car that night, that no matter what happens Nick will call me again.

And you see, in normal circumstances, I would never dream of sleeping with him on the first night, as it were. If I had looked at Nick and thought, yes, you could be The One, I would have given him my number and let him take me out a few times before even considering going to bed with him. I don't put a time limit on it, though. As far as I'm concerned you just know when it feels right, but according to Jules you have to spend thirty-six hours in their company before you sleep with them. God knows where she got that from. Probably some trashy magazine, but I suppose that's about seven dates, which sounds about right.

Oh, all right, then, maybe after four dates.

But if I stop being clinical about it, I suppose the time I decide I'm going to jump into bed with them is the time when I know, as an absolute certainty, that they are crazy about me and they aren't going to disappear.

Although I have got it wrong. But only once. That was Michael. We fell in love for two weeks, spent as much time together as we possibly could, and, although I knew I probably should have waited, it felt so right I just thought, fuck it, let's have sex. Immediately afterwards he was fine. It was only when he hadn't called me for four days – and this was the man who had called me three times a day, every day, for two weeks – that I realized something was wrong. Sure enough. He'd changed his mind. I can't even remember what shit he came out with. Something about not being ready for a relationship, blah blah blah. Usual crap. I was devastated. Devastated.

But it taught me a lesson, and the only reason I'm choosing to unlearn the lesson with Nick, is because Nick is never going to be my boyfriend, and when it's just sex, the rules change.

When it's just sex, you're allowed to be predatory, to make the first move, to entice them into bed, because it's not necessary to make them fall in love with you.

When it's just sex you're allowed to put your hand on their thigh while driving your car and say huskily, 'Will you come back to mine for coffee?'

When it's just sex you're allowed to lead them into your living room and kiss them passionately before they've even had a chance to take their coat off.

And then you're allowed to . . .

Sorry, I'm jumping ahead of myself here. Where were we? Ah, yes, in the car, listening to music, and neither of us is actually saying anything because I don't want to start just in case he tells me which tube station to drop him off at, so I keep driving, and eventually we turn into Ladbroke Grove and I have to say something, so I do.

'The tube's just down the road,' I say. Unimaginatively.

'Oh,' he says. And I smile inside.

'Do you want to come in for a coffee?' I say.

'I'd love one,' he says. And he grins.

So I park the car and I can't look at Nick because I'm very aware of his presence, of the chemistry, of this unspoken agreement we are entering into, and I just unlock my front door and we both walk in.

And you know what I love? Even though Nick isn't boyfriend material, I love the fact that he seems to feel instantly at home.

'Do you mind if I take my shoes off?' he says, and naturally I say no, although as I say it I pray he doesn't have nasty socks with holes in, or smelly feet, or something that will put me off him for ever. And I take a quick glance, and his feet, or rather his socks, look really quite nice, and I can't smell anything other than the smell of home, so I go into the kitchen to put the kettle on.

'You have incredible taste,' he says, wandering around, picking up things and putting them down. 'Really,' he reiterates. 'Such style.'

'Thank you,' I say, going through the motions of putting the kettle on, and watching curiously to see where he'll sit. If he sits on the chair, I think, I'm in trouble, because how can I manoeuvre myself into a position where he'll kiss me? Maybe I can perch on the arm of the chair, I think, watching as he seems to hover ominously by the armchair.

Phew. He seems to think twice about the chair and settles into the sofa. I kick my own shoes off, ready to curl up like a cat, bring the mugs to the coffee table, then panic about my make-up and quickly disappear into the bathroom.

I blot the shine off my nose and forehead, and think about a fresh coat of lipstick, but no, too obvious, so I just shake my hair around a bit to give it a wild, wanton look, then sashay back into the living room to put on some music.

Seduction music, I think. I need something soft, jazzy, sexy. Something that will put us both in the mood. I flick through the CDs until I find my fail safe Sinatra CD. Perfect. It always worked in the past, and I put it on and turn the volume down so it's barely throbbing in the background, then I walk over to the sofa where Nick is sipping his coffee and watching me.

'I need a woman's touch,' he says, as I curl up at the other end of the sofa, not wanting to sit too close, but knowing that I'm only a hop, skip and a touch away from the passion I'm so desperate for.

I raise an eyebrow and he laughs.

'I meant in the home,' he says, and I laugh too, then we both make big shows of drinking our coffee, although you can't really drink it, it's far too hot.

'What's your flat like, then?' I ask.

'A hovel,' he says, and he laughs.

'No, really,' I push.

'Yes, really,' he says.

'Why?' I ask, although quite frankly I'm not that surprised. Bachelor pads seem to fall into two categories. If the bachelor in question has money, it's all black leather and chrome, with nasty airbrushed pictures of sports cars on the wall and huge, fuck-off TVs and stereos. And if he, like Nick, hasn't got a pot to piss in, it will be overflowing with books and papers, and dirty clothes, and rubbish. Trust me. I know these things.

'Well,' I say, raising my mug. 'Here's to winning the lottery.'

After this we seem to relax. We talk about Sal, about her boyfriend, about us. I tell him I'm not into relationships, I've had enough of getting my heart broken and I'm not ready for anything serious.

He nods intently while I say this, and says he knows how I feel. He grins and tells me he hasn't had a serious relationship in two years, but that after his last – a miserable five-year relationship with Mary, who loved him but didn't seem to like him very much – he definitely isn't ready for commitment.

And then he looks up at me with those incredible blue eyes and says, 'But I'm very attracted to you,' and even though I'm the one who's supposed to be in control, the one who's made the decision to have a fling with him, my stomach turns over and does a little somersault and I start to feel ever so slightly sick.

There's a long silence, and then I say, 'Thank you,' because I don't know what else to say, and I can't say that I'm very attracted to him too because it sounds really naff, and anyway he must know that because why else would I have invited him back.

So we sit there in silence for a bit and then I offer him another coffee, even though I've hardly touched mine, and he shakes his head and my heart plummets.

Shit, I think. Shit, shit, shit. He's going to go home. Oh fuck. But he doesn't. He grins and says, 'You know what I'd really like?'

'No.' I shake my head.

'I'd really like a bath.'

'A bath? Are you mad?'

'I know it sounds bizarre, but I've only got a shower in my flat and I miss baths. Would you mind?'

I shake my head, wondering what the hell this is about, because this is a completely new one on me. Am I supposed to sit here and file my nails while he has a bath, or am I supposed to talk to him? What on earth am I supposed to do?

I don't have to think about it for very long because just then the phone rings.

'Hi, babe,' says Jules. 'It's me.'

'Hi,' I say guardedly, in the tone of voice that tells her this is perhaps not the best time to be calling.

'Uh oh,' she says. 'Something tells me you're not alone.'

'Mmmhmm,' I say, as Nick gets up off the sofa and turns the music down slightly.

'Who's there?' she says. 'It's a bloke, isn't it?'

'Mmmhmm,' I say again, eyes widening slightly as

Nick starts grinning manically at me, unbuttoning his shirt.

'What's going on?' she pleads, as I start giggling.

'You really want to know what's going on?' I say.

'Yes!'

'Okay,' I say, as Nick starts dancing around the room doing a bloody good imitation of a stripper, except it isn't sexy, it's very, very funny.

'Okay,' I repeat. 'There's an extremely gorgeous man jumping around my living room and taking off his clothes.'

Nick wiggles his hips in appreciation of my description of him.

'Oh ha bloody ha,' says Jules. 'Seriously. What's going on?'

'Seriously,' I say. 'He's about to take his shirt off.'

Nick takes his shirt off.

'And,' I continue, as lust starts to rise up from my groin, 'he's got a perfect washboard stomach.'

'I don't believe you,' she says, as I hold the phone out to Nick.

'Hello,' he says, as I practically salivate over the sight of his lean, muscular, naked torso. 'Who's this?'

There is a pause. 'Nick,' I hear him say, as he unbuttons the flies of his jeans, giving me minor heart failure. 'Having a bath,' he says next, and then he starts laughing as I grab the phone off him.

'What did you say, what did you say?' I beg.

'Bloody hell!' says Jules. 'Now I believe you. But who the hell is Nick?'

'It's a long story,' I say, thanking God that Nick wears boxer shorts and not something disgusting like purple

Y-fronts or those revolting briefs. 'Can I call you tomorrow?'

'Just tell me, is he naked?'

'Not yet,' I say, eyes glued to Nick, who is trying to balance on one leg as he pulls off his socks, 'but I think he will be soon.'

Nick wiggles off into the bathroom.

'Fucking hell,' I whisper quickly. 'He's gorgeous!'

'As long as you know what you're doing,' she laughs.

'Having fun,' I say. 'Something I haven't had for a while.'

'Okay,' she says. 'I'll let you go. Call me first thing, and for God's sake use a condom.'

'Right,' I say, and laugh, because Jules is the only person in the world who knows about the condom drawer – a drawer in my bedside table that's filled to bursting with condoms of all different shapes, sizes and colours, most of them, it has to be said, supplied by her.

I can hear the bathwater running, so I get up, walk through the bedroom, thanking God I had the presence of mind to make the bed this morning, and gingerly push the door open before creasing up with laughter.

Nick is sitting in the bath as the water pours in, and he's put in practically a whole bottle of bubble bath – this doesn't bother me because it means I can't see anything, which I've been dreading because I don't know him well enough to take it in my stride – and he's put a plastic shower cap on his head.

If he wasn't so damn gorgeous he'd look ridiculous. As it happens, he looks cute as hell, and I pull the loo seat down and sit on it, shaking my head.

'You really are crazy,' I say, as he rubs his face.

'No I'm not,' he says, lying back. 'This is lovely. Why don't you join me?'

'I had a bath earlier,' I say.

'So? I need someone to scrub my back.'

Oh fuck it, I think, standing up and untying my cardigan. This isn't exactly the way I'd planned it, but what have I got to lose?

Thankfully Nick doesn't watch me getting undressed. He lies back in the bath and closes his eyes, and I keep a close watch on him to check he isn't peeking. I'm not quite ready to take off all my clothes in front of him, so when I'm down to my underwear I grab a towel and go back into the bedroom.

'Libby?' he shouts as I go. 'Have you got any candles?'

I find three, and, after I've taken my bra and knickers off in the relative privacy of my bedroom, I wrap a towel around myself, light the candles, and switch the light off in the bathroom, putting the candles around the room.

Nick sits up, facing away from me, and I let the towel drop and climb in behind him in the bath.

'Here,' he says, handing me the soap over his shoulder. 'Back scrub time.'

'You just did this because you wanted a massage,' I say, soaping his back and wondering how on earth I've managed to get so intimate with someone I hardly know in such a short space of time.

'Mmm,' he murmurs. 'A bit lower. Yup, that's perfect.'

I look at my hands circling his back with soap, at the flickering candlelight picking up the definition of his spine, his shoulder blades, and when his back is covered

I put the soap on the side of the bath and slowly, smoothly rub his back.

I have my legs on either side of him, and, as I rub his back, Nick picks up the soap and starts soaping my calves. I catch my breath as I feel his big, strong hands gently soap my legs, over the knee, down to the ankles, holding my feet as he rubs them in silence.

And as we half sit, half lie in the bath, the music coming from the living room seems to take on a distinctly sexual feel, and before I even know what I'm doing I lean forward and kiss his neck. I hear him groan as my lips touch his skin, and I open my lips and taste him, sucking softly as my lips travel up to his earlobe. His hand stops circling on my leg. He's stopped moving, and everything seems to be happening very slowly.

He turns as the water sloshes around him in the bath, then looks at me through eyes glazed with lust, before kissing me softly, open lips teasing mine for what seems like hours, before finally licking my upper lip as I moan and slide my tongue into his mouth.

I'm vaguely aware that as he's kissing me he's half standing up, twisting his body round, and when he sits down again in the warm water he's facing me, his legs over my legs, his lips never leaving mine.

And as we carry on kissing, I pull the bathcap off his head and drop it over the edge of the bath, and slink my hands around his neck, pulling him closer as he drops his head and kisses my collarbone.

I shiver.

He sits back and picks up the soap again, still looking at me as if to check this is okay, which by this time it most definitely is, and very gently starts soaping my arms, my elbows, my hands, and sweet Jesus, I never knew how sensual hands could be, or how turned on I could be by someone gently slipping and sliding soap over my fingers.

And he moves the soap up my arms, on to my shoulders, then slowly circles my breasts, moving closer and closer to my nipples, which are rock hard, but not quite touching them, not yet.

Then he slides the bar of soap over my left nipple and I gasp, and look down into the water because by this time the soap has made all the bubbles disappear, and I can see his cock, thick and hard, and I slide the soap out of his hand and down the side of his cock, and it's his turn to gasp as I slide it up and down the shaft, around his balls, up around the head.

The soap slips out of my hand, and he picks it up and traces a line down my body, over my nipples, down my stomach, and across my clitoris as I close my eyes to feel these incredible feelings, and all I can think of as I reach again for his cock is that I want to feel him inside me.

I hear a slurping noise and I jerk my eyes open and Nick laughs as he holds up the plug, and it breaks the spell for a second, but just a second, because as the water slips out of the bath Nick pushes me on to my back, and, as my legs rest on either edge of the bath, he kisses his way down my body until I feel him pause between my legs, and I open my eyes and look at him, and he's looking at me as if to ask, is this okay, and I close my eyes and sigh to show him that it is.

And I feel his tongue slip in between my legs, and, as he licks, sucks, laps at my clitoris, I feel a wave of orgasm building up inside me, and after I've come, my body jerking like crazy in the confines of the bath, Nick looks at me and smiles, and I kiss him, tasting myself in his mouth, and I lead him out of the bathroom and into bed.

I slip a condom on his cock that is jerking with anticipation, and I push him on to his back and straddle him, positioning myself so I can ease him inside me, and when he's about an inch in I gasp because I really had forgotten how good this feels.

And it's perfect. The perfect fuck. Not too short, and not too long, because nothing, nothing is worse than men who think all it takes to satisfy a woman is hours and hours of deep, hard pounding. Please. I'd rather watch paint dry.

But Nick is perfect, and I love that feeling of power, being on top, being in control, and I love watching his face as he finally gives in to an orgasm.

When it's over I think he'll probably be the type to roll over and fall fast asleep, but he doesn't. He puts his arm around me and cuddles me for ages.

'That,' he says, after squeezing me very tightly, 'was lovely.'

'Good,' I say. 'I thought so too.'

'And you,' he says, kissing my nose, 'are one hell of a sexy lady.'

'I aim to please,' I laugh.

'You certainly did,' he says. 'And now I want a story.'

'A what?' I raise myself up on one arm and look at him.

'A story. I want you to tell me a bedtime story.'

'What about?'

'Anything you like.'

'But I can't think of anything.'

'Oh, for God's sake,' he sighs dramatically. 'I suppose I'll have to tell you one, then.'

'Yes, please!' I say, in a little girl voice, feeling strangely like a little girl, all safe and warm and protected, encircled in his arms.

'Once upon a time,' he starts, in a soft, low voice, 'there lived a little girl called Libby. Libby lived all by herself in a huge yellow sunflower at the bottom of a beautiful garden.'

I sigh and snuggle up closer.

'At the back of the garden,' he continues, 'was a great big house, and in the house lived Mr and Mrs Pinchnose. They were called Mr and Mrs Pinchnose because every time they went into the garden they pinched their noses because Mr and Mrs Pinchnose hated the smell of anything fresh and beautiful, but what they never knew was that it wasn't the smell of the flowers, or the trees, or the river, it was the smell of Libby.'

'Are you saying that Libby smelt?' I say indignantly, although I'm smiling.

'I'm saying that Libby smelt fresh and beautiful,' he says.

'Oh,' I say. 'That's okay, then,' and I pick up his hand and kiss it as he carries on talking, and before I know it I'm fast asleep.

Chapter Four

I hate the morning after the night before, because you never know how you stand, and even though we wake up and have sex again, I'm still not sure what will happen once we both break the spell by getting out of bed, and, in my case, going to work, so I try to put the moment off for as long as possible by snuggling up to Nick, because let's face it, it's not as if *he* has anywhere to go.

But after the fifth time the alarm goes off I have to get up or I'll be severely late for work, so I go into the kitchen to make some coffee, and Nick rolls over groaning about the sunlight.

I wrap myself up in the silk dressing gown that was a present from Jules last year, which I only ever wear if a man stays the night, so needless to say it still looks brand new, and try to fluff up my hair and wipe away the mascara from under my eyes in my powder compact mirror in the living room.

I carry a mug of coffee back into the bedroom for Nick, and stand for a while watching him. He isn't asleep, but he has his eyes closed and he's lying there, the duvet covering his legs, the rest of his body bare, with one arm slung across his eyes, and I stand there thinking, fucking hell, he may not be what I'm looking for but Jesus is he gorgeous.

And as I stand there he opens his eyes and when he sees me he holds his arms out and says, 'Come and give me a cuddle,' and as I'm lying in his arms and he's making me laugh by giving me big, punchy kisses, I'm thinking, God, I could get used to this.

No, Libby. No, you could not. He's not what you want. You really think you could spend your life in a grotty bedsit in Highgate? You think you could spend your social life in pubs drinking warm beer? You think you could forget all about your dreams of being a rich man's wife and a lady who lunches? I don't think so. No. I am not going to fall in love with this man. I'm going to be a woman of the nineties and just enjoy the sex, and so what if he happens to be affectionate and quite funny? That's just a bonus.

Nick sits up in bed and drinks his coffee while I get ready for work. He makes me laugh when I open my wardrobe, and he says, 'What on earth are those?' pointing to a load of hangers covered in tissue paper and cellophane.

'That's my dry cleaning,' I say, as he shakes his head in amazement.

'Dry cleaning? Jesus, we really do come from different worlds.'

'I suppose you don't even do ironing,' I laugh.

'Not if I can possibly help it,' he says, and then, when I'm putting my make-up on in the bathroom mirror, he comes in and sits on the edge of the bath to talk to me and, as he puts it, 'see what I'm doing'.

'What's that for?' he keeps saying, as I root around in my make-up bag and pull out yet another suspiciously alien thing – at least to his eyes.

'I dunno,' he says eventually, shaking his head as I pout at my perfect reflection. 'If you ask me you look far better without anything.'

'Now I know you're joking,' I say, because I'd never

dare leave my house without the full appliance of science.

'No, I'm serious,' he says. 'You don't need to wear all that make-up. I know there are some women who do need it because without it they look like complete dogs, but you're really pretty naturally, and you honestly do look better without.'

I don't know about you, but flattery, for me, will get anyone just about anywhere they want to go, and I could kiss him for saying that. In fact, I do. I completely forget about the make-up bit and just concentrate on the pretty bit. He says I'm pretty! He thinks I'm pretty!

By the time we leave the house and walk up to the tube station, I'm flying as high as a kite. Not that I've fallen in love, not even close, but it's just so nice to have had a night of snuggling up to someone, to have someone to talk to in the morning, to have compliments again.

But as we separate in the tube station, him to go north, me to go to Kilburn, I do feel a tiny twinge, because even though I know this isn't going to go anywhere, I don't think I can stand it if he just says, 'Bye.' I think Nick must see this in my face, because he puts his arms around me and gives me a huge hug.

'That was the nicest night I've had in ages,' he says, while my heart sinks, because surely this is the lead-in to, 'Take care.'

But no. I'm wrong.

'When can I see you again?' he says next, and, despite myself, I feel like doing a little jig on the spot.

'Umm,' I say, pulling away and digging my diary out from my bag. I flick the pages open and have a quick look. 'I'm a bit busy this week,' I say. 'So either the weekend or next week?'

Please say weekend, I think.

'Saturday?' he says.

'Great,' I say, beaming.

'Okay,' he says. 'Why don't you come to me?'

'What, and set foot in your hovel?'

Nick laughs. 'We could go out for something to eat. I'll give you a call at work to arrange a time. How's that?'

It's fine. It would have been better if he'd arranged a time there and then, because once a man says he's going to call you, even if you know you're going to see him again, you still sit and wait for his call, but hell, at least I have a firm date, if not a time, and I'm suddenly feeling a lot happier than I've felt in months.

'You look like the cat that got the cream,' says Jo, our super-trendy receptionist at the office.

'Do I?' I say innocently, but I can't help it, a huge Cheshire cat grin plasters itself to my face.

'You're in love, aren't you?' she says.

'Nope.' I shake my head. 'Definitely not. But,' and I skip away at this point, just turning back before I disappear through the doorway, 'I may well be in lust,' and I wink at her before making my way to my desk.

Do I get any work done? Do I hell. I sit and moon at my desk, looking out the window and shivering with lust at the occasional flashbacks of my passion-filled night.

And the flashbacks seem to come at the most ridiculous times. I'll be talking on the phone to a journalist, and suddenly, mid-sentence, a picture of Nick licking my neck slides into my head and I'll pause, grin and lose the plot completely.

It really isn't that I'm falling for him, it's just so

damned nice to have had a gorgeous man in my bed, to have been reminded that I am attractive, sexy, that I can still pull.

Because, to be perfectly honest, I've been starting to doubt myself these last six months. Not hugely, because there haven't been that many men I've been interested in, but I do have a tendency to fall for the ones who will never be interested in me, and the ones that fall for me are generally pretty revolting.

I can't figure out why I fall for the wrong ones. Jules can't figure it out either. I meet these men, fall desperately in love, and become friends with them in the mistaken hope that one day they'll see the error of their ways and realize they're madly attracted to me. But of course that doesn't happen. I just go out with them as friends and misinterpret every look, every sigh, every touch, and try to convince myself they're about to make a move, and each time I end up feeling like shit, because yet another man I fancy isn't interested.

The last time it happened was Simeon. I made a beeline for him at a press launch, and, because I fancied him, was the brightest, funniest, sparkiest person I could be, and naturally Simeon thought I was great.

But thinking I'm great doesn't mean he fancied me, and I set off on a mission to make Simeon feel the same way. I started by phoning him a couple of times a week, and he didn't seem to mind, he always sounded really pleased to hear from me, which is hardly surprising since I did all the talking, digging up my wittiest stories to make him laugh.

And eventually I invited him to a party, and spent the whole evening glued to his side, and he didn't seem to mind that either. In fact, he rather seemed to like it.

And gradually I forced my friendship upon him until he had no choice but to be friends with me, and soon he was phoning me as often as I was phoning him, and each time my heart would lift and I'd convince myself he was slowly starting to feel the same way.

Eventually we ended up at a party, where Simeon made a beeline for a short brunette with crappy dress sense and an American accent, and I stood on the sidelines watching this and feeling like shit.

And a week later when he phoned, full of excitement at his date with the American the evening before, I put down the phone and burst into tears, and that was when I decided I'd had enough of falling in love with men who didn't want me. I was going to let someone fall in love with me, and they'd have to treat me like a princess for me to be even the slightest bit interested.

But that's love. Lust is something completely different, and it feels like ages since I've been attracted to someone who feels the same way about me, and okay, that doesn't mean anything, it certainly doesn't mean Nick's The One, but it just makes me feel good about myself, which is good. Isn't it?

In fact, I'm feeling so good that I'm not the slightest bit stressed about my job, which is a bloody miracle, because lately I've been given more and more accounts and I have to confess that there are times when I really don't know how I'm going to cope.

My accounts? Okay, I'm currently working on Sean Moore, which you already know about. A performance artist called Rita Roberts, which is a bit peculiar because I don't tend to do the theatrical stuff as I know nothing about it; a film called *The Mystery Cup*, which you won't have heard of yet but, if I do my job properly, you'll be reading about in every paper soon; the comedian Tony Baloney; and an aspiring television presenter called Amanda Baker. I say aspiring, which isn't really fair, because she is on television, although not nearly as often as she'd like. She presents a showbiz slot on one of the daytime shows, and the minute she got her face on-screen she decided she was a star. Unfortunately, nobody seems to know who she is, and it's a bit of a catch-22. The papers won't write about her because she's a no one, but without the coverage she can't raise her profile, and it's the hardest account I've got, not just because of that, but because she's such a complete bitch.

I managed to get her into a celeb round-up where one of the nationals wanted celebs to talk about their date from hell, and you'd think she'd be over the moon, but all she did was moan about being the smallest quote in there. For God's sake, did she really expect to take precedence over Germaine Greer, Vanessa Feltz, Emma Noble and Ulrika? Well, evidently yes. The stupid cow did.

But even the fact that Amanda's coming in today for a meeting doesn't ruin my good mood, and when the receptionist buzzes me to tell me she's here, I float down to meet her, and even manage to compliment her, which seems to throw her a bit. 'I love your suit,' I lie, taking in her tele-friendly pastel trouser suit, which looks vaguely Armani-ish except I know it's not because Amanda isn't nearly successful enough to afford Armani.

'This old thing?' she says, but I can tell she's pleased.

'Come through.' I hold the door open for her, and say in my best PR voice, 'So how are you?'

'Oh, you know,' she says, running a hand through her mane of streaky blonde hair. 'Busy as ever.'

'I caught the slot last week, the one where you interviewed Tony Blackburn. It was excellent, you really are good on TV.'

'D'you think?' she says. 'I didn't look fat?'

I laugh, because, stroppy cow that she may be, she still, like every woman I know, is convinced she's fat, and yes, admittedly, television does add around ten pounds, but nevertheless she does look the part of the perfect blonde, fluffy, bimbo television presenter.

'Fat?' I say. 'You? Are you mad? You're skinny.'

'I wish,' she says, but I've done it, I've actually put her in a good mood, which may make things easier because normally we start off on the wrong foot and end up with her moaning about the lack of press coverage. Hopefully now she'll be a bit more understanding. If I weren't so keen on my job, I'd tell her she's just another bloody wannabe and I really can't be bothered, but obviously I can't do that, so I shuffle some papers around and ask what she wants to see me about.

'I really feel,' she starts, 'that now is the time we should be blitzing the papers and getting some more coverage.'

'Umm, yes,' I say, digging out the list to show her exactly who has been approached. 'Was there anything specific you had in mind?'

'Well, yes, actually,' she says. 'I noticed in *Hello!* that they've done a profile of Lorraine Kelly with her new baby, and I've just moved house and done it up, and I thought it would make a very good feature.'

'Okay,' I say, groaning inside. 'I'll ring them.' Which I will and they will sit on the other end of the phone, doubtless raising their eyes to the ceiling while I start my PR spiel about how brilliant Amanda is, and then they'll say, sorry, we've never heard of her.

'And,' she says, 'I wondered exactly who you had spoken to recently about me?'

Ah ha! Here's my perfect chance for revenge. I slide the contact sheet over to her and start speaking in my most sympathetic tone of voice. 'Last week I spoke to Femail in the *Daily Mail, Sun* Woman, the lifestyle supplement of the *Express, Bella, Best, Woman's Realm* and *Woman.* This week I spoke to *OK!, Here!* magazine, *TV Quick* and *Cosmopolitan.*'

'Oh.' Amanda's voice is very small, and, for the first time ever, and I swear, this must be down to the good mood I'm in, suddenly I feel sorry for her.

'Look,' I say. 'I know it's hard,' and I give her my speech about catch-22. 'We need to come up with an angle, really.'

'What sort of thing?' she says, and for a moment I forget I'm with a client whom I don't really like and who doesn't really like me and before I can help it I say, 'Couldn't you shag a celebrity?'

She looks horrified.

I'm horrified.

'That was a joke,' I say, trying to laugh, except I can't quite manage it and it comes out like a little strangled groan. 'Seriously, though,' I continue, 'have there been any life-changing events that we might be able to use, something that would make a good story?'

'Not like moving house, then?' she asks hopefully.

'Er, no. Not like moving house.' Like stealing, pillaging, nervous breakdowns, I'm thinking.

'Umm.' She sits there and I can almost see her brain try to kick into gear. Oops, nearly, nearly. Nope, she can't quite manage it.

'Okay,' I say. 'As a child, did you ever steal anything?'

'Are you serious?' she asks.

'Absolutely.' I nod my head very seriously.

'No. Not really. Well . . .'

'Yes?' I encourage eagerly.

'Well, I did once take an eyeliner from Boots by mistake. I meant to pay for it but I completely forgot.'

'Perfect!' I say. 'My thieving hell from top TV presenter! I can see it now.'

'Are you sure that will make a story?' she says doubtfully. 'I mean, it was only an eyeliner and I was about fourteen years old, and I wouldn't say it was hell, exactly, except I did feel terribly guilty.'

'We won't say it was an eyeliner, we'll say it was a complete set of make-up, and you won't have been fourteen, it will have happened last year, and the outcome of it was you felt so terrible, you didn't know what came over you, you went back and owned up.'

'But that's lying!' she says.

'That's PR,' I say. 'Hang on,' and I pull the phone over and dial a number. 'Keith? It's Libby from Joe Cooper PR. Fine, fine, you? Great. Listen, you know Amanda Baker from *Breakfast Break*? No, no, the showbiz slot. No, no, she does the weather. No, no, the blonde. Oh well, anyway, she's doing more and more and she's getting really big and she's just confessed the most amazing story which would be perfect for your magazine. It turns out she had the shoplifting experience from hell last year, and she feels the time is right to confess all. Yup.' I nod, listening to what he's saying. 'Yup. Perfect. Full page? Brilliant. Okay.' I scribble down the direct line of the journalist he wants to do it, and put the phone down.

'Well, Amanda,' I say. 'You've just got yourself a full

page in *Female Fancies*, with photographs and everything.'

'That's fantastic!' she says, almost breathless with excitement. 'Photos! That's brilliant! Will it be a studio shot with a professional hair and make-up person?'

'We'll sort out the details later,' I say noncommittally, thinking now would not be the time to tell her they want to take pictures of her in a chemist's, furtively slipping a make-up bag into her large, voluminous raincoat.

'And,' I say, dialling another number, 'how about some radio?'

Amanda is so impressed she can't speak. She nods.

'Mark? It's Libby from Joe Cooper PR. Listen, you know that slot about Londoners and their favourite restaurants? How about Amanda Baker from *Breakfast Break*? I'll fill you in later, yup, yup. Brilliant.' I can't be bothered to tell someone else who she is, and I knew he'd say yes because local radio will give just about anyone airtime, and it does the job because Amanda's thrilled.

'Libby,' she says, standing up and dusting imaginary dirt from her jacket. 'You are doing the most incredible job.'

I smile.

'How about making a quick call to Femail and seeing if they'll do a feature on me?'

'Er,' I stall. 'I just spoke to the commissioning editor before you arrived and I know she's in conference so I'll call her later.'

'Oh.' Her face drops slightly. 'Okay. Well, I'd better be off.' She checks her watch. 'Thank you.' And with that she gives me two air kisses on either side of my face, which throws me somewhat because she's never before offered me anything other than a limp handshake.

'Ciao,' she says, as I wince. 'I'll speak to you later,' and I know she will, because the smaller the star the bigger the pain in the arse they are.

'Libby?' says Jo, as I show Amanda to the door. 'Jules is on the line. It's about the eighth time she's called. D'you want to take it or call her back?'

I'm already running back to my desk as she finishes the sentence. 'I'll take it, I'll take it,' I scream, diving into my chair and breathlessly picking up the phone.

'Libby!' shouts Jules. 'I've been dying to speak to you, I can't believe you had a bloody meeting, I can't get any work done, who's Nick and what happened, you had sex didn't you, I know you bloody had sex, how was it, what's he like, tell me everything . . .'

'Calm down,' I laugh, lighting a cigarette and settling back in my chair for a good long chat. 'First of all you can stop planning the wedding because he's definitely not for me, but yes, we did have sex, and fucking hell, Jules, he is gorgeous.'

'Why isn't he for you? How do you know he's not for you?'

'Okay. For starters he's got no money . . .'

There's a silence on the other end of the phone.

'Next he lives in a disgusting bedsit in Highgate.'

'How do you know it's disgusting?'

'He told me. He's not looking for a relationship. He's very into politics. His idea of a good night out is down the pub with ten pints of beer.'

'Okay, okay,' sighs Jules. 'I get the picture. But Libby, just because he doesn't have money doesn't mean he's not for you. Maybe you should start lowering your expectations.'

'Jules! You know I couldn't seriously go out with someone like that. Anyway,' I say, feeling slightly guilty at admitting all this, 'it's not just the money. It's everything. We're like chalk and cheese.'

'So what happened last night, then?'

And I tell her.

Chapter Five

The high as a kite feeling lasts precisely two days. Two days of floating around beaming with love. Sorry, lust. Two days of getting very little done other than daydreaming about the events of my night with Nick. Two days of leaping every time the phone rings.

And then, when he hasn't called, I start to feel sick. Now I know I'm being ridiculous because yes, yes, I know he's not The bloody One, but that doesn't mean I don't want him to want me. I mean, Jesus, he's supposed to be madly in love with me by now, and he's definitely supposed to be phoning me.

I call Jules.

'Jules,' I moan, 'he hasn't called.'

'So?' she says pragmatically. 'He will.'

'But why hasn't he called? He said he'd call.'

'Libby, for God's sake. You sound like you're madly in love, but you keep saying this is just a fling. Flings don't call every day.'

'But just because I don't want him in that way doesn't mean I don't want him to want me.'

'Now, that,' says Jules, 'is ridiculous. Stop being so childish. Anyway, you know you're seeing him, so of course he'll call, but it will probably be on Saturday, just to confirm the time, as he said he would.'

'Okay,' I grumble.

'And,' she continues, 'you don't want him to fall in

love with you because that will only make the whole thing far more complicated.'

'Okay,' I grumble again.

'So just relax,' she finishes.

'You're right, you're right. I know you're right.'

'Naturally,' she laughs. 'I always am.'

It's a bastard isn't it, how everything changes once you've slept with someone. How, even though you know you're not going to fall for them, you still have expectations, and you'll still be disappointed in the end.

Except no, not this time. I won't be disappointed. There's no commitment, just enjoyment, and I will enjoy Nick. Really, I will.

The phone rings at one o'clock on Saturday.

'Hello?' I'm already breathless.

'Hi, babe.' It's Jules.

'Oh,' I say, the disappointment more than clear in my voice. 'Hi.'

'What are you doing now?' she asks, and I decide not to tell her that I'm sitting next to the phone willing it to ring.

'Nothing much. You?'

'Nothing. Jamie's working and I'm bored. Do you want to go shopping?'

Now that sounds more like it. A bit of retail therapy never did anyone any harm, and besides, having looked through my huge wardrobe of super-trendy clothes, I see I haven't got anything to wear for tonight. Well, it's not exactly that I haven't got anything to wear, just nothing suitable, and Nick isn't the type to appreciate my John Rocha dresses or Dolce & Gabbana trousers.

'Do you want to come and pick me up?' I say.

'No,' she says. 'You come over here and we'll hit Hampstead. How does that sound?'

'Perfect,' I say. 'See you in an hour.'

I check my bag as I leave the house. Yup. Got money, credit cards, cheque book, make-up. Shit! Nearly forgot my mobile phone, so I grab it and head down to my gorgeous car, Guzzle the Beetle, aptly named as he (and yes, I know that most cars are female but mine, with his gorgeous metallic blue coating, is most definitely male) guzzles petrol like there's no tomorrow.

And off we trundle to Jules's flat, and once again I sigh with envy as I walk in, because, thanks to being part of a couple, both with nice fat incomes – Jules is an interior designer and Jamie is a barrister – Jules lives in the flat I wish I had. A maisonette in a side road off Haverstock Hill. You walk into a huge, bright, airy living room with maple floors and floaty muslin curtains drifting on either side of french windows that lead to a large balcony. All the furniture is camel and cream, modern classics mixed with beautiful old antiques, and the canvases on the wall are huge, colourful, abstract and beautiful.

The kitchen's in the basement, and Jules spends most of her time down there. As large as the living room, the kitchen is dominated by a massive scrubbed old french pine table, with enough room left for checked yellow comfy sofas at one end. More french windows lead straight on to the garden, and the units are the ones I dream about – slightly Shaker-ish but with a modern twist. It's my favourite room in the house, and the one we always end up in, drinking huge mugs of tea at the kitchen table, or curled up on the sofa with the sun streaming in.

It does look interior-designed, but it also looks like a home, like a place where you immediately feel comfortable. I adore it, and when I arrive I do what I always do and put the kettle on, and Jules doesn't mind, I know she loves the fact that I feel almost as at home there as she does, possibly more so.

'Hi, Libby,' Jamie calls out from his study next to the kitchen.

'Hi, workie,' I call back, the shortened version of workaholic, which is what I've been calling him for years. He appears in the doorway and comes over to kiss me hello, and, even though I know I couldn't stand to be with someone who works all the time, it has to be said that I can see exactly what Jules sees in him because he is, truly, gorgeous. The only man I know who looks handsome in a wig. No, not that sort of wig, the legal barrister sort of wig.

And before I met Jamie I always thought that all barristers were pompous assholes. They were all, from my limited experience, into ballet, opera and theatre. They all spoke like they had a bagful of plums in their mouth and were as patronizing as hell.

But Jamie isn't like that. Jamie, when he isn't working, is actually a laugh. And Jamie doesn't wear pompous classically English clothes. Jamie wears faded jeans and caterpillar boots. Jamie wears midnight-blue velvet trousers and Patrick Cox loafers. Jamie smokes like a chimney and drinks like a fish. Jamie, in fact, is cool, and one night, when we were all very drunk, he confessed that if he hadn't been a barrister he would have been a pop star, which made us all choke with laughter at the time, but actually I could see that. I could see Jamie being the lead singer in a seriously hip band

and giving interviews with an insouciant toss of his head.

Jamie and I have an odd relationship, in the way that you always have slightly odd relationships with the men your girlfriends subsequently marry. Jules was my friend for years, and then Jamie came along, and yes, we hit it off immediately, but there's always that tiny bit of resentment because they took your best friend away.

But I forgave him. How could I not? And now, even though I don't see him that often, we have this lovely, teasing, almost brother–sister relationship, where he sits me down and asks about my love life and then tries to give me advice, which I almost always ignore because at the end of the day he's a bloke.

And I know what you're thinking. You're thinking that men are far better equipped to give advice when you're having man problems because they know how men think, but Jamie is a bit crap at all of that, because despite being gorgeously gorgeous, he wasn't exactly Mr Experience before Jules came along and swept him off his feet. He was far too busy building up his career, and yes, he had hundreds of admirers, but never the time to notice them.

Jules was different to all the women setting themselves up to be the perfect barrister's wife. Jules didn't wear designer clothes. Jules didn't go to the hairdresser's or have a manicure once a week. Jules didn't care about going to the best restaurants or the ballet. And, more to the point, Jules never tried to pretend she was anyone different to try to trap her man.

No, Jules has always been one of those women that men go crazy about because she has enough self-confidence to say this is me, take it or leave it. And, invariably, they take it. Or at least try to. They love the fact that she doesn't wear make-up. That her clothes, on her tiny, petite frame, are a mishmash of whatever she happens to pull out of the wardrobe that morning. That her laugh is huge and infectious, and, most of all, that she listens. She loves life, and people, and makes time for them, and even before Jamie came along men were forever falling in love with her.

I've tried to be more like Jules, but, even though there are rare occasions when I feel I'm getting close, at the end of the day I just haven't got enough self-confidence to pull it off, and they bloody know it. So they start by falling madly in love with me – with the exception, it would seem, of Nick – and they end, about three weeks later, by disappearing when they realize that I'm actually a bundle of insecurities and not the woman they thought I was at all.

But anyway, enough about me, back to Jules and Jamie. Despite Jamie spending all his time tucked away in his study, their relationship does seem to work, and what I love about going out with the two of them is that we have fun. They have fun, and it's catching.

So Jamie comes out of his study and gives me a huge kiss as I stand by the kettle and then says, 'Tea? Excellent. I need a break. So,' he says, pulling a chair out from the kitchen table, 'how's the love life?'

He always asks me this because he knows I'll have a story to tell, and, if I do say so myself, I tell my stories brilliantly. I tell them so they're sparkling, witty, amusing. I tell them so they capture people's attention and make them clutch their sides with laughter, shaking their heads and saying, 'God, Libby, you are extra-ordinary.' I tell them so people think I lead the most glamorous, exciting life in the world. Except, when I'm telling them one-on-one to Jules, I can be honest. I can tell her how lonely I am. How I spend my life wondering why I never seem to have healthy, happy relationships. How I probably wouldn't know a healthy, happy relationship if it jumped on my head and knocked me sideways.

And she listens to me quietly, and then thinks about it, and finally tells me why these men aren't right for me, and that one day someone will come along who will fall in love with me, and that the trick is to stop looking and that it will happen when I least expect it.

Which is all very well for her to say, and it's probably true, but how am I supposed to stop looking when it's the one thing I want more than anything else in the world? Well, other than winning the lottery, I suppose, but only because it would increase my pulling power a thousandfold. But seriously, I've never understood all that rubbish that married women tell you about not looking, because how can you not look when you're looking, and how can you really be happy on your own when you're not?

Sitting here in the kitchen with Jules and Jamie, I tell them my funny story about Nick, and about him performing a striptease in the living room, and about him sitting in my bath with a shower cap on, and they laugh, and I laugh with them, and Jamie shakes his head and says, 'God, Libby, what would we do without you?' and I don't take offence, I just shrug my shoulders.

'So where are you two off to today?' he ventures, standing behind Jules and rubbing her shoulders in a gesture that's so affectionate I practically sigh with craving.

'Just up the high street,' she says breezily, as he rolls his eyes to the ceiling.

'Oh, God. I know what that means. I'd better warn the bank manager.'

'No, darling,' she says, 'we're not going for me, we're going for Libby. Except I might see something I like, in which case –'

'I know, I know,' he laughs. 'So, d'you want a lift up there or are you walking?'

Jules looks at me, the disgust already written on her face because she knows exactly how I feel about walking – if God had meant us to walk he wouldn't have invented cars – and I don't have to say anything, I just give her a pleading look and she sighs an exasperated sigh and says, 'You're giving us a lift.'

We jump into Jamie's BMW, and I do what I always do and insist on sitting in the front seat so I can pretend to be married to Jamie, and Jules does what she always does and prises off her engagement ring for me to wear, and we drive up the road with my arm hanging out the window in case anyone I know should be passing, which naturally never seems to happen, and he drops us off by the station.

'Jules,' he calls out the window, just before driving off, 'can you get me some socks?'

She nods and turns to me with a sigh. 'And who said it was glamorous being married to a barrister?'

We go to Whistles, Kookai and agnès b. We mooch round Waterstone's, Our Price and David Wainwright. We ooh and aah for hours in Nicole Farhi, and finally, in a tiny little sports shop tucked away at the top of the high street, I find exactly what I'm looking for.

'You're not seriously buying those,' says Jules in horror, as I stand in the mirror with super-trendy Adidas trainers on my feet.

'Why not?' I look innocent as hell, even though I know exactly what she's going to say.

'But they're not you!' she manages in dismay. 'You're Miss aspiring Prada, Miss Gucci. You're not Miss Adidas.'

'Look,' I say to her slowly and seriously, trying to make her understand, 'let me put it this way. I'm getting tired of being Patsy, so now I want to see what it's like to be Liam for a change.'

'What are you talking about?'

'Patsy's always in Prada and Gucci, and Liam's in Adidas, so now I fancy a more casual look and these are exactly what I've been looking for.'

'But what are you going to wear them with?'

'T-shirts and jeans.'

'T-shirts and jeans!'

'Yes. T-shirts and jeans.'

'But you haven't got any T-shirts and jeans.'

'Yes I do, Jules. Don't be ridiculous. Thank you,' I say, turning to the shop assistant with my most professional tone. 'I'll take them.'

Actually that whole Patsy, Liam stuff is a load of shit, and, although Jules probably would understand, probably in fact does understand, I can't be bothered to explain it to her right now. You see, it's not that I'm trying to change myself for Nick, God no. I mean, I hardly know the guy, it's just that these somehow seem more his style, and I can hardly go to his local Highgate pub in my designer togs, can I? These are much more appropriate, and anyway I've wanted a pair for ages. Honest.

So, armed with my wonderful new trainers (and what a bargain, £54.99!), we go for a cappuccino, and as we sit down I pull my mobile phone out of my bag and ring the answering service just in case it rang and I didn't hear it, but no, the recorded voice on the end says, 'You have (pause) no (pause) new messages,' and now I'm starting to get seriously pissed off, but Jules sees what I'm feeling before I've even started really feeling it and she says, 'No. Stop it. He's going to phone,' so I relax a bit, and it's fine.

Over coffee, Jules says, 'Are you sure you're not going to get too involved?'

And I sweep her comment aside with a toss of my hair and laugh in a very grown-up, in-control sort of way and tell her she's being ridiculous, but meanwhile why the bloody hell hasn't he called? My mobile number's on my answering machine at home, and I could ring in to pick up my messages, except that if I do that I won't be able to press 1471 to find out who last called me, which is what I do automatically every time I walk in my flat, and he might be the sort of person who hates mobiles and hates leaving messages, so he might have phoned but not left a message, but Jesus Christ, Libby, SHUT UP. I'm doing my own head in.

'What makes you think I can't have a fling?' I say eventually. 'You know, sex with no strings attached?'

'Because you can't,' she says firmly.

'Now that's where you're wrong,' I say. 'I haven't done it for a while, but I've had loads of flings with men when I haven't been emotionally involved. It's just been sex. I've fancied them but I haven't liked them, or I've realized they're not for me.'

Jules sits and thinks for a minute. 'And when was the last time you did that?'

'About five years ago, but I could have done it loads of times since then.'

'So why haven't you?'

'I just haven't.'

'You don't think that perhaps we change between the ages of twenty-three and twenty-eight or nine and that what was so easy for us when we're in our early twenties becomes almost impossible when we're nearing thirty, which is why we don't do it any more?'

'What do you mean?'

'The reason women generally stop having flings, or sleeping around, or whatever you want to call it, is because they realize they can't do it, because the older they get the more they see you can't sleep with someone on a regular basis and not want more, not when you've reached an age where society, unfortunately, still tells you that you should be married and having babies.'

'No.' I shake my head. 'I think you're either the sort of person who can or the sort of person who can't, and I'm the sort of person who can.'

Jules doesn't say anything. She just looks at me.

'I am, you know,' I insist.

And she keeps looking at me. And eventually I say, 'For Christ's sake, stop looking at me,' and she shrugs and changes the subject.

And eventually at five o'clock we wander back down the high street, which I don't mind in the slightest because it's downhill and even my disgustingly unfit body can cope with practically falling down a hill, and I jump in the car and drive home, and when I walk in there have been three messages, and, as I press 'play',

I'm praying, I'm seriously praying that Nick has phoned.

The first is from my mother. 'Hello, Libby, it's me. Mum.' As if I didn't bloody know.

'C'mon, c'mon,' I urge her.

'Just calling up for a chat,' she says, 'and wondering whether you're coming for tea tomorrow. Call me later if you can, or otherwise in the morning, and if you're going out tonight have a nice time. If not, there's a really interesting documentary about magazines at nine o'clock tonight which I'll be watching with your father and – '

'Oh, shut up,' I shout at the answering machine as she finishes. Anyway, what kind of sad git does she think I am, staying in on a Saturday night? Even if there's absolutely nothing to do I'll try to go out just so that I can tell people I went out. And yes, drinking coffee at Jules's kitchen table and watching *Blind Date* and *Stars in Their Eyes* does count as going out because I've left my house, and all I need to tell people is I went to some friends for dinner.

Message number two is from Joe Cooper, which always sends me into panic mode. Not that I don't like him, I adore Joe as much as, if not more, than when we first met, but every time I get a work-related phone call on the weekend I start having anxiety attacks, convinced that something has gone terribly and irrevocably wrong, but luckily this is just Joe asking for a phone number, and he ends the message by saying he'll try to get it from someone else.

Message number three is a silence. Then the phone's put down. Shit. I pick up and dial 1471.

'Telephone number 0.1.8.1.3.4.0.2.3 . . .' Yes! I don't bother listening to the end of the number because it's a

Highgate number, and I don't know anyone else who
lives in Highgate! Yes! He rang! And it gives me the
burst of energy I need to run the bath so that I'll be
ready whenever he calls again. Yes, I know I could call
him, and I'm not playing hard to get, it's just that, having
spent so many years chasing men, I now realize it's better
not to call them. Ever. If you can possibly help it. And
that includes calling them back. Except I'm not so good
at that one.

And to make completely sure I don't give in to the
urge to call him back I jump in the bath, and then, just
as I've submerged my head under water, the phone rings
and I jump up as if I've had an electric shock and go
running into the living room, leaving a trail of sopping
wet footprints. I pick it up and, trying to sound calm and
collected and sexy as anything, say huskily, 'Hello?'

'Libby?'

'Yes?'

'It's Nick.'

Chapter Six

Oh my God, I'm having a serious clothes crisis. The trainers are great, better than great, perfect, but what the hell can I wear with them? I've tried the jeans and T-shirt, and it doesn't look quite right, and no, it's not that I'm that excited, but hell, I still want to look nice.

The bed is strewn with clothes, and eventually, right at the bottom of the wardrobe, I find a crumpled-up black T-shirt that I haven't seen for at least a year. I smell it tentatively, and okay, it's a bit musty, but I can spray perfume on it and iron it and yes! It's perfect. It hugs my body and sits perfectly around my waist, and with my black trousers it's just right. But hang on, even though I'm wearing trainers all this black looks a bit imposing. Not fresh enough, not young enough. Shit.

An hour later I settle on a white T-shirt with a babe-type logo emblazoned across the chest, my oldest, most faded, most favourite 501s, and the beloved trainers. I dig out some chunky silver earrings from the bottom of the papier mâché box I use as a jewellery box and, what the hell, stick on some chunky silver rings as well. Perfect.

I'm meeting Nick at the Flask in Highgate, a pub I vaguely remember from my teenage years, and I know I'm going to be drinking so I leave the car at home and order a minicab, and just as I'm about to leave the phone rings.

'Hello, love, it's Mum.'

As if I didn't know.

'What is it, Mum? I'm late and I'm going out.'

'Oh, that's nice. Anywhere special?'

'I've got a date.' Damn. I didn't mean to tell her. Now I'm going to get an onslaught of questions.

'How lovely!' she says, and I can almost hear her brain clicking into gear at the other end of the phone. 'Anyone nice?'

Which I know will lead to what does he do, what car does he drive, where does he live, and, basically, is he good enough for our daughter.

This is the problem with having The Suburban Parents from Hell. Not that I don't love them, I do, it's just that they've got this thing about me marrying way, way above my station, and I try not to tell them anything about my life, except sometimes things have a habit of slipping out.

'Yes, he's very nice,' I sigh, 'but I really have to go.'

'Well,' she stalls. 'You young things. I don't know, always rushing around. Dad and I were wondering if you were coming round for tea tomorrow.'

'Oh.' I'd forgotten. 'Okay,' I sigh.

'Oh, lovely dear. I've got some of your favourite chocolate marzipan cake.'

My mother thinks that my tastes are exactly the same as when I was six years old, and I don't bother telling her that these days I try to avoid chocolate marzipan cake like the plague, because it doesn't end up in my stomach, it ends up on my thighs.

'Okay, Mum. I'll see you about four?' I'm already mentally planning my day. A lazy breakfast in bed with Nick, perhaps a walk in Kenwood, and then a long kiss goodbye. Yup, if I time it perfectly I'll be able to make it to my parents in Finchley by four o'clock.

'All right, darling. What does your date do?'

'Look, Mum, I've got to go, the cab's here.'

'He's not picking you up?' There's horror in her voice.

'No, Mum. I'll see you tomorrow. Bye,' and I gently put the phone down with an exasperated sigh as the doorbell rings and the cab really does arrive.

Okay. Got everything? Clean knickers, toothbrush, make-up, moisturizer? Yup. My Prada bag's so full it's practically bursting, and I grab a jacket and run down the stairs.

And the closer we get to Highgate the more nervous I become. At Queen's Park I check my lipstick. At West End Lane I check I'm not shining. At Hampstead I flick my hair around a bit. At Kenwood I start tapping my feet and trying to ignore the driver staring at me in his rear-view mirror.

'You are going somewhere nice?' he eventually says, in a thick Eastern European accent.

'Umm, yes,' I say, because quite frankly I don't need to get into a conversation with my minicab driver and I don't like the way he's staring at me.

'You look nice,' he says.

'Thank you,' I say, in a tone of voice aimed to discourage him. It works. And then I feel guilty so when we pull up I give him a two pound tip and then I stand on the pavement for a bit, wondering what it's going to be like, and wondering where he is.

'Libby!' I look up, and there, sitting at a table outside in the large courtyard, is Nick, and as I walk over to him I feel all the tension disappear, because, after all, it's only Nick, and he looks gorgeous, he is gorgeous, and suddenly I'm beaming because everyone turned round to look at him when he shouted, and most of the women are still looking, and hey! He's with me! And then I'm standing in front of him, not sure what to do. Should I kiss him? Should I hug him? Should I just say hello? And then he leans forward and kisses me, aiming for my lips, and fool that I am I turn my head out of nervousness, so he just grazes the corner of my mouth, and he looks slightly surprised but then smiles and asks what I'd like to drink.

I can see that he's already halfway through a pint, and vodka and cranberry juice – my usual – would seem completely out of place, so I ask for half a lager and he seems pleased, and then he disappears inside to get it as I sit down and congratulate myself on such a good pull.

And he comes back grinning and puts the lager down in front of me, saying, 'I'm surprised at you, Libby. I would have thought you were a spirits sort of girl.'

And I pick up my lager and sip daintily, trying not to grimace, and say, 'When in Rome . . .'

'Ah.' He nods. 'So you'd much rather be having a gin and tonic.'

'Vodka and cranberry juice!' I say. 'Please!' Because gin and tonics, delicious as they may be, always remind me of my parents, and it's the one drink that I never order because I absolutely know that that, more than anything else, will give away my background.

Nick laughs.

'So how has your week been?' he says, and I wonder whether to tell him about Amanda and the pictures she doesn't know she's going to be doing, and I do tell him because it's a good story, and he laughs and laughs, and I'm having a good time. In fact, I'm having a much better time than I thought I would be.

You see, the thing is that since the other night, the

night I spent with Nick, every time I thought about him I thought about the sex. I never really thought about him as a person because sex objects don't need to have personalities, do they? But sitting here, in the early evening warmth, I'm surprised that Nick's so nice, so easy to be with, so laid-back.

And then Nick tells me about his week. He tells me that once again he did a mailshot, this time to eight publishers, sending them the first three chapters of his masterpiece, and that already he'd had one rejection letter saying interesting concept but 'not for us'.

'Would you ever consider going into another field?' I venture, wondering why he's bothering if he's no good at it.

'Nah.' He shakes his head. 'Well, maybe. If something interesting came along I suppose so, but this has always been my dream.'

'But how do you live?'

'What d'you mean?'

'Where do you get money from?'

'Her Majesty's Government,' he says proudly, and I blanch.

'You mean you're on the dole?'

'Yup.'

'Oh.' I'm speechless, and as I sit there wondering what to say next I think of how Jules would laugh. From Jon with his Mazda MX-5 to this. Oh dear. What the hell am I doing here?

'I don't mind,' he says, laughing at my face. 'Even though you, apparently, do.'

'It's not that I mind,' I say, and I decide not to tell him that I've never met anyone before who's on the dole. 'It's just that it seems a shame to waste your talents.'

'But I'm not wasting them. I'm waiting for them to be recognized.'

'Oh,' I say. 'Well, that's okay, then.'

'So,' he says, after our fourth drink (I got two rounds, I'm not that stingy, particularly given that he's on the dole), 'are you hungry?'

And I realize that I am. Starving.

'There's a really nice pizza place around the corner. I thought we could walk up there and have some dinner.'

'Mmm.' I nod my head vigorously. A little too vigorously, perhaps, because those lagers have gone straight to my head. 'That sounds perfect,' and we get up and start walking, and it's not round the corner, it's practically the other side of bloody London, and after about twenty minutes I say, 'Nick, where is this place?'

'Nearly there,' he says. 'God, you're hopeless.'

'I'm not,' I say, and playfully slap him, and he turns to me and grabs me, saying, 'Don't you slap me, young lady,' and I giggle as he tells me my punishment is to kiss him, and I reach up and give him a quick peck on the lips, and he stands back and smacks his lips.

'Nope,' he says. 'That wasn't enough.'

I give him another kiss, just slightly longer, and he stands there again and shakes his head, so I move over again, and this time he opens his eyes and looks at me as I'm kissing him, and before I know it it's turned into a huge, delicious, yummy snog, and my stomach turns upside-down.

And it breaks the ice – the little there was left. I don't notice the last twenty minutes of the walk because we're holding hands and stopping every few minutes to kiss each other passionately, and we're giggling like teenagers and I've forgotten all about my hunger and my aching legs, and suddenly Nick turns to me and asks how my legs are.

'They're fine,' I say, having stopped moaning about the walk the minute he kissed me.

'You don't want a piggyback?'

'You're crazy!' I laugh. 'No, I don't want a piggyback,' but before I know it he flings me over his shoulder in a fireman's lift and runs down the road, while I scream delightedly and bang his back to let me down, which is sort of what I want but only because I'm worrying that I'm too heavy, and then we're there, and you know what? I wish this walk could go on for ever because I can't remember having had this much fun in ages.

And we have a tiny cosy table in one corner with a candle in a wax-covered bottle in the centre, and everyone else in there looks exactly like Nick: young, trendy, struggling, but they're all smiling, and I wonder whether perhaps I could get used to this, this world away from the smart, posey bars and restaurants I'm used to, where the people seem to be more relaxed, unconcerned about dressing to impress, and whether Nick's way of life isn't so bad after all.

The waiter comes over to take our order, and he obviously knows Nick and there's much shaking of hands and 'good to see you's', and then Nick tells him what he wants while I sit there thinking, you should have asked me first, and then I think it really doesn't matter, and I say that I'll have a Pizza Fiorentina and a side salad, and Nick orders a bottle of house red.

As soon as the waiter goes, Nick gets a slightly serious look on his face and sighs.

'What's wrong?' I ask.

There's a silence.

'Okay,' he says finally. 'Do you think it's time we should have that talk?'

Oh shit. Shit. Shit. Shit. I knew this was too good to be true. This is the time he tells me he doesn't want to see me again.

'Well,' I say hesitantly. 'I didn't think we had anything to talk about, but if there's something on your mind perhaps you'd better get it off your chest.'

'Okay,' he nods. And then he sighs. And then he doesn't say anything and I start feeling sick.

'Look,' he says. 'The thing is,' and he stops and looks at me and then takes my hand over the table, but after about two seconds I pull away because I know I'm not going to like what he's about to say and I don't want to have my hand in his while he's saying it.

'Jesus,' he says. 'This is so difficult.'

'For Christ's sake,' I say, my nervousness giving my voice a loud, sharp edge, 'will you just say it?'

'Okay,' he nods. 'The thing is, I'm not ready for a relationship.'

I don't say anything. I don't need to. I've heard it all before.

'But,' and he looks up, 'I really like being with you.'

'So what are you saying?'

'I don't know.' He sighs and shakes his head. 'I think what I'm saying is that I need you to know that I'm not ready for commitment. I'm not really ready for a relationship. I've been single for a while, and I'm really enjoying it and I'm not ready to give that up.'

'So is this it?'

'Well, no,' he says. 'Because I really like you and I want to keep seeing you, but I just don't want you to get the wrong idea.'

'But Nick, I'm not ready for a relationship either,' I say, which is true. 'I've been single for a while and I'm in exactly the same position.' He looks relieved. 'And I know that you're not The One, and I know I'm not The One for you, but that doesn't mean we shouldn't enjoy each other.'

The relief on his face is spreading. I swear, I can practically see his shoulders relax.

'So you're okay with that?' he says.

'Absolutely.' I nod firmly. 'We like being with each other, we have lovely sex, so let's just relax and enjoy it for as long as it lasts.'

'Libby,' he says, reaching over the table and kissing me, 'you're fantastic!'

And I blush and I think to myself, there. That wasn't so bad. And at least it will stop me from falling for him. Not that I would, you understand. It's just that now I definitely won't. There'd be no point.

And we have a lovely dinner. No, that's not actually quite true, because although I can't speak for Nick I know that I hardly noticed the food, I was far too busy kissing him over the table and holding his hand under the table, but it was lovely. The evening was lovely. He was lovely.

And you know the nicest thing about it? The nicest thing was to be with a man on a Saturday night. To pretend that we were a couple. To pretend that I'm as good as the rest of the women in here, that I've got a man too, that I'm not some sad, single, lonely woman out with the girls again on a Saturday night.

You probably think I'm mad. I know Jules thinks I'm mad, because there are advantages to being single. When you're busy and sociable and meeting men and going on dates, it's the best thing in the world and you wouldn't want it any other way. But, when all your single girl-friends suddenly seem to have boyfriends and you're the only one who's on your own, it's as miserable as sin. You phone your partners in crime and ask them if they'll go to a bar with you on a Saturday night, and they apologize profusely and say they're with Steve, or Pete, or Jake, but they can meet you for a coffee in the afternoon. If you're lucky they'll glide in on their own with huge smiles on their faces and sit and regale you with tales of how wonderful He is; and if you're unlucky they'll drag Him along so you're forced to make small talk with someone you don't know, as your friend gazes into His eyes, enraptured by every boring thing He comes out with, and you make a move as quickly as is decently possible.

And you spend Saturday nights on your own or, worse, at dinner parties they've organized when more often than not they've been let down by the creepy spare man they've invited for you, so it's three couples and you on your own and you spend the whole evening feeling like shit.

But tonight I'm one of them. I belong! And you know what? I love it.

We finish dinner and walk back to Nick's flat, because it's presumed that I'll be staying, even though neither of us has mentioned it, because what, after all, does 'enjoy each other' mean, if not sex? And Nick leads me up a path to a tall, red-brick Victorian building, and there are slatted blinds on the window at the front. I can just about see through, and it doesn't look horrible, it looks lovely.

A light's been left on, and okay, it's not quite my taste,

but I can see that it's nice, not the hell hole I expected at all. And I walk through the front door and, as Nick rifles through the envelopes on a table in the hall, I put my bag down by his front door and wait.

Nick looks up and starts laughing. 'That's not mine,' he says. 'I'm upstairs.'

'Oh,' I say, flushing and picking up my bag. 'Sorry.'

And we go upstairs and he unlocks the door that really is his front door, and I walk straight into what I presume is the entire flat, and it's horrible.

Not that it's dirty, at least not on first sight, it's just that it's so messy, and untidy, and uncoordinated. There's an unmade Futon at one end, which I presume doubles as a sofa when Nick can be bothered to make it, which he evidently didn't do this morning because the duvet's still crumpled up at the bottom, and there are piles of papers and magazines everywhere. And I mean everywhere. You can hardly walk and, as I pick my way across the room, I think that the piles of papers are probably preferable to the floor, because the few bits I can see are swirly orange and brown pub carpet, and I sit gingerly on an armchair that's obviously seen better days. Far, far better days. A long time ago.

The furniture all looks as if it's been picked up at junk shops, which it undoubtedly has, and it's falling apart, and shelves have been put up haphazardly everywhere, and there are so many books that they're stacked up instead of neatly lined up like in my flat, and it's a dump.

A bloody dump.

'Would you like some tea?' Nick says, disappearing into what must be the kitchen, and I get up to follow him in there but he comes back out and says. 'Stay here. The kitchen's a mess. I'll bring it out to you,' and I wonder what the hell the kitchen can be like, and decide that as long as I'm here I'm never setting foot in it.

'Sorry it's a mess,' he says, bringing out the tea in two chipped mugs. 'I meant to tidy it today but didn't have time.'

'It's fine,' I say, racking my brain to try to come up with a compliment. 'It's exactly what a writer's flat should look like.'

'You think?' he says, obviously chuffed.

'Definitely.' I nod.

'It suits me,' he says. 'But I do need to clean it up a bit more often.'

I keep quiet and sip my tea.

And then he comes and sits next to me and starts stroking my back, and I put my tea down and lean into him and after a few minutes forget about the flat, forget about the mess, forget about everything except the feeling of his hand on my back, and I turn around to kiss him, and, I suppose, one advantage of this place is that it only takes a second to move to the Futon, and I don't even notice the state of the sheets because Nick's pulled my T-shirt up and he's undoing my bra and mmm. This is lovely.

And I unbutton my own jeans, furiously tugging them off, not wanting to waste a second, and then I watch as Nick unbuttons his, and I watch, mesmerized, as his cock stands straight out of his boxer shorts, and Nick watches me watching him stroke his cock, and then I lean forward and kiss the tip, and he groans, and I push him back so he's on his knees, and I open my lips and take the tip in my mouth, then the whole of the shaft, and he exhales very quickly.

After a while he whispers for me to stop or he'll come,

and he pulls me up and our tongues mesh together with passion, and he strokes my breasts before moving one hand down, over my pants, and it's my turn to exhale loudly, and he teases me for a while, and then he pulls the fabric aside and yes, that's it, his fingers stroking my clitoris, reaching inside me to make them wet, to help them slide, and with the other hand he circles my breasts until he reaches the nipples, and he pinches them and I moan and sink back on the bed.

And then all our clothes come off, and I can't take this any more, I insist he puts a condom on and enters me NOW, and he does and it's better, God, so much better than I remember, and as he moves in and out I suck his neck, and I wonder why it's never felt so good before, and then I stop wondering because Nick pulls me up to change position, and I look confused because why move when this feels so good, but he whispers, 'You'll see,' and he turns me around and enters me from behind, and as he does he moves one hand down to rub my clitoris at the same time, and suddenly I'm moaning in rhythm with him, and I feel the build-up and then I'm making these incredibly animalistic sounds as the most intense orgasm of my life sweeps over me.

And afterwards I'm exhausted, and I do something I've never ever done before. I fall asleep in his arms.

Chapter Seven

'So Libby dear,' says my mother, pouring the tea out of her best china teapot. 'How was last night?'

You know, it's an extraordinary thing but here I am, twenty-seven, independent, mature, sophisticated, yet the minute I step through my parents' front door I regress to being a surly teenager, and I feel the same exasperation at my parents' questions now as I did ten years ago.

'It was fine,' I say, determined to be nice, not to let them get to me.

'And?' my mother says with a smile.

'And what?' I grunt, picking up the delicate tea cup.

'And is he nice?'

'He's okay.'

'If he's just okay why are you going out with him?' she trills with laughter, and pushes her hair behind her ears – a nervous habit I've unfortunately inherited.

'I'm not going out with him,' I grunt. 'We just went out last night.'

God, I think, mentally raising my eyes to the ceiling. What would she say if I told her the truth? If I told her that yes, I went out with someone, and then we went back to his place and shagged each other senseless until we both fell asleep, and then in the morning had tea in bed (sorry, my romantic notions of breakfast in bed were slightly ambitious, given that the only things in Nick's fridge, he grudgingly admitted, were a six-pack of beer, a tub of butter and half a pack of bacon that was meant to have been eaten three months previously), then had sex again, and that I came straight here (again, we never managed that walk because Nick wanted to watch the football, so I amused myself reading back copies of *Loaded*).

'And what does he do?'

'He's a writer.'

'Ooh, a writer. How exciting. What does he write?'

She may be irritating, but I can't tell her the truth. 'He writes, er, he writes articles.'

'What sort of articles?'

'For men's magazines.'

'That's nice. He must be successful.'

'Yes. Mum?' I've just thought of something to change the subject. 'I thought you had chocolate marzipan cake.'

'Oh, silly me,' she says, standing up as I breathe a sigh of relief. 'I completely forgot. It's in the kitchen,' and she disappears while I catch Dad's eye and smile as he rolls his eyes to the ceiling.

And then Mum comes back out and says, 'Does your young man have a name?'

'He's not my young man, and yes. His name's Nick.'

'Nick,' she repeats, thinking about it. 'Nicholas. Oh, I do like the name Nicholas. Where does he live?'

'Highgate.'

'Very posh,' she says, and I think how she'd have heart failure if she saw his flat. 'He must be doing well if he can afford to live in Highgate. Has he got one of those lovely big houses, then?'

'No, Mum,' I sigh. 'No one I know lives in big houses, you know that. We all have flats.'

'Of course you do,' she says. 'So have you been there? Is it a nice flat?'

'Give her a break,' says my dad, putting down the paper. 'It's early days, isn't it, Libby?' and I nod, smiling at him with relief.

'I just worry about you,' says Mum, smoothing down her apron and sitting down. 'When I was your age I was happily married and you were three years old. I don't understand all you girls. So independent.'

'Yup. We're women of the nineties,' I say. 'And anyway I'm not bothered about getting married, I'm far too interested in my career.'

God, if only that were true.

'So how is work?' says Dad, and, as usual, I dredge up all the work stories which fascinate them both, and I tell them about Amanda, expecting them to laugh, which my dad does, except he suppresses it pretty damn quickly when he sees my mother's expression.

'That's not very nice of you, Libby. Don't you think you ought to tell her?'

'Oh, Mum,' I groan. 'It'll be fine. She'd pose naked if she thought it would get her publicity.'

'Well. You know best.' She says it with raised eyebrows, meaning I don't know best and she disapproves.

'So how's Olly?' I ask finally, knowing that the only way to put her in a truly good mood is to ask about my beloved brother, the apple of her eye.

'Being a rascal as usual,' she says. 'Loving his job, and breaking all the girls' hearts, I shouldn't wonder.'

Much as I hate to admit it, I adore my brother. Twenty-six years old, drop-dead gorgeous, he has me in fits of laughter whenever I see him, which isn't nearly as often as I'd like. He's the kind of person that everyone instantly adores, and, although I sometimes feel I ought to be jealous of that, of his easy-going nature, I'm not, and the only time I get slightly pissed off with him is when he tells me to lay off Mum.

When we were children, though, I hated him. I hated him for always being clever, and sporty, and popular. For never putting a foot wrong, for so obviously being Mum's favourite. And then, when I left home to go to university, things suddenly changed, and on my first holiday at home he stopped being an annoying little brother and started being an equal.

It helped that he began smoking as well, and we'd both lock ourselves in my room and puff furiously out the window, spraying huge amounts of sickly sweet air freshener around when we finished. He was the first person to introduce me to spliff, showing me how to take a large Rizla and sprinkle it first with tobacco, then slightly burnt bits of hash, and roll it into a joint, suspiciously similar to a super-plus Tampax.

But naturally Mum never knew. She'd shout and scream at me for drinking or smoking or coming back late at night, but Olly could do no wrong, and the older I got the more we laughed about it together, and suddenly Olly was sticking up for me and telling Mum that I hadn't been drinking, or shagging, or whatever.

And she'd listen to Olly. She'd start off on a rant, and Olly would come in and say he'd bumped into me earlier and I'd been with Susie, and she must have got the wrong end of the stick, and she'd believe him!

We even talked about sharing a flat together for a while, but then I decided that, love him as I do, I couldn't put up with his mess, so I got the flat and he got the job in Manchester.

And he's happy. He loves it there. He rents a huge flat in Didsbury, works for a large TV company as a producer, and hits all the clubs on the weekend. He doesn't have a serious girlfriend – relationship trouble must run in the family – but he has more than his fair share of flings. I call him every weekend, usually waking him from the depths of yet another killer hangover, and more often than not he has to call me back when the result of last night's session has put her make-up on and gone.

And he's the best person to sort out my love life, other than Jules. He's not as wise as Jules, but he's bloody good at giving the male perspective on things, and I've spent many hours on the phone to him working out strategies for catching the man of my dreams.

'How's his job?' I ask, because I've been a bit too caught up with my own life to call him recently.

'He's got a new programme about food,' she says proudly, puffing out her chest with pride, because television producing is something she knows about. At least she should do, the amount of TV she watches. PR, as far as she's concerned, doesn't count. She can't boast about her daughter working in PR because she's never really understood what it's all about, even though I've tried to explain it a million times, and anyway she doesn't think I should be working. She thinks I should be at home cooking delicious meals for my husband, who's out making lots of money to keep me and my ten children in the style to which she'd like me to become accustomed. Anyone would think she was living in the bloody Dark Ages. But a television producer? That's something she understands, something she has tangible evidence of, and 'my son the television producer'? It's become her catchphrase.

'Food?' I laugh. 'But Olly doesn't know the first thing about food, unless it's about takeaway curries and hamburgers.'

'It's called *The Gourmet Vegetarian*.' Evidently she's decided to ignore my last comment.

'*The Gourmet* what?' Now this I really can't believe. 'But Olly's your classic meat and two veg man.'

'I know,' she says, 'and quite frankly I don't understand all this vegetarian nonsense, I'm convinced you all do it because it's fashionable, but there it is.' And she looks at me pointedly while I glance away because any chance to get a dig in and she'll be there with a shovel.

Yes, okay, so? I was vegetarian once, for about eighteen months, and I could say that it was because of cruelty to animals, but actually it was because all my friends were doing it so I decided to do it too. And it was fine. I didn't even miss meat. But all that stuff about vegetarians being healthy is crap. Sure, it's true if you eat salads and nuts all the time, but me? I lived on bread, cheese, eggs and pastry, and I ballooned. I remember the first time I ate meat again, I was out with some friends – different ones, carnivores – and we'd gone to get Chinese takeaway and I stood in the shop, smelling all these delicious smells, and everyone was ordering sweet and sour pork and lemon chicken, and I stood there and thought, fuck it. If I have to eat stir-fried vegetables again I'm going to scream, so I didn't. I had barbecued pork spare ribs. And it was delicious. And I never looked back.

But Olly making a programme about gourmet anything is ridiculous. And I say so.

'He's already reading cookery books,' says Mum proudly, 'and you know Olly, he'll be an expert before you know it. I can't think why neither of you has inherited my cooking skills.'

'I can cook!' I practically shout.

'Libby, dear, spag bol is hardly cooking.'

'Excuse me, Mum, but, bearing in mind you've never eaten at my flat, how would you know whether I can cook or not?

'As it happens,' I continue, on a bit of a roll now, 'I'm an excellent cook.'

'Are you?' she says, sounding bored. 'So what's your best dish?'

Shit. I sit there trying to think of something and nope, the mind's gone blank.

'I can cook anything,' I bluster.

'Yes, dear,' she says, and that's it. I've had enough.

'I've got to go,' I say, standing up and going over to my dad to kiss him goodbye.

'Off so soon?' he says, lowering the newspaper again.

'Yup. You know how it is. Things to do, people to see.'

'But Libby,' says Mum, 'you've only been here five minutes.'

More like a bloody hour, and whatever it is it's about an hour too long.

'Sorry, Mum. I'll speak to you in the week,' and I dash out before she can start making me feel guilty.

I get in the minicab I called earlier and switch my mobile on immediately. Damn. No messages. But what was I expecting? That Nick would call and say he was missing me? Hardly. But then it starts to ring and Jules's number appears on the little screen and I pick up the phone.

'Where've you been?' she moans. 'Your mobile's been off. I hate it when you do that.'

'Sorry,' I say, settling back into the car seat and lighting a fag before I look up and see my mum twitching at the curtains. 'Shit. Hold on.' I haven't even told the bloody driver where we're going. 'Ladbroke Grove,' I say to him, and I wave at my mum as we crawl down the street until I'm out of view, and then I put the phone back to my ear. Mobile phones, naturally, are yet another 'modern appliance' my mother can't quite get to grips with.

'So?' she says.

'So?' I laugh.

'So how was it?'

'Amazing,' I say. 'It was so nice, he's so nice.'

'And did you stay at his?'

'Yup. And we had fantastic sex again.' I drop my voice to a whisper so the driver can't hear.

'And is his flat as disgusting as you thought?'

'Oh God, Jules,' I groan. 'Worse. Much, much worse.'

'How so?'

'Just such a bloody mess. Honestly, Jules, it's a good job this is just a fling because I couldn't live like that, I don't know how he manages.'

'Was it dirty?'

'No, although the sheets didn't exactly smell of Persil, but it was just grotty.'

'Okay. The real test is the bathroom. Doesn't matter what the rest of the flat's like as long as they've got a decent bathroom.'

Hmm. Interesting. 'Actually, the bathroom was fine. Nice, in fact. And he lied about not having a bath!'

'No stains to be seen?'

'No. Sparkling clean.'

'Thank God for that. I don't care if a man lives in a pit as long as he's clean.'

'He's definitely clean,' I say, remembering his lovely, clean, masculine smell.

'You're not in love, then?'

'God no! We ended up having a chat about things last night.' I relay the conversation, word for word, touch for touch, to Jules, who listens carefully and then says the same bloody thing as yesterday.

'You're sure you can handle it?'

'Of course! Jules, listen, if I thought he was going to be serious I'd tell you, wouldn't I?'

'Hmm.'

'But anyway, after that talk we both know exactly where we stand and it's fine.'

'As long as you don't get hurt.'

'Shut up, Jules, you know I hate that expression.'

And it's true. I do. Why do people bother saying it, I mean what's the choice? You lock yourself away in an attic and never go out because you're frightened of getting hurt? Bollocks. As far as I'm concerned you have to give every relationship your all because if you're going to get hurt, you're going to get hurt, but at least at the end of it you'll know you gave it your best shot.

Although I'm not planning to give this relationship, or fling, or whatever this is, my all, at least not when we're out of the bedroom. No, this feels good. Healthy. I'm in control, and that's something I have very little experience of. Hell, I haven't even thought of Nick since I left him. Not much. Oh, okay, not as much as I've thought about boyfriends in the past, then. Happy now?

You probably think I'm lying, but it's true, because in

the past I've thought about new boyfriends every second of every day. Well, almost. This is what I've never understood about men. No matter how crazy they are about you, they can get on with their lives, their work, their friends, and not give you a second thought. When they do think of you, which is generally when they're not thinking of anything else, they'll pick up the phone and call you, completely oblivious to the fact that you've been sitting there crying for a week because they haven't called.

Personally I think it's because men are crap at juggling. I'm not talking about juggling work and children and all that rubbish, but just doing more than one thing at once. Women can iron, watch TV, chat on the phone and answer the doorbell all at the same time, but men? Men can only do one thing at one time. Ever try chatting to a man when he's trying to park the car? Exactly. He'll ignore you because he can only concentrate on one thing at a time. So we get on with our lives while they take up space in our heads, rent-free, and they get on with their lives without giving us another thought.

And I'm not saying that our way is right. Jesus. The number of times I've wished I could stop thinking about someone and get on with work, but I can't. Once they're in your head, they're there for keeps until they either dump you or you manage to get over them. To be honest I find the whole process completely exhausting, and that's why, sitting in the car on the phone to Jules, I decide that I'm not going to do it this time. In fact, I'm fed up with talking about him, remembering him, analysing him.

'Jules, I've got to go,' I say.

'Why? Where are you going?'

'Home, but I've got to get into a bath and I'm in a minicab and I really can't talk.'

'Okay. Will you call me later?'

'Yup. Are you in?'

'Yup.'

And when I get home I jump in the bath and, as I lie there, soaking in lavender bubbles, I remind myself that I'm not going to think about Nick, but then I think, a few thoughts wouldn't hurt, so I decide to allow myself three minutes of thinking about Nick and that's it, at least for today.

So once his three minutes are up I pick up a book and start reading, and every time Nick threatens to creep back into my head (which is about once every two pages) I push him out again until I'm so immersed in the book I genuinely don't think about him, and when Jules calls me later I'm in the middle of a good Sunday night film which, I think you'll agree, is a perfectly valid reason not to talk to your best friend given that TV's normally shit on a Sunday night, and by the time I climb into bed I'm so tired I haven't got the energy to think about Nick even if I wanted to. Which I don't. Just in case you're wondering.

Chapter Eight

Sal calls the next day about the interview, and, because I'm still basking in that old post-coital glow and feeling more than a little magnanimous, I try Amanda Baker out on Sal.

'Amanda who?' she says, and I groan.

'You know, Sal,' I say. 'The showbiz reporter on *Breakfast Break*.'

'As if I'm ever up early enough to watch *Breakfast Break*.'

'She's the blonde one, very stunning.' I know already I'm on to a losing battle.

'Nope. Don't know.'

'Oh. Well, I suppose you wouldn't be interested in doing a feature on her, then?'

'Come on, Libby, you know I can't write about someone nobody knows.'

'Yeah,' I sigh. 'I know. Anyway, how's the big love of your life?'

And sure enough, her voice goes all dreamy. 'He's wonderful,' she says. 'Really, Libby, this is completely different to all of the others.'

'Which others?' I say, because truth to be told I've never heard Sal really talk about men before.

'Just all of them.'

'How long is it since you had a relationship?' I ask curiously.

'Bloody years,' she says. 'Up until now I haven't really

done relationships, I just seem to do flings. And generally with married men. Bastards.'

And we both laugh.

'What are you doing after work?' she then says, and I can tell from her voice that she's desperate to talk about Paul, to tell me every little detail about him, and, even though I know I'll be bored, you never know, I might find something out about Nick, and I don't really have any plans unless you count watching *Brookside*.

We arrange to meet at the Paradise Bar, equidistant to work and home, and I say I'll see her there at 7 p.m.

And I get a hell of a lot of work done that afternoon. I sit there phone-bashing, and I manage to persuade two journalists to write about Rita Roberts, as well as organizing the launch for Sean Moore's series. All in all, a good day's work, and the best thing about it is I hardly think about Nick at all, except to congratulate myself that I've hardly thought about him at all, if you know what I mean.

And I'm looking forward to seeing Sal. She may not be someone I see that much, but I always have a good time when I'm with her, there seems to be so much to talk about – maybe that's because we lead such separate lives, there's an awful lot to fill each other in on.

I'm really happy that she's found Paul. I've always thought that Sal would make a perfect wife and mother, because, even though she's only a year older than me, there's something incredibly warm and maternal about her, and I've never understood why she's been single for so long. She never seems to have problems attracting men, but they always run off soon afterwards, perhaps that whole maternal stuff scares them a bit. But Sal, more than anyone else, needs to be in a relationship.

She makes her own bloody marmalade, for God's sake, how could anyone resist that?

She's there when I arrive at the Paradise, sitting in a corner table at one side of the bar, and she gives me a huge hug and kiss on the cheek when I walk over.

'I'm completely starving,' she says. 'Shall we reserve a table for later in the restaurant?'

'Fine,' I say, 'I'll do it,' because I'm already standing up, and as I walk off she calls me back.

'Ask for a table for three,' she says. 'Nick's going to join us later, is that okay?'

'Oh,' I say, slightly flummoxed, because I don't know whether Sal knows about us, and why didn't he call me, and am I excited about seeing him or am I nervous and should I tell Sal and how should I act when he arrives, but fuck it, Nick's coming!

I get a drink on the way back to the table and sit down, one eye on the door to see Nick when he comes, and Sal starts telling me all about Paul.

'He's just so thoughtful,' she says. 'He keeps buying me these little presents,' and she holds out her arm to show off a beautiful silver charm bracelet. I make the appropriate oohing and aahing noises, and though I'm listening to her, I'm suddenly desperate to talk about Nick, to tell her about him, but somehow I don't quite know how to do it.

'So do you think he's The One?' I say, which is a question I always ask my girlfriends when they start going out with someone, not so much because I want to know the answer, but more because I want to know how they know, and whether I'll know too. Jules says I'm an idealist, that I have this ridiculously romantic notion of being swept off my feet and knowing instantly when I meet the man I'm going to marry, and I suppose she's right. Maybe because I've never really had long relationships, I've always thought that it would happen really quickly, that I'd meet someone, we'd fall in love, and we'd probably both know by the end of our first evening that this was It. I'm not sure how I'd know, but I'm convinced I would. The only problem with that is, as Jules keeps pointing out, I think I know with all of them.

Every time I meet someone new I ring Jules and tell her that this time it's different, this time they're different, and though I still think it I try not to tell her any more because she just starts laughing and says that she's got a very strong sense of *déjà vu*.

And, as far as Jules is concerned, you don't necessarily know when you meet the man you're going to marry. She's the only person I know who says this. Everyone else I've spoken to – and believe me, I've done my research here – says they knew. Jules hated Jamie on their first date. I remember it clearly. She met him at a party and in her drunken stupor gave him her number and promptly forgot all about him. He phoned two weeks later (two weeks! Can you imagine if she'd fancied him and had to wait two weeks!), and she didn't have a clue who he was. When he told her where they'd met, she still couldn't remember him, but she agreed to go out for dinner with him just to see whether she had met him before.

And even then she didn't remember him, which she was bloody surprised about because he was so gorgeous she was convinced she wouldn't forget a face like that. But being gorgeous does not necessarily mean you're nice, and Jamie (I've heard his side of the story now, so I've got the whole picture) was so nervous he behaved like a total idiot. He spent the whole evening talking about himself, and drank so much he ended up with his face in a plate of passion fruit sorbet. Jules was disgusted. She walked out, and refused to take his calls or accept an apology.

It was only when he turned up at her office with a huge bouquet of flowers and a very sheepish look on his face that she decided to give him a second chance, but she never, for a second, thought she'd marry him.

And that's why this whole thing with Nick is so refreshing, because I know, beyond a shadow of a doubt, that he isn't It, and normally I wouldn't bother getting involved with someone unless there was potential there, but I just need some fun right now.

'I really think he might be.' Sal answers my question. 'And I've never felt that about anyone before.'

'Really?' This is so alien to my own experience, I'm fascinated. 'You've never thought that you'd marry someone before?'

'God, no!' she laughs. 'And if you'd met them you'd see why. Nah, even the short relationships I had in my early twenties were with self-obsessed assholes. That's the difference, I've never been treated well before, and before I met Paul I didn't even know what that could be like. I think the reason this is so different is because we were friends for so long, and I never even thought about Paul as anything other than as a good mate.'

'So how did it happen?'

'I hadn't seen him for a while, and then he phoned me for a contact for a story he was doing, and we arranged to meet up for a drink. I hardly bothered making an effort, I mean it was Paul, for heaven's sake, and then, when we met, we had the most brilliant evening and suddenly at the end there was all this weird chemistry which blew my mind a bit.'

'Did you sleep with him?'

Sal starts laughing. 'You're joking! I didn't even kiss him, even though I wanted to, and I could tell he wanted to as well, but I found the whole thing really confusing.'

'So what happened then?'

'He called me the next day to thank me for a really lovely evening which, in itself, was weird, because in the past it had always been me phoning them to thank them for a lovely evening, which was actually just an excuse to phone them. And then he asked me out again, and that night something did happen, and that was that, really.

'And the weirdest thing of all is that it feels so right. I suppose it's true what they say, you never know it's right until it is, although I'm really scared of saying that out loud just in case he turns out to be a bastard, but somehow I don't think he will.'

'And you know what?' she continues, as I shake my head, 'I've never had anyone who looks after me before, and that's what I love. In the past I've always been the one cooking for them, cleaning for them, probably doing way too much for them, whereas Paul's the one who wants to do everything for me.'

'And do you love it?' I say, and grin wickedly.

Sal grins back. 'I love it. So anyway, Libby, enough about me. What about you, you've always got this fantastically tempestuous love life. Who's the latest?'

'Well, actually,' I'm just about to tell her, when I see the door open and Nick walks in. Sal sees me looking over her shoulder and turns round.

'Nick!' She stands up and waves, and he comes over to join us.

'My favourite redhead,' he says, giving her a big hug as I sit there feeling incredibly awkward and wondering what the hell I should say. And then he looks at me and I can already feel the first stirrings of lust in my groin and he grins and says, 'My favourite brunette,' and he puts his arms round me and gives me a hug too, and then he goes off to the bar to get a fresh round.

'You don't mind me asking Nick, do you?' Sal whispers once he's gone. 'It's just that we were on the phone this morning and I told him I was seeing you and when he asked if he could join us I couldn't really say no.'

I feel like jumping in the air with joy.

'That's fine,' I say. 'No problem.'

'It's really weird,' she whispers. 'I used to fancy him so much, but I don't even think he's good-looking any more, that must mean I'm in love.'

'Yup,' I say, because I can't think of anything else to say and thank God Nick chooses that moment to pull up a chair and sit down.

'So,' says Sal. 'We were just talking about Libby's love life.'

'Oh, yes?' says Nick, visibly perking up. 'What were you saying?'

'She was just going to fill me in on her latest man, and before you say anything I know you've got one, it's written all over your face. Yup, you're in love.'

Oh fuck. I can't help it. I feel a bright red, hot flush spread up from my neck until my cheeks are flaming red.

'Now I know you're in love,' she laughs, as I think, shut the fuck up.

'Now this,' grins Nick, 'I've got to hear.'

'I'm not in love,' I say forcefully. 'Definitely not.'

'Go on,' says Nick, shoving me gently and playing completely dumb. 'Tell us. You know you want to.'

'Nick's brilliant at sorting out people's love lives, aren't you, Nick?' says Sal, who, at this precise moment in time, only seems to be opening her mouth to shove her foot further in.

Nick just nods, but he's grinning, and I know he's enjoying this.

'So come on, Libby, it's not like you to be reticent.'

'Sal, I haven't got anything to talk about.'

'I don't believe you,' says Nick, as I kick him under the table.

'Ouch,' says Sal. 'What was that for?'

'Oh God, sorry,' I say, as Nick rocks back in his chair and starts roaring with laughter.

'What is going on?' Sal's now looking confused.

'Classic,' groans Nick. 'Okay. Sorry. It's just that Libby and I . . .' And he stops.

Go on, I think. What are we? Are we going out? Are we seeing one another? Are we sleeping together? What?

'Libby and I . . .' he repeats, and stops again.

'Libby and you what?' says Sal, who I'm convinced knows exactly what he's trying to say, she's just getting her revenge.

'You know, we're – ' And he tilts his head and raises his eyebrows.

'No,' she says. 'You're what?' And then she can't help it, she starts laughing. 'Oh my God,' she says. 'I feel like a total idiot.'

'It's okay,' I say. 'I should have said something.'

'Yes, you bloody should have,' she says. 'Why didn't you?'

'I didn't know how to,' I say, but in truth I didn't really want to.

'So you really did get on the other night?' she says with a smile.

'Very well,' drawls Nick, putting his arm round me and giving me a smacker on the cheek.

'Oh no. Don't start getting all lovey dovey on me.'

'Sorry,' says Nick, drawing away. 'I just can't seem to keep my hands off her.'

I sit there and smile. And smile. And smile.

And the waitress comes over to tell us there's a table waiting for us in the restaurant, so the three of us get up and walk in. Sal goes first, then me and Nick, and Nick grabs my waist as we're walking in and nuzzles my neck, whispering, 'You look gorgeous tonight,' and I smile broadly and go to sit down.

And we turn out to have a really nice evening. I like being with Nick and Sal. I like this feeling of Nick getting on with my friends, even though Sal is as much his friend as mine, possibly even more so. And more than that I like the fact that he spends most of the evening holding my hand under the table, and that he finds everything I say absolutely fascinating, even when it's not, and that he's making me feel like the most special woman in here.

We talk a bit about work, and then about people we know, and then we start sharing stories. We start with drinking stories – who can outdo the others with tales of being the most drunk, and naturally Nick wins that one. Then we do drinking and driving stories, which progresses into police stories, which forces me to reveal that once upon a time I met a guy who asked me out and then turned up at my parents' house in full police uniform – I think I win that one.

We move from there to dates from hell. Sal has us screaming with laughter when she tells us about the time she answered a Lonely Hearts ad, and they swapped photographs and the moment she set eyes on his 6′2″ hunky frame she decided she was in love, and then they met and he was 5′2″, fat and bald.

'I think he thought I wouldn't notice,' she splutters, as Nick and I separately think of stories to beat it.

Nick has a superb stalking story. A statuesque blonde (she bloody would be, wouldn't she) he picked up in a bar. He took her out a few times then decided she really wasn't very interesting, in fact, she was probably the prototype for your standard dumb blonde model, and he dumped her. She then bombarded him with phone calls, appeared at his flat every day, wrote him letters in which she told him of their wedding day plans, and eventually turned up with a kitchen knife saying if she couldn't have him, no one could.

Sal and I sit there open-mouthed.

'That's terrible!' I say. 'What the hell did you do?'

'I tried to wrestle the gun off her but I couldn't, and eventually a policeman showed up, and she held him hostage as well. He ended up getting shot, and the house was surrounded. She was put in a mental institution.' He nods his head sadly.

'Hang on,' I say. 'You said she had a knife, not a gun.'

'Did I? Oh shit.' He shrugs. 'You've got to admit, it was a good story, though.'

'You mean you made it up?' Sal's confused.

'Not exactly,' he said. 'It did happen. It just happened to Mick in *Brookside*.'

'Oh Nick,' I say, as I start laughing. 'You're hopeless.'

And when we've finished our coffees and Sal starts yawning, we get the bill and leave, and I don't bother saying anything to Nick about him staying the night because both of us know he's going to, and when Sal asks Nick if he wants a lift to the tube he just says no, and Sal gets all embarrassed again.

So we say goodbye and go back to my flat, and when I walk in there's a slight moment of awkwardness when Nick notices the flashing red light on my answer phone that tells me there've been four messages.

I could listen to them now, but I don't, and before you get the wrong idea it's not because there may be other men who are calling me, it's because of Jules. I know what Jules is like. She's probably left a message saying, 'Where are you? I hope you're not out shagging,' or 'Hope you're managing to walk properly after last night,' or 'How's the big love of your life going?', and I would die, just die, if Nick heard that.

'You've got messages,' he says, sitting down.

'Yeah,' I say nonchalantly. 'Probably my mum or Jules. Anyway, whoever it is it's too late to call them. I'll listen to them tomorrow.'

He jumps up and starts kissing my neck. 'Not calls from tall dark handsome strangers, I hope?'

'As if!' I laugh, and then I get quite serious. 'Nick,' I say, and he can tell from the tone of my voice that I have something to say, so he pulls back and says, 'Uh oh, have I been a naughty boy? I've done something wrong haven't I? What have I done?'

'No,' I laugh. 'It's just that I want you to know that while I'm sleeping with you I wouldn't sleep with anyone else.'

He nods seriously, taking it in. 'I accept that,' he says, 'and I feel the same way. I know this isn't serious between us, but I agree that as long as we're sleeping together we won't be sleeping with anyone else. And the only thing I'd add to that is that if either of us is tempted, or meets someone else, we'll talk about it, be honest with each other.'

'Perfect,' I say, as I kiss him, but even as I say the word I'm hoping that he doesn't ever tell me that, that if anyone meets someone else, or is, as he put it, 'tempted', it's me. I don't think that's too much to ask.

Chapter Nine

How can I turn down Jules's invitation to a dinner party, when Nick's sitting next to me in my flat, and can hear every word? And I can tell he can hear because he's grinning like an idiot and nodding, and it's not that I don't want to go, it's that I'm really not sure how Nick will fit in with my friends, not after meeting his the other night.

Although it has to be said that my friends would be a damn sight more welcoming than his were. Jesus, I felt like I'd been put through the mill, and I didn't come out well, which was hardly my fault.

It was, to put it nicely, a bloody nightmare. Not my cup of tea at all. I thought it was going to be just Nick and I, and then, when we met, he said he'd arranged to meet some friends of his and did I mind, and I lied and said that no, it was fine. And part of me was curious about his friends, because, even though I know Sal, I don't know any of the others, and I wanted to know who they were, what they were like.

We joined them in a pub (surprise, surbloodyprise), and from the minute we turned up I knew, from the look of the pub, that this wasn't going to be my sort of evening, because there are pubs, and there are pubs. You don't know what I'm talking about? Okay. I don't like pubs, I think I already told you that, but, on the rare occasions I do go to them, I like pubs that are either like country pubs in the middle of London (the Clifton springs to mind), pubs that are trying to be something else (the Lansdowne, which is more of a restaurant now), or pubs that have been completely redone and are clean, bright, and smart (the Queens).

Pubs I never set foot in are real pubs. The old-fashioned variety. Dark, dingy, smoky places with bottle-blonde barmaids and dodgy customers doing deals at the bar. I could mention some names, but I wouldn't want any contracts taken out on my life, and the kind of people who go to these pubs would know exactly how to deal with that sort of thing.

And this was that sort of pub, except it was even darker, dingier and smokier than the nasty pubs of my imagination, and through the haze of smoke I could see a group of people at one end – all of them stopped talking when we walked in, and they waved to Nick before giving me the once-over.

As far as I was concerned, I'd dressed down for the occasion, in my uniform of trainers, jeans and sloppy jumper. And okay, so the jumper did come from Nicole Farhi, but so what? That's casual for me. And yes, I was wearing jewellery, but it was silver, and so what if it came from Dinny Hall? Surely only those in the know would recognize that.

These women may not have been in the know, but one look at me, one look at them, and you could see, instantly, we weren't going to get on. All the people crowded round the tiny table in the pub looked like overgrown students. Big time. At least, I thought sniffily, checking them out in much the same way they were checking me out, at least my jeans are clean. Not one of the women was wearing make-up, and even though I wasn't wearing much – well, maybe a bit, but applied so it looked as if I was hardly wearing any – I could see them linger on my lipstick, and I felt like running and hiding.

And the clothes! God, the clothes. The women looked like identikit socialists – dirty jeans, DMs, and loose, shapeless jumpers with holes in them, and yes, I'm serious, even a couple of stains here and there. And, thinking about it, the men were wearing pretty much the same thing.

Oh Christ, I thought, walking up, I know I'm going to hate them, but I decided I was going to be charming and polite and make them like me, because, after all, they're Nick's friends, and I had to make an effort.

'This is Joanna,' said Nick, as a dirty blonde scowled at me.

'How do you do,' I said, holding out my arm to shake her hand. She looked at her neighbour in amazement, and hesitated with a smirk on her face before finally putting an incredibly limp hand in mine and sort of moving it vaguely, then pulling away.

'This is Pete,' and I did the same thing, except Pete didn't bother taking my hand, he just looked up from his pint and said, 'Awright?'

'Yes, thank you,' I said. 'How are you?'

He didn't say anything. Just smirked.

'Rog, Sam, Chris, Moose.'

'I'm sorry?'

'That's my name,' said Moose. 'Awright?'

Nick went off to the bar to get a fresh round of drinks, and I noticed, with more than a hint of distaste, that all the women were drinking pints, but that didn't mean I had to. No fucking way.

So I stood there awkwardly, waiting for one of the men

to offer me a stool, but no one did, they just carried on talking about Tony Blair and 'New Labour bastards', and I stood like an idiot, wishing I were anywhere else but here.

And eventually I went to the table next to them and asked if I could take a stool, and they nodded, so I perched next to Joanna and tried to be friendly.

'I love your jumper,' I lied, thinking that the best way of making friends is to offer so many compliments they can't possibly dislike you. 'Where did you get it?'

'Camden Lock,' she said, before turning away in disgust.

'So you're Libby,' said Rog, as I breathed a sigh of relief that someone was actually going to talk to me, to be nice to me. 'We've 'eard a lot about you.'

'Oh,' I said, smiling politely. 'Nice things, I hope?'

He shrugged.

'What do you do, Rog?' I ventured, careful to fit his name in the sentence because I read somewhere that when you use people's names a lot it always makes them warm to you.

He looked at me for a few seconds, then shrugged. 'Nothing.'

'Oh.' I didn't quite know what to say next. 'Well,' I carried on, 'what would you like to do?'

He shrugged again. 'Nothing.'

'You're a bloody liar,' said Joanna, and she turned to me. 'He's an artist.'

'Really?' I said. 'What do you paint?'

'Abstract.' Jesus, this is a losing battle.

'You work in PR, don't you?' said Chris, not the male variety, the female variety.

I nodded gratefully.

'Don't you think it's a complete waste of time?' she asked aggressively. 'I mean, you're not exactly helping anyone, are you, just pandering to these stupid fucking celebrities.'

'Actually, I quite enjoy it,' I bristled. 'Why, what do you do?'

'I work for Greenpeace,' she said. 'I couldn't stand a job like yours. At least with mine I know I'm making a difference to the world.'

'Why, have you been out rescuing whales?' I asked innocently.

She huffed. 'Not personally, but I have organized it.'

There was a silence as everyone looked into their drinks, but I'm sure I saw Chris look at Pete and raise her eyebrows, and I sat there miserably knowing that that look was about me.

'Do you live locally?' said Joanna, the only one in the crowd who seemed to be okay. Note that I wouldn't go as far as saying nice, just okay.

I shook my head. 'I live in Ladbroke Grove.'

'Really?' she said. 'I've got friends there. They've got this fantastic Housing Association flat, huge. Do you rent or what?'

'No, I bought it,' I said proudly.

'Oh,' she said. 'How did you afford that?'

'I saved for ages for the down payment,' I lied, knowing that if I told the truth, that my parents had helped me, they'd probably all start hissing and spitting.

'You must be loaded,' she said, and the others all looked at me, waiting to hear what I was going to say.

'Hardly,' I tried to laugh. 'I just try to be careful with money.'

'I wish I had enough money to be careful with,' she said.

'Do you work?'

'Nah.' She shook her head. 'I'm on the dole.'

And I was stuck, because I wasn't going to make the same mistake of asking what she would be doing if she wasn't on the dole.

'So,' said Moose finally. 'We were talking about New Labour. What do you reckon about them?'

'I think they're all a bunch of untrustworthy bastards,' I said firmly.

'Do you?' said Moose. 'Even Blair?'

Oh shit. What do I say now? I think Tony Blair's pretty damn nice, but somehow I suspected that wasn't the thing to say.

'Especially Blair,' I said, and thank God, they started nodding, and I felt like I'd passed some sort of test. Except unfortunately I didn't pass it for very long, and I sat there quietly as they all started talking politics, praying they weren't going to ask me for another opinion.

Nick came back, put his arm round me and whispered, 'Sorry, I had to wait for ages at the bar. Are you okay?'

What was I going to say? That I found his friends disgusting? That they were rude and nasty? That I'd rather be sitting at home watching paint dry than sitting in this revolting pub with these revolting people? I didn't have the nerve to say anything, so I just nodded, and Nick thought I was okay, and so we ended up staying, and I didn't say another word all night, which was really all right, because everyone ignored me anyway. Nick kept trying to bring me into the conversation, but it was too political for me anyway, so I sat there wondering what the fuck I was doing there.

And every time Nick asked me if I was okay, I said yes, even though I quite obviously wasn't because I was so quiet. That's the thing, you see. People think I'm hugely confident because when I'm with people I know, or people I feel comfortable with, I'm absolutely fine, but put me in a crowd of people like this, people who are hostile and unfriendly, and I just clam up.

Eventually, at around ten o'clock, I couldn't stand it any more.

'Nick,' I whispered. 'I've got a bit of a headache. Do you mind if we go?' Nick looked at me in surprise, because he'd been taking centre stage and was obviously having a great time.

'Sure,' he said. 'Why didn't you say something before?'

'I thought it might go away,' I lied. I stood up. 'Nice to meet you all,' I lied again, and as soon as we were outside I breathed a huge sigh of relief.

'You hated them, didn't you?' said Nick.

'I'm really sorry,' I said. 'I'm sure they're really nice people, but they weren't exactly friendly to me, and I didn't feel comfortable at all.'

'God, I'm sorry, Libby,' he said, and put his arms around me. 'I'm so stupid. I just kind of assume that everyone I like will get on, and I know they can be a bit funny with strangers, but I didn't expect them to be that bad. We should have left ages ago.'

'Don't worry.' I snuggled into his shoulder as we walked off down the road. 'Can we stay at mine tonight?'

Nick nodded, and I didn't feel the need to explain that after feeling so bloody insecure all evening I needed to be at home, I needed to be surrounded by my things, in my bed, feeling safe and comfortable and secure.

And that's when Jules phones.

'Hey, babe,' she says. 'Jamie and I are having people over for dinner next week, so do you want to bring the infamous Nick?'

Oh God. Nick with a bunch of barristers would be as awkward as me with a bunch of hard-line socialists. I'm about to say no, but Nick starts nodding vigorously because Jules is speaking so loud he can hear every word.

'He's sitting next to me,' I warn. 'And he's nodding, so I guess that's a yes.'

'Wednesday night, eight-thirty, casual.'

'Okay,' I say, as Nick beams, thrilled at the chance of meeting my friends.

'So I finally get to meet Jules,' he says, when I've put down the phone. 'What's she like? What's Jamie like? Who are their friends?'

And I start laughing because he always makes me laugh, and then he starts tickling me, the bastard, and I scream for him to stop even though by this time I'm more or less hysterical with laughter, and luckily he does stop because a few more seconds and I'd have wet myself, and then he gets all soppy and serious and we start kissing, and I've never made love on a sofa before but it's lovely, and I forgive him for such a shitty evening and for having such shitty friends. In fact, right now, I think I'd forgive him pretty much anything.

Casual, Jules said, which could mean anything, but I know what it doesn't mean is jeans and trainers. Nick's never seen me dressed up and I don't know what he'll think, and, although I know I look good in smarter clothes, I don't want him to think that we come from two different worlds, therefore what would be the point in carrying on. Even though it's true.

And I know that, I still know there's no future in this, but, and I feel sick admitting it, I also know that I'm starting to think about him a hell of a lot more than I used to, and I also know that I'm starting to look forward to seeing him a hell of a lot more than I used to, and I know, or at least, I think, that there's a very strong possibility that I may be slightly out of my depth here.

But I'm an adult, I can handle this, and so what if I'm starting to like him a little bit more than I'd planned, what does that mean? That I should end it because I like him? No. Exactly. I'll just carry on and maybe this is just a phase, maybe in a little while I'll go back to how I was – cool, calm, collected, free.

And I know I hated his friends, but I'm nervous as shit of him meeting mine because I so badly want him to like them, want them to like him. I suppose what I really want is approval all round, but then how could they not like him, when he's so natural, and funny, and sweet? Oh God. We'll just have to see.

So here I am, in my bedroom, and I've arranged to pick Nick up at the tube station, and there are clothes everywhere, and, bearing in mind I've completely changed my look since meeting Nick, I don't know what goes with what any more, and though I want to look smart-ish, I don't want to look middle-aged smart, if you know what I mean. I want to look smart, cool and trendy, and finally I think I've got it.

A camel-coloured print dress, hip-hugging, almost

see-through, with very high Prada strappy sandals, and I'm not sure about the shoes, they might be a bit over the top, but they make me feel beautiful and the one thing I need tonight more than anything else is a shot of confidence.

I put my make-up on carefully, only a tiny bit, just to accentuate my eyes, my lips, and when I'm ready I stand back, and I know it sounds big-headed, but God, I look amazing, I'd forgotten I could look like this, and never mind the fact that I can hardly walk in these bloody shoes, I look beautiful.

'Goodbye, Liam,' I shout triumphantly as I pick up my bag and run out of the flat, 'hello, Patsy,' and I climb into the car to go and pick up Nick.

And bless him, he's made an effort. He's not wearing his usual uniform of jeans and trainers, he's wearing chinos and brown lace-up shoes and a soft blue shirt that completely brings out the colour of his eyes, and he looks gorgeous, and God, what a difference clothes can make, because I suddenly fancy him more than ever before.

'You look amazing,' I say, as soon as he gets in. 'Where are all these clothes from?' And I practically fall out of the car with shock when I notice that not only is his shirt beautiful, it's got a very familiar polo player on the left-hand side.

'That's not Ralph Lauren!' I say, when I've finally recovered, and I know that sounds like a stupid question because it's quite obviously the Ralph Lauren symbol, but this must be a fake if Nick's wearing it.

'Yes,' he says, 'it is. So?'

'So where did you get it?'

'My mother bought me all these clothes last year, but I never wear them.'

'I know,' I laugh. 'I've never seen you in them, but Nick you look gorgeous.'

He also looks very uncomfortable. Jesus, I would marry Nick if he looked like this all the time. Well, no, I probably wouldn't. Don't get too excited, it's just a figure of speech.

And then he looks at me, and does a very slow and very sexy wolf whistle.

'Christ,' he says, taking in the outfit. 'You look unbelievable.'

'Unbelievable good or unbelievable bad?'

'Unbelievable sexy,' he says, shaking his head in disbelief, as my head threatens to swell so much it won't fit in the car. 'Why don't we not go, and I'll take you home and ravish you instead.'

And I laugh, but as I look at him I see he half means it.

'You're nervous!' I'm amazed.

'No, I'm not,' he says. A little too quickly.

'You are. Nick, why are you nervous?'

'I'm not,' and then he pauses. 'Okay. Maybe a bit.'

'Why?'

'It's the first time I'll be meeting your friends, and Jules is your best friend, and I want to make a good impression.'

He is so sweet.

'You are so sweet.'

'Don't say I'm sweet,' he growls. 'I hate that.'

'Sorry,' I say, and reach over and give him a kiss. 'But you are.'

Chapter Ten

'I thought you said you were having people over for dinner,' I say, pulling Jules aside and whispering to her furiously. 'You didn't tell me you were having a bloody party.'

'You know how it is,' she laughs. 'It was meant to be six of us, and then we invited a couple more, and then someone else phoned and asked if they could bring someone, so before we knew it there were sixteen people. Anyway, what's the problem?'

'Nothing,' I mutter, and there isn't really a problem, I just wasn't prepared for this, and somehow I thought it would be easier to introduce Nick at a dinner party, more intimate, less pressure, but I suppose, thinking about it, perhaps this is better.

'So where is he?' she says, looking around the room.

'Nick!' I call out to where Nick's already chatting to Jamie. 'Come and meet Jules.'

Jamie's smiling, so I assume whatever it is they were talking about went well, and he comes over with Nick to kiss me hello.

'Jules, Nick. Nick, Jules.' Nick holds his hand out very formally, and I have to stifle a laugh because this is not Nick's way at all, but Jules being Jules just laughs and gives him a kiss on the cheek. 'Welcome to our party,' she says. 'It's so nice to finally meet you.'

'And you,' says Nick, relaxing. 'I've heard so much about you.'

'Not half as much,' she says, winking at me, 'as I've heard about you.'

'I've heard about Tom,' he says, scooping up the grey Persian kitten who's winding his way around Nick's legs. 'Hello,' he says to Tom, stroking him under the chin as he starts purring like an engine. 'You're gorgeous, aren't you?'

'Well, Nick,' says Jules, 'you're in. Any man who likes cats is all right by me.'

'I've got two at home with my parents,' he says. 'I miss them desperately but it wouldn't be fair to have them here, I haven't got a garden.'

I look at Nick in surprise, because he never struck me as a cat sort of bloke, but I think what surprises me most is how he keeps surprising me. First the clothes that his mother bought him, and now the cats. And what's more, how come his mother has such good taste? On the rare occasions my mother buys me clothes – generally when they've been on holiday – they're disgusting. Huge voluminous T-shirts saying things like, 'My mum went to Majorca and all I got was this lousy T-shirt.' I've got about ten of them shoved away in a cupboard somewhere. I always mean to sleep in them, but I can't seem to face looking at the bloody things, never mind putting them on. But Ralph Lauren! Jesus. My mum wouldn't know Ralph Lauren if he came up and personally introduced himself.

'Libby says you're a writer,' says Jamie.

Nick nods. 'But it doesn't seem to be getting me anywhere. Unfortunately.'

'It's got to be a novel, then.'

'Yup.'

'I've always wanted to write a novel,' says Jamie. 'I

find it amazing that you have the discipline to sit down and write every day.'

'I know, everyone does, but it's getting to the stage where I might have to start looking for other work. Obviously this book is my first love, but I just don't know how much longer I can keep sending out letters only to be rejected.'

'So what sort of work would you look for?' asks Jules, as my eyes light up, because this is the first time he's ever mentioned it.

'Maybe TV work, scriptwriting, something like that.'

'You ought to meet Charles,' she says, turning to Jamie. 'Isn't he a drama producer for one of the TV companies?'

Jamie nods. 'He's the boyfriend of a friend of ours, Mara. They should be here soon, so I'll introduce you.'

'So who else is coming?' I ask.

Jules reels off a list of names, and, sure enough, they're all couples, and I thank God that this time I didn't have to turn down the invitation because I didn't want to come on my own.

'Oh, and there's a surprise for you.'

'For me?' I love surprises, even though I pretend to hate them.

'Yup.' She checks her watch. 'In fact,' she says, going to the door to answer the doorbell that's just rung, 'this could be it. Come with me.' I follow her out of the room, and the minute we're in the hallway she grabs me and whispers, 'He's gorgeous!'

'I know,' I whisper back.

'But no, I mean he's really gorgeous. So handsome! And sweet!'

'I know.' I grin happily, as the doorbell rings again.

'All right, all right,' she grumbles, running down to the front door. 'Coming!'

It's Ginny and Richard, a couple I've met before who seem very nice, but he's a bit intimidating in that barrister, legal-ish sort of way, although they've always been charming.

I stand back as they kiss Jules hello, then Richard gives me a big smile and reaches down to kiss the air on either side of my cheek. 'Libby!' he exclaims. 'How lovely to see you again!'

Ginny does the same thing, then all four of us move into the living room, as Jamie says hello, then goes off to get drinks.

'Nick!' says Richard. 'I don't believe it!' and I stand open-mouthed as Richard gives Nick a manly hug and clasps his hand in both of his. 'What on earth are you doing here?'

'I'm here with Libby,' says Nick.

'What? You and Libby?'

He nods.

'I don't believe it.' Richard turns to me. 'I haven't seen Nick in years. We were at school together.'

At school together? But I thought Richard went to . . .

'Didn't you go to Stowe?' I look at Richard, bemused.

'Most certainly did,' he nods. 'Both of us.'

'You never told me you went to Stowe,' I say to Nick, and he shrugs.

'You never asked.'

'What a small world,' says Jules, obviously delighted that her guests are getting on so well, and then the doorbell rings again.

More couples file in, some I know, but all well-spoken,

well-dressed, and very much at home standing around drinking Kir Royales and making small talk.

And there I was worrying about Nick, I think, watching him and Richard roar with laughter as they reminisce about what they used to get up to at school.

And I'm so impressed that Nick went to Stowe I completely forget about my surprise, and then the doorbell rings, and a familiar face appears in the doorway, and I'm so excited I practically spill my drink, and Jules grins as I shriek, 'Olly!' and my darling brother rushes in and scoops me up in his arms, giving me a massive hug.

'I wanted to surprise you,' he says, and I'm so happy he's here, this is so unexpected.

'What are you doing here?' I say, breathless with excitement.

'I rang him,' said Jules, 'because no party of ours would be quite the same if Olly wasn't here.'

'For God's sake, don't tell Mum,' he says. 'She'd kill me if she knew I was down and wasn't staying there.'

'Where are you staying? Will you stay with me?'

'No,' he shakes his head. 'I'm staying with Carolyn,' and then I notice the tall, tanned girl standing in the doorway.

'Carolyn.' He beckons her over. 'This is my sister, Libby.'

I shake her hand and approve immediately of her warm smile, the fact that she's so naturally pretty without make-up, her adoring look at Olly, which tells me that she is definitely not just a good friend.

'I'm so pleased to meet you,' she says. 'Olly talks about you all the time.'

'Do you work together?'

She nods. 'I'm a researcher. That's how we met.'

I look at Olly and, without Carolyn noticing, I give him an almost imperceptible nod that tells him I approve, and he grins at me.

'Oh God,' I say. 'Where's Nick?' I look around, but he's suddenly disappeared.

'Nick?' says Olly. 'Who's Nick, then? Your latest squeeze?'

And then I see Nick walk in from the kitchen and I call him over to introduce him and it turns out – another amazing fact I didn't know – that Nick's as big a Man United fan as Olly, and within minutes the pair of them are talking animatedly as if they've known each other for years.

Jules introduces Carolyn to Ginny, and then sweeps me into the kitchen to help her get the food ready.

'Everyone seems to be getting on, don't they?' she says, and I know that she was nervous, that she's always nervous before bringing together new people, but that she's such a good hostess her evenings always turn out to be fine, apart from the coupley ones I don't go to, and that's not to say they're not fine, that's just to say that I wouldn't know.

'I can't believe how Nick's fitting in.'

'Can't you?' says Jules, opening the oven and pulling out something that smells delicious. 'Why ever not?'

'God, Jules, if you'd have met his friends the other night, you would have known why not. His crowd is so completely different to ours.'

'But he's fitting in perfectly,' she says. 'He seems very comfortable.'

And it's true, he does, and I don't know why this should surprise me so much, but if anything I'd say that Nick feels even more comfortable here than I do, and these are my best friends, for God's sake. But don't get me wrong, I like it. In fact, I'd say I more than like it. I love it.

'I don't know why you keep saying there's no future in it,' says Jules, opening a cupboard door. 'I think you're perfect together.'

'But that's just your first impression, Jules. You don't know him.'

'So what do I need to know? He's handsome, obviously bright, and you seem to get on really well. What's the problem?'

How can I explain what the problem is? How can I tell her that I couldn't marry Nick because how would we live? I'd never be able to give up work, and our children would have to go to the local comprehensive, where they'd probably get in with the wrong crowd and end up taking drugs and hanging out in gangs. How can I tell her that my idea of hell would be to end up a harassed mother who had to try and be the breadwinner as well as bringing up the kids? That I'd always look a complete mess because I wouldn't have the time or the money to make an effort. That designer clothes would be something I'd only wear if someone like Jules took pity on me and gave me some hand-me-downs. That I'd have to say goodbye to the designer restaurants and bars I love so much, and on the rare occasions we went out for dinner it would have to be somewhere cheap and cheerful.

Actually, a lot of it doesn't sound so bad, but I know I'm talking myself into believing it's not so bad because I'm growing to like Nick more and more, and I'm trying to compromise, to change my lifestyle to fit into his because I have no other choice.

In fact, I haven't even been to a bloody designer restaurant or bar since before I met Nick, and okay, it's true, I don't miss them that much, but I wouldn't want to spend the rest of my life knowing that I couldn't go to them because I couldn't afford it. I may not be going now, but that's through choice.

How can I explain this to Jules when I know she wouldn't understand, particularly given that she's met Nick on her territory, when he's dressed up in clothes he never normally wears to fit in, and yes, he does fit in, but if she saw him on his territory, with his friends, doing what he likes to do, I'm sure she'd take my point. She'd have to. Wouldn't she?

'It's too long to go into,' I say. 'But I'm telling you, it's just a fling.'

'Bullshit.' She turns to look at me. 'You're my best friend, Libby, and I know you better than anyone else in the world. You may be able to get away with telling other people that you don't care about him, that it's just sex, but look at you, for God's sake. You're crazy about him.'

'What makes you say that?'

She sighs. 'It's the way you look at him, the way your face lights up every time he says something, the way you hang on his every word. Don't worry,' she says, seeing the dismay on my face. 'I don't think he knows, but I do.'

'So what do you think he thinks of me?' I can't help it. My insecurity raises its ugly head.

She shrugs. 'It's much harder to tell with men, but my guess is he probably feels the same way. The only thing that worries me is that he did say at the beginning that he wasn't looking for a relationship, and I just think you have to remember that, because you've definitely fallen for him. He may well have fallen for you too, but, if the timing's wrong, then you might get hurt.'

Timing. Jules is a big believer in timing. She always says that Jamie and she met at exactly the right time, that had it been any earlier she wouldn't have been ready for a relationship, not even with the gorgeous Jamie.

She looks at me closely and can see that what she's said has upset me, and her voice softens as she says, 'Look, Libby, I don't want to see you hurt, and I think he probably does feel the same way about you, but you have to be aware that when men say they're not ready for a relationship, nine times out of ten it means that they're not ready for a relationship, and even if you're the most wonderful woman in the world it's not going to change their minds.

'But,' she adds, almost to herself, 'there are always women who can change their minds, I suppose.'

That's what I needed to hear, and as soon as she says the words I make a decision. I'm going to be the woman who changes his mind. Except I don't share this with Jules, it's going to be my own little secret.

Jules sighs as the phone starts to ring. 'Now who the hell is calling us now?' she says, putting down the bowls and running to pick up the phone.

'Hello? Hello?' There's a pause. 'Hello? Is anyone there?' She puts the phone down and turns to me, annoyed. 'That's the fourth bloody time that's happened this week. Why do these people keep putting the phone down?'

Jamie comes rushing into the kitchen, looking startled. 'Who was that?' he asks breathlessly.

'God knows,' she says. 'I told you someone keeps ringing and putting it down when I pick up.'

'Oh,' says Jamie, as Jules picks up the bowls and leaves the room, and if I didn't know better I could swear he turns a whiter shade of pale. But no. I must be imagining it.

I bring the rest of the food into the living room and carefully put it down on the trestle table covered with a white damask tablecloth that they've set up at one end of the room.

'Mmm, this looks delicious,' says Ginny, as Jules laughs.

'This?' she says. 'It was nothing,' and I know for Jules it probably was nothing, but to anyone who didn't know it looks like a Bacchanalian feast: mounds of chicken in a curried cream sauce; a huge, whole salmon, decorated with the thinnest slices of cucumber I've ever seen; piles of couscous surrounded by ratatouille; warm potato salad sprinkled with parsley and chives; bowls of mixed leaf salads, dishes of avocado, plum tomatoes and buffalo mozzarella cheese with fresh basil sprinkled over the top.

'Wait till you see what's for pudding,' she whispers to me, and I groan in anticipation and rub my stomach.

'Don't tell me – ' I say.

'Yup,' she nods. 'Your favourite.'

'What's that?' says Nick, laughing at the expression of rapture on my face.

'Tiramisu.'

We all grab plates and tuck in, piling them high, and then small groups of people seem to gather together without thinking, so within minutes there are little clusters of people dotted around the room, friends naturally gravitating towards friends.

I sit down with Nick, Olly, Carolyn and Jamie. Jules

shouts she'll join us, but she wants to check that everyone's okay for drinks, and she waves Jamie aside when he says he'll do it, because Jules likes to be in control.

And I sit and watch Carolyn, and I watch how Nick reacts to Carolyn, because she really is very, very pretty, and I know she's going out with Olly, but I can't help that old insecurity that says that maybe Nick will fancy her, and maybe he'll fancy her more than he fancies me, and I'm waiting for him to start flirting with her, but he doesn't.

What he does is put an arm round me and rub my back, and I grin and relax, because it's a territorial thing; he's making sure everyone knows I'm with him and he's with me, and other than being polite to Carolyn he hardly seems to notice her.

'So what's all this about the gourmet vegetarian?' I say to Olly, as Carolyn laughs.

'Ridiculous, isn't it?' she says. 'Olly can't cook to save his life and here he is, producing a show about food.'

'Thank you, girls,' says Olly, in mock disgust. 'But actually I can cook.'

'Bollocks!' I say.

'I can, Libby. Tell them what I made you the other night.' He looks at Carolyn.

'He made me Chinese,' she says, trying to suppress a smile.

'Really?' Now I'm impressed. 'How on earth did you do that?'

Carolyn answers for him, which instantly makes me realize that perhaps she's not as transient as all of the other women I've heard about, that perhaps this has gone on longer than I thought, that perhaps this is serious, or at least serious in Olly terms, because, let's face it, it's all a question of relativity.

'I chopped the vegetables,' she says, winking at me, 'and Olly opened the packet of oyster sauce.'

'Ah,' says Nick. 'That's exactly how I like to do my cooking.'

'Yeah,' agrees Olly. 'It's a guy thing.'

'You've never cooked for me,' says Nick. 'Can you cook?'

''Course I can cook,' I exclaim. 'I'll make you dinner next week.'

'Damn,' says Olly. 'I needed a laugh. What a shame I'll be back in Manchester.'

I hit him.

'So how do you two know one another?' Olly gestures at Nick and I.

'We met through a friend, Sally,' says Nick.

'You don't know her,' I add.

'So how long's this been going on?'

Three months, three weeks and two days, is what I could say, but I don't, because I'm not supposed to be counting, so I don't say anything at all and I wait to hear what Nick says.

'A couple of months now?' He looks at me, and I nod.

'Serious, then?' laughs Olly.

Nick blanches slightly.

'Bit of a record for you,' continues Olly, missing the look on Nick's face.

I stand up. 'Time for seconds. Anyone coming?'

We kiss everyone goodbye, and Olly gives me a big hug and whispers, 'He's great. I'll be back in the office tomorrow afternoon, call me,' and I tell Carolyn it was nice to meet her, which it was, and, as nice a time as I've had, it's even nicer finally to have Nick to myself.

And as we walk out Nick turns to me and says, 'They were so nice! I had such a nice time!'

'Well, what did you expect from friends of mine?'

'They're just so different from the kind of people I mix with.' He looks at me. 'I suppose I didn't need to tell you that, did I?'

'Hardly,' I laugh.

'But even though they're all obviously successful, they're really down to earth.'

'Success doesn't mean you have to be pompous,' I say.

Nick walks along in silence for a while, and I can tell he's thinking about something, and I could annoy the hell out of him by saying something incredibly trite like, what are you thinking or penny for your thoughts, but I don't.

And after a while he says, 'It's not that I felt out of place, not at all, it's just sort of made me think about my life, about what I'm doing with it, about what I could be doing with it. Particularly bumping into Richard after all these years.'

I walk next to him wondering whether just to listen or to give practical advice. I mean, I've bloody read *Men are from Mars, Women are from Venus*, but this is the bit I always get confused about. I can't remember what I'm supposed to do, so I don't say anything at all, because I don't want to alienate him by doing the wrong thing.

'I don't know,' he sighs. 'I feel a bit confused at the moment.'

'Do you want to talk about it?' I say.

'I don't really know what there is to talk about,' he says, and after that he's very quiet. He's quiet all the way home, he's quiet when I make him a coffee, and we get into bed and cuddle before falling asleep. Or maybe I should say, before he falls asleep, because this worries me. Part of me thinks this is good, this is a progression, that it's not only about sex any more, that we're becoming friends, settling in, but the other part thinks, why the hell doesn't he want to have sex with me, and I can't help it, despite him being absolutely lovely to me tonight, I've got this horrible suspicion that he might be going off me.

Chapter Eleven

'He's great,' repeats Olly on the phone the next day. 'I'm really surprised.'

'Surprised? Why?'

'He's just so normal and down to earth,' Olly says, in a strange echo of what Nick said about everyone last night. 'And I think he's good for you.'

'In what way?'

'You seem really relaxed, much more so than you ever were with that other bloke, what was his name?'

'Jon?'

'Was he the poncey one with the Mazda?'

'He wasn't poncey.'

'Oh, come on, Libby, he was awful.'

'No, he wasn't.' Why the hell am I defending him? He was awful.

'Okay, he wasn't awful, but he didn't treat you well, and Nick seems much better for you.'

'It's not serious, though.'

'You can never tell whether it's serious or not,' Olly says mysteriously.

'Oh, so it's serious with Carolyn, then?'

'Did you like her?'

'I thought she was lovely.'

'Mmm. She is, isn't she?'

'Really. And Mum would love her.'

'Don't say anything. It's still early days.'

'How early?'

'About a month.'

'You go, guy! That's pretty good for you.'

'I know.'

'So do you think Nick likes me?'

'Of course he likes you. He wouldn't be with you if he didn't like you.'

'I'm a little worried because he was a bit funny with me after we left.'

'Funny how?'

'It's just that every night we're together we always have, umm' – it feels a bit weird, saying this to Olly, but what the hell, I know he'll tell me what he really thinks so I may as well be honest – 'umm, sex, and last night he was really quiet after we left and we just had cuddles and then he fell asleep, and maybe I'm being really stupid and insecure, but it seems a bit strange.'

'Women kill me,' says Olly. 'They really do. All the women I've ever met expect all men to be up and ready for sex any time, any place, any how.'

'Well, aren't they?'

'No!' he practically shouts. 'Jesus, no. Sometimes we're tired, sometimes we're stressed, sometimes we're not in the mood. Nick was under a hell of a lot of pressure last night, meeting all of us for the first time, and it's completely understandable that he just wanted to sleep.'

I breathe a sigh of relief for the first time that day. 'You don't think he's going off me?'

'Don't be so ridiculous.'

'Okay,' I say happily, 'I'm being ridiculous, then?'

'Yes, Libby, you're being ridiculous.'

That's the thing, you see. I suppose what I do is associate sex with how much someone likes me, and, if I think about it, which I don't want to do that much, every time I've broken up with someone the last night we've spent together, we haven't had sex. And okay, admittedly, there have been other problems, like they've been a bit off with me, a bit distant, but still it always comes completely out of the blue when they turn around and tell me it's over.

And every time I think, I should have known that night. I should have known when they rolled over and said they were tired or not in the mood, or stressed, but maybe Olly has a point, and I suppose it is unfair that we expect them to be up for it whenever we are.

And Nick was lovely in the morning. Okay, we didn't have sex again, but hey, it was a late night, and I know I'm being ridiculous, and insecure, and probably slightly paranoid, but Olly makes me feel better about it, so by the time Jules phones to do the post-mortem I'm feeling so okay I don't even bother mentioning it.

And she basically repeats what she said last night about Nick, the good stuff I mean, the stuff about him being nice to me and us being good together, and I drink it in, and I feel fine, and it doesn't bother me that Nick doesn't call me all morning because why would he? He's busy getting on with his life, and I'm busy getting on with mine.

At lunchtime Jo buzzes me and asks what I'm doing.

'Nothing,' I reply, looking with distaste at the smoked salmon bagel on my desk that I don't really have the stomach for.

'I want to go shopping,' she says. 'Fancy coming with me?'

'Where?' I ask, feeling that old familiar buzz at the prospect of spending some money, a feeling I haven't had in a while.

'I thought we could get a cab to St John's Wood and hit the high street.'

'St John's Wood? What the hell's in St John's Wood?'

'Joseph, for starters.'

'I'm coming.'

As a receptionist on a completely crap salary Jo really shouldn't be able to afford the clothes she wears every day, but luckily for her she has extremely wealthy parents who never seem to think twice about giving her money for her wardrobe, and, although we know we should all hate her for it, she's so nice we can't help but adore her.

And what's more she pays for the taxi.

'I'll get the one on the way back,' I say, feeling slightly guilty as she puts her Louis Vuitton purse back in her Gucci bag.

'Whatever,' she says, tripping off down the high street, and it is a bit of a revelation for me, like a mini Bond Street in North London.

'How did you discover this?' I say, itching to go into practically every shop we pass.

'My parents live round the corner,' she says, 'so I spend most of my life here. So much easier than going into town.'

She obviously does spend most of her life here because as soon as we walk into Larizia, our first stop, the girl in there says, 'Hi, Jo! How are you?' and you just know that she's probably their best customer.

On to a clothes shop a couple of doors down, where I follow her around, watching as she expertly pulls things off the racks and flings them at the sales assistant with a cheeky grin, and I perch on a chair outside the changing room, giving her the yes or the no, although to be honest pretty much everything looks fantastic on her as she's so tall and thin.

And we go into Joseph, which is a bit of a scary experience, because the woman in there looks me up and down and evidently decides I'm not good enough to bother saying hello to, so she sticks her nose up in the air and carries on ordering the sales assistant around, and I sort of want to disappear.

'Aren't you going to even look?' says Jo, and I shrug and half-heartedly look, but I can't really be bothered. I realize that it's because I haven't got anywhere to wear these clothes any more, that there wouldn't be any point in buying that 'fabulous' chiffon shirt or those 'wicked' PVC trousers, because my life with Nick just doesn't need those sorts of things.

'This isn't like you,' says Jo, pulling a gold Amex out of her purse and paying for a pile of tissue-wrapped clothes. 'What's going on?'

I shrug again, and think of explaining it to her, but then decide not to because I know what Jo would do. She'd snort with derision and tell me that you don't dress for the men in your life, you dress for yourself, and anyway what the hell was I doing going out with someone who quite clearly didn't enjoy doing the same things as me?

She wouldn't understand.

'I'm just a bit strapped for cash at the moment.' I know she won't be able to say anything after this because she feels ever so slightly guilty at having so much money from her parents, and, sure enough, she nods and drops the subject.

And when we get back to the office there's a note on my desk saying Nick called, and my heart, even after three months, etc., etc., still skips a little beat and I call him back immediately, which I know you're not supposed to do, but, as I think I may have already mentioned, I'm a bit crap at playing hard to get, and I love the sound of his voice when he picks up the phone, and all my insecurities are forgotten because he called, and he didn't just call, he called the next day.

I think you'll all agree this is a bit of a result.

'Hello, my darling,' he says.

'Hello, my darling,' I echo.

'I'm bored,' he says.

'Why don't you write?'

'I'm not in the mood.'

'Oh. What are you in the mood for?'

'You. On a silver platter. Preferably with nothing on. No, wait, with a pair of red lace crotchless knickers.'

'God, you're such a bloke!' I laugh. 'Red lace crotchless knickers? How tacky.'

'I thought I was a girl . . .'

'You are, but when it comes to sex you're very much a bloke.'

'I'm sorry about last night. I'm phoning to apologize for being so tired and for not, you know, not ravishing you like I usually do.'

'That's okay,' I say, hugging myself with happiness. 'I know that most women think all men are up for sex any time, any place, any how, but I don't think that, I know what a pressure that is for men, and it's fine if you don't feel like it.

'I didn't feel like it either,' I conclude. Lying.

'Blimey! Are you sure you're not a bloke?'

I laugh.

'I was just worried you'd get the wrong idea,' he says.

'Don't be silly,' I trill with laughter. 'It was lovely just cuddling.'

'You're so damned nice,' he says, sounding serious. 'God, how can you be this nice?'

'What d'you mean? This is just the way I am.'

'I know, but I've never met anyone like you. You're so understanding all the time, and so nice!'

'Stop saying I'm nice.' I'm grinning. I'm grinning so hard any second now I might tell him I love him. Ha! Got you. That was a joke. Of course I don't love him.

'Okay. Are you busy as well as nice?'

'No,' I lie. 'Not a lot on this afternoon.' As I say it I survey the pile of numbers I've got to call on my desk.

'What are you doing tonight?'

'Nothing planned.' Another lie. I said I'd go to the movies with Jo, but hey, it's only Jo, and it's only the movies. She'll understand. 'What about you?'

'I'm meeting Rog for a drink. I miss you, will you come with?'

Shit. Dilemma. I want to see Nick more than anything, but I honestly don't think I could stand another night with one of his vile friends.

'Umm.' I stall for time.

'Go on,' he says.

'I'd better not,' I say. 'I kind of said I might go to the movies with Jo.'

'All right,' he grumbles. 'What about later, after the movies?'

'You're thinking about sex again, aren't you?'

'I'm a bloke, Libby. I think about sex every six seconds.' I laugh.

'Why don't you come over when the movie's finished?' he says.

'Tell you what. Why don't you come over to me?'

'You really hate my flat, don't you?'

'It's not that I hate it exactly, I just prefer mine.'

'I know,' he says. 'That's the problem. So do I.'

Five minutes later Jules phones.

'I've just eaten a ton of chicken left over from last night, a ton of couscous, a whole packet of kettle crisps – the big ones – and a Mars Bar.'

'I'm still sitting here looking at a smoked salmon bagel.'

'I'm fat. I'm huge. I'm disgusting.'

'You're not fat. So you ate a lot, big deal. Anyway, it's not bad food, it's healthy.'

'Since when was a Mars Bar healthy?'

'Okay, maybe not the Mars Bar, but have a salad tonight and you'll be fine.'

'I don't think I can,' she groans. 'I haven't got any willpower. I'll have to have more chicken.'

'So you'll be good tomorrow. It'll be fine. You won't put on weight after one day of eating a lot.'

'Really?'

'Really.'

'What are you having tonight?'

'Dunno. If it makes you feel better I'll have a Chinese takeaway.'

'It makes me feel a lot better. What will you have?'

'Mmm. Let me think. How does barbecued spare ribs, chicken and cashew nuts in yellow bean sauce and rice sound to you?'

'Not nearly bad enough. What kind of rice?'

'Steamed?'

'No, make it egg fried.'

'Okay. Happy now?'

'Not yet. You can't have Chinese without having seaweed.'

'Okay. I'll have seaweed. Happy now?'

'Very happy. God, Libby, you're such a pig.' And we both start laughing.

I don't go to the movies, Jo blows me out, but I do have my Chinese, although I cheat slightly, at least I hope I do, because we've just won a new account of these supposedly unbelievable fat pills that are all the rage in America and have just come over here.

God knows what's in them, some sort of shellfish I think, and what they're supposed to do is attract all the fat you eat so instead of absorbing it it goes straight through you. We've had loads of bottles lying round the office, and I filched a couple before I left, and I know the instructions say to take two to four with a large glass of water immediately before eating, but I decide to take six just to be on the safe side.

'Bloody hell!' I look in the mirror at my pot belly, and check the packet. How bloody long does it take for these damn things to work anyway? I sit and watch TV and wait for the chance to, er, expel the fat from my body, but no, not only is having a poo the last thing my body seems to want to do, my stomach's not going down either. Shit. It's too late. Nick will just have to put up with it.

Hmm. Maybe sit-ups would work. I hook my legs under the bed, wondering why on earth I don't exercise more often, because this is easy. And one. And two. And three. And four. And five. And, Jesus, why am I puffing already? And six. And seven. And eight. And nine. And I don't think I can go on any longer.

I stand up and look in the mirror, and my face is bright red and I look seriously unfit and oh, what the hell, I think I'll have another cigarette, and just when I've lit it the doorbell rings and oh my God! Look at me! I'm a complete state.

'What have you been up to?' says Nick, kissing me hello and smoothing back my hair.

'You wouldn't want to know.'

'I think I would.'

'Exercise.'

'Urgh. Don't talk to me about exercise. I'm allergic to the bloody stuff.'

'You don't need to do it,' I say, rubbing his deliciously firm washboard stomach. 'But look at this.' I push my stomach out, figuring it's better to be upfront about it.

Nick recoils in horror. 'What. Is. That?'

'I know,' I say. 'It's awful, isn't it?'

Nick moves closer, gets down on his knees and presses one ear against my stomach. 'Yup.' He nods sagely. 'I know exactly what that is. It's a food baby.'

I start laughing.

'In fact,' he says, tapping my stomach in a doctor-ish sort of way, 'I'd say it was a Chinese food baby.'

How the hell did he know?

'How the hell do you know?'

Nick stands up and shrugs nonchalantly. 'I'm paid to know.'

I turn around and see the evidence in the kitchen. Foil cartons and white cardboard lids, which I meant to clear up because I wouldn't actually want any man in my life to know I exist almost solely on Chinese takeaways, I'd want him to think I eat ladylike things like lettuce and smoked salmon, but it's too damn late.

'Seeing as we might just about be in time to catch last orders,' says Nick, 'I thought maybe we could go out for a drink.'

'Sure!' I say enthusiastically, sitting down and pulling my trainers on. 'Where d'you fancy?'

'How about the Westbourne?'

'Great.' So it's off to the Westbourne we go, and funnily enough the Westbourne is about the first place I've been to with Nick where we both feel at home. Enough of a pub to make him relax, and trendy enough – i.e. filled with Notting Hill Trustafarians – to make me relax, so all in all a bloody good choice, I think to myself.

It's a warm night, so we sit outside at a wooden table, and, just as I think we're having a really nice time, Nick starts sighing again.

'What is it now?'

He sighs.

'Come on, Nick. There's something wrong, isn't there?'

He sighs again. And then he looks at me.

'I really like you, Libby,' he says, and my heart sinks, because I know what's coming next. What's coming next is a But.

'No, I mean I really like you. But . . .' And he stops.

'I really like you too,' I offer lamely.

'I know,' he says. 'That's what worries me.'

Oh shit. Jules got it wrong. He does know, and true to form, he's backing off. Oh God, why didn't I play harder to get, why didn't I pretend to be cool?

'I just don't know what to do.'

'I don't understand.'

'I like you more than I've liked anyone for ages. I mean, over the last year there have been several women I could have got involved with, but I didn't because I wasn't ready for a relationship, and I wasn't ready to get involved with you, but I like you so much I sort of couldn't help it.'

'Nick,' I say slowly. 'You're being very heavy about this, and this isn't what we're about. We're not having a relationship, we're just having fun, so what's wrong with that?'

'But we are having a relationship, you know that.'

There's no point in denying it because he's right.

'And what scares me is that I know you need more. I know that at some point in the not too distant future you're going to want more commitment from me, and I know, quite categorically, that I won't be able to give it to you, even though I want to, more than anything else in the world, but I'm just not ready.'

What can I say? He's right again.

He sighs.

'And I like you far too much to hurt you, and I know that inevitably I will.'

'Maybe not,' I bristle. 'Maybe I'm not as involved as you think I am.'

'Aren't you?'

I shrug. 'I don't know.'

'Look.' He takes my hand. 'You are the best person I've met in years, and if I'd met you in a year's time, or maybe even a few months, I know we could be happy together, but I can't give you what you need.' He sighs again. 'I haven't got my life together, and I can't deal with a relationship until I have. I do want to get my novel published, but I also know that I need some money, some stability, and I can't keep doing this for ever. If I had a publishing deal, or a job, then it would be different, but I need to concentrate on that right now, and it's simply not the right time for me to have a relationship.'

I think I'm going to start crying, but somehow I manage not to. I think about telling him that I don't mind, that it doesn't bother me that he doesn't have money, that I'm prepared to wait, but I know, deep down, that his mind is made up, and it really wouldn't make any difference.

'Is this it, then?' I say, in a very small voice, thinking, I knew it. I knew it when we didn't have sex.

'No,' he sighs. 'I don't know. I don't want to stop seeing you.'

'So do we carry on?' Hope. Light at the end of the tunnel.

'I don't know. I don't think we can. But I don't want to lose you.'

'You can't have it both ways,' I say, amazed at where this resolve comes from, but praying that if I tell him I'll never see him again as a friend, he'll somehow find a way to work through this, to stay with me. 'I can't be your friend,' I continue. 'I'm sorry, but I just can't.'

'I don't know what to do. What do you think?'

'I think . . .' I stop, and suddenly I feel very grown up. 'I think it's late. I think we had a late night last night and that we're both tired, and that everything seems so much worse when you're tired. I think we should go home, sleep on it, and see how things are in the morning.'

I think I said the right thing, because Nick relaxes and says, 'Maybe you're right. Okay. Shall we go?' And we do.

So we go home, and we make love, and it really is making love, it's not just sex, because it's impossibly tender and throughout it all we gaze into each other's eyes and if I didn't know better I'd say that a couple of times Nick's were swimming with tears, but it was truly beautiful, and afterwards I thought, how could he give this up? How could he say goodbye to me when we are so damn good together?

And we fall asleep cuddled up, and normally when we do that I move away after about twenty minutes because I can't stand sleeping that close to someone, I need space to sleep properly, but the next time I open my eyes his arms are still wrapped around me and it's ten to eight in the morning and I kiss him awake, thinking that last night must have been a bad dream.

We go to the tube together, but somehow it is different, even though we don't talk about last night. As we kiss goodbye Nick says to me, 'Are you okay?' and I nod.

'Are you?' I say.

'I'm still confused,' he says. 'Even more so,' and he gives me a hug, and I'm not sure I like this hug because it's so tight, so clingy, if I didn't know better I'd almost think it was the last one, but we stand there for ages, and eventually I break away and he says, 'I'll call you,' and I'm not sure what the hell is going on, but neither of us has actually said it's over, so maybe it's not, but if it isn't, then why do I feel like shit?

Chapter Twelve

I feel like shit all day. I don't start crying, but I feel as if I'm on the brink every second, and it's a bit like having a nightmare case of PMT, when you know that the tiniest thing will push you over the edge, and you're literally clinging on to sanity by your fingertips.

Of course Jules is the first person I call when I get to the office, and she listens quietly while I relay what happened, and eventually she says, 'It doesn't look good.'

'I know it doesn't bloody look good, Jules. But what's happening?'

'What do you think?'

I don't think. I know. 'I think it's over.'

'I think you're probably right, in that it's over for now, but somehow I don't think it is finally over.'

'What do you mean?'

'I think he really is confused, and that you'll need to give him space, and I could be wrong, but I think he'll come back.'

But I don't want to give him space, I want to see him, be with him, convince him that I'm right for him.

'But you can't forget what you've always said,' she continues softly, trying to ease my pain. 'You never thought he'd be The One, so maybe this is a good thing.'

'I know,' I sigh. 'But maybe I was wrong. I know it started as just a fling, but you can't sleep with someone on a regular basis that you really like and not get emotionally involved.'

Jules laughs. 'That's what I've been saying since the beginning.'

'But I really thought I could,' I groan. 'I've done it before, why can't I do it now?'

'Because things are different in your early twenties. Apart from anything else you can afford it, you've got time, but, as I said before, after about twenty-five, you can't really do it because there are other things at stake, and unfortunately every man you meet becomes a potential husband, whether you admit it to yourself or not.'

'You're right, you're right. I know you're right. But that doesn't stop it hurting.'

'I know, my darling. And it will hurt for a while, but you have to get on with your life. What are you doing tonight?'

'Nothing.'

'Right. I'm coming to pick you up at eight o'clock, and I want you in your best designer togs. We're going to Mezzo for a drink.'

'I'm really not in the mood, Jules.'

'I don't care. We're going to go out and get drunk and have some fun.'

'Can't we do it another time?'

'No way. You are not moping by yourself. Just remember who you are, Libby. Three months ago and you would have jumped at the chance to dress up and meet rich men.'

But I don't want rich men any more, I think. I want Nick, but there's no getting out of it, so I say yes and miserably put down the phone, only for it to ring again two seconds later.

'Libby? It's Sal.'

'Hi! How are you!' Just the person I need to speak to,

because she knows Nick, maybe she'll have a better idea of what's going on.

'Nick just called me,' she says. 'Are you okay?'

Shit. That means he told her it was over.

'Did he tell you it was over?'

'No. Not exactly. He just said he was confused and he didn't think it was fair to you to keep going. I don't understand.'

'Neither do I.'

'Because he said he really likes you, and if he does, then why doesn't he get his shit together?'

'Exactly.'

'God, I despair of him sometimes. He's done this too many bloody times.'

'What?'

'Every time he gets close to having a relationship he goes into panic mode and runs away.'

'You mean he's done this a lot?'

'Libby,' she says gently. 'You don't look the way Nick does and lead a life of celibacy, but, trust me, you're better off out of it. He's a lovely guy, but a complete fuck-up when it comes to commitment. You deserve better. We all do.'

I can't believe I'm hearing this, not that I blame Sal for telling me, but I never knew. I suppose I never stopped to think about him doing this to anyone else, and okay, so he mentioned he'd met a few women that he could have got involved with but didn't, but I never thought he was a serial fucking commitaphobe. Or a womanizer, when it comes to that. And I start to feel sick, sick, sick.

This is really not what I need, and I can't bloody believe that it's happened again. That once again I've been unceremoniously dumped when I thought I was in control, I thought I had a handle on things, I thought that I wouldn't get hurt. What is wrong with me? I mean, I'm a good person, I'm nice to people, and animals, and I try to treat people with respect, and what happens?

I get bloody dumped.

Over and over and over again.

'Libby?' Sal's obviously wondering whether I've deserted her because I've been so busy thinking about this I forget to say anything.

'Sorry,' I say. 'I've just had enough, Sal.'

'Libby, it's not your problem, it's his.'

'Yeah, yeah, that's what I'm always told.'

'I'm serious, Libby.'

'Libby?' Jo's shouting from reception.

'Hang on a sec,' I say to Sal. 'Yeah?'

'Nick's on the line.'

'Oh shit. Sal, it's Nick. I've gotta go.'

'Okay, and listen, I'm here if you need me, okay?'

Christ, get off the bloody phone.

'Hi.' My voice is strained when I say hello to Nick.

'Hi. I just wanted to phone to check you were okay.'

'I'm okay. Sal just phoned.'

'You don't mind me telling her?'

'Not really. Is this it, then?'

He sighs. 'I don't know. But you know, it's not you. It's me.'

I almost laugh.

'I think I might have to go into therapy or something,' he sighs.

'Good idea.' And hell, maybe I should do the same thing. Maybe if I went to see someone they'd help me understand why I keep attracting the bastards. Not that

145

Nick's a bastard, it's just that none of the men I meet seem to be available. They're either physically unavailable, in other words they're never interested in me, or they're emotionally unavailable, see Nick.

'I'd really like it if we could stay friends,' he says. 'You're incredibly important to me, Libby.'

Well, that's it, then, isn't it? He may as well have said it's over, he just didn't have the balls.

'I've got enough friends,' I say. 'Thanks.'

His voice sounds sad. 'Can I phone you?'

'If you want.' Now it's my turn to be harsh.

'Listen, take care.'

'Yup. Bye.' I put down the phone and give in. I start crying. Fuck it. I don't care that I'm at work or that everyone's looking at me, and as I sit there with my shoulders heaving a sob escapes my throat and that's it, moments later I'm crying like a baby and I get up and run to the loo, where I lock myself in a cubicle and just let go.

I hear the door open, but I don't stop. I can't stop.

'Libby? Are you okay?' It's Jo.

I try to answer her but the words don't come out, just great big hiccups and sobs.

'It's Nick, isn't it? Let me in.' She starts banging on the cubicle door, so I get up and unlock it, then sit back down on the toilet seat (closed).

'They're all bastards,' she says vehemently. 'He's not worth it.' She waits for a bit while I try to regain a bit of composure, which is hard when you've got snot running down your face and your eyes look remarkably like those of Dracula's daughter.

'I' hiccup 'know' hiccup 'it's just' hiccup 'I' hiccup, hiccup, sob, sob.

'It's okay.' She puts an arm round me, which is pretty damn difficult in the confines of the cubicle, but she manages it somehow and rubs my back and I can't help it – someone being this nice, this sympathetic, sets me off all over again.

'It's okay,' she keeps saying softly. 'It's okay.'

But it's not okay, I think. It's not okay because I've got used to having Nick around, because I love having him around. Because for the first time in ages I wasn't some sad lonely person who either had to stay in on Saturday nights, or go out on the pull with the girls because there was nothing better to do.

It's not okay because I love, loved, having sex with Nick. Because there was nothing better than waking up and rolling over only to discover that you're not on your own.

It's not okay because he made me laugh. Because I didn't have to pretend to be anything other than who I am when I was with him. Because I don't believe that stuff about finding your other half, but because I do believe that what you look for is someone who makes you a better person when you're with them, who changes you for the better, who makes you the best person you can possibly be, and because I thought I had found that in Nick.

Even though I don't think I ever quite realized it until now.

And yes, maybe you're right, maybe I'm being over-dramatic, maybe I'm blowing this up into something much bigger than it is because I'm feeling sorry for myself, but why the hell not, huh? Why the hell can't I feel like this, and, whether it's true or not, it certainly feels true right now. And it feels like shit.

And oh my God, I'm never going to wake up next to him again. And oh my God, I'm never going to look in his eyes as we're making love, and oh my God, he's going to be doing that with someone else, and probably very soon, and me? I'm going to be on my own for the rest of my bloody life.

I start sobbing again.

There's a knock on the door. It's Lisa, another PR, who sits at the desk next to mine. Jo opens the door and I hear Lisa whisper, 'Is Libby okay?'

'She's fine,' says Jo, even though I'm quite patently not.

'Is there anything I can do?' says Lisa, and I know what that means. What that means is she'd kill to know what's going on, what's happened to me, and I'm sure that already a buzz has gone round the office and they're doubtless already laying bets on what it is that's made me cry, and they probably think I've got the sack.

And I hate myself for losing it at the office. That's the thing. When you set yourself up, as I've done, as this strong independent career woman, always in control, people get very nervous when you lose it, they don't quite know how to react, and sure enough, when half an hour's passed and I've finally managed to get a grip (mostly thanks to Jo and her Murine eye drops and waterproof mascara), I walk back in with head held high and everyone stops talking and starts pretending to be very busy.

A couple of minutes after I've sat down at my desk Lisa comes over and puts a cup of tea in front of me, which I suppose is very sweet, and then she looks at me with these big concerned eyes and says, 'Are you okay?' and I nod.

'Do you want to talk about it?' she says, and I catch Jo's eye and Jo makes a face and I almost laugh, because I know, I just know, that Lisa is dying to know what it's all about.

'Thanks, Lisa,' I say. 'But there's really nothing to talk about.'

'Oh,' she says, the disappointment written all over her face, and then she leans forward conspiratorially, 'It's not the job, is it?'

'No,' I say sweetly, 'it's not the job,' and she can see she's not going to get anything more out of me, so she wanders off.

Somehow I manage to get things done today, although my voice keeps breaking in the middle of phone conversations with journalists, and I have to pretend I've got a stinking cold to explain my blocked-up nose.

Eventually I set off home, and, perhaps because I've immersed myself in work, by the time I actually leave the building I really am starting to feel a lot better, and when Jules arrives I've been so busy reading I haven't even had time to get dressed, and the first thing we do after pouring ourselves a glass of wine is sit down and make a list. Yup, that list. The list I showed you when we first met.

And you know, looking at the list I start to feel one hell of a lot better, because yes, maybe he was nice, and yes, maybe he was sweet to me, but really, how could I ever have even thought of getting seriously involved? And Jesus, the thought of spending even one more night with his revolting friends in a revolting pub turns my stomach.

I leave Jules sitting in the living room as I go and get dressed, and fuck it, I'm going to make an effort. So I pull out a Joseph dress from last season and team it with my gorgeous Prada shoes, and I put on lots and lots of make-up, and I sweep my hair up into a big beehivey-type thing, and when I walk out Jules does a wolf whistle and claps her hands.

'Hooray!' she shouts, as she leaps up and grabs me, dancing round the living room. 'We've got the old Libby back, the Libby we know and love.'

'Was I really that bad?'

'Worse!' she laughs. 'Now where are those smelly old trainers?' She looks around the room.

'They're not smelly. Why?'

'They're going in the bin.'

I panic. 'No,' I say, because the trainers remind me of Nick, and I'm not quite ready to let go of the memories. 'They're perfect for work,' I say. 'I want to keep them.'

She looks at me in horror. 'Are you serious?'

I nod.

'Have it your way.' She shrugs. 'But you look gorgeous, Libby, just like your old self.' Bless her. She doesn't mention the fact that my eyes, despite a ton of mascara and cleverly applied eyeshadow, look like pissholes in the snow.

And off we go, to Mezzo, and it's packed with City boys and glamorous girls, and we haven't been there five minutes before a group of chinless wonders send over some champagne, and okay, so they're not my type, but it's really quite nice to be in this sort of environment again, and I realize that, even though I thought I didn't miss it, I now think I did.

'So how come someone as gorgeous as you hasn't got a boyfriend?' says Ed, who is not my type at all. Tall, and stocky with a moustache, and I hate moustaches. No, actually, I despise moustaches, and he's also very, very straight.

And yes, he's probably rolling in money, and yes, I know that I'm looking for a rich man, but I don't want him to be straight, I want him to be just as comfortable at the opera as he would be at, say, a Lightning Seeds gig, and there aren't too many men around like that. In fact, it may well be that Jules nabbed the last of a dying breed, but I can still hope, can't I?

This guy Ed would probably be okay-looking without the moustache, but even if he shaved it off I just know he's too damn straight for me, but what the hell, I flick my hair around a bit and smile coyly as I say, 'How do you know I haven't got a boyfriend?'

'Oh, umm. Er. Have you?' Inspired or what?

I shake my head and suddenly feel incredibly sad. Jules sees it and grabs me.

'Excuse us, boys. We'll be back in a sec.'

We leave them moaning about why women always go off to the loo in pairs, and once we're in there she asks if I'm okay.

'I am. Really. I'm having quite a nice time. I don't know. It's just that I miss Nick.'

'What about Ed?'

'What about him?'

'Might be worth a date. He's definitely interested.'

'Nah,' I say. 'Not my type. Too straight.'

'How d'you know? Sometimes people can surprise you.'

'Okay. I'll show you.' And we go back to join them.

'So,' I say to Ed. 'Been to any good gigs lately?'

'Gigs?' He looks completely bewildered. 'Oh, ah. Gigs.

Oh yes,' and he starts laughing. 'Hilarious,' he says, over and over as I look at Jules and raise one eyebrow.

'You're very funny, Libby,' he says, although I haven't quite got the joke. 'I'd love to take you out for dinner.'

'Okay.' I shrug, not really giving a damn whether he does or not.

'May I have your number?'

Jesus, is this guy formal or what? I scrabble around in my bag for a pen, but no, once again I'm carrying a magic bag that eats pens, keys and lipsticks, and there's no pen to be found. Ed stops a passing waitress and asks for her pen, and he writes my number down carefully in a black leather wallet thing that holds small sheets of white paper and looks desperately expensive.

'I shall call you,' he says. 'And we shall go somewhere wonderful.'

I literally have to force myself not to shrug and say, 'Whatever.' Instead I smile and say, 'Lovely.'

And when we leave, which is shortly afterwards because all the emotion of this morning is starting to make me extremely tired, Ed shakes my hand and says, 'It's been an absolute pleasure meeting you. I'll ring you about dinner.' And that's it. We jump in a taxi and head home.

'I can't believe you pulled,' says Jules. 'You pulled someone on your first night as a single girl!'

'Oh, come on, Jules, he's not exactly a good pull.'

'You're blind, Libby. He was lovely, and obviously smitten with you. Are you going to have dinner with him?'

'Dunno.'

'Anyway, at least now you know there are other men out there, that it's not the end of the world.'

I know she's right, it's just that I don't want any other men at the moment, I just want Nick.

'And,' she continues, 'he'll probably take you somewhere fantastic, he's obviously loaded.'

'How can you tell?'

She looks at me in dismay. 'Libby, everything I know I learnt from you. Don't tell me you didn't notice the Rolex?'

I shake my head.

'The Hermès tie?'

I shake my head.

'The Porsche keyring?'

I shake my head.

'Maybe I will go out for dinner with him,' I say, suddenly quite liking the idea of being driven around in a Porsche. 'But just dinner. That's all.'

Jules sits there and smiles to herself, and I give her a look.

'I know you so well,' she chuckles, and I can't help it, I start laughing too.

Chapter Thirteen

The good mood lasts precisely as long as it takes me to get back to the flat. I open the front door and turn on the lights, kick off my shoes, and as I walk around I start fighting off the memories of Nick that seem to be everywhere I look.

The sofa where we curled, that first night, when he came back after Sal's get-together. The bath where he sat in that ridiculous bath hat. The bed. Oh my God. The bed.

I sink to the floor, tears streaming down my face, and I curl up, hugging my knees to my chest, crying like a baby.

Why did this have to happen to me? Why can't this work? I try to remember what Nick said, why it's ended, because it doesn't make sense. How can you like someone, I mean really like them, and still want to end it? He said it might have worked if we'd met in a few months' time, so maybe it could work now, maybe I could change his mind.

I stop thinking properly. I stand up, wipe the tears from my eyes and grab my car keys. The only thing that will make this better is seeing Nick. I have to see him. Talk to him. Make him see that this can work, that I don't care about his job, his money, because suddenly I don't. All that matters to me right now is being with him, working things out, and the only way I can do this is to go to him.

I climb in the car, filled with resolve, so intent on making this work that I forget to cry, I concentrate on manoeuvring the car through London's streets, until eventually I pull up outside Nick's flat in Highgate.

I sit for a while in the car, suddenly unsure about ringing his bell, about actually confronting him, but I'm here now, and this is the only way, and I know that I don't believe it's over, I won't believe it's over, until I can talk to him face to face, and if he sees me, if he sees what he's doing to me, he'll change his mind. He has to.

Nick takes for ever to answer the door. At one point I start turning back, feeling absolutely sick at what I'm doing, rethinking the whole thing, but just as I turn I hear a door upstairs, and then the soft clump of footsteps coming down the stairs.

The door opens and there he is. His hair mussed up, his eyes half closed with sleep, and he is obviously shocked to see me standing there.

We look at each other while I try to find the words, the words that will bring him back, but nothing comes out, and I try to blink back the tear that squeezes itself out of the corner of my right eye.

'Libby,' he whispers, as he puts his arms around me, and I can't help it. I break down, sobbing my heart out because as he stands there with his arms around me, gently rubbing my back, I know that this is pointless, that I am making a fool of myself, that nothing will change his mind.

'You'd better come upstairs,' he says eventually, gently disengaging himself and leading me upstairs by the hand, while I try to wipe my face.

We sit in silence for a while, me on the armchair, Nick on the Futon, and all I want to do is climb into the Futon with him and cuddle him, make everything okay, turn the clock back to how it was the other night. I can't believe things can change so quickly. I can't believe that I am no longer allowed to do this because it's over, and as I start to think about it the tears roll down my face again.

'God, Libby,' Nick whispers. 'I am so sorry. I never meant to hurt you.'

'I don't understand,' I blurt out. 'You said if we met in a few months it would be okay, we could be together, so I don't understand why we can't just carry on.'

Nick doesn't say anything. 'I don't care about the money,' I sniffle, my voice becoming louder, almost as if he will understand me better if I shout. 'I don't give a damn about you not having a job. We're so good together, Nick, why do you have to do this? Why can't we just carry on?'

'This is why,' he says gently. 'Because neither of us was supposed to get emotionally involved. I never wanted to cause you any pain, and it's killing me to see you like this.'

'So why are you causing me this much pain?' I look up at him, not caring that the tears are now flowing freely down my face. 'Why are you doing this to me?'

'Libby,' he says, coming over and crouching down so that his face is level with mine. 'I told you from the beginning I wasn't ready for a relationship. I knew you were getting more involved, but I tried to deny it because I knew I couldn't give you, I can't give you, what you want. I'm just not ready. I am so sorry.'

'Okay,' I snuffle, regaining some small measure of composure. 'So you can't give me what I want. So what? So now I know. Let's carry on anyway. You can't hurt me more than you already have, and now I know exactly where I stand, so I don't see why we can't keep seeing each other, not when we get on so well, when things are so good between us.' I am trying to bring him closer, to draw him in through talking to him, but it seems that the more I talk, the more distance there is between us.

'No, Libby.' He shakes his head sadly. 'I want to, but I can't put you through this again, and it will happen again, because I can't commit to anyone right now. And even though you say that it doesn't matter, I know that that's what you're looking for, and it couldn't work. Believe me,' he says softly, touching my cheek, 'if I were to commit to anyone it would be to you, but I'm just not ready.'

The tears dry up as I realize that I cannot persuade him. That his mind is made up. That now there is no doubt that it really is over. I stand up and go to the door, trying to regain some self-respect, although even I know it's a little late for that.

'I'll call you,' Nick says, walking down the stairs behind me as I head for the front door, feeling like nothing is real, like this is all a horrific nightmare. I don't bother saying anything. I just walk out and somehow manage to make it home.

'What did you do this time?' My mother's looking at me, and it's all I can do not to jump up and scream at her because this is absolutely typical, it's always my bloody fault. My mother would never stop to think that perhaps there was something wrong with these men, but oh no. It's always that I've put them off.

'Did you come on too strong?' she says, and I wish, oh how I bloody wish, I'd never mentioned anything. I wasn't planning to, really I wasn't, but then my mother seems to have some sort of psychic sixth sense, and she could see something was wrong, and before I knew it it just came out. That I'd split up with Nick. Although I ommitted the part about turning up at his flat. That's something I'm trying hard to forget.

And yes, I regret it. I regret it because I allowed him to see me at my most vulnerable. I laid all my cards on the table and he swept them away without a second glance. In the few days since it happened, I've tried not to think about it, because the only thing I feel when I remember laying myself open in the way that I did is shame. Pure and absolute shame.

'No,' I say viciously. 'I did not come on too strong. He just doesn't want a relationship, okay?'

'What do you mean, he doesn't want a relationship? Since when does any man want a relationship?' She snorts with laughter at her little joke, and I look at her, wondering when in hell my mother became such an expert at relationships? I mean, she's only ever been with my dad, for God's sake. No one else would have her.

'You know you have to play hard to get, Libby. None of this jumping into bed on the first night and being there whenever they want you.'

How the fuck would she know?

'You nineties women, I don't know.' She shakes her head. 'You all think that everything's equal now, but, when it comes to matters of the heart, it most certainly isn't. Men haven't changed: they love the thrill of the chase, and if you hand yourself over on a plate they'll lose interest. Simple as that.'

'It's not like that, Mum,' I say through gritted teeth. 'It had nothing to do with that.'

'I know you think I'm just your mum and I don't know anything, but, let me tell you, I watch Vanessa, and Ricki, and Oprah, and you girls all say the same thing, and the answer's as clear to me as anything. You have to play hard to get, it's the answer to all your problems.'

'Mum, you really don't know what you're talking about. Watching a few daytime telly shows does not make you an expert on relationships.'

'That's what you think,' she says firmly. 'And anyway I'm not saying I'm an expert, all I'm saying is that I can see what you're doing wrong.'

That's it. I've had enough. Again. 'Why is it always me who's doing something wrong?' I practically shout. 'Have you ever considered the fact that it might be men who have the problem? No, no, how stupid of me, of course it's my fault. It's always my bloody fault.'

'No need for that sort of language,' my mum says. 'But have you ever considered why you're still single at twenty-seven?'

'It's only twenty-seven, for God's sake! I'm not exactly forty, I've got years.'

My mum shakes her head sadly. 'No, Libby, you haven't, not if you want to get married and have children, and I think it's high time you stopped and had a good long look at yourself and how you are with these boyfriends.'

'You're amazing.' I shake my head in disbelief. 'Most girls my age would kill to have my life. I've got a flat, a great job, a car and plenty of disposable income. I've got a busy social life, hundreds of friends, and I meet celebrities every day.'

'Fine,' says my mother. 'Fine. But I don't see any of these celebrities proposing to you, do you?'

'Can you not see that having a man is really not that

important these days? That I'm far happier being a . . . a Singleton.'

'A what?'

'Someone who's happier being single with no attachments.'

'Libby, dear,' she says patronizingly. 'You know that's not true and I know that's not true.'

Why does she always have to have the last bloody word? And what's more, the nasty old cow is right. Well, right about me not liking being single, I really don't know about the rest of that stuff, and even if she were right, I certainly wouldn't tell her.

'Mum, let's just drop it,' I say, getting up to go.

'Oh, you can't go,' she says. 'You've only just got here. And I'm concerned about you, Libby, you look as if you've put on a bit of weight.'

Jesus Christ. Talk about knowing where to hit the weak spot. And so what if I've put on a bit of weight, it's not like I'm huge or anything, but I've always strived to be half a stone thinner, and trust my mother to notice that in the few days since that night at Nick's flat I've been eating like a pig, although I decided this morning that that was going to stop. Definitely.

'I haven't put on weight,' I say, although I know from the scales that I'm four pounds heavier.

'Okay, okay,' she sighs. 'I simply don't want you to get fat, I'm only saying it for your own good.'

'Look. I'm going.'

'Not just yet.' She stands up. 'Tell you what, I've got some of your favourite caramel cakes here, why don't I just go and get them?'

'You just told me I'd put on weight!'

'One won't hurt you,' and she bustles off.

Please tell me I'm not the only one with a completely mad, insensitive mother. Please say that all mothers are like this, that I'm not the only one who goes through hell every time she goes home to see her parents. I don't even know why I bloody go. Every weekend I'm expected for tea on Sunday, and every weekend I turn up, behave like a pissed-off teenager and run away as fast as I can.

Maybe I should do what Olly did. Maybe I should move to Manchester.

She comes back and puts a plate of caramel cakes on the table, and to piss her off I refuse them and tell her I'm on a diet.

'Have just the one,' she says. 'Look, I'll share one with you,' and she picks one up and takes a bite, handing me the other half.

'I. Don't. Want. It,' I say through gritted teeth. 'Okay?'

'Libby, I wish you wouldn't always take offence when I try to help.' She sighs and looks at me with those mournful eyes, and if I didn't know better I'd start feeling sorry for her. Fortunately, I know better.

'I'm your mother and I want what's best for you, and I'm only saying these things because I've got the benefit of experience and I can see things from a different perspective, that's all. And there's nothing I'd love more than to see you happy and with a good man.'

I huff a bit but I don't say anything, and after a while she sighs again and evidently decides to give up on this particular line of conversation.

'Spoken to Olly recently?' she asks after a long silence.

Hmm. Now this would really get to her, if I told her that yes, actually, I had just spoken to him, I'd seen him, and, not only that, I'd met his girlfriend, Carolyn. What,

Mum? You didn't know he had a girlfriend? You didn't know he was in London? Gosh. I am surprised.

But no, I couldn't do that. Much as it would satisfy me to upset Mum right now, I couldn't do it to Olly, so I just nod and say we had a chat the other day.

'Did he mention anything to you about a girlfriend?' she says, trying to sound as if she doesn't care either way, and this is a bit odd because I'm sure Olly wouldn't have told her.

'Why?' I say carefully, not wishing to be drawn into a trap.

'Oh, no reason,' she says lightly. 'Only he mentioned he was going away for the weekend and wouldn't tell me who with, so I wondered if he might have some special lady friend.'

'If he has he hasn't told me,' I lie, knowing that Olly would do his damndest to keep Carolyn away from Mum, because, as far as Mum's concerned, no one's good enough for her darling son. Not that she'd ever say it out loud, she'd just come out with the odd well-aimed dart, something like, 'It's a very interesting accent, darling. Whereabouts in London did you say she came from?' or 'I'm sure it's all the rage now, but honestly, darling, her skirt was so short you could practically see her undies.'

Believe me, I'm not making it up, she has actually said these things, and Olly does his best to ignore them, but somehow once she's said something he starts noticing it too, and Sara went out the window not long after Mum implied she was common, and Vicky? Well, even I had to admit that Vicky was a bit provocative. Dad loved her, though. Needless to say.

'I hope if he is with someone she's the right kind of girl.'

'What on earth are you talking about?'

'Olly's a good boy, he deserves someone very special, not like those other girlfriends he's paraded through here over the years.'

Bloody typical.

'Mum,' I say, standing up and giving her the obligatory peck on the cheek. 'I really am going now,' and finally, thankfully, I manage to get away.

'Right,' says Jules, curling up on my sofa, pen poised in hand. 'You have to be completely honest, and I mean completely. I want to hear everything that you're looking for.'

'But I'm not looking, Jules, I want some time out from relationships, I just want to be on my own for a bit.'

'Okay, so in that case just tell me what your dream man is like.'

I shrug. 'He's tall, about 6'1", and he's got light brown, no, make that dark brown hair.'

'Eyes?'

'Green.'

'Would he look like anyone famous? Mel Gibson?'

He'd look like Nick, I think sadly, pushing that thought away almost as quickly as it appears. 'Eugh, no. No. Let me think. Who do I like? I know!' I shout. 'Tom Berenger.'

'Who's Tom Berenger?'

'The actor, *Platoon*? *Someone to Watch Over Me*?'

Jules shakes her head, but writes his name down anyway.

'Okay,' she says. 'What else?'

'He's got to be rich, seriously rich. He'd live in one of those huge stucco houses in Holland Park, but not a flat, it would be a whole house, and he'd rattle around in it waiting for his wife and her interior designer best friend to come and redo it all.'

'Mmm,' laughs Jules. 'Now that I like the sound of.'

'He'd probably be a businessman, he'd have his own business, God knows at what, and he'd drive a Ferrari.'

'Bit flash, isn't it?'

'Okay. A Mercedes SLK.'

Jules nods and writes it down. 'Just the one car, then?'

'Good point. No, he'd have the Merc, and a Range Rover for weekends at his country pad, and he'd buy me that new BMW, you know, the sporty one, what is it, an F3 or a Z3 or something?

'He would have to wear beautiful navy suits for work, but then when he's at home he'd be in really faded 501s and polo shirts, oh, and leather trousers because he'd have a motorbike as well.'

'What kind of motorbike? A Harley?'

'Nah, way too common. An Indian.'

'Okay.' She keeps scribbling, and I hug my knees to my chest, wondering what else I can say about my dream man, because I love playing these fantasy games.

'I can't think of what else to say.' I sit and think for a while.

'Er, Libby?' Jules looks up.

'Mmm?'

'Haven't you forgotten something?'

'What?'

'His personality?'

Well, what can you say about a personality, for heaven's sake? I mean, let's face it, we all want pretty much the same thing when it comes to personality. We want someone who's intelligent. We'd quite like him to be creative, although that's not a prerequisite if you're not into that kind of stuff. We'd like someone kind. Sensitive. Oh, and how could we forget, a good sense of humour, although that's a bit of a difficult one, because, as Carrie Fisher once said in a film, everyone thinks they have good taste and a sense of humour.

We'd like someone who likes going out for dinner and going to the movies. We'd like someone who's also very happy going on a long walk in the country, then curling up by a fire, and, even though I'd never dream of actually going for a long walk in the country, it's a nice thought, and I'd definitely want someone who would, at the very least, appreciate that thought.

And, before you think I'm completely superficial, I have to say in my defence that I honestly never gave the personality a second thought, because it's kind of an unspoken thing. Of course you assume he's going to have a personality you like, otherwise you wouldn't bother in the first place.

So, finally, we end up with a list that's two pages long. A page and a half of what he looks like, where he lives, how he lives, and a few hastily scribbled lines of the personality stuff, and when we've finished Jules tucks it into my bag and says, 'I think you may have to compromise somewhat on the material side, but it always helps to write down what you think you're looking for. Now the next step is wardrobe.'

Jules goes into the kitchen, opens the fridge, and pulls a black bin liner off a roll that's nestling there, and only Jules knows me well enough to know that due to the lack of space in my kitchen the vegetable drawer in the fridge is also home to various cleaning items that I rarely get around to using.

'What's that for?' I look at her suspiciously.

'This is for Nick memorabilia.'

'But I don't have any memorabilia.' Why do I still feel a pang of sadness when his name is mentioned unexpectedly?

'What, nothing? No photos? No letters? No sweat-shirts that you borrowed and accidentally on purpose forgot to give back?'

I shake my head, and then I remember. 'Wait!' I run into the bedroom and pull a T-shirt out of the dirty linen basket, and I can't help it. I'm completely ashamed to admit that I bury my nose in it to smell Nick, since he was the last person wearing it, but try as I might I can't smell him. All I can smell is the musty odour of dirty linen.

I go back into the living room, holding the T-shirt, and gingerly hand it to Jules, who, it has to be said, accepts it even more gingerly before stuffing it in the bag.

'Are you sure that's it?' I know she doesn't believe me, but I nod.

'So this is the last reminder?'

I nod again.

She ties the bin bag tightly and takes it out the front door, putting it with the rubbish.

'I thought you liked him,' I moan, because I can't believe she's being so ruthless.

'I did like him,' she says. 'But the only way you're going to get over him properly is to remove all the evidence, and by going out with other men. Speaking of which, has that guy called?'

'Which guy?'

'Ed.'

He has called. He called the day after I met him and left a rather nervous-sounding message on my machine, which was a bit peculiar because he was so self-assured when we met. 'Hello, Libby,' he said. 'Er, it's, er, Ed here. We met last night at Mezzo. I was just wondering whether perhaps you'd, er, like to come out for dinner with me. It was lovely to meet you, and I wondered whether you might give me a call back.'

Maybe he's just one of those blokes who hate answering machines. Anyway, he left his home number, his work number and his mobile number, and he said he'd be in all day and at home that evening.

I didn't call back.

I mean, I know I said I'd have dinner with him, but I'm really not that bothered, and what would be the point? I don't fancy him, there's no stomach-churning lovely lustful feeling like I had with Nick when we first got together, like I still have when I think about Nick, and I'm sure he's a nice guy but I really can't see me getting involved with anyone right now, even if he does drive a Porsche. I just feel weary. Exhausted. That whole Nick thing has done me in, and right at this moment if I can't have him I don't want anyone.

Plus, this Ed character might not drive a Porsche anyway. He might be one of those wanky types who has a Porsche keyring to impress women he's trying to pick up in Mezzo.

'No,' I lie, shaking my head. 'He hasn't called.'

'Really?' Jules looks surprised. 'I can't believe he hasn't called, he seemed so smitten. Well, he will.'

'I really don't care.'

'I know,' she says. 'But it would do you good. He'll probably take you somewhere incredibly swanky and treat you like a princess and you'll have a good time. No one says you have to sleep with him, or even see him again for that matter, but you never know what his friends are like. You might meet the man of your dreams by being friends with him.'

'Oh, shut up, Jules, you sound just like my mother.'

And I know I will be fine, it's not like the other times I've broken up with boyfriends, when I've been so heart-broken I've cried solidly for about three weeks and not wanted to go anywhere or do anything. Okay, I had that one night from hell, but since then I've been really okay, and at least I know there's no point living on false hope. At least I know it really is over so I can move on. But I have to say that this time I feel a bit numb, still in a state of shock, really, although I don't feel that my world has ended, not completely. I suppose that the light at the end of the tunnel, though not very bright, is at least there.

They say that it never hurts as much after the first time, and I suppose there's an element of truth in that, but they also say that every time you get hurt the barriers go up a little bit higher, and you end up being hard and cynical, and not giving anything to anyone.

God that that were true.

I wish that I could be hard and cynical. That I could take things slowly, not give too much of myself, because I'd be so frightened of getting hurt that there wouldn't be any other way. But no. Every time I meet someone I dive in head first, showering them with love and atten-tion, and hoping that this time they're going to turn out to be different.

Chance would be a fine bloody thing.

I don't see the point in pretending to be something other than what you are, because if you do, at some point, you're going to have to reveal your true self, and, if it's completely different, they're going to run off screaming.

But perhaps I'm learning to hold back a little bit, perhaps that's why this isn't hurting so much, or perhaps it's because Nick wasn't, isn't, The One, and, although I was starting to like him more and more, I suppose deep down I knew I couldn't live his life, and that's why I'm really feeling okay.

But okay isn't great, and so what if I go through my CD collection once Jules has gone and pull out all the songs which I know are guaranteed to make me cry. So what if I start with REM and 'Everybody Hurts', and sob like a baby. So what if I continue with Janis Ian's 'At Seventeen', and start feeling like the biggest reject in the world. And yeah, so I stick on Everything But The Girl singing 'I Don't Want to Talk about It', but Jesus, everyone's allowed to feel a bit sorry for themselves sometimes, aren't they?

So I sit, and keep putting on CDs, and cry and cry and cry, until I'm hiccuping madly and I've got a pounding headache, and the phone rings but I don't answer it because I'm not sure whether I can disguise the fact I've been crying this time, and I really don't want to have to explain myself to anyone right now.

The machine clicks on, I hear my message, and then I hear a voice. 'Oh hello, er, Libby. It's Ed, we met the other night at Mezzo. I left you a message the other day but I thought perhaps you didn't get it, so I'm leaving you another one because I'd really love to see you.'

Once again he leaves all his numbers, and I know this

sounds bizarre, but it cheers me up a bit, the fact that someone likes me enough to leave two messages, and even though it doesn't cheer me up enough to actually pick up the phone, soon after he's finished speaking I decide that I might just call him back after all.

Chapter Fourteen

Today is the day I'm going to phone Ed. Definitely. I thought about it last night, and Jules is absolutely right, I should be going out with other men, and I know he's not really my type, but what the hell. I am, as my mother reminded me, twenty-seven years old and I suppose what it's all about is a numbers game: go out with enough men and one of them's bound to be Mr Right.

But in the meantime I've got my hands completely full at work. I'm trying to organize the launch for this TV series, and I've just finished the press release inviting all the journalists and photographers, when who should call up but Amanda Baker.

Not what I need right now at all.

'Hi, darling,' she says, which throws me ever so slightly, because she's not the sort of person I'd ever *darling*, and she's never done this to me before, but I suppose since her recent radio appearances she's forgiven me my apparent lack of work on her behalf, and now she's treating me as if we're best friends.

'I thought we could go out for lunch,' she says. 'You know, a girls' lunch. You and me.'

I'm so flummoxed I don't know what to say, so I stammer for a while, wondering what on earth is going on.

'Are you free today?' she says. 'It's just that I'm so busy at the moment, but I'd love to see you and I thought we might go to Quo Vadis.'

Now that's done it for me, because needless to say I haven't been to Quo Vadis yet, and it's one of those restaurants that you really ought to go to at least once, if only to say that you've been there.

'I'd love to,' I say. 'Shall I meet you there?'

'Perfect,' she says. 'Book the table for one fifteen. All right, darling, see you later.' And she's gone, leaving me sitting there looking at the receiver in my hand and wondering why on earth I'm supposed to book the table when she invited me?

So I'm walking round the office in a bemused fashion, asking if anyone's got the number for Quo Vadis, when Joe Cooper walks out of his office and says, 'That's very posh. How come you're going to Quo Vadis?'

'This is really odd, Joe,' I say. 'Amanda Baker just phoned and invited me out for lunch, which is completely peculiar in itself because up until pretty damn recently I was her worst enemy, and I suddenly seem to have become her best friend, and then she asked me to book the table. All a bit weird.'

Joe throws back his head with laughter. 'Libby,' he says. 'This is Amanda's trick, she's done this with every PR she's ever worked with. She starts off mistrusting you and the minute you actually get her some coverage she decides you're her best friend. Don't worry about it, look at it this way, at least it will make your life easier.'

I shrug. 'S'pose so.' And I scribble down the number on a yellow Post-it note and go to call the restaurant.

It's half past one, and I'm sitting at a window table trying to see out the stained-glass and wondering what they do when it gets really hot in here, because there aren't any window latches so they can't open the windows. I'm trying to look very cool, as if I'm someone famous, because it seems that almost everybody else in here is. I've already spotted three television presenters, two pop stars, and the people at the table next to me are talking about their latest film, and since I don't recognize them I presume they're behind the camera, as it were. And no, I'm not trying to earwig, it's just that it's bloody difficult when you're sitting on your own not to hear what the table next door is talking about when they're so close to you they're practically sitting in your lap, and where the hell is Amanda anyway?

I ask for another Kir and puff away on my fourth cigarette, when I suddenly hear a familiar 'Darling!' and look up and see Amanda kiss her way through the restaurant, greeting all the minor celebrities as if she's known them for ever, and to my immense surprise they do all know her, and I suddenly feel quite pleased that she's meeting me, and I'm even more pleased when she sweeps up to the table and gives me two air kisses before sitting down.

'Darling,' she says, evidently in a much more ebullient mood than when we last met. 'You look fab.'

'So do you,' I say. 'It's lovely to see you.'

'I thought that we really ought to get to know each other a bit better,' she says, glancing round the room as she speaks, presumably just in case she's missing anything.

She orders a sparkling mineral water from the waiter, and we sit and make small talk for a while, and then, once we've ordered – me from the set lunch menu at £15.95 and Amanda from the à la carte menu – the conversation turns, as it so often does with single women, to men.

'Well, you know' – she leans forward conspiratorially – 'my last affair was with . . .' She leans even closer and whispers the name of a well-known TV anchorman in my ear, then sits back to note my admiration, because the anchorman in question is indeed gorgeous, and I would normally tell you, but somehow I don't think Amanda would want you to know, because as well as being gorgeous he's also very married, and it wouldn't do his image any good at all.

But trust me. It's great gossip.

'So what happened?'

'He came out with all the usual shit about loving his wife but not being in love with her, and how they slept in separate beds, and he was only with her because it was good for his profile, and that he was going to leave her, he'd had enough. But of course he didn't.'

'Amazing, isn't it?' I say. 'Whenever our friends get involved with married men we hear about what they say and it's always the same and we always tell our friends that he's never going to leave her, but the minute it happens to us, the minute we meet a married man and he says he loves his wife but he's not in love with her, we believe him.'

'I know,' she laughs, but there's a tinge of bitterness in her laugh. 'I really thought I was more clever than that. I really thought that he was different, that he was going to leave.'

'So what made you realize he wasn't?'

'When I opened the pages of *Hello!* and read how excited they both were that she was pregnant again with their sixth child.'

'Jesus.' I exhale loudly and sit back. 'That must have hurt.'

'It was a killer,' she says. 'So now I'm back on the dating scene, which is hell, really, because even though I'm famous . . .'

I suppress a snort.

' . . . I just don't seem to meet any decent men. To be honest I think they're all a bit intimidated by me.'

'I can understand that,' I say.

'Really?' she says. 'Why do you think it is?'

'Oh, er. Well, because you're famous, and you're very bright, and very attractive.' I see her face fall. 'I mean, you're beautiful, and that scares a lot of men off.'

'I know,' she nods. 'You're absolutely right.'

'It's the same for me,' I say, and wait for her to ask me about my own love life, but she doesn't, and then I think how stupid I am to think a celebrity, even one as minor as Amanda, would be interested in anyone other than themselves. But fuck it. I want to talk about this. I need to talk about this. And somehow, sitting right here with this woman who's more than a stranger but not quite a friend, I find myself telling her all about it, which I suspect throws her a bit, because she's far more used to talking about herself than to listening to other people, but I can't help it. It all comes out.

'So,' I end, having spoken non-stop for the last twenty minutes, 'now there's this guy Ed pursuing me and I really don't know whether to call him, because even though he's nice enough I just can't see a future in it and I guess I'm still hung up on Nick, even though I know there's no future in that either.'

'Ed who?' Amanda asks, a flicker of interest in her eyes.

'I don't know,' I say, and I laugh, because I'm so uninterested I haven't even bothered to look at his business card. 'Hang on,' I say, fishing around in my bag. 'His card's here somewhere.'

I find my diary and pull out the card, glancing at it briefly. 'Ed McMahon.'

'You're joking!' Amanda's gasping across the table at me. 'No.' She shakes her head. 'It can't be.' She grabs the card and starts laughing as she reads it. 'Oh my God, Libby! Ed McMahon! Don't you know who he is?'

I shake my head.

'He's only one of the most eligible bachelors in Britain. I can't believe you pulled Ed McMahon and you didn't even realize who he was!'

'Who is he, then?'

'He's a financial whizzkid who everyone's talking about, because he seemed to appear out of nowhere. He's single, hugely rich and supposedly unbelievably intelligent. I've never met him, but my friend Robert knows him really well. I've been begging him to fix me up with him, but Robert keeps saying we wouldn't get on.'

'But Amanda,' I say slowly, 'have you seen him? He's not exactly an oil painting.' I laugh, although suddenly I'm slightly more interested in Ed. Not a lot, just slightly.

'So?' she says. 'With his kind of money, who cares?'

'How come, if he's so rich and so eligible, he hasn't got a girlfriend?'

'That's the odd thing,' she says. 'He doesn't seem to have much luck with women. Robert says it's because he's a bit eccentric, but I don't really know.'

'Well,' I say, 'maybe I will call him, then.'

'Call him?' Amanda snorts. 'Marry him, more like.'

By the end of our lunch, and I swear, no one is more

surprised by this than me, I've made two decisions. One is to call Ed McMahon this afternoon, and the other is that I quite like Amanda Baker. Okay, she's not someone whom I'd normally consider being friends with, but, after our bit of female bonding over lunch, I think she's quite sweet really, and as we leave I decide that I'm going to try to get her a bit more coverage, work a bit harder for her. Don't get me wrong, I'm not saying that she's my new best friend or anything, it's just that she's all right, she's one of us, if you know what I'm saying.

So I go back to the office and pull out Ed McMahon's business card again, and I sit for a while looking at it, and then I pick up the phone and dial his number.

'Hello, is Ed McMahon there, please?'

'Who may I say is calling?'

'Libby Mason.'

'And will he know what it's in connection with?'

'Yes.'

'May I tell him?'

'Tell him what?'

'What it's in connection with?'

'It's, umm. Don't worry. He'll know.' What is this, for heaven's sake? The Spanish Inquisition?

And then there's a silence, and I sit and listen to piped music for a while, and finally, just when I'm about to give up, Ed comes on the phone.

'Libby?'

'Ed?'

'Libby! I'm so delighted you phoned. I was so worried you didn't get my messages.'

'I'm sorry,' I say, 'I've been running around like a mad woman, I've been so busy.'

'Never mind, never mind. You've phoned now! I was giving up hope! When are you free for dinner?'

'I'll just look in my diary,' I say, looking in my diary. 'When were you thinking of?'

'Tomorrow night?'

Naturally there's nothing in my diary for tomorrow night, but do I really want to see this man so soon? Nah, I don't think I do, I think I'd be much happier staying in and watching the box.

'I'm sorry,' I say, sounding as if I mean it. 'But this week's horrendous. How about next week, that's looking pretty clear.'

'Oh, umm. Okay. Actually, what about the weekend? Saturday night?'

Now Saturday night's a big night. Saturday night is not a night to give up for just anyone, particularly a man I don't even fancy, but then again, he's bound to take me somewhere nice, and he may not be Nick, but he is one of the most eligible men in Britain, and I really ought to be a bit more excited about this than I am, so okay, I'm game on.

And Ed is so excited I can practically hear him jumping up and down. He takes my address and I laugh to myself, wondering what he'll make of my tiny little basement flat in grotty Ladbroke Grove, because he must live in some unbelievable mansion somewhere, but I don't really care what he thinks, and he says he'll pick me up at eight and book somewhere special.

I say goodbye and ring Jules without even putting down the phone.

'I have a date with one of the most eligible men in Britain on Saturday night!' I say, and I do add an unspoken exclamation mark at the end of my sentence, because actually I'm pretty damn pleased with myself.

'Who?'

'Ed McMahon.'

'Ed? Ed that we met?'

'Yup.'

'What do you mean, one of the most eligible bachelors in Britain?'

I repeat, word for word, what Amanda told me over lunch.

'Jesus,' she says. 'That's a result. And he sounds much more you than that Nick.'

See? Already Nick's become 'that Nick' – not someone involved in my life, someone in my past, someone who never had a future.

'In what way?'

'Oh, come on, Libby, he'll probably take you to amazing places and buy you wonderful presents and you'll love every minute of it.'

'Jules, I think you're jumping a bit ahead of yourself here. I mean, I hardly know the guy, and I certainly don't fancy him. At least, I didn't the other night.'

'Fine,' she laughs. 'Let's just wait and see.'

I wake up on Saturday and have to admit that, while I'm not exactly jumping with joy at the prospect of tonight's date with Ed, I do have slight butterflies, but I suspect that's more to do with having a date at all rather than who the date's with. And I still miss Nick.

I get all the boring chores done – dry cleaners; cleaning the flat; sorting out all the shit I don't have time for during the week – and then, after I've settled in front of the *Brookside* omnibus, I start planning what to wear.

A black suit, I decide. A suit that's smart, sophisticated, and always makes me feel fantastic. But I don't want to look too straight, even though, from what I remember, Ed would make Pall Mall look positively curvy, so I team it with very high-heeled black strappy sandals and a beautiful grey silk scarf tied softly at my neck.

And I look in the mirror and I smile to myself because I certainly look the part, even if I don't feel it inside, and I feel that I can hold my head up high and walk in anywhere feeling good.

Not that I know where Ed's planning to take me, but I'm sure it will be somewhere expensive and impressive, and whenever I go to places like that I like to feel well-armed, and the best way of feeling like that is to look fantastic, preferably in designer clothes.

And the flat looks perfect. Well, as perfect as it can look. I even bought armfuls of flowers this morning, and I have to say I'm quite proud of the place, even though I know Ed will probably never have seen anything this small. I've done away with the clutter. At least, I've swept it under the sofa and into cupboards, so it looks pristine. I've sprayed air freshener around, so it smells like a summer meadow, or so it says on the can, and okay, it wouldn't pass my mother's inspection, but I'm damn sure it would pass everyone else's.

The only thing I haven't bothered to do is change the sheets, or even shave my legs when it comes to that, because I'm absolutely sure that I will not be going to bed with Ed, or anyone else for that matter, for a while yet, and at the grand old age of twenty-seven I've realized that the best contraception of all is hairy legs.

So my outer perfection hides my lower layer of stubble

and greying Marks & Spencer knickers, but it hardly matters tonight, and I don't believe all that rubbish about you feeling more sexy when you're wearing sexy underwear. It's crap. As far as I'm concerned you feel more sexy when you've lost weight and you're having a good hair day. Simple as that.

And tonight I have lost weight (I've been practically starving myself since my mother's comment), I'm back to my usual, and I'm having a good hair day, so, when the doorbell rings at eight on the dot, I walk confidently to the door and open it with a gracious smile.

Chapter Fifteen

I don't actually see Ed for a while. All I can see, when I open the door, is the most enormous bouquet of long-stemmed creamy white roses that I've ever seen in my life, and they completely take my breath away.

No one's ever bought me flowers before, you see. I know that sounds daft, but none of my boyfriends have ever been the romantic type, and I've always longed for someone who would bring me flowers and chocolates.

I was given chocolates once by a very keen man who arrived to pick me up and handed me a box of Milk Tray. I had to give him ten out of ten for effort, but Milk Tray? They should have been Belgian chocolates, at the very least.

And Jon bought me flowers once, but it was only because I'd gone over to his flat and he'd obviously been out buying loads of flowers for himself, and I was so upset that he didn't buy me any that I threw a wobbly, and when we left the flat he stopped outside the flower shop and bought me a bunch of wilting chrysanthemums, which was hardly the point. What I remember most clearly about him doing that was his face. He was so proud of himself because he thought I'd be over the moon, but if anything it pissed me off even more.

And here, on my doorstep, is a bunch of flowers so big it hides the man standing behind, and, as I take the flowers and see Ed, my first thought is that he isn't nearly as bad as I remember him. In fact, apart from the disgusting moustache, he looks rather nice, really, and we stand there and sort of grin at one another because I'm not sure whether to kiss him or whether that would be too forward, and in the end he leans forward and gives me a kiss on the cheek and says that I look lovely.

I twirl around and he hands me the flowers and of course I invite him in. He stands in the living room and looks around and doesn't actually say anything, doesn't say how lovely it is, how clean, how pristine, which is a bit strange because most people, when they come to your house for the first time, compliment it out of politeness, even if they hate it.

I take the flowers and dig out a jug, which is the only thing I've got left since I've used up my one vase for the flowers I bought myself earlier, and as I arrange them Ed stands there rather awkwardly, so I try to make small talk with him.

'Did you find it all right?' I say, for want of something better.

'I got a bit lost,' he says. 'It's not really my neck of the woods.'

'Where do you live?'

'Regent's Park.'

'Oh, really? Whereabouts?'

'Do you know the park?'

I nod.

'Hanover Terrace.'

Jesus Christ! Hanover Terrace! That's one of those huge sweeping Regency Nash terraces that sweeps along the side of the park next to the mosque. I once met someone whose parents live there, and I know that the houses are enormous, and each has its own little mews house at the end of the garden. But maybe Ed has a flat there, maybe it's not as impressive as I think.

'Do you have a flat?'

'Er, no, actually. I have a house.'

'So you've got one of those little mews houses too?'

'Yes,' he laughs. 'But I still haven't figured out quite what to do with it. So how come you live here, Libby?'

'What, in Ladbroke Grove?'

'Yes.'

'It's the only place I can afford,' I laugh, and wait for him to smile, but he doesn't. He looks horrified.

'But it's not very safe,' he says finally. 'I don't think I'd be happy living here.'

'It's fine,' I say. 'You get used to it, and I quite like the fact that there's such a mixture of people, there's always something going on. And it's a great place to score drugs.' I can't help this last comment, it just sort of comes out and I don't know what it is but something about him being so straight makes me want to shock him.

It works.

'You take drugs?' Now he looks completely disgusted.

'I'm joking.'

'Oh.' And then, thankfully, he starts laughing. 'Hilarious,' he says. 'You're ever so funny, Libby.'

I shrug and smile, and then the flowers are in the jug and the jug is on my mantelpiece, and we're ready to go.

'Libby, I didn't say this before but you really are looking absolutely beautiful tonight.'

'Thank you.' And thank God I've learned to be gracious about receiving compliments. For years I'd say things like, 'What? In this old thing?' but now I accept compliments like the sophisticated woman I'm trying so hard to be.

'And I particularly like the scarf,' he says. 'It's beautiful.'

'What? This old thing?' I couldn't help it. It just came out.

'Is it silk?'

I nod.

'I thought so. Shall we go?'

So we walk out the front door and I can't help but grin when I see his Porsche – a midnight-blue Porsche Carrera, which would have been a convertible had I had anything to do with it, but hell, cars can always be changed, and it's still a beautiful, wonderful, sexy car.

And not only that. Ed walks round to my side first, opens the door and waits until I get in before closing it gently, and I almost want to hug myself because I can't believe I'm sitting in a Porsche with one of the most eligible men in Britain, and Jesus, what the hell did I put up with Nick for when I could have had this all along?

'I've booked a table at the River Café,' he says. 'Is that all right?'

All right? All right? It's fantastic because I haven't been – it's far too expensive for my meagre pockets – and I've heard all about it and it's the best possible choice he could have made. Plus, and this is important, it's not too straight or stuffy, in fact it's pretty damn trendy, and I think I would have been extremely upset if we'd ended up somewhere too grown up.

'I really wanted to take you to Marco Pierre White's restaurant, but I couldn't get a table,' he admits. 'I tried begging, but they were fully booked.'

'That's fine,' I say. 'The River Café is perfect. I haven't been and I really want to go.'

'Oh, good.' He smiles at me. 'I was so worried you wouldn't like it. Shall I put some music on?'

'Definitely,' I say approvingly, reaching for the CDs stacked in the glove compartment. 'You can always tell what a man's like by the music he listens to and the books he reads.'

Ed laughs. 'So what can you tell about me?'

I pull out the CDs and flick through. Oh dear. Opera and classical music. Lots and lots of opera. Wagner. Donizetti. Offenbach. Bizet. Oh God. I rifle through, praying that there's something I know, I don't even mind if it's something I don't particularly like, something like, say, Elton John or Billy Joel, but no. Nothing. So I pretend his question was a rhetorical one.

'What would you like me to put on?' Ed says.

'Well, actually,' I say, deciding to bite the bullet and be completely honest. 'I'm not really that into classical music.'

'Oh.' There's a silence. 'So what kind of music do you listen to?'

'Pretty much anything and everything,' I laugh. 'Except classical and opera.'

'But why not?'

'I don't know. I suppose I never listened to it when I was young, so I never developed an ear for it.'

'How about this one, then?' he says, reaching over and taking a CD out of my hand. '*L'Elisir d'amore*,' he says, in a perfect Italian accent, the *r*'s rolling off his tongue. 'I think you'll like this.'

He puts it on and looks at me for approval, and what can I say? It's all right, really, quite melodic, but it's opera, for God's sake, but I can't tell him this, so I just smile and tell him he made a good choice and that I like it.

And then as we stop at some traffic lights I turn my head and notice that in the car next to us – an old Peugeot 106, just in case you're interested – are two girls my age, and they're both looking enviously at the Porsche and at me, and I smile to myself and sink a little deeper into the seat because I'm quite enjoying this. Despite the music.

So I decide that I'm going to make an effort with Ed, even though I suspect he really isn't my type, but surely he could grow to be my type? Surely if he brings me flowers I could grow to like him? Fancy him? Couldn't I? I sneak a peek at him driving and feel a wave of disappointment rush over me, because he's not half as gorgeous as Nick, but then Nick isn't here, and Ed is.

'Tell me about your job, Libby,' he says, concentrating on the road, but trying to be polite.

'Not much to tell,' I say. 'I work in PR on people like Sean Moore.'

'Who?'

I look at him in amazement. 'Sean Moore. You must know who he is. He's the biggest heart-throb since, well, since Angus Deayton.'

'Oh, ha ha. I know who Angus Deayton is! He's the chap on that programme, isn't he? The news one.'

'*Have I Got News for You.*'

Ed nods vigorously. 'Yes, that's the one. Very funny show. Always try and catch it if I'm in on a Friday night.'

'And are you usually in on a Friday night?'

'Not usually,' he laughs. 'Most Friday nights I'm working late.'

'Don't you ever take time off?'

'To be honest with you I suppose I throw myself into work because I haven't met the right woman yet.'

Now this is a first. I can't believe he's telling me this on our first date. And I'm eager to hear more.

'You mean you want to settle down?'

'Definitely,' he says. 'Absolutely. That's why I bought the house in Hanover Terrace. I thought it would be a perfect home for a family and children, but at the moment I'm still rattling around in it all by myself.'

This is getting better and better. The most eligible bachelor in Britain is desperate to get married and he's taking me out! He's with me! And I can't believe his honesty, the fact that he's willing to admit he wants to get married, the fact that for the first time in my life I'm on a date with a man who doesn't appear to be allergic to commitment.

Although to be honest, I'm not sure about this whole scared of commitment business. I think it's become too handy, a useful phrase that men can bandy about whenever they feel like being assholes. And sure, I do believe there are some men who are genuinely terrified of commitment, but there aren't that many, and for the most part I think it's that they haven't met the right woman yet. Because if a man, no matter how scared he professed to be, met the woman of his dreams, he wouldn't want to let her go, would he? And sure, he might not want to actually get married, but if he were madly in love and risked losing her, he'd do it, wouldn't he?

That's what I think, anyway.

And I'm so used to playing games with men, to pretending that I'm this hard, tough, career woman who's very happy being single and really doesn't mind, no, loves having relationships which involve seeing one another twice a week if you're lucky, that I'm not quite sure what to do with someone this honest.

I decide to ask more questions. To see whether he really is for real.

'So how come you haven't married?'

'I don't know. I thought I had met the right woman, but then it turned out I hadn't, she wasn't the right one. You see, I suppose I'm quite old-fashioned. I don't understand these career girls, and yes, I think it's fine for girls to have a bit of independence, but I'm really looking for a wife. Someone who'll look after me and our children.'

'So you wouldn't want her to work once she got married?'

He shakes his head. 'Do you think that's too much to ask?'

'No,' I say firmly. 'I absolutely agree.'

'Do you?'

'Yes. I think it's appalling that women continue their careers once they've had children. A mother ought to be at home with the children. I know too many women whose kids are completely neglected because they seem to be more interested in working late at the office.'

This last bit isn't completely true, but what the hell, I know I'm on the right track and Ed's so excited he can hardly contain himself.

'Libby,' he says, taking his eyes off the road and turning to me. 'I'm jolly glad I met you. Jolly glad.' And his grin's so wide for a second I think it's going to burst off his face.

When we get to the River Café, Ed walks up to the girl standing behind the desk at the front and says, 'Hello!' in such an effusive tone I figure he must know her, but she stands there smiling awkwardly at him, which makes me think that he's this over-exuberant all the time. 'Ed McMahon!' he says. 'Table for two!'

'Oh, yes,' she says, scanning her list. 'Follow me.'

'I hope it's a good table!' he says to her. 'I asked for the best table in the restaurant. Are we by the window?'

'I'm afraid not,' she says. 'But you're as close as we could get you,' and she leads us to a table in the middle of the room.

'Oh, jolly good!' Ed says loudly in his public school accent, and I cringe slightly as I notice how other people in the restaurant are turning to look at where this voice is coming from. '*Très bien!*' he then says, in a very, very bad French accent, and I can't help it, I start giggling, because if nothing else he's certainly a character.

'Umm, you speak French?' I say, as we sit down.

'*Mais bien sûr!*' he says, and it comes out, 'May bienne soor,' and I sit there and wish he'd shut up, and then I mentally slap myself for being so nasty, because he's just a bit eccentric, that's all, and it's quite endearing in a weird sort of way, it simply takes a bit of getting used to. That's all.

And you know what? I have a really nice time. Ed's quite funny. He tells me lots of stories about investment banking, and admittedly a large part of each story goes completely over my head because investment banking is not exactly a subject I know an awful lot about, but he giggles as he tells them, and it's quite cute, not to mention infectious, and I find myself giggling with him and I'm quite surprised at how well this evening's going.

But just because he's good company doesn't mean I fancy him, but then maybe fancying someone isn't what it's all about? Maybe I've been wrong in waiting for that sweep you off your feet feeling, the feeling I had with Nick. And, let's face it, it didn't exactly work with Nick, did it, so maybe I've been looking for the wrong thing.

Here I am sitting with a man who's rich, charming, honest and wants to get married. Most women would kill to be sitting where I am right now, and okay, so he's not really my type, but maybe that could grow?

And as I sit I allow myself to imagine what it would be like kissing him. I picture his face moving closer to mine, and then, yuck! Oh God! That moustache! Yuck, yuck yuck!

'Do you cook?' I'm brought back to earth by the sound of Ed's voice, and I try to push the thought of him kissing me out of my head. Unfortunately, I don't manage to, but it lodges somewhere near the back, which is okay for now.

'I love cooking,' I say. 'But only for other people. I can never be bothered to cook for myself, but my ideal evening would be cooking for my close friends.'

'Gosh!' he says. 'You can cook too! Libby, is there anything you're not good at?'

'Sex?'

'Oh ha ha!' He rocks back in his chair, gulping with laughter. 'Hilarious!' And I sit and smile, wondering who on earth this man is, but not in a bad way, in more of an intrigued way, and the bill arrives, which is always a bit of an awkward time because I'm never too sure whether to offer, but this time I decide not to because, after all, Ed did say he was old-fashioned, and anyway with the amount of wine we've had to drink, plus the champagne he ordered at the beginning, I couldn't afford it even if I wanted to. So I sit back and watch as Ed pulls out a platinum American Express card – platinum! I've never met anyone with a platinum American Express card before! – and when the waitress takes it away I lean forward and thank him for a lovely evening.

'Libby,' he says earnestly. 'The pleasure was all mine. I think you're fantastic!' And I smile because it feels like a long time since anyone's thought that about me, and I'm not sure whether anyone's really felt that way about me, ever. I'm used to being the chaser, the one to fall head over heels in love. I'm the one who's usually sitting there thinking that they're fantastic, although I'd never dare say it for fear of scaring them off, and here's someone who not only thinks it, but has the balls to say it!

I think I could get used to this, and quite frankly if I can't have Nick, then perhaps I can settle for having someone who completely adores me. Even though he hardly even knows me.

We get back in his car and on the way back we have that whole relationship talk where they ask you why you're single, when your last relationship was and what the longest relationship you've ever had has been, and I say we have that talk but actually that's slightly wrong – I'm so busy trying to think of how to avoid saying I'm a complete nightmare in relationships because I'm so needy, paranoid and insecure that I forget to ask him anything at all.

But he doesn't seem to mind. In fact, he doesn't say anything as I tell him that I haven't met the right man yet, that I drifted apart from all my previous boyfriends, and that my longest relationship has been a year (well, okay then, nine months, but he doesn't have to know that, does he?). I do mention Nick, but I brush over it, brush over the pain that it caused, is still causing, and

I do my best to be light-hearted about it, to say it meant nothing.

Ed nods thoughtfully and if I didn't know better I'd say he was definitely sizing me up for wife material, but maybe that's a bit ridiculous of me because this is only our first date.

Do I ask him in for coffee? I'm not sure I want him to come in for coffee. I'm not entirely sure how to deal with this whole scenario, but luckily Ed pulls up outside my flat and doesn't switch the engine off so I assume he'll be whizzing home.

'Hang on,' he says, leaping out of the car. 'I'll come and get you out.' And he runs around the car and opens the door for me, and, against my better judgement perhaps, I wish my mother could see me now!

'May I see you again?' he says and, without even thinking about whether I really want to, I find myself saying yes.

'Are you free tomorrow?' he says eagerly.

'I'm afraid not,' I say, because okay, I'm only going to my parents, but tomorrow feels a bit too soon, and I know that if I were completely crazy about him I'd say of course tomorrow would be fine, but I'm still not entirely sure how I feel about this. Physically he is so not my type that I decide to give myself a few days' breathing space to think about this one.

'I could do next week, though,' I say. 'Tuesday?'

'Marvellous!' he says, without looking at his diary. 'I'll pick you up at eight, how does that sound?'

'Fine,' I say. 'And thank you, again, for a lovely evening.'

Ed walks me to my front door, and I turn awkwardly as I put my key in the lock, wondering exactly how to say goodbye, and even as I turn he's leaning down to give me two kisses on each cheek.

'Again, Libby,' he says, turning to walk back towards the car, 'the pleasure was all mine.'

Chapter Sixteen

I don't mean to say anything, really I don't, but my mother is banging on about me being single again, and before I know it it just slips out that last night I had a date with Ed McMahon, and my mother being my mother knows exactly who Ed McMahon is, and she's so shocked all the colour practically drains from her face.

'Not Ed McMahon the finance person?'

'Yes, Mum,' I say, and I can't help the hint of pride in my voice. 'Ed McMahon the finance person.'

For one ghastly minute I think she's about to hug me, but thankfully she doesn't.

'How on earth did you meet him?' she says.

'I met him at Mezzo,' I say. 'And he took my number, and he's been calling ever since.'

'Mezzo?' she says in awe, because my mother, despite never actually leaving suburbia, dreams of doing so on a regular basis, and consequently reads every style magazine on the shelves. She is what we in PR would call aspirational. 'What's it like?'

'It's fine.' I shrug. 'Big.'

'And you met Ed McMahon there? Well, Libby, all I can say is this time don't blow it.'

'I beg your pardon?'

'You heard me. Don't mess this one up. Ed McMahon's very, very rich.'

'God, Mum,' I say in disgust, 'is that all you ever think about?'

*

And the funny thing is that all day Sunday, when I think about my evening with Ed, I find myself smiling, and it's not a lustful, falling-head-over-heels type of smile, but an I-had-quite-a-nice-time-and-I'm-surprised kind of smile, and although I wouldn't go as far as saying I can't wait until Tuesday, I would say that I'm quite looking forward to it because the man's definitely got something, I'm simply not entirely sure what it is.

And I feel quite grown up about this. Sure, the fact that Ed's in his late thirties means I have to be mature when I'm with him anyway, but I feel incredibly grown up at being able to go out with someone like him, though I don't feel all those things that I did with Nick.

Even the way my mother already seems to be planning the wedding day doesn't rile me. In fact, I think it's quite funny, although I'm not planning on marrying Ed.

Obviously.

'So tell me what he's like?'

I have my mother's undivided attention.

'He's nice.'

'What do you mean, he's nice? There must be something else you can say about him.'

'Okay. He's nice, and . . .' – I watch her face closely – 'he drives a Porsche.'

She practically swoons before regaining her composure. 'A Porsche? What was it like, being driven in a Porsche?'

'Comfortable, Mum. What do you think?'

'So where did he take you?'

'The River Café.'

'Ooh. That's meant to be very expensive. What did you have?'

I tell her, and quite enjoy that she hangs on to my every word, and for once I'm getting as much attention as Olly.

'And does he want to see you again?'

I nod. 'We're going out on Tuesday.'

'That's so exciting! What are you going to wear? For heaven's sake don't wear one of those awful trouser suits you always wear. Wear something feminine. Haven't you got any nice dresses?'

I knew it was too good to last. Here we go again, Libby can't do anything right.

'My trouser suits happen to be designer, actually,' I say indignantly. 'And there's nothing wrong with them. Everyone wears them.'

'But men like feminine women,' she says defiantly. 'They like to see a nice pair of legs.'

I shake my head in amazement. 'If I didn't know better I'd say you were still living in the 1950s.'

'That's as may be,' she says with a sniff. 'But I know what men like, and I know they don't like hard, masculine, career girls.'

Before I get a chance to tell her how ridiculous she's being, the phone rings. Talk about being saved by the bell.

'Olly!' she says. 'Hello, darling. How are you?'

I stretch and put my feet on the coffee table as I flick on the TV.

'Hang on. Off!' she says to me, brushing my feet from the table, so just to piss her off I turn the volume up to drown her out.

'Libby!' she shouts. 'Turn that down. It's your brother. From Manchester.'

As if I didn't know, but I turn it down.

'How's my gorgeous boy, then?' she says, as I grimace

at the TV set. 'Oh, Dad and I are fine, but we're missing you. When are you coming down to see us? I see. No, no, don't worry, I know how busy you are. How's the series coming along? You are clever, Olly!'

'You are clever, Olly!' I mimic to myself in what I mean to be a whisper, except she hears and shoots me a filthy look.

'Your sister's here,' she says. 'Yes. Hang on. All right, my darling. I'll speak to you this week. Big kiss from Dad and I,' and she passes the phone to me.

'Hey, Oll,' I say distractedly, because I'm watching some disgusting outfits being paraded up and down a catwalk on *The Clothes Show.*

'Hey, big sis. How's it going?'

'Fine. You?'

'Yeah. Good.'

'How are your friends?'

'What?'

'You know, Oll, your friends.'

'Oh!' He starts laughing. 'You mean Carolyn?'

'Mmm hmm.'

'She's really nice. Can't quite believe it, I just really like being with her.'

'That's great, Oll.' I ignore my mum looking quizzically at me, doubtless trying to work out what we're talking about.

'How 'bout you? How's Nick?'

'Finished. Kaput. Over.'

'Oh, Libby, I'm sorry. He seemed like a really nice bloke. What happened?'

I look at my mum, who's now pretending to be immersed in dusting the side tables, but I know her ears are fully alert.

'Tell you later.'

He laughs. 'Mum's in the room, then?'

'As ever.'

'Anyone new on the scene?'

'Kind of. Had dinner with this guy last night, and he's nice, but I'm not sure he's my type.'

My mother raises an eyebrow.

'Anyway,' I continue, 'we'll see.'

'Okay. You should come up and stay here,' he says. 'Seriously, it would be so nice to spend some time with you. I haven't seen you properly, just you and me, for ages.'

'Yeah.' I nod. 'That'd be great. I'll check my diary and let you know.'

We say goodbye and I get up to go.

'What would be really nice?' My mother's pretending she's not really interested.

'I might go and stay with Olly,' I say. 'He just invited me.'

'Oh, what a good idea!' she says, suddenly beaming. 'Maybe Dad and I will come too, we could all get the train up there together. A proper family outing!'

'Hmph.' I shrug. 'Maybe.'

On Monday morning Jo buzzes me from reception.

'Jesus Christ!' she says. 'You'd better come out here.'

'Why?'

'Just come out here! Now!'

I walk through the office to the reception desk, and there, on the counter, is a forest. Well, okay, not quite a forest, but an arrangement of flowers that's so big it's threatening to take over the room.

'Jesus Christ!' I echo. 'These are for me?'

'They certainly are,' she says, the grin stretching across her face. 'Come on, come on. Open the card. Who are they from?'

I open the card with fingers that are shaking ever so slightly, and I suppose a part of me hopes they're from Nick, though I know they won't be, because flowers aren't Nick's style, plus he could never afford something like this. These must have cost a fortune.

'Dearest Libby,' I read out loud. 'Just wanted to thank you for a wonderful evening. Can't wait until Tuesday. With love, Ed.'

'Who the fuck's Ed?'

'Just an admirer,' I say breezily, skipping back into the office with the flowers and loving, loving the admiring glances I get on the way.

And I know this might sound a bit stupid, but I'd quite like to send him something in return, even though I know you're not really supposed to, and it's not because I desperately fancy him, but because he did a nice thing for me and I'd like to repay him somehow.

And I suppose if I did fancy him I wouldn't be able to do this, because I'd be far too busy playing games and playing hard to get. But number one, I don't really care if me sending something to him scares him off, and number two, I'm pretty damn sure it won't anyway. I suppose it's sod's law, isn't it? The ones that like you are never the ones you're interested in, and the ones you like are always the bastards. But Ed's different. I'm not really sure how I feel. I know that I'm not in lust with him, but I also know that I'd like to see him again. I'm just so fed up with being on my own, and Nick may not want me, but Ed certainly does, and that's a bloody nice feeling. So this is why I want to do something for him.

But what?

I go back out to Jo.

'Okay,' I sigh. 'You win. I'll tell you everything if you help me out,' and I do.

'Got it!' she says when I've finally finished, although I didn't give her the long version, I kept it as short as I possibly could. 'Send him a virtual food basket!'

'A what?'

'On the Internet! You can go to these places and send virtual flowers and food baskets, they're amazing. It's a seriously cool thing to do, and you'll probably blow his mind. Hang on. Does he have e-mail?'

'How the hell should I know?'

'Check his business card.'

So I run back and get it, and, sure enough, there at the bottom is his e-mail address.

'Okay,' says Jo. 'Let me just get someone to cover for me, then I'll show you how to do it.'

Ten minutes later Jo's sitting in front of the computer, tapping away, and there it is! A site that shows you pictures of flowers and presents which you can send to people.

'Is this going to cost anything?'

'Nah. Don't be daft. They're virtual, aren't they? That means they're not real.'

She clicks on a picture of a basket stuffed with crisps, cakes and biscuits, then over her shoulder says to me, 'What do you want to say?'

'How about, Dear Ed, thank you for your beautiful flowers. I thought you might be hungry but save the Oreos for me. They're my favourite . . . Looking forward to seeing you on Tuesday. Libby.'

'Love, Libby?' Jo asks, typing in my message.

'Oh, all right then. Love, Libby. So what happens now?'

'You just send it, and they get a message on their e-mail saying they've had a virtual delivery and it gives instructions on where to go to pick up the present.'

'That's amazing. Can I have a go?'

'What? More admirers?'

'Hmm.' Jo stands up and I sit in her place as she wanders back to reception, and ten minutes later I've sent virtual food baskets to Jules, Jamie, Olly and Sal.

Unsurprisingly, Jules calls half an hour later, and she's laughing so hard I can hardly hear her. 'That is fantastic!' she splutters. 'How in the hell did you do that?'

'More to the point, Jules, what are you doing checking your e-mail in the middle of the day? Shouldn't you be interior designing or something?'

'Should be,' she says. 'I was just getting on the Internet to try and find some suppliers of this Spanish furniture I'm looking for. Someone said they had a site on the Web, and my e-mail told me I had a delivery. It's bloody inspired, Libby! I love it!'

I tell her about the flowers and about sending the same basket to Ed, and I can hear her squealing and clapping her hands on the other end of the phone.

'Jesus, Libby!' she says. 'He's going to fall head over heels in love with you! I bet he's never met anyone like you before!'

I bet he hasn't either.

At the end of the day, just before I leave, I check my e-mail, just in case, and sure enough there's a message from EMcMhn@compuserve.com.

'Dearest Libby,' it says. 'I'm now absolutely stuffed!

What a delightful surprise, and I'm so pleased you received the flowers. I must say, no one's ever done anything like that for me before . . . Can hardly wait to see you again. Much love, Ed.'

'Cor,' says Jo, who's standing behind me, reading this over my shoulder. 'Now. He. Is. Keen.'

And I go home with a smile on my face.

I sneaked off early today, to have enough time to get ready, because I want to look good tonight and not necessarily for Ed, more for me, but I could really get used to these flowers and this general feeling of having met someone who could, possibly, adore me.

So it's face pack time, and deep conditioning hair stuff time, and new MAC lipstick time, and anyway, there's nothing wrong in trying to look the best you can possibly look, is there? Plus, Nick never appreciated the designer Libby, and it's bloody nice to dress up again, even though I'm still thinking about Nick, just not quite as often.

And again, tonight, I don't bother with the old razors, because, like Ed as I do, I can't get my head round anything physical happening between us, and even if it were to happen, there's no way it would happen tonight, so that's why, underneath my trousers (yup, trousers; my mother can go to hell), my legs are again as hairy as, well, as someone who hasn't shaved them for a week or so.

I'd like to run with this one, as it were. Not jump into bed, or jump into a relationship, but keep seeing him and see what happens. Whether I might grow to like him, whether he might turn out to be someone special, whether I could actually persuade him to shave off that bloody moustache.

And I'm pretty damned pleased with how I look tonight. A pale grey trouser suit with little pearl earrings that are really not my style at all, but they were a present from my mum a couple of birthdays ago, and flat cream suede shoes.

God. If my mother could see me now! I look like the epitome of a sophisticated young woman. Apart from the trousers, that is. I almost laugh at the sight of myself because I look more like a Sloane Ranger than Princess Diana in her early days, but this look fits with Ed, and it's quite good fun, dressing up. I sort of feel a bit like a child playing a big game. Let's pretend to be sophisticated, smart and mature. What fun! Hey ho! Jesus.

The phone rings just as I've finished applying a final coat of clear nail polish. Couldn't have gone for my beloved blues or greens – far too trendy for Ed.

'What have you eaten today?' Naturally, it's Jules.

'Nothing for breakfast. A milk chocolate Hobnob at about eleven o'clock, d'you know how many calories they are?'

'I think they're about seventy-eight.'

'Oh shit. Anyway. A Caesar salad for lunch, and an apple halfway through the afternoon.'

'That's good. You've been really good. The biscuit wasn't bad, not if you compare it to what I've had today.'

'Go on.'

'Okay. For breakfast I had a huge bowl of cornflakes. Huge. Really. Disgusting. Then at about ten o'clock I was hungry again, so I had three chocolate Bourbons. At lunch I went out with a client and had grilled vegetables swimming in olive oil to start with, then a huge plate of pasta in a creamy sauce, and then we shared a crème brûlée but she hardly ate anything, I had practically the whole thing.'

Jules is such a bloody liar. I know exactly what she's like. She probably had a tiny bowl of cornflakes. No Bourbons. Plain vegetables. A couple of mouthfuls of pasta and a taste of the crème brûlée. There's no way Jules would be as slim as she is if she really ate what she says she does. I know there are times when she's telling the truth, but I also know that most of the time she's so bloody fat-conscious she only picks at food, doesn't really eat anything. She's more than a little obsessed, which is why we have so many food phone calls a day. I don't mind, really I don't, but I wish she'd stop thinking about it quite as much as she does.

Although I suppose I'm not that much better.

But she encourages me.

Not that I wouldn't think about it at all if we didn't talk about it.

But I wouldn't think about it as much . . .

'I'm not going to have any dinner,' she says firmly. 'That's it for today. And tomorrow I'm going on a diet.'

'Oh, for God's sake, Jules!'

'What? What?'

'Never mind.' There's no point in telling her she doesn't need to lose weight, if anything she needs to put it on, because she won't believe me. The number of times we've gone out and the first thing she says to me is, 'Do I look fat?' and I look at her skinny, waif-like frame and say, 'No! Don't be ridiculous,' and she says, 'Can't you see it on my face? There? Look.' And she taps a non-existent double chin and spends the rest of the day, or evening, smoothing this invisible double chin away.

God. What it is to be a woman.

'So what are you wearing?'

I tell her.

'Mmm. Very sophis.'

'I know. It's not really me, but I couldn't turn up in something dead trendy or he'd faint.'

'You know what you are?'

'What?'

'You're a chameleon girlfriend.'

'A what?'

'I was reading an article about it. It's about women who change their image, their hobbies, pretty much everything, depending on the man they're with.'

I wish I didn't have to say this, but as usual Jules is absolutely right, and I've always done it. I've tried to change myself depending on the man of the moment, and I know it's wrong, even as I'm doing it I know it's wrong, but I can't seem to help it.

Jules has never done it, she's never had to, and once we sat down and tried to figure out why I do it – although we didn't have a name for it at the time – and the only reason we could come up with was low self-esteem.

Jules has decided that because Olly was the one who had all the glory, I never think that anyone's going to like me for myself, and that's why I always try and become someone else. If you're confused, trust me, no one's more confused about it than me.

'So tell me something else I didn't know,' I say bitterly, because, much as I love Jules, I suppose I'm slightly envious of her confidence.

'Don't take it like that,' she says, sounding wounded. 'It's fine. I'm quite jealous of it, in fact. You can wake up in the morning and think, hmm, who am I going to be today?'

I can't help it. I laugh.

'I wish I could be more like you sometimes,' she says, and I nearly fall off my chair.

'Jules! You're nuts! You'd like to be single with no self-esteem and a radar that warns off all decent men and only attracts the bastards?'

'Ed's not a bastard.'

'Not yet. Anyway, he's not good-looking enough to be a bastard.'

'And Jon was good-looking?'

'Okay, okay, so he wasn't your type. But I thought he was good-looking.'

'Listen, Jamie's back, I gotta go. Have a fantastic evening, and call me first thing.'

'Thanks, sweetie. Bye.'

'Oh, Libby?'

I put the receiver back to my ear.

'Don't do anything I wouldn't do!' and, cackling, she puts down the phone.

Now this is getting ridiculous. The doorbell rings, I open the door, and once again Ed's standing on the doorstep holding a huge bouquet of roses.

'Ed,' I say, loving this attention but not wanting to get too used to it, to take it for granted. 'You must stop buying me flowers. It's beginning to look like a florist's in here. I'm running out of vases!'

'Oh. Er. Sorry, Libby.' He looks crestfallen and I feel like a bitch.

'No, no, don't be silly. It's just that you're spoiling me, but they're beautiful. Thank you.'

He comes in and stands in the living room, as I open lots of cupboard doors, hoping that there's a vase I've forgotten about. In the end I pull a milk bottle out of the fridge and empty the milk down the sink.

And although I have to cut down the stems by about a foot, the roses actually look pretty damn nice in a milk bottle. It must be the mix of the luxury and the everyday.

A bit like me and Ed, really.

Chapter Seventeen

We go to the Ivy, and Ed seems to know an awful lot of people in there, and I'm really beginning to enjoy being with this man who's so sophisticated and yet so naïve at the same time. Because he is naïve. He's somehow slightly gauche, awkward, and it's probably his most endearing quality.

He orders champagne and, as we raise our glasses, I hear a familiar swooping voice.

'Libby! Darling!' And I turn around and there, resplendent in a tiny black dress, is Amanda. I give her the obligatory air kisses, and then she just stands there, looking at me, then at Ed, and I introduce them.

And it's quite extraordinary, because Ed stands up to shake her hand, and Amanda starts simpering like an idiot, fluttering her eyelashes and being all coy, and I'm really quite embarrassed for her, and I breathe a sigh of relief when she finally leaves.

'Who was that?'

'Amanda Baker. She's a television presenter.'

'I see. Is she famous?'

'Not as famous as she'd like to be.'

'Ha ha! That's very good, Libby. How do you know her?'

'I do her PR.'

'So you could make her famous, then?'

'It's sort of catch-22. You can't be famous without being written about, and nobody wants to write about someone who isn't famous. But I'm trying.'

'I don't watch much television, that's probably why I didn't recognize her. I only ever seem to watch the news.'

'What do you do if you're at home at night?'

'Work usually. Listen to music.'

'So if I told you I was in love with Dr Doug Ross it wouldn't mean anything to you?'

His face falls. 'Who's Dr Doug Ross?'

'Never mind,' I laugh. 'You wouldn't understand.'

The food's delicious, the champagne's delicious, and I'm loving sitting here star-spotting, although every time I whisper that another celebrity has just walked in, Ed stares at them in confusion, and it's quite amazing that he really doesn't have a clue who these people are. I mean, for God's sake, some of the people that have walked in here tonight are the biggest stars of stage and screen, and Ed's never seen them before in his life!

'Libby,' he says, when we're waiting for our coffees. 'I think you're extraordinary. I've never met anyone like you.'

'Thank you. Really? How?' I know you're not supposed to fish for compliments, but I can't help it, and after Nick I deserve to have my ego inflated a little bit.

'You're just so bright, and sparky, and full of life. I really enjoy being with you. And . . .' He pauses.

'And?' I prompt.

'Well, I'm not sure whether I should say this yet, and it probably sounds ridiculous, but I really like you.'

'That doesn't sound ridiculous.'

'No. I mean I really like you.'

'I like you too.'

'Good. And I think we might have something special here.'

I smile. I mean, what could I say? The guy hardly knows me.

'I thought you might like to see my house,' he says, on the way back.

'I'd love to!' which is true, I want to know more about him, more about where he lives, how he lives. I want to nose around his home and look for clues about who he is, whether I could be happy with him.

Please don't think I'm sounding ridiculous. It's not that I've decided he's The One or anything, but I do have a worrying tendency to, how shall I put it, plan ahead. The number of times I've sat in bed dreaming of my marriage to someone I've had one date with. And, although I don't fancy Ed, it's quite good fun dreaming about it anyway. To be honest, he wouldn't figure that strongly in this particular daydream. Nah, when I day-dream about getting married I'm far more concerned about the dress, the location, the bridesmaids. The groom tends to be a faceless person, he's really not that important.

So while I'm not planning the wedding just yet, I'd still like to see his home.

We pull up outside a sweeping terrace, and the thing I find most strange about where he lives is not the size or the grandeur, but the fact that someone his age lives there at all. I know he said he bought it as a family home, but it seems crazy to live somewhere that feels so middle-aged when you're still relatively young. And anyway, if I got married I'd want to buy a new home together, start afresh; I wouldn't want to move into the place he already lived in.

The hallway floor is one of those black and white marble numbers, and I can see that Ed's incredibly proud of his house as he flings open the doors to the most spectacular drawing room I've ever seen. Huge, airy, with stunning original mouldings on the walls and ceiling, it's completely empty.

'Umm, have you recently moved in?' I ask.

'No. I've lived here for two years!' he says.

'What about furniture?'

'I've never got around to buying any,' he says, shrugging. 'I suppose I'm waiting for my wife to come in and redecorate.'

'But you could have got an interior designer to do it.'

'I did!' he says indignantly, pointing at the swagged, pelmeted curtains.

'Oh. Right,' I say.

He leads me upstairs to his bedroom. Immaculate and huge, it leads into an enormous dressing room, lined wall to wall with cupboards, and then through to an en suite bathroom.

Next door is his study, and upstairs there's a gym, a sauna and more empty bedrooms. And more. And more. They seem to stretch on for ever, and I honestly feel as if I've stumbled into a ghost house, because it's quite clear that none of these rooms is ever used. There's no warmth in this house, it's a museum, a showpiece, and I start to feel increasingly uncomfortable here.

We go downstairs to the basement. A country-style kitchen, and I breathe a sigh of relief because next to the kitchen there are sofas, and french doors leading on to a garden. Judging by the amount of books and papers piled around the room, this is the place he lives in.

And it really is quite cosy. Not perhaps exactly as I'd

do it. I'd get rid of those dried flowers hanging from the ceiling for starters, but it's not at all bad.

Ed goes into the kitchen to make some coffee, and I sit and look around the room, deciding what I'd change if I lived here. I'd have the sofas re-covered in a bright blue and yellow chequered fabric, I'd get rid of that revolting limed kitchen table and put in an old scrubbed pine one, I'd . . .

'Do you like it?' Ed interrupts my thoughts.

'Your house?'

He nods.

'I think it's spectacular,' I say, because it undoubtedly is, but I decide against telling him it's a bit like a morgue. 'But don't you get a bit lonely rattling around in this huge place by yourself?'

'Yes,' he says, suddenly looking like a little boy lost. 'At times I do.'

And he looks so sweet I want to hug him.

He comes to sit next to me on the sofa, and the air suddenly feels a lot more oppressive, and I know he's going to kiss me, but I'm not sure I want him to. I try to avoid looking at him, keeping my eyes fixed firmly on my coffee, because I can feel he's staring at me, and I'm praying, Jesus how I'm praying, that he doesn't put his coffee cup down.

He puts his coffee cup down.

And he sneaks an arm around the back of the sofa, not yet touching me, and I want to run out of there screaming because at this moment I know as an absolute certainty that I don't want to kiss him.

This, it has to be said, is a bit of a new feeling for me. If I bother going out with someone again after a first date, then it's because I fancy them, and I spend the rest of the second date praying they'll kiss me and wondering how they'll do it.

I remember Jon didn't kiss me until date number six. On date number four I was convinced it was going to happen. We'd been to the cinema, he dropped me home, and even after he declined coffee – he said he had an early meeting – I sat in the car with my face raised expectantly. He just smiled and kissed me on each cheek.

Two dates later he cooked me dinner at his flat, and after dinner I was standing in the kitchen helping him wash up, wondering whether I'd completely misjudged the situation and thinking he was only interested in me as a friend, when suddenly he grabbed me and started kissing me, and minutes later we'd sunk to the kitchen floor in a frenzy of passion.

And I remember how desperate I was for him to kiss me, so why am I so desperate for Ed not to kiss me now?

And more to the point, what the hell am I supposed to do? Suddenly, and I'm not really sure how this happens, suddenly he's kissing me, and I wish to God I could tell you that it was lovely, that my stomach turned over with lust, that I suddenly started to fancy him . . .

It was revolting.

You know how you forget what bad kissers are like when you haven't encountered a bad kisser for years? I'd forgotten. This was like the snogs of my teenage years, with spotty boys who were trying to be grown men, who didn't have a clue.

And I wish I could pinpoint exactly what it was that was so revolting, but I can't. Too much tongue. Too much saliva. Too much moustache. Yuck. Not nice at all. So I pull away and resist the urge to wipe my mouth with my sleeve, and I think that nothing, nothing will make me kiss him again.

Not even the Porsche.

But I don't mind cuddling him, and he puts his arms round me and that's quite nice, at least it would be if I wasn't so tense at the prospect of him kissing me again.

'Libby,' he says after nuzzling my neck for a while. 'I think I'd better take you home.'

What? What? He's supposed to ask me to stay the night and I'm supposed to turn him down. What is this? He's supposed to be dying of lust for me, every fibre in his body aching for me. He's not supposed to want to take me home.

I know, I know. Never mind the fact that I don't want him, he's still supposed to want me. But at least it means I won't have to kiss him again.

We get in the car, and this time Ed keeps a hand on my thigh all the way back, but the funny thing is it's not sexual somehow, more proprietorial, and, although I wish he'd take it off, I'm not quite sure how to tell him, so I do an awful lot of shuffling around and crossing and uncrossing my legs, but the hand stays.

'When can I see you again?' he says, walking me to the front door of my flat and insisting on holding my hand.

'Well, I'm a bit busy this week,' I say.

'Oh.' His face falls. 'Actually, I wanted to invite you to a ball.'

'A ball? What kind of ball?' My mother's voice echoes in my head: go out with him because you never know what his friends are like.

'Some friends of mine in the country are having their

annual ball. I think you'd really like them, and I'd love you to come.'

'When is it?'

He tells me it's the weekend after next, and I tell him that I'd love to come.

'Do you have anything to wear?'

'I'm sure I've got something.'

'Look, I hope you don't think this too forward of me, but I'd really like to buy you something special. Would you allow me to?'

What am I, stupid? As if I'm going to turn this down.

'If you're sure,' I say.

'Absolutely. Why don't we go shopping on Saturday?'

My brain starts ticking quickly. Shopping. Daytime. No public displays of affection, therefore no kissing.

'That sounds lovely.'

'Great! I'll see you on Saturday.' His arms encircle my waist and his head moves in again, so I give him a few pecks on the lips, which aren't too bad really, and then with a mysterious smile I move away and go into my flat.

Quite well handled, if I say so myself.

But once I'm home, back in the safety of my flat, I start thinking about that kiss, and then, I can't help it, I start thinking about Nick kissing me, about how it made me feel, and that leads to other memories of Nick, and before I know it I'm sitting on my sofa with tears streaming down my cheeks, and Jesus Christ, haven't there been enough tears recently to last me a lifetime?

I miss him. I can't help it. I just miss him. And Ed, nice as he is, isn't Nick and never will be.

But it's funny how sometimes a little cry makes you feel a whole hell of a lot better, and when I've finished I feel sort of resigned. I know that it's over with Nick, and I know that I don't feel the same about Ed, but maybe love doesn't have to be about lust, maybe I could learn to love Ed. Maybe.

'Nah. I don't think there's any point.'

'But he's so nice, Jules! Maybe it could grow.'

'Libby, when he kissed you, you felt sick. What could grow, exactly?'

'I don't know,' I huff. 'Maybe I need to get used to his kissing.'

'Then go for it.'

'God, you're no help at all.'

'Well, what am I supposed to say? I tell you not to bother and you say he's really nice, so I tell you to keep seeing him and you tell me I'm not helping. I can't win with you.'

'Sorry,' I grumble, curling my feet up under me on the sofa in Jules's kitchen.

'So what's going on now?' Jamie walks in, bends down and gives me a kiss on the cheek before ruffling Jules's hair as he heads to put the kettle on, and something about this affectionate gesture suddenly makes me feel incredibly lonely.

I want this too. I want someone who will adore me so much that they cannot even walk past me without touching me in some way. I want someone who will worship me, even when – as Jules is now – I'm sitting around in fluffy slippers with no make-up on and hair scraped back.

I'm sick and tired of being on my own. Most of the time I'm fine. Some of the time I even quite enjoy it. But at this precise moment in time I'm fed up with it. I've had enough. I'm twenty-seven years old and I deserve to be with someone. I deserve to live in a beautiful house, not a grotty little flat in Ladbroke Grove. I deserve to be with someone who brings me flowers and buys me presents. I deserve to be in a couple, someone's other half.

'More man problems?' Jamie says from the other end of the kitchen.

'Naturally,' I say. 'Isn't it always?'

Jamie brings three mugs of coffee over and sits down. 'Jules said you'd been out with Ed McMahon. Bit of a catch, I'd say.'

'I know,' I moan. 'But I don't fancy him.'

'Ah,' says Jamie. 'That could be a problem. But he's meant to be a nice guy. Maybe you need to give it time.'

'Tell him about the kissing.' Jules prods me.

I tell him about the kissing. I even tell him about the tongues, saliva and moustache bit.

Jamie makes a face. 'I've got to be honest, Libs, it doesn't sound good.'

'And meanwhile,' Jules interrupts, 'he's taking her shopping for a ballgown on Saturday.'

'Look on the bright side,' Jamie says. 'At least you'll get a designer outfit out of it.'

On Friday afternoon another bouquet arrives. This is getting silly. And what's even more ridiculous is that I'm becoming so used to getting flowers from Ed that I'm beginning to take them a little bit for granted. And my flat's looking less like a florist's and more like Kew Gardens every day.

God, will you listen to me?

Sorry, sorry, sorry. It's typical, isn't it? For twenty-seven years I've wanted someone who adores me and now I've found that person I just can't seem to get excited. Why can't I fancy him? Why can't I make myself fancy him? Maybe I can. Let's just see what happens on Saturday.

In the meantime I'm not going to send him anything else because quite frankly I'm not entirely sure whether I should be encouraging him. Not until I'm a bit more clear about how I feel, anyway.

And then a very peculiar thing happens. Just after the flowers arrive the phone rings.

'Libby? It's Nick.'

'Nick who?' I'm so distracted by the flowers I'm not quite thinking straight.

'What do you mean, Nick who? Thanks a lot. It wasn't that long ago, surely.'

'Nick!' My heart starts pounding. Perhaps he's changed his mind. Perhaps he's ringing because he misses me so much he's realized he's made a terrible mistake. Perhaps it will all be okay.

'Libby!'

'Oh my God! I'm so sorry! I was distracted. Hi!' I'm fighting to sound as normal as possible, and it's a hard struggle, but I think I'm winning.

'Hello, my darling. I was just sitting here doing nothing and I was thinking about you so I thought I'd phone and see how you are.'

He called me darling! He was thinking about me!

'I'm absolutely great,' I say, with conviction, because of course, now that he's phoned, I am. 'How are you?'

'Oh, you know. Usual. Trying to write but can't seem to concentrate. Plus, I'm still trying to get over the most mind-blowing hangover.'

'Where did you go? Anywhere nice?' I feel a huge twinge of jealousy at the thought that Nick might have been with another woman, and I pray that he wasn't, that he was somewhere dull. My prayers, for once, are answered.

'Just down the pub with Moose and that lot.'

Thank God. At least I know he couldn't have fancied any of those awful women. God. Moose. Those friends. I suddenly remember that awful night, and, as I remember how awkward I felt, how out of place, I realize that even though I adored Nick, I couldn't have done it. I couldn't have continued with that lifestyle, and suddenly I feel like laughing, because for the first time I realize I won't ever have to go to a pub with Moose and that lot again. And not only that, I'll never have to sleep in that filthy bedsit again. And I realize that for the first time in my life I might actually be able to stay friends with an ex-lover, and that for the first time in my life I want to stay friends with an ex-lover. And I really don't want anything more from him. Honestly.

'A heavy session?' I laugh, thrilled at this feeling of being set free.

'A very heavy session,' he groans. 'But I'm paying for it now. So what have you been up to? I've been thinking about you.'

'Have you? That's nice. I've been very busy, actually. Everything's going really well.'

There's a short silence before Nick asks, 'How's your love life?'

'Umm. Well . . .' Oh fuck it. Why not? 'I've sort of met someone.'

There's a long silence.

'That's great, Libby!' he says finally, but if I didn't

know better I'd say he didn't think it was great at all.
'Who is he?'

'Just a guy. I don't know whether it's anything serious,'
I say. 'Really, nothing to write home about, but he's nice,
he treats me well.'

'What does he do?'

'Investment banker.'

Nick groans. 'So he can afford to take you to all the
places I never could?'

'Yup!' I say, and laugh.

'I knew you hated me not having money,' Nick says
suddenly.

'No, I didn't, Nick. I just hated staying the night in
your disgusting bedsit.'

We both laugh.

'I suppose now you're staying the night in Buck-
ingham Palace?'

'Hanover Terrace, actually.' I don't bother mentioning
the fact that I don't even like kissing my new man, let
alone thinking about going to bed with him.

'Seriously, Libby,' he says. 'I'm really happy that you've
found someone.'

'Are you?'

'Well, okay then, not really. Well, sort of. I am happy,
but I'm also really sorry that things didn't work out with
us.'

This conversation seems to be going in a very strange
direction, but I think it's okay, I think that I'm over
Nick, that we probably both have regrets but that it's
time to move on.

'I know,' I say. 'So am I, but, let's face it, we weren't
exactly a match made in heaven.'

There's a silence.

'I mean,' I continue, 'I think you're lovely, and I'd love to have you as my friend, but in hindsight we should probably never have been together.'

'You're probably right,' he sighs. 'And anyway, I couldn't handle a relationship right now.'

'I know,' I laugh. 'That's what you said when you dumped me.'

'I didn't dump you! We just . . . parted.'

'A bit like the Red Sea?'

'Exactly.'

'And what about you, Nick?' I don't really want to ask this question, I don't really want to know, but I can't help it. 'How's your love life?'

'Terrible.' Thank you, thank you, thank you, God.

'No women, then?'

'Nah. Not since you.'

'You must be getting withdrawal symptoms.'

'I'm fine. I'm being very introverted and doing lots of thinking about love and life and all that stuff.'

'Come up with any conclusions yet?'

'Yes. I've concluded that I'm completely screwed up.'

'So tell me something else I didn't know.'

'Thanks!' Indignant tone.

'Pleasure!' Light and breezy tone.

'So are we friends now?' A cautious tone.

'Of course! I'd love to be friends with you.'

'Does that mean we could get together for a drink sometime?'

'As long as it's not with your disgusting friends.'

Nick laughs. 'No. Just you and me.'

'That would be lovely.'

'Okay. Listen, I'll call you next week and we'll sort something out.'

'Fine. I've gotta go, Nick, there's another call for me.'

'Okay. God, it's so nice to hear your voice, Libby. I've missed you.'

'I've missed you too.'

I ring Jules immediately to tell her that Nick called, but as soon as she picks up the phone I can hear there's something wrong. Her voice is sounding flat, she doesn't sound as bright as she normally does, and I mentally kick myself for not thinking of her first.

'Jules?' I venture. 'Is everything okay?'

I hear a long sigh.

'What's the matter?'

'God, Libby,' she sighs. 'I'm really worried. About Jamie.'

'Jamie? What on earth are you worried about with Jamie?'

'I know this sounds crazy, and I know he works all the time, but the last couple of weeks he's been working late in the office, and last night I called him and there was no reply. When he got home I casually asked him if he went out, but he said no, he'd been in his office all night.'

'So? He'd probably gone to the loo or something.'

'For three hours? And that's not everything. He's been a bit distant lately but I tried to ignore it and when I did ask him if there was something the matter he said his mind was on a case and he was really busy.'

'Jules, you're not telling me you think he's having an affair, are you? You're crazy, Jamie would never do that.'

'I thought I was going mad,' Jules says slowly, 'but suddenly I've started remembering that over the last few weeks the phone's rung a few times and it's been put down when I've answered.'

'So? Probably a wrong number.'

'I know something's wrong, Libby. I can't explain it, it's almost like a sixth sense. I feel him distancing himself, and I'm sure he's met someone else.'

'Jules, you're being ridiculous. I saw you together just the other day and you're still the perfect couple, and he still obviously adores you. Are you sure you're not imagining it? Jamie's hardly the type to have an affair. Jesus, Jules. I don't know what to say. I mean, how could he possibly be having an affair? Are you sure you're not going through an early menopause or something?'

'I don't know. Look, I've got to go. I haven't decided what to do yet but I'll fill you in.'

I put down the phone, wondering whether Jules is going mad, whether Jamie would be unfaithful, trying to imagine what she must feel like. There isn't anything I can do, other than help out with some amateur sleuthing if she asks, but Jules isn't the type to start following Jamie around in sunglasses and a wig. She isn't the type to tap his phone calls or to trick him into revealing the truth.

I would be rifling through his pockets, checking his credit card statements, but Jules, despite her suspicions, won't really want to know. She'll blind herself to it, hoping that it will go away. But Jesus Christ, how could Jamie, *Jamie*, be having an affair?

Over the next few days Jules tries to change the subject when I ask how things are. 'Fine,' she says guardedly, and I know that there's no point in pushing her to talk about it. That she'll talk about it when she's ready, and that the only thing I can do is be there for her when she decides to open up.

But I'll tell you this. If Jamie is having an affair I'll

kill him. Even the thought of him causing Jules pain makes me so angry I want to go storming into his chambers now and kick the living daylights out of him. How could he? How dare he?

I seems as if a weight has suddenly descended on to my shoulders, and, if I feel like this, how in the hell must Jules be feeling?

Chapter Eighteen

'So you're actually going out with him?'

Amanda and I are once again having lunch, this time at Daphne's, and she's still treating me like her best friend, and I can't figure out why we're having lunch again so soon after the last one, but she phoned up and suggested it and anything to get me out of the office for a while.

Not that I don't enjoy work. I love my job. But recently I've found myself dreaming more and more about not having to work. Leading a life of luxury. Lunching at Daphne's and shopping at Joseph every day. Heaven.

And of course it doesn't help actually having lunch in Daphne's, because we're surrounded by the proverbial ladies who lunch, all immaculate in their little designer suits with their Gucci bags and perfectly streaked blonde hair. They all look as if they spend a large part of every day at the hairdresser's or the manicurist's, and I feel like an old trollop in my Episode suit that's trying very hard to be Armani, and my Pied à Terre shoes that would like to come back in another life as a pair of Stephane Kélians.

'I'm not sure I'd say that,' I say. 'We're just sort of seeing one another.'

'I think he's really quite sexy,' says Amanda in a dreamy sort of voice while I look at her in horror.

'What? That moustache? Sexy?'

'I don't mind moustaches,' she says. 'Not if they have

that much money. But surely if you're seeing him you must find him sexy?'

I shrug, because I'm not sure I want to tell Amanda about him kissing me, I'm not sure I trust her.

'Libby?' she pushes.

'I don't really know,' I say eventually. 'I'm not sure how I feel about him, but he treats me well and he's taking me out on Saturday to buy me an outfit for this ball he's taking me to. To be honest, I'm just enjoying being spoiled, no one's ever done anything like this for me before.'

'He's taking you shopping?' Her eyes are wide.

I nod.

'Where are you going to go?'

'I don't know. You're probably the best person to ask. Where will I find a black tie type dress?'

'Unlimited budget?'

'Well, not quite,' I laugh. 'But something nice.'

'Why don't you go to Harvey Nichs? They've got a decent evening wear department, and if you don't find anything you like there, then they've got all the designer concessions.'

'Excellent idea. Harvey Nichs it is.'

'And I have to tell you, Libby, if you decide you don't want him, I'll have him.'

I laugh, but then I look up and realize that Amanda's not laughing with me. She has this sort of strange smile on her face, and Jesus Christ, she's not bloody joking. Oh well, if I decide I don't want him she can have him. With pleasure. And am I going mad or might the fact that she wants him be making me want him just a teeny bit more?

On the way back to the office – I get a cab, on expenses,

naturally – I decide that I could quite like Ed. Maybe I could even fancy him, and maybe the fact that I'm not thinking about him that much when I'm not with him is a good thing, maybe it means this is a proper relationship, not just lust, or the equivalent to a teenage crush. Because quite frankly I'm sick of falling madly in love and spending twenty-four hours a day thinking about them and crying with misery when they don't phone. I'm sick of being the kind of girl who, when they say jump, asks how high. I'm sick of always, always being the one to fall in love and get hurt. And maybe this is how it should be, getting on with my life and not putting all my energies into a relationship.

So when Saturday arrives I'm feeling okay about this. So, fine. I'm not crazy about him, but I am sort of looking forward to seeing him, and I think maybe this could work, maybe he could grow on me, so what I've done, in the days that have passed since my lunch with Amanda, is try to picture Ed as being much worse than he actually is. I know that might sound a bit bizarre, but I've pictured him as really ugly, his moustache as really big, his laugh really braying, and that way I'm hoping that I won't be disappointed when I open the door, that I'll actually be pleasantly surprised.

And you know what? It bloody works! I open the door and Ed is far, far better than I remember him, and I grin as I take the flowers – lilies this time – and reach up and give him a kiss on the lips.

Not tongues, okay? I want to enjoy this feeling of appreciating him for a little while, and I'm not ready to take it further. Not just yet.

'I've really looked forward to seeing you,' he says, putting his arms around me and giving me a hug.

'Good,' I say, as I hug him back.

I break away and he says, 'So have you thought where to go?'

'Does Harvey Nichols sound okay?'

'Fine, fine,' he says. 'I don't really know anything about women's clothes, but if that's the place to go, then we'll go there. Have you had breakfast?'

I shake my head.

'Why don't I take you out for breakfast first?'

'Fine.'

We drive up to Knightsbridge, park the car, and Ed takes me for yummy scrambled eggs and freshly squeezed orange juice, and I sit there watching all the beautiful people, thinking, I'm okay, I fit, I'm part of a couple.

Because it's very obvious that Ed and I are together. He sits gazing at me as I eat, stroking my face, my hair, and I bask in this adoration because it's so completely new for me. He refuses to let me pay, and quite frankly I'm feeling a bit ridiculous offering, and when we leave he takes my hand and I follow meekly, loving this submissive role of being a wealthy-woman-who-lunches-in-waiting.

I think we actually look a pretty good couple. Ed in his casual but still oh-so-smart polo shirt, crisp dark blue jeans and brown suede Gucci loafers (of course I bloody noticed them, what do you think I am, blind or something?), and me in my camel silk trousers, brown mock-croc loafers and white linen shirt. Unfortunately, I haven't yet acquired lots of chunky gold Italian-style jewellery to complete the look, but I know we look like a young wealthy couple out shopping, we look like we totally belong in Knightsbridge, we look like we do this every Saturday.

And it gets better! In the evening wear department in Harvey Nichols, Ed walks around silently looking at clothes as the sales assistant – a middle-aged woman – bustles around showing me dresses. 'Would your husband like this one?' she says at one point, and Ed overhears while I almost faint in alarm, because you should never, ever, bring up the M word, you should never even allow the M word to be mentioned by anybody else when you're with your new boyfriend, but Ed just smiles at me, a very tender, affectionate smile, and I can't help it. I grin back.

'I can see my *wife* in something like this,' Ed says, and my heart turns over, and then it stops completely when I see what he's picked out. It's a twin-set taffeta suit. The jacket's navy, with a nipped in waist and a flared peplum skirt, and the skirt's probably mid-calf length. It is absolutely disgusting. It's the sort of thing my mother would wear.

'Umm, I don't think that's quite me, actually,' I say, turning away.

'Would you just try it on?' he says. 'For me?'

'Okay.' I shrug, and take the outfit into the changing room. Jesus Christ, I look like my mother, and I wouldn't be caught dead in anything like this. I poke my head round the curtain. 'Ed, I don't think this is quite, er, me.'

'Let me see. Come out here.'

I walk out with shoulders stooped, stomach pressed out, trying to look as disgusting as the suit, hoping to put him off.

'You really hate it, don't you?' he laughs.

'I really hate it.'

'I think it's rather nice.'

'Ed. . . .' I say in a warning tone.

'Okay, okay. If you don't like it, then we'll find something else.'

Eight more disgusting taffeta numbers and I'm beginning to lose heart. This was supposed to be fun, but Ed keeps making me try on these revolting, middle-aged, nasty outfits, and I'm beginning to seriously rethink this whole thing.

And then finally we leave the evening wear department, and, just as we're walking through the designer section, Ed stops and walks over to Donna Karan. There, on a dummy, is the most beautiful shimmering black dress I've ever seen. Long sleeved, it swoops at the front and sweeps down to the floor in the most gorgeous, slinky, sexy way.

We both stand there for a while, admiring this dress, and then Ed turns to the assistant, who's hovering behind us, a bright smile on her face.

'Do you have this in a twelve?' he says, bless him, because he's remembered my size.

'Certainly, sir,' she says, and smiles at me as she goes to get the dress.

And finally I feel like a princess. Actually, make that a queen. I stand straight and proud, admiring the way the dress cleverly hugs, but not too tightly, my figure, how it makes me look slim and tall, elegant and sophisticated. I imagine how I'd look with my hair swept up in a chic chignon, with high strappy sandals tripping off my feet, with tiny little diamond studs sparkling in my ears, oops, jumping ahead of myself here. Where on earth would I get diamond studs from?

I walk out of the changing room, and both Ed and the sales assistant gasp.

'You look beautiful!' Ed whispers, as the sales girl

just nods in agreement, and it's not like those times when sales girls say you look lovely and you know that they say it to everyone, no matter how shit they look; I can see from this girl's face that she's as thrilled as I am with how the dress looks, and Jesus Christ, this dress has to be mine.

'That's the dress!' Ed says, and I beam as I admire myself in the full-length mirror.

'I love it!' I say. 'It's the most beautiful thing I've ever worn.'

Ed turns to the sales assistant. 'Do you take American Express?'

I go back into the changing room, and I can't help myself, when I finally tug the dress off I sneak a quick look at the price.

And I almost faint.

£1,500.

Jesus Christ. What the hell should I do? I don't think Ed realizes how much it is, and I can't let him spend this money on me, that's absurd. That's the most ridiculous amount of money I've ever seen in my whole life.

The sales assistant pops her head round, smiles at me and takes the dress as I try to look confident, even though I'm standing there in my greying M&S bra and knickers, and then the dress has gone, and I figure that if Ed has a problem with it, he'll tell me, because he's going to find out soon enough how much it is.

I finish getting dressed and walk out of the changing room, and Ed's sitting in a chair with a big grin on his face. By his feet is a bag, floaty wisps of tissue paper peeking out from the top.

'There you are, my darling,' he says, handing me the bag. 'A beautiful dress for my beautiful Libby.'

'But Ed,' I say, flushing because I can't believe he's done this, and I start to say something about the price, but he stops me.

'I don't want to hear another word about it,' he says, so I reach up and kiss him.

'Thank you,' I say. 'No one's ever bought me anything so wonderful before.'

'It's my pleasure,' he says. 'Now. What about shoes? Do you have shoes?'

I nod firmly. 'Yes,' I say. 'I've got the perfect shoes.'

'So do you need anything else?' he says. 'While we're here, what about stockings, or a cape?'

'Ed,' I say. 'It's fine. I don't need anything else.'

'So do you have plans for the rest of the day?'

I know what he means. He means this evening. And you know what? Fuck it. I don't mind spending the rest of my Saturday with him, evening included. I mean, Jesus Christ, for £1,500 it's the very least I can do.

We go back to Ed's house, and you know this time, the second time, it doesn't seem quite so cold and forbidding. I'm beginning to feel quite at home: I even offer to make tea while Ed makes some business calls. While I'm pottering in the kitchen, opening cupboards to find out where everything is, I'm starting to think that I could live in a house like this. I could, in fact, live in this house.

Oh, for God's sake, Libby! Stop it!

But anyway, this feels very cosy. Very *coupley*. Unbelievable, bearing in mind I hardly know this guy, but I do feel very comfortable with him, surprisingly so, and whether this is because I'm not in love with him and he, I suspect, is crazy about me, I don't know, but it's a nice feeling, really. Bit of a new one for me.

Ed comes down when he's finished his calls and puts his arms around me in the kitchen, and this time I have to kiss him again, I really can't get out of it, and while I can't say it's exactly amazing, I think it's a bit better than last time. I'm sure it's a bit better than last time. Maybe it's just a question of getting used to it. Maybe it will get better and better.

'Mmm,' Ed says, burying his face in my neck. 'You're so delicious, I could eat you up.'

'Speaking of eating,' I say brightly, 'have you got any biscuits?'

Ed looks crestfallen.

'Cakes?' I say hopefully. 'Anything?'

'Oh dear,' he says. 'I'm really sorry, Libby, I don't have anything at all.'

'Toast?'

'Nothing. Look, wait here, I'll be back in a jiffy.'

In a jiffy? In a jiffy? Who the hell says in a jiffy? Before I have a chance to stop him, because I'm not really hungry, it was just a diversionary tactic, Ed's grabbed his keys and disappeared out the door.

So what do I do? In normal circumstances I'd do what every girl would do left alone in her new man's house and start rifling. I'd normally be shuffling papers around, looking for evidence of previous girlfriends, opening drawers, looking in briefcases, but somehow I just instinctively know that Ed's so honest he doesn't have anything to hide and I'd be half relieved and half disappointed at not finding anything, so what I do at this present moment is pick up the phone and ring Jules. But I lower my voice just in case he should come back, because I wouldn't want him to think I'd be so rude as to use his phone without asking.

'Jules, it's me.'

'Hi, babe. Back home already? So? What d'you get? What d'you get?'

'No, I'm not at home, I'm at his.'

'Oh. Is he there?'

'No, he's gone out to get something to eat.'

'So?'

'Jules. You. Are. Not. Going. To. Believe. This.'

'What? What? Tell me, what?'

'He has just spent . . .' I pause for a bit of dramatic build-up.

'What? What?' Jules is practically shouting.

'One. Thousand. Five. Hundred. Pounds.'

'Aaaaaaaargh!' Jules screams and drops the phone, and I can hear her doing her little Indian warrior dance in the background.

She comes back to the phone while I sit there laughing. 'Yesssss!' she says. 'Yessssss!'

'He has bought me the most stunning dress you have ever seen in your entire life, and it's a Donna Karan and I love it and I can't believe he spent that much money on me and you've never seen anything like this dress, and can you believe how much it was, can you believe he spent that much on me!' I pause to take a breath.

'Fucking hell!' says Jules. 'Donna Karan? Fucking hell.'

'I know, I know. Unbelievable.'

'So did you kiss him to thank him?'

'Yes, I did, as it happens.'

'And?'

'And it wasn't so bad.'

'Oh my God! This is it! You're going to fall madly in love with him and marry him and we're going to be your poverty-stricken friends who aren't good enough to be seen with you.'

I know what I should say here. I should say that she's being ridiculous, that of course I'm not going to marry him, that I've only just met him, for heaven's sake, but instead I find myself saying that they're not poverty-stricken at all, and of course they're good enough to be seen with me.

'So you promise you won't forget me when you're living in Hanover Terrace with your maid and your butler and everything?'

'Jules!' I admonish with a laugh, and then, in what I have to say is a very gracious tone, 'Stop being so silly.'

'So what's Ed getting to eat?'

'Biscuits, I think.'

'Hmm. I've just had four chocolate Hobnobs.'

'Milk or plain?'

'Milk. But I think it's okay because I only had a small salad for lunch, so it sort of balances out.'

'And is everything okay now with you and Jamie?'

She sighs. 'I don't know. He's been better recently, but I still think that something's wrong, but maybe you were right. Maybe I was just imagining it. Anyway, he's been bringing me the most stunning flowers, so we'll just have to see.'

'I told you!' I laugh. 'Jamie would never hurt you,' and before I can carry on I hear the front door slam, and I quickly whisper bye and put the phone down as quietly as I can.

Ed walks in holding a cardboard box in one hand, one of those boxes you get at upmarket patisseries for cakes and things, and in the other is a plastic bag.

'Ed? What have you been doing?'

'I didn't know what you like, so I bought loads of things I thought you might.'

'Give me that box!' I snatch the box in a most unladylike fashion, and tear off the ribbon to reveal tiny little chocolate eclairs, marzipan animals, strawberry tarts, vanilla slices oozing crème anglaise.

'Ed! You've bought enough to feed an army!' But I'm licking my lips as I say it, and when I look up Ed seems very pleased with himself because he can see how excited I am at the prospect of overdosing on all this cream.

'I got these as well,' he says, offering the bag, and inside are packets of chocolate-chip cookies, Swiss butter biscuits and those fancy oatmeal and chocolate numbers that you find only in very smart supermarkets.

'Ed!' I start laughing. 'I can't believe how much food you've bought.'

'You do like cream?' he says, sounding worried.

'Like it? I love it. God, I'm going to get fat being with you.'

'I wouldn't mind,' he says, putting the bag down and clasping me round the waist. 'I'd still think you were perfect.'

Now surely this man is way too good to pass up?

Ed doesn't eat the cream cakes. Nor does he touch the biscuits. It's only when I've eaten so much I feel absolutely sick that I realize this, and when I ask him why he's not eating he tells me he's not hungry, and at that precise moment I know that this man would do anything in the world for me, and I understand what an incredibly powerful feeling that is. I hope I don't blow it by – sick cow that I sometimes am – pushing him to see exactly how much he will take.

But we have a nice evening. To be honest I would be happy staying in, but we're still in the getting-to-know-you stages, and we're not quite ready for cosy, coupley evenings in, and as far as I'm concerned those only happen once you've slept together, and, lovely as I'm beginning to think Ed is, I'm still not ready to sleep with him. Not yet.

So instead of curling up on the sofa and watching a video, we jump in the car and whizz down to the Screen on Baker Street to watch a film, and Ed insists on buying me a huge bucket of popcorn, even though the very thought of food is enough to make me sick after all that sugar, but it's sweet of him to do it.

And the strangest thing of all is that he is so intent on making me happy, on making sure that I'm all right during every single second that I'm in his company, on really looking after me in a way that no other man has ever done before, that I start thinking that maybe he could be The One after all.

Chapter Nineteen

The strangest thing happens later that week. Ed rings me at work and before I know it I've agreed to schlep up to the City to meet him for a quick drink after work.

I get the tube to Moorgate, busily trying to follow the directions he'd given me on the phone, because West London might be fine, but as far as the City's concerned I may as well be from Spain.

People are milling about, looking as if they all know exactly where they're going, all wearing a uniform of dark suits and umbrellas, and I feel as if I've stepped into an alien world, because even the streets here are a world away from Kilburn or Ladbroke Grove, and there's a palpable buzz in the air, you can almost smell the money.

Eventually I find Ed's office, and go through to a smart reception with the ubiquitous black leather sofas and huge glass bowls of lilies on a large polished beech desk.

'May I help you?' says the girl behind the desk.

'I'm here to see Ed McMahon,' I say.

'Your name?'

'Oh. Sorry. Libby.'

She smiles and picks up the phone, and a few seconds later directs me through to Ed's office.

I walk down the corridors, past meeting rooms filled with people deep in concentration, and eventually walk into a huge, open-plan room, with desks and people everywhere. The noise is almost deafening, and everyone seems to be on the phone, which is a bit like being at Joe Cooper, but this is so much bigger.

I stand there for a few seconds, unsure where to go, and then a girl catches my eye, smiles and says, 'You look lost.'

'I am,' I say, smiling back. 'I'm looking for Ed McMahon?'

She points me to the other end of the room, to three offices with closed doors, and I knock on the door with Ed's name on it and wait for a few seconds until he opens it.

He's on the phone. His jacket's off, his sleeves are rolled up, and he's evidently having an argument with someone. He doesn't smile, just gestures me in and points to a chair, still talking to the person on the other end of the phone.

I sit and watch him, and suddenly I realize what authority he must have. I had never before thought of Ed as a powerful man, but, listening to his voice, I understand why he has reached the heights he has reached, and why he deserves, at least from his associates, an air of deference.

Because they are deferential. As I'm sitting there, Ed puts down the phone, kisses me, then walks to the door and shouts for someone to come into his office.

A middle-aged man, smartly dressed, walks in, and you can see, instantly, that he is intimidated by Ed. Ed gives him instructions on a deal he is brokering, a deal which, thanks to that last phone call, now appears to be problematic, and the man – Peter – murmurs that he will get on to it immediately.

And I can't help it. I'm impressed. If you really must know, I'm damned impressed. And it is at precisely this moment that I decide that perhaps this isn't such a big mistake after all.

The phone's ringing as I walk in the door, but for a while I have no idea who it is, because all I can hear is sobbing.

'Hello? Hello? Who is this?'

'It's me,' and between the hiccups and the sobs I recognize Jules's voice and my face drains of colour as I slowly sit down.

'Jules? What's the matter?'

'I . . .' She can't speak.

'I'm coming over,' I say, and bang down the phone, grab my keys and head out the door.

Jules looks terrible. Her eyes are so puffy they've almost disappeared, and what little I can see of them is red raw. I walk in and put my arms around her, and she leans her head on my shoulder and collapses into a fresh round of tears.

Eventually the tears dissipate into hiccups, and I lead Jules, her shoulders heaving, into the kitchen and sit down on the sofa with my arm around her. I don't say anything, I just wait for her to talk.

'I don't know what to do,' she says eventually, her pain almost breaking my heart. 'I don't know what to do.'

'What's happened?' Gentle, soothing tone of voice.

'He's gone,' she says, as the tears start flowing again. 'I don't know what to do.'

An hour later, after countless tears, I have the full story, and it makes me feel sick. Sick, frightened and angry. I had always thought Jules and Jamie were the perfect couple. They had the marriage I aspired to have, the life I had always wanted. They had fulfilled a dream, and now that dream was lying in shreds around our feet.

Jamie, it seems, had walked in last night and said that they needed to talk. Jules had sat there with pounding heart as he told her that he had a confession, that he wasn't going to tell her, but that it was only fair that she should know. He said that he loved her, that he would never do anything to hurt her, and that he didn't know what had come over him.

He said that he had been having an affair with Laura, a lawyer he had met, but that it wasn't meant to be an affair – they had only slept together three times and he had felt so guilty that it was now over.

He said he was telling her because it was over, and because if anything it had made him realize how important Jules was. He couldn't live with himself any more, with the guilt, and he hoped she would forgive him, and it would never happen again.

And Jules, apparently, sat there speechless, too shocked to say anything, feeling as if he had walked in and physically kicked her in the stomach.

After the shock came anger, at which point Jules ran to their bedroom and ripped open the cupboard doors, throwing his clothes into a heap and screaming at him to get out.

Jamie had started crying, trying to put his arms around her and telling her that he loved her, that he couldn't live without her, but Jules kept screaming at him to go. She spent the night pacing round the flat, and now anger has been replaced by desolation, and this is why she does not know what to do.

'I hate him,' she sobs, as she finishes. 'I absolutely bloody hate him,' and I feel helpless as I try to comfort her, try to ease her pain.

'Jules,' I say eventually, as once again the crying subsides. 'Are you sure this is over, between you two, I mean? Shouldn't you try and talk about things, give this time?'

There is a silence, and then: 'I don't know. I don't know what to do.'

'He said it was over with this Laura,' and Jules winces at the mention of her name, but I continue nevertheless, 'and he loves you, and is it really worth throwing away your marriage because of a mistake?'

'A huge bloody mistake,' she says. 'I don't know if I can forgive him, if I can ever trust him again.' And I sit there as she lets out the anger, lets out the pain, and I think, if this marriage is over, then perhaps I can no longer believe in the dream at all.

'Oll! What are you doing here?' I fling my arms around Olly, and he scoops me off the ground and swings me round.

'Sorry, sis,' he laughs. 'I seem to have a nasty habit of surprising you at the moment.'

'It's not nasty,' I say. 'It's lovely!' And it's just what I need to lift my spirits, because I've been feeling almost as emotionally wrecked as Jules. It sounds crass to say that her pain is my pain, but it's just so fucking awful watching her crumple, and I'm trying to be there for her, trying to look after her, and I'm not complaining, but God, it's tiring.

My mum stands in the living room watching Olly and I, her face beaming because her beloved son is back home this weekend.

'How long are you down for?'

'Just this weekend, but then I'm coming down soon for a couple of weeks because we're shooting a load of stuff in London, when I'll move the team to the London offices.'

'He's going to stay here, aren't you, Olly?' says my mum proudly. 'It'll be just like old times having you back here again.'

'Only if you promise to make a fuss of me and spoil me,' says Olly, with a cheeky grin.

'Oh, you,' says my mother grinning, flicking a dish-cloth at Olly's legs.

'I've only been here five minutes,' he says to me, 'and already she's trying to feed me up. I think Mum thinks I haven't eaten since the last time I walked out of this house.'

'It's not that I think you haven't eaten,' Mum says. 'It's just what you've been eating that concerns me.'

Olly and I catch each other's eye, and we both suppress a grin because there was no way Mum meant a double entendre, and it's probably just the way our sick minds work anyway, but I know we're both thinking the same very rude thing.

'All that junk food, Olly. You need some good old-fashioned home-cooking.'

'Mmmmmm,' says Olly, rubbing his stomach. 'Does that mean . . .' He looks at her hopefully.

'Roast beef and Yorkshire pudding tonight. Your favourite.'

'Thanks, Mum! What's for pudding?'

'What do you think?'

'Not spotted dick?'

She nods and smiles a very self-satisfied smile, at least in my eyes, and Olly leaps up and gives her a hug.

'Mum, have I ever told you you're the best?'

'Oh, it's nice to see you, Olly.'

I sit there and watch them and wonder how in the hell he does it. How he manages never to put a foot wrong in her eyes. How he teases her and she loves it. He never gets her back up, never upsets her. And part of me, I suppose, is slightly envious of that. Not that I'd want that sort of relationship with her – God no – but I do sometimes wish I had a mother with whom I did have that sort of relationship.

Like Jo, for instance, at work. I know that she and her mum get on like a house on fire. As far as Jo's concerned, her mum's a friend who just happens to have given birth to her. They go out shopping together, have dinner together, and whenever Jo has a problem the first person she'll turn to for help is her mother.

And I've seen Jo's mother. Tall, *soignée*, elegant, she's so warm and friendly she just makes everyone fall in love with her. I remember the first time she came into the office to meet Jo for lunch. All the men banged on about how gorgeous she was, and all the women sighed and said they wished they had a mother like that. Especially me.

I'd die if my mother came into the office. Seriously. I'd want the ground beneath me to open and swallow me up. She'd be an embarrassment. The suburban housewife from hell who wouldn't know what to say to my colleagues or how to say it.

I sigh as she bustles into the kitchen to make some tea, and I settle back into the sofa with Olly.

'So how's Carolyn?'

'She's fine,' he says.

'Still going strong?'

'Yeah, I know. Amazing. It's still going strong.'

'So what's her secret?'

'I don't know really . . .' Like a man would ever take the time to analyse, but then Olly surprises me. 'I think the thing is that she doesn't make any demands on me. Usually after a few weeks women start expecting things from you. They want to see you more and more often, and then they get pissed off when you're out with the boys, stuff like that. But Carolyn's really laid-back. She's happy to get on with her own life, and it's just really comfortable and relaxed, because I know she doesn't expect to see me all the time.'

'So how often are you seeing her?'

'Well, actually,' he laughs, 'I suppose I am seeing her a lot, but that's because she's so easy to be with. And when I'm not with her she's out with her friends.'

'That's brilliant, Olly,' I say, and I wonder whether I could ever be more like Carolyn, whether I could be laid-back, low-maintenance, but then I suppose I am like that with Ed. I'm really not that bothered about where he is when he's not with me, so maybe I've become a Carolyn after all.

'And you really like her?'

'I really like her. So what about you, Libby? What's going on with men in your life? Any action?'

'Yes, there is. Remember I told you about that guy I had dinner with?'

'Yup.'

'I'm still seeing him, and he's really nice.'

'Tell me about him.'

'His name's Ed, he's thirty-nine – '

'Thirty-nine? Isn't that a bit old for you?'

'Nah, I like older men.' As it happens I've never liked older men before, but there's something quite sophisticated about being the sort of woman who likes older men, and if I'm ever going to get the lifestyle I want I'm going to have to go for older men, because no one my age would have enough money.

'So go on.'

'He's an investment banker . . .'

Olly lets out a high whistle. 'Shit. He must be loaded.'

'He is,' I say, smiling happily. 'But more importantly he's really nice to me, he treats me like a queen.'

'You really like him?'

'Ye-es,' I say. 'I do really like him. The only thing is I'm not sure how much I fancy him, but I think I'm beginning to, so that's okay.'

Shit. My bloody mother overheard that last bit.

'You don't know whether you fancy him? *Fancy* him? I've never heard anything so ridiculous, Libby. Since when do you have to fancy someone? It's not about fancying someone, it's about liking them and getting on with them. None of that fancying stuff lasts anyway, and do you think in my day we married people because we fancied them? D'you think I *fancied* your father?'

Olly and I both grimace. Not a thought I particularly want to dwell on, I have to say.

'It's Ed McMahon, Olly,' my mother says. 'He's very rich and very nice, and Libby's worried about whether she fancies him or not. Honestly. I just don't know what to do with you sometimes.'

'How do you know he's very nice?' I taunt. 'You've never met him, he could be a complete bastard for all you know.' Like Jamie, I think. And, much as I hate to admit it, I think that my mother may be right, because Jules fancied Jamie. Jules thought she'd have a happy ending. Maybe it's not about fancying after all.

'I won't have that language in my house, Libby, and I've heard he's very nice.'

'Oh right. Of course. Because you do mix in the same social circles.'

My mother harrumphs and walks back into the kitchen.

'What was all that about?' Olly's looking confused.

'You know Mum. She's decided that come hell or high water I'm going to marry Ed, because he's rich and because she can boast to all her friends.'

'Uh oh,' he says. 'Sounds like you're in trouble. So when am I going to meet this Ed?'

My mother's back in the room, evidently having forgotten my last sarcastic remark.

'Ooh, I'd love to meet him too,' she says, eyes brightening at the thought, any sarcasm forgiven.

'I think it's a little bit early on to start introducing him to my parents,' I say, feeling physically sick at the thought.

'I don't think so,' she says. 'If he's as nice as you say he is then he'd be delighted to meet us.'

I know how her mind works. She wants to meet him so she can drop it into the conversation at one of her ghastly coffee mornings. I can hear her now. 'Had a marvellous time last night with Libby's new boyfriend. Ed McMahon. Yes, *that* Ed McMahon. Oh well, he obviously adores Libby, I think,' and I can hear her lowering her voice, 'I think we might be making plans soon . . .'

'I don't think so, Mum,' I say. 'Look, Olly, I've got to go.' Even the added attraction of Olly being there doesn't make me want to stay in this house a second longer than is absolutely necessary. 'Why don't you come with me and we can have a drink?'

'Olly's staying here,' my mum says firmly. 'And where are you going that's so important?'

'To Ed's,' I lie, knowing that this will be the one thing she won't try to stop.

'How lovely,' she trills. 'Ask him if he'd like to come over for dinner.'

'Yeah, really,' I mutter, kissing her goodbye.

And when I get home there's a long, rambly message on my machine from Ed, and I ring him back, and he's so pleased to hear from me it's really sweet. And he asks me about my day, and I tell him I've just got back from my parents. Ed says he'd love to meet my parents.

'You are joking?'

'Of course not. Why would I joke about something like that?'

'Oh. Funnily enough my mum was saying the same thing.'

'Well, there you are, then. Why don't we all go out for dinner this week?'

'Ed,' I say slowly, not quite knowing what to say next. 'Let's just wait until after the ball, okay?'

'Fine, fine. But I would like to meet them.'

'Umm, don't you think that, umm, it might be a little soon? I mean, we haven't been seeing each other very long.'

'Libby,' he says calmly. 'When it's right, it's right,' and in a flood of confusion I say goodbye.

What the fuck does that mean, when it's right, it's right? What was he saying? Was he saying that he loves me? Was he saying that I'm The One? Do I feel the same way about him?

Normally I'd talk this through with Jules, but the only

thing we talk about now on the phone is Jamie, and what she's going to do. But I need to know if she's okay, so I put my life on hold for the time being and call her. Her machine picks up and I start talking, and then she picks up the phone.

'How are you feeling?' I venture, surprised and incredibly relieved that she sounds almost, almost, like her normal self.

'Not great,' she says. 'But better than I was.'

'Have you spoken to him?'

'I've left the machine on and he's been leaving pleading messages. I can't face speaking to him just yet, I've still got a lot to think about.

'So you think you might give him another chance?'

'I don't know. I can't believe what he's done, I can't believe how much this hurts, but you were right the other night, I have to think about the marriage, think about whether it's worth throwing it all away and starting again.'

'Jules, do you still love him?'

'Of course I still love him. That's the bloody problem.'

Selfish as I may be, I still need to talk to someone about my life, so I phone Sal. And I know I've been remiss, I haven't really made an effort with her recently, but that's kind of what happens when men get in the way. You suddenly find that a few weeks, or sometimes months, have gone by, and you've been meaning to speak to your friends, but somehow you've been too busy trying to build a relationship.

'Libby!' she says. 'What a surprise!'

'Hi, Sal. How are you?'

'Never mind about me, how are you?'

'Fine, fine.'

'You're okay, then?'

'Umm.' I'm missing something here. 'Okay about what?'

'Well, Nick and all that.'

'Oh God, yes. Actually I've met someone new. Sort of.'

'You're kidding! That's fantastic! Tell me everything!'

So I start to tell her, except I give her the short version, and then I get to the bit about him saying when it's right, it's right, and I hear Sal audibly draw her breath in.

'Jesus!' she says, after a short silence.

'I know. But what d'you think it means?'

'I think it means he's in love with you! Libby, that's so exciting! Ed McMahon's in love with you!'

'He hasn't actually said that.'

'Yet . . .'

'Well, yes. Yet. And maybe he meant something else.'

'Like what?' Sal splutters.

And truth to be told I can't actually think of anything else.

'Listen,' she says eventually. 'I know this may well not be your thing, and Nick's coming, but presumably if you're going out with Ed that won't bother you any more, and it's just that a few of us are meeting up tonight at the Clifton, and I don't know why I didn't think of you earlier, but d'you want to come?'

I suddenly have an inspired thought. 'Sal, my brother Olly's in London this weekend. If he's still here, can he come too?'

''Course he can.'

'And it's fine with Nick. It will be really lovely to see him.'

But after I put the phone down I'm not so sure. First

of all I'm no longer the sort of woman who goes to pubs, although admittedly I would make an exception for the Clifton, being as it is one of the few truly country-style pubs in St John's Wood, not to mention the whole of London. And I'm not too sure I do want to see Nick.

I mean, yes, it was lovely talking to him on the phone the other day, but seeing him's another matter entirely, and I really don't know how I'll feel about him. In fact, if I'm really honest with you, I really don't know whether I want to know. If you see what I mean.

Because as long as I don't see him I can pretend it's okay. I can settle for Ed, because I don't have to face physically what I may never have again. I know that one look into Nick's eyes, and it will bring all the pain back again, and I'm not sure I can deal with that.

But I suppose I'll have to deal with it sooner or later, and who knows? I may be pleasantly surprised and discover that my feelings for him are on the wane.

And pigs might fly.

Oh, what the hell, it's not as if I've got anything better to do. I ring Olly and yes, he's still in London, and yes, Mum's beginning to get on his nerves a bit, and yes, yes, yes, he'd love to come out for a drink tonight.

I give Olly the details and arrange to meet him there, and once I've put down the phone I look at myself in my jeans and sloppy jumper, and I decide that, as befits a woman of my recently acquired social standing, I will dress up. I will be smart casual. I will blow Nick's socks off.

Yeah, yeah, yeah, I know. It's that old story again. Nick said he didn't want me any more, but if I look completely incredible maybe he'll change his mind, and, even though I'm with Ed now, I want to show Nick what he's missing out on, what he could have had, what someone else is now getting.

Or not, as the case may be, but Nick doesn't need to know that.

What to wear, what to wear? I rifle through my clothes, and eventually pull out some wide-legged navy trousers, which I team with navy J. P. Tod's shoes and a thin cream cashmere sweater.

Oops, sorry, I forgot to mention that I went on a bit of a shopping spree recently. It's Ed, you see. I can hardly go out with him to the smartest restaurants in London in all my old clothes, so I've bitten the bullet, pushed my overdraft to the very back of my head, and been hitting Joseph in a major, major fashion. (And no, couldn't face the woman in the St John's Wood store, so I went up to Brompton Cross. Much nicer. They treated me like a human being.)

And, er, I probably shouldn't admit this, but on the way back from Joseph I happened to pass Emporio Armani – well, it wasn't exactly on the way back, more of a slight detour, but that's beside the point – and went in just to look, and I came out with masses of stuff. Armfuls. Fortunes.

I felt slightly sick for a while, but I'm Ed McMahon's girlfriend . . . almost. I have to look the part. And anyway, I justified to Jo when she sat there open-mouthed listening to how much I'd spent (and Jo spends money like it's going out of fashion, so imagine how much I had to spend to shock her), it's only money. I mean, for God's sake, we're only here for about ninety years if we're lucky, so nothing really matters very much, and certainly not money.

Yup. This is the outfit. Nick will have heart failure.

*

I walk in the pub, and it's a bit like *déjà vu*, because sitting at a table on the other side of the bar are Sal and Paul, the gorgeous Kathy with an equally gorgeous and evidently new man by her side called Jared, and Nick.

And when I see Nick my heart does begin to beat a little faster because – and I know it hasn't been that long – I really had forgotten quite how blue his eyes are, and just how gorgeous his smile is.

He stands up and gives me a huge bear hug, and there's something incredibly sweet and painful about hugging this body that up until recently I knew so well, and I can't help myself, those old loins start stirring and I don't want to let go. Ever.

No! Stop it, Libby! Nick is not for you. Nick has no money. Remember Moose. Remember the bedsit. I remember, and my heart slows down. It slows down even more when I think of the Porsche and the house in Hanover Terrace.

Nick stands back and looks at me, giving me a wolf whistle and a cheeky grin.

'Cor,' he says. 'If I didn't know better I'd say I was having a drink with Tara Palmer-Tomkinson.'

'Don't say that!' I slap him lightly. 'I don't look anything like her!'

'You do tonight,' he says. 'You're all sophisticated and sexy. Verrrrrry nice.'

'You like my new look, then?'

'Mmm,' he says. 'I could definitely get used to it.'

I almost laugh when I think of how I only ever wore jeans and trainers with Nick because I thought that's what he wanted. Almost, but not quite, because Jules's description of me as a chameleon girlfriend is still in my mind, and I don't want to think about the fact that I might be doing it again.

'Hi, sorry I'm late.' Olly walks in, and I give him a kiss, then introduce him round the table. I can see Kathy's eyes light up as she shakes his hand, and bless Olly, he barely even seems to notice her. This is when I realize that it really must be serious with Carolyn, because, up until he met her, Kathy would have been just his type.

'Nick! Good to see you again!' Nick stands up and they give each other a really warm, claspy sort of handshake – the sort of handshake that men give each other when they really like one another – and for a fleeting moment I wonder whether Olly will have this sort of relationship with Ed.

God, why am I even worrying about it? I mean, Ed's a nice bloke. He's nice to me. What's not to like?

'I was just saying that Libby looks fantastic,' says Nick.

'Yeah. You do look nice. Very smart.' Olly seems to notice what I'm wearing for the first time. 'That looks expensive. Had a pay rise?'

Nick chuckles as I blush. 'No. It's courtesy of my overdraft facility.'

'Who wants what?' Olly goes off to the bar to get the drinks, and I start chatting to Sal and Paul.

But while I'm chatting to them I keep feeling Nick's eyes on me, and I can feel myself holding in my stomach, straightening my back, tossing my hair around as I laugh in what I hope is a sexy and mysterious way.

And then there's a break in the conversation and Nick leans over to me. 'You must be happy with this bloke,' he says. 'You're glowing.'

'Am I?'

'Yes. You look like you're going to explode soon, a sort of thermo-nuclear reaction.'

'Is that supposed to be a compliment?'

'It is a compliment.'

'Okay. Well, thanks.'

'And no food babies tonight, then?' He looks at my stomach and I laugh, and suddenly I'm swept back to that night in my flat when Nick knelt down and rubbed my stomach, and I feel this incredible yearning, and I meet his eyes which are watching me curiously, and I suddenly think that this is exactly what he intended.

He wanted to remind me of what we had, what it was like, and I don't know why he's doing this because he was the one who said he didn't want me, and as far as I'm concerned Nick is now a closed chapter. Or closing, anyway.

I change the subject.

'So how's the book coming along?'

'Finished!' he says, thanking Olly for the pint that's just been placed in front of him. 'I'm about to send the finished manuscript off to a load of literary agents. I've had it with publishers. I don't think they even bother to read the bloody thing, so I'm going the agent route.'

'Good luck,' I say, and I mean it. 'What do you think will happen?'

'I don't know,' he says. 'But unless I win the lottery very soon, I'm going to have to do something about a job.'

There, you see? He did it again. Brought up the lottery. Made me think instantly of the first night we got it together, when we talked about what we'd do if we won the lottery.

'So go on,' he says. 'Tell me everything you've bought in the last week.'

'What?'

'You said you'd been shopping. I want to know exactly what you bought and where you got it from.'

I start to laugh. 'Jesus, Nick. I'd forgotten what a girl you are.'

'It's not that I'm a girl,' he says. 'It's just that I know the way to a girl's heart.'

Chapter Twenty

'Darling, I'm leaving now.'

'Okay, I'll see you in a little while.'

I put down the phone to Ed and ring Jules.

'I feel awful,' she says, as soon as she picks up the phone. 'I completely forgot about the ball. Are you excited?'

'Jules, my darling, I didn't expect you to remember, you've got far too much to think about.'

'I'll be fine,' she says. 'It's just weird being in this huge flat on my own. I feel a bit lost, I don't know what to do with myself.'

'Look, I can cancel tonight. Why don't I come over? We can do face packs and girly things.'

'That's so sweet of you, but no. I'm a big girl now and I can cope, and anyway I wouldn't ruin your date. I'll make some supper and have an early night. God knows this is exhausting me. It feels like I haven't slept for years.'

I want so desperately for her and Jamie to get back together. I know he's done an appalling thing, he's betrayed her utterly and completely, but I also know, or at least I think I know, that for men sex doesn't have to mean an emotional commitment. That for many men it's simply physical gratification, and that Jamie, despite having made a major fuck-up, has admitted it's over. And I wonder whether three fucks, to put it crudely, are worth a marriage, are worth throwing away a man who might not be perfect, but who loves her, despite everything, and who is a good husband, will be a good father.

And I want them to get back together because I want to regain the equilibrium in our friendship, selfish as that may be. You see Jules has always been the strong one. Jules has been the one to whom I turn in times of pain, and, now that she is turning to me, I am not sure that I am strong enough, or wise enough, to give her the advice she needs.

And I miss the easy banter of our friendship, although I hate to say, despite sounding completely exhausted, the more we talk the more Jules sounds like her old self. Maybe she's just putting on a very good act, but things are almost like they used to be.

'So did you ask him?' she says.

'I couldn't. How could I ask him whether or not we would be staying the night?'

Because for the last few days I have been terrified of this. The ball is in a country house in Midhurst, and I phoned the AA, who said it was about an hour and a half's drive from London, so does that mean we'll be driving back, or does it mean we're staying there, and if we are staying are we staying in the same room, or will they have organized separate rooms for us, and I'm really not sure I'm ready for this yet.

'You are such a wimp!' says Jules. 'What are you going to do?'

'I don't know. I've packed clean knickers and a toothbrush just in case, but I don't want to be forced into a situation where I have to have sex with him before I'm ready.'

'Don't you mean, make lurrrve,' she shrieks, giggling.

'Oh, Jules! Be serious.'

'Okay, okay. Sorry. Look, Libby, I doubt very much whether Ed will force you into anything, he's far too much of a gentleman, so I would assume that if you are staying the night you will definitely have separate bedrooms.'

'You really think so?'

'I really think so. Anyway, have you got a nightie or what?'

'I couldn't spend any more money, Jesus, do you know how much I've spent recently?'

'Yup.'

'So I'm just taking a T-shirt.'

'I hope it covers your bum. You might have to get up in the middle of the night and wander down dark, frosty corridors looking for the loo.'

'Do you really think I hadn't thought of that?'

'You're going to have a brilliant time. Think of your gorgeous dress.'

'Okay, okay. You're right. I will have a brilliant time. I'll ring you tomorrow, either way. Are you sure you're going to be okay tonight?'

'I'm sure,' she says. 'Slowly getting used to enjoying the single life again. It's reminding me how jealous I am of your life.'

'Oh yeah, really – you'd just love to be living in my tiny flat, fending off the bastards, trying to find Mr Right.'

'First of all, I may well be single again. Secondly, my self-esteem's taken the biggest knocking it's ever had and I'm not sure I'll ever feel the same, and thirdly, I thought I had found a decent man. It looks like we are pretty damn similar after all.'

Shit. Why did I have to say that? I've unwittingly brought the conversation back round to Jamie.

'I'm sorry,' Jules says after a pause. 'I didn't mean that. I still feel so hurt. Look, I'd better go. Have a wonderful time tonight, and let me know how it went tomorrow.'

'Are you sure?'

'Sure that you should have a wonderful time or sure that you should let me know tomorrow? On both counts I'm sure.'

'No, are you sure you don't want to carry on talking?'

'No, Libby. I'm tired of talking about Jamie. I need a break.'

'Okay. Just look after yourself.'

'What am I, an invalid?'

'You know what I mean.'

'I do know, and I can't tell you how much easier this is, having you there. I couldn't go through this without you, Libby, I really couldn't.'

'You know I love you.' There are tears filling my eyes.

'I know. And I love you too. Oh, and by the way. Give him one for me,' she says, with a faint hint of laughter that brings a smile to my face, because at least I know we've ended the conversation on a good note.

I put the phone down and it rings again immediately. Who the hell is it now?

I might have guessed.

'Ringing to remind you, darling, that if it's a sit-down dinner you work your way in from the outside of the cutlery.'

What the fuck does my mother think I am? Ten years old?

'I can't believe you're ringing to tell me that.' I shake

my head, trying to stifle the urge simply to tell her to fuck off.

'I'm only trying to help, Libby,' she says indignantly. 'I don't want you showing me up.'

'You? You? What on earth has anything got to do with you? You're not coming.'

'I know, but you're still your mother's daughter.'

'Oh, for God's sake.'

'And have you taken a hot-water bottle? You know how these country mansions can get very draughty at night.'

Typical. In the past, if ever my mother has had an inkling of me sleeping with a boyfriend before at least six months, she's gone bananas, and now she's practically encouraging it, and it's been, what? Two weeks?

'No, Mum,' I sigh wearily. 'I'm sure they'll have central heating. Look, I really have to go.'

'All right, darling. Have a wonderful time, and ring me tomorrow and tell me everything.'

'Yeah, Mum. I will.'

As if.

Thank God, no flowers this time. And Ed doesn't say I look beautiful, because I'm just in my everyday clothes, my Donna Karan special in a zipped-up hanging cover, and I know this may sound crazy, but Ed seems ever so slightly nervous, which I find odd in a man who's so wealthy and sophisticated.

'Are you nervous?' I venture, as we set off from Ladbroke Grove.

'A little.' He turns to me and grins. 'Are you?'

'A little. But why are you nervous?'

He shrugs. 'I really want you to like my friends, that's all.'

Thank God for that. For one horrible minute there I thought he was worried about his friends liking me, worried that they might see beyond my designer dress to the not-nearly-good-enough suburban girl lurking just beneath the surface.

I know my mother spent her whole life telling me this is what she was raising me for, but the truth is I'm not sure how comfortable I am around these people, and, chameleon woman that I so evidently am, I've raised my accent a few notches just to make absolutely sure I fit in.

And for a second, as we drive through Putney, I think that actually I'd be much happier going to the pub with Nick, although I know that isn't strictly true.

I suppose, what I'd really like is a man who can fit into both worlds. Who's just as happy going to a smart ball, as going to the local Italian pizza joint (not pubs, never pubs). But if I really have to make a choice, then I'd have to choose the ball.

Wouldn't I?

God, would you listen to me? My entire life I've dreamt of finding a man like Ed, and now I have I'm starting to think that maybe I don't want this after all. Which is ridiculous. Because I've always wanted this, and I will make this work. I bloody will.

After a while Ed puts some music on – classical, naturally, and we sit there in this comfortable silence, and it is comfortable, and this feels so much nicer than the times I've spent with men in the past, desperately trying to think of something to say to fill the silences.

And finally we take an exit off the A3 and wind our

way down country roads, as Ed tells me about the ball they had last year, and how wonderful it was, except that he didn't have anyone to share it with then, and how happy he is that I'm with him now.

We pull off the road and eventually come to a halt outside a pair of tall, black iron gates, and Ed speaks into an intercom, the gates open, and we're on a magnificent sweeping driveway, and I'm so impressed, and suddenly so nervous I can hardly speak.

Ed gets out of the car and comes round to open the door for me, which is really rather stupid because it's not like I can't get out of the car myself, but Ed seems to think this is the way to treat women, and as I take his hand and step out of the car I feel somewhat princess-like, and we both turn as a couple come walking out of the huge, heavy oak front door.

'Ed!' says the petite, blonde woman, who turns out to be Sarah, one half of Sarah and Charlie, and I'm quite surprised because she's not in designer togs at all. In fact, and I know it's only four o'clock, she looks a bit of a mess.

'Sarah!' he says, giving her a kiss on each cheek as she looks interestedly over his shoulder at me, standing there awkwardly smiling because I'm not sure what else to do.

He shakes hands with Charlie and turns to me.

'This is – '

'Libby,' says Sarah warmly, coming over to shake my hand. 'I am so delighted to meet you. We've heard all about you.'

'We certainly have,' echoes Charlie, coming over to give me a huge kiss on the cheek. 'Let me take your bags.'

Uh oh. Here it is. That bedroom moment. And I don't know why, but I'm vaguely disappointed that there isn't a butler or someone to carry my bags. I mean, if you're going to live in a place this stately, you may as well do it properly.

Charlie and Ed lag behind as Sarah leads me up this, well, the only word for it would be magnificent, staircase, as I wonder what on earth I'm going to do.

'So how long have you known Ed?' She turns with a warm smile.

'Not long,' I venture. 'Only a few weeks.'

'He seems to be completely smitten.' She winks, stops and opens a door. 'We thought you might like this bedroom.'

I walk in, mouth wide open, because I can't believe how beautiful it is. There's a huge oak four-poster bed, and for a moment I'm so taken in with the splendour of the damn thing I forget to think, fuck! Double bed.

'We've put Ed next door,' she whispers, as the men approach. 'We weren't sure . . .' She tails off as I breathe a sigh of relief and grin.

'That's perfect,' I say, feeling as though I want to hug her. 'Thank you.'

She puts a hand gently on my arm and squeezes it. 'I completely understand,' she says. 'It must be terribly daunting for you, having to meet all these strange people.'

'You're not strange,' I say, smiling, and she laughs.

'Come down when you're ready,' she says. 'We'll have tea.' She turns and goes, and Ed comes in and gives me a hug.

'She's lovely,' I say into his shoulder.

'I know,' he says. 'I knew you'd like them.'

And then, naturally, insecurity hits.

'Do you think they liked me?'

'Of course they liked you,' he guffaws. 'How could they not?'

Thankfully he doesn't then expect me to engage in a passionate embrace, he just lets me go and says, 'Shall we go down for tea in fifteen minutes?'

'Sure,' I say, nodding, and Ed leaves the room and closes the door behind him.

I bounce up and down on the bed a few times, because this is what they do in the films when they walk into a fabulously sumptuous bedroom, and then I wonder what it is I'm supposed to do for the next fifteen minutes. I hang my dress in the wardrobe and then touch up my make-up, and there are still ten minutes to go, and no television to pass the time.

But on the side table I discover a host of glossy women's magazines, and I'm leafing through them, about to read an article on how women know When It's Right, when I hear a soft knock on the door, and Ed and I walk down for tea.

I'm introduced first to a large blue and yellow parrot squawking in a cage in the corner of the living room. Charles, 'the cynical parrot', as he's described, has apparently perfected his speech when it comes to insults, but the only thing he says as I bend down to cluck at him is 'Have a cup of tea,' and, relieved, I leave him to go and meet everyone else in the room.

I suppose I was half expecting to hate his friends. I knew they were all much older than me – and, judging by Sarah and Charlie, who must be in their forties, most of them are, but I also thought they'd be those really English county types, who would look down their noses and be incredibly snotty to someone like me, but I was completely wrong.

We walk into the room and I'm dreading it, but as Sarah introduces me as 'Ed's friend', with, incidentally, no special emphasis on the 'friend', everyone is just incredibly friendly, and no one is nearly as smart or as intimidating as I'd feared.

In fact, I'd go as far as saying they all seemed very down to earth, and the only thing I found strange was mixing with people who were almost old enough to be my parents, but I'm mature enough to handle that.

I don't want to embarrass myself by scoffing, so I settle into an old sofa (and, not wishing to sound like my mother, but haven't they heard of Dustbusters? Couldn't they have hoovered, somehow, the dog hairs off the sofa?) and nibble daintily at a cucumber sandwich as Julia (one half of Julia and David) sits next to me and makes small talk.

'It's lovely to see Ed with someone,' she says finally, after we've discussed PR versus being a housewife, which is what she is, we've both agreed that the grass is always greener, how she'd kill for my 'exciting, glamorous' lifestyle, and how I think hers sounds like complete bliss.

'We're so used to Ed turning up on his own to these annual balls, and he's such a good chap, we've always wondered why he's never found himself someone lovely,' she continues. 'But now, it seems, he has.'

I laugh. 'Well, I don't know about that. It's very new. We're really just, umm, friends, right now.'

'But from what I hear Ed's quite serious about you.'

Should she be quite so candid? I mean, she hardly knows me.

I smile again. 'We shall see,' I say mysteriously, because I don't know quite what else to say.

I notice that the men seem to be on one side of the room, presumably discussing business, because occasionally I hear the odd 'equity', 'made a mint', 'gilt-edged securities', while the women sit on my side of the room talking about the best places to shop in 'town'. Town being London.

'You're ever so lucky, Libby,' says Sarah, moving to sit closer to me. 'Libby lives in London,' she explains to the rest of the women. 'We have to make a particular journey whenever we want to buy anything special.'

'Where do you live?' says a youngish woman who, I think, is called Emily, but I can't quite remember.

'Ladbroke Grove,' I say, wishing I could say Regent's Park, or Knightsbridge, or Chelsea, and at the same time wishing it didn't matter, wishing I didn't still feel I had to impress these people. Among my friends I'm pretty damn proud of living in Ladbroke Grove, because it's trendy, but here, with Ed's friends, I know it's not even nearly good enough.

'How lovely,' says Julia. 'That's bang next door to Notting Hill, isn't it, and there are so many wonderful places in Notting Hill. Tell me, do you go to the Sugar Club?'

'Yes,' I say, my face lighting up because I have actually been there. Once. 'I go there all the time.'

'Lucky you,' they all coo. 'Having all those wonderful places right on your doorstep.'

And then the talk disintegrates into schools that their children go to, so I put down my cup of tea and wander on to the terrace, and sitting on the low brick wall that looks out on to sweeping gardens I wonder what Nick would think if he could see me now.

I turn as a hand rubs my back, and Ed leans down and plants a kiss on my cheek, and what's really sweet about this is that it's in full view of all his friends, but he doesn't seem to mind, and I think about all the men who have warned me about public displays of affection, and I look at Ed and wonder whether, if he was a bastard to me like all the others, I might like him better.

Except the thing is that I'm feeling very comfortable here, with his friends, and I think I am growing to like him more, for obviously hinting that we would want separate bedrooms, for not having sex as the first and only thing on his mind, for introducing me to this incredible lifestyle, for treating me like a goddess.

'Do you want to go for a walk?' he says. 'I could show you the grounds.'

I nod and link my arm through his, and his face lights up at my spontaneous display of tenderness, and he strokes my hand through his elbow. 'I don't want you to get cold,' he says. 'Shall I go and get your jacket?'

'Don't worry.' I lean up and give him a kiss on the cheek, 'I'll be fine.'

At seven o'clock everyone disappears to their respective bedrooms to get ready, all having been given strict instructions to be downstairs at eight thirty.

And so much for cold, draughty corridors and seeking bathrooms. My room is lovely and warm, and I have an en suite bathroom, which Sarah has filled with delicious smelling bubble baths and soft, thick towels.

I soak for ages, right up until the water is practically

cold, and grin to myself as I think where I am, who I'm with, and when I start shivering I consider running some more hot water in the bath, but don't, because they probably won't have enough to go round, and I get out, carefully, so as not to soak the floor, and go into the bedroom to try and reposition the dressing table mirror to give me enough light to do my make-up perfectly.

And finally, at 8.30 p.m., when I've just clipped on the tiny diamanté studs, which, I'm sure, if you didn't look that closely, you might mistake for the real thing, there's a knock on my door and Ed's standing there in a dinner jacket.

Neither of us says anything for a while. I'm just so impressed with the difference black tie can make on a man. He looks, well, the word that springs to mind is powerful. He looks like a real man, and that's when I realize that up until now I've only ever been out with boys, and something about him looking like a real man makes me feel incredibly feminine, and eventually Ed is the first to speak.

'You look beautiful,' he whispers. 'Absolutely beautiful. Stunning. You'll be the most beautiful woman at the party.'

There. He said it, didn't he? Woman. Not girl.

'You look lovely yourself,' I say, grinning. 'All dark and sexy and mysterious.' I don't mention that the moustache ruins the effect somewhat, because I think I might just about be getting used to it . . . as long as it doesn't get too close to me.

And we walk down the staircase, my hand resting gently on his arm, and maybe I'm imagining it, but I do seem to be wearing the most stunning dress here, and we walk down to meet all those upturned faces, doubtless wondering who this girl is with Ed, and I do feel, for perhaps the first time in my life, truly, truly, beautiful.

We have an incredible evening. And though I can safely say that the people are slightly older than those I would normally socialize with, they are all so warm and friendly that after a while I start to forget the age difference.

The champagne helps of course.

And God, the champagne. And the food. And the thousands of tiny white fairy lights sprinkled around the trees surrounding the terrace. And the music. And the fact that I am high on the champagne, on the glamour, on the excitement of being at a party that truly looks like something you would see in a Hollywood movie, or perhaps because of the British accents, in a Merchant Ivory film.

It feels like the kind of party that I would only ever go to once in my life, because it is all so magical, and so beautiful, and so special, it could never be re-created. Except, of course, with Ed there would be parties like this all the time.

And the more champagne I drink – which, let me tell you, is a hell of a lot, because every time my glass is half empty a waiter-type person appears at my side as quietly as a ghost and refills it – the more attractive Ed becomes.

And at around one o'clock in the morning I'm thinking, yes. Yes. Tonight's the night. I'm going to do it tonight. And I think that perhaps this whole sex thing has become such an issue because it's been hanging over my head, because I've been so worried about it, and that if we got it out of the way it would all be fine, because it's bound to be better than I expect. Isn't it?

Ed's trying to stifle a yawn, and I laugh and put my arms around him, kissing him on the forehead, saying, 'it's past your bedtime, isn't it, old man?'

And he snuggles up to me, smiling sleepily. 'I'm not old.'

'Okay. Older-than-me-man.'

'That's better. I'm fine. You're not ready for bed. I'm really happy staying up a bit longer. *Ce n'est pas un problème.*'

Oh shut up with the bloody French, Ed. You're about to ruin the moment. But of course I don't say this. I say: 'You mean a minute longer, don't you?'

'You're right,' he laughs. 'I am pretty tired.'

'Come on.' I take him by the hand and pull him to his feet. 'I'm putting you to bed.'

Now I know I could have said I'm taking you to bed, but that would have been too obvious, wouldn't it? That would have made him realize tonight is the night, and then we would have both had to walk upstairs knowing that once we made it into the room we were about to, as Jules put it, make lurrve, and halfway up we probably would have started throwing up with nerves or something.

So we say goodnight to Sarah and Charlie, and wave apologetically to people like Julia, who we can just about make out over the sea of heads, and we walk upstairs, me leading Ed by the hand. My heart's pounding, I can't believe I'm about to do it, and part of me wants – and God oh God, please don't think I sound like a total prostitute for saying this – part of me wants to give him something, to thank him for all he's done for me.

Ed stops outside his bedroom door and puts his arms around me.

'You are the most beautiful woman I've ever seen,' he says, pulling me close. 'What are you doing with me?'

And the way he says it makes my heart open, and I reach up to kiss him on the lips, and when I pull back I smile and say, 'Would you stay with me tonight?' and my voice is a bit shaky because Ed is so old-fashioned. I do suddenly think, once the words are out, that he might take me for a brazen hussy, and I'd have to say goodbye to my new-found lifestyle.

'Are you sure?' he whispers back. 'I don't mind sleeping on my own. In fact, I wasn't expecting –'

And I cut him off with a kiss as I, rather spectacularly I have to admit, open my bedroom door with one hand and pull him gently in with the other.

Chapter Twenty-one

Sometimes I feel so angry that I think I'm going to scream. It's like a deep well of anger, resentment, fury, whatever, and I have to concentrate incredibly hard, because at any moment it's all going to come flooding out and I'm just going to completely lose control.

This is how I feel this morning. Ed's sitting next to me, we've just driven past Guildford on our way back home, and I want to kill him. He keeps giving me these worrying glances, and putting his hand on my leg with a reassuring squeeze, and every time he does it I want to hit him.

And I know I'm being a bitch. I know I'm behaving like a spoilt brat who hasn't got what she wanted, but the more disgusting I am to him, the more he looks at me with these sad puppy-dog eyes, the worse I become.

So what was his terrible crime?

The sex was crap.

A joke.

Make that a complete farce.

I mean, here's this guy that's supposed to be one of the most eligible bachelors in the country, who has, he says, been out with people, and all I can say is he hasn't got a damn clue.

Not a clue.

And I'm furious with him for it, which I know is completely unfair, but I can't help it.

So okay, you're probably now dying to hear just how

bad it was, so fine. I'll tell you, but before you think I'm being a total cow, just put yourself in my position, and ask yourself whether you might not be feeling exactly the same way.

I pulled Ed into my room and started kissing him, and the kiss wasn't brilliant, still way too much saliva if you must know, so I stopped kissing him on the mouth and started to plant tiny kisses over his cheek and down his neck, which is when I realized what it is about him that somehow turns me off.

It's his smell. Not BO, or anything like that, but just his natural body smell. It seems to be kind of sour, not massively pleasant, so I decided I'd better keep my tongue firmly in my mouth from there on in.

I know, I know. I should have stopped there. I should have realized that sexual chemistry quite obviously hadn't grown, at least not for me, but I kept going, thinking that Julia Roberts admitted in *Pretty Woman* that she never kissed the men she slept with (up until Richard Gere, of course, and who could blame her?), therefore I could have sex with Ed without having to kiss him either.

And because I didn't want to taste his skin, Ed obviously thought that these strange bird-like pecks I was giving him were the way to turn me on, so he started doing the same thing to me, at which point I promptly stopped, because it didn't feel the least bit sensuous, or sexy, or anything other than bloody irritating.

And then he said, 'Do you want to use the bathroom to get undressed?' which was a bit odd, because I thought in the heat of the moment he would just rip my clothes off, but I went into the bathroom anyway with my T-shirt. When I came out Ed was lying in bed with the duvet tucked up under his chin, and my first instinct was to run far, far away.

But, being the determined woman I am, I squashed that instinct flat, and gingerly climbed into bed beside him. He cuddled up to me and started kissing me again, and I thought, this will be okay, I can do this.

And after a while I moved my hand down and felt the very thing that I had been completely dreading.

Y-fronts.

So I prised them off as gently as I could, given the fact that he had an enormous erection, and Ed started squeezing – actually, perhaps kneading would be a more accurate description – my breasts through my T-shirt, and he did it for so long that I figured I may as well take my T-shirt off myself, which I did, and then he carried on kneading, and I have to say I was about as turned on as a loaf of bread.

And then, before I knew it, Ed was on top of me, and, even though penetration was now the very last thing on my mind, I reached for a condom and put it on for him, because, although he tried, he didn't seem to know what to do with it. Then he was inside me, and there was a look of pure bliss on his face, and he started moving a bit, and then, I kid you not, about six seconds later he groaned very loudly and collapsed on top of me.

And I lay there fuming.

Absolutely fucking fuming.

And while I was staring at the ceiling with his huge weight on top of me and thinking that this, without doubt, was the worst sex I'd ever had, the worst sex it was possible to have, Ed moved his face above mine, grinning like a Cheshire cat, and said, 'That was wonderful, darling.'

And then he must have seen that my face was completely blank, and he kissed me and said, 'Was that okay?'

Well no, actually, it wasn't bloody okay. It was abysmal, and maybe I should have been more ladylike about it, maybe I should have just nodded, rolled over and gone to sleep, but I couldn't, I was just too damn frustrated, and disappointed, and angry.

So that's what I said.

And Ed rolled off me, looking as if he were going to cry, and this in itself made me even more furious, because he's not exactly a child, and how could a man of his age be so completely pathetic in bed?

But he didn't say anything, so I just kept ranting about how sex is a two-way street, and did he really think I would get turned on by ten minutes kneading my breasts, and hadn't he ever heard of the clitoris, and premature ejaculation wasn't exactly enjoyable, especially given that I'd had no foreplay whatsoever, and come to that, did he even know what the word 'foreplay' meant.

And the more I ranted – because by this time I was really getting into it – the more upset he looked. Eventually, when I finished, he tried to put his arms round me and say sorry, but I just stormed off and went into the bathroom.

I sat on the loo seat, wishing to Christ I could talk to Jules. After a while I got a bit cold, so I went back into the bedroom, and Ed was sitting on the edge of the bed with his head hung low. He looked up and sighed.

'I really am sorry,' he started. 'I feel awful, it's just that I suppose I'm not terribly experienced, but if you help me I can learn, you can show me what to do. I really do think that we can work this out if we're both willing.'

I harrumphed a bit and said that I didn't want to be his teacher, but then I started to feel really nasty, so after a while I said okay, we could work through this, and I got back into bed and allowed Ed to cuddle me, and, I suppose, we both fell asleep.

But the thing is I thought I'd feel better about it this morning, but I don't. I feel worse. Because while I don't believe that sex is the most important thing in a relationship, it has to be, at least, okay. I mean, I know that sex with Nick was completely fantastic, but I also know that it's very rarely like that, and that as long as it's good, you can get by.

And Ed probably is right, I probably could teach him what to do, what I like, but the fact of the matter is he's awkward. Awkward about his body, awkward about my body. Just gauche, and even if, say, technically he learns the right moves, it's never going to be silkily smooth and sensual and delicious.

And this morning I start thinking about what sex was like with Nick, and of course the more I think about how good it was, the more I start to resent Ed, and this is why we're driving home in a thick, tense silence.

Not that Sarah and Charles would have been able to tell. At least, I hope not, because they were so charming and so hospitable. I think, this morning, when we all met up over breakfast, I managed to hide the fact that I'd had the night from hell. When we said goodbye and I thanked them for everything, Sarah gave me a big hug and said we'd have to come up again.

So we hardly say a word on the way back, and when we reach my flat Ed brings my bag inside and says, 'Can I call you later?' and I shrug and say, 'S'pose so,' behaving like a six-year-old, and he just looks incredibly sad and gives me a kiss on the cheek.

And the minute he's gone I pick up the phone and ring, naturally, Jules, ignoring the three messages on my answering machine from my mother begging me to ring her as soon as I get back.

'Uh oh,' she says, hearing how flat my voice is. 'Start at the beginning.'

'Just tell me first,' I say. 'Any news from Jamie?'

'Well, yes,' she says slowly. 'He called last night sounding absolutely miserable, so I said he could come over this evening and talk about it.'

'You're kidding!' I gasp. 'Are you going to forgive him?'

'I want to see what he has to say first,' she says, 'because I know that even if I may be able to forgive him, I'll never be able to forget, and I still don't know if I'll ever be able to trust him again, and if you don't have trust, what is there?'

'Love?' I venture softly.

'Yes,' she sighs. 'There is that. Anyway, enough about me. Tell me everything about last night.'

I try and forget how pissed off I am, and start at the beginning, describing everything to her, in graphic detail, what the people were like, what they were wearing, the atmosphere, the music, the champagne.

And then I get to the bit about going to bed and I stop.

'Go on,' she prompts. 'You did it, didn't you?'

'In a manner of speaking.'

'Please don't tell me it was awful,' she groans. 'I couldn't cope.'

'It was awful,' I shriek. 'No. I take that back. It was worse than awful. The worst experience of my life.' And

I tell her, exactly as I told you, what happened, and when I've finished speaking there's a silence.

'Hello?' I say. 'Are you still there?'

'Hang on. I'm thinking.'

'What are you thinking? Don't say that lust can grow, because I honestly don't think I can go through that again.'

'Okay,' Jules sighs. 'I don't think that lust can grow, but I do think that he's obviously inexperienced, and that can be resolved. But,' she adds ominously, 'I also think that you mustn't try to talk yourself round this one.'

'What do you mean?'

'I mean, don't ignore this and just carry on living out your fantasy.'

'So you think I should end it?'

'No, that's not what I'm saying. What I'm saying is just be aware of how you're feeling now, because I worry that sometimes you jump in and do things that you know aren't right, just because you really want them to be right. And I don't mean that this isn't right, I just mean don't try to whitewash over the things that aren't.'

And as she talks I can see my fantastic fantasy life slipping away, and I don't want it to slip away, I want to marry a rich man, someone like Ed, I want to live in a house in Hanover Terrace, but I also see the point that Jules is making. Even if I don't like it much.

'So what should I do now?'

'You don't have to do anything. Just wait and see what happens. But Libby, you don't have to be with this man. You don't have to make a lifelong decision after three weeks, that's all I'm saying. If it doesn't work out, fine. You'll move on.'

And I can see that she's absolutely right, except it's bloody hard to not think about the life you've always wanted when it's right there, at your fingertips. And okay, I have been spending rather a large amount of time recently thinking about how I'd redecorate Hanover Terrace, and maybe it isn't very healthy, but it's a damn sight better than thinking about how to avoid nights down the pub drinking pints with your mates.

'But do you think it is going to work out?'

'What do you want me to say, Libby?'

I want her to say yes, everything's going to be fine. I want her to tell me that Jamie was a crap lover when she first met him and that he then became the best in the world. I want her to tell me that it is entirely possible that Ed will become as good, as perfect, as I once thought Jamie was. As I still think it is possible for a man to be. Just not Jamie. Which is all slightly ridiculous, really, given that this morning I was more than ready to dump Ed and never see him again.

'I just want you to say what you really think.'

'God, you're high-maintenance sometimes. I've already told you. Look, do you want to come over?'

'Nah. I'm going to stay in and watch the box.' I pause. 'Unless you want me to.'

'No. Don't worry about it. I should get ready for Jamie coming over anyway. Mentally steel myself and all that. But don't worry about Ed, it will all work out.'

'Okay, thanks. Isn't that what I'm supposed to be saying to you?'

At five o'clock, just as the movie I've been watching finishes, the phone rings ... again. And again I don't pick up the phone because it's probably my mother, who hasn't stopped ringing all day, and even though she hasn't left any more messages, every time she puts the phone down I dial 1471 and it's her bloody number.

I just can't face talking to her right now. I wouldn't know what to say, and actually I'm grateful as hell that there's been good TV on all day, because I haven't had to think about Ed, or last night.

But this time it's Ed on the phone, and as I hear his little worried voice I start feeling really bad, so I pick up the phone, and before he has a chance to say anything I apologize.

'I can't believe those things I said to you,' I say, more than a touch sheepishly. 'I feel like a complete bitch, and especially after you took me to such a wonderful party and you've been so incredibly sweet to me.' I pause for a while. 'I completely understand if you don't want to see me again.'

'Of course I want to see you again!' splutters Ed. 'I was phoning to apologize myself because I know last night was awkward, and I was just phoning to tell you that I'm willing to do anything, *anything* to make this relationship work. And I know that the physical side is very important to you, and I feel so ashamed that I'm so inexperienced, but I promise you, Libby, I'll learn. I even went out today and bought *The Joy of Sex*.'

How could I have been so nasty?

'Have you started reading it yet, or are you just looking at the pictures?'

'No, no, I'm reading it, and I think I can learn how to, umm, well, satisfy you.'

'Oh, Ed,' I say, amazed at the lengths to which this man will go to make me happy. 'You do satisfy me, and last night I was just in a really bad mood, and I'm sure we'll be fine.'

'I think so too,' he says, and I can hear from the relief in his voice that he really does. 'You probably want to be on your own tonight, don't you?'

'Why? What were you thinking?' Umm, hello? Libby? You did want to stay on your own tonight. God, why am I such a complete pushover?

'I just wondered, perhaps, whether you wanted to come over and have supper. It would just be nice to see you and, sort of, make up for last night.'

'Okay,' I find myself saying. 'I'll come over at eight, how's that?'

'Do you want me to come and pick you up?'

'Don't worry,' I say, thinking I'm going to organize my own transport because I definitely won't be staying the night. 'I'll make my own way there.'

Why am I going over there? I can't believe I'm about to go back and spend the evening with the man I wanted to kill just a few hours ago. But I so badly want this to work, and I'm not angry any more, and he obviously is trying, poor thing. He must have died, going up to a cash desk to pay for *The Joy of Sex*, but look at the effort he's making. I have to try as well, and I think he's right about every relationship needing work, and I'm willing to work at it. I really am.

'I love you.'

A million things go through my mind. How much I wanted Jon to tell me he loved me, but he never did. How I've felt like saying it to so many men so many times in the past, but how I've never dared because I've known as an absolute certainty that should the L word come from my lips, they would have scarpered. How I have spent years looking for someone who treats me like a queen and tells me he loves me. Except I never thought it would happen with someone like Ed.

And in all my fantasies when the tall, dark, faceless but presumably handsome love of my life tells me he loves me, I melt into his arms, murmuring, 'I love you too.'

But I really don't know what to say.

'I know this might seem odd, Libby,' Ed says, holding my hand across the table, 'because I know we haven't known each other very long, but my mother always said when it's right, it's right, and I know that you are the right woman for me. And I know things haven't been great, but I also know that we can work them out, so you might not be able to say that you love me too, which is fine, because I know that you will.'

'I love you too.' What else can I say? And the fact of the matter is, I may not love him, but I love the idea of loving him, and I think, for the moment, that might be enough. And Ed looks so happy I think his smile may well burst off his face.

'I really do love you,' he says again. 'And you make me so happy.'

How can I not spend the night after this?

I walk upstairs, knowing that I have to try everything in my power to make this work, especially when I take in, once again, the softness of the carpets, the size of the bedroom, the grandeur of the swagged curtains, because I want this. This is exactly what I have always dreamt of.

And this time Ed seems to discover that nipples are an erogenous zone. That the clitoris is not just a useless body part. That I quite like soft, sweeping strokes down my stomach.

Okay, it's not perfect. He's still slightly clumsy, awkward, and he keeps on saying, 'Is this okay? What about this? Do you like this?' And I try to show him by moving his hand, nodding, whispering back to him because he keeps asking me in a very loud voice, and it seems to be destroying the atmosphere somewhat, but eventually he slightly seems to get the hang of it.

And well before there is any question of actually having full-blown sex, I find that if I close my eyes and concentrate very hard, it starts to feel nice, and, although I wouldn't normally be so selfish as to just lie there and not do anything while someone is slowly stroking my clitoris and asking if it's okay, I do feel that after last night I deserve at least the chance of an orgasm, and, after what seems like hours, I feel a familiar warmth as the tingling feeling spreads up through my body, and I have an orgasm. I actually have an orgasm.

I open my eyes and smile at Ed, who's looking half pleased with himself and half worried, and he says, 'Did you, umm, well. Was that?'

And I nod, and he exhales loudly as I laugh, and plant a soft kiss on his lips.

'Thank goodness for that,' he says, and that's when I think that maybe sex will get better, maybe it won't be so bad, and I pull him on top of me and guide him inside me, and okay, if the truth be known I still can't quite handle kissing him, or licking him, or burying my nose in his neck, but it's a hell of a lot better than last night.

I think we make it to twelve seconds. Not that it matters, because after my orgasm I can quite happily go to sleep, but I want to do this for him, because he is so sweet, because he is trying so hard.

We lie in bed afterwards, talking softly, and I am so pleased I gave him another chance.

'How did you learn all that in a day?' I ask, eventually.

'I speed-read *The Joy of Sex*,' he chuckles.

'You mean you didn't do any work today?'

'Of course not. This is far more important. You're far more important.'

And I snuggle into his shoulder, just loving this feeling of being loved so much.

'Libby?'

'Hmm?' I'm almost asleep.

'I think perhaps it's time I met your parents.'

I'm now wide awake.

'Umm. Why? Don't you think it's a bit soon?'

'Not if we're serious about one another, and I'm certainly serious about you.'

Jesus, the thought of my parents meeting Ed makes me feel sick. My mother would go into Hyacinth Bucket overdrive, and I'd want to die.

'Umm, well, er.' I struggle, unsuccessfully, to think of an excuse.

'Don't you want them to meet me?'

'Of course!' I lie. And it's not them meeting him that's the problem, it's him meeting them. I don't want Ed to see who I really am, who I'm trying so hard to leave behind. 'I just think it's a bit soon, that's all.'

'I think it's a good idea,' he says, with a mysterious smile, and suddenly I think, shit! He's going to ask me to marry him! But it's much too soon for that, and even Ed wouldn't jump in this early on, I mean for God's sake, he hardly knows me.

And this is something of a worry, because he really doesn't know me, and it has crossed my mind that perhaps Ed isn't really bothering to get to know me. That perhaps he thinks I will make a suitable wife, a good mother, that perhaps he's not really interested in the rest, because he's already pigeonholed me, but that's very cynical of me, and I'm sure that isn't the case. He loves me, for Christ's sake, he must really feel it.

'Okay. We'll sort something out,' I say vaguely, praying he'll forget about it.

'Great,' he says, reaching out for his diary on the bedside table. Fuck. 'What about Wednesday?'

'I'll have to check with them,' I say, already knowing that my parents will definitely be busy on Wednesday. At least if I have anything to do with it. 'I'll let you know.'

'They could come here for dinner,' he says. 'We could cook.'

'But you can't cook.'

'Okay. Well, you can cook and I can help you.'

See what I mean? He's already got me cooking, already placed me in the role of wife. Maybe I'm being ridiculous. After all, it does make sense that I should cook. Not that I'm the best cook in the world, as you already know, but I can probably follow a recipe a damn sight better than Ed.

'Okay,' I say. 'Maybe.'

'I love you, Libby Mason,' he says, kissing me before closing his eyes.

'I love you too.'

Chapter Twenty-two

'Are you entirely sure you know what you're doing?'

'Not in the slightest,' I groan. 'In fact, I think this may well be a nightmare come true.'

'I'm glad I'm not the only one having her nightmare come true,' Jules sighs.

Jamie did go over to see Jules that night. She said she opened the door and her very first feeling was this overwhelming maternal urge, because Jamie looked terrible.

'He'd lost so much weight,' she said. 'He obviously hadn't been eating a thing.'

He'd looked haggard, and miserable, and just completely downtrodden. Jules invited him in and took him into the kitchen, where she'd spent all day cooking his favourite meal, so the smell of oxtail stew would permeate the air and make him realize just what he had thrown away. Or not. She hadn't, at that point, decided.

Jamie naturally commented on the food, but Jules didn't offer him any. She offered him a cup of tea instead, knowing that he prefers coffee. He said he didn't want anything.

He sat there, on the sofa, with his head in his hands, and when he eventually raised his eyes he looked at her pleadingly and said, 'I miss you so much, Jules. I love you so much. I don't want to be without you.'

And somehow this seemed to empower Jules, who suddenly felt she was in control, who discovered this pool of strength lurking within, and, looking at him, decided that she would make him suffer.

She was still unsure as to whether she would take him back, but the only certainty she had was that, whatever her decision, she was going to make him pay.

So she told him that he had hurt her beyond measure. That he had broken down every belief she had ever had about marriage. That he had destroyed every dream she had ever had about her future. Their future.

Jamie didn't say a word.

She said that it was still far too early for her to make a decision about whether he could move back in. Too early to decide even whether she wanted to see him at the moment.

And Jamie apologized, repeatedly, and hung his head in shame.

She said she needed more time, and Jamie nodded and silently left. He turned to kiss her just as he was walking out the door, and Jules moved her head so he ended up kissing air.

'But Jesus, Libby,' she says, when she has finished telling me this, as we are pushing the trolley round Sainsbury's, me once again, having crept out of work slightly earlier than usual, 'it was so hard. So fucking hard. All I wanted to do was rewind the clock and make things okay.'

'So do you think they will be okay?'

'Who knows? All I do know is I won't be ready to take him back until he's suffered nearly as much as I have.' She pauses. 'And I've got this bloody work do I've got to go to tonight, which Jamie was supposed to come to, and I'm dreading it.'

'Do you have to go?'

'Unfortunately, yes. Too many good contacts to pass up. Anyway,' she continues, sighing, and attempting to smile, 'tell me again why you decided to go through with this.'

'This' being Ed meeting my parents.

'Because, Jules,' I say in a mock exasperated tone, 'it's going to happen sooner or later, and I may as well get it out of the way now.'

'But it's your parents.' Jules knows my parents. My parents, in fact, love Jules. They think she is the perfect woman, and many's the time my mother has compared me to Jules, with me, naturally, falling short. And Jules likes my parents – how could she not when every time she's been to their house my mother's clucked around her like a mother hen, going on about how thin she is and how much she needs feeding up.

And I've tried to tell Jules how completely awful my mother is, but she still thinks she's nice, which I suppose I might do as well if she wasn't my mother. Well, maybe not, but I can see that parents always seem a hell of a lot better if they're not yours.

'You don't think Ed's going to take your father for a walk round the garden after dinner and ask for your hand in marriage, do you?' she jokes as I throw a bag of spinach in the basket.

Actually, that's exactly what I had been thinking, and I can't believe that Jules thought it too. I turn to her in amazement 'Do you think he might do that? Really?'

She shrugs. 'Do you?'

'It had crossed my mind. Damn. I need chocolate for the chocolate mousse but I forgot what kind of chocolate.'

'Bourneville,' she says, throwing a couple of big bars in the basket. 'So what would you say?'

And suddenly I know exactly what I would say. 'I think I'd say yes.'

She gasps and stops dead in her tracks. 'Yes? Are you serious? You hardly know the guy.'

'But as you've always said, Jules, when it's right, it's right.'

'I never said that.'

'Oh, well, okay. But someone did. And I really do think it's right.'

'So, the sex is crap, him speaking French irritates you beyond belief, and you think you could spend the rest of your life with this man?'

'Jules!' I admonish firmly. 'The sex isn't crap. Okay, it wasn't great the first time, but it's much better now,' and, incidentally, given that I've now stayed at Ed's every night since Sunday, we've had plenty of time to practise, 'and the French annoys me a bit, but not that much, and yes, I can imagine spending the rest of my life with this man.'

As it happens, that's not strictly true, because my fantasies haven't yet reached beyond the wedding day, but what a wedding I've been planning! I've worked it all out, from my Bruce Oldfield dress, to my bridesmaids, to the admiring looks of all the people I've ever known, because this will be no small wedding, this will be the wedding of the century.

Jules shakes her head. 'Listen, Libby, I know things don't appear to have worked out with Jamie, but at least I loved him. I mean I really really loved him. Are you sure you know what you're doing?'

'Jules, for God's sake. It's highly unlikely that he will actually propose tonight, so I think we're both jumping ahead of ourselves here, and anyway even if we did get engaged we'd definitely have a long engagement.'

'How long? The chicken's down here.' She wheels the trolley down aisle eight.

'A year.'

'Promise?'

'Promise.'

Jules drops me home so I can pick up my recipe books, and I ring Mum once she's gone, just to check she's got the right address. Her voice is all fluttery and excited on the phone.

'Are you sure my green suit will be all right?'

'Mum, it doesn't matter what you wear, we're only staying in.'

'But, darling, I want to make a good impression.'

'It really doesn't matter, Mum. Your green suit will be fine.'

'Should Dad wear a tie?'

'No, Mum,' I sigh. 'He doesn't have to wear a tie.'

'I thought perhaps you might like me to bring some salmon mousse to start with. I made it anyway for us this morning, and I thought maybe we could bring it with.'

'You think I can't cook, don't you?'

'No, darling. I'm just trying to help.'

'Forget it, Mum, I've got all the food sorted out.'

'Are you sure?'

'Yes, Mum, I'm sure.'

'It's no trouble – '

'Mum!' Why, oh why, did I ever decide to go ahead with this?

*

Did I mention that Ed gave me the spare keys yesterday and told me to keep them?

I let myself into his house, lugging the bags of shopping, and go down to the kitchen. There's something very eerie about being in a house this size all by myself, so I turn on the lights and retune his radio to Virgin (it was, unsurprisingly, tuned to Radio 3), and rearrange a few things to make it a bit more cosy.

I must talk to him about getting the sofas re-covered.

I open the recipe books to the pages I've bookmarked and start to read. I went through them last night and picked out a Jules special which I'd scribbled down on the corner of a page for the main course, and a Delia special for pudding. I had a bit of a panic about starters, but Jules said I should try bruschetta, so I've got the ciabatta, garlic and tomatoes, and she says all I have to do is toast the bread, rub it with garlic and olive oil, and arrange tomatoes, olives and fresh basil on top, and the bonus is it's completely idiot-proof.

So there I am, boiling the spinach, seasoning the chicken breasts, making a total mess of the kitchen but trying my damndest to clear up as I go, because that, they say, is the mark of a true cook, when the phone rings.

Now there's something very weird about being in your boyfriend's house on your own and having the phone ring, and for a minute my heart stops, because what if it were another woman leaving a sultry, sexy message?

But then I remember I'm at Ed's, and Ed completely adores me, and the very last thing on earth I have to worry about is other women. And the machine picks up while I stop everything to hear who it is.

'Libby? Are you there? Pick up the phone.'

It's Ed.

'Hi, darling. I'm here cooking.'

'Yummy. What are you making?'

'It's a surprise.'

'Have you got everything you need?'

'Yup. I went shopping with Jules.'

'Which reminds me. I must meet Jules again properly. We ought to all go out for dinner sometime.'

'That would be great,' I say, not saying anything more about the separation, or about Jamie, because Ed doesn't need to know, although dinner is a brilliant idea, and I would love Jules to get to know Ed, even though now isn't the right time. But I need her approval more than anyone else's, and even though Jules was there the night we met, she didn't exactly talk to him, and I really want her to see how right for me he is. I'm just praying they get back together, so things can get back to normal. For all of us.

'I've got some things to do in the office and then I'll be home. Gosh, I must tell you, it's very nice indeed having someone to come home to. I'll be walking through the door to all sorts of nice cooking smells. We must do this more often.'

'You mean get me round to cook a meal for when you get home?' I laugh, because I'm joking.

'Exactly,' he says. 'Nothing like a home-cooked meal.'

'I'll have you know I had to leave work early to get this done. This won't be a regular occurrence or I'll get the sack.'

'I'd look after you,' he says. 'You wouldn't need to work.'

'Now that,' I say, unable to believe my luck, 'is exactly what a girl like me needs to hear.'

I'm not entirely sure how to squeeze all the water out of the spinach, plus, what the hell does blanching mean anyway? I boiled it for fifteen minutes, and I stuck it through a colander and put it in the dish with the chicken breasts on top. Jules's recipe says use four large chillies, and I forgot the chillies in Sainsbury's so had to stop at a corner shop and sod's law they didn't have any big chillies, only the tiny ones, so I figured four small chillies would equal one big one, so I chop up the chillies and throw them in the sauce.

But the chocolate mousse is easy. I whip the egg whites until my arm is so stiff it's painful, and, although I haven't got a clue what a bain-marie is, I melt the chocolate, butter and sugar in a saucepan, and stir it into the egg whites. (What exactly is folding?)

Jules said make the bruschetta just before they arrive. Ed isn't home yet, and it's quarter to eight, which means my parents will be here any minute, so I stick the bread under the grill and start piling all the used dishes into the sink to wash.

The doorbell goes. I check my watch and it's ten to. Trust my parents to be early. I go to the door and here they are, Mum and Dad, standing on the doorstep. Mum grins expectantly, and Dad looks ever so uncomfortable in a suit and tie. Yes, she obviously forced him to wear a tie.

'Where's Ed,' Mum says in a stage whisper.

'He'll be home any minute. He's stuck in the office. Come in.' I kiss them both on the cheek, and step aside as they walk in, my mother, apparently, struck speechless for the first time in her life by the size of the hallway, while I smugly lead the way down to the kitchen.

'It's wonderful,' she whispers. 'Look, Dad,' she says, nudging my father, 'he's got real marble tops in the kitchen. This must have cost a fortune!'

'Do you want the guided tour?' I can't help myself, I want to feel smug for a little while longer. 'Come on, take your coats off and I'll show you round.'

'Do you think we ought?' says my mother. 'Shouldn't we wait until Ed gets home?'

'Don't worry. It's fine,' I say, as I hang the coats in the cloakroom, which, incidentally, is about the size of my parents' bedroom.

And I lead them around the house, while they ooh and aah over the rooms, and even my father, a man not exactly known for his conversational skills, admits it's beautiful.

'It's not beautiful,' admonishes my mother. 'It's a palace,' and then she turns to me, and you're not going to believe it but she actually has tears in her eyes. 'Oh, Libby,' she says, clasping her hands together as a tear threatens to trickle down her cheek. 'I'm so happy for you.'

'I'm not married to the guy, Mum,' I say.

'Not yet,' offers my dad, whose grin now matches my mother's.

'You'd better not mess this one up,' says my mum, opening Ed's cupboard doors and inspecting his clothes. 'You'll have me to answer to if you do.'

'Mum, can't you give it a rest just for tonight?'

'Yes, dear,' echoes my father as I look at him in amazement. 'Don't give her a hard time.'

My mother looks at both of us as if she doesn't know

what we're talking about, then shakes her head and goes to look at the curtains. 'Fully lined,' she mutters to herself. 'Must have cost a fortune with all these fancy swags.'

'Shall we go downstairs?' The last thing I want is for Ed to catch us snooping round his bedroom, so we troop downstairs and I make them both gin and tonics while we sit and attempt to make small talk.

'I must say you seem very at home here,' my mum sniffs. 'You know where everything is.'

I decide not to answer.

'But I'm not sure I like these sofas,' she continues, because she has to find fault in something. 'I think I'd have them re-covered.'

'I like them,' I say firmly. 'I wouldn't touch them.'

'Oh well,' she sighs. 'Takes all sorts. So what are we having for dinner?'

'Bruschetta followed by, shit! shit! shit! shit!'

I leap up as my mother sniffs again. 'Is that burning I can smell, Libby?'

Fuck. Fuck, shit, and fuck again. I open the oven door to reveal eight lumps of chárcoal steaming away, and I groan because I know exactly what my mother's going to say. I don't even have to go back into the dining area to hear her say it, because there she is, right behind me.

'I knew I should have brought the salmon mousse,' she says.

And saved by the bell, or key turning in the lock in this case, we all freeze as Ed comes bounding down the stairs calling, 'Helloooo? Hellooo? Anyone home?'

He sniffs as he walks into the kitchen but obviously decides to refrain from commenting – so much, I think, for coming home to good old-fashioned home-cooking –

and immediately shakes hands with my mother and father.

'Thank you so much for coming,' he says, his public school accent suddenly sounding ridiculously loud and affected next to my parents' suburban-but-trying-hard-to-escape accents, but he doesn't seem to notice, so I decide not to make an issue out of it.

Besides, I know they drive me up the wall but they are my parents, and I suppose, if I'm pushed, I'd have to admit that I do love them.

'Thank you so much for having us,' says my mother, and I can't say I'm exactly surprised to notice that her accent has also gone up a few notches. Not in my estimation, I have to add.

'No, no, it's nothing. Think nothing of it. Can I give you a top-up?'

'Why thank you,' says my mother, patting, yes, actually patting her hair as she holds out her glass. 'That would be splendid.'

Splendid? Splendid? Since when has the word 'splendid' been a part of my mother's vocabulary? Even my dad looks slightly taken aback, and as I catch his eye he does his customary eye roll to the ceiling and I have to stifle the giggles.

'Did you find the house all right?' says Ed. 'Did you drive?'

'We didn't have any problems, did we Da – ' She stops, having just realized that it's not quite the done thing to refer to Dad as Dad in the company of someone like Ed. 'Alan?'

For a second there I wonder who she's talking about, because I don't think I've ever heard her call my dad anything but Dad.

'No, Jean,' says my dad, putting a tiny emphasis on the word 'Jean', because he seems to think it's as odd as I do. 'No worries.'

My mother gives my father a curt shake of the head, which my father and I understand to mean, don't say phrases like that, but Ed doesn't notice, and just hands them back their glasses.

'Da – Alan, don't have another one. You're driving.'

'Oh, what a shame,' says Ed. 'I've got a lovely wine for dinner. I thought, as this was a special occasion, I'd open the 1961 Mouton Rothschild for dinner. You'll have some, won't you, Mrs Mason?'

'Oh, call me Jean,' my mother giggles. 'Everyone else does.'

'*Mais bien sûr*,' chuckles Ed along with my mother. 'Jean.' And I want to kill him, except my mother seems enormously impressed with these three words of craply accented French.

'Ooh,' she exclaims. 'You speak French?'

' *Juste un peu*,' Ed laughs. '*Et vous?*'

'*Moi?*' My mother thinks this is the funniest thing she's ever said, and I go back to the stove to avoid watching any longer. Christ. Why oh why did I ever agree to this?

'Would you like to sit down at the table?' I say, in my most gracious hostess manner, because I figure the sooner I serve, the sooner we'll be finished, and the sooner they can go.

And obviously the bruschetta is a bit of a non-starter, as it were, so I bring the chicken to the table with rice and vegetables, and everyone holds their plate up as I serve them and Ed goes to bring the wine up from the cellar.

'He's absolutely charming,' whispers my mother hurriedly, the minute he's left the room, still speaking in her 'posh' voice. 'And perfect for you.'

And, despite myself, I breathe a sigh of relief, because finally someone, albeit only my mother, whose opinion I take as much notice of as William Hague's, someone has given me their seal of approval, has told me exactly what I wanted to hear. That Ed is perfect for me.

And Ed comes back, opens the wine, and my Mum and Dad sit there watching us, waiting for one of us to start before picking up their knife and fork. Eventually I pick up my fork, so my mother picks up hers and takes the first mouthful.

I swear, I've seen cartoons where people go bright red and smoke starts pouring from their ears when they've eaten something hot, but I never thought it actually happened in real life.

Everyone stops, forks halfway to their mouths, and we all just stare at my mother as she drops her fork and sits there gasping, flapping her hands around.

'Here, here,' says my father, holding up the wine glass because that's the only liquid on the table, and my mother gulps the whole thing down in one. 'What's the matter?' says my father. 'Did it go down the wrong way?'

Now there are tears streaming down my mother's face, and for God's sake, isn't she just overreacting a little bit? She's trying to speak but can't seem to get the words out, so she points to the food, furiously shaking her head.

'Mrs Mason?' Ed's jumped up and gone over to her, terribly concerned, and I wonder how it is my mother always manages to make herself the centre of attention.

'Jean?' he continues. 'Can I get you anything? Is it the food?'

My mother nods.

'Perhaps I'd better taste it,' says Ed, going back to his plate and gingerly taking a tiny amount on his fork while I feel more and more of a failure. He tastes it, sits for precisely two seconds while it hits his tastebuds, then jumps up and runs to the kitchen, and the next thing I hear is the sound of the tap running.

'What is the problem?' I practically shriek, taking a forkful of food. 'My cooking isn't that bad,' and, while my father's still comforting my mother and Ed's still in the kitchen, I take a mouthful.

Aaaaaaaaargh!!!!!!!

I run into the kitchen, shove Ed out of the way and lean under the sink, sticking my entire mouth under the water. It feels like my mouth is about to burn off, and I stay there for about three minutes, and the only good thing is that right at this moment I'm not thinking about the embarrassment, I'm far too busy thinking about cooling down my mouth.

Eventually, when I'm fairly certain there's no permanent damage and I think I can talk again, I walk back to face the music.

'What did you put in that?' My mother's face is puce.

'I only put four chillies in.'

'That's not four chillies,' she says. 'What kind of chillies?'

'Well the recipe said four large ones, but I couldn't get them so I put sixteen small ones in.'

'Sixteen?' Ed looks at me in horror as my father starts giggling.

'What? What? What's the problem? Four small chillies equals one large one.'

My mother's looking at me as if she can't believe I'm her daughter.

'Libby,' she says, after nudging my father, who quickly stops laughing and tries to make his face serious, 'small chillies are four times the strength of large ones.'

'Oh goodness,' says Ed, looking slightly disconcerted. 'I thought you said you could cook?'

'I can cook!' I say. 'But how was I to know that about chillies?'

'I'm sorry, darling,' he says, kissing me on the forehead, which seems to perk my mother up no end. 'I know you can cook. What about pudding?'

I fling my napkin on the table and go to fetch the chocolate mousse, and the minute I open the fridge door I know it's a complete disaster. It's basically just a big glass bowl of chocolate-coloured slop, and I don't even bother bringing it to the table. I just tip the bowl so the whole lot slides into the dustbin.

'Umm,' I say, coming back to the table. 'There's been a bit of a problem with pudding.'

'You know what I really fancy?' says Ed. 'I'd really like a Chinese takeaway,' and my parents both say what a brilliant idea, as I sit there too embarrassed to say anything.

And half an hour later there we sit, my parents in their smartest clothes, at the table that I've beautifully laid with table mats, Irish linen napkins and even flowers in the centre, surrounded by tinfoil tubs of Chinese food, and it really isn't so bad, although I know my mother will never let me live this one down.

Ed seems to keep the evening going by telling my

parents all about his investment banking, and my parents look completely riveted, although I'm sitting there half proud of him for making sure there are no uncomfortable silences and half bored to tears.

But my parents don't seem to mind. Actually, make that my mother doesn't seem to mind. My mother's sitting there listening to every word, smiling encouragingly and making all the right noises in all the right places, while my father just looks slightly uncomfortable, but then I suppose my father doesn't say much at the best of times.

And finally Ed and I see them to the door, while my mother makes big eyes at me, and I know she's simply dying to get me on the phone to do the post-mortem, and presumably to have a go at me about the chillies, and Ed is as charming as he always is and walks them to their car, and thank God it's over.

Chapter Twenty-three

'I'm really not that interested,' Jules says, getting up to make another cup of tea.

'But Jules!' I make a face. 'You said he's tall, handsome, sexy and funny. How can you not be interested?'

She turns and faces me. 'Libby, I still love Jamie. I don't know what's going to happen with us, but the one thing I do know is that I don't want anyone to confuse the issue further.'

'But it's only one night, for God's sake. And you don't have to do anything. Anyway, you did give him your number.'

She sighs and runs her fingers through her hair. 'I know,' she moans. 'I didn't know what else to say when he asked. Jesus. You go to a work party expecting to stay for twenty minutes, and some bloody bloke comes along who would have been exactly your type if you weren't married, and . . . I don't know. I'm not interested in going out on a date with him. I just didn't know what else to say.'

'One date isn't going to hurt you. And if you and Jamie don't get back together, at least you'll know there are other men out there.'

'But I'm not sure I want other men.'

'You did say that, what was his name? Paul?' She nods. 'Paul was the first man you'd met since you'd been married that you'd found attractive.'

'But that doesn't mean I want to sleep with him.'

304

'Who said anything about sleeping with him?'

'Go out with him, then.'

'Oh, why did he have to bloody phone,' she moans, bringing a fresh pot of tea over to the sofa. 'Why couldn't he have been like all those men you used to meet who'd take your number and never phone?'

'Because he's not a bastard,' I say, smirking. 'And anyway. You never know. You might have a nice time.'

'I've just finished the interview with the *Mail*, and I was passing so I thought I'd pop in and see if you wanted to have a coffee?'

Amanda, as usual, looks a vision of B-list loveliness, in a hot-pink trouser suit with chunky gold earrings, and a huge pair of Jackie O sunglasses, and evidently she's enjoying her new-found fame. Well, fame-ish, because Amanda has been 'stepping out' with one of television's brightest actors thanks to me, and suddenly the papers are taking a huge interest in her.

There's no question of there being any romance, because once the actor in question is away from the cameras he's as camp as Amanda's suit, but naturally he's spent his whole life in the closet, and the news that he's gay wouldn't exactly help his status as a heartthrob.

So I organized that Amanda should accompany him to a film première, and the cameras flashed away, and Amanda even stopped to tell a journalist that they had no comment to make on their relationship, which was as good as telling them they were shagging, and it made page three the next day in several of the tabloids.

And she, of course, is over the moon. They've now been written about as TV's most glamorous couple, her haircut has been analysed over and over again by the women's pages, and his macho masculine image has been more than confirmed in the public eye.

The *Telegraph* even phoned me last week and asked if they could do a feature on Amanda, which, as far as she's concerned, is the mark of true fame, and now I really do seem to have become her best friend.

I have to speak to her every day because the calls requesting interviews, photo-shoots, soundbites, have been coming in thick and fast, and I really am starting to like her more, even though I know our friendship is a transient one, and I still have to slightly watch my guard.

'I'm so busy setting up your interviews,' I laugh, extending my cheek for her to air kiss. 'I'm not sure.'

'Amanda! Darling!' Joe Cooper walks out of his office and gives Amanda a huge kiss. 'What do you think of all the coverage our Libby is getting for you?'

'It's wonderful!' she gushes. 'You're doing the most amazing job. I came in to see if Libby would go for a coffee with me.' She tells Joe that the *Telegraph* interview went fantastically, and Joe says of course I can go, so off we trot, Amanda still in her sunglasses, despite the weather being distinctly overcast.

And on our way to the Italian caff round the corner, which is the only place around here, a woman stops dead in her tracks when she sees us. She walks over and taps Amanda on the arm.

'Excuse me?' she says. 'But aren't you Amanda Baker?'

Amanda nods graciously.

'Oh, I love you on TV. I watch you every morning.'

'Why thank you,' says Amanda, fishing around in her bag. 'Would you like a signed picture?' And while I look on in amazement Amanda draws out a large glossy black and white photograph of herself as the woman stares in delight.

'To?' says Amanda, pausing regally as she looks at the woman.

'Jackie,' she says. 'Oh, I can't wait to tell my friends I've met you, and you're much more beautiful in the flesh.'

'Thank you,' says Amanda, scribbling away as the woman thanks her profusely and scuttles off.

'Jesus,' I say. 'Does that happen a lot?'

'All the time,' she sighs. 'It drives me mad.'

But of course it doesn't drive her mad. She loves every minute of it. This is exactly what she's been waiting for, and she knows that, now she's got it, the mark of true stardom is to complain about it.

We order cappuccinos at the bar and sit down by the window, and Amanda finally takes her sunglasses off, and checks the room just to see if anyone's looking at her, but of course the Italian waiters are here all day, and don't have a chance to watch breakfast television.

'So,' she says, running her fingers through her perfectly coiffed hair. 'How are you?'

'Really well,' I say. 'Actually, I'm extremely well.'

'Oh? How are things going with Mr McMahon?'

And I find myself telling her that he met my parents, and that everything's almost perfect, and that I think I may well have found myself Mr Right.

'You'd better hang on to him,' she says, when I've finished. 'Because there are plenty of women who'd love to get their hands on Ed McMahon.'

She doesn't say she's one of those women, but then I suppose she doesn't have to. It's written all over her face, and the fact that she would so obviously love to have a shot at him makes me even more determined to make this work. To be Mrs Ed McMahon.

Oh? Did you think I might keep my name? Don't be ridiculous. There's no cachet in ringing up Nobu to book a table under the name Libby Mason, but there's a hell of a lot of cachet in booking a table as Ed McMahon's wife. It's like those tests they do every few months on news magazine shows. Mr and Mrs Joe Bloggs ring up the ten top restaurants in town and ask for a table for two that night, only to be told they're fully booked for the next three months. And then one of the researchers rings up, saying that Elizabeth Hurley and Hugh Grant are flying in, and they know it's short notice but could these same restaurants possibly squeeze them in, and naturally the restaurants fall over themselves to accommodate them, and say of course, whatever time would suit them.

Not that I'm suggesting that Ed McMahon is in the same league as Elizabeth and Hugh, but anyone worth their salt ought to know who he is. And Jules did ask me whether I'd feel the same way if he were, say, Ed McMahon, welder, but I got out of that one by saying that what he does is part and parcel of who he is, so I honestly couldn't answer that one.

Although I think you know what the answer is.

And when I get back to the office there's a message from Jules and a message from my mother. I ring Mum first, who can hardly contain her excitement, and spends twenty minutes telling me how wonderful he is, and how he's the best catch I'll ever have, and how she can see he adores me, and thank God she doesn't mention the cooking.

Just as I'm about to pick up the phone to ring the *Telegraph* to check they're happy with the interview and sort out the photo-shoot, my phone rings again (trust me, the life of a PR is all about phone calls, personal or otherwise), and it's my father.

'What's wrong, Dad?' My father never, ever calls me. In fact, it took me a while to recognize his voice, so rarely does he actually speak.

'I just thought I'd phone to thank you for last night.'

'Oh! Well, Mum already phoned. Did you enjoy it?'

'Yes. It was very nice. Are you happy with him, Libby?'

What is this? First my father phones me at work, and then he asks me about the state of my relationship. I need to get to the bottom of this.

'Why, Dad?'

'I know that your mother's over the moon because he's obviously very wealthy and very keen on you, but I just wondered whether you were very serious.'

'You didn't like him, did you, Dad?' My heart sinks.

'Do you want me to be honest?'

'Yes.' No.

'I think he's obviously smitten with you. In material terms he could probably give you everything you needed. But . . .' And he stops.

'Go on, Dad.'

'Well, it's just that I'm not entirely sure he's for you.'

'Why not?'

He sighs. 'Nothing that I can exactly put my finger on, but I wanted to make sure you were happy, because I want what's best for you.'

'And you don't think he is?' I have a feeling my dad wants to say more, but he doesn't, and I don't push him.

'If you're happy, Libby, then I'm happy.'

'I'm happy, Dad. Honestly.'

'Good. All right, darling, that's all. We'll see you on Sunday?'

'See you then. Bye, Dad.'

'Bye.'

What was all that about? Well, I knew my dad didn't feel comfortable last night, and I knew that he was falling asleep during all Ed's stories, and I'll even go so far as to admit that even I find Ed boring sometimes, but he does have other redeeming qualities, and nobody can keep you amused all the time. Can they?

I've already spoken to Jules twice today, but I want to know what she thinks of this strange conversation with my dad, plus she'd better have returned Paul's call, so I ring her mobile because I know she's on her way to a client.

'My Dad hates him.'

'You're joking!' she gasps. 'Did he say that?'

'Well, no. Not exactly. But he didn't have to.' And I tell her what he did say.

'Hmm. Could just be parental concern. I mean, Ed is quite a lot older than your other boyfriends, so maybe he's just worried about you.'

'What's Ed being older got to do with anything?'

'Okay. Point taken. I'd tell you what I thought of Ed, and you know I'd be entirely honest. In fact, I've just had a brilliant idea. You know that guy Paul? Why don't the four of us go out for dinner? I couldn't face seeing him on my own, it's too like a date, but I could cope if you were there too, and then I could suss out Ed as well.'

'Fantastic!' I say, and it is, even though it will feel completely weird without Jamie, but at least this way Jules will definitely see this guy again. I'm trying to fight Jamie's corner, but I don't think there's any harm in lining up a reserve, just in case. 'When can you make it?'

'Friday night?'

'Perfect.'

'Libby? Delivery again for you.' It's Jo on the internal phone.

'Don't tell me yet more flowers.'

'Nah. This one's more mysterious. Come and see.'

I go to reception, where there's a large plastic Gucci carrier bag, and my heart, I swear, misses a beat, because we don't handle Gucci's PR (chance would be a fine bloody thing), so why is there a bag from Gucci with my name on it?

Jo rubs her hands together squealing, 'Open it, open it,' so I do, but first I pull out the card and read out loud: 'To my darling Libby, for making such an effort last night. I love you. Ed.'

'Oh my God,' Jo squeals. 'What's in the bloody bag?'

I slowly tear off the tissue paper, and open a drawstring fabric bag with Gucci printed on it, and pull out a chocolate-brown leather Gucci bag. The one with bamboo handles. The one I've always wanted.

'You. Are. So. Fucking. Lucky,' says Jo.

'You've got one of these!' I say, stroking the leather that's as soft as butter.

'Yeah, but I had to pay for it. £310.'

'You're joking!' Now it's my turn to squeal.

'I can't believe your boyfriend bought you a Gucci bag!'

'Jesus Christ. Neither can I!'

Naturally, I have to phone Jules again, and, although

she is excited, there's something about her voice, something slightly reserved, that makes me question her until she tells me what she's really thinking.

'I'm worried that it's almost like he's buying you.'

'Don't be ridiculous,' I snort, still stroking my gorgeous new acquisition. 'Three hundred quid for him is like three quid for the rest of us.'

'Still,' she says. 'Lavishing presents on you would make it very difficult for you to leave.'

'But I'm not going to leave,' and for the first time I'm beginning to get slightly pissed off with Jules, which never, ever happens.

'God, I'm sorry,' she says. 'I'm being a complete killjoy. It's fantastic and I'm jealous, that's all.'

'It is gorgeous,' I say, smiling. 'You really will be jealous when you see it.'

'It's the one in *Tatler* this month, isn't it? The one that all the It Girls are supposed to have.'

'Yup. That's the one.'

'You lucky cow. 'Course I'm jealous, and I can't wait to meet him on Friday.'

'Good. And I can't wait to meet Paul. Oh, and just in case you don't recognize me I'll be the one with the Gucci bag.'

We get to Sartoria first, having found a parking space almost immediately, which is a bit of a miracle in the West End, and I order a Kir, which is what I've taken to ordering these days because it fits my new image as the smart, sophisticated partner of Ed McMahon.

And in case you're wondering, I'm wearing a brown leather skirt that I picked up yesterday, because, much as I love my trousers, Ed has now grudgingly admitted that he completely adores women in skirts, so it's the least I can do to please him, and it does happen to look rather spectacular with my new Gucci bag. (Okay, okay, I'll stop now, I just had to mention it one more time.)

Ed sits next to me and holds my hand under the table, and every few minutes he kisses me on the lips, which, nice as it is to be so adored, is beginning to irritate me ever so slightly. I did try and extract my hand, but then he got that sad puppy-dog look on his face again, and I felt guilty, so I placed my hand back in his and gave him a reassuring squeeze.

And then Jules and Paul arrive (it sounds so wrong, Jules and Paul), and Ed stands up to shake their hands and say how lovely it is to see Jules again, while Paul stands there awkwardly waiting to be introduced to me.

Paul seems . . . he seems nice, which I know is pretty nondescript, but, despite being everything that Jules described, he's just not Jamie, and I really don't know whether I could get used to this man.

We sit and make small talk about how wonderful the restaurant is, and how we've all heard how marvellous the food is, and when the waiter comes to take our order Ed can't decide and he asks me to choose for him, which I do and which I love – this gesture of trust and intimacy.

And Ed is at his most charming, asking lots of questions, not, thank God, telling his bloody investment banking stories, and I'm praying and praying that Jules loves him.

I do get slightly exasperated when most of Ed's hors d'oeuvre ends up on his moustache, because this happened the other night as well, and I had to nudge him while I thought my parents weren't looking and gesture to wipe the food off. Tonight I'm feeling more confident, and I want Jules to see how close we are, so I pick up my napkin, raise my eyes to the ceiling and wipe the food off, and while Ed looks a bit sheepish, he's also delighted that I'm looking after him so well.

There is a moment when Jules is talking about someone she works with who's driving her mad by constantly changing her mind, and whom she describes as 'mercurial'.

'Umm, excuse me?' Ed interrupts her.

'Yes?' She stops in mid-flow.

'I don't think "mercurial" is the word you mean.'

Jules stopped dead in her tracks. 'Umm. I think it is,' she says slowly.

'I don't think it is. What did you mean?'

Jules looks at him as if he's mad, which I have to say, I think he is rather, because even I'm wary of challenging Jules when she's on a roll.

'Flighty. Constantly changing,' she says. 'A person who suffers from mood swings.'

'As far as I'm aware, mercurial means of mercury, i.e. liquid, flowing.'

'I think you'll find it can also mean constantly changing,' she says, and from the tone of her voice I pray that Ed backs down.

'Please don't think me rude, but I think you'll find *The Oxford English Dictionary* defines it as "of or containing mercury",' Ed persists, while I want to die with embarrassment.

'Actually,' says Paul, jumping in to save the day, 'I think you'll find you're both right. As far as I can remember, mercurial means both of or containing mercury, and volatile.'

'And Paul's a surgeon,' I say, trying to break the ice,

'therefore frighteningly clever, so I think we'll all have to agree with him.'

Thank God, it does break the ice somewhat, but from thereon in the atmosphere is slightly less convivial than it has been, and every now and then I see Jules shooting him daggers when she thinks neither of us is looking.

'Well, I must say,' Ed exclaims as we're about to order coffee, evidently having completely missed the implication of his near-argument with Jules. 'It's lovely to meet Libby's closest friend.'

'Thank you,' says Jules. 'And it's lovely to meet you.' This bit was said through gritted teeth. 'Has Libby met your closest friends?'

And that's when I realize that apart from Sarah and Charlie and the people at the party in the country, not only have I not met any of Ed's friends, I haven't even heard about any. Everyone he talks about seems to be a colleague through work, and isn't this a bit strange? I look at Ed to see what he says.

'Ha, ha,' he laughs. Umm, was there a joke? 'I don't really have many friends.'

'I can't think why not,' mutters Jules, as I kick her under the table. 'But you must have a few,' she pushes, in a light tone of voice.

'Oh, yes. Yes. Charlie and Sarah of course. Libby's met them. And, umm. Well. I suppose I work so hard I haven't really had time to make that many friends.'

I can see that Ed's slightly flummoxed, so I interject with: 'Charlie and Sarah were lovely. I told you all about them, remember?'

Jules nods. 'I just wondered what you did socially before you met Libby.'

'I'm not a hugely social creature, ha ha,' says Ed. 'I'm either in the office or at home.'

'You must be delighted you've met Libby, then,' says Paul with a smile.

'Oh, I am,' he says, beaming at me with relief at being let off the hook. 'I am.' And he leans over and kisses me on the lips.

'I'm just going to the ladies' room. Jules?'

'I'll come,' she says, putting her napkin on the chair as we stand up and walk down to the loo.

'Well? What d'you think?' The words are out of her mouth before the door is even shut.

'He's lovely,' I say. 'A really nice guy.'

'I know,' she sighs, reapplying some lipstick. 'But it's not the same, is it?'

'Well, no. I suppose it's not.'

'Oh Gawd,' she says. 'What am I going to do?'

'Are you planning on doing anything?' I look at her in amazement.

'I don't want to,' she says. 'But, and I know this sounds weird, but I kind of feel that if I were to be unfaithful as well, then we'd be equal, and then I could forgive him.'

'Are you sure that's what you want to do?'

'No. I don't really want to do it. But I think it's the only way. Anyway, enough about me. Ed. He obviously adores you.'

'I know that! But what do you think of him?'

'Do you want me to be completely honest?'

Suddenly I'm not so sure, because I don't want to fall out with Jules, not with my best friend, but I know it's not going to be good news, and I don't think I could stand to argue with her.

I shrug.

'Look,' she says, calming down. 'We haven't exactly got off to a great start. I didn't appreciate that whole mercurial business, so right at this moment I can't think of a great many positive things to say, but I can see that he's treating you incredibly well, and for that I'm grateful.'

'You really don't like him?'

'I don't know. I'd need to spend more time with him. But the main thing is that you're happy.'

'You will like him, you know,' I say. 'He's really a sweetheart once you get past all the pompous shit.'

'You mean you can get past the pompous shit?'

'Oh, Jules!' I give her a hug. 'Please be happy for me. He's treating me better than anyone I've ever met.'

'That's what I'm scared of,' she says into my shoulder. 'I'm just scared that you've fallen for the way he's treating you, rather than for the man himself.'

We disengage and it's my turn to reapply some lipstick. 'I don't think that's the case,' I say, painting on my top lip. 'I really don't.'

'Okay,' she says, smiling at me in the mirror. 'If you say so, then I believe you.'

'Did you like them?'

'Yes,' says Ed slowly, on the way back to his place.

'Did you like Jules?'

'She's certainly feisty,' he says.

'You didn't like her, did you?'

'Of course I did,' he says, reaching over to give me a kiss as we stop at a red light. 'She's your best friend, so I have to like her.'

I'm not sure that's entirely what I wanted to hear, plus

I don't really believe him, but I'm sure they'll both get over it. I'm sure everything will be fine. It has to be.

We park the car and get out, and just as we're walking to the front door Ed suddenly turns and grabs me, enveloping me in a huge hug.

'I was going to wait,' he says, 'and do this properly. But I think I should probably ask you now. Will you marry me?'

These are the words I've waited my whole life to hear, so why isn't my heart soaring into the night sky? Why am I not dancing up the terrace with joy? Why do I feel so completely and utterly normal?

'Okay,' I say eventually, watching Ed's expression turn from worried into rapturous.

'You will?'

'I will.'

'You'll be my wife?'

'Yes.'

'Oh goodness. I think we need to celebrate this with champagne.'

So we go inside and as I sit on the sofa watching Ed open the champagne I wonder why this feels like the biggest anti-climax of my life. And even when he brings me the glass and sits next to me to cuddle me, I still don't feel ecstatically happy, but then maybe no one feels like this? Maybe the whole thing is a bit like a Hollywood film, the passionate love thing, the feeling of ecstasy when you're proposed to? Maybe none of it really exists, and, even if it did, this feeling of being grounded is so much safer, in some ways more real, and I definitely prefer being the loved rather than the lover, I'm much more in control.

And after we've celebrated for a while I pick up the

phone and wake up my parents to tell them the good news.

My mother screams. Literally. Screams.

'She's getting married,' she then shrieks at my father. 'Oh, Libby, I don't know what to say I'm so excited and I can't believe it you're getting married and oh my good Lord I never thought I'd see the day and you're marrying Ed McMahon and he's so eligible and you've got him . . .' I swear I'm not making this up, she doesn't take a breath.

Nor does she add, 'Wait until I tell the neighbours,' but I know that's what she's thinking.

And Dad comes on the phone and just says, 'Congratulations, darling. I'm very happy for you,' and then I pass the phone to Ed and I can hear my mother shrieking delight at Ed, and finally we put the phone down and I think about calling Jules, because, after my parents, she should be the first person in the world to know, but somehow I'm not so sure I want to tell her when I'm with Ed, I think I'd rather tell her when I'm on my own, so I leave that call until tomorrow morning and we go to bed.

Chapter Twenty-four

I didn't sleep all that well last night. Ed and I 'made lurrve', and, although it's getting better, in some ways it's getting worse. His technique has improved immeasurably, but I now know exactly what he's going to be doing – I did try telling him that perhaps he ought to vary the routine a little bit, and then he got upset and said it felt like I was criticizing him. I tried to explain that even though he read up on sex in a textbook, the act itself shouldn't feel like a textbook, and it wasn't a criticism, it would just sometimes be nice if he surprised me, rather than going through exactly the same motions every time.

Ed apologized, and then I felt guilty, especially because this was the night we got engaged, so I apologized. Within minutes he was asleep, while I lay awake in his bed for hours, trying to get a grip on the situation. And yes, I was happy, but I lay there thinking that it all still felt a bit like a dream, and I couldn't quite get used to the fact that this was for life. That this man sleeping beside me would be the only man ever to sleep beside me for the rest of my life.

But Ed looked so sweet when he was fast asleep. I watched him for ages, and suddenly, at about three in the morning, I felt it. A huge burst of joy that spread up through my body, and that was when it hit me. I'm getting married! Me! Libby Mason! I'm going to be a wife! I'm never going to have to worry about being sad, lonely and single again!

I crept out of bed and walked around the house, opening all the doors and going into all the empty rooms, standing in them and grinning, knowing that all this was officially mine. And then I went into the gym and started leaping around a bit, until I realized that the whole house was shaking and I might wake Ed, and I didn't want to wake Ed. This was my moment. Oh my God! I'm getting married!

I went downstairs and made myself a cup of tea, and sat curled up on the sofa, still grinning manically at the prospect of living in this spectacular house. Of never having to shop in high street chains again. Of showing off my huge house to Jules. And Sally. And Nick.

Jesus Christ! What will Nick say? I'd like him to be happy for me, but I'd also like him to be just a little bit jealous. I want him to have a few regrets, to help my ego, I suppose.

I sat for a while thinking of all the people I'd want to know, and then I decided to make a bit of an engagement party list, except I couldn't find any paper and I was getting kind of sleepy by then anyway, so eventually I went back up and climbed into bed beside Ed, and finally, at 5.45 a. m., just as the birds were singing, I drifted off to sleep with a smile still on my face.

'I couldn't do it!' says Jules, when I ring her the next morning. 'Paul came back here for coffee, and it was awful, Libby. It was so weird, sitting here drinking it and knowing that he was going to make a pass, and I was completely dreading it, so I kept getting up for biscuits, and sugar, and things, and it was awful.'

'Well? Did you do it?'

'No!' she practically screams. 'He tried to kiss me and I panicked! I started blabbing about how I hadn't been separated for very long and I wasn't sure I was ready and I couldn't do this. Oh, Libby. I feel such a total failure.'

'What did he say?'

'What could he say? He was really sweet, and kissed me on the cheek and said he'd call me again but that he understood and he wasn't in any hurry.'

'Do you still think that you'll be sleeping with him to get back at Jamie?'

'Oh shit. I don't know. I know that last night I couldn't, but now, this morning, I just don't know.'

'Jules, do you really think it's going to help, getting back at Jamie?'

'At least we'll be equal, but I don't know if I can go through with it.'

'So are you going to see Paul again?'

'He probably won't phone me now anyway. What do you think? Do you think he'll call?'

'Of course he will, and by the way I'm getting married.'

'But what should I do when he calls?'

'Jules? Did you hear what I just said?'

'No. What?'

'I'm getting married!'

There's a long silence.

'Jules?'

'Oh my God!'

'I know! Can you believe it? Ed proposed when we got home last night.'

'And you didn't call me? You cow! Why didn't you call me?'

'I wanted to tell you when I was alone. So. Aren't you going to congratulate me?'

'I can't believe it,' she says. 'When? When are you actually going to do it?'

'We never got round to talking about it. But don't worry, I do want to be engaged for about a year.'

'Promise?'

'Promise. Jules, aren't you happy for me?'

'God, Libby. I'm over the moon. Are you with Ed tonight?'

'Nah. I'm having a night off. Just want to chill out on my own tonight.'

'You mean I can't tempt you with a Marks & Sparks dinner and a selection of bridal magazines from which to choose your dress?'

'You've kept your bridal magazines?'

'Libby, I keep everything. I've got stacks and stacks of them, plus loads of info on hotels for the reception and everything.'

'You've got me. I'm coming. Shall I come straight from work?'

'Yup. I'll get the champagne on ice. Damn. I wish Jamie were here.'

Thank God. That's the first time she's given any indication that she misses him. 'I know,' I say. 'Me too.'

By lunchtime I think I've told the world, and, though personal calls are normally frowned upon at work (not that you'd know it, the number of times I speak to Jules), Joe said it was fine to make a few this morning, and he sent Jo out to buy champagne so we could have a mini office celebration.

That's what I love about this job: everyone here is so laid-back that they'll jump on any excuse to have a knees-up. Joe is genuinely delighted for me, although, and I know this is paranoia striking, I hope it's not because he wants to get rid of me.

'Will we be saying goodbye to you?' he says, pouring some more champagne into my glass.

'You can't get rid of me that easily,' I laugh, 'I'll be here for at least another year.'

'We'll be doing your PR next,' he says, grinning. 'Setting up features on the glamorous charity-supporting wife of Ed McMahon.'

I laugh. Although it's not a bad idea. And charity work would be a good thing to do, because other than shop, meet friends for lunch and eventually look after our children, how will I fill my days?

What bliss. I mean, I may well carry on working for a bit, maybe until I have children, but it won't be serious slogging work for peanut money. Maybe I'll work here part time, say, two days a week, and maybe I'll join some snazzy charity committee and organize fashion lunches and things. God. I'm almost tempted to leave now.

Everyone at work keeps congratulating me, and the champagne's going straight to my head, when Jo – who's been rushing back and forth to pick up the phone in between swigging champagne and chatting away – shouts, 'Libby, Nick's on the phone. D'you want to call him back?'

'No, I'll take it.' I run to my desk, away from the hubbub, and pick up the phone.

'Hi, Nick!'

'Congratulations. Sal just told me.'

Is it my imagination or does, ha ha, his voice sound just a teensy bit flat? Not that it bothers me any more, talking to Nick, not now that I've got Ed.

'I know. Thanks. Can you believe it, me, getting married?'

'Well, no. Not really. It seems like only yesterday that we were going out.'

Oh. I see. Now, all of a sudden, we were 'going out'. Before, we were just sort of seeing one another.

'As my mother always says, when it's right, it's right.'

'And he's right?'

'Yup.'

'I'm really happy for you, Libby. I hope he knows how lucky he is.'

'Oh, he does,' I laugh, because it's clear that Nick does have at least some regrets, which is always nice to hear when you were the one that was, to put it unceremoniously, dumped.

'Good. Listen, I can't stay on. I just wanted to say congratulations. I really hope you'll be happy, Libby. You deserve to be.'

'Nick! This isn't like you. What's all this stuff about how lucky Ed is and how I deserve to be happy?' I can't help it. The champagne seems to have loosened my tongue.

Nick laughs. 'I'm sorry. I've been thinking about you recently, and I suppose part of me kind of regrets things not working out.'

'Ah ha!' I say. 'I'll always be the one that got away.'

'Yes,' he says seriously. 'I suspect you will. Anyway, I really must go, but we should get together soon. Maybe you and I could celebrate, for old times' sake.'

'As long as you promise not to make a pass.'

'That's going to be a hard one,' he says, and I can hear from his voice that he's smiling. 'But I can promise I won't make more than one.'

'Perfect,' I say. 'One pass will do wonders for the ego,' as indeed will this entire conversation, although naturally I keep that thought to myself. 'I'll call you when things have settled down a bit, how's that?'

'That would be lovely. Oh, and give my love to Jules and Jamie.'

Yet another one who doesn't know about Jamie. I put down the phone, thinking it was a shame it didn't work out with Nick. He seemed to fit in so well, so much better than Ed in some ways, and God knows there was certainly passion there. But Nick could never have given me the life I wanted, and anyway it's not lust that's important. It's not even whether someone fits in with my friends that matters. It's whether someone fits in with me, and Ed does.

I know Jules has loads of magazines, but I can't help myself. I have to sneak out mid-afternoon and buy three more, because Jules got married ages ago and fashions change, even in wedding dresses, and I want to know exactly what's in now.

And although I make all the calls I have to make and speak to all the people I have to speak to, those magazines perch in a plastic bag on the corner of my desk just whispering my name all afternoon. In the end I take them into the loo and sit on the closed seat, leafing through quickly, but dying to study every page, every dress.

And when I come back from the loo I idly doodle a few

designs on my pad, dreaming about walking down the aisle while all my friends gasp at my incredible beauty and tiny waist, because in my fantasies I will have lost a stone by my wedding day, and I will of course be the most beautiful bride they've ever seen.

And then I think about engagement rings, and I go round the office to all the women who are married or engaged, and insist upon trying on their rings to see what sort suits my hand. Deborah has a beautiful antique emerald-cut emerald surrounded by tiny pavé diamonds, which looks incredible except I wouldn't have an emerald, I'd have to have a huge fuck-off diamond, and those pavé diamonds surrounding it are far too small, and, as I joke to Deborah while I inspect the ring on the third finger of my left hand, I can still move my hand around far too easily.

Becs has a pear-shaped diamond, which is more like it, and I quite like it being pear-shaped, although maybe I'd have one pear-shaped and two round ones on either side.

'Where are you thinking of getting it?' Becs says, laughing at me as I parade around the office with my hand splayed in front of me.

'Give me a chance!' I laugh. 'I only got engaged a few hours ago! Isn't there some sort of rule on how much a man should spend on an engagement ring? Isn't it something like six months' salary or something?'

'Six months!' she shrieks. 'In your dreams, love! It's one month, which still means your ring will cost a bloody fortune, given that you're marrying Ed McMahon.'

Jesus. I'm marrying Ed McMahon! It hits me again and I whoop round the office telling everyone again that I'm marrying Ed McMahon, until they're all completely sick of me and Joe tells me to shut up or go home, and I would have gone home, except I think I've been going home early a bit too often lately, so I skulk back to my desk and do a few more weddingy doodles until it actually is time to leave.

Jules staggers down the stairs under the weight of two cardboard boxes.

'They're in there,' she announces as she drops them on the floor in the kitchen. 'But first,' and she beckons me towards the door with her finger and grabs my hand.

'Where are we going?'

She's pulling me upstairs, and we end up in the spare room, where she clambers on a chair and opens a cupboard at the top, pulling out a large white box.

I gasp. 'It's your wedding dress, isn't it?'

'Yup,' she says, lifting off the lid and carefully unwrapping the layers of tissue paper. 'I thought you might like to try it on.'

'Are you sure?'

'Go on. Let's see what kind of a bride you'll make.'

I whip off my clothes and Jules helps me into the dress. It's not exactly a perfect fit – in fact, we don't even bother attempting to do up the tiny row of buttons at the back – but it gives me the bride effect, and we both stand there giggling as she shows me how to do those tiny measured steps down the aisle.

'Let me practise the stairs,' I say, walking regally on to the landing, shoulders back, head held high, staring at myself in awe as I pass the mirror.

And eventually we kick off our shoes (don't worry, the wedding dress has been safely packed away again) and curl up on the sofas to work our way through the magazines.

'You can't have that one,' Jules says in horror, as I show her this fairy-tale meringue dress with layers and layers of stiff tulle shooting out from a tiny boned waist. 'You'll look like a huge cream puff.'

'Oh, thanks a lot. Are you trying to tell me I'm fat?'

'Yeah, really.' She raises her eyes to the ceiling. 'You? Fat? Hardly. I'm just saying that those dresses are really unflattering. I think you should go for something much more simple. Remember my motto – '

'Yeah, yeah, yeah. Less is more.'

'Exactly. I can see you in something really elegant and sophisticated. Here. What about something like this?' She slides her magazine over to my lap and points to a stunning ivory sheath.

'Mmm,' I say, trying to imagine my head superimposed on to the model's. 'That is gorgeous.'

'Very sophis,' she says.

'Mmm. But what about bridesmaids?'

'You could do something similar but on a smaller scale. Maybe knee length or something, in a different colour.'

'Oh God. Colours. What colour?'

Two hours later we're groaning after a major pig-out, and at our feet are piles of pages I've torn out for ideas.

'You really are going to marry him, aren't you?' Jules says suddenly.

'What? Did you think this was all a joke?'

'Not a joke, but I just . . .'

'Jules, I really am going to marry him.'

'Okay, but let me ask you one question. Are you in love with him?'

I pause. 'Yes. Well. I love him.'

'That's not what I asked,' she says. 'Are you in love with him?

'Jules,' I say slowly, as if I'm talking to a child because I really want her to understand what I'm about to say. 'You were incredibly lucky with Jamie, or at least, we all thought so at the time. You seemed to have found someone who was gorgeous, bright, funny, who adored you, who was your best friend, and whom you completely fancied. You thought you'd found the perfect man, and it didn't work out.'

'Thanks,' she says bitterly. 'Rub it in, why don't you.'

'I didn't mean it like that,' I say. 'All I'm trying to say is that you thought you'd found the recipe for a lifetime of happiness, and it still didn't work out. Maybe what I have with Ed would work out. And maybe the fact that it isn't the same as it was with you and Jamie isn't such a bad thing, because at least I'm going into this with my eyes open.'

'You mean you're having to compromise.'

'Well, yes, but I do sort of think you have to compromise. Not on everything, but I think the most important thing is to look for a good man. A man who will look after you, who will be a good husband, a good father to your children. Someone who can be your best friend, who will see you through the ups and downs.'

'But you have to fancy them.'

'Of course you have to fancy them,' I say. 'But that's not nearly as important as the other things, because the fancying thing, the lust thing, always goes, and once it does you're left with nothing. But if you've chosen someone you're really compatible with, then you'll always be friends, and friendship is the most important thing.'

'So you don't fancy Ed, but you like him as a friend?'

I sigh. 'No. That's not what I'm saying. I do fancy Ed, but it's not that out of control feeling of frenzied lust that I felt about, say, Jon. Even with Nick I started to feel out of control towards the end . . .'

'That was because you really fell for him.'

'But don't you see that this is really what I want? That I prefer being in control? That I've found someone who will always adore me, and whom I will always be friends with. And although I fancy him, the sex isn't the most important thing.'

'That's because it's crap.'

'It bloody is not crap.'

'That's what you said.'

'That was at the beginning,' I grumble. 'It's much better now.'

'But it's not as good as Nick.'

'But that's my whole point,' I sigh in exasperation. 'Nick wasn't for me. Sex isn't everything, and yes, the sex with Nick was amazing, but nothing else was.'

'Yes, it was. You got on fantastically.'

'Well, okay, we did. But why are we talking about Nick? This isn't about Nick, it's got nothing to do with him. This is about what we look for in a partner.'

'I'm just worried that you might be compromising a little too much, and I could understand it if you were thirty-seven or something, but you're twenty-seven, and it just seems a bit young to be making these sorts of compromises.'

'Jules, I do love him, and I know he's very good for me, and it doesn't feel like a compromise to me. I can see how you'd think that, but I promise you, it's not. He's everything I've ever wanted.'

'In terms of wealth,' she says with a sniff.

'No. Not only that. I can really see us together.'

'I'm sorry, I just don't want to see you making a big mistake. Marriage is such a huge step, you have to be completely sure.'

'I am completely sure. I know that, because being involved with men I'm completely crazy about has only ever made me miserable.'

'You'll never know now, will you?'

'Know what?'

'Whether you'd find someone whom you could fall completely in love with without being miserable; someone who'd feel the same way about you. This is it, Libby. No more men. No more adventures. No more getting excited over dates with someone you really like.'

'Yes, and no more tears. No more feeling like a piece of shit when you've been dumped yet again. No more sitting at home crying while you're waiting for the phone to ring. No more being on that bloody awful dating scene. Jules, I promise you this is right. Ed is exactly what I've always looked for and I know I'll be happy. Anyway, I can't see why you're getting so uptight. It's not like we're walking down the aisle next week. I've already told you that we're going to be engaged for about a year.'

'Okay, okay. I'm sorry. I really am happy for you, Libby, I simply want to be absolutely sure that you know what you're doing. You're going to be spending the rest of your life with Ed.'

'I know,' I say happily. 'Let's get back to the wedding. So what colours do you think the bridesmaids' dresses should be?'

Chapter Twenty-five

'Where's Ed?' My mother's bright smile is disappearing as she stands on the doorstep looking over my shoulder.

'He had to work. Sorry,' I say, pushing past her into the house, which isn't strictly true – I couldn't face another Ed and my family scenario.

'Jesus, Mum. What's all this?'

The dining table has been laid with my mother's best china that only ever seems to see the light of day once a year, and, peering through the clingfilm that covers the dishes, I can see my mother's completely gone to town.

'Obviously it's a waste of time,' she says, reaching down and tightening the clingfilm covering a plate of bridge rolls in the centre of the table. 'I thought Ed would be with you and I didn't want him to think we didn't know how to provide a nice tea.'

'Mum, tea is tea, with maybe a cake or some scones or something. This is enough to feed an army. What have you got here?' I pull back some more clingfilm to find piles of tiny Danish pastries, and more to reveal a huge chocolate cake. Thank God Ed isn't here. Thank God he can't see my mother in all her suburban glory.

'Oh well,' I say, taking a pastry, 'I'm starving.'

My mother sighs. 'I was so looking forward to seeing Ed again. I thought we could all celebrate together.'

The doorbell rings and I look up. 'Who's that?'

'What am I going to tell Elaine and Phil?' she says,

walking to the door as I sink into the sofa in disbelief. My mother's invited her bloody bridge partners, presumably to show off her new wealthy son-in-law-to-be.

'Hello, Libby,' says Elaine, walking over at the same time as looking round the room. 'Congratulations. Where's the lucky man?'

'Working,' I say ungraciously, as she leans down to kiss my cheek.

'That's a pity,' booms Phil, walking into the living room. 'We were looking forward to meeting the famous Ed McMahon. Well done, girl. You've struck lucky there.'

I force a pained smile on to my face as I nod.

'Where's Alan?' says Phil. 'In the garden?'

My mother raises her eyes to the ceiling and nods. 'With his rose bushes, as usual,' and Elaine gives a tinkling laugh.

'At least your Alan does the gardening,' says Elaine. 'My Phil wouldn't know what a rose bush looks like.'

'Thank you, Elaine,' says Phil. 'And who does all the DIY, then, I'd like to know?'

'I know, dear. You are wonderful with a drill, I'll give you that.'

Phil's chest puffs out like a pigeon. 'I'll go and see if Alan needs a hand,' he says, as he leaves the room.

And the doorbell rings again. I look at my mother with raised eyebrows, as she goes to answer it.

'Diane! Ken!' I hear her exclaim, and then I have to strain my ears to hear her voice, which drops down to what my mother thinks is a whisper. 'Ed's not here. I'm so sorry, he had to work. You know how it is, being such a successful financier. Never mind,' and her voice goes back to its normal booming self. 'We've got a lovely tea.'

'Libby!' says Ken, as if he's surprised to see me there. 'Ay ay.' He nudges me and winks. 'What's all this about being a millionaire's wife, then?'

'Ken,' warns Diane. 'Leave the poor girl alone. She's probably fed up with all these people going on about it.' I give her a grateful smile.

'We've heard all about him,' she then, unbelievably, continues, taking off her tweed Country Casuals jacket. 'Jean told us all about the house. He sounds wonderful. Aren't you a lucky girl?'

Why do I feel like a six-year-old around my parents' friends?

My mother comes over to me and prods me with her elbow.

'Yes,' I say, smiling. 'I'm a very lucky girl.'

'Lovely bag,' Diane then twitters, as she turns and sees my beloved Gucci, which is dumped next to the sofa. 'That's not yours, Jean, is it?'

'No. It's Libby's,' says my mum, who turns to me. 'Looks expensive?' Said as a question.

'Yes. It's very expensive. Ed bought it for me.'

'Not one of those Pucci ones, is it?' Diane says, walking over and – can you believe this – actually opening my bag to look at the label. 'Oh!' she giggles. 'I meant Gucci.'

'Ed bought you a Gucci bag?' Now my mother's seriously impressed. I nod. 'That Tara whatsername's got one of those.'

'Tara?' Diane stands racking her brains for a neighbour/member of the bridge club called Tara.

'You know, Diane, that girl in all the papers. Tara Thompson Parker.'

'It's Tara Palmer-Tomkinson, actually,' I say through gritted teeth.

'That's the one,' Elaine says brightly from the dining table, where she's looking at all the goodies. 'Goodness, Jean, look at this spread. You must have worked so hard.'

'It was nothing,' says my mum proudly. 'No trouble.'

'Oooh, look at that cake.' Elaine removes some tinfoil for a peek. 'Did you do that yourself?'

'Of course. I'd never serve a store-bought cake,' says my mother. 'You know how much I love baking.'

Christ. I wish Olly were here. My mother on her own is bad enough, but with her ridiculous, twittering friends it's just a total nightmare.

'You'll have to start cooking for your fiancé now,' Elaine says, smiling at me, while my mother snorts merrily away. 'What?' says Elaine, looking at my mother. 'She'll have to get used to entertaining all his friends.'

'Unfortunately for Libby, she didn't inherit my cooking skills,' says my mother, who then proceeds to describe the food the other night, in great detail, while Elaine and Diane tut tut and give me disbelieving looks and I want to kill them. All of them. And in my mother's case I'd make it particularly tortuous.

'I hear there are some wonderful cooking courses around,' Diane says innocently, when they've finished laughing at me. 'Maybe you should try that Pru Leith school. They're meant to be very good.'

Oh please shut up. All of you.

'Maybe,' I find myself saying.

'What a pity your Ed isn't here,' Elaine says, after the awkward silence that followed. 'We were so looking forward to meeting him.'

'I know,' I say, and then, I can't help it, it just comes out in a massively sarcastic tone: 'He would have loved you.'

My mother looks at me in horror. 'Libby!'

'I'm really sorry,' I say, and I am, I honestly didn't mean to say that. 'I didn't mean that to come out the way it did.'

Elaine does a perfect impersonation of my mother's sniff, while Diane pats my knee and smiles. 'Don't worry,' she says. 'You must be under a lot of pressure, marrying someone like Ed.'

'Mum,' I mumble. 'Mum, can I use the phone?'

'Go on,' she sighs. 'Take it upstairs,' and I think even she is grateful to see the back of me for a few minutes.

'Jules. This is hell. I am going through living hell.'

'Where are you?'

'At my bloody parents with their bloody friends, who are all taking the piss out of my cooking.'

'Do you have to stay?'

I sigh. 'For about an hour. Listen, what do you think about an engagement party?'

'Hmm. What about an engagement dinner?'

'What, instead of a party?'

'Well, you can always have a party later, but, seeing as Ed doesn't have that many friends, why don't you have a small dinner somewhere and introduce him to everyone? Otherwise you're going to have to go out with everyone separately, and this way you can get all the introductions out of the way.'

'Yeah. Good idea. So have like an introductory dinner, and then have the party?'

'Yup, because it will be a bit weird to have the party when no one's met him.'

'When should I do it?'

'Sooner the better.'

'Should I just ring everyone and see when they're free?'

'Yeah. We could do next week if you want. Any night except Tuesday.'

'Wednesday?'

'Fine. Who else will you ask?'

'Sally and Paul. Olly and Carolyn.'

'He's still with her, then?'

'Mmm hmm.'

'Oh good. I really liked her. Who else?'

'Well, how many do you think? Should it be everyone or just the inner circle?'

'Just the inner circle, I think. What about Nick?'

Is that really a good idea? 'Do you think he'll come?'

'Yes. Plus you're always saying you're still friends.'

'But then I need a woman for him. I know! Jo from work! They'd get on.' Actually, I'm not sure that they would, which is why I'll ask her. Jo, like me, would never demean herself by going out with someone with no money whatsoever.

'Okay. Then you can ask those friends of Ed,' says Jules. 'What were their names?'

'Charlie and Sarah. Hmm. Don't know. Maybe not. They were really nice but they're quite a bit older, I'm not sure they'd fit in.'

'Fine. Well have one dinner for your friends and another for Ed's.' And then she stops and sighs.

'What's the matter, Jules?'

'Oh, I don't know,' she says. 'It's just that . . . well, it's just that it's going to be so weird celebrating this without Jamie. You know, being with all these people I know and being on my own.'

'You could ask him,' I say hesitantly.

'No way,' she says firmly. 'I'm not going to let him turn up and pretend to everyone that everything's fine.'

'Are you sure?'

'No.' She attempts a laugh. 'But I'm still not going to ask him.'

'Libby!' My mum's standing at the bottom of the stairs shouting for me.

'Shit, gotta go. The dragon's screaming.'

'Call me later.'

'Yup.'

'So when will you have the engagement party?' Elaine's got a smudge of egg mayonnaise on her chin, and I'm quite enjoying the fact that no one's noticed, or if they have, they haven't bothered to say anything.

'We haven't really discussed it and by the way you seem to have left half your sandwich on your chin.'

Her eyes widen as she hurriedly wipes her chin with a paper napkin.

'Sorry,' I say cheerfully, enjoying her embarrassment, 'but I always think you should tell people things like that.'

'Yes. Er. Thank you.'

'So what sort of party will it be?' says Diane loudly, over the sound of the football, which Phil insisted on turning on, so Phil, Ken and my dad are huddled by the TV while 'the girls' – as Phil called us – are on the suite on the other side of the room.

'I don't know, but I think we'll probably have it at home.'

'Hanover Terrace,' my mum adds smugly.

'I know dear,' says Diane. 'You already told me.'

'I just can't believe my daughter's going to be living in Hanover Terrace,' she says, almost crying with the sheer joy of it. 'It's not a house, it's a mansion.'

'I hope he's got good security.' Elaine obviously feels left out. 'Those sorts of houses are forever getting burgled.'

'There wouldn't be anything to take,' jokes my mother, 'the house is practically empty.'

'So you'll be redecorating, then?' says Elaine, as I nod. 'How exciting. I noticed they had some lovely suites in John Lewis the other day.'

'Libby won't be buying anything in John Lewis,' says my mother, as I look at her, wondering what on earth she's on about. 'She'll be doing her shopping at Harrods, thank you very much.'

Diane and Elaine look impressed.

'Actually,' I say, 'I think Harrods is a bit old-fashioned for me. I'm planning on going to the Conran Shop.'

'The Conran Shop?' say Diane and Elaine in unison.

'You can't buy those modern new-fangled things in the Conran Shop!' explains my mother. 'They might look nice but I'll tell you this, Libby, they're not comfortable.'

'And when was the last time you went to the Conran Shop?' I offer.

'Two days ago,' shouts my father. It's half-time. 'She decided she ought to learn a bit more about how the other half live.'

Elaine and Diane giggle politely, while my mother pretends to smile at the same time as shooting daggers at my father.

'We just happened to be passing,' she says, 'so we thought we'd have a look and see what all the fuss was about.'

341

'Passing?' I say, an evil smile on my lips. 'Was that before or after lunch at Daphne's?'

She gives me a stony look.

'I think I'll just use the phone again.' I stand up and make a move to go upstairs, and, as my mother's about to protest, I add: 'I'm calling Ed. Is that okay?'

'Oh yes,' she simpers. 'Of course. Do give him our love.'

'Right.' I walk on up to their room and sit on their bed to make the call.

'Hello, sweetieloviedarling!' Ed exclaims. 'I miss you.'

'What are you doing?'

'Working, but I've nearly finished. Are you coming over later?'

'I'll leave here in a minute, then I'll come.'

'How are your parents?'

'A pain. As usual.'

'Libby! Don't say that about them. They're your parents.'

'Sorry,' I grumble. 'It's just that they've got their friends round, and it's all a bit much for me. What are we doing tonight?' I'm hoping that we'll be going out somewhere swish, because I haven't worn my new designer outfit for nothing.

'Sundays are always a bit difficult. I thought maybe we could go to the cinema? Or perhaps we could rent a video and watch it at home.'

'Oh. I thought we were going out for dinner.'

'Not on a Sunday, I think. Is that all right? Do you want to go out? I could always book somewhere.'

'Don't worry,' I say. 'I'm happy staying in.

'I'll make sure everything's *magnifique*,' he booms. 'What would you like to eat? I'll go shopping now before you get here.'

'I don't mind, Ed. Anything. I'm pretty full after tea here.'

'Smoked salmon? Scrambled eggs? Pasta?'

'Anything, Ed. Really. I don't mind.'

'All right, my darling. I can't wait to see you and I love you very very much.'

'I know,' I sigh. 'I love you too.'

I walk back into the living room and everyone turns to look at me.

'Well?' says my mother.

'Well what?' I positively sneer.

'Well what did he have to say?'

'Oh. He said he was really sorry he couldn't be here, and he was particularly sorry he missed the bridge rolls and he can't wait to see you soon.'

My mother sighs and turns, smiling, to Elaine and Diane. 'I can't tell you how lovely it is to have such a charming son-in-law.'

'He's not your son-in-law yet,' I mutter.

'Speaking of which,' my mother says, grabbing the opportunity, 'when are you thinking of actually setting a date?'

'We haven't talked about it, but don't worry, I'm sure you'll be the first to know.'

'I always think summer weddings are lovely,' says Elaine.

'I'll bear it in mind. I'm sorry, everyone, but I must go. Ed's waiting for me.'

I walk round the room and perfunctorily kiss all the guests goodbye, and my mother sees me to the door.

'You could have been a bit nicer to our guests,' she hisses on the doorstep.

'You could have made it a bit less obvious that you'd

invited them round to show off your daughter's boyfriend.'

'Not boyfriend. Fiancé', she says. 'And anyway. I didn't invite them round to show Ed off to them. I owed them, and I completely forgot you and Ed were supposed to be coming round.'

'Which is why they were all so upset when he wasn't here.'

My mother folds her arms and looks at me. 'Honestly, Libby. Most girls would be over the moon to be engaged to Ed McMahon, but you just seem to be in a permanent bad mood. I can't think what's the matter with you. Anyone would think you didn't want to be engaged to one of the most eligible men in the country.'

'What are you wearing?' I've just disengaged from one of Ed's smothering hugs, and I look down to see these worn-out shabby old carpet slippers that are exactly like the worn-out shabby old carpet slippers my grandfather used to wear.

'My slippers,' he says in a bemused tone. 'They're my favourite slippers. Don't you like them?'

'Ed! They're old man slippers. They're awful!'

Once again he gets that sad puppy-dog expression on his face, and this time it just irritates the fuck out of me.

'Ed, sometimes I think you're a sixty-year-old trapped in a younger man's body.'

'What do you mean?'

'It's only that sometimes you seem so middle aged.' Shit, I think I've pushed this one a bit too far. 'I'm sorry,' I say, putting my arms around him and kissing him, which, thank God, removes the expression. 'It's just that you aren't old and sometimes you behave a bit like an old fuddy-duddy.'

'I'll throw them away,' he says, kicking off the offensive slippers and carrying them to the dustbin. 'There!' He closes the lid of the bin. 'All gone. Happy now?'

'Yes,' I snort, although it's not just about the slippers, and I do genuinely worry that Ed lives in another world. That he doesn't really have a clue what's going on, that I really am forcing myself to be compatible with someone who's too damn straight for me.

Would you listen to me?

'I'm in a bit of a bad mood. I'm sorry, darling. My parents seem to have that effect on me.'

'I don't like Libby when she's grumpy,' he says, sitting next to me on the sofa and pursing his lips for a kiss. I dutifully kiss him and he grins at me. 'I like Libby when she's happy.'

'I'll try to be happy,' I say, and smile.

'That's better,' he says, kissing me again and then kissing my neck and stroking my hair, and I know what this means. Yup. Move number two is hand up to my breast.

'Mmm,' he says into my hair. 'Libby smells sexy.'

And then move number three is hand under the jumper, hand under the bra, bra strap undone (amidst much fumbling, I'll have you know).

'Shall we go to bed?' Ed says as he's pulling off my jumper.

'Why? What's wrong with the sofa?' I say.

'Oh no!' He looks horrified. 'If we're going to play bouncy castles we have to do it in bed.'

'Right. Bouncy castles. In bed. Okay.' And I pick up my jumper and walk up the stairs, wondering how I'm supposed to be turned on by the words 'bouncy castles'. Wondering whether sex is ever going to improve with a man who refers to a fuck as 'playing bouncy castles'. Whether 'bouncy castles' is as dirty as it's ever going to get.

And for a second there I do think about Nick. Well, okay. A few seconds, actually. I think about how sexy he was, how it was fucking, how it wasn't playing anything other than very dirty indeed, how incredibly turned on I was by the fact that we fucked our way all over his flat and all over mine.

Oh, and did I mention that once we did it in the car? Bit embarrassing, that one. It was at King's Cross. We'd stopped off to get the late-night papers one Saturday night, and both of us started feeling really horny once we got back in the car. An hour later there was a knock on the steamed-up window, and I rolled it down breathlessly to find a policeman standing there.

'Everything all right, madam?' he said, smirking.

'Oh yes. Fine.'

'It's just that you've been here for an hour and this isn't the safest place, you know. All sorts of strange people here.'

'Oh. Er. Sorry.'

'Kissing your boyfriend goodnight, were you?' The smirk got bigger. Bloody cheek.

But no. Enough about Nick. Where was I? Oh yes. Playing 'bouncy castles' with Ed. In bed. Which is fine. Not great. Not even good. Just okay. And for your information I do have an orgasm, but I suppose if someone, anyone, rubs long enough in the right place it's bound to happen, isn't it?

I try to do something different. I think it might be

quite nice to go on top for a change, and, as I clamber on top and guide him inside me, Ed looks completely baffled.

'What are you doing?' he booms.

'Just trying something new,' I whisper back.

'Are you sure about this, darling?'

'Ed, shut up. You're destroying the moment.'

'Sorry,' he booms again. I give him a look.

I move on top of him for about a minute, and then he starts shaking his head and pulls me off him. 'Sorry, darling,' he says. 'I don't think I like that at all,' and then he gets back into his favoured missionary position and starts pounding away, while I look at the ceiling and try to picture my wedding dress.

'That was gorgeous,' he says, when he's finished.

'Mmm? Good,' I murmur, halfway down the aisle once again.

'Libby? Was it, umm, good for you?'

'Yes, Ed. It was lovely,' I lie, turning to kiss him as he gives me a grateful smile.

Ed gets up to go to the bathroom, and when he comes back I tell him about my idea for an introductory pre-engagement-party dinner. I do say it was mine, because I'm not entirely sure what reaction I'd get if he knew Jules came up with the idea.

'Excellent idea,' he says. 'I'll take everyone out for dinner.'

'Don't be silly,' I say. 'Everyone will pay for themselves.'

He looks at me in horror. 'Libby, you can't invite people out for dinner and then expect them to pay. That's very bad form.'

'Are you sure?'

'I wouldn't have it any other way.'

'Okay,' I say, shrugging. 'If you don't mind.' I tell him who I think we should invite and he says fine. And what's more, he doesn't even ask who Nick is.

Chapter Twenty-six

Much as I hate to admit that my mother's ever right about anything, I can see that she does seem to have a point, that bit about me being in a bad mood, but the problem is the only time I'm really in a bad mood, other than when I'm at my parents' of course, is when I'm with Ed.

I just don't understand why all of a sudden he seems to irritate me, and there seems to be a bit of a pattern developing which is beginning to worry me. Ed constantly smothers me with affection, attention and love, and the more he smothers me the more claustrophic I find it. Eventually I snap at him, and then he gets that look, and then I have a bit of breathing space, until I feel so guilty at hurting him I apologize and then he starts smothering me all over again.

You would think, given that I am one of the most self-aware people I know, that there would have been a book written about this syndrome, but I've flicked through all the usual ones, and I can't find anything that pertains to this particular problem.

And the thing is, maybe it isn't a problem. Maybe deep down I don't believe I deserve to be happy, so now that I have found a really good man who treats me well, I'm deliberately trying to sabotage it because I don't think I deserve someone who treats me well.

Or maybe he just irritates me.

But I don't want to consider that as an option because

it's just too damn easy. It's too damn easy to say that I am irritated with Ed because he is an irritating person. And if I admitted that, then I couldn't marry him, and I so badly want to marry him, I so badly want this to work.

I suppose I've never had anyone treat me like this before, worship me in the way Ed does, want to do anything to make me happy, and I suspect I just don't know how to deal with it. Sometimes I feel as if I'm almost testing Ed. The more loving and giving he is to me, the more it pisses me off, the more I push him away. Sometimes I think I'm just seeing how far I can push him, because when, eventually, he dumps me, as he'd have to if I continued treating him the way I have been, then I can turn around and say, 'See? I told you so?' Because everyone else has always dumped me eventually, and maybe part of me expects that, so in a sick sort of way I'm trying to create that situation.

I know it sounds complicated, but it makes sense to me. I ran it by Jules the other night, and she nodded in all the right places, but then didn't say anything at the end, so I just went into overdrive explaining why I was so convinced this was the case.

'Are you absolutely sure you should be engaged to him?' was all she said.

'Absolutely,' I said, as I tried to explain that the only way out of this one, as far as I could see, was to work through it, and work through it with him. There would be no point in breaking off the engagement, being single again and then trying to deal with it. I have to be in it, experiencing it right now if I'm ever going to come through and learn how to really love.

Although I suspect learning how to really love isn't an issue for me. I've always felt that I've had masses of love to give. Before Ed I was always the one doing the smothering. I'd do whatever I could to make myself indispensable to whoever was the current man in my life. And I was always the one who drove them away. I suppose it's a bit like that old Groucho Marx saying – I wouldn't want to join any club that would have me as a member.

Perhaps the main issue, for me now, is actually learning how to be loved. All the men with whom I've been involved before Ed treated me appallingly, and the worse they treated me, the more I wanted to make them change, the more I'd shower love, affection and attention on them.

Much like Ed is doing to me.

God. I feel like I'm having a breakthrough. That's exactly what's happening. The roles have been reversed, and I'm doing to Ed exactly what has always been done to me. I remember Jon growing more and more distant. I remember him turning round at the end of the evening and saying, 'I'm sorry, do you mind if you don't stay the night, I'd just really like to be on my own.' I remember covering Jon with kisses as he became less and less affectionate.

Thank God I've realized this now. Before it's too late. Because I will work this one through, and I will walk down that aisle if it's the last thing I ever do.

'So come on, then, sis. Tell me all about him.'

'Olly, you're going to be meeting him in about six hours. You'll see for yourself.'

'He's definitely a big hit with Mum, but I'm never sure if that's a good sign or not.'

'Tell me about it. Has Dad said anything to you?'

Is it my imagination or does Olly suddenly sound

slightly shifty? 'Nah,' he says. 'You know what Dad's like. Conversation isn't exactly his bag.'

I laugh.

'Wait until they meet Carolyn,' I say. 'Then you'll know just what I've been going through.'

'I know,' he sighs. 'I think I'm going to have to get it over with. I've told them about her, so now Mum's driving me mad.'

'Ha ha! Good. Shit, someone needs me. Listen, I've gotta go, but you'll be there on time, won't you?'

'Yup. I'll see you then.'

'All right, darling. Bye.' I put the phone down and turn to Jo, who's been making worried faces at me while I've been chatting. 'What's the matter, Jo?'

'You're going to kill me,' she says. 'I'm really, really sorry.'

'Please don't tell me you can't come,' I say slowly.

'I'm really sorry,' she says, wincing. 'My friend Jill called to check I was coming to her birthday party, and I completely forgot, and she went bananas when I said I couldn't make it, I'm so sorry.'

'Don't worry,' I sigh, completely pissed off but not enough to shout about it, because I probably would have done the same thing. It's what single women do. We'll make arrangements, and then if something better comes up, i.e. some event where we're more likely to meet Mr Right, we'll cancel our first arrangements without even thinking about whether we're upsetting anyone.

And I'm not upset, it's just that the numbers are now uneven, and who the hell will I put with Nick? Thankfully, my phone rings, so Jo takes the opportunity to slink back to reception while I sigh a 'hello' into the receiver.

352

'Darling! It's me.' Now 'me' could be any number of me's, but in this case I know, instantly, it's Amanda Baker, and a lightbulb in my head switches on.

'Amanda! I was just going to call you! I know this is incredibly short notice, but basically, umm' – time for a little white lie here – 'Ed and I decided to get together with a few friends this evening and I know how horribly busy you are, but I really want you to come. I can't believe you called, I was literally, just this second, picking up the phone to call you.'

'How lovely!' she exclaims, as I wait with bated breath. 'Actually, I'm not doing anything tonight. I was going to have a bath and give myself lots of face packs and things, but I'd love to come out for dinner with Ed McMahon. And you.'

'Wonderful!' I exclaim, mustering up some enthusiasm from somewhere. 'That's great!'

'Just tell me,' she interrupts, 'is it going to be couple hell?'

I laugh. 'Sort of. But there is a single man there, although I don't think he's your type.'

'That's okay, as long as I'm not the only single person there.'

'Nope. Don't worry,' and, as I tell her where to be and at what time, I breathe a sigh of relief because I never have to be ashamed of being single again.

I remember clearly all those times I'd turn down invitations to dinner parties because I'd always be the only person on my own, and those times I'd turn up to find I'd been fixed up with someone awful, and how inferior I felt to those cosy couples, how I vowed I'd never go again until I had a partner.

And now I do, and I never have to ask those questions,

and even though my friends said I was being ridiculous, how could I possibly feel inferior to them just because I was single, even though I believed them at the time, as I put down the phone to Amanda, I realize, and I know this is not exactly a nice thing to realize, but I realize that I do feel slightly superior to her. I've got a partner. A fiancé. I'm now, officially, a grown-up.

Jules says there are three things that make you a grown-up: radiator cabinets, gin, vodka and whisky in the house, and making your bed every morning. But I disagree with her. I think you're officially a grown-up when you've got another half. When you don't have to live in fear of other couples. When you don't have to feel you're not good enough.

I make sure that Ed and I are early, the first to arrive, and we order champagne as we sit down. Ed kisses me and tells me how beautiful I am. Just as the champagne arrives, so does Jules, followed swiftly by Olly and Carolyn.

Ed kisses Jules, and shakes hands with the others, telling Olly how delighted he is to meet him, having heard so much about him.

'We're all thrilled Libby's finally settling down,' Olly says, winking at me. 'We're just slightly surprised at how quick it's all been.'

'Ha ha!' laughs Ed. 'I'm surprised myself, but when it's right, it's right.'

Right.

'So where's Jamie, then?' Olly asks, looking at Jules quizzically. 'Got a big case on again, I suppose?'

Jules manages to pull off a shrug that looks genuine to everyone but me, but then again I'm the only one who knows the truth. 'You know how it is,' she says with a sad smile. 'Bloody barristers.'

'You could have asked him, you know,' I whisper, sidling up to her and pulling her to one side.

'I know,' she says. 'And he phoned today, and I so nearly asked him, but he hasn't suffered enough. Not yet.'

'So what did you say?'

'Well, I told him you were having an engagement do tonight, and I think he thought I was going to invite him, but I changed the subject.'

'How do you feel?'

'Lonely as hell.'

I put my arm around her shoulders and give her a squeeze, and then I hear, 'Libby!' and Sal comes bustling through the restaurant. 'I'm so excited for you!' she says, throwing her arms around me and giving me a huge hug. 'Paul and Nick are parking the car. They'll be here any second.' She looks at the others, who are now standing by the side of the table making small talk, and seems to do a double-take when she sees Ed. 'Is that him?' she says finally, sounding surprised.

'Yes. Why? You sound surprised.'

She shakes her head. 'Sorry. God, I'm really sorry, Libby. It's just that, he's, well, he's not really what I would have thought you'd go for.'

'You mean he's not good-looking?'

She leans forward and whispers, 'I thought you hated moustaches.'

'I do,' I whisper back. 'I'm working on it.'

'You must think I'm really rude. He looks lovely. It's just that I've only ever really seen you with,' and she stops, checking that no one hears as she mouths 'Nick' at me.

355

'And?'

'And I suppose I assumed that was your type.'

'Sal, I don't have a type. I never have had a type. And Ed's lovely. You'll see.'

'Of course he is!' she says, squeezing my arm. 'He's marrying you, so he has to be!'

'Ed?' I call over to get his attention. 'Come and meet Sal.'

Ed walks over, smiling, and extends a hand, looking a bit taken aback when Sal reaches up and gives him a hug. 'Lovely to meet you,' she says. 'We've heard all about you, except I suppose you're sick of hearing that, aren't you?'

Ed chuckles. 'Not at all. Not at all. And how do you know Libby?'

As Sal's explaining, I see Paul walk into the restaurant with Nick at his heels, and for a second my heart catches in my throat. He's in his old chinos with his DMs and a scruffy old raincoat, but he looks so familiar, so gorgeous, that for a second I think I'm going to start crying.

'Libby. You look lovely,' he says, giving me a sedate kiss on each cheek. 'Congratulations.'

'I'm so pleased you're here, Nick,' I say, and I am. 'I was a bit worried about, well, you know.'

'Don't be silly. We're friends, aren't we? I wouldn't miss this for anything. I'm dying to know what the infamous Ed's like.' Nick turns and sees Ed talking to Sally.

'That's not him, is it? Please tell me that's not him.'

'Nick! What do you mean? Why not?'

'Libby, he's old enough to be your grandfather.'

'Crap,' I laugh, suddenly remembering Nick's sense of humour. 'He's only ten years older than me.'

'Nice tache,' Nick says. 'Hmm, I've always fancied one of those.'

'Oh shut up.' I slap him. 'Anyway, hopefully he won't have it for much longer.'

'If I were you I'd wait until he's asleep, then shave it off. The less painful the better.'

'I might just do that,' I laugh. 'Come and meet him.'

'Umm, is there a reason you've left an empty seat beside me?' Nick leans over the table to me. 'Has my personal hygiene problem become that bad?'

I laugh. 'No. Amanda Baker's coming. She's late, she should be here any minute.'

'Amanda Baker?' Nick's eyes widen. 'Here? Tonight? Sitting next to me? Phwooargh.'

'I might have known you'd know who she is,' I laugh. 'You're the only person I know who watches daytime TV on a regular basis.'

'When it comes to Amanda Baker,' he drools, 'the word salivate comes to mind. Is she my blind date, then?'

'No,' I say sternly, suddenly feeling slightly nauseous, because what if they do get on? What if Amanda decides Nick's just her type? I'm not sure I could cope with that, seeing Nick and Amanda together. Oh shit. What have I done here?

'Speak of the devil,' whispers Nick, as Amanda sashays towards the table.

'Libby!' she kisses me, then kisses Ed, moving back round the table to sit next to Nick. 'I'm so sorry I'm late,' she says. 'I had to do another bloody interview.' She waits for someone to comment on the fact that she's famous, but no one does, until Nick steps in to fill the void.

'I watch you all the time on TV,' he says. 'I never realized you were a friend of Libby.'

'Yes. Do you like the show?' Her face lights up, happy at being given the opportunity to talk about herself.

Jules rolls her eyes at me as I suppress a giggle, but I watch Amanda very carefully, and, although she's obviously delighted at having found a fan, I can't hear a glimmer of flirtation in her voice, or a flicker of interest. I look up to catch Jules watching me watching her, and Jules raises an eyebrow as I shrug and turn to Ed, who's got his hand on my knee.

'Are you enjoying yourself?' he asks, pursing up for a kiss. I kiss him and nod.

'Are you?'

He smiles. 'Of course,' and looks round the table. 'Who would like some more champagne?'

'Yes, please,' says Sal, proffering her glass. 'I'll never say no to a bit of fizz.'

Ed refills her glass, then says, 'Do you know Amanda?'

'We haven't met,' says Sal, as Amanda looks up at the mention of her name. 'Hello. I'm Sally Cross.'

'How do you do,' says Amanda, a distracted look on her face. 'Sally Cross. That's a familiar name. Have we met before?'

'No, I don't think so,' says Sal.

'What do you do? Are you in TV?'

Sal explains her job, and Amanda's voice immediately warms up. A journalist! Another potential hit to get a feature written about herself! They start talking shop, and after a few minutes Amanda stops in mid-flow and taps Nick on the shoulder, 'Sorry, but could we swap places for a bit, it's just that it's so rude talking across you.'

Nick shrugs and stands up, and Amanda pushes past him to sit in his recently vacated seat, as she carries on talking about her career as a presenter.

'How's the book going?' Olly shouts over to Nick.

Nick taps the side of his nose mysteriously. 'All sorts of things going on, but can't talk about them.

'Yet,' he adds.

Olly laughs. 'You mean that we're actually going to be able to read it soon?'

'Time will tell,' says Nick, in his Mystic Meg voice.

'You're an author?' Ed, for the first time this evening, is showing an interest in Nick.

'Aspiring,' Nick says with a smile.

'You're not published, then?'

'Not yet. But things are looking hopeful.'

'What sort of a book have you written?'

'Oh, usual thriller, cloak and dagger type stuff.'

'So if you're not published you must do other work.'

'Nope. The only other work I do is walk to the dole office and back.'

'Oh ha ha! Very funny.' Ed's laughing, and Nick looks at him peculiarly.

'Yes, well, I'm glad you think it's funny. Unfortunately, it's not a joke.'

'Oh gosh!' Ed colours a deep red. 'I'm terribly sorry. I thought, I assumed you were joking.'

'I wouldn't joke about a thing like that.'

'I've never met anyone on the dole before,' says Ed, digging himself deeper and deeper as far as I'm concerned. Nick catches my eye, and I can't help it, I shrug and raise my eyes to the ceiling.

'Well, there are plenty of us about,' Nick says, as I decide to step in and help the conversation change course.

'Come on, Nick, tell us what your book's about.'

'You wouldn't be interested,' he says.

'Yes, yes! We would.' Jules joins in with me, and for the next ten minutes Nick holds centre stage as he details the plot for us, while I sit there absolutely staggered, because it is brilliant! Seriously, it is one of the most original ideas I've heard for ages, and I wish I'd listened to him before. I can't believe that no one's already done it.

'That sounds fantastic!' says Olly, who by now is also listening in. 'You shouldn't have any trouble getting that published.'

'I agree,' says Paul. 'I'd buy it.'

'I hope you will,' laughs Nick, who's puffed up with pride at the positive reaction to his story. 'I expect all of you to contribute to my royalty payments.'

Amanda and Sal have finished their shop talk, and Amanda taps Ed on the shoulder. 'Binky Donnell says hello,' she says, smiling, 'and congratulations.'

'Binky Donnell!' exclaims Ed, his eyes lighting up. 'There's a name I haven't heard in a while. How is the old rascal?'

Nick nudges me and mouths, 'Rascal?' I kick him under the table, but I can see that even Jules has a smirk on her face.

'He's lovely,' she says. 'I had dinner with Binky and Bunny last week.'

Nick nudges me again and this time I can't help myself, I start giggling, and I honestly can't believe I'm going to marry someone who has friends called Binky and Bunny.

'I can't believe you're going to marry someone who has friends called Binky and Bunny,' Nick mutters, when he's finally recovered.

'Oh I see,' I say, 'and Moose is so much better?'

'At least Moose is cool,' Nick says, mock indignantly. 'Binky and Bunny don't exactly have much street cred.'

'How do you know? For all you know Binky drives a vintage Harley, and Bunny's a blonde bombshell rock chick.'

'With long floppy ears?'

'Quite possibly,' I snort, and we both collapse with laughter again, completely unnoticed by Ed and Amanda, who are now shrieking with delight at having so many people in common. More power to them, as far as I'm concerned.

Even Jules shoots me an odd look, and I just shrug, more than happy that Ed's found something in common with at least one of my friends, even if Amanda isn't exactly a friend.

Olly and Carolyn are chatting away to Sal and Paul, and as far as I can tell the evening's a success. Everyone's had a chance to meet Ed, they all seem to be getting on, and okay, so not everyone's really had a chance to talk to Ed, but then that's always the problem with large groups of people at dinner, isn't it? Olly, for example, has barely exchanged words with Ed, but at least they've met, and it's a starting point. On the other hand, maybe they should have a bit more of a chat.

When the coffee arrives I get up and go to see Olly at the other end of the table.

'Why don't you talk to Ed a bit? Get to know him?'

Olly sighs. 'Libby, I'm not sure what I'd have to say to him.'

'Olly! That's not very nice. This is the man I'm marrying. You could make an effort. How do you know you wouldn't have anything to say to him?'

'Okay, you're right. But I've heard him across the table and . . .' He pauses.

'And what?'

'Nothing.' He sighs. 'Anyway. He's deep in conversation with your friend Amanda. I don't want to interrupt.'

'Okay,' I say warily. 'Maybe you and Carolyn will come over for dinner with us?'

'Maybe,' he says distractedly. 'Look, let's talk about this tomorrow, shall we?'

'God, Oll. Anyone would think you'd taken an instant dislike to him.'

'Libby, we'll talk about it tomorrow.'

Chapter Twenty-seven

'So what did you think?' We're driving back home, and much as I hate to admit it I'm actually far more worried about what my friends thought of Ed, but I won't be able to get the low-down until tomorrow morning, so in the meantime I want to know if Ed liked them, if he approved, if he can see them fitting into our lives.

'It was a great success.' He smiles indulgently at me.

'No, I meant what did you think of my friends?'

And it suddenly occurs to me that this is an important conversation. That before now I would quite happily have sacrificed my friends for a man, but that I would never dream of doing that now, and that Ed's opinion matters far more than I ever dreamt. And not because I want him to like them, but that whatever he says will be a reflection of who he is, and that if he doesn't get it right, if he fails to approve, I'm not sure I'll ever be able to see him in the same light again.

'Oh, they were great fun,' he says finally. 'Especially Amanda. I definitely approve of Amanda.'

'It's not about approval, Ed,' I say slowly. 'It's about liking the people whom I love. And Amanda isn't exactly a friend, more of a work colleague, and the only reason you liked her was because you both know so many of the same people, and that's probably because Amanda's such a bloody networker.'

'Libby! That's not nice.'

'Sorry,' I mutter. 'But it's true. Anyway, what did you think of Olly?'

'I didn't really talk to him,' Ed says truthfully, 'so we'll have to have him over for dinner, I think. Soon.'

'Yup, okay. But he's nice, isn't he? Is he what you expected?'

'I didn't expect anything, and he seems awfully nice.'

'What about Sal and Paul? Did you like them?'

'Well,' he pauses. 'I'm not sure I'm that happy about you being friends with tabloid journalists.'

'What? Are you serious?'

'Well, yes. I wouldn't mind if they were on the *FT*, but their paper's such rubbish. I don't think they're, well, suitable really.'

I can feel an argument coming on.

'What do you mean, suitable?'

'Darling, I'm not sure I trust them, that's all.'

'But you don't even bloody know them.'

'Don't swear at me, Libby.'

'Sorry. But they're two of the nicest people I know. I can't believe you're judging them by their jobs. And their paper isn't exactly sleazy, plus they don't do news, they don't doorstep people or anything like that.'

'Still,' he says, looking quickly at me. 'Oh, maybe you're right. I'm just being a judgemental old fuddy-duddy, but I do have to say I was very surprised that you are friendly with someone like that Nick fellow. How on earth do you know him?'

'Nick. Not that Nick fellow.' My voice is becoming more and more strained. 'I know him through Sal. Why?'

'Ah,' he nods. 'That makes sense.'

How dare he. How dare he. How dare he.

'What. Makes. Sense?' The words, if Ed bothered to

listen, are dangerously slow coming out of my mouth.

'He's terribly scruffy. So unkempt. Not the sort of person I'd have thought you'd associate with at all.'

'But you hardly said two words to him.'

'But Libby, please. Look at the chap, what does he think he looks like? Those shabby clothes, and as for that business about being on the dole . . . I think it's best if you don't see him again.'

'I can't believe you're saying this. I can't believe you're sitting here' – incidentally, I'm now spluttering with rage – 'I can't believe you're trashing my friends. And most of all, I cannot believe how incredibly superficial you're being. You have judged all my friends either by their appearance or by their jobs, and I would have thought that you are old enough to know better. Evidently unlike you' – this last bit said through gritted teeth – 'I choose my friends because of who they are, and not because of how much money they have or which bloody public school they went to.'

I run out of steam then and sit there shaking with anger, and we don't say a word to one another the whole way back.

There have been times, in the past, when I've introduced boyfriends to friends and my friends haven't liked them, and I've been furious with those friends, furious with them for not seeing what I see, for having the temerity to tell me the truth, and yes, I've fallen out with people over it. But this time I can't see a grain of truth in what Ed is saying. I cannot see that my friends are bad people because they don't have as much money as he would like, because they do not dress in immaculate designer clothing, because they do not socialize with Binky and Bunny fucking Donnell.

And as we get out of the car outside Ed's house, I wonder whether I'm being too hard. Whether perhaps Nick's clothes are a bit shabby, whether Sal and Paul are perhaps not altogether my cup of tea, whether it would be a huge hardship for me to cut them out of my life, and the truth is that I really don't know. I don't know whether to compromise on this and try to forget about it and accept that they are not the sort of people the wife of Ed McMahon should be socializing with. I just don't know what to think any more.

We get undressed in stony silence, and, after I have climbed into bed and turned my back to Ed, he says he's sorry.

I ignore him.

He touches my shoulder and I shrug off his hand, and he says, again, that he's sorry.

'I didn't mean to hurt you,' he says. 'And you're right. I was wrong. I've been far too judgemental. Libby, my darling, I really am sorry.'

And I turn to him and there are tears in his eyes, and I can see that he is sorry, so when he starts stroking my leg I accept his apology, but I don't feel anything. Completely numb. And when he thinks he's done enough foreplay and is ready to enter me, I still don't feel anything. And then he's inside me, pounding away on top of me, and this time I don't think about walking down the aisle, I just lie there with a strange pain in my chest, and this pain moves higher and higher, and suddenly I'm crying.

Huge, great heaving sobs. Like a child. And I push Ed off and run into the bathroom, locking the door, and look at myself in the mirror for a long time.

I have never felt so lonely in my life.

*

Despite myself, as soon as I get to the office the next morning I pick up the phone and ring Sal.

'Well? What did you think?'

'He's lovely!' exclaims Sal, and I start to relax.

'Really? You liked him?'

'He's very charming. Of course. You two look good together.'

'God, Sal. I am so pleased to hear that.'

'Why? Did you think I wouldn't?'

'No.' Yes. 'It's just that it's important to me what my friends think.'

'Did he like us, then?'

'Yes! He thought you were lovely!' And as I say it I recognize the insincerity. My voice has exactly the same inflection as Sally's.

'I'm ringing up to thank you for last night.' Why do I suddenly feel that Nick is playing a larger and larger role in my life? I mean, it's over. Finished. I'm getting married to someone else, yet suddenly I seem to be speaking to Nick, or seeing him, far more often than ever before.

'Did you enjoy it?'

'It was lovely to see you,' he says warmly. 'Especially looking so glowing and happy.'

'Am I?' I'm surprised. I never dreamt Ed had that effect on me.

'Very much so,' he laughs. 'You're really going through with this?'

What does that mean? 'We haven't set the date yet,' I say. 'And it doesn't really feel real at the moment.'

'I suppose you're waiting until you've got that rock on your finger for it all to sink in,' he says in a strange tone, which can only mean one thing. He's jealous. But then it hits me, what he's just said. The ring.

Oh God. The ring. The diamond that will make it all true. The diamond that will mean there's no going back. Because suddenly I'm not so sure, and suddenly I remember Jules's words: that this isn't about falling in love with love, or wanting to get married for the sake of being married, or getting excited about walking down the aisle, or living in Hanover Terrace, or any of those things. This is about spending the rest of my life with Ed, and as I think that I remember last night, and how I felt looking in the mirror, and I feel an icy dagger of fear splinter my heart.

No. I'm not going to think about this. I wrap the dagger in a fantasy of white ivory lace, and surround it with images of my vast designer wardrobe, and start to feel slightly better.

'Just how big do you think the rock should be?'

'At least five carats, Libby.' Nick sounds exasperated but jokey, like he used to. 'And that's just the one in the middle. It will basically have to be so big, no one will be able to look at your finger without wearing sunglasses.'

I chuckle. 'That sounds like the one for me.'

'So you're really going to do it?' he says, sounding suddenly serious.

''Course!' I say indignantly. 'I don't go around getting engaged to every man I meet.'

'You're telling me,' he laughs.

I want to ask Nick what he thought of Ed, but I have a horrible feeling that Nick will tell the truth, which is why he hasn't volunteered the information himself, and I don't want to know. As far as I'm concerned my doubts are just pre-wedding nerves, but even so I don't want anyone else to corroborate them.

It isn't as if I shouldn't be nervous. Surely every bride feels this way? Aren't there people who become completely terrified the night before the wedding, who, despite being madly in love, suddenly doubt that they're doing the right thing? That's all that these feelings are, I realize with relief. It is perfectly natural for me to be doubting this. Everything's going to be fine.

Jo runs in and tells me Sean Moore's here for the meeting, so I say goodbye to Nick and spend the rest of the morning talking to Sean Moore, his agent and Joe Cooper about his publicity campaign. I do well. I think they're all happy with the work I've been doing, and when we're finished there's a message from Jules.

I don't call her back. Not yet. I go out for lunch with Jo and try to forget about everything, because right at this moment I feel that it's all getting a bit much for me. So we go to the Italian café and order milky cappuccinos, and tuna salad on toasted baps, and we sit there and gossip about everyone at work, and by the time I step back into the office at half past two I feel human again.

So when Jules calls again mid-afternoon I'm in a good mood, and I'm totally unprepared for what she's about to say.

'Libby, you might hate me for saying this, but after last night I've just got to.'

'Go on. What is it?'

'Look, I'm only saying this because I love you and I don't want to see you make a mistake.'

'Get to the point, Jules.'

'Okay, okay. The thing is, I'm just really concerned that you haven't thought this through. You've been swept up in a whirlwind of excitement, and I'm worried that you haven't actually thought about the reality of it.'

'Jules, you've said all this to me before. I know what I'm doing.'

'Okay, fine. But I'm going to say it again, and I really want you to listen to me. Marriage is for life. It's not just about having a spectacular wedding day, it's about spending the rest of your life with that person, for better or worse. You can't just turn around and decide you're not compatible and walk away. What about children? If you have children Ed will want to send them to Eton, and would you really want your children brought up away from you? There are so many other things to consider, and I'm just so frightened that you haven't thought this through.'

I start to feel sick, and immediately jump on the defensive. 'What about you, then? If marriage is for life, how come you keep saying that Jamie has to suffer and you don't know whether you'll take him back? If you really believe what you're saying, then you'll do anything to save your own marriage, and that includes forgiving Jamie.'

There's a long silence, and then I hear a catch in her throat as she says softly, 'I'm trying.'

'What?'

'I do believe what I just said, and all I've been thinking about is that I have to find it in my heart to forgive him, because I love him, because he's my husband, and because I don't want to live without him.'

'Thank God,' I practically scream.

'That doesn't mean everything's fine,' she says slowly. 'It's not, and I don't know if it will ever be fine again, but I'm going to tell him to come home.'

'Yes!' I punch the air. 'Thank God you've seen sense.'

'Libby,' she says, 'stop changing the subject. You need to know that marriage is not a fairy-tale. This has been the most nightmarish fucking thing that's ever happened to me, but I'm willing to work at it.

'Look,' she continues. 'I'm not saying that Ed's not for you, or that you can't marry him, but all I'm saying is you have to have more time. Marriage isn't easy. God knows I know that now. Anything that's irritating you slightly now will magnify a thousandfold once you're married. I think you need to be very sure. You need some time out on your own to think about this, to think about spending. The. Rest. Of. Your. Life. With. Ed.'

There's a silence while I digest what she's just said, because, even though she's said it before, it never hit home. I came up with arguments to refute it, but now I see that she's right. That this, marriage, means I'll never have another flirtation again. I'll never be with anyone else again. I'll be sleeping with Ed, and only Ed, for the rest of my life. And I remember last night again, and I exhale deeply.

'Libby? Are you still there?'

'Yes.' My voice sounds small. 'I think you're right.'

'I'm not saying this isn't it,' she says, sounding relieved, 'I'm just saying you need to be one hundred per cent sure.'

'I know.' My voice still sounds small. 'So what do I do?'

Jules tells me to tell Ed I've got a pitch coming up, and that everyone will be expected to work late for the next few days, and that I'll miss him desperately but I need to prove myself with this one because since I've met Ed I've barely concentrated on work, and if I don't do this I'll be in big trouble.

And as she says it I know that even though it's going to be difficult to tell him – I can already see his sad puppy-dog expression – it's a vaguely credible excuse, and she's right, I don't need weeks to think about this, just a few days on my own.

'Jules? Thanks. Really.'

'Don't be ridiculous. That's what best friends are for.'

But I still feel nervous as hell as I'm driving over to Ed's that night. I have nothing with me. No set of clean underwear, no change of clothes for tomorrow, no make-up bag, and I can see that Ed notices this as soon as he opens the door.

'Darling? Where are your things?'

I can't lie, I can't tell him they're in the car, and, even though I hadn't planned on saying this quite so soon, I haven't got much choice, have I?

'I'm not staying tonight,' I say, and, predictably enough, he looks crestfallen.

'Is something the matter?' I can already see the fear in his eyes, and a wave of sympathy sweeps over me.

'Don't be silly, darling. Nothing's the matter. But I'd love a cup of tea.'

Anything to stall for time.

We go into the kitchen and as I sit at the counter in silence Ed turns to me and asks worriedly, 'There is something wrong, isn't there?'

'I already told you. No. There's nothing wrong. It's just that I'm in big trouble at work, and we've got a pitch coming up and I'm going to be working really hard the next few days, so I don't think I'm going to be able to spend much time with you.'

Ed is visibly relieved as he puts the tea in front of me. 'Is that all, darling? Don't worry about work. I'll look after you anyway and you know I won't want you working once we're married, so why don't you just hand in your notice?'

'I love my job,' I say indignantly, suddenly realizing that, at the moment, I do. 'I don't want to give it up quite yet. Although,' I add as an afterthought, 'it's very sweet of you to offer. I feel that I need to prove myself with this. You do understand, don't you?' I sip the tea.

'I suppose so,' he says sadly. 'But I will see you, won't I?'

'God, I hope so,' I lie, reaching up and giving him a kiss, then pulling away just as I feel Ed getting passionate, because the last thing I want is to have sex tonight. I look at my watch. 'Jesus, I've got to get back. Everyone's working late tonight in a frenzy.'

'You mean you're going back to the office now?'

'I'm so sorry, darling,' I say, grabbing my bag. 'But they'll sack me if I'm not there. You'd better not call because the switchboard will be closed, but if there's anything urgent I'll leave the mobile on. I'll call you tomorrow,' and I give him another peck and run out the door.

I catch Marks & Sparks off the Edgware Road just as they're about to close, but the security man is taken in by my pleading looks and winning smile, and he lets me in with a shake of his head.

Freedom. I feel free. I can eat whatever I want tonight, and I'm going to be in my flat for the whole night and refuse to answer the phone. I'm going to do what I want, when I want, and already I feel as if a load has been lifted. For the next few days I am completely free.

I run down the aisles throwing things in a basket. Mini pitta breads, taramasalata, hummus, olives. I chuck in a packet of smoked salmon and some mini chicken tikkas. Fuck it. I'm having a blow-out. I hesitate over some vegetables, then decide they're far too healthy, so it's back to the deli section via the party section, where I can't help but be tempted by some gorgeous looking canapés.

And I dash up to the one remaining till that's open, and while the girl adds up my stuff I grab a handful of chocolate bars and add them to the pile.

Then back in the car and on to Ladbroke Grove, but not before stopping at the video store. And while I'm in the video store trying to decide between *Sleepless in Seattle* and *Sleepers*, my mobile rings and Ed's number flashes up on the screen. I press the busy button on the phone, and poor Ed gets my answer phone, and I know it's mean, but I don't want to have to deal with him right now. I just want to be on my own.

I choose *Sleepers*. The last thing I need is to watch a slushy romantic love story where the hero is gorgeous (if you're into Tom Hanks, that is, which I happen to be), and I whizz off home via the off-licence, where I treat myself to a very expensive (that means more than £4.99) bottle of claret.

Home. Wonderful, fantastic home. As I'm unloading the bags the phone rings, and I hear Ed's voice on my machine.

'Sweetieloviedarling, I tried your mobile but you're not answering. I just wanted to ring and say that I miss you and I love you and I can't wait for us to get married. Don't worry about work, and I'll call you tomorrow. I love you very, very much.'

'Fuck off,' I mutter, as I pop the chicken tikka in the microwave to heat it up.

And the phone rings again.

'Libby, darling. It's Mum.' As if I didn't know. 'You're obviously out, probably having a wonderful time with Ed. Dad and I were just saying we hadn't heard from you for a few days and wondered how you are. Perhaps you and Ed would like to come over for supper next week? Oh well, you know how I hate talking into these little machines. If you don't get back too late give me a ring. Well. Ah. If you come back. If not, call me in the morning. Bye, bye, darling.'

'And you can fuck off too,' I shout, my mouth full of pitta bread, as I gather up my food and collapse on to the sofa.

Chapter Twenty-eight

Thank God. It's Saturday morning and I've managed to avoid Ed since Thursday night. Okay, I know it's only one day, but I told Jo to tell him I was in a meeting when he called, and then yesterday, at around three o'clock when I knew he'd be at work, I rang his answer machine at home and told him I missed him and that I was fine, but really busy, and I'd have to work on Saturday but I'd call him in the evening, and maybe we could get together on Sunday.

Not that I am missing him. That's what's so extraordinary. I've loved having two nights in at home by myself. I haven't picked up the phone once, I've just pottered around, watching TV, reading magazines. I even attempted a bit of DIY and hung some pictures that have been propped up on top of the radiator since I moved in.

I thought that these 'days off', as Jules put them, would be a time of reflection. I thought I'd be sitting around analysing every aspect of our relationship and trying to work out whether Ed is The One, whether I do want to spend the rest of my life with him, but actually I haven't even thought about him. I've been far too busy being happy by myself.

Which I suppose is slightly worrying in itself.

So when the phone rings on Saturday morning, again I leave it because I've assumed it's Ed, but of course I leave the volume up just in case it's someone important like, well, I suppose like Jules, because really she's the only person I feel like talking to at the moment, not to mention the only person who really needs me right now.

Jamie moved back in two days ago. Jules was trying to be cold, trying to let him know that they couldn't simply pick up where they left off, but, as she admitted to me in a whisper while Jamie was downstairs, 'God, Libby, it's so nice to have him home,' and her coldness towards him is warming up by the minute. Make that the second.

And I know, she knows, it won't be forgotten about, and the strangest thing of all is that, hearing this, I started kind of rethinking the whole marriage thing. Not that I don't want to get married, it's just that maybe it isn't the happy ending. Maybe the marriage is just the beginning. Maybe getting married isn't going to be the answer to my prayers after all.

I mean, Jesus, it wasn't exactly the answer to Jules's prayers now, was it?

It isn't Jules. It's Nick.

I trip over the rug and stub my toe on the coffee table as I'm rushing to the phone to pick it up before Nick rings off and I pick up the phone shouting, 'Shit!'

'Is that any way to greet your second-favourite man? If I piss you off that much why bother picking up the phone at all?'

'Ouch,' I say, rubbing my toe. 'I just stubbed my toe.'

'Have you looked out the window?'

'No. Why? Are you sitting on my railings?'

He chuckles. 'Nope. But it's a beautiful day. Far too nice to be staying inside. What are you doing?'

Like I even have to think about it. 'Nothing. Absolutely nothing.'

'Not spending the day with your fiancé, then?'

'Nope. He thinks I'm spending the day in the office.'

'Oops. Do I smell trouble on the West London front?'

'Nah, not really. I just needed a bit of space. Anyway, why are you asking?'

'Just wondered if you wanted to come out to play.'

'What kind of play?'

'Not that kind of play,' he laughs. 'Although now you mention it – '

'What do you want to do?' I resist all temptation to flirt.

'I thought maybe we could go for a walk on the heath, then window shop in Hampstead, maybe have lunch or something.'

'That sounds fantastic!' It does. 'I'd love to.' I would.

'Great! How about I'll meet you outside the cinema on South End Green.'

'Okay. Give me an hour.' I look at my watch. 'I'll see you at twelve.'

'See you then.'

And for the first time in what feels like ages I don't have to worry about what to wear. I don't have to worry about 'looking the part', or being accepted, or wearing designer gear. I sling on my jeans that haven't seen the light of day since I met Ed, pull on some trainers and inch on a tight, white, V-necked T-shirt. If I were with Ed, I'd loop a cardigan stylishly around my shoulders, but, seeing as it's Nick, I tie it round my waist and to be honest it's far more comfortable that way, at least I don't have to worry about it falling off.

I slap on a bit of make-up – because even though this isn't a romantic assignation, I wouldn't be caught dead leaving the house without something on – toss my hair around a bit and that's it. I'm ready.

And when I reach the cinema at noon, Nick's already there, sitting on the steps outside reading the *Guardian*, occasionally looking up and closing his eyes as the sun bathes his face in warmth.

There's a girl leaning against a lamp-post trying to look as if she's also basking in sunlight, but as I approach I watch her sneaking looks at Nick, who is looking, it has to be said, decidedly gorgeous.

'Libby!' He stands up and flings his arms around me, giving me a smacker on the cheek, and as we walk off down the road he keeps an arm casually around my shoulders, and maybe this should make me feel uncomfortable, but there's nothing sexual, nothing intimate, it's just the mark of a good friend, and I laugh as I put my arm around his waist and give him a squeeze, instantly remembering the hard contours of his body, the way he looks when he is naked.

But then I remember I am the property of another, and I move away from him slightly, just enough for him to remove his arm, and I link arms with him instead, which feels much safer.

'Come on, come on,' he urges, marching next to me. 'If I'd known you were such a snail I wouldn't have asked you to come for a walk.'

'We can't go for a walk yet,' I say in horror. 'It's practically lunchtime and I haven't had any breakfast. I'm starving.'

'Okay. Shall we hit the high street?'

'To the high street we shall go,' and giggling together we march up Downshire Hill.

'God, this is beautiful,' I say halfway up the hill,

stopping to peer into the windows of a tiny, cottagey whitewashed house.

'Mmm,' agrees Nick. 'This is one of my favourite roads in the whole of London. If I had money I'd definitely buy a house here.'

'Money?' I look at him with horror. 'But Nick! You're forgetting. You don't want money. In fact, if I remember correctly, you'd give it all to the bloody politicians.'

'Ah,' he says, nodding sagely. 'Yes, that is correct. I did once say I would give my lottery win to the bloody politicians, but of course I'd save a few million for myself.'

'You've changed your tune.'

'Yes, well. As you keep saying, I'm really a girl, and isn't it a woman's prerogative to change her mind?'

I laugh. 'Are you quite sure you're not gay?'

'Never!' he exclaims loudly in a Winston Churchill voice. 'When there are so many gorgeous women around.' He leers at me and tries to pinch my bum as I shriek with laughter and run off.

'Wait, wait,' he calls, and I stop and grin at him as he lopes towards me. 'I am sorry m'lady for insulting you by partaking of your bottom.'

'You're forgiven,' I say, 'just don't make a habit of it.' And then I get this flashback of Nick kissing my breasts, down to my stomach, and I shiver, horrified that I'm still thinking about it, that the memory of it, in the presence of the man himself, is definitely turning me on. I shake my head to try and dislodge the memory, but of course Nick is here, with me, so it doesn't really go away, just moves to the back of my mind, which seems to be fairly safe for now.

We walk past the police station, past a café, and as we

pass the furniture shop on the corner I stop Nick and drag him to the window.

'It's gorgeous,' I sigh. 'Can we have a look?'

'Yes. Let's go in and look at all the things we could never afford.' And then his face falls. 'I mean, me. Sorry. I keep forgetting that you can probably afford the whole shop. A thousand times over.'

'Not yet, I can't. Come on.' I drag him in by the hand. 'Let's drool.'

I sigh with delight over the ethnic furniture, and shriek with horror at the prices.

'They want £970 for that piece of Indian tat?' says Nick very loudly, as he looks at the price of a coffee table.

'Sssh. Keep your voice down,' I whisper, noting that the sales assistants' eyes are following us around the shop. Just as we walk out, Nick says, loud enough for the entire shop to hear, 'You know Simon bought the very same table in India for £3.20. And what's more, he thought he was ripped off.'

'You are incorrigible,' I laugh, as we step outside.

'But really,' he insists. 'Those prices are laughable. And they do probably buy it in India for nothing. Think of all those poor people struggling in India, and thinking they're getting a bargain by selling their handcrafted stuff for a fiver.'

'Hmm.' I can see he has a point. 'Are you getting on your political high horse again? I just want to be warned.'

'Nah,' he says, 'the weather's far too lovely to get on any horse. Much more fun walking.'

We continue up the hill, idly chatting about this and that, and then I remember how mysterious he was the other night about the book, and what's happening with it, and I ask him again if he'll tell me.

'Can't.' He shakes his head. 'It's a secret.'

'Oh, pleeeeeeeeeeaaaaaaase,' I plead, looking up at him hopefully. 'I'll be your best friend.'

'Nope.'

'What about if we exchange secrets?'

Now he looks interested. 'You mean you tell me one, then I'll tell you?'

He stops walking and turns to look at me. Now he's interested. 'Okay, I'll do a deal with you. You tell me a secret, and if I think it's good enough I'll tell you. How's that?'

'Okay, deal.' And I stand there desperately trying to think of a secret, but I can't think of any. I could tell him that I cried during sex the other night, but I don't want him to know that, it wouldn't be fair on Ed, and anyway it isn't really a secret. But I don't really have secrets. And then I think of something.

'I've got one, but you have to promise you'll never tell anyone.'

'I promise.'

'It's really stupid.'

'Libby! Just tell me.'

'Okay. When I'm driving in my car I talk to myself.'

'So? Loads of people talk to themselves.'

'But I do it in an American accent.'

'You're kidding!'

I shake my head.

'Give me an example.'

I shake my head again.

'Oh, go on, just give me an idea of what you say, what you talk about.'

Reluctantly, it has to be said, I stand in the middle of Hampstead High Street and in a crap American accent I say, 'Did you have a good time tonight? Yeah, it was rilly cool.'

And Nick collapses with laughter.

'I can't believe that,' he splutters, and I start laughing too. 'You are seriously weird.'

'I am not. I bet loads of people do that.'

'Not in an American accent. Go on, do some more.' He wipes the tears from his eyes.

So I do a little bit more, and soon the pair of us are clutching each other to stop from falling down, and I'm holding my stomach because I'm laughing so hard it's hurting.

And when we recover I say, 'Your turn. Now tell me about the book.'

'No way. Your secret wasn't big enough.'

'What? You're joking! You loved my secret.'

'Only because it demonstrates what a completely weird person you are. It isn't that big a secret.'

'You bastard.' I hit him.

'Wanna try again?'

'Nope. You're not getting any more secrets out of me. Now I really am starving, what about here?' We're standing outside a café with tables dotted on the pavement, and I watch a couple leave a tip, then stand up.

'Quick, quick.' Nick grabs me by the hand. 'We must have that table.'

I order a salade niçoise, and Nick has an egg and bacon baguette, but by the end of the meal we're feeding each other our respective meals, making a huge mess, and giggling like children.

And Nick insists on paying, which I feel slightly guilty

about, because he really doesn't have much money, but he won't hear of accepting anything from me, and then we leave and walk up, past Whitestone Pond, and on to the heath.

And the weather is beautiful. It's a hot, hazy, lazy summer's day, and everyone's smiling, and this is London at its best, it's why I wouldn't live anywhere else.

After a while, kicking through the long grass until we're on open spaces, Nick says why don't we sit down and sunbathe for a bit, and I put my bag down, kick off my shoes and fold my arms behind my head, just listening to the birds and watching the trees blow slowly in the soft, occasional breeze.

'So,' I say eventually, when we've been lying there for a bit in silence. 'What did you think of Ed?' I don't know why I ask this question, but I suppose I think he'll echo Sal and say he seemed like a nice guy. I'm certainly not expecting what comes next. If I had been, I would never have asked.

'Do you want the truth?' Nick says seriously, and I shrug.

'I think he's awful,' Nick says slowly, while I look at him with a smile because he's obviously joking.

He's not joking.

'I think he is absolutely horrific,' he says, and there isn't even the merest hint of a smile. 'Not only is he far too old for you, he's also far too straight for you. He's pompous, arrogant, and he doesn't fit into any aspect of your life. He treats you like some sort of trophy girlfriend, sorry, fiancée, with patronizing comments and pats on the head, and he has completely ignored who you really are because he's just not interested. He probably cannot believe his luck that someone like you would even look at him.

'And to be honest,' he continues, while I sit open-mouthed in shock. 'I can't believe you would even look at him. I think he is quite possibly one of the most awful men I have ever met, and all I can think is that you've had some sort of mental block, because you would have to be absolutely crazy to even look at him, let alone consider marrying him.'

I'm about to scream at him, to shout 'How dare you,' to splutter with indignation, and fury, and rage, but I don't. Nick just looks at me, waiting for a reaction, and I feel my eyes well up, and suddenly I'm crying. Hiccuping huge sobs, and before I know it Nick has his arms around me, and he's rubbing my back in great big circular motions, and I'm soaking his shoulder with my tears.

'Sssh, sssh,' he's saying. 'It's okay. It's all going to be okay.' And this makes me cry even more, because, even though I don't want to be influenced by what Nick has just said, I know he's right. He's absolutely fucking right.

And eventually I calm down, and pull away and try to smile through my tears, finally absolutely sure that I have to end this with Ed, that I cannot go through with it, and Nick smiles at my wobbly smile, and Christ only knows how this happens, but we're kissing.

It's not that I kiss Nick, or that he kisses me, it just happens. One minute I'm smiling at him and the next second I'm locked into his arms.

His lips are on mine, and they're soft, and warm, and then, before I even register what's happening, my tongue takes on a life of its own and slips into his mouth, and he pushes me back on the grass and a moan escapes me, from somewhere deep down, and I want his kiss to swallow me up.

We can't stop. Neither of us. Not even when a group of teenagers walks past and starts catcalling and shouting things. I am lost in this kiss, in Nick, and I want it to go on for ever.

Does it sound clichéd to say that everything disappears? That it's as if there is nothing else on this planet except me, and Nick, and the feelings that are churning up inside me, feelings that I had honestly forgotten I ever had? That if we had not been in a public place there is no question that we would have ended up having sex? That when Nick's hand disappeared up my T-shirt to gently rub my breasts I would have let him carry on for ever had it not been for my sense of decorum?

But we have to stop. Eventually. And as we pull apart and look at one another, my hands fly up to my mouth. 'Oh my God,' I whisper. 'What have I done.'

I am not the sort of person who is unfaithful, and, before you argue with me, I consider kissing someone, when you are engaged, going out with, or married to someone else, unfaithful.

Many years ago I caught Matthew, an old boyfriend, with someone else. When I say caught, I don't mean that I walked in on them, interrupting coitus, as it were. I mean that I was in the wrong place at the wrong time (or perhaps you would argue the right place at the right time), and that Matthew had no idea I would be there, and that I saw him kissing someone else.

It was a crowded party, and yes, admittedly, I was far too young to be getting serious with anyone, let alone Matthew. I stood there and watched them, frozen with horror, and I thought that my heart was actually going to break. Many years ago Matthew argued that it was only a kiss, that she was no one, that they hadn't even petted, let alone slept together, so what was the big deal about. But I vowed, there and then, that I would never do that. I decided that if ever I were in a relationship that made me so unhappy I was looking for emotional or physical gratification outside that relationship, I would first discuss it with my partner, and together we would try and work it out.

Of course I now know, thanks to Jamie, that nothing is quite as easy as that. I have surprised myself with the way I seem to have forgiven Jamie committing what I have always considered to be the cardinal sin, but there again, as Jamie confessed, it was simply physical gratification, which, although I don't condone, I can sort of understand.

But the thing that's worrying me now, the thing that I could never have predicted, is what on earth you are supposed to do when your feelings are unfaithful?

Chapter Twenty-nine

I didn't expect to be quite so upset, but I cried all night. I cried for the loss of my fantasies, for the loss of my dreams. And I cried at the memory of what it is like to be alone.

Last night, drowning in tears, Nick rang, and this time I didn't pick up the answer phone. He left a message – in other circumstances I would say a very sweet message – saying that he'd had a lovely time, and that he was sorry for compromising me, and that he hoped he hadn't offended me, but if I wanted to call him he would be there.

But I don't want to call him. I don't want to confuse the issue any further, and the only issue that's important right now is Ed.

Ed. I called him. Last night. I managed to calm down enough to pretend there was nothing wrong, although the first thing he asked was whether I had a cold because I sounded sniffly. He told me he loves me very, very much, and he said he'd missed me desperately, and we arranged to meet this evening

He wants to take me out for dinner, a romantic evening, just the two of us, and I nearly broke down when he said this, because he doesn't have a clue what I'm going to say to him tonight.

I could have told him on the phone, but even I'm not that much of a bitch. I have to be brave, I have to do this face to face, and I feel physically sick at the very thought.

And then, at the end of the conversation, he said, 'Darling, I think it's time we went shopping for a ring,' and I didn't say anything. I couldn't say anything, and when I said we'd talk about it tonight, he sounded worried.

I feel like I've been drugged. I suppose that crying all night does that to you. You move as if in slow motion, your head too thick and fuzzy to think clearly, and eventually I ring Jules, because I can't do this on my own. I need to tell her what happened yesterday, to describe my feelings.

She knows instantly that something's wrong, and orders me over there immediately. They have a lunch with friends, but she sends Jamie off by himself, not, however, before I have a chance to see them together, to see how they are post-trauma. Jamie is being extra affectionate towards her, and, although I can see she is trying to resist, when he puts his arms around her to say goodbye she leans into him and the expression on her face is one of relief.

And when he leaves she sits me down and makes me milky sweet tea without saying anything, just waits for me to start.

Haltingly I start to tell her about Nick, and when I've finished she doesn't say anything for a while, so I start blabbering and everything comes out in a big rush.

'I can't marry him,' I say, tears already filling my eyes. 'I can't. He's not what I want, and more importantly I'm not what he wants. Nick's right. I've realized that all this time he's been trying to turn me into the investment banker's wife, and that's not me, it never will be, and I never laugh with Ed, and you were right about everything, about me falling for the fantasy, and even though

I know it was an appalling thing to do with Nick I think something like that had to happen to jolt me back to reality, and the thing is I'm seeing Ed tonight, and he's not a bad person, and I do genuinely think he adores me, and I just don't know what to say to him or how to say it, because however I put it it's going to destroy him.' I stop, taking a deep breath.

Jules still doesn't say anything, so I carry on. 'And you know the worst thing is that I don't love him, I don't think I even like him that much, and I know I was wrong to get into that with Nick, but you see kissing him, Nick I mean, has made me understand just how much is missing with Ed, I mean our sex life is crap. Really. Awful.'

I never thought I'd be able to stay in a relationship where the sex was awful. I always assumed I was one of those women with a high sex drive who would disappear out the door if they were crap, but I suppose it's amazing what you'll talk yourself into when you want something so desperately. That's it. I can't believe how desperately I wanted to get married.

'I know it's hard,' Jules says finally. 'But you're doing the right thing. Everything I've said to you is finally sinking in, and yes, Ed is a lovely guy, but he's not for you, and thank God you've seen that now rather than a year into the marriage.'

I nod sadly.

'Do you think you would have actually gone through with it?'

'I don't know.' I shrug sadly. 'I think I just wanted to get married, but I'm sure at some point, even if it hadn't been for Nick, I would have realized all this. I think I've probably known it for a while, but I didn't have the heart to admit it to myself because he's the first man who's wanted to marry me and on paper he has everything I've ever wanted.'

'Does this mean you've finally understood that money isn't everything?' Jules grins, and I smile back.

'Not everything,' I say. 'But all this means is that I'll have to make it myself.'

'Which is a far healthier attitude.'

'Yeah. I know.'

'So you're going to tell him tonight?'

'Oh God.' I sink my face into my hands. 'This is going to be the hardest thing I've ever done.'

Jules looks worried. 'But you have to,' she says firmly. 'You have to be very honest and say that you won't make him happy.'

'So I put the blame on myself rather than on him?'

She nods. 'Isn't that what men always do?'

I stay at Jules's all morning, and by lunchtime I'm starting to feel much better. Until, that is, three o'clock approaches and I know that I've got to face my parents for tea.

Jules gives me a hug at the door and wishes me luck, and says I must call her when it's done, and I drive straight to my parents, feeling this cloud of dread hanging over me, and wondering how on earth to tell my parents.

My mother, being the witch that she is, can see something's wrong as soon as I walk in.

'You look like you've been crying,' she says, stepping in for a closer look. 'I hope everything's all right with you and Ed. What's the matter?'

'Nothing,' I mutter, going into the living room and moving aside the newspaper in front of my father's face so I can kiss him hello.

My mother follows me in. 'I know something's wrong, dear,' she says firmly. 'You may as well tell us now, get it out of the way, but I must say that I do hope it's nothing to do with Ed.'

'Uh oh,' says my father, shuffling his feet into his slippers. 'Girl talk. I'll leave you two alone, shall I? I'll be out in the garden.'

'Come on, then, out with it.'

'Leave me alone, Mum. I don't want to talk about it.'

'Have you two had a lovers' tiff? I shouldn't worry about that, it'll blow over.'

I sit there with my arms crossed, staring at the mute television picture, and refuse to speak as my mother perches on the edge of the armchair and mimics my pose.

'I hope it's nothing serious,' she says, and before she has a chance to say anything more I stand up and march outside, 'I'm going to see what Dad's done in the garden,' I shout over my shoulder as I step through the french windows.

My dad's dead-heading the roses, and I stand next to him as he hands me the dead-heads in silence. My dad and I have never exactly had long conversations, but I know that the only way to do this is to tell him first – yet I don't know how to tell him, I don't know which words to use.

'Is it Ed, then?' my dad says slowly, not looking at me, just reaching up to a particularly high branch.

'Yes.'

'Is it over?'

'Yes. Well. Not yet. But it will be tonight.'

My dad just nods and carries on.

'D'you think I'm doing the right thing?'

My dad stops and finally looks at me.

'I couldn't tell you this before. I couldn't even tell your mother, not when she was so excited about having a rich son-in-law, but he wasn't for you, Libby. He wouldn't have made you happy.'

'You didn't like him, did you, Dad?'

'It wasn't that I didn't like him,' my dad says slowly. 'It was just that he lives in a completely different world, and I worried that he didn't really approve of you the way you are, that he was trying to change you into something else.'

God, I never realized my dad was that perceptive.

'And I didn't think you loved him,' he continues, walking over to the bench at the end of the garden and sitting down before I join him.

'You see, the thing is,' he says after we've both sat for a while in the sunshine, 'the thing is that love is really the most important thing. I know it's hard for you to see it now' – he chuckles quietly – 'but when I first laid eyes on your mother I thought she was fantastic, and I've never stopped loving her, not for a second. Oh yes, we've had our rough patches, and she can be a bit of an old battleaxe at times, but I still love her. That in-love feeling at the beginning settles down into a different, familiar sort of love, but it has to be there right from the start, otherwise it just won't work.'

He looks at me and smiles. 'You didn't love Ed. I could see that, but I couldn't say anything as long as you thought he was making you happy.' He sighs, stands up and stretches before saying, 'Do you want me to tell your mother?'

An hour later I'm sitting at the kitchen table watching my mother still wiping the tears from her eyes.

'What am I going to tell everyone?' she sniffles. 'How could you do this to me?'

I shrug, not bothering to reply.

'You know, Libby, you may not find another man who treats you like Ed treated you.'

'But Mum,' I sigh, 'I don't love him. I'm never going to love him.'

'And since when was that important? As I've said to you before, Libby, it's far more important to find a good man, and Ed is definitely a good man.'

'But you and Dad were in love when you met.'

'Pfff.' She rolls her eyes. 'It was so long ago I can't remember, but I'm sure it was about the same as you and Ed.'

'Dad told me when he first saw you he thought you were fantastic.'

Her face lights up and she beams as she says, 'Did he? Oh well, I suppose I was a bit of a looker in those days.'

'And he said you were madly in love.' Okay, artistic licence here.

My mother practically simpers. 'He was terribly handsome himself, your father. When he was young.'

'You see?' I persist. 'I've never thought Ed is terribly handsome, and I've never felt madly in love with him, but I tried to pretend that that was okay, that I didn't need more, but now I've realized that I do. And I'm really sorry that Ed won't be your son-in-law, but you should want what's best for me, and it isn't him. I'm sorry, but it just isn't.'

My mother opens her mouth as if she's about to say something, but, wonder of wonders, she doesn't seem able to think of anything to say, anything to prove me wrong. For once in my life I think she sees my point, and I think it's rendered her completely speechless.

So finally, after my traumatic afternoon, I head home in preparation for an even more traumatic evening, and maybe this is slightly sick, but I make far more of an effort tonight. I wear a biscuit-coloured jumper and taupe trousers, and I'm tempted to carry the Gucci bag, but I don't, just in case he asks for it back. I do my make-up very slowly, making sure everything's perfectly blended, making sure I look my absolute best.

I'm ready well before the appointed hour, and pour a stiff vodka to steel myself, to provide me with Dutch courage, and I phone Jules for some moral support.

'You'll be fine,' she tells me. 'You need to be strong and know that you are doing the right thing.'

So when the doorbell goes at seven thirty, I walk towards it feeling strong, feeling calm, in control, but as soon as I open the door and see Ed standing on the doorstep, already looking crestfallen, I know that this really is going to be, as I predicted, one of the hardest things I've ever had to do.

But I also know, looking at his face, that I have to do it. That there is no going back. That I will not be tempted, even for an instant, to take the easy route and stay in this relationship, not even for one more night.

Ed leans forward and gives me a kiss, and I turn my head so he catches the corner of my mouth, and I look away quickly, so I don't have to see the confused expression on his face.

'You look beautiful,' he says. 'I've missed you,' and he tries to pull me in for a kiss but I breeze away to pick up my coat.

'Shall we go?' I say, and I see that he doesn't understand; that he knows he's missing something, only he's not entirely sure what it is.

We walk out to the car in silence, and as I climb into the passenger seat I try to remember all the details of this Porsche, because the chances are this will be the last time I'm ever in one. Ed turns on the engine and as we drive he keeps shooting me these worried glances, and I seem to have forgotten the art of making conversation, because I just can't think of anything to say to him.

'Poor Libby,' Ed says finally, as we pull up to some traffic lights, 'I can see you're exhausted. They've obviously been working you far too hard.'

And I should feel something other than pity, but in that instant I do pity him, and I am enormously irritated by the fact that he cannot see what is blindingly obvious: that there is something drastically wrong, and that it's about to get a hell of a lot worse.

'I'm fine,' I say. 'Really. There are just some things I need to talk about with you.'

There! The sad puppy-dog expression! Just as I predicted. Ed finally seems to cotton on to the fact that this isn't just my problem, this somehow involves him as well, and for the rest of the car journey he doesn't say a word. He puts some music on, bloody opera at that, and after a while I lean forward and switch it off, muttering that I've got a headache.

We get out of the car and go into the restaurant, and I am constantly aware that Ed is gazing at me with that ridiculous bloody expression. We sit down and Ed orders me a Kir, and then looks at me, waiting for me to say the words I now think he knows he's going to hear, the words he's terrified of hearing.

I'm not hungry. Really. Food is the very last thing on my mind, but the waiter brings the menu, and I have to make a pretence of looking at it and admiring the dishes, and eventually I order a green salad to start with, and penne as a main course, although right now I do not have a clue how I will manage to pass any food between my lips at all.

We sit in awkward silence, Ed looking at me, me looking at the other diners in the restaurant, wondering how they can be so normal, so happy, so coupley, when I am about to break this man's world apart.

And eventually, after much sighing and spluttering, I manage to get the first sentence out.

'Ed, we need to talk.'

He doesn't say anything. Still. Just looks at me.

I sigh a bit more, and lapse into silence for a few more seconds, moving a few bits of lettuce around my plate, then, putting down my knife and fork. I pick them up again, sigh, and put them down, pushing my hair back with my hands.

'Ed,' I say softly. 'This isn't working.'

And he looks at me. Silently.

'This. Us. I'm not happy. I don't think I'm what you're looking for.'

And he looks at me. Silently.

Now I expected arguments. I expected Ed to tell me that nothing in life is easy, least of all relationships, and that things need to be worked at, and that he would be willing to do anything to save this relationship, and perhaps my voice would become louder as I tried to explain that there is no point in working at it because I have made up my mind.

But I wasn't expecting this. Silence.

'I think you're wonderful,' I say, going to take his hand to reinforce the point, but Ed moves his hand away, which shocks me slightly. I sit back and try again. 'You are an incredible man. You are loving, giving, you have so many wonderful qualities, but I'm not the right woman for you.'

At least I didn't say I'm not ready for a relationship, which is what you're always supposed to say in these circumstances, isn't it? Not that it makes any difference. No matter what the words are, the sentiments are the same: I don't love you enough to stay with you.

'You will meet someone one day who is perfect for you,' I say earnestly, although even as I'm saying these words they sound patronizing as hell, 'and I wish it were me. I wish I could be the woman you want me to be, but I can't.'

And he looks at me.

The waiter comes over and says, 'Is everything okay?', and Ed ignores him, still looking at me, but I force a smile and tell him it's fine but we're not that hungry, and he raises an eyebrow, takes the plates away.

And from thereon in it is quite possibly the most awkward, uncomfortable, desperately sad evening I have ever spent. We sit there, Ed and I, in silence, Ed still looking at me, and me still looking around the restaurant, and when the bill finally comes we stand in silence and walk outside and into his car.

'Umm, I think it's probably a good idea for me to come back now and get my stuff.' It could have waited, but I want this over, I want to be out of this, I don't want anything of mine to remain entangled with Ed's life.

So we go back to his house and Ed waits downstairs while I throw my nightdress, toothbrush, the few bits and pieces I had left there, into a bag, and when I come downstairs I find Ed sitting in the kitchen staring into space.

He looks at me, stands up and walks outside to the car, and this time he doesn't even attempt to use music to fill the silence that is becoming more and more oppressive by the second. And when, finally, we pull up outside my house, I look at him sadly, and twist his key off my keyring. 'You'd better have this back,' I say, and he nods.

'Can I call you?' I say, not because I want to call him, but because I can't just climb out of the car and say goodbye. Because I have never been in this position before, and I have absolutely no idea how to end this cleanly, how to, in fact, end this at all. Ed shrugs, and then, evidently having thought about it, shakes his head, and we sit there for a while, both of us presumably feeling like shit, and then I reach over, kiss him on the cheek, and get out of the car.

He still hasn't uttered a word.

And later that night, while I'm lying in bed crying, because I never realized how much it would hurt to cause that much pain to someone who loves you, it suddenly strikes me that the reason Ed didn't say anything, at all, all evening, was because he was holding back the tears.

Chapter Thirty

I don't bother getting up the next day. I ring the office at half past nine and croakily tell Jo I think I've picked up some kind of bug, and then burrow back under the duvet and sleep for another hour.

At half ten I wrap myself up in the duvet and collapse on the sofa, and for the next hour and a half I watch crap daytime television to take my mind off the fact that I am on my own again, and that I have been a complete fool.

Because how can you tell your friends that you were so desperate to get married you said yes to the first candidate that asked, even when you didn't feel anything for him other than mild irritation and occasional bursts of friendship?

How do you say that you have spent the past few months planning, in meticulous detail, your wedding day, without giving a second thought to what lies beyond?

How can they understand that, despite my independence and so-called career, I was swept away by a fantasy, seduced by a lifestyle, and that I am evidently far more shallow than even I ever dreamt?

The day passes in a bit of a blur. I try not to think about it too much, which is bloody difficult, because when I do I just feel enormously sad, and when Jo rings from the office and says I've had an urgent message to call Amanda, I think, fuck it, at least it will take my mind off things.

'Amanda? It's Libby.'

'Darling!' she exclaims. 'Poor you! They told me you were ill and I said it could wait, but your receptionist insisted on disturbing you at home.'

A likely bloody story. Jo would never insist on something like that, and I know that Amanda would have demanded that they give her my number.

'I'm okay,' I croak. 'Just a bit under the weather.'

'You'll be fine soon,' she says breezily. 'It's just that I had a message from *Cosmo* this morning about wanting to interview me, and I wondered whether you could ring them back and set it up.'

She rang me at home for that? When she could quite easily have picked up the phone herself and called, but then again, I suppose Amanda has to pretend she's a megastar, and hence cannot talk to anyone personally.

'Sure,' I sigh wearily. 'I'll ring them tomorrow.'

'Great!' she enthuses. 'Oh, and by the way, I had such a lovely time the other night. You're so lucky, getting engaged! To Ed McMahon!'

'Actually,' I groan, knowing that if I don't tell her now she'll be furious when she eventually finds out, 'actually it's all off.'

I think she stops breathing.

'Amanda? Are you still there?'

'Yes. Sorry. It's just that you two seemed so perfect together.'

'Well, we weren't.'

'But you're still together, surely, just not getting married yet?'

'No. It's over. Finished.'

'Oh my God, poor, poor you. No wonder you're not at work. Are you okay?'

'I'm fine, and anyway, it wasn't his decision, it was mine.'

'You're kidding?' She's laughing.

'No. Why?'

'You dumped Ed McMahon?' she splutters. 'Are you completely mad?'

'Jesus, Amanda, if you think he's so great, why don't you go out with him?'

There's another silence.

'Sorry,' I mumble. 'I didn't mean to be rude. He's just not for me, that's all.'

'Right. Right. I completely understand. Oh well, plenty more fish in the sea,' and a few seconds later she tells me her call waiting's going and she'd better answer it, so we say goodbye.

For a few minutes after I put the phone down I feel pretty damn awful. I mean, what if this is the last opportunity I'm ever going to have to get married? Maybe I have done the wrong thing. But then I remember his sad expression, his moustache, his habit of speaking French, and I know that I could never have gone through with it. Not for all the money in the world.

Later that afternoon, when Jules has left the fourth message of the day, I pick up the phone and she says she's coming over to check I'm okay.

'You look terrible,' she says, as I open the door, still in pyjamas.

'Thanks,' I mutter. 'What did you expect?'

'Sorry, I just didn't think you'd be this upset. You look like you've been crying for weeks.'

'That's how I feel.'

'Come here,' she says, giving me a big hug, and when

we pull apart I put the kettle on and make some tea, and we sit down as I give her all the details.

'I can understand how hard this is for you, but now you've got to get on with your life, and look on the bright side. You'll never make the same mistake again.'

'I know,' I sigh. 'It's just that he seemed so hurt, he seemed to be in so much pain, and I don't think I've ever caused anyone that much pain before, and that hurts me.'

'You were, as the saying goes, cruel to be kind. Far better to have done it now, you know that.'

'Yes. I do know that. Oh God, now I've got to start going to parties again and getting back into that bloody singles scene.'

'It's the best way of getting over someone.'

'But I really don't want anyone else. I just want to be alone for a while.'

'What about Nick?'

I shake my head. 'I'm not ready for anything. And Nick isn't what I'm looking for either. Although,' and for the first time in what feels like days, a glimmer of a smile crosses my face, 'although it might be worth it again for the sex.'

'Don't you dare!' admonishes Jules. 'You're not getting into that whole just a fling business again.'

'Jules?' I sink back into the sofa and start giggling, 'You know what? Thank God I'll never have to sleep with Ed again.'

Jules starts to laugh. 'Was it really that bad?'

'No,' I say. 'It was worse.'

We carry on talking about it, and Jules makes me cups of tea, and generally treats me like an invalid, but I start to feel better, and as we talk I realize that, however upset I am, my foremost feeling is one of relief.

And then suddenly, unexpectedly, the doorbell interrupts our conversation, and we both jump. Jules looks at me and whispers, 'Are you expecting anyone?'

'No,' I whisper back. 'Shit, I hope it's not Ed.'

'Do you want me to get it?' she says, as I nod and settle back into the sofa, knowing that whoever it is Jules will send them packing, and praying that it isn't Ed, come to change my mind.

She comes back into the living room and right behind her, literally on her heels, is the very last person I expect to see right now. Nick.

Fuck.

He looks embarrassed. I want to die. I look like shit. My hair hasn't seen a brush since sometime early yesterday evening, I have no make-up on, save smudges of mascara underneath my eyes, and my winceyette pyjamas are hardly the stuff you'd want anyone other than your best friend to see. Ever.

'Umm. Hi,' he says, as I wonder what the hell he's doing here and what the hell right he has to look so gorgeous when I look so terrible, and why the hell I didn't make an effort today just in case.

But what is he doing here?

'What are you doing here?'

Before he has a chance to answer, Jules, grinning broadly, has slipped her coat on and is already inching out the door. 'Gosh, is that the time?' she says. 'Must be off. I'll call you later,' and with that she's gone.

'So?' I persist. 'What are you doing here?'

'I was in the neighbourhood and just happened to be

passing, so I thought I'd drop a note in to apologize for what I said.'

'What were you doing in this neighbourhood?'

'Umm.' I can see him desperately trying to think of something, and I watch him as his eyes flick around the room, looking for help. 'Umm, I was dropping a video back.'

'You borrowed a video from Ladbroke Grove when you live in Highgate?'

'Oh, okay. So what? So I called your office and they said you were ill and I thought I'd come and see if you were okay, and I feel so guilty about all that stuff I said, and everything else, well. Umm. You know . . .'

'There was no need to lie about it.'

'Nice pyjamas,' he says, as I flush with embarrassment and tuck my legs underneath me to hide the faded knees (I told you they were old).

'Oh shut up and leave me alone,' I harrumph. 'Are you going to sit down or what?'

He sits. 'So,' he says, drumming on his knees, 'how are you? You don't look ill, but,' and he peers at me closely, 'you do look a little bit awful.'

'Did you come here specifically to insult me or was there another reason?' I say, forgetting quite how terrible I look because quite frankly I no longer give a damn.

'Sorry, sorry. Anyway. I bought you a present.' He fishes around in the pocket of his overcoat and, with a flourish, brings out a jar of Nutella.

'Nick! That's my favourite!' I'm already salivating as I reach out and grab it from him.

'I didn't want to bring you flowers,' he says, grinning sheepishly. 'That would be far too predictable. Anyway, that's my apology for the other day. I really am sorry, I just couldn't help myself.'

'S'okay,' I say, already undoing the cap and digging my index finger into the Nutella, sucking it clean, making noises of ecstasy.

'That's disgusting,' Nick says, watching me. 'Can't you use a spoon or something?'

I hold the jar out to him. 'Want some?' and he grins as he digs his index finger into the jar too.

'So,' he says eventually, 'everything okay with Ed?'

'What do you mean?' I ask slowly.

'Well, it's just . . . after Saturday . . . I . . . well. I just wondered if everything was okay.'

I sit for a few seconds debating whether or not to tell him, but I know he'll find out sooner or later, so he may as well hear it from me.

I take a deep breath. 'Actually, no. It's not.'

Nick raises an eyebrow questioningly.

'It's over.'

'Oh my God,' he says, genuinely shocked. 'Not because of me? Not because of what I said?'

'No, you arrogant bastard, not because of you. Well, maybe a bit because of you, because I realized that you were right. Everything you said was true. He isn't what I want and in the long term I don't think it would work out.'

'Jesus, Libby. I'm really sorry.'

'Yeah, you look it.'

'No, really. I am. I don't know what to say.'

'There's nothing to say. It's fine. I'm fine. It's just one of those things.'

'Do you want to talk about it?'

'There's nothing really to say. I kind of got swept away

in a fantasy without thinking about what the implications were, and luckily I realized in time.'

'Is Ed okay?'

'I don't know. I told him last night and he didn't say anything.'

'What? Nothing?'

'Nope. Just sat there not saying a word all evening.'

'Jesus,' Nick exhales loudly. 'Poor bastard.'

'I know. I feel like a total bitch.'

'No, you're not a bitch, Libby. At the end of the day you were just being cruel to be kind.'

'Funny, that's exactly what Jules said.'

'But it's true, and he'll get over it, he'll find someone else. You will too, you know.'

'Forget it.' I shake my head vehemently. 'That's it. I'm taking a vow of celibacy. The last thing in the world I need right now is men.'

'Even me?' I look up, and even though Nick is gorgeous, even though I do fancy him, I'll probably always fancy him, I know that I can't deal with this right now, that the last thing I need is to get involved with Nick on the rebound, so I shake my head sadly as I look him in the eye and try to smile.

'No,' I say softly. 'Even you.'

Olly phones the next day.

'I heard,' he says. 'Mum called me this morning to tell me how upset she is. Are you okay?'

'I'm fine, Oll,' I say. 'I still feel a bit bruised, but actually I'm starting to feel relief.'

Olly starts laughing. 'I didn't want to say anything at the time but he was awful, you know.'

'What?'

'Oh, come on. I can say it now, but he was a pompous old fart.'

I can't handle hearing this from someone else I love. Sorry, not that I love Nick, but this is all a bit much for me. 'Oll! Don't be so nasty. He wasn't that bad. Jesus, we only broke up a few days ago.'

'Libby, I've never said this about any of your boyfriends in the past, but if you'd have married him I think I would have disowned you.'

I'm truly, truly shocked. 'Did you really feel that strongly?'

'Sorry, Libby, but not only was he fuck ugly, he was arrogant too. His only saving grace, as far as I can see, is his money. Oh, and the fact that he adored you.'

I wince as the reality hits home. 'Do you think everyone felt the same way?'

'I wouldn't like to hazard a guess. Look, I'm sorry if you're upset by this, but it's over now, I didn't think you'd mind me being honest.'

'No,' I sigh. 'I don't. I just feel really stupid, but you know, Oll, he really wasn't a bad guy.'

'Okay, fine. But he wasn't for you.'

'No. I know that now. So has Mum forgiven me yet?'

'Nah. You know Mum. It'll take her about ten years to stop blaming you for finishing with Ed McMahon.'

'God, she's annoying. You'd think she'd have a bit of sympathy.'

'Well, if it's any consolation she did say that she understood how you felt.'

'You're kidding!'

'I know. I was as surprised as you. I think she's dreading telling the neighbours, but, from what she was saying, I think she knows that it wasn't really right. She started banging on about her and Dad, and how in love they were. The woman's finally gone completely round the bend.'

'Oh, Oll,' I laugh. 'You will never know how relieved I am.'

Chapter Thirty-one

It's been a month, and I really feel fine now. I've redis-
covered my career, and no one at work can believe quite
how hard I've been working, or quite how much I've
achieved, but Jesus, isn't that the best way of getting
over being single again?

And okay, so my evenings are slightly harder. Not that
I want to be with Ed, it's just that I find myself at a loss
for things to do, although my friends have been fantastic,
and everyone's been inviting me to everything, and the
best thing about going out with my friends again is that
I know there's absolutely no possibility of me bumping
into Ed. Ever.

Because now that I'm single again I've realized that I
was living a total fantasy with Ed. I was wearing clothes
I never thought I'd wear, going to places I never thought
I'd go, and generally behaving in a way that absolutely,
one hundred per cent, was not me. You see, although I
always thought that was the lifestyle I wanted, now that
I've had a taste I know that I never again want to pretend
to be something I'm not.

It is, however, a bit weird having to readjust to being
single. Having to plan my diary meticulously so I'm not
sitting at home every night eating takeaways, but I'd
much rather be making the effort than be with Ed.

Although I'm still slightly thrown when Amanda rings
me at work one day and out of the blue asks me if I'd
mind if she went out with Ed.

'No, no,' I say, in a falsely enthusiastic voice. 'That's fine.'

'Are you sure you don't mind?' she says, and I know that, even if I did, it wouldn't make a blind bit of difference to her. They're probably perfectly suited, and Amanda's a far better social climber than I'll ever be, although my social aspirations seem to have gone down a peg or five.

'I'm delighted,' I say, wondering whether they've already gone out, but I don't have to wonder very long, because later that afternoon Jo runs in brandishing the *Daily Express* and the late edition of the *Standard*.

'Okay,' she says, perching her long legs on the edge of my desk. 'Take a deep breath. Are you ready?'

I nod, and Jo opens the *Express* first and places it on my desk in front of me, and there, in Features, is a piece on London's new It couples. And taking pride of place with a large colour photograph are Amanda Baker and Ed McMahon. The picture is obviously a paparazzi, and I note with interest how Amanda has perfected the pissed-off look and the pose of holding her hand in front of her face to pretend she doesn't want to be photographed.

'Jesus,' I gasp. 'That was quick work.'

'Wait,' laughs Jo. 'It gets better,' and with that she flings the *Standard* on top of the *Express* and opens it to the front page of the Homes and Property section, and in the Homes Gossip section is another picture of Amanda.

'Breakfast Break presenter Amanda Baker,' Jo reads out loud, 'is selling her interior designed one-bedroom flat in Primrose Hill, where near neighbours include Liam Gallagher and Patsy Kensit, and Harry Enfield. The estate agent has revealed she is moving to Hanover

Terrace to be with her new love, Ed McMahon The flat has a picturesque roof terrace, and a beautifully presented aspect, and is now on the market at £185,000 through agents blah blah blah.' Jo stops and checks to see how I'm taking it.

'Fucking hell,' I splutter. 'When the fuck did all this happen?'

Jo shrugs. 'Dunno, but thank God you got out of it when you did. I mean, please. Look at that picture of Ed. Look at that tache. How could you?' And I examine the picture in the *Express* again and start to laugh. 'I know.' I shrug my shoulders. 'What the hell was I thinking?'

Joe Cooper comes out of his office and sees us laughing, and he walks over to see what all the fuss is about.

'Are you okay with this?' he says, looking at me intently. 'If there's any problem I'll put someone else on her account.'

'No,' I laugh. 'I'm fine. I'm just bloody relieved it's not me in there.'

'What are you doing on Saturday night?' Sal sounds excited.

'Noth-ing,' I say slowly, always wary of committing myself before I know what I'm committing myself to. 'Why?'

'We're having a party and you must come. Paul and I were talking the other night about how nobody has house parties any more, in fact nobody even has parties.'

'You're right, weird isn't it.'

'Yup, so we've decided to have one. The biggest, loudest, fuck-off party you've ever been to.'

I can already feel my own excitement rising at the

prospect of a proper party, something to dress up for, something to look forward to.

'Are you having it in your place?' I'm picturing Sal's house in Clapham, her double reception room, the french doors opening on to a large garden.

'Yup, of course. Paul spent last weekend building a barbecue, and we're going to have a bar with Sea Breezes and Martinis, and I've got to go out this afternoon and buy a load of fairy lights to string up in the trees.'

I squeal with excitement. 'Who's coming? Who's coming?'

'Everyone!' she shrieks. 'No, but wait. I haven't finished. Paul's got a friend who's a DJ, and he's coming and bringing his recordy deck thingy to do all the music properly.'

'Not techno rubbish?'

'Nah, for us old things? Nope, he says it's serious funk with a strong seventies flavour.'

'Excellent, my favourite. What time will it start?'

'We thought around eight, and most people probably won't turn up until later, but I definitely want the hard core of close friends there early. Seriously, Libby, there'll be so much food and drink, and so many people, we think we're on to a bit of a winner.'

'How many people?'

'We've got about eighty on the list, but everyone wants to bring friends because they're all saying the same thing, that no one has parties any more.'

'Sal, I cannot even begin to tell you how excited I am.' And it's true. I am.

On Saturday afternoon I do something I haven't done for ages: I start getting ready for the party at three in the afternoon, and, even though it brings back shades of my teenage years, I'm loving every minute of it.

I wash my hair in the shower, then smear a hot wax treatment all over it, cover it in a hot towel and spend the next hour chatting to Jules while it does its stuff.

I use an apricot facial scrub, then three different face packs, all of which I leave on for twenty minutes, and by the time I've finished my face is so tight and shiny you can almost see your reflection in it.

I dash out to the newsagent's and return with an armful of glossy magazines, because, chameleon woman that Jules so rightly once said I am, I haven't yet decided who I'm going to be tonight. Am I going to be sophisticated, trendy, funky or aloof? Do I slick back my hair, wear it in a spiky pony-tail, or have it loose and tousled around my shoulders? Should I stagger in heels, glide in pumps, or stomp in trainers?

Flicking through the magazines, I have a wild impulse to pluck my eyebrows into perfect, sardonic arches, so, grabbing the tweezers, I do just that, marvelling at the difference it makes to my face, and wondering what else I can do to achieve model perfection.

At last, at precisely half past seven, I'm done. I survey myself in the mirror, in my floaty chiffon floor-length dress covered in a dusky flower print, demure until I walk, when the front slit sweeps aside revealing my newly tanned legs (I bought the fake stuff this morning and much to my amazement it left me with smooth brown legs, and no orange stripes). Flat strappy sandals complete the look, and I scoop my hair up into a messy pony-tail, figuring I can always loosen it later, should I find someone to loosen it for.

I'm tempted to drive, but I'm planning to really let my

hair down this evening (excuse the pun), and call a minicab instead. I make him stop outside the off-licence so I can run in and get beer. I would normally have brought wine, but Sal warned me off, saying they were stuffing three huge dustbins with ice, and beer would be more appropriate.

There are only a handful of other people there when I arrive, and no one I recognize, but there's a buzz of excitement in the air already, and we all grin at each other and shake hands, chattering about how wonderful the weather is, and what a beautiful evening to have a party.

And the garden looks spectacular. Paul waves to me from behind the barbecue, the coals still jet-black, and behind him are makeshift wooden shelves, lined with what I can only assume must be Jello shots.

The trees surrounding the garden are all covered with tiny white fairy lights, but, as Sal says, as she shows me what they've done, we won't get the full effect until later. I say hi to Jools, the DJ, a scarily trendy and rather gorgeous bloke who's testing his system, too caught up in his music to notice the guests, other than to wave hello.

'I can't believe what you've done,' I say, after Sal and I have knocked back a delicious lime Jello shot together. 'This is amazing.'

'Do you think everyone will turn up?' She shoots me a worried glance before looking around the garden. 'I mean, hardly anyone's here yet.'

'Don't worry.' I check my watch. 'It's only 8.45. People will start rolling in any minute now.'

And sure enough, as if by magic, people do start

arriving, and within an hour the garden is heaving, literally heaving, and the nicest thing about it is that, even though I don't know more than a handful of people, everyone feels like my closest friend, and I'm having a whale of a time dancing with some guy called Dave who isn't really my type but who's a bloody good dancer, and I know that I haven't had this much fun in ages.

And then Sal runs in and switches on the lights, and Paul moves around the garden, lighting the torches that have been strategically placed in the flower beds around the edge, and the whole night seems to take on a magical quality, and it does feel like the kind of night when anything could happen.

Soon there are crowds of people dancing, and although we're outside there's no breeze, and it's so hot I can feel beads of perspiration dotted on my forehead, and eventually I shout to Dave that I'm going to get a drink, and he nods, grins, and turns to dance with the girl behind him.

The only drink to quench my thirst right now is good old tap water, so I push through the party-goers until I'm in Sal's tiny kitchen, and, leaning panting against the sink, I reach for a glass and gulp it down in about two seconds.

'John Travolta has nothing on you.' I jump and with my hand on my heart I turn to see Nick lounging in the doorway with a big grin on his face.

'I hope you're not still in insulting mode,' I say suspiciously.

'No!' He looks aghast. 'I was serious. I never realized you were such a good dancer.'

I shrug, secretly flattered. 'How long have you been here?'

'Not long. We got here about fifteen minutes ago. Just in time to see those hips move.'

I laugh self-consciously before asking, 'We?' And then I notice her. Tall, skinny, cropped dark hair in that perfect gamine cut that you can only have when you are tremendously beautiful and live in Notting Hill, and of course she is tremendously beautiful, and I hate her. Instantly. Not that I'm jealous, in fact I'm happy that Nick has found someone. Well, okay. Maybe happy would be a bit of an over-exaggeration, and why does she have to be so bloody beautiful?

'Hi,' she smiles, and fuck. Her teeth are perfect. If I didn't know better I'd think she stepped straight out of an American advert for toothpaste. 'I'm Cat.' Great. This gets better. I shake her hand warily, and trying to be polite ask, 'Is that your real name?'

'No.' She shakes her head and laughs. 'My real name's Sophie, but everyone used to tell me I looked like a cat at school and the name stuck.' As I take in her cat-like almond-shaped eyes, I note that her voice is immaculately polished, that lazy insouciant tone that immediately marks her out as a member of the upper classes. Or, at the very least, upper middle. I don't feel good enough, and I can't believe a friend of Nick is making me feel inadequate. Not that she's unfriendly, but she's so gorgeous I feel like a dumpy fraud, and I wish, instantly, that I had worn something more like her, a plain vest top with baggy combat trousers and trainers.

Nick smiles at me, waiting to see what I'll say next, probably proud as punch that he can show off his new girlfriend and she can be that gorgeous. Well, fuck you, I think, smiling at him graciously as I say, 'I mustn't leave Dave alone for too long,' and with that I sweep past them, ignoring his odd look at me, and go back into the garden.

Dave's still dancing with the other girl, and I tap him on the shoulder and grin at him as he turns, holds my hips, and moves his body perfectly in tune with mine. Over his shoulder I see Nick and Cat walk into the garden, and I throw my head back with laughter to prove I'm having a fantastic time, because Nick's looking at me and quite frankly he can go screw himself. Or Cat. Which he probably will be doing later.

Fuck.

Why does this bother me so much? Why do I care? After all, I was the one who turned him down. This time. And I really, really don't want a relationship right now, and even if I did the last person I'd be interested in would be Nick. So why can't I take my eyes off the two of them, giggling together in the corner? Why do I feel a stab of jealousy when I remember how he used to do that with me? Why is he making her laugh and not me?

I resolve that there's only one solution to this dilemma, and that is to get drunk. Very, very drunk. I down my next Sea Breeze in one, much to Paul's astonishment, and then instantly start on another one. That's it. Much better.

Nick who?

I lose track of time, but soon the world suddenly becomes slightly hazy, and I know that I've probably had enough. More, and I'd run the risk of getting into bed only to have an attack of the deadly bedspins or, worse, throw up at the party. This is just perfect: hazy, friendly, just enough to make me happy. Who cares. I've got no problems other than who to dance with next.

Nick who?

Sal comes up and grabs me. 'Did you see her?'

'See who?'

'Cat?'

I nod.

'She's gorgeous, isn't she? Who would have thought it.'

'Yeah, who would have bloody thought it,' and I give Sal a drunken kiss on the cheek and go staggering off to the barbecue, not that I'm hungry, it's just that drinking on an empty stomach is not exactly clever, and I know that if I don't have something to eat, anything, I really won't be very well at all.

I tear at a chicken kebab, not really tasting it, and, as I throw the stick merrily over my shoulder, I see Nick standing by himself on the other side of the garden, and when I catch his eye he starts walking over to me, so I head off in the other direction and make myself very busy flirting with a group of men I've never seen before, who seem more than happy to make me feel welcome.

Ha! That will show him. Nick has skulked off, presumably to find his precious Cat.

The party's in full throttle at two in the morning, despite the neighbours' complaints, but gradually people have started disappearing, and I haven't seen Nick for ages and I'm slightly drunk and very tired and actually I'm now wondering how I'm going to get home.

I go inside, to the living room at the front of the house, which is pitch black and empty, and, bumping into the coffee table en route, I finally make it to the sofa and slump down.

'Fuck!'

'Fuck!' I jump back up to hear rustling, then footsteps, then the light's switched on.

'Libby? What are you doing?'

'What am I doing? What the hell are you doing?' I'm looking at Nick suspiciously as he starts to laugh, and it sobers me up instantly.

'I was just lying down for a bit. In the dark. I know you still have a soft spot for me but did you really have to leap on top of me to prove it?'

'I didn't,' I grumble, sitting down again. 'I didn't know you were there. Anyway. Where's Cat?'

'Gone. She's off to some other party.'

'Why didn't you go too?'

'Her friends are far too Notting Hill for me. You know, they're all those bloody awful Trustafarians and I can't stand them.'

I look at him strangely. 'So how do you . . . I mean, do you find it difficult . . . well . . .'

Now it's Nick's turn to look at me strangely. 'What? What are you talking about? Libby, you're pissed.'

'No, no.' I shake my head to clear it. 'I mean, if you don't like her friends, well, it's just that I can't see her getting on with yours, you know, Moose and that lot, and, well . . .' I stumble into silence.

'Libby, what the fuck are you on about, all this friends stuff? Cat's always had bloody awful friends. Apart from the old ones, that is. Some of her friends at school were completely gorgeous when they were fourteen.'

I still don't understand, and then it slowly dawns on me. 'Cat's not your . . .'

'Sister? Yes. Why? What did you think?' And then he sees exactly what I thought and he roars with laughter.

'God, Libby. You are fantastic. Cat? My girlfriend?' and he snorts with laughter again.

'Well, how was I to know?' I go on the defensive because what else can I do?

'I don't know,' Nick splutters, wiping the tears from his eyes. 'I just, well. Even if she wasn't my sister she wouldn't be my type.'

'No?' I resist the urge to ask him what would be his type.

'No. Look, how are you getting home? You're not driving, are you?'

'No.'

'Thank Christ for that. If you get a cab I'll come with you to check you get home okay, then I'll take it on home.'

'Okay.' Actually, with a bit of a shock I realize that I'm not sure it is okay. I'm not sure that I want him to go back to his home, but maybe I'm just drunk.

Nick calls a cab, and when it arrives we hug Sal and Paul goodbye and stumble into the back seat, and I pretend to look out the window for a bit, but the only thing I'm concentrating on is keeping my breathing as normal as possible, because the fact that it's so dark in here, so quiet, and that there is a gorgeous, sexy man sitting inches away from me, is making it very, very difficult to pretend that the only thing on my mind right now is friendship.

'Nearly there,' he says, as the cab turns from Holland Park into Ladbroke Grove, and I smile and lean my forehead against the window, and wonder how I can prolong this evening, how I can make him stay, without putting myself on the line by actually asking him.

And then we're outside my house, and we just sit and

look at one another as the cab driver taps his fingers impatiently on the wheel.

'Shit,' Nick says suddenly, slapping his palm on his forehead. 'I knew there was something I forgot to tell you.'

'What?'

'It's a long story.'

The cab driver, who's listening, sighs, and I say, 'Do you want to come in? You can always call another cab.'

'Great!' he says, reaching into his pocket and pulling some money out. 'I'll get this,' and he follows me inside the door.

Nick closes the front door behind me, and stands in front of the light switch, so as I fumble to turn on the lights I don't feel anything. Except Nick's hand. He grabs my wrist and doesn't say anything, and we stand in the darkness, just listening to the sound of one another's breathing and is it my imagination or does the breathing become heavier, slower?

And then Nick takes my hand, and possibly the darkness makes it feel like it's happening in slow motion, and he places it on his cheek, and I can't help myself, I start stroking his cheek, and then I'm tracing his lips, unable to see anything, but knowing his face so well from memory, and then his lips are open and he's gently sucking my finger, fingers, into his mouth.

I gasp, and Nick pulls me very gently towards him, and our mouths find one another's in the darkness and Nick leans back against the wall, holding me tightly, kissing me slowly, sensually, until I think my legs are going to give way.

And then very gently he moves around and, holding one arm out to guide him, falls slowly on to the sofa, pulling me with him, and within seconds my dress is around my waist, and I am moaning softly as he gently teases me with his tongue.

And the only thing that's going through my mind is how did I do without this for so long, how could I have ever settled for anything less?

Nick's hand moves up my thigh, stroking, gliding, as I groan into his neck and softly bite the skin there, and I reach down for his belt buckle and listen as his belt clicks undone, and I unzip the zipper of his trousers and stroke the length of his hard-on, and he inhales sharply before kissing me again.

We move to the bedroom, and we make slow, languorous, passionate love, and as he enters me, just at that moment before he starts moving inside me, three words enter my head: I've come home. It's difficult to explain, but there is something so familiar, so comfortable, so right about this moment, it suddenly feels like I am exactly where I should be, at exactly the right time, with exactly the right person.

I'm far too busy losing myself in the moment to dwell on this any further, and after we have made love, after we have murmured to each other and are lying in bed, side by side, with Nick's arm around my shoulders, gently stroking my hair, I remember he had said he had something to tell me.

I lean over and kiss him gently on the nose. 'So what was it you had to tell me, then?' I whisper.

Nick opens his eyes. 'Actually, there are two things.'

'And they are?'

Nick pulls his arm out from under me and sits up in bed, turning to look at me as he takes my hand. 'Libby,' he says seriously, while I start to get worried. 'I know you're probably not ready to hear this, but the thing is, well . . .' He stops.

'Yes?' I prompt, not having a clue what he is going to say.

'Well, the thing is that I think I might be in love with you . . .' My mouth falls open, and he gulps before continuing. 'I'm not entirely sure because I don't think I've ever been in love before and it's a bit of a new feeling for me, but it's just that I haven't been able to stop thinking about you, and I don't know whether it was just the timing last time, that I wasn't ready, but now I think I am, and you may not even want me, but I just had to say something, because every morning when I wake up you're the first thing on my mind, and every night before I go to sleep you're the last person I think of, and I have no idea what you are going to say but I wanted you to know.'

And I sit there, my heart racing at hearing these words, at hearing them from Nick, at seeing the expression in his eyes which are glistening with emotion, and I know he means it. I know that he is in love with me, and not the way that Ed loved me, not for my potential, or because I would make a good wife, or for any of those other superficial reasons, but for me. He loves me for who I am.

And suddenly I realize that although I've never thought about being in love with Nick before, all the right ingredients are there. I fancy him. I like him. He's my friend. He makes me laugh. I love being with him. And I start to feel all sort of warm and glowy, and screw the other stuff. Screw the stuff about him having no money, and living in a bedsit, and not being what I thought I wanted. I'm just going to go with this and see where it ends up. I mean, no one says I have to marry the guy, for God's sake.

And anyway. I no longer think that marriage is the be-all and end-all. Not by a long shot. Not after Jules and Jamie, and as she put it the other day. 'It's a long hard struggle, but I think we'll get there.' I'm not sure I'm ready for that struggle. Not yet.

'Nick,' I say, leaning down to kiss him. 'No one's ever said that to me before. If I'm being really honest, I don't know how I feel about you yet, I think it's still a little early for me to talk about love, but I know that I do love being with you, and I'd like to give it a shot. Just being together, I mean, and seeing where it goes.'

Relief spreads over his face.

'So,' I say curiously, after we've snuggled up and kissed for a few minutes. 'What was the other thing?'

'Other thing?'

'You said you had two things to tell me.'

'Oh yes. That. It's nothing major,' and he grins. 'I've got a publishing deal!'